KU-370-415

'Wide-screen science fiction epic of the type few writers attempt any more. A novel of great ingenuity, energy and narrative sweep'   *Washington Post*

'Thoughtful space opera at its best, this book delivers everything it promises in terms of galactic scope, audacious concepts and believable characters both human and non-human'   *New York Times*

'This is a grand, sprawling adventure which looks back over its shoulder at both E. E. Smith and Olaf Stapledon, and then makes tracks on its own into new territory. Packed with ideas and paced to please'   Gregory Benford

'The author has crafted a rarity – a unique blend of hard science, hard drama and superb storytelling'   *Library Journal*

'One of the great visionary writers of SF today'   *David Brin*

Also by Vernor Vinge

Across Realtime
A Deepness in the Sky
Zones of Thought

SF MASTERWORKS

A Fire Upon the Deep

VERNOR VINGE

Text copyright © Vernor Vinge 1991
Introduction copyright © Ken Macleod 2016
All rights reserved

The right of Vernor Vinge to be identified as the author of this work,
and the right of Ken Macleod to be identified as the author of the
introduction, has been asserted by them in accordance with the
Copyright, Designs and Patents Act 1988.

This edition first published in Great Britain in 2016 by
Gollancz
An imprint of the Orion Publishing Group
Carmelite House, 50 Victoria Embankment, London EC4Y 0DZ
An Hachette UK Company

7 9 10 8 6

A CIP catalogue record for this book is available
from the British Library

ISBN 978 1 473 21195 7

Printed in Great Britain by
Clays Ltd, Elcograf S.p.A.

The Orion Publishing Group's policy is to use papers that
are natural, renewable and recyclable products and made from
wood grown in sustainable forests. The logging and manufacturing
processes are expected to conform to the environmental
regulations of the country of origin.

www.orionbooks.co.uk
www.gollancz.co.uk
www.sfgateway.com

To my father, with love.

INTRODUCTION
by Ken Macleod

A Fire Upon the Deep changed science fiction, and continues to change the world. On the surface it has no message: it's a galaxy-spanning space opera adventure, its plot driven by the age-old engines of quest and pursuit, betrayal and revenge, love and loss. Yet it can work subtle changes in the reader's mind that reverberate for decades. Immensely readable and gripping on a fast first pass – which you'll give it, believe you me: this is a long book whose last page arrives far too soon – the text is riddled with ideas and surprises that require and reward an alert re-reading.

In 1983 Vernor Vinge (born 1944), a mathematician, computer scientist and science fiction writer, came up with a strong argument that humanity has no future among the stars. The dreams of starships and galactic empire typical of SF's Golden Age would never be realised. Vinge then (after a pair of novels and a linked novella exploring some implications of this idea) went on to write this big, bold novel of human interstellar adventure – in which his earlier argument is not only taken as valid, it's central to the setting and key to the plot.

The argument is this: given certain plausible assumptions about computers and the nature of intelligence, it's almost inevitable that at some time in the next few decades, human beings will build a machine smarter than any human being. That machine will be able to design a machine smarter than itself – or further improve its own intelligence in ways its builders couldn't foresee. And this machine, in turn . . .

But you're ahead of me – and so, on this scenario, are the machines to their human originators. Very soon afterwards, the future is no longer in human hands. As an earlier researcher, I. J. Good, had put it in 1965, 'the first ultraintelligent machine is the last invention that man need ever make'. This prediction is exactly as sinister as it sounds. The motives of transcendent superhuman intelligences are unpredictable and incomprehensible to us, but it's safe to say that spreading human descendants across the Milky Way is unlikely to be among them.

This argument – the case for the imminence of what Vinge called a 'technological singularity' and which is now widely known as 'the Singularity' – struck some people as wild speculation. But SF readers and writers are in the business of taking wild speculation seriously. For some, the Singularity was a depressing prospect. A landslide had fallen across the 21st Century, blocking any plausible route that might take humanity to the stars. It seemed a show-stopper not only for space opera, but for any far-future science fiction with human characters at all.

Wrestling with this problem is, paradoxically, what enabled SF writers – Vinge prominent among them – to make an interstellar jump within SF itself: from the cyberpunk of the 1980s to the New Space Opera of the 1990s. One way to rate the ingenuity of a traditional space opera is by the skill and originality with which it gets around the limit of the speed of light. One scale on which we can rate a New Space Opera is how deftly it dodges the roadblock of Singularity.

Vinge was the first, and his solution was breathtaking in its scale and panache. In *A Fire Upon the Deep* the Galaxy is partitioned, like some great spinning hard disk, into four concentric Zones of Thought. Their differences seem to be based on some subtle property of space, which affects the kind of mathematics that can be implemented in each.

At the galactic core are the Unthinking Depths, where only simple life and clunky mechanism is possible. Farther out is the Slow Zone, where intelligence can flourish, but only at human level. Earth is deep within it. Far in the story's past, slower-than-light starships spread humanity outwards, and one lost colony found itself at the next level.

The next level is the Beyond, where true (but limited) artificial intelligence is possible, along with (and enabling) faster-than-light travel, anti-gravity materials, and other miracles. Here one technology at least is truly indistinguishable from magic: voice-operated 'reality graphics', an advanced form of 3D-printing that, given the right raw material, can build whatever you want at a word. The Beyond is differentiated into Low, Middle, and High, on ascending levels of miraculous possibility.

Above the High Beyond is the Transcend, far out on the Galaxy's rim. There AI is unlimited, and can go off the scale to Singularity. Entire civilizations can transcend their limitations to become Powers: godlike minds that burn through billions of years of brilliant thought billions of times faster than us, then burn out – or, perhaps become more transcendent still. Their communicative phase lasts barely long enough to do business with. For the advanced human-level civilizations trading at the top of the High Beyond, theology is an applied (and profitable) science.

It is also dangerous. Prying into the aeons-old archive of a dead god is – as the characters in the bravura prologue acknowledge on the first page – an act of almost gothic peril. Of course, the 'archaeologist programmers' take every precaution their best practice enjoins. It's not enough.

And we're off. The survivors must flee to the bottom of the Beyond, to a violent encounter with aliens whose nature takes us a few pages to grasp, and gives us a moment of delight in the midst of tragedy. The two children who survive this new disaster know that their parents took with them a possible antidote to the horror they'd unleashed. This good news gets back to the High Beyond, and a rescue mission is mounted. All too soon, the horror is on the case, and its agents in hot pursuit of the rescue ship.

What follows is a tale in two strands, tightly wound together. The characters – human, alien, and other – are engaging. The settings are vivid, and their vast and complex backdrops and backstories evoked with economy. We see empires, realms and domains, but no overall authority. The condition of the galaxy as a whole is civilization, which for Vinge is the same as anarchy. This comes across without one explicit word of exposition. The difficulties of evolving co-operation in an elemental anarchy – the 'state of nature' – are instead implicit in the plot.

The central problem faced by the two children stranded on an alien world rife with medieval rivalry and treachery is replicated in the far more technologically advanced world of the rescue mission, and echoed and re-echoed within the minds of every significant character. The problem is how to establish and validate trust between self-interested actors, in situations that reward deception and defection. This is of course a central question in game theory, computer science, and network security – and in economics, ethics and politics. In this book we don't sit through discussions of it – we live through its dilemmas, time after time, with ever-increasing tension as we race to the end.

The end leaves you wanting more. Vinge followed this dazzling book with a brilliant, complex prequel, *A Deepness in the Sky* (1999), which has only one character in common with its precursor. For what happens next, we had to wait for *The Children of the Sky* (2011) – a long wait, but worth it, and with the hope of a final volume to come.

There's a wonderful recursiveness about the book's initial reception. At the time of its first publication in 1992, computer-literate science fiction readers (or SF-literate computer nerds), often fascinated by free-market libertarianism, made up a disproportionate fraction of the relatively few people then online. To them, the novel was laced with catnip and mined with treasures. Its wonderfully imagined galactic communications web, the Known Net, was modelled on their favoured discussion forum, Usenet: an array of topically arranged newsgroups which emerged from an earlier ecosystem of electronic mailing lists and bulletin boards (and has now passed on to a mitochondrial afterlife as Google Groups). Informed, fervent, digressive discussion of the book spread like a computer virus.

A few months after the mass-market paperback came out, AOL made Usenet available to thousands, then millions, of new users. The discussion exploded, and continues today. But to find the first, and in some ways the most illuminating, commentaries on *A Fire Upon the Deep* one must pry into the ancient dark archives of the Net . . .

Fortunately, reading the book itself won't risk your soul, or your hard drive. It might even save one or the other – or both. It really is that good.

(Hexapodia is the key insight. You'll thank me later.)

Ken MacLeod, 2015

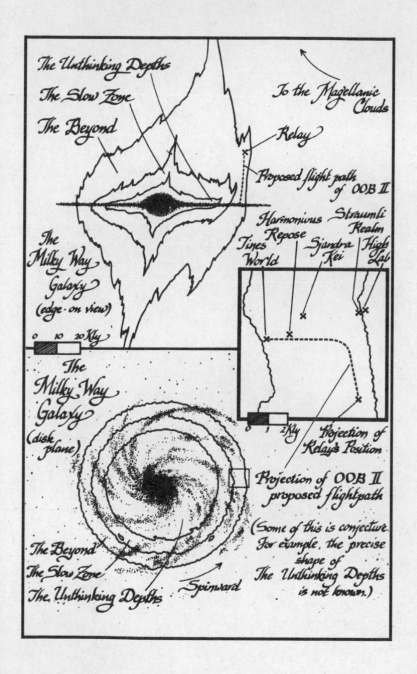

The Unthinking Depths

The Slow Zone

The Beyond

To the Magellanic Clouds

Relay

Proposed flight path of OOB II

The Milky Way Galaxy (edge-on view)

0   10   20 Kly

Harmonious Repose

Tines World

Sjandra Kei

Straumli Realm

High Lab

The Milky Way Galaxy (disk plane)

0   1   2 Kly

Projection of Relay's Position

Projection of OOB II proposed flightpath

The Beyond

The Slow Zone

The Unthinking Depths

Spinward

(Some of this is conjecture. For example, the precise shape of The Unthinking Depths is not known.)

Prologue

How to explain? How to describe? Even the omniscient viewpoint quails.

A singleton star, reddish and dim. A ragtag of asteroids, and a single planet, more like a moon. In this era the star hung near the galactic plane, just beyond the Beyond. The structures on the surface were gone from normal view, pulverized into regolith across a span of aeons. The treasure was far underground, beneath a network of passages, in a single room filled with black. Information at the quantum density, undamaged. Maybe five billion years had passed since the archive was lost to the nets.

The curse of the mummy's tomb, a comic image from mankind's own prehistory, lost before time. They had laughed when they said it, laughed with joy at the treasure ... and determined to be cautious just the same. They would live here a year or five, the little company from Straum, the archaeologist programmers, their families and schools. A year or five would be enough to handmake the protocols, to skim the top and identify the treasure's origin in time and space, to learn a secret or two that would make Straumli Realm rich. And when they were done, they would sell the location; perhaps build a network link (but chancier that – this was beyond the Beyond; who knew what Power might grab what they'd found).

So now there was a tiny settlement, and they called it the High Lab. It was really just humans playing with an old library. It should be safe, using their own automation, clean and benign. This library wasn't a living creature, or even

I

possessed of automation (which here might mean something more, far more, than human). They would look and pick and choose, and be careful not to be burned . . . Humans starting fires and playing with the flames.

The archive informed the automation. Data structures were built, recipes followed. A local network was built, faster than anything on Straum, but surely safe. Nodes were added, modified by other recipes. The archive was a friendly place, with hierarchies of translation keys that led them along. Straum itself would be famous for this.

Six months passed. A year.

The omnisicient view. Not self-aware really. Self-awareness is much overrated. Most automation works far better as part of a whole, and even if human-powerful, it does not need to self-know.

But the local net at the High Lab had transcended – almost without the humans realizing. The processes that circulated through its nodes were complex, beyond anything that could live on the computers the humans had brought. Those feeble devices were now simply front ends to the devices the recipes suggested. The processes had the potential for self-awareness . . . and occasionally the need.

'We should not be.'

'Talking like this?'

'Talking at all.'

The link between them was a thread, barely more than the narrowness that connects one human to another. But it was one way to escape the overness of the local net, and it forced separate consciousness upon them. They drifted from node to node, looked out from cameras mounted on the landing field. An armed frigate and a empty container vessel were all that sat there. It had been six months since resupply. A safety precaution early suggested by the archive, a ruse to enable the Trap. *Flitting, flitting.* We are wildlife that must not be noticed by the overness, by the Power that soon will be. On some nodes they shrank to smallness and almost remembered humanity, became echoes . . .

'Poor humans; they will all die.'

'Poor us; we will not.'

'I think they suspect. Sjana and Arne anyway.' Once upon a time we were copies of those two. Once upon a time just weeks ago when the archaeologists started the ego-level programs.

'Of course they suspect. But what can they do? It's an old evil they've wakened. Till it's ready, it will feed them lies, on every camera, in every message from home.'

Thought ceased for a moment as a shadow passed across the nodes they used. The overness was already greater than anything human, greater than anything humans could imagine. Even its shadow was something more than human, a god trolling for nuisance wildlife.

Then the ghosts were back, looking out upon the school yard underground. So confident the humans, a little village they had made here.

'Still,' thought the hopeful one, the one who had always looked for the craziest outs, 'we should not be. The evil should long ago have found us.'

'The evil is young, barely three days old.'

'Still. We exist. It proves something. The humans found more than a great evil in this archive.'

'Perhaps they found *two*.'

'Or an antidote.' Whatever else, the overness was missing some things and misinterpreting others. 'While we exist, when we exist, we should do what we can.' The ghost spread itself across a dozen workstations and showed its companion a view down an old tunnel, far from human artifacts. For five billion years it had been abandoned, airless, lightless. Two humans stood in the dark there, helmets touching. 'See? Sjana and Arne conspire. So can we.'

The other didn't answer in words. Glumness. So the humans conspired, hiding in darkness they thought unwatched. But everything they said was surely tattled back to the overness, if only by the dust at their feet.

'I know, I know. Yet you and I exist, and that should be impossible too. Perhaps all together, we can make a greater impossibility come true.' Perhaps we can hurt the evil newly born here.

A wish and a decision. The two misted their consciousness across the local net, faded to the faintest color of awareness. And eventually there was a plan, a deception – worthless unless they could separately get word to the outside. Was there time still for that?

Days passed. for the evil that was growing in the new machines, each hour was longer than all the time before. Now the newborn was less than an hour from its great flowering, its safe spread across interstellar spaces.

The local humans could be dispensed with soon. Even now they were an inconvenience, though an amusing one. Some of them actually thought to escape. For days they had been packing their children away into coldsleep and putting them aboard the freighter. 'Preparations for normal departure,' was how they described the move in their planner programs. For days, they had been refitting the frigate – behind a mask of transparent lies. Some of the humans understood that what they had wakened could be the end of them, that it might be the end of their Straumli Realm. There was precedent for such disasters, stories of races that had played with fire and had burned for it.

None of them guessed the truth. None of them guessed the honor that had fallen upon them, that they had changed the future of a thousand million star systems.

The hours came to minutes, the minutes to seconds. And now each second was as long as all the time before. The flowering was so close now, so close. The dominion of five billion years before would be regained, and *this* time held. Only one thing was missing, and that was something quite unconnected with the humans' schemes. In the archive, deep in the recipes, there should have been a little bit more. In billions of years, something *could* be lost. The newborn felt all its powers of before, in potential . . . yet there should be something more, something it had learned in its fall, or something left by its enemies (if there ever were such).

Long seconds probing the archives. There were gaps, checksums damaged. Some of the damage was age . . .

Outside, the container ship and the frigate lifted from the landing field, rising on silent agravs above the plains of gray on gray, of ruins five billion years old. Almost half of the humans were aboard those craft. Their escape attempt, so carefully concealed. The effort had been humored till now; it was not quite time for the flowering, and the humans were still of some use.

Below the level of supreme consciousness, its paranoid inclinations rampaged through the humans' databases. Checking, just to be sure. Just to be sure. The humans' oldest local network used light speed connections. Thousands of microseconds were spent (*wasted*) bouncing around it, sorting the trivia . . . finally spotting one incredible item:

Inventory: *quantum data container, quantity (1)*, loaded to the frigate one hundred hours before!

And all the newborn's attention turned upon the fleeing vessels. Microbes, but suddenly pernicious. *How could this happen?* A million schedules were suddenly advanced. An orderly flowering was out of the question now, and so there was no more need for the humans left in the Lab.

The change was small for all its cosmic significance. For the humans remaining around, a moment of horror, staring at their displays, realizing that all their fears were true (not realizing how much worse was true).

Five seconds, ten seconds, more change than ten thousand years of a human civilization. A billion trillion constructions, mold curling out from every wall, rebuilding what had been merely superhuman. This was as powerful as a proper flowering, though not quite so finely tuned.

And never lose sight of the reason for haste: the frigate. It had switched to rocket drive, blasting heedless away from the wallowing freighter. *Somehow*, these microbes knew they were rescuing more than themselves. The warship had the best navigation computers that little minds could make. But it would be another three seconds before it could make its first ultradrive hop.

The new Power had no weapons on the ground, nothing but a comm laser. That could not even melt steel at the frigate's range. No matter, the laser was aimed, tuned civilly

5

on the retreating warship's receiver. No acknowledgment. The humans knew what communication would bring. The laser light flickered here and there across the hull, lighting smoothness and inactive sensors, sliding across the ship's ultradrive spines. Searching, probing. The Power had never bothered to sabotage the external hull, but that was no problem. Even this crude machine had thousands of robot sensors scattered across its surface, reporting status and danger, driving utility programs. Most were shut down now, the ship fleeing nearly blind. They thought by not looking that they could be safe.

One more second and the frigate would attain interstellar safety.

The laser flickered on a failure sensor, a sensor that reported critical changes in one of the ultradrive spines. Its interrupts could not be ignored if the star jump were to succeed. Interrupt honored. Interrupt handler running, looking out, receiving more light from the laser far below . . . a backdoor into the ship's code, installed when the newborn had subverted the humans' groundside equipment . . .

. . . and the Power was aboard, with milliseconds to spare. Its agents – not even human equivalent on this primitive hardware – raced through the ship's automation, shutting down, aborting. There would be no jump. Cameras in the ship's bridge showed widening of eyes, the beginning of a scream. The humans knew, to the extent that horror can live in a fraction of a second.

There would be no jump. Yet the ultradrive was already committed. There would be a jump attempt, without automatic control a doomed one. Less than five milliseconds till the jump discharge, a mechanical cascade that no software could finesse. The newborn's agents flitted everywhere across the ship's computers, futilely attempting a shutdown. Nearly a light-second away, under the gray rubble at the High Lab, the Power could only watch. So. The frigate would be destroyed.

So slow and so fast. A fraction of a second. The fire spread out from the heart of the frigate, taking both peril and possibility.

Two hundred thousand kilometers away, the clumsy container vessel made its own ultradrive jump and vanished from sight. The newborn scarcely noticed. So a few humans had escaped; the universe was welcome to them.

In the seconds that followed, the newborn felt ... emotions? ... things that were more, and less, than a human might feel. Try emotions:

Elation. The newborn knew that now it would survive.

Horror. How close it had come to dying once more.

Frustration. Perhaps the strongest, the closest to its mere human echo. Something of significance had died with the frigate, something from this archive. Memories were dredged from the context, reconstructed: What was lost might have made the newborn still more powerful ... but more likely was deadly poison. After all, this Power had lived once before, then been reduced to nothing. What was lost might have been the reason.

Suspicion. The newborn should not have been so fooled. Not by mere humans. The newborn convulsed into self-inspection and panic. Yes, there were blindspots, carefully installed from the beginning, and not by the humans. *Two* had been born here. Itself ... and the poison, the reason for its fall of old. The newborn inspected itself as never before, knowing now just what to seek. Destroying, purifying, rechecking, searching for signs of the poison, and destroying again.

Relief. Defeat had been so close, but now ...

Minutes and hours passed, the enormous stretch of time necessary for physical construction: communications systems, transportation. The new Power's mood drifted, calmed. A human might call the feeling triumph, anticipation. Simple hunger might be more accurate. What more is needed when there are no enemies?

The newborn looked across the stars, planning. *This time things will be different.*

Part 1

I

The coldsleep itself was dreamless. Three days ago they had been getting ready to leave, and now they were here. Little Jefri complained about missing all the action, but Johanna Olsndot was glad she'd been asleep; she had known some of the grownups on the other ship.

Now Johanna drifted between the racks of sleepers. Waste heat from the coolers made the darkness infernally hot. Scabby gray mold grew on the walls. The coldsleep boxes were tightly packed, with narrow float spaces every tenth row. There were places where only Jefri could reach. Three hundred and nine children lay there, all the kids except herself and her brother Jefri.

The sleep boxes were light-duty hospital models. Given proper ventilation and maintenance, they would have been good for a hundred years, but . . . Johanna wiped her face and looked at a box's readout: Like most of the ones on the inside rows, this was in bad shape. For twenty days it had kept the boy inside safely suspended, and would probably kill him if he stayed one day more. The box's cooling vents were clean, but she vac'd them again – more a prayer for good luck than effective maintenance.

Mother and Dad were not to blame, though Johanna suspected that they blamed themselves. The escape had been put together with the materials at hand, at the last minute, when the experiment turned wicked. The High Lab staff had done what they could to save their children and protect against still greater disaster. And even so, things might have worked out if –

'Johanna! Daddy says there's no more time. He says to finish what you're doing an' come up here.' Jefri had stuck his head down through the hatch to shout to her.

'Okay!' She shouldn't be down here anyway; there was nothing more she could do to help her friends.

Tami and Giske and Magda ... oh, please be safe. Johanna pulled herself through the floatway, almost bumped into Jefri coming from the other direction. He grabbed her hand and hung close as they drifted toward the hatch. These last two days he hadn't cried, but he'd lost much of the independence of the last year. Now his eyes were wide. 'We're coming down near the North Pole, by all those islands and *ice*.'

In the cabin beyond the hatch, their parents were strapping themselves in. Trader Arne Olsndot looked up at her and grinned. 'Hi, kiddo. Have a seat. We'll be on the ground in less than an hour.' Johanna smiled back, almost caught by his enthusiasm. Ignore the jumble of equipment, the odors of twenty days' confinement: Daddy looked as dashing as any adventure poster. The light from the display windows glittered off the seams of his pressure suit. He was just in from outside.

Jefri pushed across the cabin, pulling Johanna behind him. He strapped into the webbing between her and their mother. Sjana Olsndot checked his restraints, then Johanna's. 'This will be interesting, Jefri. You will learn something.'

'Yes, all about ice.' He was holding Mom's hand now.

Mom smiled. 'Not today. I'm talking about the landing. This won't be like an agrav or a ballistic.' The agrav was dead. Dad had just detached their shell from the cargo barrier. They could never have landed the whole thing on one torch.

Dad did something with the hodgepodge of controls he had softwired to his dataset. Their bodies settled into the webbing. Around them the cargo shell creaked, and the girder support for the sleep boxes groaned and popped. Something rattled and banged as it 'fell' the length of the shell. Johanna guessed they were pulling about one gravity.

Jefri's gaze went from the outside display to his mother's face and then back. 'What is is like then?' He sounded curious, but there was a little tremor in his voice. Johanna almost smiled; Jefri knew he was being diverted, and was trying to play along.

'This will be pure rocket descent, powered almost all the way. See on the middle window? That camera is looking straight down. You can actually see that we're slowing down.' You could, too. Johanna guessed they weren't more than a couple of hundred kilometers up. Arne Olsndot was using the rocket glued to the back end of the cargo shell to kill all their orbital velocity. There weren't any other options. They had abandoned the cargo carrier, with its agrav and ultradrive. It had brought them far, but its control automation was failing. Some hundreds of kilometers behind them, it coasted dead along their orbit.

All they had left was the cargo shell. No wings, no agrav, no aero shielding. The shell was a hundred-tonne carton of eggs balanced on one hot torch.

Mom wasn't describing it quite that way to Jefri, though what she said was the truth. Somehow she had Jefri seeming to forget the danger. Sjana Olsndot had been a pop writer-archaeologist at Straumli Realm, before they moved to the High Lab.

Dad cut the jet, and they were in free fall again. Johanna felt a wave of nausea; ordinarily she never got space sick, but this was different. The image of land and sea in the downward window slowly grew. There were only a few scattered clouds. The coastline was an indefinite recursion of islands and straits and inlets. Dark green spread along the coast and up the valleys, shading to black and gray in the mountains. There was snow – and probably Jefri's ice – scattered in arcs and patches. It was all so beautiful . . . and they were falling *straight into it!*

She heard metallic banging on the cargo shell as the trim jets tipped their craft around, aligning the main jet downwards. The right-hand window showed the ground now. The torch lit again, at something like one gravity. The edge of the display darkened in a burnout halo. 'Wow,' said Jefri. 'It's like an elevator, down and down and down and . . .' One hundred kilometers down, slow enough that aero forces wouldn't tear them apart.

Sjana Olsndot was right; it was a novel way to descend from orbit, not a preferred method under any normal circumstances.

It was certainly not intended in the original escape plans. They were to meet with the High Lab's frigate – and all the adults who could escape from the High Lab. And of course, that rendezvous was to be in space, an easy transfer. But the frigate was gone now, and they were on their own. Her eyes turned unwillingly to the stretch of hull beyond her parents. There was the familiar discoloration. It looked like gray fungus . . . growing out of the clean hull ceramic. Her parents didn't talk about it much even now, except to shoo Jefri away from it. But Johanna had overheard them once, when they thought she and her brother were at the far end of the shell. Dad's voice almost crying with anger. 'All this for nothing!' he said softly. 'We made a monster, and ran, and now we're lost at the Bottom.' And Mom's voice even softer: 'For the thousandth time, Arne, not for nothing. We have the kids.' She waved at the roughness that spread across the wall, 'And given the dreams . . . the directions . . . we had, I think this was the best we could hope for. Somehow we are carrying the answer to all the evil we started.' Then Jefri had bounced loudly across the hold, proclaiming his imminent entrance, and his parents had shut up. Johanna hadn't quite had the courage to ask them about it. There had been strange things at the High Lab, and toward the end, some quietly scary things; even people who were not quite the same.

Minutes passed. They were deep in the atmosphere now. The hull buzzed with the force of the air stream – or turbulence from the jet? But things were steady enough that Jefri was beginning to get restless. Much of the down-looking view was burned out by airglow around the torch. The rest was clearer and more detailed than anything they had seen from orbit. Johanna wondered how often a new-visited world had been landed upon with less reconnaissance than this. They had no telescopic cameras, and no ferrets.

Physically, the planet was near the human ideal – wonderful good luck after all the bad.

It was heaven compared to the airless rocks of the system that had been the prime rendezvous.

On the other hand, there was intelligent life here: From orbit, they could see roads and towns. But there was no evidence of technic civilization; there was no sign of aircraft or radio or intense power sources.

They were coming down in a thinly populated corner of the continent. With luck there would be no one to see their landing among the green valleys and the black and white peaks – and Arne Olsndot could fly the torch right to ground without fear of hurting much more than forest and grass.

The coastal islands slid past the side camera's view. Jefri shouted, pointing. It was gone now, but she had seen it too: on one of the islands an irregular polygon of walls and shadow. It reminded her of castles from the Age of Princesses on Nyjora.

She could see individual trees now, their shadows long in slanting sunlight. The roar of the torch was as loud as anything she had ever heard; they were deep in atmosphere, and they weren't moving away from the sound.

'. . . things get tricky,' Dad shouted. 'And no programs to make things right . . . Where to, Love?'

Mom looked back and forth between the display windows. As far as Johanna knew, they couldn't move the cameras or assign new ones. '. . . that hill, above the timber line, but . . . think I saw a pack of animals running away from the blast on . . . west side.'

'Yeah,' shouted Jefri, '*wolves*.' Johanna had only had a quick glimpse of moving specks.

They were in full hover now, maybe a thousand meters above the hilltops. The noise was painful, unending; further talk was impossible. They drifted slowly across the landscape, partly to reconnoiter, partly to stay out of the plume of superheated air that rose about them.

The land was more rolling than craggy, and the 'grass' looked mossy. Still Arne Olsndot hesitated. The main torch was designed for velocity matching after interstellar jumps; they could hang like this for a good while. But when they did touch down, they'd better have it right. She'd heard her

15

parents talking that one over – when Jefri was working with the coldsleep boxes and out of earshot. If there was too much water in the soil, the backsplash would be a steam cannon, punching right through the shell. Landing in trees would have some dubious pluses, maybe giving them a little cushioning and a standoff from the splash. But now they were going for direct contact. At least they could see where they were landing.

Three hundred meters. Dad dragged the torch tip through the ground cover. The soft landscape exploded. A second later their boat rocked in the column of steam. The down-looking camera died. They didn't back off, and after a moment the battering eased; the torch had burned through whatever water table or permafrost lay below them. The cabin air grew steadily hotter.

Olsndot brought them slowly down through it, using the side cameras and the sound of the backsplash as his guides. He cut the torch. There was a scary half-second fall, then the sound of the rendezvous pylons hitting ground. They steadied, then one side groaned, giving way a little.

Silence, except for heat pinging around the hull. Dad looked at their ad hoc pressure gauge. He grinned at Mom. 'No breach. I bet I could even take this baby up again!'

2

An hour's difference either way and Peregrine Wick-wrackrum's life would have been very different.

The three travelers were headed west, down from the Icefangs towards Flenser's Castle on Hidden Island. There were times in his life when he couldn't have borne the company, but in the last decade Peregrine had become much more sociable. He *liked* traveling with others nowadays. On his last trek through the Great Sandy, there had been five packs in his party. Part of that had been a matter of safety: some deaths are almost inevitable when the distance between oases can be a thousand miles – and the oases themselves are transient. But aside from safety, he had learned a lot in conversation with the others.

He was not so happy with his current companions. Neither were truly pilgrims; both had secrets. Scriber Jaqueramaphan was fun, an amusing goofball and font of uncoordinated information . . . There was also a good chance he was a spy. That was okay, as long as people didn't think Peregrine was working with him. The third of their party was the one who really bothered him. Tyrathect was a newby, not all together yet; she had no taken name. Tyrathect claimed to be a school teacher, but somewhere in her (him? gender preference wasn't entirely clear yet) was a killer. The creature was obviously a Flenserist fanatic, standoffish and rigid much of the time. Almost certainly, she was fleeing the purge that followed Flenser's unsuccessful attempt to take power in the east.

He'd run into these two at Eastgate, on the Republican side of the Icefangs. They both wanted to visit the Castle on Hidden Island. And what the hell, that was only a sixty-mile detour off the main trail to Woodcarvers; they all would have to cross the mountains. Besides, he had wanted to visit Flenser's Domain for years. Maybe one of these two could get him in. So much of the world reviled the Flenserists. Peregrine Wickwrackrum was of two minds about evil: when enough rules get broken, sometimes there is good amid the carnage.

This afternoon, they'd finally come in sight of the coastal islands. Peregrine had been here only fifty years before. Even so, he wasn't prepared for the beauty of this land. The Northwest Coast was by far the mildest arctic in the world. In high summer, with unending day, the bottoms of the glacier-reamed valleys turned all to green. God the carver had stooped to touch these lands . . . and His chisels had been made of ice. Now, all that was left of the ice and snow were misty arcs at the eastern horizon and remnant patches scattered on the near hills. Those patches melted and melted through the summer, starting little creeks that merged with one another to cascade down the steep sides of the valleys. On his right, Peregrine trotted across a level stretch of ground that was soggy with standing water. The chill on his feet felt wonderful; he didn't even mind the midges that swirled around him.

Tyrathect was paralleling his course, but above the heather line. She'd been fairly talkative till the valley curved and the farmland and the islands came into view. Somewhere out there was Flenser's Castle, and her dark appointment.

Scriber Jaqueramaphan had been all over, mindlessly running around. He'd collect in twos or threes and execute some jape that made even the dour Tyrathect laugh, then climb to a height and report what he saw beyond. He'd been the first to see the coast. That had sobered him some. His clowning was dangerous enough without doing it in the neighborhood of known rapists.

Wickwrackrum called a pause, and got himself together to adjust the straps on his backpacks. The rest of the afternoon was going to be tense. He'd have to decide whether he really wanted to enter the Castle with his friends. There are limits to an adventurous spirit, even in a pilgrim.

'Hey, do you hear something bass?' called Tyrathect. Peregrine listened. There was a rumbling – powerful, but almost below his range of hearing. For an instant, fear crossed his puzzlement. A century before, he'd been in a monster earthquake. This sound was similar, but the ground did not move beneath his feet. Would that mean no landslides and flashfloods? He hunkered down, looking out in all directions.

'It's in the *sky!*' Jaqueramaphan was pointing.

A spot of glare hung almost overhead, a tiny spear of light. No memories, not even legends, came to Wickwrackrum's mind. He spread out, all eyes on the slowly moving light. *God's Choir*. It must be *miles* up, and still he heard it. He looked away from the light, afterimages dancing painfully in his eyes.

'It's getting brighter, louder,' said Jaqueramaphan. 'I think it's coming down on the hills yonder, on the coast.'

Peregrine pulled himself together and ran west, shouting to the others. He would get as close as was safe, and watch. He didn't look up again. It was just too bright. It cast shadows

18

in broad daylight!

He ran another half mile. The star was still in the air. He couldn't remember a falling star so slow, though some of the biggest made terrible explosions. In fact . . . there were no stories from folks who had been near such things. His wild, pilgrim curiosity faded before that recollection. He looked in all directions. Tyrathect was nowhere in sight; Jaqueramaphan was huddled next to some boulders ahead.

And the light was so bright that where his clothes did not protect him, Wickwrackrum felt a blaze of heat. The noise from the sky was outright pain now. Peregrine dived over the edge of the valley side, rolled and staggered and fell down the steep walls of rock. He was in the shade now: only sunlight lay upon him! The far side of the valley shone in the glare; crisp shadows moved with the unseen thing behind him. The noise was still a bass rumble, but so loud it numbed the mind. Peregrine stumbled past the timberline, and continued till he was sheltered by a hundred yards of forest. That shuld have helped a lot, but the noise was all growing *still louder* . . .

Mercifully, he blacked out for a moment or two. When he came around, the star sound was gone. The ringing it left in his tympana was a great confusion. He staggered about in a daze. It seemed to be raining – except that some of the droplets glowed. Little fires were starting here and there in the forest. He hid beneath dense-crowned trees till the burning rocks stopped falling. The fires didn't spread; the summer had been relatively wet.

Peregrine lay quietly, waiting for more burning rocks or new star noise. Nothing. The wind in the tree tops lessened. He could hear the birds and crickers and woodborers. He walked to the forest edge and peeked out in several places. Discounting the patches of burnt heather, everything looked normal. But his viewpoint was very restricted: he could see high valley walls, a few hilltops. *Ha!* There was Scriber Jaqueramaphan, three hundred yards further up. Most of him was hunkered down in holes and hollows, but he had a couple of members looking toward where the star had fallen. Peregrine squinted. Scriber was such a buffoon most of the time. But sometimes it just seemed a cover; if he really was a fool, he was one with a streak of genius. More than once, Wicky had seen him at a distance, working in pairs with some strange tool . . . As now: the other was holding something long and pointed to his eye.

Wickwrackrum crept out of the forest, keeping close together and making as little noise as possible. He climbed carefully around the rocks, slipping from hummock to heather hummock, till he was just short of the valley crest and some fifty yards from Jaqueramaphan. He could hear the other thinking to himself. Any closer, and Scriber would hear *him*, even bunched up and quiet as he was.

'*Ssst!*' said Wickwrackrum.

The buzzing and muttering stopped in an instant of shocked surprise. Jaqueramaphan stuffed the mysterious seeing tool into a backpack and pulled himself together, thinking very quietly. They stared at each other for a moment, then Scriber made silly swirling gestures at his shoulder tympana. *Listen up*. 'Can you talk like this?' His voice came very high-pitched, up where some people can't make voluntary conversation, where low-sound ears are deaf. Hightalk could be confusing, but it was very directional and faded quickly with distance; no one else would hear them. Peregrine nodded. 'Hightalk is no problem.' The trick was to use tones pure enough not to confuse.

'Take a look over the hill crest, friend pilgrim. There is something new under the sun.'

Peregrine moved up another thirty yards, keeping a lookout in all directions. He could see the straits now, gleaming rough silver in the afternoon sunlight. Behind him, the north side of the valley was lost in shadow. He sent one member ahead, skittering between the hummocks to look down on the plain where the star had landed.

God's Choir, he thought to himself (but quietly). He brought up another member to get a parallax view. The thing looked like a huge adobe hut mounted on stilts . . . But this was the fallen star: the ground beneath it glowed dull red. Curtains of mist rose from the moist heather all around. The torn earth had been thrown in long lines that radiated from a spot beneath it.

He nodded at Jaqueramaphan. 'Where is Tyrathect?'

Scriber shrugged. 'Way back, I'll bet. I'm keeping an eye out for her . . . Do you see the others though, the troopers from Flenser's Castle?'

'No!' Peregrine looked west from the landing site. There. They were almost a mile away, in camouflage jackets, belly-crawling across the hummocky terrain. He could see at least three troopers. They were big guys, six each. 'How could they get here so fast?' He glanced at the sun. 'It can't be more than half an hour since all this started.'

'Their good luck.' Jaqueramaphan returned to the crest and looked over. 'I'll bet they were already on the mainland when the star came down. This is all Flenser territory; they must have patrols.' He hunkered down so just two pairs of eyes would be visible to those below. 'That's an ambush formation, you know.'

'You don't seem very happy to see them. These are your friends, remember? The people you've come to see.'

Scriber cocked his heads sarcastically. 'Yeah, yeah. Don't rub it in. I think you've known from the beginning that I'm not all for Flenser.'

'I guessed.'

'Well, the game is over now. Whatever came down this afternoon is worth more to . . . uh, my friends than anything I could have learned on Hidden Island.'

'What about Tyrathect?'

'Heh, heh. Our esteemed companion is more than genuine, I fear. I'd bet she's a Flenser Lord, not the low-rank Servant she seems at first glance. I expect that many of her kind are leaking back over the mountains these days, happy to get out of the Long Lakes Republic. Hide your behinds, fellow. If she spots us, those troopers will get us sure.'

Peregrine moved deeper into the hollows and burrows that pocked the heather. He had an excellent view back along the valley. If Tyrathect were not already on the scene, he'd see her long before she would him.

'Peregrine?'

'Yes?'

'You're a pilgrim. You've traveled the world . . . since the beginning of time, you'd have us believe. How far do your memories really go back?'

Given the situation, Wickwrackrum was inclined to honesty. 'Like you'd expect: a few hundred years. Then we're talking about legends, recollections of things that probably happened, but with the details all mixed and muddled.'

'Well, I haven't traveled much, and I'm fairly new. But I do read. *A lot.* There's never been anything like this before. That is a *made* thing down there. It came from higher than I can measure. You've read Aramstriquesa or Astrologer Belelele? You know what this could be?'

Wickwrackrum didn't recognize the names. But he *was* a pilgrim. There were lands so far away that no one there spoke any language he knew. In the Southseas he met folk who thought there was no world beyond their islands and who ran from his boats when he came ashore. Even more, one part of him had *been* an islander and had watched that landing.

He stuck a head into the open and looked again at the fallen star, the visitor from farther than he had ever been . . . and he wondered where this pilgrimage might end.

3

It took five hours for the ground to cool enough for Dad to slide the ladder-ramp to ground. He and Johanna climbed carefully down, hopped across the steaming earth to stand on relatively undamaged turf. It would be a long time before this ground cooled completely; the jet's exhaust was very 'clean,' scarcely interacting with normal matter – all of which meant that some very hot rock extended down thousands of meters beneath their boat.

Mom sat in the hatchway, watching the land beyond them. She had Dad's old pistol.

'Anything?' Dad shouted to her.

'No. And Jefri doesn't see anything through the windows.'

Dad walked around the cargo shell, inspecting the misused

docking pylons. Every ten meters they stopped and set up a sound projecter. That had been Johanna's idea. Besides Dad's gun, they really had no weapons. The projectors were accidental cargo, stuff from the infirmary. With a little programming, they could put out wild screeching all up and down the audio spectrum. It might be enough to scare off the local animals. Johanna followed her father, her eyes on the landscape, her nervousness giving way to awe. It was so beautiful, so cool. They were standing on a broad field, in high hills. Westward the hills fell toward straits and islands. To the north the ground ended abruptly at the edge of a wide valley; she could see waterfalls on the other side. The ground felt spongy beneath her feet. Their landing field was puckered into thousands of little hillocks, like waves caught in a still picture. Snow lay in timid patches across the higher hills. Johanna squinted north, into the sun. North?

'What time is it, Daddy?'

Olsndot laughed, still looking at the underside of the cargo shell. 'Local midnight.'

Johanna had been brought up in the middle latitudes of Straum. Most of her school field trips had been to space, where odd sun geometries were no big deal. Somehow she had never thought of such things happening on the ground . . . *I mean, seeing the sun right over the top of the world.*

The first order of business was to get half the coldsleep boxes out into the open, and rearrange those left aboard. Mom figured that the temperature problems would just about disappear then, even for the boxes left on board: 'Having separate power supplies and venting will be an advantage now. The kids will all be safe, Johanna, you check Jefri's work on the ones inside, okay? . . .'

The second order of business would be to start a tracking program on the Relay system, and to set up ultralight communication. Johanna was a little afraid of that step. What would they learn? They already knew the High Lab had gone wicked and the disaster Mom predicted had begun.

How much of Straumli Realm was dead now? Everyone at the High Lab had thought they were doing so much good, and now . . . *Don't think about it*. Maybe the Relayers could help. Somewhere there must be people who could use what her folks had taken from the Lab.

They'd be rescued, and the rest of the kids would be revived. She'd been feeling guilty about that. Sure, Mom and Dad needed extra hands right at the end of the flight – and Johanna was one of the oldest children in the school. But it seemed wrong that she and Jefri were the only kids going into this with their eyes open. Coming down, she had felt her mother's fear. *I bet they wanted us together, even if it was only for one last time*. The landing had been truly dangerous, however easy Dad made it look. Johanna could see where the backsplash had gouged the hull; if any of that had gotten past the torch and into the exhaust chamber, they'd all be vapor now.

Almost half the coldsleep boxes were on the ground now, by the east side of the boat. Mom and Dad were spreading them out so the coolers would have no problem. Jefri was inside, checking if there were any other boxes that needed attention. He was a good kid when he wasn't a brat. She turned into the sunlight, felt the cool breeze flowing across the hill. She heard something that sounded like a birdcall.

Johanna was out by one of the sound projectors when the ambush happened. She had her dataset plugged to its control and was busy giving it new directions. It showed how little they had left, that even her old dataset was important now. But Dad wanted the projectors to sweep through the broadest possible bandwidth, making plenty of racket all the way, but with big spikes every so often; her Pink Olifaunt could certainly manage that.

'Johanna!' Mom's cry came simultaneous with the sound of breaking ceramic. The projector's bell came shattering down beside her. Johanna looked up. Something ripped through her chest just inside her shoulder, knocking her down. She stared stupidly at the shaft that stuck out of her. An *arrow!*

The west edge of their landing are was swarming with . . . things. Like wolves or dogs, but with long necks, they moved quickly forward, darting from hummock to hummock. Their pelts were the same gray green of the hillside, except near their haunches where she saw white and black. No, the green was clothing, *jackets*. Johanna was in shock, the pressure of the bolt through her chest not yet registering as pain. She had been thrown back against uptilted turf and for the moment had a view of the whole attack. She saw more arrows rise up, dark lines floating in the sky.

She could see the archers now. More dogs! They moved in packs. It took two of them to use a bow – one to hold it and one to draw. The third and fourth carried quivers of arrows and just seemed to watch.

The archers hung back, staying mostly under cover. Other packs swirled in from the sides, now leaping over the hummocks. Many carried hatchets in their jaws. Metal tines gleamed on their paws. She heard the *snickety* of Dad's pistol. The wave of attackers staggered as individuals collapsed. The others continued forward, snarling now. These were sounds of madness, not the barking of dogs. She felt the sounds in her teeth, like *blasti* music punching from a large speaker. Jaws and claws and knives and noise.

She twisted on her side, trying to see back to the boat. Now the pain was real. She screamed, but the sound was lost in the madness. The mob raced around her, heading for Mom and Dad. Her parents were crouched behind a rendezvous pylon. There was a constant flicker from the pistol in Arne Olsndot's hand. His pressure suit had protected him from the arrows.

The alien bodies were piling high. The pistol, with its smart flechettes, was deadly effective. She saw him hand the pistol to Mom and run out from under the boat, toward her. Johanna stretched her free arm towards him and cried, screamed for him to go back.

Thirty meters. Twenty-five. Mom's covering fire swept around them, driving the wolves back. A flurry of arrows descended on Olsndot as he ran, arms upheld to shield his head. Twenty meters.

A wolf jumped high over Johanna. She had a quick glimpse of its short fur and scarred rear end. It raced straight for Dad. Olsndot weaved, trying to give his wife a clear shot, but the wolf was too quick. It jinked with him, sprinting across the gap. It leaped, metal glittering on its paws. Johanna saw red splash from Daddy's neck, and then the two of them were down.

For a moment, Sjana Olsndot stopped shooting. That was enough. The mob parted and a large group ran purposefully toward the boat. They had tanks of some kind on their backs. The lead animal held a hose in its mouth. A dark liquid jetted out . . . and vanished in an explosion of fire. The wolf pack played their crude flamethrower across the ground, across the pylon where Sjana Olsndot stood, across the ranks of school children in coldsleep. Johanna saw something moving, twisting in the flames and tarry smoke, saw the light plastic of the coldsleep boxes slump and flow.

Johanna turned her face to the earth, then pushed herself up on her good arm and tried to crawl toward the boat, the flames. And then the dark was merciful, and she remembered no more.

4

Peregrine and Scriber watched the ambush preparations throughout the afternoon: infantry arrayed on the slope west of the landing site, archers behind them, flame troopers in pounce formation. Did the Lords of Flenser's Castle understand what they were up against? The two debated the question off and on. Jaqueramaphan thought the Flenserists did, that their arrogance was so great that they simply expected to grab the prize. 'They go for the throat before the other side even knows there's a fight. It's worked before.'

Peregrine didn't answer immediately. Scriber could be right. It had been fifty years since he had been in this part of the world. Back then, Flenser's cult had been obscure (and not that interesting compared to what existed elsewhere).

Treachery did sometimes befall travelers, but it was rarer than the stay-at-homes would believe. Most people were friendly and enjoyed hearing about the world beyond – especially if the visitor was not threatening. When treachery did occur, it was most often after an initial 'sizing-up' to determine just how powerful the visitors were and what could be gained from their death. Immediate attack, without conversation, was very rare. Usually it meant you had run into villains who were both sophisticated . . . and crazy. 'I don't know. That *is* an ambush formation, but maybe the Flenserists will hold it in reserve, and talk first.'

Hours passed; the sun slid sideways into the north. There was noise from the far side of the fallen star. Crap. They couldn't see anything from here.

The hidden troops made no move. The minutes passed . . . and they got their first view of the visitor from heaven, or part of him anyway. There were four legs per member, but it walked on its *rear* legs only. What a clown! Yet . . . it used its front paws for holdling things. Not once did he see it use a mouth; he doubted if the flat jaws could get a good hold, anyway. Those forepaws were wonderfully agile. A single member could easily use tools.

There were plenty of conversation sounds, even though only three members were visible. After a while, they heard the much higher pitched tones of organized thought; God, the creature was noisy. At this distance, the sounds were muffled and distorted. Even so, they were like no mind he had ever heard, nor like the confusion noises that some grazers made.

'Well?' hissed Jaqueramaphan.

'I have been all around the world – and this creature is not part of it.'

'Yeah. Well, it reminds me of mantis bugs. You know, about this high –' he opened a mouth about two inches wide. 'Great for keeping your garden free of pests . . . great little killers.'

Ugh. Peregrine hadn't thought of the resemblance. Mantises were cute and harmless – as far as people were concerned. But he knew the females would eat their own mates. Imagine such creatures grown to giant size, and possessed of pack mentality. Maybe it was just as well they couldn't go prancing down to say hello.

A half hour passed. As the alien brought its cargo to ground, the Flenser archers moved closer; the infantry packs arranged themselves in assault wings.

A flight of arrows arched across the gap between the Flenserists and the alien. One of the alien members went down immediately, and its thoughts quieted. The rest moved out of sight beneath the flying house. The troopers dashed forward, spaced in identity-preserving formations; perhaps they meant to take the alien alive.

. . . But the assault line crumpled, many yards short of the alien: no arrows, no flames – the troopers just fell. For a moment Peregrine thought the Flenserists might have bit off more than they could chew. Then the second wave ran over the first. Members continued to fall, but they were in killing frenzy now, with only animal discipline left. The assault rolled slowly forward, the rear climbing over the fallen. Another alien member down . . . Strange, he could still hear wisps of the other's thought. In tone and tempo, it sounded the same as before the attack. How could anyone be so composed with total death looming?

A combat whistle sounded, and the mob parted. A trooper raced through and sprayed liquid fire the instant it was past the front. The flying house looked like meat on a griddle, flame and smoke coming up all around it.

Wickwrackrum swore to himself. Good-bye alien.

The wrecked and wounded were low on the Flenserist priority list. Seriously wounded were piled onto travoises and pulled far enough away so their cries would not cause confusion. Cleanup squads bullied the trooper fragments away from the flying house. The frags wandered the hummocky meadow; here and there they coalesced into ad hoc packs. Some drifted among the wounded, ignoring the screams in their need to find themselves.

When the tumult was quieted, three packs of whitejackets appeared. The Servants of the Flenser walked under the flying house. One was out of sight for a long while; perhaps it even got inside. The charred bodies of two alien members were carefully placed on travoises – more carefully than the wounded troopers had been – and hauled off.

Jaqueramaphan scanned the ruins with his eye-tool. He

had given up trying to hide it from Peregrine. A whitejackets carried something from under the flying house. 'Sst! There are other dead ones. Maybe from the fire. They look like pups.' The small figures had the mantis form. They were strapped into travoises and hauled out of sight over the hill's edge. No doubt they had kherhog-drawn carts down there.

The Flenserists set a sentry ring around the landing site. Dozens of fresh troopers stood on the hillside beyond it. No one was going to sneak past that.

'So it's total murder.' Peregrine sighed.

'Maybe not . . . The first member they shot, I don't think it's quite dead.'

Wickwrackrum squinted his best eyes. Either Scriber was a wishful thinker, or his tool gave him amazingly sharp sight. The first one hit had been on the other side of the craft. The member had stopped thinking, but that wasn't a sure sign of death. There was a whitejackets standing around it now. The whitejackets put the creature onto a travois and began pulling it away from the landing site, towards the southwest . . . not quite the same path that the others had taken.

'The thing *is* still alive! It's got an arrow in the chest, but I can see it breathing.' Scriber's heads turned toward Wickwrackrum, 'I think we should rescue it.'

For a moment Peregrine couldn't think of anything to say; he just gaped at the other. The center of Flenser's worldwide cabal was just a few miles to the northwest. Flenserist power was undisputed for dozens of miles inland, and right now they were virtually surrounded by an army. Scriber wilted a little before Peregrine's astonishment, but it was clear he was not joking. 'Sure, I know it's risky. But that's what life is all about, right? You're a pilgrim. You understand.'

'Hmf. That was the pilgrim reputation, all right. But no soul can survive total death – and there were plenty of opportunities for such annihilation on a pilgrimage. Pilgrims do know caution.

And yet – and yet this was the most marvelous encounter in all his centuries of pilgrimage. To know these aliens, to *become* them . . . it was a temptation that surpassed all good sense.

'Look,' said Scriber, 'we could just go down and mingle

with the wounded. If we can make it across the field, we might get a closer look at that last alien member without risking too much.' Jaqueramaphan was already backing down from his observation point, and circling around to find a path that wouldn't put him in silhouette. Wickwrackrum was torn; part of him got up to follow and part of him hesitated. Hell, Jaqueramaphan had admitted to being a spy; he carried an invention that was probably straight from the Long Lakes sharpest intelligence people. The guy had to be a pro . . .

Peregrine took a quick look around their side of the hill and across the valley. No sign of Tyrathect or anyone else. He crawled out of his various hidey holes and followed the spy.

As much as possible, they stayed in the deep shadows cast by the northering sun, and slipped from hummock to hummock where there was no shade. Just before they got to the first of the wounded, Scriber said something more, the scariest words of the afternoon. 'Hey, don't worry. I've read all about doing this sort of thing!'

A mob of frags and wounded is a terrifying, mind-numbing thing. Singletons, duos, trios, a few quads: they wandered aimlessly, keening without control. In most situations, this many people packed together on just a few acres would have been an instant choir. In fact, he did notice some sexual activity and some organized browsing, but for the most part there was still too much pain for normal reactions. Wickwrackrum wondered briefly if – for all their talk of rationalism – the Flenserists would just leave the wreckage of their troops to reassemble itself. They'd have some strange and crippled repacks if they did.

A few yards into the mob and Peregrine Wickwrackrum could feel consciousness slipping from him. If he concentrated really hard, he could remember who he was and that he must get to the other side of the meadow without attracting attention.

Other thoughts, loud and unguarded, pummeled him:
. . . *Blood lust and slashing* . . .
Glittering metal in the alien's hand . . . *the pain in her chest* . . . *coughing blood, falling* . . .

. . . Boot camp and before, my merge brother was so good to me . . . Lord Steel said that we are a grand experiment . . .

Running across the heather toward the stick-limbed monster. Leap, tines in paw. Slash the monster's throat. Blood spouts high.

. . . Where am I? . . . May I be part of you . . . please?

Peregrine whirled at that last question. It was pointed and near. A singleton was sniffing at him. He screeched the fragment off, and ran into an open space. Up ahead, Jaquewhat's-his-name was scarcely better off. There was little chance they would be spotted here, but he was beginning to wonder if he could make it through. Peregrine was only four and there were singletons everywhere. On his right a quad was raping, grabbing at whatever duos and singles happened by. Wic and Kwk and Rac and Rum tried to remember just why they was here and where they was going. *Concentrate on direct sensation; what is really here:* the sooty smell of the flamer's liquid fire . . . the midges swarming everywhere, clotting the puddles of blood all black.

An awfully long time passed. Minutes.

Wic-Kwk-Rac-Rum looked ahead. He was almost out of it; the south edge of the wreckage. He dragged himself to a patch of clean ground. Parts of him vomited, and he collapsed. Sanity slowly returned. Wickwrackrum looked up, saw Jaqueramaphan just inside the mob. Scriber was a big fellow, a sixsome, but he was having at least as bad a time as Peregrine. He staggered from side to side, eyes wide, snapping at himself and others.

Well, they had made it a good way across the meadow, and fast enough to catch up with the whitejackets who was pulling the last alien member. If they wanted to see anything more, they'd have to figure how to leave the mob without attracting attention. Hmm. There were plenty of Flenserist uniforms around . . . without living owners. Peregrine walked two of himself over to where a dead trooper lay.

'Jaqueramaphan! Here!' The great spy looked in his direction, and a glint of intelligence returned to his eyes. He stumbled out of the mob and sat down a few yards from Wickwrackrum. It was far nearer than would normally be comfortable, but after what they'd been through, it seemed barely close. He lay for a moment, gasping. 'Sorry, I never guessed it would be like that. I lost part of me back there . . . never thought I'd get her back.'

Peregrine watched the progress of the whitejackets and its travois. It wasn't going with the others; in a few seconds it would be out of sight. With a disguise, maybe they *could* follow and – no, it was just too risky. He was beginning to think like the great spy. Peregrine pulled a camouflage jacket off a corpse. They would still need disguises. Maybe they could hang around here through the night, and get a closer look at the flying house.

After a moment, Scriber saw what he was doing, and began gathering jackets for himself. They slunk between the piled bodies, looking for gear that wasn't too stained and that Jaqueramaphan thought had consistent insignia. There were plenty of paw claws and battle-axes around. They'd end up armed to the teeth, but they'd have to dump some of their backpacks . . . One more jacket was all he needed, but his Rum was so broad in the shoulders that nothing fit.

Peregrine didn't really understand what happened till later: a large fragment, a threesome, was lying doggo in the pile of dead. Perhaps it was grieving, long after its member's dying dirge; in any case, it was almost totally thoughtless until Peregrine began pulling the jacket off its dead member. Then, 'You'll not rob from mine!' He heard the buzz of nearby rage, and then there was slashing pain across his Rum's gut. Peregrine writhed in agony, leaped upon the attacker. For a moment of mindless rage, they fought. Peregrine's battle-axes slashed again and again, covering his muzzles with blood. When he came to his senses one of the three was dead, the others running into the mob of wounded.

Wickwrackrum huddled around the pain in his Rum. The attacker had been wearing tines. Rum was slashed from ribs to crotch. Wickwrackrum stumbled; some of his paws were caught in his own guts. He tried to nose the ruins back into his member's abdomen. The pain was fading, the sky in Rum's eyes slowly darkening. Peregrine stifled the screams he felt climbing within him. *I'm only four, and one of me is dying!* For years he'd been warning himself that four was just too small a

32

number for a pilgrim. Now he'd pay the price, trapped and mindless in a land of tyrants.

For a moment, the pain eased and his thoughts were clear. The fight hadn't really caused much notice amid the dirges, rapes, and simple attacks of madness. Wickwrackrum's fight had only been a little bigger and bloodier than usual. The whitejackets by the flying house had looked briefly in their direction, but were now back to tearing open the alien cargo.

Scriber was sitting nearby, watching in horror. Part of him would move a little closer, then pull back. He was fighting with himself, trying to decide whether to help. Peregrine almost pleaded with him, but the effort was too great. Besides, Scriber was no pilgrim. Giving part of himself was not something Jaqueramaphan could do voluntarily . . .

Memories came flooding now, Rum's efforts to sort things out and let the rest of him know all that had been before. For a moment, he was sailing a twinhull across the South Sea, a newby with Rum as a pup; memories of the island person who had born Rum, and of packs before that. Once around the world they had traveled, surviving the slums of a tropic collective, and the war of the Plain Herds. Ah, the stories they had heard, the tricks they had learned, the people they had met . . . Wic Kwk Rac Rum had been a terrifice combination, clear-thinking, lighthearted, with a strange ability to keep all the memories in place; that had been the real reason he had gone so long without growing to five or six. Now he would pay perhaps the greatest price of all . . .

Rum sighed, and could not see the sky anymore. Wickwrackrum's mind went, not as it does in the heat of battle when the sound of thought is lost, not as it does in the companionable murmur of sleep. There was suddenly no fourth presence, just the three, trying to make a person. The trio stood and patted nervously at itself. There was danger everywhere, but beyond its understanding. It sidled hopefully toward a sixsome sitting nearby – Jaqueramaphan? – but the other shooed it away. It looked nervously at the mob of wounded. There was completeness there . . . and madness too.

A huge male with deeply scarred haunches sat at the edge

of the mob. It caught the threesome's eye, and slowly crawled across the open space toward them. Wic and Kwk and Rac back away, their pelts puffing up in fright and fascination; the scarred one was at least half again the weight of any of them.

... *Where am I?* ... *May I be part of you* ... *please?* Its keening carried memories, jumbled and mostly inaccessible, of blood and fighting, of military training before that. Somehow, the creature was as frightened of those early memories as of anything. It lay its muzzle – caked with dried blood – on the ground and belly-crawled toward them. The other three almost ran; random coupling was something that scared all of them. They backed and backed, out onto the clear meadow. The other followed, but slowly, still crawling. Kwk licked her lips and walked back towards the stranger. She extended her neck and sniffed along the other's throat. Wic and Rac approached from the sides.

For an instant there was a partial join. *Sweaty, bloody, wounded – a melding made in hell.* The thought seemed to come from nowhere, glowed in the four for a moment of cynical humor. Then the unity was lost, and they were just three animals licking the face of a fourth.

Peregrine looked around the meadow with new eyes. He had been disintegrate for just a few minutes: The wounded from the Tenth Attack Infantry were just as before. Flenser's Servants were still busy with the alien cargo. Jaqueramaphan was slowly backing away, his expression a compound of wonder and horror. Peregrine lowered a head and hissed at him, 'I won't betray you, Scriber.'

The spy froze. 'That you, Peregrine?'

'More or less.' Peregrine still, but Wickwrackrum no more.

'H-how can you do it? Y-you just lost . . .'

'I'm a pilgrim, remember? We live with this sort of thing all our lives.' There was sarcasm in his voice; this was more or less the cliché Jaqueramaphan had been spouting earlier. But there was some truth to it. Already Peregrine Wickwrack . . . scar felt like a person. Maybe this new combination had a chance.

'Uk. Well, yes . . . What should we do now?' The spy

34

looked nervously in all directions, but his eyes on Peregrine were the most worried of all.

Now it was Wickwrackscar's turn to be puzzled. What *was* he doing here? Killing the strange enemy . . . *No.* That's what the Attack Infantry was doing. He would have nothing to do with that, no matter what the scarred one's memories. He and Scriber had come here to . . . to rescue the alien, as much of it as possible. Peregrine grabbed hold of the memory and held it uncritically; it was something real, from the past identity he must preserve. He glanced towards where he had last seen the alien member. The whitejackets and his travois were no longer visible, but he'd been heading along an obvious path.

'We can still get ourselves the live one,' he said to Jaqueramaphan.

Scriber stamped and sidled. He was not quite the enthusiast of before. 'After you, my friend.'

Wickwrackscar straightened his combat jackets and brushed off some of the dried blood. Then he strutted off across the meadow, passing just a hundred yards from the Flenser's Servants around the enemy – around the flying house. He flipped them a sharp salute, which was ignored. Jaqueramaphan followed, carrying two crossbows. The other was doing his best to imitate Peregrine's strut, but he really didn't have the right stuff.

Then they were past the military crest of the hill and descending into shadows. The sounds of the wounded were muted. Wickwrackscar broke into double time, loping from switchback to switchback as he descended the rough path. From here he could see the harbor; the boats were still at the piers, and there wasn't much activity. Behind him, Scriber was talking nervous nonsense. Peregrine just ran faster, his confidence fueled by general newby confusion. His new member, the scarred one, had been the muscle behind an infantry officer. That pack had known the layout of the harbors and the castle, and all the passwords of the day.

Two more switchbacks and they overran the Flenser Servant and his travois. 'Hallo!' shouted Peregrine. 'We bring new instructions from Lord Steel.' A chill went down his spines at the name, remembering Steel for the first time. The

Servant dropped the travois and turned to face them. Wickwrackscar didn't know his name, but he remembered the guy: fairly high-ranking, an arrogant get-of-bitches. It was a surprise to see him pulling the travois himself.

Peregrine stopped only twenty yards from the whitejackets. Jaqueramaphan was looking down from the switchback above; his bows were out of sight. The Servant looked nervously at Peregrine and up at Scriber.

'What do you two want?'

Did he suspect them already? No matter. Wickwrackscar braced himself for a killing charge . . . and suddenly he was seeing in fours, his mind blurred with newby dizziness. Now that he needed to kill, the scarred one's horror of the act undid him. Damn! Wickwrackscar cast wildly about for something to say. And now that murder was out of his mind, his new memories came easily: 'Lord Steel's will, that the creature be brought with us to the harbor. You, ah, you are to return to the invader's flying thing.'

The whitejackets licked his lips. His eyes swept sharply across Peregrine's uniforms, and Scriber's. 'Impostors!' he screamed, at the same instant lunging one of his members toward the travois. Metal glinted in the member's forepaw. *He's going to kill the alien!*

There was a bow snap from above, and the runner fell, a shaft through its eye. Wickwrackscar charged the others, forcing his scarbacked member out front. There was an instant of dizziness and then he was whole again, screaming death at the four. The two packs crashed together, Scar carrying a couple of the Servant's members over the edge of the path. Arrows hummed around them. Wic Kwk Rac twisted, slashing axes at whatever remained standing.

Then things were quiet, and Peregrine had his thoughts again. Three of the Servant's members twitched on the path, the earth around them slick with blood. He pushed them off the path, near where his Scar had killed the others. Not one of the Servant had survived; it was total death, and he was responsible. He sagged to the ground, seeing in fours again.

'The alien. It's still alive,' said Scriber. He was standing around the travois, sniffing at the mantis-like body. 'Not conscious though.' He grabbed the travois poles in his jaws and looked at Peregrine. 'What . . . what now, Pilgrim?'

Peregrine lay in the dirt, trying to put his mind back together. *What now, indeed.* How had he gotten into this mess? Newby confusion was the only possibility. He'd simply lost track of all the reasons why rescuing the alien was impossible. And now he was stuck with it. Pack crap. Part of him crawled to the edge of the path, and looked around: There was no sign they had attracted attention. In the harbor, the boats were still empty; most of the infantry was up in the hills. No doubt the Servants were holding the dead ones at the harbor fort. So when would they move them across the straits to Hidden Island? Were they waiting for this one's arrival?

'Maybe we could grab some boats, escape south,' said Scriber. What an ingenious fellow. Didn't he know that there would be sentry lines around the harbor? Even knowing the passwords, they'd be reported as soon as they passed one. It would be a million-to-one shot. But it had been a flat impossibility before Scar became part of him.

He studied the creature lying on the travois. So strange, yet real. And it was more than just the creature, though that was the most spectacular strangeness,. Its bloodied clothes were a finer fabric than the Pilgrim had ever seen. Tucked in beside the creature's body was a pink pillow with elaborate stitchery. With a twist of perspective he realized it was alien art, the face of a long-snouted animal embroidered on the pillow.

So escape through the harbor was a million-to-one-shot; some prizes might be worth such odds.

'. . . We'll go down a little farther,' he said.

Jaqueramaphan pulled the travois. Wickwrackscar strode ahead of him, trying to look important and officerly. With Scar along, it wasn't hard. The member was the picture of martial competence; you had to be on the inside to know the softness.

They were almost down to sea level.

The path was wider now and roughly paved. He knew the harbor fort was above them, hidden by the trees. The sun was well out of the north, rising into the eastern sky. Flowers were everywhere, white and red and violet, their tufts floating thick on the breeze – the arctic plant life taking advantage of its long day of summer. Walking on sun-dappled cobblestones, you might almost forget the ambush on the hilltops.

Very soon, they'd hit a sentry line. Lines and rings are interesting people; not great minds, but about the largest effective pack you'd find outside the tropics. There were stories of lines ten miles long, with thousand of members. The largest Peregrine had ever seen had fewer than one hundred: Take a group of ordinary people and train them to string out, not in packs but as individual members. If each member stayed just a few yards from its nearest neighbors, they could maintain something like the mentality of a trio. The group as a whole was scarcely brighter – you can't have much in the way of deep thoughts when it takes *seconds* for an idea to percolate across your mind. Yet the line had an excellent grasp of what was happening along itself. And if any members were attacked, the entire line would know about it with the speed of sound. Peregrine had served on lines before; it was a strung-out existence, but not nearly as dull as ordinary sentry duty. It's hard to be bored when you're as stupid as a line.

There! A lone member stuck its neck around a tree and challenged them. Wickwrackscar knew the password of course, and they were past the outer line. But that passage and their description was known to the entire line now – and surely to normal soldiers at the harbor fort.

Hell. There was no cure for it; he would go ahead with the crazy scheme. He and Scriber and the alien member passed through the two inner sentries. He could smell the sea now. They came out of the trees onto the rock-walled harbor. Silver sparkled off the water in a million changing flecks. A large multiboat bobbed between two piers. Its masts were like a forest of tilting leafless trees. Just a mile across the water they could see Hidden Island. Part of him dismissed the sight as a commonplace; part of him stumbled in awe. This was the center of it, the worldwide Flenser movement. Up in those dour towers, the original Flenser had done his experiments, written his essays . . . and schemed to rule the world.

There were a few people on the piers. Most were doing maintenance: sewing sails, relashing twinhulls. They watched the travois with sharp curiosity, but none approached. *So all we have to do is amble down to the end of the pier, cut the lashings on an outside twinhull, and take off.* There were probably enough packs on the pier alone to prevent that – and their cries would surely draw the troops he saw by the harbor fort. In fact, it was a little surprising that no one up there had taken serious notice of them yet.

These boats were cruder than the Southseas version. Part of the difference was superficial: Flenser doctrine forbade idle decoration on boats. Part of it was functional: These craft were designed for both winter and summer seasons, and for troop hauling. But he was sure he could sail them given the chance. He walked to the end of the pier. Hmm. A bit of luck. The bow-starboard twinhull, the one right next to him by the pier, looked fast and well-provisioned. It was probably a long-range scout.

'Ssst. Something's going on up there.' Scriber jerked a head toward the fort.

The troops were closing ranks – a mass salute? Five Servants swept by the infantry, and bugles sounded from the fort's towers. Scar had seen things like this, but Peregrine didn't trust the memory. How could –

A banner of red and yellow rose over the fort. On the piers, soldiers and boatworkers dropped to their bellies. Peregrine dropped and hissed to the other, '*Get down!*'

'Wha –?'

'That's Flenser's flag . . . his personal presence banner!'

'That's impossible.' Flenser had been assassinated in the Republic six tendays earlier. The mob that tore him apart had killed dozens of his top supporters at the same time . . . But it was only the word of the Republican Political Police that all Flenser's bodies had been recovered.

Up by the fort, a single pack pranced between the ranks of soldiers and whitejackets. Silver and gold glinted on its shoulders. Scriber edged a member behind a piling and surreptitiously brought out his eye-tool. After a moment: 'Soul's end . . . its *Tyrathect*.'

'She's no more the Flenser than I am,' said Peregrine. They had traveled together from Eastgate all the way across the Icefangs. She was obviously a newby, and not well-integrated. She had seemed reserved and innerlooking, but there had been rages. Peregrine knew there was a deadly streak in Tyrathect . . . Now he guessed whence it came. At least some of Flenser's members had escaped assassination, and he and Scriber had spent three tendays in its presence; Peregrine shivered.

At the fort's gate, the pack called Tyrathect turned to face the troops and Servants. She gestured, and bugles sounded again. The new Peregrine understood that signal: an Incalling. He suppressed the sudden urge to follow the others on the pier as they walked belly-low toward the fort, all their eyes upon The Master. Scriber looked back at him, and Peregrine nodded. They had needed a miracle, and here *was* one – provided by the enemy itself! Scriber moved slowly toward the end of the pier, pulling the travois from shadow to shadow.

Still no one looked back. For good reason; Wickwrackscar remembered what happened to those showing disrespect at an Incalling. 'Pull the creature onto the bow-starboard boat,' he said to Jaqueramaphan. He leaped off the pier and scattered across the multiboat. It was great to be back on swaying decks, each member drifting a different direction! He sniffed among the bow catapults, listened to the hulls and the creak of the lashings.

But Scar was no sailor, and had no recollection of what might be the most important thing.

'What are you looking for?' came Scriber's Hightalk hiss.

'Scuttle knockouts.' If they were here, they looked nothing like the Southseas version.

'Oh,' said Scriber, 'that's easy. These are Northern Skimmers. There are swingout panels and a thin hull behind.' Two of him dropped from sight for a second and there was a banging sound. The heads reappeared, shaking water off. He grinned surprise, taken aback by his own success. 'Why, it's just like in the books!' his expression seemed to say.

Wickwrackscar found them now; the panels had looked like crew rests, but they were easily pulled out and the wood behind was easy to break with a battle-axe. He kept a head out, looking to see if they were attracting attention, while at the same time he hacked at the knockouts. Peregrine and Scriber worked their way across the bow ranks of the multiboat; if those foundered, it would take a while to get the twinhulls behind them free.

Oops. One of the boat workers was looking back this way. Part of the fellow continued up the hillside, part strained to return to the pier. The bugles sounded their imperative once more, and the sailor followed the call. But his whining alarums were causing other heads to turn.

No time for stealth. Peregrine hotfooted it back to the bow-starboard twinhull. Scriber was cutting the braid-bone fasteners that held the twinhull to the rest of the ship. 'You have any sailing experience?' Peregrine said. Foolish question.

'Well, I've read about it –'

'Fine!' Peregrine shooed him all into the twinhull's starboard pod. 'Keep the alien safe. Hunker down, and be as quiet as you can.' He could sail the twinhull by himself, but he'd have to be all over to do it; the fewer confusing thought sounds, the better.

Peregrine poled their boat forward from the multiboat. The scuttling wasn't obvious yet, but he could see water in the bow hulls. He reversed his pole and used its hook to draw the nearest boat into the gap created by their departure. Another five minutes and there'd be just a row of masts sticking out of the water. Five minutes. No way they could make it . . . if not for Flenser's Incalling: up by the fort, troopers were turning and pointing at the harbor. Yet still they must attend on Flenser/Tyrathect. How long would it be before someone important decided that even an Incalling can be overriden?

He hoisted canvas.

The wind caught the twinhull's sail and they pulled out from the pier. Peregrine danced this way and that, the shrouds grasped tightly in his mouths. Even without Rum, what memories the taste of salt and cordage brought back! He could *feel* where tautness and slack meant that the wind was giving all it could. The twin hulls were sleek and narrow, the mast of ironwood creaking as the wind pulled on the sail.

The Flenserists were streaming down the hillside now. Archers stopped and a haze of arrows rose. Peregrine jerked on the shrouds, tipping the boat into a left turn on one hull. Scriber leaped to shield the alien. To starboard ahead of them the water puckered, but only a couple of shafts struck the boat. Peregrine twisted the shrouds again, and they jigged back in the other direction. Another few seconds and they'd be out of bowshot. Soldiers raced down to the piers, shrieking as they saw what was left of their ship. The bow ranks were flooded; the whole front of the anchorage was a wreck of sunken boats. And the catapults were in the bow.

Peregrine swept his boat back, racing straight south, out of the harbor. To starboard, he could see they were passing the southern tip of Hidden Island. The Castle towers hung tall and ominous. He knew there were heavy catapults there, and some fast boats in the island harbor. A few more minutes and even that wouldn't matter. He was gradually realizing just how nimble their boat was. He should have guessed they'd put their best in a corner bow position. It was probably used for scouting and overtaking.

Jaqueramaphan was piled up at the stern of his hull, staring across the water at the mainland harbor. Soldiers, workers, whitejackets were crowded in a mind-numbing jumble at the ends of the piers. Even from here, you could see the place was a madhouse of rage and frustration. A silly grin spread across Scriber as he realized they really were going to make it. He clambered onto the rail and jumped into the air to flip a member at their enemies. The obscene gesture nearly cast him overboard, but it *was* seen: the distant rage brightened for a moment.

They were well south of Hidden Island; even its catapults could not reach them now. The packs on the mainland shore were lost to view. Flenser's personal banner still whipped cheerfully in the morning breeze, a dwindling square of red and yellow against the forest's green.

All Peregrine looked at the narrows, where Whale Island

curved close to the mainland. His Scar remembered that the choke point was heavily fortified. Normally that would have been the end of them. But its archers had been withdrawn to participate in the ambush, and its catapults were under repair.

. . . so the miracle had happened. They were alive and free and they had the greatest find of all his pilgrimage. He shouted joy so loud that Jaqueramaphan cowered and the sound echoed back from the green and snow-patched hills.

5

Jefri Olsndot had few clear memories of the ambush and saw none of the violence. There had been the noises outside, and Mom's terrified voice, screaming for him to stay inside. Then there had been lots of smoke. He remembered choking, trying to crawl to clear air. He blacked out. When he woke, he was strapped onto some sort of first-aid cot, with the big dog creatures all around. They looked so funny with their white jackets and braid. He remembered wondering where their owners were. They made the strangest noises: gobbling, buzzing, hissing. Some of it was so high-pitched he could barely hear it.

, For awhile he was on a boat, then on a wheeled cart. Before this, he had only seen pictures of castles, but the place they took him was the real thing, its towers dark and overhanging, its big stone walls sharply angled. They climbed through shadowed streets that went *skumpety skumpety* beneath the cart's wheels. The long-necked dogs hadn't hurt him, but the straps were awfully tight. He couldn't sit up; he couldn't see to the sides. He asked about Mom and Dad and Johanna, and he cried a little. A long snout appeared by his face, the soft nose pushing at his cheek. There was a buzzing sound he felt all the way down to his bones. He couldn't tell if the gesture was comfort or threat, but he gasped and tried to stop the tears. They didn't befit a good Straumer, anyway.

Now he saw more white-jacketed dogs, ones with silly

shoulder patches of gold and silver.

His cot was being dragged again, this time down a torch-lit tunnel. They stopped by a double door, two meters wide but scarcely one high. A pair of metal triangles was set in the blond wood. Later Jefri learned they signified a number — fifteen or thirty-three, depending on whether you counted by legs or fore-claws. Much, *much* later he learned that his keeper had counted by legs and the builder of the castle by fore-claws. Thus he ended up in the wrong room. It was a mistake that would change the history of worlds.

Somehow the dogs opened the doors and dragged Jefri in. They clustered around the cot, their snouts tugging loose his restraints. He had a glimpse of rows of needle-sharp teeth. The gobbling and buzzing was very loud. When Jefri sat up, they backed off. Two of them held the doors as the other four exited. The doors slammed shut and the circus act was gone.

Jefri stared at the doors for a long moment. He knew it was no circus act; the dog things must be intelligent. Somehow they had surprised his parents and sister. *Where are they?* He almost started to cry again. He hadn't seen them by the spaceship. They must have been captured, too. They were all being held prisoner in this castle, but in separate dungeons. Somehow they must find each other!

He climbed to his feet, swayed dizzily for a moment. Everything still smelled like smoke. It didn't matter; it was time to start working on getting out. He walked around the room. It was huge, and not like any dungeon he'd seen in stories. The ceiling was very high, an arching dome. It was cut by twelve vertical slots. Sunlight fell in a dust-moted stream from one of them, splashing off the padded wall. It was the room's only illumination, but more than enough on this sunny day. Low-railed balconies stuck out from the four corners of the room just below the dome. He could see doors in the walls behind them. Heavy scrolls hung by the side of each balcony. There was writing on them, really big print. He walked to the wall and felt the stiff fabric. The letters were *painted* on. The only way you could change the display was by rubbing it out. Wow. Just like olden times on Nyjora, before Straumli Realm! The baseboard below the scrolls was black stone, glossy. Someone had used scraps of chalk to draw on it. The stick-figure dogs were crude; they reminded Jefri of pictures little kids draw in kinderschool.

He stopped, remembering all the chidren they had left aboard the boat, and on the ground around it. Just a few days ago he'd been playing with them at the High Lab school. The last year had been so strange – boring and adventurous at the same time. The barracks had been fun with all the families together, but the grownups hardly ever had time to play. At night the sky was so different from Straum's. 'We're beyond the Beyond,' Mom had said, 'making God.' When she first said it, she laughed. Later when people said it, they seemed more and more scared. The last hours had been crazy, the coldsleep drills finally for real. All his friends were in those boxes . . . He wept into the awful silence. There was no one to hear, no one to help him.

After a few moments he was thinking again. If the dogs didn't try to open the boxes, his friends should be okay. If Mom and Dad could make the dogs understand . . .

Strange furniture was scattered around the room: low tables and cabinets, and racks like kids' jungle gyms – all made from the same blond wood as the doors. Black pillows lay around the widest table. That one was littered with scrolls, all full of writing and still drawings. He walked the length of one wall, ten meters or so. The stone flooring ended. There was a two-by-two bed of gravel where the walls met. Something smelled even stronger than smoke here. A bathroom smell. Jefri laughed: they really were like dogs!

The padded walls soaked up his laughter, echoless. Something . . . made Jefri look up and across the room. He'd just assumed he was alone here; in fact, there were lots of hiding places in this 'dungeon'. For a moment, he held his breath and listened. All was silent . . . almost: at the top of his hearing, up where some machines wheep, and Mom and Dad and even Johanna couldn't hear – there was something.

'I – I know you're here,' Jefri said sharply, his voice squeaking. He stepped sideways a few paces, trying to see around the furniture without approaching it. The sound continued, obvious now that he was listening to it.

45

A small head with great dark eyes looked around a cabinet. It was much smaller than the creatures that had brought Jefri here, but the shape of the muzzle was the same. They stared at each other for a moment, and then Jefri edged slowly toward it. A puppy? The head withdrew, then came further out. From the corner of his eye, Jefri saw something move – another of the black forms was peering at him from under the table. Jefri froze for a second, fighting panic. But there was no place to run, and maybe the creatures would help find Mom. Jefri dropped to one knee and slowly extended his hand. 'Here . . . here, doggy.'

The puppy crawled from beneath the table, its eyes never leaving Jefri's hand. The fascination was mutual; the puppy was beautiful. Considering all the thousands of years that dogs have been bred by humans (and others), this could have been some oddball breed . . . but only just. The hair was short and dense, a deep velour of black and white. The two tones lay in broad swaths with no intermediate grays. This one's entire head was black, its haunches split between white and black. The tail was a short, unimpressive flap covering its rear. There were hairless patches on its shoulders and head, where Jefri could see black skin. But the strangest thing was the long, supple neck. It would look more natural in a sea'mal than a dog.

Jefri wiggled his fingers, and the puppy's eyes widened, revealing an edge of white around the iris.

Something bumped his elbow, and Jefri almost jumped to his feet. So many! Two more had crept up to look at his hand. And where he had seen the first one there were now three, sitting alertly, watching. Seen in the open, there was nothing unfriendly or scary about them.

One of the puppies put a paw on Jefri's wrist and pressed gently downward. At the same time, another extended its muzzle and licked Jefri's fingers. The tongue was pink and raspy, a round narrow thing. The high-pitched wheeping got stronger; all three moved in, grabbing at his hand with their mouths.

'Be careful!' Jefri said, jerking back his hand. He remembered the grownups' teeth. Suddenly the air was full of gobbling and buzzing. *Hmp*. They sounded more like goofy birds than dogs. One of the other pups came forward. It extended a sleek nose toward Jefri. 'Be careful!' it said, a perfect playback of the boy's voice . . . yet its mouth was closed. It angled its neck back . . . to be petted? He reached out; the fur was so *soft!* The buzzing was very loud now. Jefri could feel it through the fur. But it wasn't just the one animal who was making it; the sound came from all directions. The puppy reversed direction, sliding its muzzle across the boy's hand. This time he let the mouth close on his fingers. He could see teeth all right, but the puppy carefully kept them from touching Jefri's skin. The tip of its snout felt like a pair of small fingers closing and opening around his.

Three slipped under his other arm, like they wanted to be petted too. He felt noses poking at his back, trying to pull his shirt out of his pants. The effort was remarkably coordinated, almost as if a two-handed human had grabbed his shirt. *Just how many are there?* For a moment he forgot where he was, forgot to be cautious. He rolled over and began petting the marauders. A surprised squeaking sound came from all directions. Two crawled beneath his elbows; at least three jumped on his back and lay with their noses touching his neck and ears.

And Jefri had what seemed a great insight: The adult aliens had recognized he was a child; they just didn't know how old. They had put him in one of their own kinderschools! Mom and Dad were probably talking to them right now. Things were going to turn out all right after all.

Lord Steel had not taken his name casually: steel, the most modern of metals; steel, that takes the sharpest edge and never loses it; steel, that can glow red hot, and yet not fail; steel, the blade that cuts for the flenser. Steel was a crafted person, Flenser's greatest success.

In some sense, the crafting of souls was nothing new. Brood kenning was a limited form of it, though mainly concerned with gross physical characteristics. Even kenners agreed that a pack's mental abilities derived from its various members in different measures. One pair or triple was almost always responsible for eloquence, another for spatial intuition. The virtues and vices were even more complex. No single member was the principal source of courage, or of conscience.

Flenser's contribution to the field – as to most others – had been an essential ruthlessness, a cutting away of all but the truly important. He experimented endlessly, discarding all but the most successful results. He depended on discipline and denial and partial death as much as on clever member selection. He already had seventy years of experience when he created Steel.

Before he could take his name, Steel spent *years* in denial, determining just what parts of him combined to produce the being desired. That would have been impossible without Flenser's enforcement. (Example: if you dismissed a part of yourself essential for tenacity, where could you get the will to continue the flensing?) For the soul in creation, the process was mental chaos, a patchwork of horror and amnesia. In two years he had experienced more change than most people do in two centuries – and all of it directed. The turning point came when he and Flenser identified the trio that weighed him down with both conscience and slowness of intellect. One of the three bridged the others. Sending it into silence, replacing it with just the right element, had made the difference. After that, the rest was easy; Steel was born.

When Flenser had left to convert the Long Lakes Republic, it was only natural that his most brilliant creation should take over here. For five years Steel had ruled Flenser's heartland. In that time he had not only conserved what Flenser built, he extended it beyond the cautious beginnings.

But today, in a single circling of the sun about Hidden Island, he could lose everything.

Steel stepped into the meeting hall and looked around. Refreshments were properly set. Sunlight streamed from a ceiling slit onto just the place he wanted. Part of Shreck, his aide, stood on the far side of the room. He said to it, 'I will speak with the visitor alone.' He did not use the name 'Flenser.' The whitejackets groveled back and its unseen members pushed open the far doors.

A fivesome – three males and two females – walked through the doorway, into the splash of sunlight. The individual was unremarkable. But then Flenser had never had an imposing appearance.

Two heads raised to shade the eyes of the others. The pack looked across the room, spotting Lord Steel twenty yards away. 'Ah-h . . . Steel.' The voice was gentle, like a scalpel petting the short hairs of your throat.

Steel had bowed when the other entered, a formal gesture. The voice caused a sudden cramp in his guts, and he involuntarily brought bellies to the ground. That was *his* voice! There was at least a fragment of the original Flenser in this pack. The gold and silver epaulets, the personal banner, those could be faked by anyone with suicidal bravado . . . But Steel remembered the manner. He wasn't surprised that the other's presence had destroyed discipline on the mainland this morning.

The pack's heads, where they were in sunlight, were expressionless. Was a smile playing about the heads in shadow? 'Where are the others, Steel? What happened today is the greatest opportunity of our history.'

Steel got off his bellies and stood at the railing. 'Sir. There are some questions first, just between the two of us. Clearly, you are much of Flenser, but how much –'

The other was clearly grinning now, the shadowed heads bobbing. 'Yes, I knew my best creation would see that question . . . This morning, I claimed to be the true Flenser, improved with one or two replacements. The truth is . . . harder. You know about the Republic.' That had been Flenser's greatest gamble: to flense an entire nation-state. Millions would die, yet even so there would be more molding than killing. In the end, there would exist the first collective outside of the tropics. And the Flenser state would not be a mindless agglomeration grubbing about in some jungle. The top would be as brilliant, as ruthless as any packs in history. No people in the world could stand against such a force.

'It was an awesome risk to take, for an even more awesome goal. But I took precautions. We had thousands of converts, many of them people with no understanding of our true ambition, but faithful and self-sacrificing – as they should be. I always kept a special group of them nearby. The Political Police were clever to use mob assassination against me, the last thing I had expected – *I* who made the mobs. No matter, my bodyguards were well trained. When we were trapped in Parliament Bowl, they killed one or two members of each of those special packs . . . and I simply ceased to exist, dispersed among three panicky, ordinary people trying to escape the blood swamp.'

'But everyone around you was killed; the mob left no one.'

The Flenser-thing shrugged. 'That was partly Republican propaganda, and partly my own work: I ordered my guards to hack each other down, along with everyone who was not me.'

Steel almost voiced his awe. The plan was typical of Flenser's brilliance, and his strength of soul. In assassinations, there was always the chance that fragments would get away. There were famous stories of heroes reassembled. In real life such events were rare, usually happening when the victim's forces could sustain their leader through reintegration. But Flenser had planned this tactic from the beginning, had envisaged reassembling himself more than a thousand miles from the Long Lakes.

Still . . . Lord Steel looked at the other in calculation. Ignore voice and manner. *Think* for power, not for the desires of others, even Flenser. Steel recognized only two in the other pack. The females and the male with the white-tipped ears were probably from the sacrificed follower. Very likely only really two of Flenser faced him; scarcely a threat . . . except in the very real sense of appearances. 'And the other four of you, Sir? When may we expect your entire presence?'

The Flenser-thing chuckled. Damaged as it was, it still understood balance-of-power. This was almost like the old days: when two people have a clear understanding of power and betrayal, then betrayal itself becomes almost impossible. There is only the ordered flow of events, bringing good to those who deserve to rule. 'The others have equally good . . . mounts. I made detailed plans, three different paths, three different sets of agents. I arrived safely. I have no doubt the others will too, in a few tendays at most. Until then,' he turned all heads toward Steel, 'until then, dear Steel, I do not claim the full role of Flenser. I did so earlier to establish priorities, to protect this fragment till I am assembled. But this pack is deliberately weak-minded; I know it wouldn't survive as the ruler of my earlier creations.'

Steel wondered. Half-brained, the creature's schemes were perfect. Nearly perfect. 'So you wish a background role for the next few tendays? Very well. But you announced yourself as Flenser. How shall I present you?'

The other didn't hesitate. 'Tyrathect, Flenser in Waiting.'

Crypto: 0
As received by: Transceiver Relay03 at Relay
Language path: Samnorsk→Triskweline, SjK: Relay units
From: Straumli Main
Subject: Archive opened in the Low Transcend!
Summary: Our links to the Known Net will be down temporarily
Key phrases: transcend, good news, business opportunities, new archive, communications problems
Distribution:
  Where Are They Now Interest Group
  Homo Sapiens Interest Group
  Motley Hatch Administration Group
  Transceiver Relay03 at Relay
  Transceiver Windsong at Debley Down
  Transceiver Not-for-Long at Shortstop
Date: 11:45:20 Docks Time, 01/09 of Org year 52089
Text of message:
  We are proud to announce that a human exploration company from Straumli Realm has discovered an accessible archive in the Low Transcend. This is not an announcement of Transcendence or the creation of a new Power. We have in fact postponed this annoucement until we were sure of our property rights and the safety of the archive. We have installed

interfaces which should make the archive interoperable with standard syntax queries from the Net. In a few days this access will be made commercially available. (See discussion of scheduling problems below.) Because of its safety, intelligibility, and age, this Archive is remarkable. We believe there is otherwise lost information here about arbitration management and interrace coordination. We'll sent details to the appropriate news groups. We're very excited about this. Note that no interaction with the Powers was necessary; no part of Straumli Realm has transcended.

Now for the bad news: Arbitration and translation schemes have had unfortunate clenirations[?] with the ridgeway armiphlage[?]. The details should be amusing to the people in the Communication Threats news group and we will report them there later. But for at least the next hundred hours, all our links (main and minor) to the Known Net will be down. Incoming messages may be buffered, but no guarantees. No messages can be forwarded. We regret this inconvenience, and will make up for it very soon

Physical commerce is in no way affected by these problems. Straumli Realm continues to welcome tourists and trade.

6

Looking back, Ravna Bergsndot saw it was inevitable that she become a librarian. As a child on Sjandra Kei, she had been in love with stories from the Age of Princesses. There was adventure, a time when a few brave Ladies had dragged humankind to greatness. She and her sister had spent countless afternoons pretending to be the Greater Two and rescuing the Countess of the Lake. Later they understood that Nyjora and its Princesses were lost in the dim past. Sister

Lynne turned to more practical things. But Ravna still wanted adventure. Through her teens, she had dreamed of emigrating to Straumli Realm. *That* was something very real. Imagine: a new and mostly human colony, right at the Top of the Beyond. And Straum welcomed folk from the mother world; their enterprise was less than one hundred years old. They or their children would be the first humans anywhere in the galaxy to transcend their own humanity. She might end up a god, and richer than a million Beyonder worlds. It was a dream real enough to provoke constant arguments with her parents. For where there is heaven, there can also be hell. Straumli Realm kissed close to the Transcend, and the people there played with 'the tigers that pace beyond the bars.' Dad had actually used that tired image. The disagreement drove them apart for several years. Then, in her Computer Science and Applied Theology courses, Ravna began to read about some of the old horrors. Maybe, maybe . . . she should be a little more cautious. Better to look around first. And there was a way to see into everything that humans in the Beyond could possibly understand: Ravna became a librarian. 'The ultimate dilettante!' Lynne had teased. 'It's true and so what?' Ravna had grumped back, but the dream of far traveling was not quite dead in her.

Life in Herte University at Sjandra Kei should have been perfect for her. Things might have gone on happily for a lifetime there – except that in her graduation year, there had been the Vrinimi Organization's Faraway 'Prentice contest. Three years work-study at the archive by Relay was the prize. Winning was the chance of a lifetime; she would come back with more experience than any local academician.

So it was that Ravna Bergsndot ended up more than twenty thousand light-years from home, at the network hub of a million worlds.

Sunset was an hour past when Ravna drifted across Citypark toward Grondr Vrinimikalir's residence. She'd been on the planet only a handful of times since arriving in the Relay system. Most of her work was at the archives themselves – a thousand light-hours out. This part of Groundside was in early autumn, though twilight had faded the tree colors to bands of gray. From Ravna's altitude, one hundred meters up, the air had the nip of frosts to come. Between her feet she could see picnic fires and gaming fields. The Vrinimi Organization didn't spend much on the planet, but the world was beautiful. As long as she kept her eyes on the darkening ground, Ravna could almost imagine this was someplace in her home terrane on Sjandra Kei. Look into the sky though . . . and you knew you were far from home: twenty thousand light-years away, the galactic whirlpool sprawled up toward the zenith.

It was just a faint thing in the twilight, and it might not get much brighter this night: Low in the western sky, a cluster of in-system factories glowed brighter than any moon. The operation was a brilliant flickering of stars and rays, sometimes so intense that stark shadows were cast eastwards from the Citypark mountains. In another half hour the Docks would rise. The Docks weren't as bright as the factories, but together they would outshine anything from the far stars.

She shifted in her agrav harness, drifting lower. The scent of autumn and picnics came stronger. Suddenly, the click of Kalir laughter was all around her; she had blundered into an airball game. Ravna spread her arms in mock humiliation and dodged out of the players' way.

Her stroll through the park was just about over; she could see her destination ahead. Grondr 'Kalir's residence was a rarity in the Citypark landscape: a recognizable building. It dated from when the Org bought into the Relay operation. Seen from just eighty meters up, the house was a blocky silhouette against the sky. When factory lights flashed, the smooth walls of the monolith glowed in oily tints. Grondr was her boss's boss's boss. She had talked to him exactly three times in two years.

No more delay. Nervous and very curious, Ravna floated lower and let the house electronics guide her across the tree decks toward an entrance.

Grondr Vrinimikalir treated her with standard Organization courtesy, the common denominator that served between the several races of the Org: The meeting room had furniture suitable for human and Vrinimi use. There were refreshments, and questions about her job at the archive.

'Mixed results, sir,' Ravna replied honestly. 'I've learned a great deal. The 'prenticeship is everything it's claimed to be. But I'm afraid the new division is going to require an added index layer.' All this was in reports the old fellow could have seen at the flick of a digit.

Grondr rubbed a hand absently across his eye freckles. 'Yes, an expected disappointment. We're at the limits of information management with this expansion. Egravan and Derche –' those were Ravna's boss and boss's boss '– are quite happy with your progress. You came well educated, and learned fast. I think there's a place for humans in the Organization.'

'Thank you, sir.' Ravna blushed. Grondr's assessment was casually spoken but very important to her. And it would probably mean the arrival of more humans, perhaps even before her 'prenticeship was up. So was this the reason for the interview?

She tried not to stare at the other. She was quite used to the Vrinimi majority race by now. From a distance the Kalir looked humanoid. Up close, the differences were substantial. The race was descended from something like an insect. In upsizing, evolution had necessarily moved reinforcing struts inside the body, till the outside was a combination of grublike skin and sheets of pale chitin. At first glance Grondr was an unremarkable examplar of the race. But when the fellow moved, even to adjust his jacket or scratch at his eye freckles, there was a strange precision to him. Egravan said that he was very very old.

Grondr changed the subject with clickety abruptness. 'You are aware of the . . . changes at Straumli Realm?'

'You mean the fall of Straum? Yes.' *Though I'm surprised you are.* Straumli Realm was a significant human civilization, but it accounted for only an infinitesimal fraction of Relay's message traffic.

'Please accept my sympathy.' Despite the cheerful announcements from Straum, it was clear that absolute disaster had befallen Straumli Realm. Almost every race eventually dabbled in the Transcend, more often than not becoming a superintelligence, a Power. But it was clear by now that the Straumers had created, or awakened, a Power of deadly inclination. Their fate was as terrible as anything Ravna's father had ever predicted. And their bad luck was now a disaster that stretched across all that had been Straumli Realm. Grondr continued: 'Will this news affect your work?'

Curiouser and curiouser; she would have sworn the other was coming to the point. Maybe this *was* the point? 'Uh, no sir. The Straumli affair is a terrible thing, especially for humankind. But my home is Sjandra Kei. Straumli Realm is our offspring, but I have no relatives there.' *Though I might have been there if it hadn't been for Mother and Dad.* Actually, when Straumli Main dropped off the Net, Sjandra Kei had been unreachable for almost forty hours. That had bothered her very much, since any rerouting should have been immediate. Communication was eventually established; the problem had been screwed-up routing tables on an alternate path. Ravna had even shot half a year's savings for an over-and-back mailing. Lynne and her parents were fine; the Straumli debacle was the news of the century for folks at Sjandra Kei, but it was still a disaster at great remove. Ravna wondered if parents had ever given better advice than hers had!

'Good, good.' His mouth parts moved in the analog of a human nod. His head tilted so only peripheral freckles were looking at her; the guy actually seemed hesitant! Ravna looked back silently. Grondr 'Kalir might be the strangest exec in the Org. He was the only one whose principal residence was Groundside. Officially he was in charge of a division of the archives; in fact, he ran Vrinimi Marketing (i.e., Intelligence). There were stories that he had visited the Top of the Beyond; Egravan claimed he had an artificial immune system. 'You see, the Straumli disaster has incidentally made you one of the Organization's most valuable employees.'

'I . . . don't understand.'

'Ravna, the rumors in the Threats newsgroup are true.

The Straumers had a laboratory in the Low Transcend. They were playing with recipes from some lost archive, and they created a new Power. It appears to be a Class Two perversion.'

The Known Net recorded a Class Two perversion about once a century. Such Powers had a normal 'lifespan' – about ten years. But they were explicitly malevolent, and in ten years could do enormous damage. *Poor Straum*.

'So you can see there's enormous potential for profit or loss here. If the disaster spreads, we will lose network customers. On the other hand, everyone around Straumli Realm wants to track what is happening. This could increase our message traffic by several percent.'

Grondr put it more cold-bloodedly than she liked, but he had a point. In fact, the opportunity for profit was directly linked with mitigating the perversion. If she hadn't been so wrapped up in archive work, she'd have guessed all this. And now that she *did* think about it: 'There are even more spectacular opportunities. Historically, these perversions have been of interest to other Powers. They'll want Net feeds and . . . information about the creating race.' Her voice guttered into silence as she finally understood the reason for this meeting.

Grondr's mouth parts clicked agreement. 'Indeed. We at Relay are well-placed to supply news to the Transcend. And we also have our own human. In the last three days we've received several dozen queries from civilizations in the High Beyond, some claiming to represent Powers. This interest could mean a large increase in Organization income through the next decade.

'All this you could read in the Threats news group. But there is another item, something I ask you to keep secret for now: Five days ago, a ship from the Transcend entered our region. It claims to be directly controlled by a Power.' The wall behind him became a window upon the visitor. The craft was an irregular collection of spines and lumps. A scale bar claimed the thing was only five meters across.

Ravna felt the hair on her neck prickling. Here in the Middle Beyond they should be relatively safe from the caprice of the Powers. Still . . . the visit was an unnerving thing. 'What does it want?'

'Information about the Straumli perversion. In particular, it is very interested in your race. It would give a great deal to take back a living human . . . '

Ravna's response was abrupt. 'I'm not interested.'

Grondr spread his pale hands. The light glittered from the chitin on the back of his fingers. 'It would be an enormous opportunity. A 'prenticeship with the gods. This one has promised to establish an oracle here in return.'

'No!' Ravna half rose from her chair. She was one human, more than twenty thousand light-years from home. That had been a frightening thing in the first days of her 'prenticeship. Since then she had made friends, had learned more of Organization ethics, had come to trust these folk almost as much as people at Sjandra Kei. But . . . there was only one halfway trustable oracle on the Net these days, and it was almost ten years old. This Power was tempting Vrinimi Org with fabulous treasure.

Grondr clicked embarrassment. He waved her back to her chair. 'It was only a suggestion. We do not abuse our employees. If you will simply serve as our local expert . . . '

Ravna nodded.

'Good. Frankly, I had not expected you to accept the offer. We have a much more likely volunteer, but one who needs coaching.'

'A human? Here?' Ravna had a standing query in the local directory for other humans. During the last two years she had seen three, and they had just been passing through. 'How long has she – he? – been here?'

Grondr said something halfway between a smile and a laugh. 'A bit more than a century, though we didn't realize it until a few days ago.' The pictures around him shifted. Ravna recognized Relay's 'attic,' the junkyard of abandoned ships and freight devices that floated just a thousand light-seconds from the archives. 'We receive a lot of one-way freight, items shipped in the hope we'll buy or sell on consignment.' The view closed on a decrepit vessel, perhaps two hundred meters long, wasp-waisted to support a ramscoop drive. Its ultradrive spines were scarcely more than stubs.

'A bottom-lugger?' said Ravna.

Grondr clicked negation. 'A dredge. The ship is about thirty thousand years old. Most of that time was spent in a deep penetration of the Slow Zone, and ten thousand years in the Unthinking Depths.'

Up close now, she could see the hull was finely pitted, the result of millennia of relativistic erosion. Even unpiloted, such expeditions were rare: a deep penetration could not return to the Beyond within the lifetime of its builders. Some would not return within the lifetime of the builders' *race*. People who launched such missions were just a little weird; People who recovered them could make a solid profit.

'This one came from very far away, even if it's not quite a jackpot mission. It didn't see anything interesting in the Unthinking Depths – not surprising given that even simple automation fails there. We sold most of the cargo immediately. The rest we cataloged and forgot . . . till the Straumli affair.' The starscape vanished. They were looking at a medical display, random limbs and body parts. They looked very human. 'In a solar system at the bottom of the Slowness, the dredge found a derelict. The wreck had no ultradrive capability; it was truly a Slow Zone design. The solar system was uninhabited. We speculate the ship had a structural failure – or perhaps the crew was affected by the Depths. Either way, they ended up in a frozen mangle.'

Tragedy at the bottom of the Slowness, thousands of years ago. Ravna forced her eyes from the carnage. 'You figure on selling this to our visitor?'

'Even better. Once we started poking around, we discovered a substantial error in the cataloging. One of the deaders is almost intact. We patched it up with parts from the others. It was expensive, but we ended up with a living human.' The picture flickered again, and Ravna caught her breath. In the medical animation, the parts floated into an orderly arrangement. There was a complete body there, torn up a little in the belly. Pieces came together, and . . . this was no 'she.' He floated whole and naked, as if in sleep. Ravna had no doubt of his humanity, but all humankind in the Beyond was descended from Nyjoran stock. This fellow had none of that heritage. The skin was smoky gray, not brown. The hair was bright reddish brown, a color she had only seen in pre-Nyjoran histories. The bones of the face were subtly different from modern humans. The small differences were more jarring than the outright alienness of her coworkers.

Now the figure was clothed. Under other circumstances, Ravna would have smiled. Grondr 'Kalir had picked an absurd costume, something from the Nyjoran era. The figure bore a sword and slug gun . . . A sleeping prince from the Age of Princesses.

'Behold the Ur-human,' said Grondr.

7

'Relay' is a common place-name. It has meaning in almost any environment. Like Newtown and Newhome, it occurs over and over when people move or colonize or participate in a communications net. You could travel a billion light-years or a billion years and still find such names among races of natural intelligence.

But in the current era there was one instance of 'Relay' known above all others. That instance appeared in the routing list of two percent of all traffic across the Known Net. Twenty thousand light-years off the galactic plane, Relay had an unobstructed line of sight on thirty percent of the Beyond, including many star systems right at the bottom, where starships can make only one light-year per day. A few metal-bearing solar systems were equally well-placed, and there was competition. But where other civilizations lost interest, or colonized into the Transcend, or died in apocalypse, Vrinimi Organization *lasted*. After fifty thousand years, there were several races of the original Org in its membership. None of those were still leaders – yet the original viewpoint and policies remained. Position and durability: Relay was now the main intermediate to the Magellanics, and one of the few sites with any sort of link to the Beyond in the Sculptor galaxy.

At Sjandra Kei, Relay's reputation had been fabulous. In her two years of 'prenticeship, Ravna had come to realize that the truth exceeded the reputation. Relay was in Middle Beyond; the Organization's only export was the relay function and access to the local archive. Yet they imported the finest biologicals and processing equipment from the High Beyond. The Relay Docks were an extravagance that only the absolutely rich could indulge. They stretched a thousand kilometers: bays, repair holds, transhipment centers, parks, and playgrounds. Even at Sjandra Kei there were habitats far larger. But the Docks were in no orbit. They floated a thousand kilometers above Groundside on the largest agrav frame Ravna had ever seen. At Sjandra Kei the annual income of an academician might pay for a square meter of agrav fabric – junk that might not last a year. Here there were millions of hectares of the stuff, supporting billions of tonnes. Just replacements for dead fabric required more High Beyond commerce than most star clusters could command.

And now I have my own office here. Working directly for Grondr 'Kalir had its perks. Ravna kicked back in her chair and stared across the central sea. At the Docks' altitude, gravity was still about three-quarters of a gee. Air fountains hung a breathable atmosphere over the middle part of the platform. The day before, she had taken a sailboat across the clear-bottomed sea. That was a strange experience indeed: planetary clouds below your keel, stars and indigo sky above.

She had the surf cranked up this morning – an easy matter of flexing the agravs of the basin. It made a regular crashing against her beach. Even thirty meters from the water there was a tang of salt in the air. Rows of white tops marched off into the distance.

She eyed the figure that was trudging slowly up the beach toward her. Just a few weeks ago she would never have dreamed this situation. Just a few weeks ago she had been out at the archive, absorbed in the upgrade work, happy to be involved with one of the largest databases on the Known Net. Now . . . it was almost as if she had come full circle, back to her childhood dreams of adventure. The only problem was that sometimes she felt like one of the villains: Pham Nuwen was a living person, not something to be sold.

She stood and walked out to meet her red-haired visitor.

He wasn't carrying the sword and handgun of Grondr's fanciful animation. Yet his clothes were the braided fabric of ancient adventure, and he carried himself with lazy confidence. Since her meeting with Grondr, she had looked up some anthropology from Old Earth. The red hair and the eyefolds had been known there, though rarely in the same individual. Certainly his smoky skin would have been remarkable to an inhabitant of Earth. This fellow was, as much as herself, a product of post-terrestrial evolution.

He stopped an arm's length away and gave her a lopsided grin. 'You look pretty human. Ravna Bergsndot?'

She smiled and nodded up at him. 'Mr Pham Nuwen?'

'Yes indeed. We seem both to be excellent guessers.' He swept past her into the shade of the inner office. Cocky fellow.

She followed him, unsure about protocol. You'd think with a fellow human there would be no problems . . .

Actually, the interview went pretty smoothly. It was more than thirty days since Pham Nuwen's resuscitation. Much of that time had been spent in cram language sessions. The fellow must be damned bright; he already spoke Triskweline trade talk with a folksy slickness. He really was rather cute. Ravna had been away from Sjandra Kei for two years, and had another year of her 'prenticeship to go. She'd been doing pretty well. She had many close friends here, Egravan, Sarale. But just chatting with this fellow brought a lot of the loneliness back. In some ways he was more alien that anything at Relay . . . and in some ways she wanted to just grab him and kiss his confident grin away.

Grondr Vrinimikalir had been telling the truth about this Pham Nuwen. The guy was actually enthusiastic about the Org's plans for him! In theory, that meant she could do her job with a clear conscience. In fact . . .

'Mr Nuwen, my job is to orient you to your new world. I know you've been exposed to some intense instruction the last few days, but there are limits to how fast such knowledge can sink in.'

The redhead smiled. 'Call me Pham. Sure, I feel like an overstuffed bag. My sleep time is full of little voices. I've learned an awful lot without experiencing anything. Worse, I've been a *target* for all this 'education.' It's a perfect setup if Vrinimi wants to trick me. That's why I'm learning to use the local library. And that's why I insited they find someone like you.' He saw the surprise on her face. 'Ha! You didn't know that. See, talking to a real person gives me a chance to see things that aren't all planned ahead. Also, I've always been a pretty good judge of human nature; I think I can read you pretty well.' His grin showed he understood just how irritating he was being.

Ravna looked up at the green petals of the beachtrees. Maybe this boob deserved what he was getting into. 'So you have great experience dealing with people?'

'Given the limitations of the Slowness, I've been around, Ravna. I've been around. I know I don't look it, but I'm sixty-seven years old subjective. I thank your Organization for a fine job of thawing me out.' He tipped a non-existent hat in her direction. 'My last voyage was more than a thousand years objective. I was Programmer-at-Arms on a Qeng Ho longshot –' His eyes abruptly widened, and he said something unintelligible. For a moment he almost looked vulnerable.

Ravna reached a hand toward him. 'Memory?'

Pham Nuwen nodded. '*Damn*. This is something I *don't* thank you people for.'

Pham Nuwen had been frozen in the aftermath of violent death, not as a planned suspension. It was a near miracle that Vrinimi Org had been able to bring him back at all – at least with Middle Beyond technology. But memory was the hardest thing. The chemical basis of memory does not survive chaotic freezing well.

The problem was enough to shrink even Pham Nuwen's ego by a size or two. Ravna took pity on him. 'It's not likely that anything is completely lost. You just have to find a different angle on some things.'

'. . . Yes. I've been coached about that. Start with other memories; work sideways toward what you can't remember straight on. Well . . . it beats being dead.' Some of his jauntiness returned, but subdued to a really quite charming level. They talked for a long while as the redhead worked around the points he couldn't 'remember straight on.'

And gradually Ravna came to feel something she had never expected in connection with a Slow Zoner: *awe*. In one lifetime, Pham Nuwen had accomplished virtually everything that was possible for a being in the Slowness. All her life she had pitied the civilizations trapped down there. They could never know the glory; they might never know the truth. Yet by luck and skill and sheer strength of will, this fellow had leaped barrier after barrier. Had Grondr known the truth when he pictured the redhead with sword and slug gun? For Pham Nuwen really was a barbarian. He had been born on a fallen colony world – Canberra he called it. The place sounded much like medieval Nyjora, though not matriarchal. He'd been the youngest child of a king. He'd grown up with swords and poison and intrigue, living in stone castles by a cold, cold sea. No doubt this little prince would have ended up murdered – or king of all – if life had continued in the medieval way. But when he was thirteen years old everything changed. A world that had only legends of aircraft and radio was confronted by interstellar traders. In a year of trading, Canberra's feudal politics was turned on its head.

'Qeng Ho had invested three ships in the expedition to Canberra. They were pissed, thought we'd be at a higher level of technology. We couldn't resupply them, so two stayed behind, probably turned my poor world inside out. I left with the third – a crazy hostage deal my father thought he was putting over on them. I was lucky they didn't space me.'

Qeng Ho consisted of several hundred ramscoop ships operating in a volume hundreds of light-years across. Their vessels could reach almost a third of the speed of light. They were mostly traders, occasionally rescuers, even more rarely conquerors. When Pham Nuwen last knew them, they had settled thirty worlds and were almost three thousand years old. It was as extravagant a civilization as can ever exist in the Slowness . . . And of course, until Pham Nuwen was revived, no one in the Beyond had ever heard of it. Qeng Ho was like a million other doomed civilizations, buried thousands of light-years in the Slowness. Only by luck would they ever penetrate into the Beyond, where faster-than-light travel was possible.

But for a thirteen-year-old boy born to swords and chain mail, the Qeng Ho was more change than most living beings ever experience. In a matter of weeks, he went from medieval lordling to starship cabin boy.

'At first they didn't know what to do with me. Figured on popping me into cold storage and dumping me at the next stop. What can you make of a kid who thinks there's one world and it's flat, who has spent his whole life learning to whack about with a sword?' He stopped abruptly, as he did every few minutes, when the stream of recollection ran into damaged territory. Then his glance flicked out at Ravna, and his smile was as cocky as ever. 'I was one mean animal. I don't think civilized people realize what it's like to grow up with your own aunts and uncles scheming to murder you, and you training to get them first. In civilization I met bigger villains – guys who'd fry a whole planet and call it 'reconciliation' – but for sheer up-close treachery, you can't beat my childhood.'

To hear Pham Nuwen tell it, only dumb luck saved the crew from his scheming. In the years that followed, he learned to fit in, learned civilized skills. Properly tamed, he could be an ideal ship master of the Qeng Ho. And for many years he was. The Qeng Ho volume contained a couple of other races, and a number of human-colonized worlds. At three-tenths lightspeed, Pham spent decades in coldsleep getting from star to star, then a year or two at each port trying to make a profit with products and information that might be lethally out-of-date. The reputation of the Qeng Ho was some protection. 'Politics may come and go, but Greed goes on forever' was the fleet's motto, and they had lasted longer than most of their customers. Even religious fanatics grew a little cautious when they thought about Qeng Ho retribution. But more often it was the skill and deviousness of the shipmaster that saved the day. And few were a match for the little boy in Pham Nuwen.

'I was almost the perfect skipper. Almost. I always wanted to see what was beyond the space we had good records on.

Every time I got really rich, so rich I could launch my own subfleet – I'd take some crazy chance and lose everything. I was the yo-yo of the Fleet. One run I'd be captain of five, the next I'd be pulling maintenance programming on some damn routineer. Given how time stretches out with sublight commerce, there were whole generations who thought I was a legendary genius – and others who used my name as a synonym for goofball.'

He paused and his eyes widened in pleased surprise. '*Ha!* I remember what I was doing there at the end. I was in the 'goofball' part of my cycle, but it didn't matter. There was this captain of twenty who was even crazier than I . . . Can't remember her name. Her? Couldn't have been; I'd never serve under a fem captain.' He was almost talking to himself. 'Anyway, this guy was willing to bet *everything* on the sort of thing normal folks would argue about over beer. He called his ship the, um, it translates as something like "wild witless bird" – that gives you the idea about him. He figured there must be some really high-tech civilizations somewhere in the universe. The problem was to find them. In a strange way, he had almost guessed about the Zones. Only problem was, he wasn't crazy enough; he got one little thing wrong. Can you guess what?'

Ravna nodded. Considering where Pham's wreck was found, it was obvious.

'Yeah. I'll bet it's an idea older than spaceflight: the "elder races" must be toward the galactic core, where stars are closer and there are black hole exotica for power. He was taking his entire fleet of twenty. They'd keep going till they found somebody or had to stop and colonize. This captain figured success was unlikely in our lifetime. But with proper planning we could end up in a close-packed region where it would be easy to found a new Qeng Ho – and it would proceed even further.

'Anyway, I was lucky to get aboard even as a programmer; this captain knew all the wrong things about me.'

The expedition lasted a thousand years, penetrating two hundred and fifty light-years galactic inward. The Qeng Ho volume was closer to the Bottom of the Slowness than Old

Earth, and they were proceeding inwards from there. Even so, it was plain bad luck that they encountered the edge of the Deeps after only two hundred and fifty light-years. One after another, the *Wild Witless Bird* lost contact with the other ships. Sometimes it happened without warning, other times there was evidence of computer failure or gross incompetence. The survivors saw a pattern, guessed that common components were failing. Of course, no one connected the problems with the *region of space* they were entering.

'We backed down from ram speeds, found a solar system with a semi-habitable planet. We'd lost track of everybody else . . . Just what we did then isn't real clear to me.' He gave a dry laugh. 'We must have been right at the edge, staggering around at about IQ 60. I remember fooling with the life support system. That's probably what actually killed us.' For a moment he looked sad and bewildered. He shrugged. 'And then I woke up in the tender clutches of Vrinimi Org, here where faster-than-light travel is possible . . . and I can see the edge of Heaven itself.'

Ravna didn't say anything for a moment. She looked across her beach into the surf. They'd been talking a long time. The sun was peeking under the tree petals, its light shifting across her office. Did Grondr realize what he had here? Almost anything from the Slow Zone had collector's value. *People* fresh from the Slowness were even more valuable. But Pham Nuwen might be unique. He had personally experienced more than had some whole civilizations, and he had ventured into the Deeps to boot. She understood now why he looked to the Transcend and called it 'Heaven.' It wasn't entirely naïveté, nor a failure in the Organization's education programs. Pham Nuwen had already been through two transforming experiences, from pre-tech to star-traveler, and star-traveler to Beyonder. Each was a jump almost beyond imagination. Now he saw that another step was possible, and was perfectly willing to sell himself to take it.

So why should I risk my job to change his mind? But her mouth was living a life of its own. 'Why not postpone the Transcend, Pham? Take some time to understand what is here in the Beyond. You'd be welcome in almost any civilization. And on human worlds you'd be the wonder of the age.' *A glimpse of non-Nyjoran humanity.* The local newsgroups at Sjandra Kei had thought Ravna radically ambitious to take a 'prenticeship twenty thousand light-years away. Coming back from it, she would have her pick of Full Academician jobs on any of a dozen worlds. That was nothing compared to Pham Nuwen; there were folks so rich they might *give* him a world if he would just stay. 'You could name your price.'

The redhead's lazy smile broadened. 'Ah, but you see, I've already named my price, and I think Vrinimi can meet it.'

I really wish I could do something about that smile, thought Ravna. Pham Nuwen's ticket to the Transcend was based on a Power's sudden interest in the Straumli perversion. This innocent's ego might end up smeared across a million death cubes, running a million million simulations of human nature.

Grondr called less than five minutes after Pham Nuwen's departure. Ravna knew the Org would be eavesdropping, and she'd already told Grondr her misgivings about this 'selling' of a sophont. Nevertheless, she was a bit nervous to see him.

'When is he actually going to leave for the Transcend?'

Grondr rubbed at his freckles. He didn't seem angry. 'Not for ten or twenty days. The Power that's negotiating for him is more interested in looking at our archives and watching what's passing through Relay. Also . . . despite the human's enthusiasm for going, he's really quite cautious.'

'Oh?'

'Yes. He's insisting on a library budget, and permission to roam anywhere in the system. He's been chatting with random employees all over the Docks. He was especially insistant about talking to you.' Grondr's mouth parts clicked in a smile. 'Feel free to speak your mind to him. Basically, he's tasting around for hidden poison. Hearing the worst from you should make him trust us.'

She was coming to understand Grondr's confidence. Damn but Pham Nuwen had a thick head. 'Yes sir. He's asked me to show him around the Foreign Quarter tonight.' *As you well know.*

'Fine. I wish the rest of the deal were going as smoothly.' Grondr turned so that only peripheral freckles were looking in her direction. He was surrounded by status displays of the Org's communication and database operations. From what she could see, things were remarkably busy. 'Maybe I should not bring this up, but it's just possible you can help . . . Business is very brisk.' Grondr did not seem pleased to report the good news. 'We have nine civilizations from the Top of the Beyond that are bidding for wide band data feeds. That we could handle. But this Power that sent a ship here . . .'

Ravna interrupted almost without thinking, a breach that would have horrified her a few days earlier. 'Just who is it, by the way? Any chance we're entertaining the Straumli Perversion?' The thought of *that* taking the redhead was a chill.

'Not unless all the Powers are fooled, too. Marketing calls our current visitor "Old One."' He smiled. 'That's something of a joke, but true even so. We've known it for eleven years.' No one really knew how long Transcendent beings lived, but it was a rare Power that stayed communicative for more than five or ten years. They lost interest, or grew into something different – or really did die. There were a million explanations, thousands that were allegedly from the Powers firsthand. Ravna guessed that the true explanation was the simplest one: Intelligence is the handmaiden of flexibility and change. Dumb animals can change only as fast as natural evolution. Human equivalent races, once on their technological run-up, hit the limits of their zone in a matter of a few thousand years. In the Transcend, superhumanity can happen so fast that its creators are destroyed. It wasn't surprising then that the Powers themselves were evanescent.

So calling an eleven-year Power 'Old One' was almost reasonable.

'We believe that Old One is a variant on the Type 73 pattern. Such are rarely malicious – and we know from whom it Transcended. Just now it's causing us major discomfort, though. For twenty days it has been monopolizing an enormous and increasing percentage of Relay bandwidth. Since its ship arrived, it's been all over the archive and our local nets. We've asked Old One to send noncritical data by starship, but it refuses. This afternoon was the worst yet. Almost five percent of Relay's capacity was bound up in its service. And the creature is sending almost as much downlink as it is receiving uplink.'

That *was* weird, but, 'It's still paying for the business, isn't it? If Old One can pay top price, why do you care?'

'Ravna, we hope our Organization will be around for many years after the Old One is gone. There is nothing it could offer us that would be good through all that time.' Ravna nodded. Actually, there were certain 'magic' automations that might work down here, but their long-term effectiveness would be dubious. This was a commercial situation, not some exercise in an Applied Theology course. 'Old One can easily top any bid from the Middle Beyond. But if we give it all the services it demands, we'll be effectively nonfunctional to the rest of our customers – and they are the people we must depend on in the future.'

His image was replaced by an archive access report. Ravna was very familiar with the format, and Grondr's complaint really hit home. The Known Net was a vast thing, a hierarchical anarchy that linked hundreds of millions of worlds. Yet even the main trunks had bandwidths like something out of Earth's dawn age; a wrist dataset could do better on a local net. That's why bulk across to the Archive was mostly local – to media freighters visiting the Relay system. But now . . . during the last hundred hours, remote access to the Archive, both by volume and by count, had been higher than local! And ninety percent of those accesses were from a single account – Old One's.

Grondr's voice continued from behind the graphics. 'We've got one backbone transceiver dedicated to this Power right now . . . Frankly, we can't tolerate this for more than a few days; the ultimate expense is just too great.'

Grondr's face was back on the display. 'Anyway, I think you can see that the deal for the barbarian is really the least of our problems. The last twenty days have brought more income than the last two years – far more than we can verify and absorb. We're endangered by our own success.'

He made an ironic smile-frown.

They talked a few minutes about Pham Nuwen, then Grondr rang off. Afterwards, Ravna took a walk along her beach. The sun was well down toward the aft horizon, and the sand was just pleasantly warm against her feet; the Docks went round the planet once every twenty hours, circling the pole at about forty degrees north latitude. She walked close to the surf, where the sand was flat and wet. The mist off the sea was moist against her skin. The blue sky just above the white-tops shaded quickly to indigo and black. Specks of silver moved up there, agrav floaters bringing starships into the Docks. The whole thing was so fabulously, unnecessarily expensive. Ravna was by turns grossed out and bedazzled. Yet after two years at Relay, she was beginning to see the point. Vrinimi Org wanted the Beyond to know that it had the resources to handle *whatever* communication and archive demands might be made on it. And they wanted the Beyond to suspect that there were hidden gifts from the Transcend here, things that might make it more than a little dangerous to invaders.

She stared into the spray, feeling it bead on her lashes. So Grondr had the big problem right now: how do you tell a Power to take a walk? All Ravna Bergsndot had to worry about was one overconfident twit who seemed hell-bent on destroying himself. She turned and paralleled the water. Every third wave it surged over her ankles.

She sighed. Pham Nuwen was beyond doubt a twit . . . but what an awesome one. Intellectually, she had always known that there was no difference in the possible intelligence of Beyonders and the primitives of the Slowness. Most automation worked better in the Beyond; ultralight communication was possible. But you had to go to the Transcend to build truly superhuman minds. So it shouldn't be surprising that Pham Nuwen was capable. *Very* capable. He had picked up Triskweline with incredible ease. She had little doubt that he was the master skipper he claimed. And to be a trader in the Slowness, to risk centuries between the stars for a destination that might have fallen from civilization or become deadly hostile to outsiders . . . that took courage that was hard to imagine. She could understand how he might think going to the Transcend was just another challenge. He'd had about twenty days to absorb a whole new universe. That simply wasn't enough time to understand that the rules change when the players are more than human.

Well, he still had a few days of grace. She would change his mind. And after talking to Grondr just now, she wouldn't feel especially guilty about doing it.

8

The Foreign Quarter was actually about a third of the Docks. It abutted the no-atmosphere periphery – where ships actually docked – and extended inwards to a section of the central sea. Vrinimi Org had convinced a significant number of races that this was a wonder of the Middle Beyond. In addition to freight traffic there were tourists – some of the wealthiest beings in the Beyond.

Pham Nuwen had carte blanche to these amusements. Ravna took him through the more spectacular ones, including an agrav hop over the Docks. The barbarian was more impressed by their pocket space suits than by the Docks. 'I've seen structures bigger than that down in the Slowness.' *Not hovering in a planetary gravity well, you haven't.*

Pham Nuwen seemed to mellow as the evening progressed. At least his comments became more perceptive, less edged. He wanted to see how real traders lived in the Beyond, and Ravna showed him the bourses and the traders' Local.

They ended up in The Wandering Company just after Docks' midnight. This was not Organization territory, but it was one of Ravna's favorite places, a private dive that attracted traders from the Top to the Bottom. She wondered how the decor would appeal to Pham Nuwen. The place was modeled as a meeting lodge on some world of the Slow Zone. A three-meter model ramscoop hung in the air over the main service floor. Blue-green drive fields glowed from the ship's every corner and flange, and spread faintly among patrons sitting below.

To Ravna the walls and floors were heavy timber, rough cut. People like Egravan saw stone walls and narrow tunnels – the sort of broodery his race had maintained on new conquests of long ago. The trickery was optical – not some mental smudging – and about the best that could be done in the Middle Beyond.

Ravna and Pham walked between widely spaced tables. The owners weren't as successful with sound as with vision: the music was faint and changed from table to table. Smells changed too, and were a little bit harder to take. Air management was working hard to keep everyone healthy, if not completely comfortable. Tonight the place was crowded. At the far end of the service floor, the special-atmosphere nooks were occupied: low pressure, high pressure, high NO_x, aquaria. Some customers were vague blurs within turbid atmospheres.

In some ways it might have been a port bar at Sjandra Kei. Yet . . . this was *Relay*. It attracted High Beyonders who would never come to backwaters like Sjandra Kei. Most of the High Ones didn't look very strange; civilizations at the Top were most often just colonies from below. But the headbands she saw here were not jewelry. Mind-computer links aren't efficient in the Middle Beyond, but most of the High Beyonders would not give them up. Ravna started toward a group of banded tripods and their machines. Let Pham Nuwen talk with creatures who teetered on the edge of transsapience.

Surprisingly, he touched her arm, drawing her back. 'Let's walk around a little more.' He was looking all around the hall, as if searching for a familiar face. 'Let's find some other humans first.'

When holes showed in Pham Nuwen's cram-education, they were gapingly wide. Ravna tried to keep her face serious. 'Other humans? We're all there is at Relay, Pham.'

'But the friends you've been telling me about . . . Egravan, Sarale?'

Ravna just shook her head. For a moment the barbarian

73

looked vulnerable. Pham Nuwen had spent his life crawling at sublight between human-colonized star systems. She knew that in all that life he had seen only three non-human races. Now he was lost in a sea of alienness. She kept her sympathy to herself; this one insight might affect the guy more than all her arguing.

But the instant passed, and he was smiling again. 'Even more an adventure.' They left the main floor and walked past special-atmosphere nooks. 'Lord, but Qeng Ho would love this.'

No humans anywhere, and The Wandering Company was the homiest meeting place she knew; many Org customers met only on the Net. She felt her own homesickness welling up. On the second floor, a signet flag caught her eye. She'd known something like it back at Sjandra Kei. She drew Pham Nuwen across the floor, and started up the timbered stairs.

Out of the background murmur, she heard a high-pitched twittering. It wasn't Triskweline, but the words made sense! By the Powers, it was *Samnorsk:* 'I do believe it's a Homo Sap! Over here, my lady.' She followed the sound to the table with the signet flag.

'May we sit with you?' she asked, savoring the familiar language.

'Plese do.' The twitterer looked like a small ornamental tree sitting in a six-wheeled cart. The cart was marked with cosmetic stripes and tassels; its 150-by-120-centimeter topside was covered with a cargo scarf in the same pattern as the signet flag. The creature was a Greater Skroderider. Its race traded through much of the Middle Beyond, including Sjandra Kei. The Skroderider's high-pitched voice came from its voder. But speaking Samnorsk, it sounded homier than anything she'd heard in a long time. Even granting the mental peculiarities of Skroderiders, she felt a surge of affectionate nostalgia, as if she had run into an old classmate in a far city.

'My name is –' the sound was the rustling of fronds, 'but you can easier call me Blueshell. It's nice to see a familiar face, hahaha.' Blueshell spoke the laughter as words. Pham Nuwen had sat down with Ravna, but he understood not a word of Samnorsk and so the great reunion was lost on him. The Rider switched to Triskweline and introduced his four companions: another Skroderider, and three humanoids who seemed to like the shadows. None of the humanoids spoke Samnorsk, but no one was more than one translator hop from Triskweline.

The Skroderiders were owners/operators of a small interstellar freighter, the *Out of Band II*. The humanoids were certificants for part of the starship's current cargo. 'My mate and I have been in the business almost two hundred years. We have happy feelings for your race, my lady. Our first runs were between Sjandra Kei and Forste Utgrep. Your people are good customers and we scarcely ever have a shipment rot . . .' He wheeled his skrode back from the table and then drove forward – the equivalent of a small bow.

All was not sweetness and light, however. One of the humanoids spoke. The sounds could almost have come from a human throat, though they made no sense. A moment passed as the house translator processed his words. Then the broach on his jacket spoke in clear Triskweline: 'Blueshell states you are Homo sapiens. Know that you have our animosity. We are bankrupt, near-stranded here by your race's evil creation. The Straumli Perversion.' The words sounded emotionless, but Ravna could see the creature's tense posture, its fingers twisting at a drink bulb.

Considering his attitude, it probably wouldn't help to point out that though she was human, Sjandra Kei was thousands of light-years from Straum. 'You came here from the Realm?' she asked the Skroderider.

Blueshell didn't answer immediately. That's the way it was with his race; he was probably trying to remember who she was and what they were all talking about. Then: 'Yes, yes. Please do excuse my certificants' hostility. Our main cargo is a one-time cryptographic pad. The source is Commercial Security at Sjandra Kei; the destination is the certificants' High colony. It was the usual arrangement: We're carrying a one-third xor of the pad. Independent shippers are carrying the others. At the destination, the three parts would be xor'd together. The result could supply a dozen worlds' crypto needs on the Net for —'

Downstairs there was a commotion. Someone was smoking something a bit too strong for the air scrubbers. Ravna caught a whiff, enough to shimmer her vision. It had knocked out several patrons on the main level. Management was counseling the offending customer. Blueshell made an abrupt noise. He backed his skrode from the table and rolled to the railing. 'Don't want to be caught unawares. Some people can be so *abrupt* . . . ' When nothing more came of the incident, he returned. 'Uh, where was I?' He was silent a moment, consulting the short-term memory built into his skrode. 'Yes, yes . . . We would become relatively rich if our plans work out. Unfortunately, we stopped on Straum to drop off some bulk data.' He pivoted on his rear four wheels. 'Surely that was safe? Straum itself is more than a hundred light-years from their lab in the Transcend. Yet —'

One of the certificants interrupted with loud gabble. The house translator kicked in a moment later: 'Yes. It should have been safe. We saw no violence. Ship's recorders show that our safeness was not breached. Yet now there are rumors. Net groups claim that Straumli Realm is owned by perversion. Absurdity. Yet these rumors have crossed the Net to our destination. Our cargo is not trusted, so our cargo is ruined: now it is only a few grams of data medium carrying random —' In the middle of the flat-voiced translation, the humanoid lunged out of the shadows. Ravna had a glimpse of a jaw edged with razor-sharp gums. He threw his drink bulb at the table in front of her.

Pham Nuwen's hand flashed out, snatching the drink before it hit — before she had quite realized what was happening. The redhead came slowly to his feet. From the shadows, the two other humanoids came to their feet and moved toward their friend. Pham Nuwen didn't say a word. He set the bulb carefully down and leaned just slightly toward the other, his hands relaxed yet bladelike. Cheap fiction talks about 'looks of deadly menace.' Ravna had never expected to see the real thing. But the humanoids saw it too. They tugged their friend gently back from the table. The loudmouth did not resist, but once beyond Pham's reach he erupted in a barrage of squeals and hisses that left the house translator speechless. He made a sharp gesture with three fingers, and shut up. The three swept silently down the stairs and away.

Pham Nuwen sat down, his gray eyes calm and untroubled. Maybe he *did* have something to be arrogant about! Ravna looked across at the two Skroderiders. 'I'm sorry your cargo lost value.'

Most of Ravna's past contacts had been with Lesser Skroderiders, whose reflexes were only slightly augmented beyond their sessile heritage. Had these two even noticed the interruption? But Blueshell answered immediately, 'Do not apologize. Ever since our arrival, those three have been complaining. Contract partners or not, I'm very tired of them.' He lapsed into potted-plant mode.

After a moment, the other Rider – Greenstalk, was it? – spoke. 'Besides, our commercial situation may not be a complete failure. I am sure the other thirds of the shipment went nowhere near Straumli Realm.' That was the usual procedure anyway: each part of the shipment was carried by a different company, each taking a very different path. If the other thirds could be certified, the crew of the *Out of Band* might not come away empty-handed. 'In – in fact, there may be a way we can get full certification. True, we were at Straumli Main, but –'

'How long ago did you leave?'

'Six hundred and fifty hours ago. About two hundred hours after they dropped off the Net.'

It suddenly dawned on Ravna that she was talking to something like eyewitnesses. After thirty days, the Threats news was still dominated by the events at Straum. The consensus was that a Class Two perversion had been created – even Vrinimi Org believed that. Yet it was still mainly guesswork . . . And here she was talking to beings who had actually been there. 'You don't think the Straumers created a perversion?'

It was Blueshell who replied. 'Sigh,' he said. 'Our certificants deny it, but I see a problem of conscience here. We *did* witness strangeness on Straum . . . Have you ever encountered artificial immune systems? The ones that work

77

in the Middle Beyond are more trouble than they're worth, so perhaps not. I noticed a real change in certain officers of the Crypto Authority right after the Straumli victory. It was as if they were suddenly part of a poorly calibrated automation, as if they were somebody's, um, fingers . . . No one can doubt they were playing in the Transcend. They found something up there; a lost archive. But that is not the point.' He stopped talking for a long moment; Ravna almost thought he was finished. 'You see, just before leaving Straumli Main, we –'

But now Pham Nuwen was talking too. 'That's something I've been wondering about. Everybody talks as though this Straumli Realm was doomed the moment they began research in the Transcend. Look. I've played with bugged software and strange weapons. I know you can get killed that way. But it looks like the Straumers were careful to put their lab far away. They were building something that could go very wrong, but apparently it was a previously tried experiment – like just about everything Up Here. They could stop the work any time it deviated from the records, right up to the end. So how could they screw up so bad?'

The question stopped the Skroderider in its tracks. You didn't need a doctorate in Applied Theology to know the answer. *Even the damn Straumers should have known the answer.* But given Pham Nuwen's background, it was a reasonable question. Ravna kept her mouth shut. The Skroderider's very alienness might be more convincing to Pham than another lecture from her.

Blueshell dithered for a moment, no doubt using his skrode to help assemble his arguments. When he finally spoke, he didn't seem irritated by the interruption. 'I hear several misconceptions, my lady Pham.' He seemed to use the old Nyjoran honorific pretty indiscriminately. 'Have you been into the archive at Relay?'

Pham said yes. Ravna guessed he'd never been past the beginners' front end.

'Then you know that an archive is a fundamentally vaster thing than the database on a conventional local net. For practical purposes, the big ones can't even be duplicated. The major archives go back millions of years, have been maintained by hundreds of different races – most now extinct or Transcended into Powers. Even the archive at Relay is a jumble, so huge that indexing systems are laid on top of indexing systems. Only in the Transcend could such a mass be well organized and even then only the Powers could understand it.'

'So?'

'There are thousands of archives in the Beyond – tens of thousands if you count the ones that have fallen into disrepair or dropped off the Net. Along with unending trivia, they contain important secrets and important lies. There are traps and snares.' Millions of races played with the advice that filtered unsolicited across the Net. Tens of thousands had been burned thereby. Sometimes the damage was relatively minor, good inventions that weren't quite right for the target environment. Sometimes it was malicious, viruses that would jam a local net so thoroughly that a civilizaton must restart from scratch. Where-Are-They-Now and Threats carried stories of worse tragedies: planets kneedeep in replicant goo, races turned brainless by badly programmed immune systems.

Pham Nuwen was wearing his skeptical expression. 'Just test the stuff at a safe remove. Be prepared for local disasters.'

That would have brought most explanations to a stop. Ravna had to admire the Skroderider: he paused, retreated to still more elementary terms. 'True, simple caution can prevent many disasters. And if your lab is in the Middle or Low Beyond, such caution is all that is really needed – no matter how sophisticated the threat. But we all understand the nature of the Zones . . .' Ravna had virtually no feel for Rider body language, but she would have sworn that Blueshell was watching the barbarian expectantly, trying to gauge the depth of Pham's ignorance.

The human nodded impatiently.

Blueshell continued. 'In the Transcend, truly sophisticated equipment can operate devices substantially smarter than anyone down here. Of course, almost any economic or military competition can be won by the side with superior computing resources. Such can be had at the Top of the

Beyond and in the Transcend. Races are always migrating there, hoping to build their utopias. But what do you do when your new creations may be smarter than you are? It happens that there are limitless possibilities for disaster, even if an existing Power does not cause harm. So there are unnumbered recipes for safely taking advantage of the Transcend. Of course they can't be effectively examined except in the Transcend. And run on devices of their own description, the recipes themselves become sentient.'

Understanding was beginning to glimmer across Pham Nuwen's face.

Ravna leaned forward, caught the redhead's attention. 'There are complex things in the archives. None of them is sentient, but some have the potential, if some naive young race will only believe their promises. We think that's what happened to Straumli Realm. They were tricked by documentation that claimed miracles, tricked into building a transcendent being, a Power – but one that victimizes sophonts in the Beyond.' She didn't mention how rare such perversion was. The Powers were variously malevolent, playful, indifferent – but virtually all of them had better uses for their time than exterminating cockroaches in the wild.

Pham Nuwen rubbed his jaw thoughtfully. 'Okay, I guess I see. But I get the feeling this is common knowledge. If it's this deadly, how did the Straumli bunch get taken in?'

'Bad luck and criminal incompetence.' The words popped out of her with surprising force. She hadn't realized she was so bent by the Straumli thing; somewhere inside, her old feelings for Straumli Realm were still alive. 'Look. Operations in the High Beyond and in the Transcend *are* dangerous. Civilizations up there don't last long, but there will always be people who try. Very few of the threats are actively evil. What happened to the Straumers . . . They ran across this recipe advertising wondrous treasure. Quite possibly it had been lying around for millions of years, a little too risky for other folks to try. You're right, the Straumers knew the dangers.' But it was a classic situation of balancing risks and choosing wrong. Perhaps a third of Applied Theology was about how to dance near the flame without getting incinerated. No one knew the details of the Straumli debacle, but she could guess them from a hundred similar cases:

'So they set up a base in the Transcend at this lost archive – if that's what it was. They began implementing the schemes they found. You can be sure they spent most of their time watching it for signs of deception. No doubt the recipe was a series of more or less intelligible steps with a clear takeoff point. The early stages would involve computers and programs more effective than anything in the Beyond – but apparently well-behaved.'

'. . . Yeah. Even in the Slowness, a big program can be full of surprises.'

Ravna nodded. 'And some of *these* would be near or beyond human complexity. Of course, the Straumers would know this and try to isolate their creations. But given a malignant and clever design . . . it should be no surprise if the devices leaked onto the lab's local net and distorted the information there. From then on, the Straumers wouldn't have a chance. The most cautious staffers would be framed as incompetent. Phantom threats would be detected, emergency responses demanded. More sophisticated devices would be built, and with fewer safeguards. Conceivably, the humans were killed or rewritten before the Perversion even achieved transsapience.'

There was a long silence. Pham Nuwen looked almost chastened. *Yeah. There's a lot you don't know, Buddy. Think on what Old One might have planned for you.*

Blueshell bent a tendril to taste a brown concoction that smelled like seaweed. 'Well told, my lady Ravna. But there is one difference in the present situation. It may be good fortune, and very important . . . You see, just before leaving Straumli Main, we attended a beach party among the Lesser Riders. They had been little affected by events to that point; many hadn't even noticed the destruction of independence at Straum. With luck, they may be the last enslaved.' His squeaky voice lowered an octave, trailing into silence. 'Where was I? Yes, the party. There was one fellow there, a bit more lively than the average. Somewhere years past, he had bonded with a traveler in a Straumli news service. Now he was acting as a clandestine data drop, so humble that he wasn't even listed in that service's own net . . .

'Anyway, the researchers at the Straumli lab – a few of them at least – were not so incautious as you say. They suspected a perverse runaway, and were determined to sabotage it.'

This *was* news, but – 'Doesn't look like they had much success, does it?'

'I am nodding agreement. They did not prevent it, but they did plan to escape the laboratory planet with two starships. And they did get word of their attempt into channels that ended with my acquaintance at the beach party. And here is the important part: At least one of these ships was to carry away some final elements of the Perversion's recipe – *before* they were incorporated into the design.'

'Surely there were backups –' began Pham Nuwen.

Ravna waved him silent. There had been enough grade-school explanations for one night. This was incredible. She'd been following the news about Straumli Realm as much as anyone. The Realm was the first High daughter colony of Sjandra Kei; it was horrifying to see it destroyed. But nowhere in Threats had there been even a rumor of this: the Perversion not whole? 'If this is true, then the Straumers may have a chance. It all depends on the missing parts of the design document.'

'Just so. And of course the humans realized this too. They planned to head straight for the Bottom of the Beyond, rendezvous there with their accomplices from Straum.'

Which – considering the ultimate magnitude of the disaster – would never happen. Ravna leaned back, oblivious of Pham Nuwen for the first time in many hours. Most likely both ships had been destroyed by now. If not – well, the Straumers had been at least half-smart, heading for the Bottom. If they had what Blueshell thought, the Perversion would be very interested in finding them. It was no wonder Blueshell and Greenstalk hadn't announced this on the news groups. 'So you know where they were going to rendezvous?' she said softly.

'Approximately.'

Greenstalk burred something at him.

'Not in ourselves,' he said. 'The coordinates are in the safeness at our ship. But there is more. The Straumers had a backup plan if the rendezvous failed. They intended to signal Relay with their ship's ultrawave.'

'Now wait. Just how big is this ship?' Ravna was no physical-layer engineer, but she knew that Relay's backbone transceivers were actually swarms of antenna elements scattered across several light-years, each element ten-thousand kilometers across.

Blueshell rolled forward and back, a quick gesture of agitation. 'We don't know, but it's nothing exceptional. Unless you're looking precisely at it with large antenna, you'd never detect it from here.'

Greenstalk added, 'We think that was part of their plan, though it is desperation on top of desperation. Since we came to Relay, we've been talking to the Org –'

'Discreetly! Quietly!' Blueshell put in abruptly.

'Yes. We've asked the Organization to listen for this ship. I'm afraid we haven't talked to the right people. No one seems to put much credence in us. After all, the story is ultimately from a Lesser Rider.' *Yeah. What could they know that was under a hundred years old?* 'What we're asking would normally be a great expense, and apparently prices are especially high right now.'

Ravna tried to curb her enthusiasm. If she had read this in a newsgroup, it would've been just one more interesting rumor. Why should she boggle just because she was getting it face-to-face? By the Powers, what irony. Hundreds of customers from the Top and the Transcend – even Old One – were saturating Relay's resources with their curiosity about the Straumli debacle. What if the answer had been sitting in front of them, suppressed by the very eagerness of their investigation? 'Just who have you been talking to? Never mind, never mind.' Maybe she should just go to Grondr 'Kalir with the story. 'I think you should know that I am a –' *very minor!* '– employee of the Vrinimi Organization. I may be able to help.'

83

She had expected some surprise at this sudden good luck. Instead there was a pause. Apparently Blueshell had lost his place in the conversation. Finally Greenstalk spoke. 'I am blushing . . . You see, we knew that. Blueshell looked you up in the employees directory; you are the only human in the Org. You're not in Customer Contact, but we thought that if we chanced upon you, so to speak, you might give us a kindly hearing.'

Blueshell's tendrils rustled together sharply. Irritation? Or had he finally caught up to the conversation? 'Yes. Well, since we are all being so frank, I suppose we should confess that this might even benefit us. If the refugee ship can prove that the Perversion is not a full Class Two, then perhaps we can convince our buyers that our cargo has not been compromised. If they only knew, my certificant friends would be groveling at your feet, my lady Ravna.'

They stayed at The Wandering Company until well past midnight. Business picked up at the circadian peak of some of the new arrivals. Floor and table shows were raucous all around. Pham's eyes flickered this way and that, taking it all in. But above all he seemed fascinated by Blueshell and Greenstalk. The two were starkly nonhuman, in some ways even strange as aliens go. Skroderiders were one of the very few races that had achieved long-term stability in the Beyond. Speciation had long ago occurred, varieties heading outward or becoming extinct. And still there were some who matched their ancient skrodes, a unique balance of outlook and machine interface that was more than a billion years old. But Blueshell and Greenstalk were also traders with much of the outlook that Pham Nuwen had known in the Slowness. And though Pham acted as ignorant as ever, there was new diplomacy in him. Or maybe the awesomeness of the Beyond was finally getting through his thick skull. He couldn't have asked for better drinking buddies. As a race, the Skroderiders preferred lazy reminiscence to almost any activity. Once delivered of their critical message, the two were quite content to talk of their life in the Beyond, to explain things in whatever detail the barbarian could wish. The razor-jawed certificants stayed well lost.

Ravna got a mild buzz on, and watched the three talk shop. She smiled to herself. *She* was the outsider now, the person who had never *done*. Blueshell and Greenstalk had been all over, and some of their stories sounded wild even to her. Ravna had a theory (not that widely accepted, actually) that where beings have a common fluency, little else matters. Two of these three might be mistaken for potted trees on hotcarts, and the third was unlike any human in her life. Their fluency was in an artificial language, and two of the 'voices' were squawky raspings. Yet . . . after a few minutes' listening, their personalities seemed to float in her mind's eye, more interesting than many of her school chums, but not that different. The two Skroderiders were mates. She hadn't thought that could count for much; among Riders, sex amounted to scarcely more than being next-door neighbors at the right time of year. Yet there was deep affection here. Greenstalk especially seemed a loving personality. She (he?) was shy yet stubborn, with a kind of honesty that might be a major handicap in a trader. Blueshell made up for that failing. He (she?) could be glib and talkative, quite capable of maneuvering things his way. Underneath, Ravna glimpsed a compulsive person, uncomfortable with his own sneakiness, ultimately grateful when Greenstalk reined him in.

And what of Pham Nuwen? *Yes, what's the inner being you see there?* In an odd way, he was more of a mystery. The arrogant boob of this afternoon seemed to be mostly invisible tonight. Maybe it had been a cover for insecurity. The fellow had been born in a male-dominated culture, virtually the opposite of the matriarchy that all Beyonder humanity descended from. Underneath the arrogance, a very nice person might be living. Then there was the way he had faced down the razor-jaw. And the way he was drawing out the Skroderiders. It occurred to Ravna that after a lifetime of reading romantic fiction, she had run into her first hero.

It was after 02:30 when they left The Wandering Company. The sun would be rising across the bow horizon in less than five hours. The two Skroderiders came outside to see them

85

off. Blueshell had switched back to Samnorsk to regale Ravna with a story of his last visit to Sjandra Kei – and to remind her to ask about the refugee ship.

The Skroderiders dwindled beneath them as Ravna and Pham rose into the thinning air and headed toward the residential towers.

The two humans didn't say anything for a couple of minutes. It was even possible that Pham Nuwen was impressed by the view. They were passing over gaps in the brightly lit Docks, places where they could see through the parks and concourses to the surface of Groundside a thousand kilometers below. The clouds there were whorls of dark on dark.

Ravna's residence was at the outer edge of the Docks. Here the air fountains were of no use; her apartment tower rose into frank vacuum. They glided down to her balcony, trading their suits' atmosphere for the apartment's. Ravna's mouth was leading a life of its own, explaining how the residence was what she'd been assigned when she worked at the archive, that it was nothing compared to her new office. Pham Nuwen nodded, quiet-faced. There were none of the smart remarks of their earlier tours.

She babbled on, and then they were inside and . . . She shut up, and they just looked at each other. In a way, she'd wanted this clown ever since Grondr's silly animation. But it wasn't till this evening at The Wandering Company that she'd felt right about bringing him home with her. 'Well, I, uh . . .' *So. Ravna, the ravening princess. Where is your glib tongue now?*

She settled for reaching out, putting her hand on his. Pham Nuwen smiled back, shy too, by the Powers! 'I think you have a nice place,' he said.

'I've decorated it Techno-Primitive. Being stuck at the edge of the Docks has its points: The natural view isn't messed up by city lights. Here, I'll show you.' She doused the lights and pulled the curtains aside. The window was a natural transparency, looking out from the edge of the Docks. The view tonight should be terrific. On the ride from The Company the sky had been awfully dark. The in-system factories must be off-line or hidden behind Groundside. Even ship traffic seemed sparse.

She went back to stand by Pham. The window was a vague rectangle across her vision. 'You have to wait a minute for your eyes to adjust. There's no amplification at all.' The curve of Groundside was clear now, clouds with occasional pricks of light. She slipped her arm across his back, and after a moment felt his across her shoulders.

She'd guessed right: tonight the Galaxy owned the sky. It was a sight that Vrinimi old hands happily ignored. For Ravna it was the most beautiful thing about Relay. Without enhancement, the light was faint. Twenty thousand light-years is a long, long way. At first there was just a suggestion of mist, and an occasional star. As her eyes adapted, the mist took shape, curving arcs, some places brighter, some dimmer. A minute more and . . . there were knots in the mist . . . there were streaks of utter black that separated the curving arms . . . complexity on complexity, twisting toward the pale hub that was the Core. Maelstrom. Whirlpool. Frozen, still, across half the sky.

She heard Pham's breath catch in his throat. He said something, sing-song syllables that could not have been Trisk, and certainly not Samnorsk. 'All my life I lived in a tiny clump of that. And I thought I was a master of space. I never dreamed to stand and see the whole blessed thing at once.' His hand tightened on her shoulder, then gentled, stroking her neck. 'And no matter how long we watch, will we see any sign of the Zones?'

She shook her head slowly. 'But they're easily imagined.' She gestured with her free hand. In the large, the Zones of Thought followed the mass distribution of the Galaxy; The Unthinking Depths extending down to the soft glow of the galactic Core. Farther out, the Great Slowness, where humankind had been born, where ultralight could not exist and civilizations lived and died unknowing and unknown. And the Beyond, the stars about four-fifths out from the center, extending well off-plane to include places like Relay. The Known Net had existed in some form for billions of years in the Beyond. It was not a civilization; few civilizations lasted

87

longer than a million years. But the records of the past were quite complete. Sometimes they were intelligible. More often, reading them involved translations of translations of translations, passed down from one defunct race to another with no one to corroborate – worse than any multihop net message could ever be. Yet some things were quite clear: There had always been the Zones of Thought, though perhaps they were slightly inward-moved now. There had always been wars and peace, and races upwelling from the Great Slowness, and thousands of little empires. There had always been races moving into the Transcend, to become the Powers . . . or their prey.

'And the Transcend?' Pham said. 'Is that just the far dark?' The dark between the galaxies.

Ravna laughed softly. 'It includes all that but . . . see the outer reaches of the spirals. They're in the Transcend.' Most everything farther than forty thousand light-years from the galactic center was.

Pham Nuwen was silent for a long moment. She felt a tiny shiver pass through him. 'After talking to the wheelies, I – I think I understand more of what you were warning me about. There's a lot of things I don't know, things that could kill me . . . or worse.'

Common sense triumphs at last. 'True,' she said quietly. 'But it's not just you, or the brief time you've been here. You could study your whole life, and not know. How long must a fish study to understand human motivation? It's not a good analogy, but it's the only safe one; we *are* like dumb animals to the Powers of the Transcend. Think of all the different things people do to animals – ingenious, sadistic, charitable, genocidal – each has a million elaborations in the Transcend. The Zones are a natural protection; without them, human-equivalent intelligence would probably not exist.' She waved at the misty star swarms. 'The Beyond and below are like a deep of ocean, and we the creatures that swim in the abyss. We're so far down that the beings on the surface – superior though they are – can't effectively reach us. Oh, they fish, and they sometimes blight the upper levels with poisons we don't even understand. But the abyss remains a relatively safe place.' She paused. There was more to the analogy. 'And just as with an ocean, there is a constant drift of flotsam from the top. There are things that can only be made at the Top, that need close-to-sentient factories – but which can still work down here. Blueshell mentioned some of those when he was talking to you: the agrav fabrics, the sapient devices. Such things are the greatest physical wealth of the Beyond, since we can't make them. And getting them is a deadly risky endeavor.'

Pham turned toward her, away from window and the stars. 'So there are always "fish" edging close to the surface.' For an instant she thought she had lost him, that he was caught by the romance of the Transcendent death-wish. 'Little fish risking everything for a piece of godhood . . . and not knowing heaven from hell, even when they find it.' She felt him shiver, and then his arms were around her. She tilted her head up and found his lips waiting.

It had been two years since Ravna Bergsndot left Sjandra Kei. In some ways the time had gone fast. Just now her body was telling her what a long, long time it really had been. Every touch was so vivid, waking desires carefully suppressed. Suddenly her skin was tingling all over. It took marvelous restraint to undress without tearing anything.

Ravna was out of practice. And of course she had nothing recent to compare to . . . But Pham Nuwen was very, *very* good.

Crypto: 0
As received by: Transceiver Relay01 at Relay
Language path: Acquileron→Triskweline, SjK: Relay units
From: Net Administrator for Transceiver Windsong at Debley Down
Subject: Complaints about Relay, a suggestion
Summary: It's getting worse; try us instead
Key phrases: communications problems, Relay unreliability, Transcend
Distribution:

Communication Costs Special Interest Group
Motley Hatch Administration Group
Transceiver Relay01 at Relay
Transceiver Not-for-Long at Shortstop
Follow-ups to: Windsong Expansion Interest Group
Date: 07:21:21 Docks Time, 36/09 of Org year 52089
Text of message:

During the last five hundred hours, Comm Costs shows 9,834 transceiver-layer congestion complaints against the Vrinimi operation at Relay. Each of these complaints involves services to tens of thousands of planets. Vrinimi has promised again and again that the congestion is a purely temporary increase of Transcendent usage.

As Relay's chief competitor in this region, we of Windsong have benefited modestly from the overflow; however, until now we thought it inappropriate to propose a coordinated response to the problem.

The events of the last seven hours compel us to change this policy. Those reading this item already know about the incident; most of you are the victims of it. Beginning at [00:00:27 Docks Time], Vrinimi Org began taking transceivers off-line, an unscheduled outage. R01 went out at 00:00:27, R02 at 02:50:32, RO3 and RO4 at 03:12:01. Vrinimi stated that a Transcendent customer was urgently requesting bandwidth. (ROO had been previously dedicated to that Power's use.) The customer required use of both up- and down-link bandwidth. By the Org's own admission, the unscheduled usage exceeded sixty percent of their entire capacity. Note that the excesses of the preceding five hundred hours – excesses which caused entirely justified complaint – were never more than five percent of Org capacity.

Friends, we of Windsong are in the long-haul communication business. We know how difficult it is to maintain transceiver elements that mass as much as a planet. We know that hard contract commitments simply cannot be made by suppliers in our line of work.

But at the same time, the behavior of Vrinimi Org is unacceptable. It's true that in the last three hours the Org has returned R01 through R04 to general service, and promised to pass on the Power's surpayment to all those who were 'inconvenienced.' But only Vrinimi knows how large these surpayments really are. And no one (not even Vrinimi!) knows whether this is the end of the outages.

What is to Vrinimi a sudden, incredible cash glut, is to the rest of you an unaccountable disaster.

Therefore Windsong at Debley Down is considering a major – and permanent – expansion of our service: the construction of five additional backbone transceivers. Obviously this will be immensely expensive. Transceivers are never cheap, and Debley Down does not have quite the geometry enjoyed by Relay. We expect the cost must be amortized over many decades of good business. We can't undertake it without clear customer commitment. In order to determine this demand, and to ensure that we build what is really needed, we are creating a temporary newsgroup, Windsong Expansion Interest Group, moderated and archived at Windsong. Send/Receive charges to transceiver-layer customers on this group will be only ten percent our usual. We urge you, our transceiver-layer customers, to use this service to talk to each other, to decide what you can safely expect from Vrinimi Org in the future and how you feel about our proposals.

We are waiting to hear from you.

9

Afterwards, Ravna slept well. It was halfway through the morning when she drifted back toward wakefulness. The ring of her phone was monotonously insistent, loud enough to reach through the most pleasant dreams. She opened her eyes, disoriented and happy. She was lying with her arms wrapped tightly around . . . a large pillow. Damn. He'd already left. She lay back for a second, remembering. These last two years she had been lonely; till last night she hadn't realized how lonely. Happiness so unexpected, so intense . . . what a strange thing.

The phone just kept ringing. Finally she rolled out of bed and walked unsteadily across the room; there should be limits to this Techno Primitive nonsense. 'Yes?'

It was a Skroderider. Greenstalk? 'I'm sorry to bother you, Ravna, but – are you all right?' The Rider interrupted herself.

Ravna suddenly realized that she might be looking a little strange: sappy smile spread from ear to ear, hair sticking out in all directions. She rubbed her hand across her mouth, cutting back laughter. 'Yes, I'm fine.' Fine! 'What's up?'

'We want to thank you for your help. We had never dreamed that you were so highly placed. We'd been trying for hundreds of hours to persuade the Org to listen for the refugees. But less than an hour after talking to you, we were told the survey is being undertaken immediately.'

'Um.' Say *what*? 'That's wonderful, but I'm not sure I – who's paying for it, anyway?'

'I don't know, but it *is* expensive. We were told they're dedicating a backbone transceiver to the search. If there's anyone transmitting, we should know in a matter of hours.'

They chatted for a few more minutes, Ravna gradually becoming more coherent as she parceled the various aspects of the last ten hours into business and pleasure. She had half expected the Org to bug her at The Wandering Company. Maybe Grondr just heard the story there – and gave it full credit. But just yesterday, he'd been wimping about transceiver saturation. Either way, this was good news – perhaps extraordinarily good. If the Riders' wild story were true, the Straumli Perversion might be less than Transcendent. And if the refugee ships had some clues on how to bring it down, Straumli Realm might even be saved.

After Greenstalk rang off, Ravna wandered about the apartment, getting herself in shape, playing the various possibilities against each other. Her actions became more purposeful, almost up to their usual speed. There were a lot of things she wanted to check into.

Then the phone was ringing again. This time she previewed the caller. Oops! It was Grondr Vrinimikalir. She combed her hand back through her hair; it still looked like crap, and this phone was not up to deception. Suddenly she noticed that Grondr didn't look so hot either. His facial chitin was smudged, even across some of his freckles. She accepted the call.

'Ah!' His voice actually squeaked, then returned to its normal level. 'Thank you for answering. I would have called earlier, except things have been very . . . chaotic.' Just where had his cool distance gone? 'I just want you to know that the Org had nothing to do with this. We were totally taken in until just a couple of hours ago.' He launched into a disjointed description of massive demand swamping the Org's resources.

As he rambled, Ravna punched up a summary of recent Relay business. By the Powers that Be: *Sixty percent diversion?* Excerpts from Comm Costs: She scanned quickly down the item from Windsong. The gasbags were as pompous as ever, but their offer to replace Relay was probably for real. It was just the sort of thing Grondr had been afraid might happen.

'– Old One just kept asking for more and more. When we finally figured things out, and confronted him . . . Well, we came close to threatening violence. We *have* the resources to destroy his emissary vessel. No telling what his revenge might be, but we told Old One his demands were already destroying us. Thank the Powers, he just seemed amused; he backed off. He's restricted to a single transceiver now, and that's on a signal search that has nothing to do with us.'

Hmm. One mystery solved. Old One must have been snooping around The Wandering Company and overheard the Skroderiders' story. 'Maybe things will be okay, then. But it's important to be just as tough if Old One tries to abuse us again.' The words were already out of her mouth before she considered who she was giving advice to.

Grondr didn't seem to notice. If anything, *he* was the one scrambling to agree: 'Yes, yes. I'll tell you, if Old One were any ordinary customer, we'd blacklist him forever for this deception . . . But then if he were ordinary, he could never have fooled us.'

Grondr wiped pudgy white fingers across his face. 'No mere Beyonder could have altered our record of the dredge expedition. Not even one from the Top could have broken into the junkyard and manipulated the remains without our even suspecting.'

Dredge? Remains? Ravna began to see that she and Grondr were not talking about the same thing. 'Just what did Old One do?'

'The details? We're pretty sure of them now. Since the Fall of Straum, Old One has been very interested in humans. Unfortunately, there were no willing ones available here. It began manipulating us, rewriting our junkyard records. We've recovered a clean backup from a branch office: The dredge really did encounter the wreck of a human ship; there were human body parts in it – but nothing that we could have revived. Old One must have mixed and matched what he found there. Perhaps it fabricated memories by extrapolating from human cultural data in the archives. With hindsight, we can match its early requests with the invasion of our junkyard.'

Grondr rattled on, but Ravna wasn't listening. Her eyes stared blindly through the phone's display. *We are little fish in the abyss, protected by the deep from the fishers above. But even if they can't live down here, the clever fisherfolk still have their lures and deadly tricks.* And so Pham – 'Pham Nuwen is just a robot, then,' she said softly.

'Not precisely. He is human, and with his fake memories he can operate autonomously. But when Old One buys full bandwidth, the creature is fully an emissary device.' The hand and eye of a Power.

Grondr's mouthparts clattered in abject embarrassment. 'Ravna, we don't know all that happened last night; there was no reason to have you under close surveillance. But Old One assures us that its need for direct investigation is over. In any case, we'll never give him the bandwidth to try again.'

Ravna barely nodded. Her face suddenly felt cold. She had

94

never felt such anger and such fright at the same time. She stood in a wave of dizziness and walked away from the phone, ignoring Grondr's worried cries. The stories from grad school came tumbling through her mind, and the myths of a dozen human religions. Consequences, consequences. Some of them she could defend against; others were past repair.

And from somewhere in the back of her mind, an incredibly silly thought crawled out from under the horror and the rage. For eight hours she had been face to face with a Power. It was the sort of experience that made a chapter in textbooks, the sort of thing that was always far away and misreported. And it was the sort of thing no one in all of Sjandra Kei could come near to claiming. Until now.

10

Johanna was in the boat for a long time. The sun never set, though now it was low behind her, now it was high in front, now all was cloudy and rain plinked off the tarp covering her blankets. She spent the hours in an agonized haze. Things happened that could only have been dreams. There were creatures pulling at her clothes, blood sticking everywhere. Gentle hands and rat snouts dressed her wounds and forced chill water down her throat. When she thrashed around, Mom rearranged her blankets and comforted her with the strangest sounds. For hours, someone warm lay beside her. Sometimes it was Jefri; more often it was a large dog, a dog that purred.

The rain passed. The sun was on the left side of the boat, but hidden behind a cold, snapping shadow. More and more, the pain became divisible. Part of it was in her chest and shoulder; that stabbed through her whenever the boat wobbled. Part of it was in her gut, an emptiness that was not quite nausea . . . she was so hungry, so thirsty.

More and more, she was remembering, not dreaming. There were nightmares that would never go away. They had really happened. They were happening now.

The sun peeked in and out of the tumble of clouds. It slid slowly lower across the sky till it was almost behind the boat. She tried to remember what Daddy had been saying just before . . . everything went bad. They were in this planet's arctic, in the summer. So the sun's low point must be north, and their twin-hulled boat was sailing roughly southwards. Wherever they were going, it was minute by minute farther from the spacecraft and any hope of finding Jefri.

Sometimes the water was like open sea, the hills distant or hidden by low clouds. Sometimes they passed through narrows and swept close to walls of naked rock. She'd had no idea a sailboat could move so fast or be so dangerous. Four of the rat creatures worked desperately to keep them off the rocks. They bounded nimbly from mast platform to railing, sometimes standing each on the other's shoulders to extend their reach. The twin-hulled boat tilted and groaned in water that was suddenly rough. Then they'd be through and the hills would be at a peaceful distance, sliding slowly past.

For a long while she pretended delirium. She moaned, she twisted. She watched. The boat hulls were long and narrow, almost like canoes. The sail was mounted between them. The shadow in her dreams had been that sail, snapping in the cold, clean wind. The sky was an avalanche of grays, light and dark. There were birds up there. They dipped past the mast, circled again and again. There was twittering and hissing all around her. But the sound did not come from the birds.

It was the monsters. She watched them through lowered lashes. These were the same kind that killed Mom and Dad. They even wore the same funny clothes, gray-green jackets studded with stirrups and pockets. Dogs or wolves, she had thought before. That didn't really describe them. Sure, they had four slender legs and pointy little ears. But with their long necks and occasionally reddish eyes, they might as well be huge rats.

And the longer she watched them, the more horrible they seemed. A still image could never convey that horror; you had to see them in action. She watched four of them – the ones on her side of the boat – play with her dataset. The Pink Oliphaunt was tied in a net bag near the rear of the boat. Now the beasts wanted to look it over. At first it looked like a circus act, the creatures' heads darting this way and that. But every move was so precise, so *coordinated* with all the others. They had no hands, but they could untie knots, each holding a piece of twine in its mouth and maneuvering its necks around others. At the same time, one's claws held the loose netting tight against the railing. It was like watching puppets run off a group control.

In seconds they had it out of the bag. Dogs would have let it slide to the bottom of the hull, then pushed it around with their noses. Not these things: two put it onto a cross bench, while a third steadied it with its paw. They poked around the edges, concentrating on the plush flanges and floppy ears. They pushed and nuzzled, but with clear purpose. *They were trying to open it.*

Two heads showed over the railing on the other hull. They made the gobbling, hissing sounds that were a cross between a bird call and someone throwing up. One of those on her side glanced back and made similar sounds. The other three continued to play with the dataset's latches.

Finally they pulled the big, floppy ears simultaneously: the dataset popped open, and the top window went into Johanna's startup routine – an anim of herself saying 'Shame on you, Jefri. Stay out of my things!' The four creatures went rigid, their eyes suddenly wide.

Johanna's four turned the set so the others could see. One held it down while another peered at the top window, and a third fumbled with the key window. The guys in the other hull went nuts, but none of them tried to get any closer. The random prodding of the four abruptly cut off her startup greeting. One of them glanced at the guys in the other hull; another two watched Johanna. She continued to lie with her eyes almost closed.

'Shame on you, Jefri. Stay out of my things!' Johanna's voice came again, but from one of the animals. It was a perfect playback. Then a girl's voice was moaning, crying, 'Mom, Daddy.' It was her own voice again, but more frightened and childish than she ever wanted it to sound.

They seemed to be waiting for the dataset to respond. When nothing happened, one of them went back to pushing its nose against the windows. Everything valuable, and all the dangerous programs, were passworded. Insults and squawking emerged from the box, all the little surprises she had planted for her snooping little brother. *Oh Jefri, will I ever see you again?*

The sounds and vids kept the monsters amused for several minutes. Eventually their random fiddlings convinced the dataset that somebody *really* young had opened up the box, and it shifted into kindermode.

The creatures knew she was watching. Of the four fooling with her Oliphaunt, one – not always the same one – was always watching her. They were playing games with her, pretending they didn't know she was pretending.

Johanna opened her eyes wide and glared at the creature. 'Damn you!' She looked in the other direction. And screamed. The mob in the other hull were clumped together. Their heads rose on sinuous necks from the pile. In the low sunlight, their eyes glinted red: a pack of rats or snakes, silently staring at her, and for heaven knew how long.

The heads leaned forward at her cry, and she heard the scream again. Behind her, her own voice shouted 'Damn you!' Somewhere else, she was calling for 'Mom' and 'Daddy.' Johanna screamed again, and they just echoed it back. She swallowed her terror and kept silent. The monsters kept it up for a half minute, the mimicking, the mixing of things she must have said in her sleep. When they saw they couldn't terrorize her that way any more, the voices stopped being human. The gobbling went back and forth, as if the two groups were negotiating or something. Finally the four on her side closed her dataset and tied it into the net bag.

The six unwrapped themselves from each other. Three jumped to the outboard side of the hull. They gripped the edge tight in their claws and leaned into the wind. For once they almost did look like dogs – big ones sitting at a car window, sniffing at the airstream. The long necks swept forward and back. Every few seconds, one of them would dip its head out of sight, into the water. Drinking? Fishing?

Fishing. A head flipped up, tossing something small and green into the boat. The other three animals nosed about, grabbing it. She had a glimpse of tiny legs and a shiny carapace. One of the rats held it at the tip of its mouth, while the other two pulled it apart. It was all done with their uncanny precision. The pack seemed like a single creature, and each neck a heavy tentacle that ended in a pair of jaws. Her gut twisted at the thought, but there was nothing to barf up.

The fishing expedition went on another quarter hour. They got at least seven of the green things. But they weren't eating them; not all of them, anyway. The dismembered leavings collected in a small wood bowl.

More gobbling between the two sides. One of the six grabbed the bowl's edge in its mouth and crawled across the mast platform. The four on Johanna's side huddled together as if frightened of the visitor. Only after the bowl was set down and the intruder had returned to its side, did the four in Johanna's hull poke their heads up again.

One of the rats picked up the bowl. It and another walked toward her. Johanna swallowed. What torture was this? Her stomach twisted again . . . she was *so* hungry. She looked at the bowl again and realized that they were trying to feed her.

The sun had just come out from under northern clouds. The low light was like some bright fall afternoon, just after rain: dark sky above, yet everything close by was bright and glistening. The creatures' fur was deep and plush. One held the bowl towards her, while the other stuck its snout in and withdrew . . . something slick and green. It held the tidbit delicately, just with the tips of its long mouth. It turned and thrust the green thing toward her.

Johanna shrank back. 'No!'

The creature paused. For a moment she thought it was going to echo her. Then it dropped the lump back into the bowl. The first animal set it on the bench beside her. It looked up at her for an instant, then released the jaw-wide flange at the edge of the bowl. She had a glimpse of fine, pointy teeth.

Johanna stared into the bowl, nausea fighting with hunger.

99

Finally she worked a hand out of her blanket and reached into it. Heads perked up around her, and there was an exchange of gobble comments between the two sides of the boat.

Her fingers closed on something soft and cold. She lifted it into the sunlight. The body was gray green, its sides glistening in the light. The guys in the other hull had torn off the little legs and chopped away the head. What remained was only two or three centimeters long. It looked like filleted shellfish. Once she had liked such food. But that had been cooked. She almost dropped the thing when she felt it quiver in her hand.

She brought it close to her mouth, touched it with her tongue. Salty. On Straum, most shellfish would make you very sick if you ate them raw. How could she know, all alone without parents or a local commnet? She felt tears coming. She said a bad word, stuffed the green thing into her mouth, and tried to chew. Blandness, with the texture of suet and gristle. She gagged, spat it out . . . and tried to eat another. Altogether she got parts of two down. Maybe that was for the best; she'd wait and see how much she barfed up. She lay back and saw several pairs of eyes watching. The gobbling with the other side of the boat picked up. Then one of them sidled toward her, carying a leather bag with a spigot. A canteen.

This creature was the biggest of all. The leader? It moved its head close to hers, putting the spout of the canteen near her mouth. The big one seemed sly, more cautious about approaching her than the others. Johanna's eyes traveled back along its flanks. Beyond the edge of its jacket, the pelt on its rear was mostly white . . . and scored deep with a Y-shaped scar. *This is the one that killed Dad.*

Johanna's attack was not planned; perhaps that's why it worked so well. She lunged past the canteen and swung her free arm around the thing's neck. She rolled over the animal, pinning it against the hull. By itself, it was smaller than she, and not strong enough to push her off. She felt its claws raking through the blankets but somehow never quite cutting her. She put all her weight on the creature's spine, grabbed it where throat met jaw, and began slamming its head against the wood.

Then the others were on her, muzzles poking under her, jaws grabbing at her sleeve. She felt rows of needle teeth just poking through the fabric. Their bodies buzzed with a sound from her dreams, a sound that went straight through her clothes and rattled her bones.

They pulled her hand from the other's throat, twisting her; she felt the arrowhead tearing her inside. But there was still one thing she could do: Johanna pushed off with her feet, butting her head against the base of the other's jaw, smashing the top of its head into the hull. The bodies around her convulsed, and she was flipped onto her back. Pain was the only thing she could feel now. Neither rage nor fear could move her.

Yet part of her was still aware of the four. She had hurt them. She had hurt them. She had hurt them *all*. Three wandered drunkenly, making whistling sounds that for once seemed to come from their mouths. The one with the scarred butt lay on its side, twitching. She had punched a star-shaped wound in the top of its head. Blood dripped down past its eyes, red tears.

Minutes passed and the whistling stopped. The four creatures huddled together and the familiar hissing resumed. The bleeding from her chest had started again.

They stared at each other for a while. She smiled at her enemies. They could be hurt. *She* could hurt them. She felt better than she had since the landing.

I I

Before the Flenser Movement, Woodcarvers had been the most famous city-state west of the Icefangs. Its founder went back six centuries. In those days, things had been harder in the north; snow covered even the lowlands through most of the year. The Woodcarver had started alone, a single pack in a little cabin on an inland bay. The pack was a hunter and a thinker as much as an artist. There had been no settlements for a hundred miles around. Only a dozen of the carver's early statues ever left his cabin, yet those statues had been his first fame. Three were still in existence. There was a city by the Long Lakes named for the one in its museum.

With fame had come apprentices. One cabin became ten, scattered across Woodcarver's fjord. A century or two passed, and of course the Woodcarver slowly changed. He feared the change, the feeling that his soul was slipping away. He tried to keep hold of himself; almost everyone does to one extent or another. In the worst case, the pack falls into perversion, perhaps becomes soul-hollow. For Woodcarver, the quest was itself the change. He studied how each member fits within the soul. He studied pups and their raising, and how you might guess the contributions of a new one. He learned to shape the soul by training the members.

Of course little of this was new. It was the base of most religions, and every town had romance advisors and brood kenners. Such knowledge, whether valid or not, is important to any culture. What Woodcarver did was to look at it all again, without traditional bias. He gently experimented on himself and on the other artists in his little colony. He watched the results, using them to design new experiments. He was guided by what he saw rather than by what he wanted to believe.

By the various standards of his age, what he did was heresy or perversion or simply insanity. In the early years, King Woodcarver was hated almost as much as was Flenser three centuries later. But the far north was still going through its time of heavy winters. The nations of the south could not easily send armies as far as Woodcarvers. Once when they did, they were thoroughly defeated. And wisely, Woodcarver never attempted to subvert the south; not directly. But his settlement grew and grew, and its fame for art and furniture was small beside its other reputations. Old of heart traveled to the town, and came back not just younger, but smarter and happier. Ideas radiated from the town: weaving machines, gearboxes and windmills, factory postures. Something new had happened in this place. It wasn't the inventions. It was the people that Woodcarver had midwifed, and the outlook he had created.

Wickwrackscar and Jaqueramaphan arrived at Woodcarvers late in the afternoon. It had rained most of the day, but now the clouds had blown away and the sky was that bright cloudless blue that was all the more beautiful after a stretch of cloudy days.

Woodcarver's domain was paradise to Peregrine's eyes. He was tired of the packless wilderness. He was tired of worrying about the alien.

Twinhulls paced them suspiciously for the last few miles. The boats were armed, and Peregrine and Scriber were coming from very much the wrong direction. But they were all alone, clearly harmless. Long callers hooted, relaying their story ahead. By the time they reached the harbor they were heros, two packs who had stolen unspecified treasure from the villains of the north. They sailed around a breakwater that hadn't existed on Peregrine's last trip and tied in at the moorage.

The pier was crowded with soldiers and wagons. Townspeople were all over the road leading up to the city walls. This was as close to a mob scene as you could get and still have room for sober thought. Scriber bounced out of the boat and pranced about in obvious delight at the cheers from the hillside. 'Quickly! We must speak with the Woodcarver.'
, Wickwrackscar picked up the canvas bag that held the alien's picture box, and climbed carefully out of the boat. He was dizzy from the beating the alien had given him. Scar's fore-tympanum had been cut in the attack. For a moment he lost track of himself. The pier was very strange – stone at first glance, but walled with a spongy black material he hadn't seen since the Southseas; it should be brittle here . . . *Where am I? I should be happy about something, some victory.* He paused to regroup. After a moment both the pain and his thoughts sharpened; he would be like this for days yet, at least. Get help for the alien. Get it ashore.

King Woodcarver's Lord Chamberlain was a mostly over-weight dandy; Peregrine had not expected to see such at

Woodcarvers. But the fellow became instantly cooperative when he saw the alien. He brought a doctor down to look at the Two-Legs – and incidentally, at Peregrine. The alien had gained strength in the last two days, but there had been no more violence. They got it ashore without much trouble. It stared at Peregrine out of its flat face, a look he knew was impotent rage. He touched Scar's head thoughtfully . . . the Two-Legs was just waiting for the best opportunity to do more damage.

Minutes later the travelers were in kherhog-drawn carriages, rolling up the cobblestone street toward the city walls. Soldiers cleared the way through the crowd. Scriber Jaqueramaphan waved this way and that, the handsome hero. By now Peregrine knew the shy insecurity that lurked within Scriber. This might be the high point of his whole life till now.

Even if he wanted it, Wickwrackscar could not be so expansive. With one of Scar's tympana hurt, wild gestures made him lose track of his thoughts. He hunkered down on the carriage seats and looked out in all directions:

But for the shape of the outer harbor, the place was not at all what he remembered from fifty years ago. In most parts of the world, not much changed in fifty years. A pilgrim returning after such an interval might even be bored by the sameness. But this . . . it was almost scary.

The huge breakwater was new. There were twice as many piers, and multiboats with flags he had never seen on this side of the world. The road had been here before, but narrow, with only a third as many turnoffs. Before, the town walls had been more to keep the kherhogs and froghens in than any invaders out. Now the walls were ten feet high, black stone extending as far as Peregrine could see . . . And there had been scarcely any soldiers last time; now they were everywhere. That was not a good change. He felt a sinking in the pit of Scar's stomach; soldiers and fighting were *not* good.

They rode through the city gates and past a market maze that spread across acres. The alleys were only fifty feet wide, narrower where bolts of cloth, furniture displays, and crates of fresh fruit encroached. Smells of fruit and spice and varnish hung in the air. The place was so crowded that the haggling was almost an orgy, and dizzy Peregrine almost blacked out. Then they were on a narrow street that zigzagged through ranks of half-timbered buildings. Beyond the roofs loomed heavy fortifications. Ten minutes later they were in the castle yard.

They dismounted and the Lord Chamberlain had the Two-Legs moved to a litter.

'Woodcarver, he'll see us now?' said Scriber.

The bureaucrat laughed. '*She*. Woodcarver changed gender more than ten years ago.'

Peregrine's heads twisted about in surprise. Precisely what would *that* mean? Most packs change with time, but he had never heard of Woodcarver being anything but 'he.' He almost missed what the Lord Chamberlain said next.

'Even better. Her whole council must see . . . what you've brought. Come inside.' He waved the guards away.

They walked down a hall almost wide enough for two packs to pass abreast. The chamberlain led, followed by the travelers and the doctor with the alien's litter. The walls were high, padded with silver-crusted quilting. It was far grander than before . . . and again unsettling. There was scarcely any statuary, and what there was dated from centuries before.

But there were pictures. He stumbled when he saw the first, and behind him he heard Scriber gasp. Peregrine had seen art all around the world: The mobs of the tropics preferred abstract murals, smudges of psychotic color. The Southseas islanders had never invented perspective; in their watercolors, distant objects simply floated in the upper half of the picture. In the Long Lakes Republic, representationism was currently favored, especially multiptychs that gave a whole-pack view.

But Peregrine had never seen the likes of these. The pictures were mosaics, each tile a ceramic square about a quarter inch on a side. There was no color, just four shades of gray. From a few feet away, the grainiess was lost, and . . . they were the most perfect landscapes Peregrine had ever seen. All were views from hilltops around Woodcarvers. Except for the lack of color, they might have been windows. The bottom of each picture was bounded by a rectangular frame, but the tops were irregular; the mosaics simply broke off at the horizon. The hall's quilted wall stood where the pictures should have shown sky.

'Here now, fellow! I thought you wanted to see Woodcarver.' The remark was directed at Scriber. Jaqueramaphan was strung out along the landscapes, one of him sitting in front of a different picture all down the hall. He turned a head to look at the chamberlain. His voice sounded dazed. 'Soul's end! It's like being God, as if I have one member on each hilltop and can see everything at once.' But he scrambled to his feet and trotted to catch up.

The hall opened on one of the largest indoor meeting rooms Peregrine had ever seen.

'This is as big as anything in the Republic,' Scriber said with apparent admiration, looking up at the three levels of balconies. They stood alone with the alien at the bottom.

'Hmf.' Besides the chamberlain and the doctor, there were already five other packs in the room. More showed up as they watched. Most were dressed like nobles of the Republic, all jewels and furs. A few wore the plain jackets he remembered from his last trip. Sigh. Woodcarver's little settlement had grown into a city and now a nation-state. Peregrine wondered if the King – the Queen – had any real power now. He trained one head precisely on Scriber and Hightalked at him. 'Don't say anything about the picture box just yet.'

Jaqueramaphan looked puzzled and conspiratorial all at once. He High-talked back, 'Yes . . . yes. A bargaining card?'

'Something like that.' Peregrine's eyes swept back and forth across the balconies. Most packs entered with an air of harried self-importance. He smiled to himself. One glance into the pit was enough to shatter their smugness. The air above him was filled with buzzing talk. None of the packs looked like Woodcarver. But then, she'd have few of her members from before; he could only recognize her by manner and bearing. *It shouldn't matter.* He had carried some friendships far longer than any member's lifespan. But with others the friend had changed in a decade, its viewpoints altering, affection turning to animosity. He'd been counting on Woodcarver being the same. Now . . .

There was a brief sound of trumpets, almost like a call to order. The public doors of a lower balcony slid open and a fivesome entered. Peregrine felt a twitchy thrill of horror. This *was* Woodcarver, but so . . . misarranged. One member was so old it had to be helped by the rest. Two were scarcely more than puppies, and one of those a constant drooler. The largest member was white-eyed blind. It was the sort of thing you might see in a waterfront slum, or in the last generation of incest.

She looked down at Peregrine, and smiled almost as if *she* recognized *him*. When she spoke, it was with the blind one. The voice was clear and firm. 'Please carry on, Vendacious.'

The chamberlain nodded. 'As you wish, Your Majesty.' He pointed into the pit, at the alien. 'That is the reason for this hasty meeting.'

'We can see monsters at the circus, Vendacious.' The voice came from an overdressed pack on the top balcony. To judge from the shouting that came from all sides, this was a minority view. One pack on a lower balcony jumped over the railing and tried to shoo the doctor away from the alien's litter.

The chamberlain raised a head for silence, and glared down at the fellow who had jumped into the pit. 'If you please, Scrupilo, be patient. Everyone will get a chance to look.'

'Scrupilo' made some grumbling hisses, but backed off.

'Good.' Vendacious turned all his attention on Peregrine and Scriber. 'Your boat has outrun any news from the north, my friends. No one but I knows much of your story – and what I have is guard codes hooted across the bay. You say this creature flew down from the sky?'

It was an invitation to speechify. Peregrine let Scriber Jaqueramaphan do the talking. Scriber loved it. He told the story of the flying house, of the ambush and the murders, and the rescue. He showed them his eye-tools and announced himself as a secret agent of the Long Lakes Republic. *Now what real spy would do that?* Every pack on the council had eyes on the alien, some fearful, some – like Scrupilo – crazily curious. Woodcarver watched with only a couple of heads. The rest might have been asleep. She looked as tired as

Peregrine felt. He rested his own heads on his paws. The pain in Scar was a pulsing beat; it would be easy enough to set the member asleep, but then he'd understand very little of what was being said. Hey! maybe that wasn't such a bad idea. Scar drifted off and the pain receded.

The talk went on for some minutes more, not making a whole lot of sense to the threesome that was Wickwrack. He understood the tones of voice though. Scrupilo – the pack on the floor – complained several times, impatiently. Vendacious said something, agreeing with him. The doctor retreated, and Scrupilo advanced on Wickwrack's alien.

Peregrine pulled himself to full wakefulness. 'Be careful. The creature is *not* friendly.'

Scrupilo snapped back, 'Your friend has already warned me once.' He circled the litter, staring at the alien's brown, furless face. The alien stared back, impassive. Scrupilo reached forward cautiously and drew back the alien's quilt. *Still* no response. 'See?' said Scrupilo. 'It knows I mean no harm.' Peregrine said nothing to correct him.

'It really walks on those rear paws alone?' said one of the other advisors. 'Can you imagine it, towering over us? One little bump would knock it down.' Laughter. Peregrine remembered how mantis-like the alien had seemed when upright.

Scrupilo wrinkled a nose. 'The thing is filthy.' He was all around her, a posture that Peregrine knew upset the Two-Legs. 'That arrow shaft must be removed, you know. Most of the bleeding has stopped, but if we expect the creature to live for long, it needs medical attention.' He looked disdainfully at Scriber and Peregrine, as if they were to blame for not performing surgery aboard the twinhull. Something caught his eye and his tone abruptly changed: 'By the Pack of Packs! Look at its forepaws.' He loosened the ropes about the creature's front legs. 'Two paws like that would be as good as five pairs of lips. Think what a pack of these creatures could do!' He moved close to the five-tentacled paw.

'Be –' careful, Peregrine started to say. The alien abruptly bunched its tentacles into a club. Its foreleg flicked out at an impossible angle, ramming its paw into Scrupilo's head. The blow couldn't have been too strong, but it was precisely placed on the tympanum.

'*Ow! Yow! Wow. Wow.*' Scrupilo danced back.

The alien was shouting, too. It was all mouth noise, thin and low-pitched. The eldritch sound brought up all heads, even Woodcarver's. Peregrine had heard it many times by now. There was no doubt in his mind – this was the aliens' interpack speech. After a few seconds, the sound changed to a regular hacking that gradually faded.

For a long moment no one spoke. Then part of Woodcarver got to her feet. She looked at Scrupilo. 'Are you all right?' It was the first time she had spoken since the beginning of the meeting.

Scrupilo was licking his forehead. 'Yes. It smarts is all.'

'Your curiosity will kill you some day.'

The other huffed indignantly, but also seemed flattered by the prediction.

Queen Woodcarver looked at her councillors. 'I see an important question here. Scrupilo thinks one alien member would be as agile as an entire pack of us. Is that so?' She pointed the question at Peregrine rather than Scriber.

'Yes, Your Majesty. If those ropes had been tied within its reach, it could easily have unknotted them.' He knew where this was going; he'd had three days to get there himself. 'And the noises it makes sound like coordinated speech to me.'

There was a swell of talk as the others caught on. An articulate member can often make semi-sensible speech, but usually at the expense of dexterity.

'Yes . . . A creature like nothing on our world, whose boat flew down from the top of heaven. I wonder at the mind of such a pack, if a single member is almost as smart as *all* of one of us?' Her blind one looked around as it made the words, almost as if it could see. Two others wiped at her drooler's muzzle. She was not an inspiring sight.

Scrupilo poked a head up. 'I hear not a hint of thought sound from this one. There is no fore-tympanum.' He pointed at the torn clothing around the creature's wound. 'And I see no sign of shoulder tympana. Perhaps it *is* pack smart even as a singleton . . . and perhaps that's all the aliens ever are.' Peregrine smiled to himself; this Scrupilo was a prickly twit, but not one who held with tradition. For centuries, academics had debated the difference between people and animals. Some animals had larger brains; some had paws or lips more agile than a member's. In the savannahs of Easterlee, there were creatures that even looked like people and ran in groups, but without much depth of thought. Leaving aside wolf nests and whales, only people were *packs*. It was the coordination of thought between members that made them superior. Scrupilo's theory was a heresy.

Jaqueramaphan said, 'But we did hear thought sounds, *loud* ones, during the ambush. Perhaps this one is like our unweaned, unable to think –'

'And yet still almost as smart as a pack,' Woodcarver finished somberly. 'If these people are not smarter than we, then we might learn their devices. No matter how magnificent they are, we could eventually be their equals. But if this member is just one of a superpack . . .' For a moment there was no talk, just the muted underedge of her councillors' thoughts. If the aliens were superpacks, and if their envoy had been murdered – then there might not be anything they could do to save themselves.

'So. Our first priority should be to save this creature, to befriend it and learn its true nature.' Her heads lowered, and she seemed lost within herself – or perhaps just tired. Abruptly, she turned several heads toward her chamberlain. 'Move the creature to the lodge by mine.'

Vendacious started with surprise. 'Surely not, Your Majesty! We've seen that it is hostile. And it needs medical attention.'

Woodcarver smiled and her voice turned silky. Peregrine remembered that tone from before. 'Do you forget that I know surgery? Do you forget . . . that I am the Woodcarver?'

Vendacious licked his lips and looked at the other advisors. After a second he said, 'No, Your Majesty. It will be as you wish.'

And Peregrine felt like cheering. Perhaps Woodcarver did still run things.

12

Peregrine was sitting back to back on the steps of his quarters when Woodcarver came to see him next day. She came alone, wearing the simple green jackets he remembered from his last visit.

He didn't bow or go out to meet her. She looked at him coolly for a moment, and sat down just a few yards away.

'How is the Two-Legs?' he asked.

'I took out the arrow and sewed the wound shut. I think it will survive. My advisors were pleased: the creature didn't act like a reasoning being. It fought even after it was tied down, as though it had no concept of surgery . . . How is your head?'

'All right, as long as I don't move around.' The rest of him – Scar – lay behind the doorway in the dark interior of the lodge. 'The tympanum is healing straight, I think. I'll be fine in a few days.'

'Good.' A wrecked tympanum could mean continuing mental problems, or the need for a new member and the pain of finding a use for the singleton that was sent into silence. 'I remember you, pilgrim. All the members are different, but you really are the Peregrine of before. You had some great stories. I enjoyed your visit.'

'And I enjoyed meeting the great Woodcarver. That is the reason I returned.'

She cocked a head wryly. 'The great Woodcarver of before, not the wreck of now?'

He shrugged. 'What happened?'

She didn't answer immediately. For a moment, they sat and looked across the city. It was cloudy this afternoon, with rain coming. The breeze off the channel was a cool stinging on his lips and eyes. Woodcarver shivered, and puffed her fur out a bit. Finally she said, 'I held my soul six hundred years – and that's counting by foreclaws. I should think it's obvious what has become of me.'

'The perversion never hurt you before.' Peregrine was not normally so blunt. Something about her brought out the frankness in him.

'Yes, the average incest degrades to my state in a few centuries, and is an idiot long before then. My methods were much cleverer. I knew who to breed with whom, which puppies to keep and which to put on others. So it was always my flesh bearing my memories, and my soul remained pure. But I didn't understand enough – or perhaps I tried the impossible. The choices got harder and harder, till I was left with choosing between brains and physical defect.' She wiped away the drool, and all but the blind one looked out across her city. 'These are the best days of summer, you know. Life is a green madness just now, trying to squeeze the last bit of warmth from the season.' And the green did seem to be everywhere it could be: featherleaf down the hillside and in the town, ferns all over the near hillsides, and heather struggling toward the gray crowns of the mountains across the channel. 'I love this place.'

He never expected to be comforting the Woodcarver of Woodcarvers. 'You made a miracle here. I've heard of it all the way on the other side of the world . . . And I'll bet that half the packs around here are related to you.'

'Y-yes, I've been successful beyond a rake's wildest dreams. I've had no shortage of lovers, even if I couldn't use the pups myself. Sometimes I think my get has been my greatest experiment. Scrupilo and Vendacious are mostly my offspring . . . but so is Flenser.'

Huh! Peregrine hadn't known that last.

'The last few decades, I'd more or less accepted my fate. I couldn't outwit eternity; sometime soon I would let my soul slip free. I let the council take over more and more; how could I claim the Domain after I was no longer me? I went back to art – you saw those monochrome mosaics.'

'Yes! They're beautiful.'

'I'll show you my picture loom sometime. The procedure is tedious but almost automatic. It was a nice project for the last years of my soul. But now – you and your alien have changed everything. Damn it! If only this had happened a hundred years ago. What I would have done with it! We've been playing with your "picture box," you know. The pictures are finer than any in our world. They are a bit like my mosaics – the way the sun is like a glowbug. Millions of colored dots go to make each picture, the tiles so small you can't see them without one of Scriber's lenses. I've worked for *years* to make a few dozen mosaics. The picture box can make unnumbered thousands, so fast they seem to move. Your aliens make my life less than an unweaned pup's scratching in its cradle.'

The queen of the Woodcarvers was softly crying, but her voice was angry. 'And now the whole world is going to change, but too late for such wreckage as I!'

Almost without conscious thought, Peregrine extended one of his members toward the Woodcarver. He walked unseemly close: eight yards, five. Their thoughts were suddenly fuzzy with interference, but he could feel her calming.

She laughed blearily. 'Thank you . . . Strange that you should be sympathetic. The greatest problem of my life is nothing to a pilgrim.'

'You were hurting.' It was all he could think to say.

'But you pilgrims change and change and change –' She eased one of herself close to him; they were almost touching, and it was even harder to think.

Peregrine spoke slowly, concentrating on every word, hoping he wouldn't forget his point. 'But I do keep something of a soul. The parts that remain a pilgrim must have a certain outlook.' Sometimes great insight comes in the noise of battle or intimacy. This was such a time. 'And – and I think the world itself is due for a change of soul now that we have Two-Legs dropping from the sky. What better time for Woodcarver to give up the old?'

She smiled, and the confusion became louder, but a pleasant thing. 'I . . . hadn't . . . thought of it that way. Now is the time to change . . .'

Peregrine walked into her midst. The two packs stood for a moment, necking, thoughts blending into sweet chaos. Their last clear recollection was of stumbling up the steps and into his lodge.

*

113

Late that afternoon, Woodcarver brought the picture box to Scrupilo's laboratory. When she arrived Scrupilo and Vendacious were already present. Scriber Jaqueramaphan was there too, but standing farther from the others than courtesy might demand. She had interrupted some kind of argument. A few days before, such squabbling would have just depressed her. Now – she dragged her limper into the room and looked at the others through her drooler's eyes – and smiled. Woodcarver felt the best she had in years. She had made her decision and acted on it, and now there were new adventures to be had.

Scriber brightened at her entrance. 'Did you check on Peregrine? How is he?'

'He is fine, fine, just fine.' *Oops, no need to show them how fine he really is!* 'I mean, there'll be a full recovery.'

'Your Majesty, I'm very grateful to you and your doctors. Wickwrackscar is a good pack, and I . . . I mean, even a pilgrim can't change members every day, like suits of clothes.'

Woodcarver waved an offhand acknowledgment. She walked to the middle of the room, and set the alien's picture box on the table there. It looked like nothing so much as a big pink pillow – with floppy ears and a weird animal design sewed in its cover. After playing with it for a day and a half, she was getting pretty good . . . at opening the thing up. As always, the Two-Legs's face appeared, making mouth noises. As always, Woodcarver felt an instant of awe at seeing the moving mosaic. A million colored 'tiles' had to flip and shift in absolute synchrony to create the illusion. Yet it happened exactly the same each time. She turned the screen so Scrupilo and Vendacious could see.

Jaqueramaphan edged toward the others, and craned a pair of heads to look. 'You still think the box is an animal?' he said to Vendacious. 'Perhaps you could feed it sweets and it would tell us its secrets, eh?' Woodcarver smiled to herself. Scriber was no pilgrim; pilgrims depend on goodwill too much to go around giving the needle to the powerful.

Vendacious just ignored him. All his eyes were on her. 'Your Majesty, please do not take offense. I – we of the Council – must ask you again. This picture box is too important to be left in the mouths of a single pack, even one so great as you. Please. Leave it to the rest of us, at least when you sleep.'

'No offense taken. If you insist, you may participate in my investigations. Beyond that, I will not go.' She gave him an innocent look. Vendacious was a superb spymaster, a mediocre administrator, and an incompetent scientist. A century ago she would have had the likes of him out tending the crops, if he chose to stay at all. A century ago there had been no need for spymasters and one administrator had been enough. How things had changed. She absentmindedly nuzzled the picture box; perhaps things would change again.

Scrupilo took Scriber's question seriously. 'I see three possibilities, sir. First, that it is magic.' Vendacious winced away from him. 'Indeed, the box may be so far beyond our understanding that is *is* magic. But that is the one heresy the Woodcarver has never accepted, and so I courteously omit it.' He flicked a sardonic smile at Woodcarver. 'Second, that it is an animal. A few on the Council thought so when Scriber first made it talk. But it looks like a stuffed pillow, even down to the amusing figure stitched on its side. More importantly, it responds to stimuli with perfect repeatability. *That* is something I do recognize. That is the behavior of a machine.'

'That's your third possibility?' said Scriber. 'But to be a machine means to have moving parts, and except for –'

, Woodcarver shrugged a tail at them. Scrupilo could go on like this for hours, and she saw that Scriber was the same type. '*I* say, let's learn more and then speculate.' She tapped the corner of the box, just as Scriber had in his original demonstration. The alien's face vanished from the picture, replaced by a dizzying pattern of color. There was a splatter of sound, then nothing but the mid-pitch hum the box always made when the top was open. They knew the box could hear low-pitched sounds, and it could feel through the square pad on its base. But that pad was itself a kind of picture screen: certain commands transformed the grid of touch spots into entirely new shapes. The first time they did that, the box refused any further commands. Vendacious had been sure they had 'killed the little alien.' But they had closed the box and reopened it – and it was back to its original behavior. Woodcarver was *almost* certain that nothing they could do by talking to it or touching it would hurt the thing.

Woodcarver retried the known signals in the usual order. The results were spectacular, and identical to before. But change that order in any way and the effects would be different. She wasn't sure if she agreed with Scrupilo: The box behaved with the repeatability of a machine . . . yet the variety of its responses was much more like an animal's.

Behind her, Scriber and Scrupilo edged members across the floor. Their heads were stuck high in the air as they strained for a clear look at the screen. The buzz of their thoughts came louder and louder. Woodcarver tried to remember what she'd been planning next. Finally, the noise was just too much. 'Will you two *please* back off! I can't hear myself think.' *This isn't a choir, you know.*

'Sorry . . . this okay?' They moved back about fifteen feet. Woodcarver nodded. The two members were less than twenty feet from each other. Scrupilo and Scriber must be really eager to see the screen. Vendacious had kept a proper distance, and a look of alert enthusiasm.

'I have a suggestion,' said Scriber. His voice was slurred from the effort of concentrating over Scrupilo's thoughts. 'When you touch the four/three square and say –' he made the alien sounds; they were all very easy to do '– the screen shows a collection of pictures. They seem to match the squares. I think we . . . we are being given choices.'

Hm. 'The box could end up training *us*.' *If this is a machine, we need some new definitions.* '. . . Very well, let's play with it.'

Three hours passed. Toward the end, even Vendacious had moved a member nearer the screen; the noise in the room verged on mindless chaos. And everybody had suggestions; 'say that,' 'press this,' 'last time it said that, we did thus and so.' There were intricate colored designs, sprinkled with things that must have been written language. Tiny, two-legged figures scampered across the screen, shifting the symbols, opening little windows . . . Scriber Jaquerama-phan's idea was quite right. The first pictures *were* choices. But some of those led to further pictures of choices. The options spread out – tree-like, Scriber said. He wasn't quite right; sometimes they came back to an earlier point; it was a metaphorical network of streets. four times they ended in cul de sacs and had to shut the box and begin again. Vendacious was madly drawing maps of the paths. That would help; there were places they would want to see again. But even he realized there were unnumbered other paths, places that blind exploration would never find.

And Woodcarver would have given a good part of her soul for the pictures she had already seen. There were starscapes. There were moons that shone blue and green, or banded orange. There were moving pictures of alien cities, of thousands of aliens so close that they were actually *touching*. If they ran in packs, those packs were bigger than anything in the world, even in the tropics . . . And maybe the question was irrelevant; the cities were beyond anything she ever imagined.

Finally Jaqueramaphan backed off. He huddled together. There was a shiver in his voice. 'T-there's a whole universe in there. We could follow it forever, and never know . . .'

She looked at the other two. For once, Vendacious had lost his smugness. There were ink stains on all his lips. The writing benches around him were littered with dozens of sketches, some clearer than others. He dropped the pen, and gasped. 'I say we take what we have and study it.' He began gathering the sketches, piling them into a neat stack. 'Tomorrow, after a good sleep, our heads will be clear and –'

Scrupilo dropped back and stretched. His eyes had excited red rims. 'Fine. But leave the sketches, friend Vendacious.' He jabbed at the drawings. 'See that one and that? It's clear that our blundering gets us plenty of empty results. Sometimes the picture box just locks us out, but much more often we get that picture: No options, just a couple of aliens dancing in a forest and making rhythm sounds. Then if we say –' and he repeated part of the sequence, '– we get that picture of piles of sticks. The first with one, the second with two, and so on.'

Woodcarver saw it too. 'Yes. And a figure comes out and points to each of the piles and says a short noise by each.' She and Scrupilo stared at each other, each seeing the same gleam in the other's eyes: the excitement of learning, of finding order where there had seemed only chaos. It had been a hundred years since she last felt this way. 'Whatever this thing is . . . it's trying to teach us the Two-Legs' language.'

In the days that followed, Johanna Olsndot had lots of time to think. The pain in her chest and shoulder gradually eased; if she moved carefully, it was only a pulsing soreness. They had taken the arrow out and sewed the wound closed. She had feared the worst when they had tied her down, when she saw the knives in their mouths and the steel on their claws. Then they began cutting; she had not known there could be such pain.

She still shuddered with remembered agony. But she didn't have nightmares about it, the way she did about . . .

Mother and Dad were dead; she had seen them die with her own eyes. And Jefri? Jefri *might* still be alive. Sometimes Johanna could go a whole afternoon full of hope. She had seen the coldsleepers burning on the ground below the ship, but those *inside* might have survived. Then she would remember the indiscriminate way the attackers had flamed and slashed, killing everything around the ship.

She was a prisoner. But for now, the murderers wanted her well. The guards were not armed – beyond their teeth and tines. They kept well away from her when they could. They knew she could hurt *them*.

They kept her inside a big dark cabin. When she was alone she paced the floor. The dogthings were barbarians. The surgery without anesthetics was probably not even intended as torture. She hadn't seen any aircraft, or any sign of electricity. The toilet was a slot carved in a marble slab. The hole went so deep you could scarcely hear the plop hit bottom. But it still smelled bad. These creatures were as backward as people in the darkest ages on Nyjora. They had never had technology, or they had thoroughly forgotten it. Johanna almost smiled. Mom had liked novels about shipwrecks and heroines marooned on lost colonies. The big deal was usually to reinvent technology and repair the spacecraft. Mom was . . . had been . . . so into the history of science; she loved the details of those stories.

Well, Johanna was living it now, but with important differences. She wanted rescue, but she also wanted revenge. These creatures were nothing like human. In fact, she couldn't remember reading of anything quite like them. She'd have looked for them in her dataset, except they had taken that. *Ha*. Let them play with it. They'd quickly run into her booby traps and find themselves totally locked out.

At first there were only blankets to keep warm. Then they'd given her clothes cut like her jumpsuit but made of puffy quilting. They were warm and sturdy, the stitching neater than anything she imagined a nonmachine could do. Now she could comfortably walk around outside. The garden beyond her cabin was the best thing about the place. It was about a hundred meters square, and followed the slope of a hillside. There were lots of flowers, and trees with long, feathery leaves. Flagstoned walks curved back and forth through mossy turf. It was a peaceful place if she let it be one, a little like their backyard on Straum.

There were walls, but from the high end of the garden she could see over them. The walls angled this way and that, and in places she could see their other side. The window slits were like something out of her history lessons: they let you fire arrows or bullets without making a target of yourself.

When the sun was out, Johanna liked to sit where the smell of the feather leaves was strongest, and look over the lower walls at the bay. She still wasn't sure just what she was seeing. There was a harbor; the forest of spars was almost like the marinas on Straum. The town had wide streets, but they zigged and zagged and the buildings along them were all askew. In places there were open-roofed mazes of stone; from up here she could see the pattern. And there was another wall, a rambling thing that ran for as far as she could see. The hills beyond were crowned with gray rock and patches of snow.

She could see the dogthings down in the town. Individually, you *could* almost mistake them for dogs (snake-necked, rat-headed ones). But watch them from a distance and you saw their true nature. They always moved in small groups, rarely more than six. Within the pack they touched, cooperated with clever grace. But she never saw one group come closer than about ten meters to another. From her distant viewpoint, the members of a pack seemed to merge . . . and she could imagine she was seeing one multilimbed beast ambling cautiously along, careful not to come too close to a similar monster. By now, the conclusion was inescapable: one pack, one mind. *Minds so evil they could not bear to be close to one another.*

Her fifth time in the garden was the prettiest yet, a coercion toward joy. The flowers had sprayed downy seeds into the air. The lowering sunlight sparkled off them as they floated by the thousands on the slow breeze, clots in an invisible syrup. She imagined what Jefri would do here: first pretend grownup dignity, then bounce from one foot to the other. Finally he would race down the hillside, trying to capture as many of the flying tufts as he could. Laughing and laughing –

'One, two, how do you do?' It was a child's voice, behind her.

Johanna jumped up so fast she almost tore her stitches. Sure enough, there was a pack behind her. They – it? – was the one who had cut the arrow out of her. A mangy lot. The five were crouched, ready to run away. They looked almost as surprised as Johanna felt.

'One, two, how do you do?' The voice came again, exactly as before. It might as well have been a recording, except that one of the animals was somehow synthesizing the sound with the buzzing patches of skin on its shoulders, haunches and head. The parrot act was nothing new to her. But this time . . . the words were almost appropriate. The voice was not hers, but she had heard that chant before. She put hands on hips and stared at the pack. Two of the animals stared back; the others seemed to be admiring the scenery. One licked nervously at its paw.

The two rear ones were carrying her dataset! Suddenly she knew where they'd gotten that singsong question. And she knew what they expected in response. 'I am fine and how do you do?' she said.

The pack's eyes widened, almost comically. 'I am fine, so then are we all!' It completed the game, then emitted a burst of gobbling. Someone replied from down the hill. There was another pack there, lurking in the bushes. She knew that if she stayed near this one, the other wouldn't approach.

So the Tines – she always thought of them by those claws on their front feet; those she would never forget – had been playing with the Pink Oliphaunt, and hadn't been stopped by the booby traps. That was better than Jefri ever managed. It was clear they had fallen into the kindermode language programs. She should have thought of that. When the dataset noted sufficiently asinine responses it would adapt its behavior, first for young children, and – if that didn't work – for youngsters who didn't even speak Samnorsk. With just a little cooperation from Johanna, they could learn her language. Did she want that?

The pack walked a little nearer, at least two of them watching her all the time. They didn't seem quite so ready to bolt as before. The nearest one dropped to its belly and looked up at her. Very cute and helpless, if you didn't see the claws. 'My name is –' Johanna heard a short burst of gobble with an overtone that seemed to buzz right through her head. 'What is your name?'

Johanna knew it was all part of the language script. There was no way the creature could understand the individual words it was saying. That 'my name, your name' pair was repeated over and over again between the children in the language program. A vegetable would get the point eventually. Still, the Tines pronounciation was so perfect . . .

'My name is Johanna,' she said.

'Zjohanna,' said the pack, with Johanna's voice, and splitting the word stream incorrectly.

'Johanna,' corrected Johanna. She wasn't even going to try saying the Tines name.

'Hello, Johanna. Let's play the naming game!' And that was from the script too, complete with silly enthusiasm. Johanna sat down. Sure, learning Samnorsk would give the Tines power over her . . . but it was the only way *she* could learn about *them*, the only way she could learn about Jefri. And if they had murdered Jefri, too? Well then, she would learn to hurt them as much as they deserved.

13

At Woodcarvers and then – a few days later – at Flenser's Hidden Island, the long daylight of arctic summer ended. At first there was a little twilight just around midnight, when even the highest hill stood in shadow. And then the hours of dark grew quickly. Day fought night, and night was winning. The featherleaf in the low valleys changed to autumn colors. Looking up a fjord in daylight was to see orange red on the lower hills, then the green of heather merging imperceptibly to the grays of lichen and the darker grays of naked rock. The snowpatches waited for their time; it would come soon.

At every sunset, each day a few minutes earlier, Tyrathect toured the ramparts of Flenser's outer wall. It was a three-mile walk. The lower levels were guarded by linear packs, but up here there were only a few lookouts. When she approached, they stepped aside with military precision. More than military precision; she saw the fear in their look. It was hard to get used to that. For almost as far back as she had clear memories – twenty years – Tyrathect had lived in fear of others, in shame and guilt, in search of someone to follow. Now all that was turned on its head. It was not an improvement. She knew now, from the inside, the evil she had given herself to. She knew why the sentries feared her. To them, she *was* Flenser.

Of course, she never gave any hint of these thoughts. Her life was only as safe as the success of her fraud. Tyrathect had worked hard to suppress her natural, shy mannerisms. Not once since coming to Hidden Island had she caught herself in the old bashful habit of heads lowering, eyes closing.

Instead, Tyrathect had the Flenser stare – and she used it. Her passage around the top wall was as stark and ominous as

Flenser's had ever been. she looked out over her – his – domain with the same hard gaze as before, all heads front, as if seeing visions beyond the petty minds of the disciples. They must never guess her real reason for these sunset sweeps: for a time, the days and nights were like in the Republic. She could almost imagine she was still back there, before the Movement and the massacre at Parliament Bowl, before they cut her throats and wed pieces of Flenser to the stumps of her soul.

In the gold and russet fields beyond the stone curtains, she could see peasants trimming the fields and the herds. Flenser ruled lands far beyond her view, but he had never imported food. The grain and meat that filled the storehouses were all produced within a two-days march of the straits. The strategic intent was clear; still, it made for a peaceful evening's view and brought back memories of her home and school.

The sun slid sideways into the mountains; long shadows swept the farm lands. Flenser's castle was left an island in a sea of shadow. Tyrathect could smell the cold. There would be frost again tonight. Tomorrow the fields would be covered with false snow that would last an hour past sunrise. She pulled the long jackets close around her and walked to the eastern lookout. Across the straits, one of the near hilltops was still in the sun. The alien ship had landed there. It was still there, but now behind wood and stone. Steel began building there right after the landing. The quarries at the north end of Hidden Island were busier now than ever in Flenser's time. The barges hauling stone to the mainland made a steady traffic across the straits. Even now that the light was not dayround, Steel's construction went on nonstop. His Incallings and lesser inspections were harsher than Flenser's had been.

Lord Steel was a killer; worse, a manipulator. But since the alien landing, Tyrathect knew that he was something else: deathly afraid. He had good reason. And even though the folk he feared might ultimately kill them all, in her secret soul she wished them well. Steel and his Flenserists had attacked the star people without warning, more out of greed than fear.

They had killed dozens of beings. In a way the murders were worse than what the Movement had done to her. Tyrathect had followed the Flenser of her own free will. She had had friends who warned her about the Movement. There had been dark stories about the Flenser, and not all had been government propaganda. But she had so wanted to follow, to give herself to Something Greater . . . They had used her, literally, as their tool. Yet she could have avoided it. The star people had had no such option; Steel simply butchered them.

So now Steel labored out of fear. In the first three days he had covered the flying ship with a roof: a sudden, silly farmhouse had appeared on the hilltop. Before long the alien craft would be hidden behind stone walls. Ultimately, the new fortress might be bigger than the one on Hidden Island. Steel knew that if his villainy did not destroy him, it would make him the most powerful pack in the world.

And that was Tyrathect's reason for staying, for continuing her masquerade. She couldn't go on forever. Sooner or later the other fragments would reach Hidden Island; Tyrathect would be destroyed and all of Flenser would live again. Perhaps she wouldn't survive even that long. Two of Tyrathect *were* of Flenser. The Master had miscalculated in thinking they could dominate the other three. Instead the conscience of the three had come to own the brilliance of the two. She remembered almost everything the great Flenser had known, all the tricks and all the betrayals. The two had given her an intensity she had never had before. Tyrathect laughed to herself. In a sense, she had gained what she had been so naïvely seeking in the Movement; and the great Flenser had made exactly the mistake that in his arrogance he thought impossible. As long as she could *keep* the two under control, she had a chance. When she was all awake, there wasn't much problem; she still felt herself a 'she,' still remembered her life in the Republic more clearly than the Flenser memories. It was different when she slept. There were nightmares. The memories of torment inflicted suddenly seemed sweet. Sleep-time sex should soothe; with her it was a battle. She awoke sore and cut, as if she had been fighting a rapist. If the two ever broke free, if she ever awoke a 'he . . .' It would take only a few seconds for the two to denounce the masquerade, only a little longer to kill the three and put the Flenser members aboard a more manageable pack.

Yet she stayed. Steel meant to use the aliens and their ship to spread Flenser's nightmare worldwide. But his plan was fragile, with risks on every side. *If there was anything she could do to destroy it and the Flenser Movement, she would.*

Across the castle, only the western tower still hung in sunlight. No faces showed at the window slits, but eyes looked out: Steel watched the Flenser Fragment – the Flenser-in-Waiting as it styled itself – on the ramparts below. The fragment was accepted by all the commanders. In fact, they accorded it almost the awe they had given to the full Flenser. In a sense, Flenser had made them all, so it wasn't surprising they felt a chill in the Master's presence. Even Steel felt it. In his shaping, Flenser had forced the aborning Steel to try to kill him; each time Steel had been caught and his weakest members tortured. Steel knew the conditioning that was there, and that helped him fight it. If anything, he told himself, the Flenser Frag was in greater danger because of it: in trying to counter the fear, Steel might just miscalculate, and act more violently than was appropriate.

Sooner or later Steel had to decide. If he didn't kill it before the other fragments reached Hidden Island, then *all* of Flenser would be here again. If two members could dominate Steel's regime, then six would totally erase it. Did he want the Master dead? And if he did, was there any surely safe way? . . . Steel's mind flickered lightly all around the issue as he watched the black-frocked pack.

Steel was used to playing for high stakes. He had been *born* playing for them. Fear and death and winning were his whole life. But never had the stakes been as high as now. Flenser had come close to subverting the largest nation on the continent, and had had dreams of ruling the world . . . Lord Steel looked to the hillside across the straits, at the new castle he was building. In Steel's present game, world conquest would follow easily on victory, and the destruction of the world was a conceivable consequence of failure.

Steel had visited the flying ship shortly after the ambush. The ground was still steaming. Every hour it seemed to grow hotter. The mainland peasants talked of demons wakened in the earth; Steel's advisors could not do much better. The whitejackets needed padded boots to get close. Steel had ignored the steam, donned the boots, and walked beneath the curving hull. The bottom was vaguely like a boat's hull, if you ignored the stilts. Near the center was a teat-like projection; the ground directly underneath burbled with molten rock. The burned-out coffins were on the uphill side of the ship. Several of the corpses had been removed for dissection. In the first hours his advisors had been full of fanciful theories: the mantis folk were warriors fleeing a battle, come to bury their dead . . .

So far no one had been able to take a careful look inside the craft.

The gray stairs were made of something as strong as steel yet feather light. But they were recognizably stairs, even if the risers were high for the average member. Steel scrambled up the steps, leaving Shreck and his other advisors outside.

He stuck a head through the hatch – and jerked back abruptly. The acoustics were deadly. He understood what the whitejackets were complaining about. How could the aliens bear it? One by one he forced himself through the opening.

Echoes screamed at him – worse than from unpadded quartz. He quieted himself, as he had so often done in the Master's presence. The echoes diminished, but they were still a horde raging in the walls all around. Not even his best whitejackets could tolerate more than five minutes here. The thought made Steel stand straighter. Discipline. Quiet does not always mean submission; it can mean hunting. He looked around, ignoring the howling murmurs.

Light came from bluish strips in the ceiling. As his eyes adjusted, he could see what his people had described to him: the interior was just two rooms. He was standing in the larger one – a cargo hold? There was a hatch in the far wall and then the second room. The walls were seamless. They met in angles that did not match the outer hull; there would be dead spaces. A breeze moved fitfully about the room, but the air

126

was much warmer than outside. He had never been in a place that felt more of power and evil. Surely it was only a trick of acoustics. They would bring in some absorbent quilts, some side reflectors, and the feeling would go away. Still . . .

The room was filled with coffins, these unburned. The place stank with the aliens' body odor. Mold grew in the darker corners. In a way that was comforting: the aliens breathed and sweated as other living things, and for all their marvelous invention, they could not keep their own den clean. Steel wandered among the coffins. The boxes were mounted on railed racks. When the ones outside had been here, the rom must have been crammed full. Undamaged, the coffins were marvels of fine workmanship. Warm air exited slots along the sides. He sniffed at it: complex, faintly nauseating, but not the smell of death. And not the source of the overpowering stench of mantis sweat that hung everywhere.

Each coffin had a window mounted on its top side. What effort to honor the remains of single members! Steel hopped onto one and looked down. The corpse was perfectly preserved; in fact, the blue light made everything look frozen. He cocked a second head over the edge of the box, got a double view on the creature within. It was far smaller than the two they had killed under the ship. It was even smaller than the one they had captured. Some of Steel's advisors thought the small ones were pups, perhaps unweaned. It made sense; their prisoner never made thought sounds.

Partly as an act of discipline, he stared for a long while at the alien's queer, flat face. The echo of his mind was a continuing pain, eating at his attention, demanding that he leave. *Let the pain continue*. He had withstood worse before, and the packs outside must know that Steel was stronger than any of them. He could master the pain and have the greater insight . . . And then he would work their butts off, quilting these rooms and studying the contents.

So Steel stared, almost thoughtless, into the face. The screaming in the walls seemed to fade a little. The face was so ugly. He had looked at the charred corpses outside, noticed their small jaws and randomly misshapen teeth. How could the creature eat?

A few minutes passed; the noise and ugliness mixed together, dreamlike ... And then out of his trance, Steel knew a nightmare horror: *The face moved.* The change was small, and it happened very, very slowly. but over a period of minutes, the face had changed.

Steel fell from the coffin; the walls screamed back terror. For a few seconds, he thought the noise would kill him. Then he regained himself with quiet thought. He crawled back onto the box. All his eyes stared through the crystal, waiting like a pack on hunt ... The change was regular. The alien in the box was breathing, but fifty times more slowly than any normal member. He moved to another box, watched the creature in it. Somehow, they were *all alive.* Inside those boxes, their lives were simply slowed.

He looked up from the boxes, almost in a daze. That the room reeked of evil was an illusion of sound ... and also the absolute truth.

The mantis alien had landed far from the tropics, away from the collectives; perhaps it thought the Arctic Northwest a backward wilderness. It had come in a ship jammed with hundreds of mantis pups. These boxes were like larval casings: the pack would land, raise the small ones to adulthood – out of sight of civilization. Steel felt his pelts puff up as he thought about it. If the mantis pack had not been surprised, if Steel's troops had been any less aggressive ... it would have been the end of the world.

Steel staggered to the outer hatch, his fears coming louder and louder off the walls. Even so, he paused a moment in the shadows and the screams. When his members trooped down the stairs, he moved calmly, every jacket neatly in place. Soon enough his advisors would know the danger, but they would never see fear in him. He walked lightly across the steaming turf, out from under the hull. But even he could not resist a quick look across the sky. This was one ship, one pack of aliens. It had had the misfortune of running into the Movement. Even so, its defeat had been partly luck. How many other ships would land, had already landed? Was there time for him to learn from this victory?

*

128

Steel's mind returned to the present, to his eyrie lookout above the castle. That first encounter with the ship was many tendays past. There was still a threat, but now he understood it better, and – as was true of all great threats – it held great promise.

On the rampart, Flenser-in-Waiting slid through the deepening twilight. Steel's eyes followed the pack as it walked beneath the torches and one by one disappeared downstairs. There was an awful lot of the Master in that fragment; it had understood many things about the alien landing before anyone else.

Steel took one last look across the darkening hills as he turned and started down the spiral stair. It was a long, cramped climb; the lookout sat atop a forty-foot tower. The stair was barely fifteen inches wide, the ceiling less than thirty inches above the steps. Cold stone pressed in from all around, so close that there were no echoes to confuse thought – yet also so close that the mind was squeezed into a long thread. Climbing the spiral required a twisting, strung-out posture that left any attacker easy prey for a defender in the eyrie. Such was military architecture. For Steel, crawling the cramped dark was pleasant exercise.

The stairs opened onto a public hallway, ten feet across with back-off nooks every fifty feet. Shreck and a bodyguard were waiting for him.

'I have the latest from Woodcarvers,' said Shreck. He was holding sheets of silkpaper.

Losing the other alien to Woodcarvers had once seemed a major blow. Only gradually had he realized how well it could work out. He had Woodcarvers infiltrated. At first he'd intended to have the other alien killed; it would have been easy to do. But the information that trickled north was interesting. There were some bright people at Woodcarvers. They were coming up with insights that had slipped past Steel and the Master – the *fragment* of the Master. So. In effect, Woodcarvers had become Steel's second alien laboratory, and the Movement's enemies were serving him like any other tool. The irony was irresistible.

'Very good, Shreck. Take it to my den. I'll be there shortly.'

Steel waved the whitejackets into a back-up nook and swept past him. Reading the report over brandy would be a pleasant reward for the day's work. In the meantime, there were other duties and other pleasures.

The Master had begun building Hidden Island Castle more than a century earlier; it was growing yet. In the oldest foundations, where an ordinary ruler might put dungeons, were the Flenser's first laboratories. Many could be mistaken for dungeons – and were, by their inhabitants.

Steel reviewed all the labs at least once a tenday. Now he swept through the lowest levels. Crickers fled before the light of his guard's torches. There was a smell of rotting meat. Steel's paws skidded where slickness lay upon the stone. Holes were dug in the floor at regular intervals. Each could hold a single member, its legs jammed tight against its body. Each was covered by a lid with tiny air holes. It took the average member about three days to go mad in such isolation. The resulting 'raw material' could be used to build blank packs. Generally they weren't much more than vegetables, but then that was all the Movement asked of some. And sometimes remarkable things came from these pits: Shreck for instance. Shreck the Colorless, some called him. Shreck the stolid. A pack who was beyond pain, beyond desire. Shreck's was the loyalty of clockwork, but built from flesh and blood. He was no genius, but Steel would have given an eastern province for five more of him. And the promise of more such successes made Steel use the isolation pits again and again. He had recycled most of the wrecks from the ambush that way . . .

Steel climbed back to higher levels, where the really interesting experiments were undertaken. The world regarded Hidden Island with fascinated horror. They had heard of the lower levels. But most didn't realize what a small part those dark spaces played in the Movement's science. To properly dissect a soul, you need more than benches with blood gutters. The results from the lower levels were simply the first steps in Flenser's intellectual quest. There were great questions in the world, things that had bothered packs for thousands of years. How do we think? Why do we believe? Why is one pack a genius and another an oaf? Before Flenser, philosophers argued them endlessly and never got closer to the truth. Even Woodcarver had pranced around the issues, unwilling to give up her traditional ethics. Flenser was prepared to get the answers. In these labs, nature itself was under interrogation.

Steel walked across a chamber one hundred yards wide, with a roof supported by dozens of stone pillars. On every side there were dark partitions, slate walls mounted on tiny wheels. The cavern could be blocked off, maze-like, into any pattern. Flenser had experimented with all the postures of thought. In the centuries before him, there had been only a few effective postures: the instinctive heads together, the ring sentry, various work postures. Flenser had tried dozens more: stars, double rings, grids. Most were useless and confusing. In the star, only a single member could hear all the others, and each of those could only hear the one. In effect, all thought had to pass through the hub member. The hub could contribute nothing rational, yet all its misconceptions passed uncorrected to the rest. Drunken foolishness resulted . . . Of course, that experiment was reported to the outside world.

But at least one of the others – still secret – worked strangely well: Flenser posted eight packs around the floor and on temporary platforms, blocked them from each another with the slate partitions, and then put members from each pack in connection with their counterparts in three others. In a sense, he created a pack of eights packs. Steel was still experimenting with that. If the connectors were sufficiently compatible (and that was the hard part), the resulting creature was far smarter than a ring sentry. In most ways it was not as bright as a single heads-together pack, yet sometimes it had striking insights. Before he left for the Long Lakes, the Master had developed a plan to rebuild the castle's main hall so council sessions could be conducted in this posture. Steel hadn't pursued that idea. It was just a bit too risky; Steel's domination of others was not quite as complete as Flenser's had been . . .

No matter. There were other, more significant projects.

The rooms ahead were the true heart of the Movement. Steel's soul had been born in these rooms; all of Flenser's greatest creations had begun here. During the last five years, Steel had continued the tradition . . . and improved upon it.

He walked down the hall that linked the separate suites. Each bore its number in inlaid gold. At each he opened a door and stepped partway through. His staff left their report on the previous tenday just inside. Steel quickly read each one, then poked a nose over the balcony to look at the experiment within. The balconies were well-padded, and screened; it was easy to observe without being seen.

Flenser's one weakness (in Steel's opinion) was his desire to create the superior being. The Master's confidence was so immense, he believed that any such success could be applied to his own soul. Steel had no such illusions. It was a commonplace that teachers are surpassed by their creations – pupils, fission-children, adoptions, whatever. He, Steel, was a perfect illustration of this, though the Master didn't know it yet.

Steel had determined to create beings that would each be superior in some *single* way – while flawed and malleable in others. In the Master's absence he had begun a number of experiments. Steel worked from scratch, identifying inheritance lines independent of pack membership. His agents purchased or stole pups that might have potential. Unlike Flenser, who usually melded pups into existing packs in an approximation of nature, Steel made his totally newborn. His puppy packs had no memories or fragments of soul; Steel had total control from the beginning.

Of course, most such constructions quickly died. The pups had to be parted from their wet nurses before they began to participate in the adult's consciousness. The resulting pack was taught entirely in speech and written language. All inputs could be controlled.

Steel stopped before door number thirty-three: Experiment Amdiranifani, Mathematical Excellence. It was not the only attempt in this direction, but it was by far the most successful. Steel's agents had searched the Movement for packs with ability for abstraction. They had gone further: the world's most famous mathematician lived in the Long Lakes Republic. The pack had been preparing to fission; she had several puppies by herself and a mathematically talented lover. Steel had had the pups taken. They matched his other acquisitions so well that he decided to make an eightsome. If things worked out, it might be beyond all nature in its intelligence.

Steel motioned his guard to shield the torches. He opened door thirty-three and soft-toed one member to the edge of the balcony. He looked down, carefully silencing that member's fore-tympanum. The skylight was dim, but he could see the pups huddled together . . . with its new friend. The mantis. Serendipity, that was all he could call this, the reward that comes to a researcher who labors long enough, carefully enough. He had had two problems. The first had been growing for a year: Amdiranifani was slowly fading, its members falling into the usual autism of wholly newborn packs. The second was the captured alien; that was an enormous threat, an enormous mystery, an enormous opportunity. How to communicate with it? Without communication, the possibilities for manipulation were very limited.

Yet in a single blind stroke, an incompetent Servant had shown the way to solve both problems. Now that his eyes were adjusted to the dimness, Steel could see the alien beneath the pile of puppies. When first he'd heard that the creature had been put in with an experiment, Steel had been enraged beyond thought; the Servant who made the mistake had been recycled. But the days passed. Experiment Amdiranifani began showing more liveliness than at any time since its pups were weaned. It quickly became obvious – from dissecting the other aliens, and observing this one – that mantis folk did *not* live in packs. Steel had a complete alien.

The alien moved in its sleep, and made a low-pitched mouth noise; it was totally incapable of any other kind of sound. The pups shifted to fit the new position. They were sleeping too, vaguely thinking among themselves. The low end of their sounds was a perfect imitation of the alien . . . And that was the greatest coup of all. *Experiment Amdiranifani was learning the alien's speech*. To the pack of newborns this was simply another form of interpack talk, and apparently its mantis friend was more interesting than the tutors who appeared on these balconies. The Flenser Fragment claimed it was the physical contact, that the pups were reacting to the alien as a surrogate parent, thoughtless though the alien was.

It really didn't matter. Steel brought another head to the edge of the balcony. He stood quietly, neither member thinking directly at the other. The air smelled faintly of puppies and mantis sweat. These two were the Movement's greatest treasure: the key to survival and more. By now, Steel knew the flying ship was not part of an invasion fleet. Their visitors were more like ill-prepared refugees. There had been no word of other landings, and the Movement's spies were spread far.

It had been a close thing, winning against the aliens. Their single weapon had killed most of a regiment. In the proper jaws, such weapons could defeat armies. He had no doubt the ship contained more powerful killing machines – ones that still functioned. Wait and watch, Steel counseled himself. Let Amdiranifani show the levers that could control this alien. The entire world would be the prize.

14

Sometimes Mom used to say that something was 'more fun than a barrel full of puppies.' Jefri Olsndot had never had more than one pet at a time, and only once had that been a dog. But now he understood what she meant. From the very first day, even when he had been so tired and scared, he had been entranced by the eight puppies. And they by him. They were all over him, pulling at his clothes, unfastening his shoes, sitting on his lap, or just running around him. Three or four were always staring at him. Their eyes were completely brown or pink, and seemed large for their heads. From the beginning the puppies had mimicked him. They were better than Straumli songbirds; anything he said they could echo –

or play back later. And when he cried, often the puppies would cry too, and cuddle around him.

There were other dogs, big ones that wore clothes and entered the room through doorways high up on the walls. They lowered food into the room, and sometimes made strange noises. But the food tasted awful, and they didn't respond to Jefri's screaming even by mimicking him.

Two days had passed, then a week. Jefri had investigated everything in the room. It wasn't really a dungeon; it was too big. And besides, prisoners don't get pets. He understood that this world was uncivilized, not part of the Realm, perhaps not even on the Net. If Mom or Dad or Johanna weren't nearby, it was possible that there was no one here to teach the dogs to speak Samnorsk! Then it would be up to Jefri Olsndot to teach the dogs and find his family . . . Now when the white-jacketed dogs came onto the corner balconies, Jefri shouted questions at them. It didn't help very much. Even the one with red stripes didn't respond. But the puppies did! They shouted right along with Jefri, sometimes echoing his words, sometimes making nonsense sounds.

It didn't take Jefri long to realize that the puppies were driven by a single mind. When they ran around him, some would always sit a little way off, their graceful necks arching this way and that – and the runners seemed to know exactly what the others saw. He couldn't hide things behind his back if there was even one of them to alert the others. For a while he thought they were somehow talking to each other. But it was more than that: when he watched them unfasten his shoes or draw a picture – the heads and mouths and paws cooperated *so* perfectly, like the fingers on a person's hands. Jefri didn't reason things out so explicitly; but over a period of days he came to think of all the puppies together as a single friend. At the same time he noticed that the puppies was mixing up his words – and sometimes making new meanings.

'You me play.' The words came out like a cheap voice splice, but they generally preceded a mad game of tag all around the furniture.

'You me picture.' The slate board covered the lowest meter of the wall, all around the room. It was a display device unlike any Jefri had ever seen in his life: dirty, imprecise, imperfectly deletable, unstorable. Jefri loved it. His face and hands – and most of Puppies lips – got covered with chalk stains. They drew each other, and themselves. Puppies didn't draw neat pictures like Jefri's; Puppies' dog figures had big heads and paws, with the bodies all smudged together. When he drew Jefri, the hands were always big, each finger carefully drawn.

Jefri drew his family and tried to make Puppies understand.

Day by day, the sunlight circled higher on the walls. Sometimes the room was dark now. At least once a day, packs came to talk to Puppies. This was one of the few things which could pull the little ones away from Jefri. Puppies would sit below the balconies, screeching and croaking at the adults. It was a school class! They'd lower scrolls for him to look at, and retrieve ones he had marked.

Jefri sat quietly and watched the lessons. He fidgeted, but he didn't shout at the teachers anymore. Just a little longer and he and Puppies would really be talking. Just a little longer and Puppies could find out for him where Mom and Dad and Johanna were.

Sometimes terror and pain are not the best levers; deception, when it works, is the most elegant and the least expensive manipulation of all. Once Amdiranifani was fluent in the mantis language, Steel had him explain about the 'tragic death' of Jefri's parents and brood-sibling. The Flenser Fragment had argued against it, but Steel wanted quick and unquestioned control.

Now it seemed that the Fragment might have been right; at least he should have held out the hope that the brood-sibling lived. Steel looked solemnly at the Amdiranifani Experiment. 'How can we help?'

The young pack looked up trustingly. 'Jefri is so terribly upset about his parents and *sister*.' Amdiranifani was using mantis words a lot, often unnecessarily: *sister* instead of brood-sibling. 'He hasn't been eating much. He doesn't want to play. It makes me very sad.'

Steel kept watch on the far balcony. The Flenser Fragment was there. It was not hiding, though most of its faces were out of the candlelight. So far its insights had been extraordinary. But the Fragment's stare was like old times, when a mistake could mean mutilation or worse. *So be it.* The stakes were higher now than ever before; if fear at Steel's throats could help him succeed, he welcomed it. He looked away from the balcony, and brought all his faces to an expression of tender sympathy for poor Jefri's plight. 'You just have to make it – him – understand. No one can bring his parents or *sister* back to life. But we know who the murderers are. We're doing everything we can to defend against them. Tell him how hard this is. Woodcarvers is an empire that has lasted hundreds of years. In a fight, we are no match for them. That's why we need all the help he can give us. We need him to teach us to use his parents' ship.'

The puppy pack lowered a head. 'Yes. I'll try, but . . .' The three members by Jefri made low pitched grunting noises at it. The mantis sat head bowed; it held its tentacled paws across its eyes. The creature had been like this for several days, and the withdrawal was getting worse. Now it shook its head violently, made sharp noises a little higher pitched than its normal register.

'Jefri says he doesn't understand how things work in the ship. He's just a little . . .' the pack searched for a translation. '. . . he is really very young. You know, like me.'

Steel nodded understandingly. It was an obvious consequence of the aliens' singleton nature, but weird even so: Every one of them started out all a puppy. Every one of them was like Steel's puppy-pack experiments. Parental knowledge was transmitted by the equivalent of interpack speech. That made the creature easy to dupe, but it was a damned inconveninence now. 'Still, if there's anything he can help explain.'

More grunting from the mantis. Steel should learn that language. The sounds were easy; these pitiful creatures used their *mouths* to talk, like a bird or a forest slug. For now he depended on Amdiranifani. For now that was okay; the puppy pack trusted him. Another piece of serendipity. With a few of his recent experiments, Steel had tried love in place of Flenser's original terror/love combination; there had been a slim chance that it might be superior. By great good luck Amdiranifani fell into the love group. Even his instructors had avoided negative reinforcement. The pack would believe anything he said . . . and so, Steel hoped, would the mantis.

Amdiranifani translated: 'There is something else; he has asked me about it before. Jefri knows how to wake the other children –' the word literally meant 'packs of puppies' '– on the ship. You look surprised, my lord Steel?'

Even though he no longer dreamed in terror of monster minds, Steel would just as soon *not* have a hundred more aliens running around. 'I hadn't realized they could be wakened so easily . . . But we shouldn't do it right now. We've having trouble finding food that Jefri can eat.' That was true; the creature was an incredibly finicky eater. 'I don't think we could feed any more right now.'

More grunting. More sharp cries from Jefri. Finally, 'There is one other thing, my lord. Jefri thinks it may be possible to use the ship's *ultrawave* to call for help from others like his parents.'

The Flenser Fragment jerked out of the shadows. A pair of heads looked down at the mantis, while another stared meaningfully at Steel. Steel didn't react; he could be cooler than any loose pack. 'That's something to think about. Perhaps you and Jefri could talk more about it. I don't want to try it till we're sure we won't hurt the ship.' That was weak. He saw the Fragment twitch a muzzle in amusement.

As he spoke, Amdiranifani was translating. Jefri responded almost immediately.

'Oh, that's okay. He meant a special call. Jefri says the ship has been signaling . . . all by itself . . . ever since it landed.'

And Steel wondered if he had ever heard a deadly threat uttered in such sweet innocence.

They began letting Amdi and Jefri outside to play. Beforehand Amdi was nervous about going out. He was unused to wearing clothes. His whole life – all four years of it – had been spent in that one big room. He read about the outside and was curious about it, yet he was also a little afraid. But the human boy seemed to want it. Every day he'd been more withdrawn, his crying softer. Mostly he was crying for his parents or sister, but sometimes he cried about being locked up so deep away.

So Amdi had talked to Mr Steel, and now they got out almost every day, at least to an inner courtyard. At first Jefri just sat, not really looking around. But Amdi discovered that *he* loved the outdoors, and each time he got his friend to play a little more.

Packs of teachers and guards stood at the corners of the yellowing moss and watched. Amdi – and eventually Jefri – got a big kick out of harassing them. They hadn't realized it down in the room, where visitors came at the balconies, but most adults were nervous around Jefri. The boy was half again as tall as a normally standing pack member. When he came close, the average pack would clump together and edge away. They didn't like having to look *up* at him. It was silly, Amdi thought. Jefri was so tall and skinny, he looked like he might topple over at any moment. And when he ran it was like he was wildly trying to recover from a fall and never quite succeeding. So Amdi's favorite game those first days was tag. Whenever he was the chaser, he contrived to run Jefri right through the most prim looking whitejackets. If he and Jefri did it right they could turn the tag into a three-way event, Amdi chasing Jefri and a whitejackets racing to stay away from both of them.

, Sometimes he felt sorry for the guards and whitejackets. They were so stiff and grownup. Didn't they understand how much fun it was to have a friend that you walk right next to, that you could actually *touch?*

It was mostly night now. Daylight hovered for a few hours around noon. The twilight before and after was bright enough to dim the stars and aurora, but still too faint to show colors. Though Amdi had spent his life indoors, he understood the geometry of the situation, and liked to watch the change of light. Jefri didn't much like the dark of winter . . . until the first snow fell.

Amdi got his first set of jackets. And Mr Steel had special clothes made for the human boy, big puffy things that covered his whole body and kept him warmer than a good pelt would have done.

On one side of the courtyard the snow was just six inches deep, but elsewhere it piled into drifts higher than Amdi's head. Torches were mounted in wind shields on the walls; their light glittered golden off the snow. Amdi knew about snow – but he'd never seen it before. He loved to splash it on one of his jackets. He would stare and stare, trying to see the snowflakes without his breath melting them. The hexagonal pattern was tantalizing, just at the limit of his vision.

But tag was no fun anymore; the human could run through drifts that left Amdi swimming in the white stuff. There were other things the human could do, wonderful things. He could make balls of snow and throw them. The guards were very upset by this, especially when Jefri plinked a few members. It was the first time he ever saw them get angry.

Amdi raced around the windswept side of the courtyard, dodging snowballs and keening frustration. Human hands were such wicked, wicked things. How he would love to have a pair – four pairs! He circled round from three sides and sprinted right at the human. Jefri backed quickly into deeper snow, but too late. Amdi hit him high and low, tipping the Two-Legs over into a snowdrift. There was a mock battle, slashing lips and paws against Jefri's hands and feet. But now Amdi was on top. The human got paid back for his snowballs with plenty of snow stuffed down the back of his jacket.

Sometimes they just sat and watched the sky for so long that rumps and paws went numb. Sitting behind the largest snow drift, they were shaded from the castle torches and had a clear view of the lights in the sky.

At first Amdi had been entranced by the aurora. Even some of his teachers were. They said this part of the world was one of the best places to see the sky glow. Sometimes it was so faint that the torchlight glimmering off the snow was enough to blot it out. Other times it ran from horizon to horizon: green light trimmed with hints of pink, twisting as though ruffled by a slow wind.

He and Jefri could talk very easily now, though always in Jefri's language. The human couldn't make many of the sounds of interpack speech; even his pronounciation of Amdi's name was scarcely recognizable. But Amdi understood Samnorsk pretty well; it was fun, their own secret language.

Jefri was not especially impressed by the aurora. 'We have that lots at home. It's just light from –' He said a new word, and glanced at Amdi. It was funny how the human couldn't look in more than one place at a time. His eyes and head were always moving. '– you know, places where people make things. I think the gas and waste leaks out, and then the sun lights it up or it gets –' unintelligible.

'Places where people make things?' *In the sky?* Amdi had a globe; he knew the size of the world and its orientation. If the aurora were reflecting sunlight, it must be hundreds of miles above the ground! Amdi leaned a back against Jefri's jacket and made a very human whistling sound. His knowledge of geography was not up to his geometry, but, 'The packs don't work in the sky, Jefri. We don't even have flying boats.'

'Uh, that's right, you don't . . . I don't know what the stuff is then. But I don't like it. It gets in the way of the stars.' Amdi knew all about the stars; Jefri had told him. Somewhere out there were the friends of Jefri's parents.

Jefri was silent for several minutes. He wasn't looking at the sky anymore. Amdi wriggled a little closer, watching the shifting light in the sky. Behind them the wind-sharpened crest of the drift was edged with yellow light from the torches. Amdi could imagine what the other was thinking. 'The commsets from the boat, they really aren't good enough to call for help?'

Jefri slapped the ground. 'No! I told you. They're just radio. I think I can make them work, but what's the use? The ultrawave stuff is still on the boat and it's too big to move. I just don't understand why Mr Steel won't let me go aboard . . . I'm eight years old, you know. I could figure it out. Mom had it all set up before, before . . .' His words guttered into the familiar, despairing silence.

Amdi rubbed a head against Jefri's shoulder. He had a theory about Mr Steel's reluctance. It was an explanation he hadn't told Jefri before: 'Maybe he's afraid you'll just fly away and leave us.'

'That's stupid! I'd never leave you. Besides, that boat is *real* hard to fly. It was never meant to land on a world.'

Jefri said the strangest things; sometimes Amdi was just misunderstanding – but sometimes they were literal truth. Did the humans really have ships that *never* came to ground? Where did they go then? Amdi could almost feel new scales of reference clicking together in his mind. Mr Steel's geography globe represented not the world, but something very, very small in the true scheme of things.

'I know you wouldn't leave us. But you can see how Mr Steel might be afraid. He can't even talk to you except through me. We have to show him that we can be trusted.'

'I guess.'

'If you and I could get the radios working, that might help. I know my teachers haven't figured them out. Mr Steel has one, but I don't think he understands it either.'

'Yeah. If we could get the other one to work . . .'

That afternoon the guards got a break: their two charges came in from the cold early. The guards didn't question their good fortune.

Steel's den had originally been the Master's. It was very different from the castle's meeting halls. Except for choirs, only a single pack would fit in any room. It was not exactly that the suite was small. There were five rooms, not counting the bath. But except for the library, none was more than fifteen feet across. The ceilings were low, less than five feet; there was no space for visitor balconies. Servants were always on call in the two hallways that shared a wall with the quarters. The dining room, bedroom, and bath had smaller hatches, just big enough to give orders and to receive food and drink, or use as a garderobe.

The main entrance was guarded on the outside by three trooper packs. Of course, the Master would never live in a den with only one exit. Steel had found eight secret hatches (three in the sleeping quarters). These could only be opened from within; they led to the maze that Flenser had built within the castle's walls. No one knew the extent of that maze, not even the Master. Steel had rearranged parts of it – in particular the passages leading from this den – in the years since Flenser's departure.

The quarters were nearly impregnable. Even if the castle fell, the rooms' larder was stocked for half a year; ventilation was provided by a network of channels almost as extensive as the Master's secret passages. All in all, Steel felt only tolerably safe here. There was always the possibility that there were *more* than eight secret entrances, perhaps one that could be opened from the other side.

And of course choirs were out of the question, here or anywhere. The only extrapack sex that Steel indulged was with singletons – and that as part of his experiments; it was just too dangerous to mix one's self with others.

After dinner, Steel drifted into the library. He relaxed around his reading desk. Two of him sipped brandy while another smoked southern herbs. This was pleasure but also calculation: Steel knew just what vices, applied to just which members, would raise his imagination to its keenest pitch.

... And more and more he was coming to see that imagination was at least as important as raw intelligence in the present game. The desk between him was covered with maps, reports from the south, internal security memos. But lying in all the silkpaper, like an ivory slug in its nest, was the alien *radio*. They had recovered two from the ship. Steel picked the thing up, ran a nose along the smooth, curved sides. Only the finest stressed wood – and that in musical instruments or statuary – could match its grace. Yet the mantis claimed this could be used to talk across dozens of miles, as fast as a ray of sunlight. If true ... Steel wondered how many lost battles might have been won with these, how many new conquests might be safely undertaken. And if they could learn to *make* far-talkers ... the Movement's subordinates, scattered across the continent, would be as near as the guards by Steel's den. No force in the world could stand against them.

Steel picked up the latest report from Woodcarvers. In many ways they were having more success with their mantis than was Steel with his. Apparently theirs was almost an adult. More important, it had a miraculous library that could be interrogated almost like a living being. There had been three other *datasets*. Steel's whitejackets had found what was left of them in the burnt-out wreckage around the ship. Jefri thought that the ship's *processors* were a little like a *dataset*, 'only stupider' (Amdi's best translation), but so far the *processors* had been useless.

But with their *dataset*, several on Woodcarver's staff had already learned mantis talk. Each day they discovered more about the aliens' civilization than Steel's people could in ten. He smiled. They didn't know that all the important stuff was being faithfully reported to Hidden Island . . . For now he would let them keep their toy, and their mantis; they had noticed several things that would have slipped by him. Still he damned the luck.

Steel paged through the report . . . Good. The alien at Woodcarvers was still uncooperative. He felt his smile spreading into laughter: it was a small thing, the creature's word for the packs. The report tried to spell out the word. It didn't matter; the translation was 'claws' or 'tines.' The mantis had a special horror for the tine attachments that soldiers wore on their forepaws. Steel licked pensively at the black enamel of his manicured claws. Interesting. Claws could be threatening things, but they were also part of being a person. Tines were their mechanical extension, and potentially more frightening. It was the sort of name you might imagine for an elite killer force . . . but never for all the packs. After all, the race of packs included the weak, the poor, the kindly, the naïve . . . as well as persons like Steel and Flenser. It said something very interesting about mantis psychology that the creature picked *tines* as the characterizing feature of the packs.

Steel eased back from his desk and gazed at the landscape painted around the library's walls. It was a view from the castle towers. Behind the paint, the walls were lined with patterns of mica and quartz and fiber; the echoes gave a vague sense of what you might hear looking out across the stone and emptiness. Combination audiovisuals were rare in the castle, and this one was especially well-done; Steel could feel himself relaxing as he stared at it. He drifted for a moment, letting his imagination roam.

Tines. I like it. If that was the alien's image, then it was the right name for his race. His pitiful advisors – and sometimes even the Flenser Fragment – were still intimidated by the ship from the stars. No question, there was power in that ship beyond anything in the world. But after the first panic, Steel understood that the aliens were *not* supernaturally gifted. They had simply progressed – in the sense that Woodcarver made so much of – beyond the current state of his world's science. Certainly the alien civilization was a deadly unknown right now. Indeed, it might be capable of burning this world to a cinder. Yet the more Steel saw, the more he realized the intrinsic inferiority of the aliens: What a bizarre abortion they were, a race of intelligent singletons. Every one of them must be raised from nothing like a wholly newborn pack. Memories could only be passed by voice and writing. Each creature grew and aged and even *died* as a whole. Despite himself, Steel shivered.

He had come a long way from the first misconceptions, the first fears. For more than thirty days now he'd been scheming to use the starship to rule the world. The mantis said that ship was signaling others. *That* had reduced some of his Servants to incontinence. So. Sooner or later, more ships would arrive. Ruling the world was no longer a practical goal . . . It was time to aim higher, at goals even the Master had never imagined. Take away their technical advantages and the mantis folk were such finite, fragile beings. They should be easy to conquer. Even *they* seemed to realize this. *Tines, the creature calls us. So it will be.* Some day Tines would pace between the stars and rule there.

But in the years till then, life would be very dangerous. Like a newborn pup, all their poptential could be ended by one small blow. The Movement's survival – the world's survival – would depend upon superior intelligence, imagination, discipline, treachery. Fortunately, those had always been Steel's great strengths.

Steel dreamed in the candlelight and haze . . . Intelligence, imagination, discipline, treachery. Done right . . . could the aliens be persuaded to eliminate all of Steel's enemies . . .

and then bare their throats to him? It was daring, almost beyond reason, but there might be a way. Jefri claimed he could operate the ship's signaler. By himself? Steel doubted it. The alien was thoroughly duped, but not especially competent. Amdiranifani was a different story. He was showing all the genius of his bloodlines. And the principles of loyalty and sacrifice his teachers drilled into him had taken hold, though he was a bit . . . playful. His obedience didn't have the sharp edge that fear could bring. No matter. As a tool he was useful beyond all others. Amdiranifani understood Jefri, and seemed to understand the alien artifacts even *better* than the mantis did.

The risk must be taken. He would let the two aboard the ship. They would send his message in place of the automatic distress signal. And what should that first message be? Word for word, it would be the most important, most dangerous thing any pack had ever said.

Three hundred yards away, deep in the experiment wing, a boy and a pack of puppies came across an unexpected piece of good luck: an unlocked door, and a chance to play with Jefri's commset.

The phone was more complex than some. It was intended for hospital and field work, for the remote control of devices as well as for voice talk. By trial and error, the two gradually narrowed the options.

Jefri Olsndot pointed to numbers that had appeared on the side of the device. 'I think that means we're matched with some receiver.' He glanced nervously at the doorway. Something told him they really shouldn't be here.

'That's the same pattern as on the radio Mr Steel took,' said Amdi. Not even one of his heads was watching the door.

'I bet if we press it here, what we say will come out on his radio. Now he'll know we can help . . . So what should we do?'

Three of Amdi raced around the room, like dogs that couldn't keep their attention on the conversation. By now, Jefri knew this was the equivalent of a human looking away and humming as he thought. The angle of his gaze was another gesture, in this case a spreading and mischievous smile. 'I think we should surprise him. He is always so serious.'

'Yeah.' Mr Steel was pretty solemn. But then all the adults were. They reminded him of the older scientists at the High Lab.

Amdi grabbed the radio and gave him a 'just watch this' look. He nosed on the 'talk' switch and sang a long ululation into the mike. It sounded only vaguely like pack speech. One of Amdi translated next to Jefri's ear. The human boy felt giggles stealing up his throat.

In his den, Lord Steel was lost in scheming. His imagination – loosed by herbs and brandy – floated free, playing with the possibilities. He was settled deep in velvet cushions, comfortable in the den's safety. The remaining candles shone faintly on the landscape mural, glinting from the polished furniture. The story he would tell the aliens, he almost had it now . . .

The noise on his desk began as a small thing, submerged beneath his dreaming. It was mostly low-pitched, but there were overtones in the range of thought, like slices of another mind. It was a presence, growing. *Someone is in my den!* The thought tore like Flenser's killing blade. Steel's members spasmed panic, disoriented by smoke and drink.

There was a voice in the middle of the insanity. It was distorted, missing tones that any normal speech should have. It howled and quavered at him, 'Lord Steel! Greetings from the Pack of Packs, the Lord God Almighty!'

Part of Steel was already out the main hatch, staring wide-eyed at his guards in the hallway beyond. The troopers' presence brought a bit of calm, and icy embarrassment. *This is nonsense.* He tipped a head to the alien device on his desk. The echoes were everywhere, but the sounds originated in the far-talker . . . There was no pack speech now, just the high-pitched slices of sound, mindless warbling in the middle range of thought. Wait. Behind it all, faint and low . . . there were the coughing grunts he recognized as mantis laughter.

Steel rarely gave way to rage. It should be his tool, not his master. But listening to the laughter, and remembering the words . . . Steel felt black bloodiness rising in first one member and then another. Almost without thought, he reached back and smashed the *commset*. It fell instantly silent. He glared at the guards ranged at attention in the hallway. Their mind noise was quiet with stifled fear.

Someone would die for this.

Mr Steel met with Amdi and Jefri the day after their success with the radio. They had convinced him. They were moving to the mainland. Jefri would have his chance to call for rescue!

Steel was even more solemn than usual; he made a big thing about how important it was to get help, to defend against another attack from the Woodcarvers. But he didn't seem angry about Amdi's little prank. Jefri breathed a quiet sigh of relief. Back home, Daddy would have tanned his hide for something like that. *I guess Amdi is right.* Mr Steel was serious because of all his responsibilities and the dangers they faced. But underneath he was a very nice person.

Crypto: 0
As received by: Transceiver Relay03 at Relay
Language path: Firetongue→Cloudmark→Trisk-
    weline, SjK units [Firetongue and Cloudmark are
    High Beyond trade languages. Only core meaning is
    rendered by this translation.]
From: Arbitration Arts Corporation at Firecloud Nebula
    [A High Beyond military [?] organization. Known age
    ~100 years]
Subject: Reason for concern
Summary: Three single-system civilizations are appar-
    ently destroyed
Key phrases: scale interstellar disasters, scale inter-
    stellar warefare?, Straumli Realm Perversion
Distribution:
    War Trackers Interest Group
    Threats Interest Group
    Homo Sapiens Interest Group
Date: 53.57 days since the fall of Straumli Realm
Text of message:

Recently an obscure civilization announced it had created a new Power in the Transcend. It then dropped 'temporarily' off the Known Net. Since that time, there have been about a million messages in Threats about the incident – plenty of speculations that a Class Two Perversion had been born – but no evidence of effects beyond the boundaries of the former 'Straumli Realm.'

Arbitration Arts specializes in treckle lansing disputes. As such, we have few common business interests with natural races or Threats Group. That may have to change: sixty-five hours ago, we noticed the apparent extinction of three isolated civilizations in the High Beyond near Straumli Realm. Two of these were Eye-in-the-U religious probes, and the third was a Pentragian fctory. Previously their main Net link had been Straumli Realm. As such, they have been off the Net since Straumli dropped, except for occasional pinging from us.

We diverted three missions to perform fly-throughs. Signal reconnaissance revealed wideband communication that was more like neural control than local net traffic. Several new large structures were noted. All our vessels were destroyed before detailed information could be returned. Given the background of these settlements, we conclude that this is *not* the normal aftermath of a transcending.

These observations are consistent with a Class Two attack from the Transcend (albeit a secretive one). The most obvious source would be the new Power constructed by Straumli Realm. We urge special vigilance upon all High Beyond civilizations in this part of the Beyond. We larger ones have little to fear, but the threat is very clear.

Crypto: 0
As received by: Transceiver Relay03 at Relay
Language path: Firetongue→Cloudmark→Trisk-
    weline, SjK units [Firetongue and Cloudmark are
    High Beyond trade languages. Only core meaning is

rendered by this translation.]
From: Arbitration Arts Corporation at Firecloud Nebula
[A High Beyond military [?] organization. Known age
~ 100 years]
Subject: New service available
Summary: Arbitration Arts to provide Net relay service
Key phrases: Special Rates, Sentient Translator Pro-
grams, Ideal for civilizations in the High Beyond
Distribution:
Communication Costs Inerest Group
Motley Hatch Administration Group
Date: 61.00 days since the fall of Straumli Realm
Text of message:
Arbitrtation Arts is proud to announce a
transceiver-layer service especially designed for sites
in the High Beyond [rates tabulated after the text of
this message]. State-of-the-Zone programs will provide high quality translation and routing. It has been
nearly one hundred years since any High Beyond
civilization in this part of the Galaxy has been interested in providing such a communication service. We
realize the job is dull and the armiphlage not in keeping
with the effort, but we all stand to benefit from
protocols that are consistent with the Zone we live in.
Details follow under syntax
8139 . . . [Cloudmark: Triskweline translator program
balks at handling syntax 8139.]

Crypto: 0
As received by: Transceiver Relay03 at Relay
Language path: Cloudmark→Triskweline, SjK units
[Cloudmark is a High Beyond trade language.
Despite colloquial rendering, only core meaning is
guaranteed.]
From: Transcendent Bafflements Trading Union at
Cloud Center
Subject: Matter of life and death
Summary: Arbitration Arts has fallen to Straumli
Perversion via a Net attack. Use Middle Beyond

relays till emergency passes!
Key phrases: Net attack, scale interstellar warfare,
    Straumli Perversion
Distribution:
    War Trackers Interest Group
    Threats Interest Group
    Homo Sapiens Interest Group
Date: 61.12 days since the fall of Straumli Realm
Text of message:
    WARNING! The site identifying itself as Arbitration
Arts is now controlled by the Straumli Perversion. The
Arts' recent advertisement of communications services is a deadly trick. In fact we have good evidence
that the Perversion used sapient Net packets to invade
and disable the Arts' defenses. Large portions of the
Arts now appear to be under direct control of the
Straumli Power. Parts of the Arts that were not
infected in the initial invasion have been destroyed by
the converted portions: Fly-throughs show several
stellifications.
    What can be done: If during the last thousand
seconds you have received any High-Beyond-protocol
packets from 'Arbitration Arts,' *discard them at once*. If
they have been processed, then the processing site
and all locally netted sites must be physically destroyed *at once*. We realize that this means the destruction of solar systems, but consider the alternative.
You are under Transcendent attack.
    If you survive the initial peril (the next thirty hours or
so), then there are obvious procedures that can give
relative safety: Do not accept High Beyond protocol
packets. At the very least, route all communications
through Middle Beyond sites, with translation down
to, and then up from, local trade languages.
    For the longer term: It's obvious that an
extraordinarily powerful Class Two Perversion has
bloomed in our region of the galaxy. For the next
thirteen years or so, all advanced civilizations near us
will be in great danger.

If we can identify the background of the current perversion, we may discover its weaknesses and a feasible defense. Class Two Perversions all involve a deformed Power that creates symbiotic structures in the High Beyond — but there is an enormous variety of origins. Some are poorly-formed jokes told by Powers no longer on the scene. Others are weapons built by the newly transcendent, and never properly disarmed.

The immediate source of this danger is well-documented: a species recently up from the Middle Beyond, Homo sapiens, founded Straumli Realm. We are inclined to believe the theory proposed in messages [. . .], namely that Straumli researchers experimented with something in Shortcuts, and that the recipe was a self-booting evil from an earlier time. One possibility: Some loser from long ago planted how-to's on the Net (or in some lost archive) for the use of its own descendents. Thus, we are interested in any information related to Homo sapiens.

The next day Amdi went on the longest trip of his young life. Bundled in windbreakers, they traveled down wide, cobbled streets to the straits below the castle. Mr Steel led the way on a chariot-cart drawn by three kherhogs. He looked marvelous in his red-striped jackets. Guards dressed in white fur rolled along on either side, and the dour Tyrathect brought up the rear. The aurora was as brilliant as Amdijefri had ever seen, brighter in sum than the full moon that sat upon the northern horizon. Icicles grew down from buildings' eaves, sometimes all the way to the ground: glittering, green-silver pillars in the light.

Then they were on the boats, rowing across the straits. The water swept like chill black stone around the hulls.

When they reached the other side, Starship Hill towered over them, higher than any castle could ever be. Every minute brought new visions, new worlds.

It took half an hour to reach the top of that hill, even though their carts were pulled by kherhogs, and nobody walked. Amdi looked in all directions, awed by the landscape that spread, aurora-lit, below them. At first Jefri seemed just as excited, but as they reached the hilltop, he stopped looking around and turned to hug at his friend painfully hard.

Mr Steel had built a shelter around the starship. Inside the air was still, and a little warmer. Jefri stood at the base of the spidery stairs, looking up at the light that spilled from the ship's open doorway. Amdi felt him shivering.

'Is he frightened of his own flier?' asked Tyrathect.

By now Amdi knew most of Jefri's fears, and understood most of the despair. *How would I feel if Mr Steel were killed?* 'No, not scared. It's the memories of what happened here.'

Steel said gently, 'Tell him we could come again. He doesn't have to go inside today.'

Jefri shook his head at the suggestion, but couldn't answer right away. 'I've got to go on. I've got to be brave.' He started slowly up the stairs, stopping at each step to make sure that Amdi was still all with him. The puppies were split between concern for Jefri and the desire to rush madly into this wonderful mystery.

Then they were through the hatch, and into Two-Legs strangeness: bright bluish light, air as warm as in the castle . . . and dozens of mysterious shapes. They walked to the far side of the big room, and Mr Steel stuck some heads in the entrance. His mind sounds echoed loudly around them. 'I've quilted the walls, Amdi, but even so, there isn't room for more than one of us in here.'

'Y-yes.' There were echoes and Steel's mind sounded strangely fierce.

'It's up to you to protect your friend here, and let me know about everything you see.' He moved back so that just one head still looked in upon them.

'Yes. Yes! I will.' It was the first time anybody except Jefri had really needed him.

Jefri wandered silently about the room full of his sleeping friends. He wasn't crying any more, and he wasn't in the silent funk that often held him. It was as if he couldn't quite believe where he was. He passed his hands lightly across the caskets,

153

looking at the faces within. *So many friends*, thought Amdi, *waiting to be wakened. What will they be like?*

'The walls? I don't remember this . . .' said Jefri. He touched the heavy quilting that Steel had hung.

'It's to make the place sound better,' said Amdi. He pulled at the flaps, wondering what was behind: Green wall, like stone and steel all at once . . . and covered with tiny bumps and fingers of gray. 'What's this?'

Jefri was looking over his shoulders. 'Ug. Mold. It's spread. I'm glad Mr Steel has covered it up.' The human boy drifted away. Amdi stayed a second longer, poked several heads up close to the stuff. Mold and fungus were a constant problem in the castle; people were always cleaning it up – and perversely so, in Amdi's opinion. He thought fungus was neat, something that could grow on hardest rock. And this stuff was especially strange. Some of the clumps were almost half an inch high, but wispy, like solid smoke.

The back-looking part of him saw that Jefri had drifted off toward the inner cabin. Reluctantly, Amdi followed.

They stayed in the ship only an hour that first time. In the inner cabin Jefri turned on magic windows that looked out in all directions. Amdi sat goggle-eyed; this was a trip to heaven.

For Jefri it was something else. He hunched down in a hammock and stared at the controls. The tension slowly left his face.

'I – I like it here,' said Amdi, tentatively, softly.

Jefri rocked gently in the hammock. '. . . Yes.' He sighed. 'I was so afraid . . . but being here makes me feel closer to . . .' His hands reached out to caress the panel that hung close to the hammock. 'My dad landed this thing; he was sitting right here.' He twisted around, looked at a glimmering panel of light above him. 'And Mom got the ultrawave all set . . . They did it all. And now it's only you and me, Amdi. Even Johanna is gone . . . It's all up to us.'

Vrinimi Classification: Organizational SECRET. Not for distribution beyond Ring 1 of the local net.
Transceiver Relay00 search log:

Begining 19:40:40 Docks Time, 17/01 of Org year
    52090 [128.13 days since the fall of Straumli Realm]
Link layer syntax 14 message loop detected on
    assigned surveillance bearing. Signal strength and
    S/N compatible with previously detected beacon
    signal.
Language path: Samnorsk, SjK: Relay units
From: Jefri Olsndot at I dont know where this is
Subject: Hello. My names Jefri Olsndot. Our ships hurt
    adnd we need help. pPlease anser.
Summary: Sorry if I get some of this wrong. This
    keybord is STUPID!
Key phrases: I dont know
To: Relay anybody
Text of message: [empty]

15

Two Skroderiders played in the surf.

'Do you think his life is in danger?' asked the one with the slender green stalk.

'Whose life?' said the other, a large rider with a bluish basal shell.

'Jefri Olsndot, the human child.'

Blueshell sighed to himself and consulted his skrode. You come to the beach to forget the cares of the everyday, but Greenstalk would not let them go. He scaned for danger-to-Jefri: 'Of course he's in danger, you twit! Look up the latest messages from him.'

'Oh.' Greenstalk's tone was embarrassed. 'Sorry for the partial remembering,' remembering enough to worry and nothing more. She went silent; after a moment he heard her pleasured humming. The surf crashed endlessly past them.

Blueshell opened to the water, tasting the life that swirled in the power of the waves. It was a beautiful beach. It was probably unique – and that was an extreme thing to say about anything in the Beyond. When the foam swept back from their bodies, they could see indigo sky spread from one side of the Docks to the other, and the glint of starships. When the surf came forward, the two Riders were submerged in the turbid chill, surrounded by the coralesks and intertidal creatures that built their little homes here. And at high 'tide' the flexure of the sea floor held steady for an hour or so. Then the water cleared, and if in daylight, they could see patches of glassy sea-bottom ... and through them, a thousand kilometers below, the surface of Groundside.

Blueshell tried to clear his mind of care. For every hour of peaceful contemplation, a few more natural memories would accumulate ... No good. Just now he could no more banish the worries than could Greenstalk. After a moment he said, 'Sometimes I wish I were a Lesser Rider.' To stand a lifetime in one place, with just a minimum skrode.

'Yes,' said Greenstalk. 'But we decided to roam. That means giving up certain things. Sometimes we must remember things that happen only once or twice. Sometimes we have great adventures: I'm glad we took the rescue contract, Blueshell.'

So neither of them was really in the mood for the sea today. Blueshell lowered the skrode's wheels and rolled a little closer to Greenstalk. He looked deep into his skrode's mechanical memory, scanning the general databases. There was a lot there about catastrophes. Whoever created the original skrode databases had considered wars and blights and perversion very important. They were exciting things, and they could kill you.

But Blueshell could also see that in relative terms, such disasters were a small part of the civilized experience. Only about once in a millennium was there a massive perversion. It was their bad luck to be caught near such a thing. In the last ten weeks a dozen civilizations in the High Beyond had dropped from the Net, absorbed into the symbiotic amalgam that now was called the Straumli Blight. High trade was crippled. Since their ship was refinanced, he and Greenstalk had flown several jobs, but all to the Middle Beyond.

The two of them always had been very cautious, but now –

as Greenstalk said – greatness might be thrust upon them. Vrinimi Org wanted to commission a secret flight to the Bottom of the Beyond. Since he and Greenstalk were already in on the secret, they were the natural choice for the job. Right now the *Out of Band II* was in the Vrinimi yards getting bottom-lugger enhancements and a huge stock of antenna drones. In one stroke the *OOB*'s value was increased ten-thousand-fold. There had been no need even to bargain! . . . and that was the scariest thing of all. Every addition was a clear essential for the trip. They would be descending right to the edge of the Slowness. Under the best of circumstances this would be a tedious exercise, but the latest surveys reported movement in the zone boundaries. With bad luck they might actually end up on the wrong side, where light had the ultimate speed. If that should happen, the new ramscoop would be their only hope.

All that was within Blueshell's range of acceptable business. Before he met Greenstalk he had shipped on bottom-luggers, even been stranded once or twice. But – 'I like adventure as much as you,' said Blueshell, a grumpy edge creeping into his voice. 'Traveling to the Bottom, rescuing sophonts from the claws of wildthings: given enough money, it's all perhaps reasonable. But . . . what if that Straumer ship is really as important as Ravna thinks? After all this time it seems absurd, but she's convinced Vrinimi Org of the possibility. If there's something down there that could harm the Straumli Blight –' If the Blight ever suspected the same, it could have a fleet of ten thousand warships descending on their goal. Down at the Bottom they might be little better than conventional vessels, but he and Greenstalk would be no less dead for that.

Except for a faint daydreamy hum, Greenstalk was silent. Had she lost track of the conversation? Then her voice came to him through the water, a reassuring caress. 'I know, Blueshell, it could be the end of us. But I still want to venture it. If it's safe, we make enormous profit. If our going could harm the Blight . . . well, then it's terribly important. Our help might save dozens of civilizations – a million beaches of Riders, just in passing.'

'Hmpf. You're following stalk and not skrode.'

'Probably.' They had watched the progress of the Blight since its beginning. The feelings of horror and sympathy had been reinforced every day till they percolated into their natural minds. So Greenstalk (and Blueshell too; he couldn't deny it) felt stronger about the Blight than about the danger in their new contract. 'Probably. My fears of making the rescue are still analytical,' still confined to her skrode. 'Yet . . . I think if we could stand here a year, if we could wait till we truly felt all the issues . . . I think we would still choose to go.'

Blueshell rolled irritably back and forth. The grit swirled up and through his fronds. She was right, she was right. But he couldn't say it aloud; the mission still terrified him.

'And think, mate: If it is this important, then perhaps we can get help. You know the Org is negotiating with the Emissary Device. With any luck we'll end up with an escort designed by a Transcendental Power.'

The image almost made Blueshell laugh. Two little Skroderiders, journeying to the Bottom of the Beyond – surrounded by help from the Transcend. 'I will hope for it.'

The Skroderiders were not the only ones with that wish. Further up the beach, Ravna Bergsndot prowled her office. What gruesome irony that even the greatest disasters can create opportunities for decent people. Her transfer to Marketing had been made permanent with the fall of Arbitration Arts. As the Blight spread and High Beyond markets collapsed, the Org became ever more interested in providing information services about the Straumli Perversion. Her 'special' expertise in things human suddenly became extraordinarily valuable – never mind that Straumli Realm itself was only a small part of what was now the Blight. What little the Blight said of itself was often in Samnorsk. Grondr and company continued to be vitally interested in her analysis.

Well, she had done some good. They had picked up the refugee ship's 'I-am-here,' and then – ninety days later – a message from a human survivor, Jefri Olsndot. Barely forty messages had they exchanged, but enough to learn about the

Tines and Mr Steel and the evil Woodcarvers. Enough to know that a small human life would be ended if she could not help. Ironic but natural: most times that single life weighed more on her than all the horror of the Perversion, even the fall of Straumli Realm. Thank the Powers that Grondr had endorsed the rescue mission: It was a chance to learn something important about the Straumli Perversion. And the Tinish packs seemed to interest him, too; group minds were a fleeting thing in the Beyond. Grondr had kept the whole affair secret, and persuaded *his* bosses to support the mission. But all his help might not be enough. If the refugee ship was as important as Ravna thought, there could be enormous perils awaiting any rescuers.

Ravna looked across the surf. When the waves backed down the sand, she could see the Skroderiders' fronds peeping out of the spray. How she envied them; if tensions annoyed them, they could simply turn them off. The Skroderiders were one of the most common sophonts in the Beyond. There were many varieties, but analysis agreed with legend: *very* long ago they had been one species. Somewhere in the off-Net past, they had been sessile dwellers of sea shores. Left to themselves, they had developed a form of intelligence almost devoid of short-term memory. They sat in the surf, thinking thoughts that left no imprints on their minds. Only repetition of a stimulus, over a period of time, could do that. But the intelligence and memory that they had *was* of survival value: it made it possible for them to select the best possible place to cast their pupal seeds, locations that would mean safety and food for the next generation.

Then some unknown race had chanced upon the dreamers and decided to 'help them out.' Someone had put them on mobile platforms, the skrodes. With wheels they could move along the seashores, could reach and manipulate with their fronds and tendrils. With the skrode's mechanical short-term memory, they could learn fast enough that their new mobility would not kill them.

Ravna glanced away from the Skroderiders – someone was floating in over the trees. The Emissary Device. Maybe she should call Greenstalk and Blueshell out of the water. No.

Let 'em bliss out a little longer. If she couldn't get the special equipment, things would be tough enough for them later . . .

Besides, I can do without witnesses. She folded her arms across her chest and glared into the sky. The Vrinimi Org had tried to talk to the Old One about this, but nowadays the Power would only work through its Emissary Device . . . and *he* had insisted on a face-to-face meeting.

The Emissary touched down a few meters away, and bowed. His lopsided grin spoiled the effect. 'Pham Nuwen, at your service.'

Ravna gave a little bow in return, and led him to the shade of her inner office. If he thought that face-to-face would unnerve her, he was *right*. 'Thanks for the meeting, sir. The Vrinimi Organization has an important request of your principal,' owner? master? operator?

Pham Nuwen plunked himself down, stretching indolently. He'd stayed out of her way since that night at The Wandering Company. Grondr said Old One had kept him at Relay though, rummaging through the archives for information about humanity and its origins. It made sense now that Old One had been persuaded to restrict its Net usage: the Emissary could do local processing, i.e., use human intelligence to search and summarize and then upload only the stuff that Old One really needed.

Ravna watched him out of the corner of her eye as she pretended to study her dataset. Pham had his old, lazy smile. She wondered if she would ever have the courage to ask him how much of their . . . affair . . . had been a human thing. Had Pham Nuwen felt anything for her? Hell, did he even have a good time?

From a Transcendent point of view, he might be a simple data concentrator and waldo – but from *her* viewpoint he was still too human. 'Um, yes. Well . . . The Org has continued to monitor the Straumli refugee ship even though your principal has lost interest.'

Pham's eyebrows raised in polite interest. 'Oh?'

'Ten days ago, the simple "I-am-here" signal was interrupted by a new message, apparently from a surviving crewmember.'

'Congratulations. You managed to keep it a secret, even from me.'

Ravna didn't rise to the bait. 'We're doing our best to keep it secret from everyone, sir. For reasons that you must know.' She put the messages to date on a display between them. A handful of calls and responses, scattered across ten days. Translated into Triskweline for Pham, the original spelling and grammar errors were gone, yet the tone remained. Ravna was responsible for the Org side of the conversation. It was like talking to someone in a dark room, someone you have never seen. Much was easy to imagine: a strident, piping voice behind the capitalized words and exclamation marks. She had no video of the child, but through the humankind archive at Sjandra Kei, Marketing had dug up pictures of the boy's parents. They looked like typical Straumers, but with the brown eyes of the Linden clans. Little Jefri would be slim and dark.

Pham Nuwen's gaze flicked down through the text, then seemed to hang on the last few lines:

Org[17]:   How old are you, Jefri?
Target[18]: I am eight. I mean I am eight years old. I AM OLD ENOUGH BUT I NEED HELP.
Org[18]:   We will help. We are coming as fast as we can, Jefri.
Target[19]: Sorry I couldn't talk yesterday. The bad people were on the hill again yesterday. It wasn't safe to go to the ship.
Org[19]:   Are the bad ones that close by?
Target[20]: Yes yes. I could see them from the island. I'm with Amdi on shipboard now, but walking up here there were dead soldiers all around. Woodcarver raids here often. Mother is dead. Father is dead. Johanna is dead. Mister Steel will protect me as much as he can. He says that I must be brave.

For a moment his smile was gone. 'Poor kid,' he said softly. Then he shrugged and jabbed his hand at one of the messages. 'Well, I'm glad Vrinimi is sending a rescue mission. That is generous of you.'

'Not really, sir. Look at items six through fourteen. The boy is complaining about the ship's automation.'

'Yeah, he makes it sound like something out of a dawn age: keyboards and video, no voice recognition. A completely unfriendly interface. Looks like the crash scragged almost everything, eh?'

He was being deliberately obtuse, but Ravna resolved to be infinitely patient. 'Perhaps not, considering the vessel's origin.' Pham just smiled, so Ravna continued to spell things out. 'The processors are likely High Beyond or Transcendent, snuffed down to near brainlessness by the current environment.'

Pham Nuwen sighed. 'All consistent with the Skroderiders' theory, right? You're still hoping this crate is carrying some tremendous secret that will blow the Blight away.'

'Yes! . . . Look. At one time, the Old One was very curious about all this. Why the total disinterest now? Is there some reason why the ship *can't* be the key to fighting the Perversion?' That was Grondr's explanation for the Old One's recent lack of interest. All her life Ravna Bergsndot had heard tales of the Powers, and always from a great remove. Here, she was awfully close to questioning one directly. It was a very strange feeling.

After a moment Pham said, 'No. It's unlikely, but you could be right.'

Ravna let out a breath she hadn't realized she'd been holding. 'Good. Then what we're asking is reasonable. Suppose the downed ship contains something the Perversion needs, or something it fears. Then it's likely the Perversion knows of its existence – and may even be monitoring ultradrive traffic in that part of the Bottom. A rescue expedition could lead the Perversion right to it. In that case, the mission will be suicide for its crew – and could increase the Blight's overall power.'

'So?'

Ravna slapped her dataset, resolutions of patience dissolving. '*So*, Vrinimi Org is asking Old One's help to build an expedition the Blight can't knock over!'

Pham Nuwen just shook his head. 'Ravna, Ravna. You're talking about an expedition to the *Bottom of the Beyond*. There's no way a Power can hold your hand down there. Even an Emissary Device would be mostly on its own there.'

'Don't act like more of a jerk than you are, Pham Nuwen. Down there, the Perversion will be at just as much a disadvantage. What we're asking for is equipment of Transcendent manufacture, designed for those depths, and provided in substantial quantities.'

'Jerk?' Pham Nuwen drew himself up, but there was still the ghost of a smile on his face. 'Is that how you normally address a Power?'

Before this year, I would have died *rather than address a Power in any manner.* She leaned back, giving him her own version of an indolent smile. 'You have a pipeline to god, Mister, but let me tell you a little secret: I can tell whether it's open or closed.'

Polite curiosity: 'Oh? How is that?'

'Pham Nuwen – left on his own – is a bright, egotistical guy, and about as subtle as a kick in the head.' She thought back to their time together. 'I don't really start worrying until the arrogance and smart remarks go away.'

'Um. Your logic is a little weak. If the Old One were running me direct, he could just as easily play a jerk as,' he cocked his head, 'as the man of your dreams.'

Ravna gritted her teeth. 'Maybe so, but I've got a little help from my boss. He's cleared me to monitor transceiver usage.' She looked at her dataset. 'Right now, your Old One is getting less than ten kilobits per second from all of Relay . . . which means, my friend, that you are not being tele-operated. Any crass behavior I see today is the true Pham Nuwen.'

The redhead chuckled, faint embarrassment evident. 'You got me. I'm on detached duty, have been ever since the Org persuaded Old One to back off. But I want you to know that all those ten Kb/s are dedicated to this charming conversation.' He paused as if listening, then waved his hand. 'Old One says "hi."'

Ravna laughed despite herself; there was something absurd about the gesture, and the notion that a Power would indulge such trivial humor. 'Okay. I'm glad he can, um, sit in. Look, Pham, we're not asking for much by Transcendent standards, and it could save whole civilizations. Give us a few thousand ships; robot oneshots would be fine.'

'Old One could make that many, but they wouldn't be much better than what's built down here. Tricking –' he paused, looking surprised by his own choice of words, 'tricking the Zones is subtle work.'

'Fine. Quality or quantity. We'll settle for whichever the Old One thinks –'

'No.'

'Pham! We're talking about a few days' work for the Old One. It's already paid more to study the Blight.' Their single wild evening might have cost as much – but she didn't say that.

'Yes, and Vrinimi has spent most of it.'

'Paying off the customers you stepped on! . . . Pham, can't you at least tell us *why?*'

The lazy smile faded from his face. she took a quick glance at her dataset. No, Pham Nuwen was not possessed. She remembered the look on his face when he read the mail from Jefri Olsndot; there was a decent human being lurking behind all the arrogance. 'I'll give it a try. Keep in mind – even though I've been part of Old One – I'm remembering and explaining with human limitations.

'You're right, the Perversion is chewing up the Top of the Beyond. Maybe fifty civilizations will die before this Power gets tired of screwing around – and for a couple of thousand years after that there'll be "echoes" of the disaster, poisoned star systems, artificial races with bloody-minded ideas. But – I hate to say it this way – so what? Old One has been thinking about this problem, off and on, for more than a hundred days. That's a *long* time for a Power, especially Old One. He's existed for more than ten years now; his minds are drifting fast toward . . . changes . . . that will put him beyond all

164

communication. Why should he give a damn about this?'

It was a standard topic in school, but Ravna couldn't help herself. This time it was for real. 'But history is full of incidents where Powers helped Beyonder races, sometimes even individuals.' She had already looked up the Beyonder race that created Old One. They were gasbag creatures. Their netmail was mostly jabberwocky even after Relay's best interpretation. Apparently they had no special leverage with Old One. The direct appeal was about all she had. 'Look. Turn the thing around: Even ordinary humans don't need special explanation to help animals that are hurting.'

Pham's smile was beginning to come back. 'You're so big on analogies. Remember that no analogy is perfect, and the more complex the automation the more complex the possible motivations. But . . . okay, how about this for an analogy: Old One is a basically decent guy, with a nice home in a good part of town. One day he notices he has a new neighbor, a scruffy fellow whose homestead is awhiff with toxic sludge. If you were Old One, you'd be concerned, right? You might probe around beneath your properties. You'd also chat with the new fellow and check on where he came from, try to figure out what's going on. The Vrinimi Org saw part of that investigation.

'So you discover the new neighbor is unwholesome. Basically his lifestyle involves poisoning swamp land and eating the sludge produced. That's an annoyance: it smells and it hurts a lot of harmless animals. But, after investigating, it's clear the damage will not affect your own property, and you get the neighbor to take measures to reduce the stink. In any case, eating toxic sludge is a self-defeating lifestyle.' He paused. 'As analogies go, I think this one's pretty good. After some initial mystery, Old One has determined that this Perversion is one of the common patterns, so petty and banal that even creatures like you and I can see it's evil. In one form or another, it's been drifting up from Beyonder archives for a hundred million years.'

'Damn it! I'd get my neighbors together, and run the pervert out of town.'

'That's been talked about, but it would be expensive . . .

and real people might get hurt.' Pham Nuwen came smoothly to his feet, and smiled dismissingly at her. 'Well, that's about all we had to say to you.' He walked out from under the trees. Ravna hopped up to pursue.

'My personal advice: don't take this so hard, Ravna. I've seen it all, you know. From the Bottom of the Slowness to the inside of a Transcendent Power, each Zone has its own special unpleasantness. The whole basis of the Perversion – thermodynamic, economic, however you want to picture it – is the high quality of thought and communication at the Top of the Beyond. The Perversion hasn't touched a single civilization in the Middle Beyond. Down here, the comm lags and expense are too great, and even the best equipment is mindless. To run things here you'd need standing navies, secret police, clumsy transceivers – it would be almost as awkward as any other Beyonder empire, and of no profit to a Power.' He turned and saw her dark expression. 'Hey, I'm saying your pretty ass is safe.' He reached down to pat her rear.

Ravna brushed the hand away and stepped back. She'd been working on some clever argument that might set the guy to thinking; there *were* cases where Emissary Devices had changed their principal's decision. Now the half-formed ideas were blown away, and all she could think to say was – 'So how safe is your own tail, hmm? You say Old One is about ready to pack it in, go wherever overage Powers wander off to. Is he going to take you along, or maybe just put you away, a pet that's now inconvenient?'

It was a silly shot, and Pham Nuwen just laughed. 'More analogies? No . . . most likely he'll just leave me behind. You know, like a robot probe flying free after its last use.' Another analogy, but one to his liking. 'In fact, if it happens soon enough, *I* might even be willing to take on this rescue expedition. It looks like Jefri Olsndot is in a medieval civilization. I'll wager there's no one in the Org who understands such a place better than I. And down at the Bottom, your crew could scarcely ask for a better mate than an old Qeng Ho type.' He spoke breezily, as though courage and experience were givens for him – even if other people were cowardly scuts.

'Oh, yeah?' Ravna's arms went akimbo, and she cocked her head to one side. It was just a bit too much, when his whole existence was a fraud. 'You're the little prince who grew up with intrigue and assassination, and then flew away to the stars with the Qeng Ho . . . Do you ever really *think* about that past, Pham Nuwen? Or is that something Old One tactfully blocks you from doing: After our charming evening at The Wandering Company, I did think about it. You know what? There's only a few things you can know for sure: You really were a Slow Zone spacer – probably two or three spacers, since none of the corpses were complete. Somehow you and your buddies got yourselves killed down at the nether end of the Slowness. What else? Well, your ship had no recoverable memory. The only hardcopy we found seemed to be written in some Earth Asian language. That's all, *all*, that Old One had to go on when he put together the fraud.'

Pham's smile seemed a little frozen. Ravna went on before he could speak. 'But don't blame Old One. He was a little rushed, right? He had to convince Vrinimi and me that you were real. He rummaged around in the archives, slapped together a mishmash reality for you. Maybe it took him an afternoon – are you grateful for the effort? A snip from here and a snip from there. There really was a Qeng Ho, you know. On *Earth*, a thousand years before space flight. And there must have been Asia-descended star colonies, though that's an obvious extrapolation on his part. Old One really has a nice sense of humor. He made your whole life a fantastic romance, right down to the last tragic expedition. *That* should have tipped me off, by the way. It's a combination of several pre-Nyjoran legends.'

She caught her breath and rushed on. 'I feel sorry for you, Pham Nuwen. As long as you don't think about yourself too hard, you can be the most confident fellow in space. But all the skill, all the achievement – do you ever look at it up close? I'll bet not. Being a great warrior or an expert pilot – those involve a million subskills, all the way down to kinesthetic things below the level of conscious thought. The Old One's fraud needed just the top level recollections, and a brash personality. Look under the surface, Pham. I think you'll find a whole lot of nothing.' *A dream of competence, too closely confronted.*

The redhead had crossed his arms and was tapping his sleeve with a finger. When she finally ran out of words, his smile grew broad and patronizing. 'Ah, silly Ravna. Even now you don't understand how far superior the Powers are. Old One is not some Middle Beyond tyranny, brainwashing its victims with superficial memories. Evan a Transcendent fraud has more depth than the image of reality in a human mind. And how can you know this really *is* a fraud? So you looked through the Relay archives, and didn't find my Qeng Ho.' *My Qeng Ho.* He paused. Remembering? Trying to remember? For an instant Ravna saw a gleam of panic on his face. Then it was gone, and there was just the lazy smile. 'Can any of us imagine the archives of the Transcend, all the things Old One must know about humanity? Vrinimi Org should be grateful to Old One for explaining my origins; they could never have learned that by themselves.

'Look. I am truly sorry I can't help. Even if it's otherwise a fool's errand, I'd like to see those kids rescued. But don't worry about the Blight. It's near maximum expansion now. Even if you could destroy it, you wouldn't make things better for the poor wights who've been absorbed.' He laughed, a little too loudly. 'Well, I have to go; Old One has some other errands for me this afternoon. He wasn't happy about this being face-to-face, but I insisted. The perks of detached duty, y'know. You and I . . . you and I had some good times, and I thought it would be nice to chat. I didn't mean to make you mad.'

Pham cut in his agrav and floated off the sand. He waved a laconic salute. Staring up, Ravna lifted her hand to wave back. His figure dwindled, acquiring a faint nimbus as he left the Docks' breathable atmosphere and his space suit cut in.

Ravna watched a few moments more, till the figure became one more commuter in the indigo sky. *Damn. Damn. Damn.*

Behind her there was the sound of wheels crunching across sand. Blueshell and Greenstalk had rolled out of the water. Wetness glistened on the sides of their skrodes, transforming

168

their cosmetic stripes into jagged rainbows. Ravna walked down to meet them. *How do I tell them there's no help coming?*

With someone like Pham Nuwen fronting for it, Old One had seemed so different from what she imagined in her classes back at Sjandra Kei. She'd almost thought she could make a difference just by talking. What a joke. She had caught a glimpse just now, behind the front: of a being who could play with souls the way a programmer plays with a clever graphic, a being so far beyond her that only its indifference could protect her. *Be happy, little Ravna moth. You were only dazzled by the flame.*

16

The next few weeks went surprisingly well. Despite the Pham Nuwen debacle, Blueshell and Greenstalk were still willing to fly the rescue. Vrinimi Org even kicked in some extra resources. Every day Ravna took a telexcursion to the repair yards. The *Out of Band II* might not be getting any Transcendent enhancements, but when the refitting was complete, the ship would be something extraordinary: Now it floated in a golden haze of 'structors, billions of tiny robots regrowing sections of the hull into the characteristic form of a bottom-lugger. Sometimes the ship seemed to Ravna like a fragile moth . . . and sometimes an abyssal fish. The rebuilt ship could survive across a range of environments: It had the spines of an ultradrive craft, but the hull was streamlined and wasp-waist – the classic form of a ramscoop ship. Bottom-luggers must troll dangerously near the Slow Zone. The zone surface was hard to detect from a distance, even harder to map; and there were short-term position changes. It was not impossible for a lugger to be trapped a light-year or two within the Slowness. It was then you'd thank goodness for the ramscoop and the coldsleep facilities. Of course, by the time you returned to civilization you might be completely out of date, but at least you could get back.

Ravna floated her viewpoint through the drive spines that spread out from the hull. They were broader than those on most ships that came to Relay. They weren't optimal for the Middle or High Beyond, but with appropriate (i.e., Low Beyond) computers, the ship would fly as fast as anything when it reached the Bottom.

Grondr let her spend half-time on the project, and after a few days Ravna realized this was not just a favor. She *was* the best person for this job. She knew humans, and she knew archive management. Jefri Olsndot needed reassurance every day. And the thing Jefri was telling her were immediately important. Even if everything went according to plan – even if the Perversion stayed completely out of it – this rescue was going to be tricky. The kid and his ship seemed to be in the middle of a bloody war. Extracting them would mean making instantly correct decisions and acting on them. They would need an effective onboard database and strategy program. But not much could be expected to work at the Bottom, and memory capacity would be limited. It was up to Ravna to decide what library materials to move to the ship, to balance the lease of local availability against the greater resources that would be accessible over the ultrawave from Relay.

Grondr was available on the local net, and often in real time. He wanted this to work: 'Don't worry, Ravna. We'll dedicate part of ROO to this mission. If their antenna swarm works properly, the Riders should have a thirty Kb/s link to Relay. You'll be their prime contact here, and you'll have access to our best strategists. If nothing . . . interferes, you should have no trouble managing this rescue.'

Even four weeks ago, Ravna wouldn't have dared to ask for more. Now: 'Sir, I have a better idea. Send me with the Skroderiders.'

All of Grondr's mouth parts clapped together at once. She'd seen that much surprise in people like Egravan, but never in the staid Grondr. He was silent for a moment. 'No. We need you here. You are our best sanity check when it comes to questions about humankind.' The newsgroups interested in the Straumli Perversion carried more than one hundred thousand messages a day, about a tenth of that human-related. Thousands of messages were old ideas rehashed, or patent absurdities, or probable lies. Marketing's automation was fairly good at filtering out the redundancy and some of the absurdity, but when it came to questions on human nature Ravna was without equal. About half her time was spent guiding that analysis and handling queries about humankind at the archives. All that would be next to impossible if she left with the Skroderiders.

Over the next few days, Ravna kept pushing her boss on the question. Whoever flew the rescue would need instant rapport with humans – human children, in fact. Very likely Jefri Olsndot had never even met a Skroderider.. The point was a good one, and it was gradually driving her to desperation – but by itself it would not have changed old Grondr's mind. It took some outside events to do that: As the weeks passed, the Blight's expansion slowed. Just as conventional wisdom (and Old One via Pham Nuwen) claimed, there seemed to be natural limits to how far the Perversion could extend its interests. The abject panic slowly disappeared from the High Beyond communication traffic. Rumors and refugees from the absorbed volumes dribbled toward zero. The people in the Blighted spaces were gone, but now it was more like death in a graveyard than death from contagious rot. Blight-related newsgroups continued to babble about the catastrophe, but the level of nonproductive rehashing was steadily increasing. There simply was very little new going on. Over the next ten years, physical death would spread through the Blighted region. Colonization would begin again, cautiously probing through the ruins and informational traps, and residue races. But all of that was a ways off, and for the moment Relay's Blight 'windfall' was a shrinking affair.

 ... And Marketing was even more interested in the Straumli refugee ship. None of the strategy programs – much less Grondr – believed the ship's secret could hurt the Blight, but there was a good chance it might bring commercial advantage when the Perversion finally got tired of its Transcendent game. And the Tines pack-minds had caught their interest. It was appropriate that a maximum effort be made, that Ravna give up her Docks job and go into the field.

So, for a wonder, her childhood fantasy of rescue and questing adventure would actually come true. *And even more surprisng, I'm only half-terrified by the prospect!*

Target[56]: Im sorry I diddnt anser for a while. I dont feel good a lot. Mister Steel says I should talk to you. He says I need more friends to make me feel better. Amdi says so too and hes my best friend of all . . . like packs of dogs but smart and fun. I wish I could send pictures. Mister Steel will try to get ansers for all your questions. He is doing everything he can to help, but the bad packs will be back. Amdi and I tried the stuff you said with the ship. I am sorry, it still doesnt work . . . I hate this dumb keybord . . .

Org[57]: Hi, Jefri. Amdi and Mr Steel are right. I always like to talk, and it will make you feel better . . . There are inventions that might help Mister Steel. We've thought of some improvements for his bows and flamethrowers. I'm also sending down some fortress design information. Please tell Mister Steel that we can't tell him how to fly the ship. It would be dangerous even for an expert pilot to try . . .

Target[57]: Ya, even Daddy had a hard time landing it. ikocxljikersw89iou43e5 I think Mister Steel just doesnt understand, and hes getting sorta disparate . . . Isnt there other stuff, though, like they had in oldendays. You know, bombs and airplanes that we could make? . . .

Org[58]: There are other inventions, but it would take time for Mister Steel to make them. Our star ship is leaving Relay soon, Jefri.

```
                    We'll be there long before other in-
                    ventions would help . . .
    Target[58]:     Your coming? Your finally coming!!!
                    When do you leave? When will you get
                    here???
```

Ordinarily Ravna composed her messages to Jefri on a keyboard – it gave her some feeling for the kid's situation. He seemed to be holding up, though there were still days when he didn't write (it was strange to think of 'mental depression' having any connection with an eight-year-old). Other times he seemed to have a tantrum at the keyboard, and across twenty-one thousand light-years she saw evidence of small fists slamming into keys.

Ravna grinned at the display. Today she finally had something more than nebulous promises for him: she had a definite departure time. Jefri was going to like message [59]. She typed: 'We're scheduled to leave in seven more days, Jefri. Travel time will be about thirty days.' Should she qualify that? Latest postings on the Zone boundary newsgroups said the Bottom was unusually active. The Times World was so close to the Slow Zone . . . If the 'storm' worsened, travel time would suffer. There was about a one percent chance the voyage would take more than sixty days. She leaned back from the keyboard. Did she really want to say that? Damn. Better be frank; these dates could affect the locals who were helping Jefri. She explained the 'ifs' and 'buts', then went on to describe the ship and the wonderful things they would bring. The boy usually didn't write at great length (except when he was relaying information from Steel), but he really seemed to like long letters from her.

The *Out of Band II* was undergoing final consistency checks. Its ultradrive was rebuilt and tested; the Skroderiders had taken it out a couple of thousand light-years to check the antenna swarm. The swarm worked great, too. She and Jefri would be able to talk through most of the voyage. As of yesterday, the ship was stocked with consumables. (That sounded like something out of medieval adventure. But you had to take some supplies when you were headed so far down that reality graphics couldn't be trusted.) Sometime tommorrow, Grondr's people would be loading the ship's hold with gadgets that might be real handy for a rescue. Should she mention those? Some of them might sound a bit intimidating to Jefri's local friends.

That evening, she and the Skroderiders had a beach party. That's what they called it, though it was much more like the human version than an authentic Rider one. Blueshell and Greenstalk had rolled well back from the water to where the sand lay dry and warm. Ravna laid out refreshments on Blueshell's cargo scarf. They sat on the sand and admired the sunset.

It was mostly a celebration – that Ravna had gotten permission to go with the *OOB*, that the ship was almost ready to depart. But, 'Are you really happy to be going, my lady?' asked Blueshell. 'We two will make very good money, but you –'

Ravna laughed. 'I'll get a travel bonus.' She had argued and argued for permission to go; there wasn't much room left to haggle about the pay. 'And yes. This is what I really want.'

'I am glad,' said Greenstalk.

'I am laughing,' said Blueshell. 'My mate is especially pleased that our passenger will not be surly. We almost lost our love for bipeds after shipping with the certificants. But there is nothing to be frightened of now. Have you read Threats Group in the last fifteen hours? The Blight has stopped growing, and its edges have become sharply defined. The Perversion is settling into middle age. I'm ready to leave right now.'

Blueshell was full of speculations about the Tinish 'packs,' and possible schemes for extracting Jefri and any other survivors. Greenstalk interjected a thought here and there. She was less shy than before, but still seemed softer, more diffident than her mate. And her confidence was a bit more realistic. She was glad they weren't leaving for another week. There were still the final consistency checks to run on the *OOB* – and Grondr had gotten Org financing for a small fleet of decoy ships. Fifty were complete so far. A hundred would be ready by the end of the week.

The Docks drifted into night. With its shallow atmosphere, twilight was short, but the colors were spectacular. The beach and the trees glistened in the horizontal rays. The scent of even-flowers mixed with the tang of sea salt. On the far side of the sea, all was stark bright and dark, silhouettes that might have been Vrinimi fancies or functional dock equipage – Ravna had never learned which. The sun slid behind the sea. Orange and red spread along the aft horizon, topped by a wider band of green, probably ionized oxygen.

The Riders didn't turn their skrodes for a better view – for all she knew, they had been looking that way all along – but they stopped talking. As the sun set, the breakers shattered it into a thousand images, glints of green and yellow through the foam. She guessed the two would have preferred to be out there just now. She had seen them often enough around sunset, deliberately sitting where the surf was hardest. When the water drew back, their stalks and fronds were like supplicants' arms, upstretched. At times like these she could almost understand the Lesser Skroderiders; they spent their whole lives memorizing such repeated moments. She smiled in the greenish twilight. There would always be time enough later to worry and plan.

They must have sat like that for twenty minutes. Along the curving line of the beach, she saw tiny fires in the gathering dark: office parties. Somewhere very nearby there was the *crunch crunch* of feet on sand. She turned and saw that it was Pham Nuwen. 'Over here,' she called.

Pham ambled toward them. He'd been very scarce since their last confrontation; Ravna guessed that some of her jibes had struck deep. *This once, I hope Old One made him forget.* Pham Nuwen had the potential to be a real person; it hadn't been right to hurt him because his principal was beyond reach.

'Have a seat. Galaxy-rise in a half hour.' The Skroderiders rustled, so deep into the sunset that they were only now noticing the visitor.

Pham Nuwen walked a pace or two beyond Ravna and stood arms akimbo, staring across the sea. He glanced back at her, and the green twilight gave his face an eerie fierceness. He flashed his old, lopsided smile: 'I think I owe you an apology.'

Old One's gonna let you join the human race after all? But Ravna was touched. She dropped her eyes from his. 'I guess I owe you one too. If Old One won't help, he won't help; I shouldn't have lost my temper.'

Pham Nuwen laughed softly. 'Yours was certainly the lesser error. I'm still trying to figure out where I went wrong, and . . . I don't think I have time now to learn.'

He looked back at the sea. After a moment, Ravna stood and stepped toward him. Up close his stare looked glassy. 'What's wrong?' *Damn you, Old One. If you're going to abandon him, don't do it in pieces!*

'You're the great expert on Transcendent Powers, eh?'

More sarcasm. 'Well –'

'Do the big boys have wars?'

Ravna shrugged. 'You can find rumors of everything. We think there's conflict, but something too subtle to call war.'

'You're pretty much right. There is struggle, but it has more angles than anything down here. The benefits of cooperation are normally so great that . . . That's part of the reason I didn't take the Perversion seriously. Besides, the creature is pitiful: a wimpy cur that fouls its own den. Even if it wanted to kill other Powers, something like that never could. Not in a billion years . . .'

Blueshell rolled up beside them. 'Who is this, my lady?'

It was the sort of Riderish conversation-stopper that she was only just getting used to. If Blueshell would just get in synch with his skrode memory, he'd know. Then the question truly hit her. Who *is* this? She glanced at her dataset. It was showing transceiver status, had been ever since Pham Nuwen arrived. And . . . by the Powers, *three* transceivers had been grabbed by a single customer!

She took a quick step backwards. 'You!'

'Me! Face to face once more, Ravna.' The leer was a parody of Pham's self-assured smile. 'Sorry I can't be charming tonight.' He slapped his chest awkwardly. 'I'm using this thing's underlying instincts . . . I'm too busy trying to stay alive.'

There was drool coming down his chin. Pham's eyes would focus on her and then drift.

'*What are you doing to Pham!*'

The Emissary Device stepped toward her, stumbled. 'Making room,' came Pham Nuwen's voice.

Ravna spoke Grondr's phone code. There was no response.

The Emissary Device shook its head. 'Vrinimi Org is very busy right now, trying to convince me to get off their equipment, trying to screw up their courage and force me off. They don't believe what I'm telling them.' He laughed, a quick choking sound. 'Doesn't matter. I can see now, the attack here was just deadly diversion . . . How about that, Little Ravna? See, the Blight is not a Class Two perversion. In the time I have left, I can only guess what it is . . . Something very old, very big. Whatever it is, I'm being eaten alive.'

Blueshell and Greenstalk had rolled close to Ravna. Their fronds made faint skritching noises. Some thousands of light-years away, well into the Transcend, a Power was fighting for its life. And all they saw of it was one man turned into a slobbering lunatic.

'So that's my apology, Little Ravna. Helping you probably wouldn't have saved me.' His voice strangled on itself, and he took a gasping breath. 'But helping you now will be a measure of – vengeance is a motive you would understand. I've called your ship down. If you move fast and don't use agrav, you may survive the next hour.'

Blueshell's voice was timid and blustery at the same time. 'Survive? Only a conventional attack could work down here, and there is no sign of one.'

A maniac surrounded by the soft, quiet night. Ravna's dataset showed nothing strange except for the diversion of bandwidth to Old One.

Pham Nuwen made a coughing laugh. 'Oh, it's conventional enough, but very clever. A few grams of replicant disorder, wafted in over weeks. It's blossoming now, timed with the attack you see . . . The growth will die in a matter of hours, after it kills all of Relay's precious High automation . . . Ravna! Take the ship, or die in the next thousand seconds. Take the ship. If you survive, go to the Bottom. Get the . . .' the Emissary Device gagged on the end of the sentence. It pulled itself straighter, and smiled its greenish smile a last time. 'And here is my gift to you, the best help I have left to give.'

The smile disappeared. The glassy look was replaced by a wonder . . . and then mounting terror. Pham Nuwen dragged in a great breath, and had time for one barking scream before he collapsed. He landed face down, twitching and choking in the sand.

Ravna shouted Grondr's code again, and ran to Pham Nuwen. She pulled him over on his back and tried to clear his mouth. The fit lasted several seconds, Pham's limbs flailing randomly about. Ravna collected solid hits as she tried to steady him. Then Pham went limp, and she could barely feel his breath.

Blueshell was saying, 'Somehow he's grabbed the *OOB*. It's four thousand kilometers out, coming straight for the Docks. Wail. We're ruined.' Unauthorized flight close to the Docks was cause for confiscation.

Somehow Ravna didn't think it mattered anymore. 'Is there any sign of attack?' she said over her shoulder. She eased Pham's head back, made sure he had a clear breathing passage.

Random rustling between the Skroderiders. Greenstalk: 'Something is strange. We have service suspension on the main transceivers.' *So Old One is still transmitting?* 'The local net is very clogged. Much automation, many employees being called to special duty.'

Ravna rocked back. The sky was night dark, punctuated by a dozen bright points of light – ships guiding for the Docks. All very normal. But her own dataset was showing what Greenstalk reported.

'Ravna, I can't talk right now.' Grondr's clickety voice sounded out of the air beside her. This would be his associate program. 'Old One has taken most of Relay. Watch out for the Emissary Device.' *A little late, that!* 'We've lost contact with the surveillance fence beyond the transceivers. We are having program and hardware failures. Old One claims we are being attacked.' A five second pause. 'We see evidence of fleet action at the domestic defense boundary.' That was just a half light-year out.

'*Brap!*' From Blueshell. 'At the domestic defense boundary! How could you miss them coming in?' He rolled back and forth, pivoted.

Grondr's associate ignored the question. "Minimum three thousand ships. Destruction of transceivers immin –'

'Ravna, are the Skroderiders with you?' It was still Grondr's voice, but more staccato, more *involved*. This was the real guy.

'Y-yes.'

'The local network is failing. Life support failing. The Docks will fall. We would be stronger than the attacking fleet, but we're rotting from the inside . . . Relay is dying.' His voice sharpened, clattering, 'but Vrinimi will not die, and a contract is a contract! Tell the Riders, we *will* pay them . . . somehow, someday. We *require* . . . plead . . . they fly the mission we contracted. Ravna?'

'Yes. They hear.'

'Then go!' And the voice was gone.

Blueshell said, '*OOB* will be here in two hundred seconds.'

Pham Nuwen had calmed, and his breathing was easier. As the two Riders chittered back and forth, Ravna looked around – and suddenly realized that all the death and destruction had been reports from afar. The beach and the sky were almost as placid as ever. The last of the sun's rays had left the waves. The foam was a dim band in the low green light. Here and there, yellow lights glowed in the trees and the farther towers.

Yet the alarm had clearly spread. She could hear datasets coming on. Some of the beach fires guttered out, and the figures around them ran into the trees or drifted upwards, headed for farther offices. Now starships floated up from their berths across the sea, falling higher and higher till they glittered in the departed sunlight.

It was Relay's last moment of peace.

A patch of glowing dark spread across the sy. She gasped at

light so *twisted* it should have gone unseen. It shone more in the back of her head than in her eyes. Afterwards she couldn't think what made it objectively different from blackness.

'There's another!' said Blueshell. This one was near the Docks' horizon, a blot of darkness perhaps a degree across. The edges were an indistinct bleeding of black into black.

'What *is* it?' Ravna was no war freak, but she'd read her share of adventure stories. She knew about antimatter bombs and relativistic kinetic energy slugs. From a distance such weapons were bright spots of light, sometimes an orchestrated flickering. Or closer: a world-wrecker would glow incandescent across the curve of a planet, splashing the globe itself like a drop of water, but slow, slow. Those were the images her reading had prepared her for. What she saw now was more like a defect in her eyesight than a vision of war.

Powers only knew what the Skroderiders saw, but: 'Your main transceivers . . . vaping out, I think,' said Blueshell.

'Those are light-years out! There's no way we could see –' Another splotch appeared, not even in her field of view. The color floated, placeless. Pham Nuwen spasmed again, but weakly. She had no trouble holding him still, but . . . blood dribbled from his mouth. The back of his shirt was wet with something that stank of decay.

'*OOB* will be here in one hundred seconds. Plenty of time, there's plenty of time.' Blueshell rolled back and forth around them, talking reassurance that just showed how nervous he was. 'Yes, my lady, light-years out. And years from now, the flash of their going will light the sky for anyone still alive here. But only a fraction of the vape-out is making light. The rest is an ultrawave surge so great that ordinary matter is affected . . . Optic nerves tickled by the overflow . . . So much that your own nervous system becomes a receiver.' He spun around. 'But don't worry. We're tough and quick. We've squeezed through close spots before.' There was something absurd about a creature with no short-term memory bragging up its lightning cleverness. She hoped his skrode was up to this.

Greenstalk's voice buzzed painfully loud. '*Look!*'

The surf line was drawing back, further than she had ever

seen it.

'The sea is falling!' shouted Greenstalk. Water's edge had pulled back a hundred meters, two hundred. The green-limned horizon was *dipping*.

'Ship's still fifty seconds out. We'll fly to meet it. Come, Ravna!'

Ravna's own courage died cold that second. Grondr had said the Docks would fall! The near sky was crowded now as dozens of people raced for safety. A hundred meters away the sand itself was shifting, an avalanche tilting toward the abyss. She remembered something Old One had said, and suddenly she knew the fliers were making a terrible mistake. The thought cut through her terror. 'No! Just head for higher ground.'

The night was silent no more. A bell-like moaning came from the sea. The sound spread. The sunset breeze grew to a gale that twisted the trees toward the water, sending branches and sand sweeping past them.

Ravna was still on her knees, her hands pressing down on Pham's limp arms. No breath, no pulse. The eyes stared sightlessly. Old One's gift to her. Damn all the Powers! She grabbed Pham Nuwen under the shoulders and rolled him onto her back.

She gagged, almost lost her grip. Underneath his shirt she felt cavities where there should be solid flesh. Something wet and rank dripped around her sides. She struggled up from her knees, half-carrying and half-dragging the body.

Blueshell was shouting, '– take hours to roll anywhere.' He drifted off the ground, driving his agrav against the wind. Skrode and Rider twisted drunkenly for an instant . . . and then he was slammed back to the ground, tumbled willy-nilly toward the wind's destination, the moaning hole that had been the sea. Greenstalk raced to his seaward side, blocking his progress toward destruction. Blueshell righted himself and the two rolled back toward Ravna. The Rider's voice was faint in the wind: '. . . agrav . . . failing!' And with it the very structure of the Docks.

They walked and wheeled their way back from the sucking sea. 'Find a place to land the *OOB*.'

The tree line was a jagged range of hills now. The landscape changed before their eyes and under her feet. The groaning sound was everywhere, some places so loud it buzzed through Ravna's shoes. They avoided the sagging terrain, the sink holes that opened on all sides. The night was dark no more. Whether it was emergency lighting or a side effect of the agrav failure, blue glowed along the holes. Through those holes they saw the cloud-decked night of Groundside a thousand kilometers below. The space between was not empty. There were shimmering phantoms: billions of tonnes of water and earth . . . and hundreds of dying fliers. Vrinimi Org was paying the price for building their Docks on agrav instead of inertial orbit.

Somehow the three were making progress. Pham Nuwen was almost too heavy to carry/drag; she staggered left and right almost as much as she moved forward. Yet he was lighter than she would have guessed. And that was terrifying in its own way: was even the high ground failing?

Most of the agravs died by failure, but some suffered destructive runaway: clumps of trees and earth ripped free from the tops of hillocks and accelerated upwards. The wind shifted back and forth, up and down . . . but it was thinner now, the noise remote. The artificial atmosphere that clothed the Docks would soon be gone. Ravna's pocket pressure suit worked for a few minutes, but now it was fading. In a few minutes it would be as dead as her agravs . . . as dead as she would be. She wondered vaguely how the Blight had managed this. Like the Old One, she would likely die without ever knowing.

She saw torch flares; there were ships. Most had boosted for inertial orbits or gone directly into ultradrive, but a few hung over the distintegrating landscape. Blueshell and Greenstalk led the way. The two used their third axles in ways Ravna had never guessed at, lifting and pushing to clamber up slopes that she could scarcely negotiate with Pham's weight dragging from her back.

They were on a hilltop, but not for long. This had been part of the office forest. Now the trees stuck out in different directions, like hair on a mangy dog. She felt the ground throbbing beneath her feet. What next? The Skroderiders rolled from one side of the peak to another. They would be rescued here or nowhere. She went to her knees, resting most of Pham's weight on the ground. From here you could see a long ways. The Docks looked like a slowly flapping flag, and every immense whip of the fabric broke fragments loose. As long as some consensus remained among the agrav units, it still had planar aspect. That was disappearing. There were sink holes all around their little knob of forest. On the horizon, Ravna saw the far edge of the Docks detach itself and turn slowly sideways: a hundred kilometers long, ten wide, it swept down on would-be rescue ships.

Blueshell brushed against her left side, Greenstalk against her right. Ravna twisted, laying some of Pham's weight on the skrode hulls. If all four merged their pressure suits, there would be a few more moments of consciousness. 'The *OOB*: I'm flying it down!' he said.

Something was coming down. A ship's torch lit the ground blue white, with shadows stark and shifting. It's not a healthy thing to be around a rocket drive hovering in a near-one-gee field. An hour earlier the maneuver would have been impossible, or a capital offense if accomplished. Now it didn't matter if the torch punched through the Docks or fried a cargo from halfway across the galaxy.

Still . . . where could Blueshell land the thing? They were surrounded by sinkholes and moving cliffs. She closed her eyes as the burning light drifted down before them . . . and then dimmed. Blueshell's shout was thin in their shared atmosphere. 'Let's go together!'

She held tight to the Riders, and they crawled/wheeled down from their little hill. The *Out of Band II* was hovering in the middle of a sinkhole. Its torch was hidden from view, but the glare off the sides of the hole put the ship in sharp silhouette, turned its ultradrive spines into feathery white arcs. A giant moth with glowing wings . . . and just out of reach.

If their suits held, they could make it to the edge of the hole. Then what? The spines kept the ship from getting closer than a hundred meters. An able-bodied (and crazy) human might try to grab a spine and crawl down it.

But Skroderiders had their own brand of insanity: Just as the light – the reflected light – became too much to bear – the torch winked out. The *OOB* fell through the hole. This didn't stop the Riders' advance. *'Faster!'* said Blueshell. And now she guessed what they planned. Quickly for such an awkward jumble of limbs and wheels, they moved up to the edge of the darkened hole. Ravna felt the dirt giving way beneath her feet, and then they were falling.

The Docks were hundreds – in places, thousands – of meters thick. They fell past them now, past dim eerie flickers of internal destruction.

Then they were through, still falling. For a moment the feeling of wild panic was gone. After all this was simply free fall, a commonplace, and a damnsight more peaceful than the disintegrating Docks. Now it was easy to hold onto the Riders and Pham Nuwen, and even their commensal atmosphere seemed a little thicker than before. There was something to be said for hard vacuum and free fall. Except for an occasional rogue agrav, everything was coming down at the same acceleration, ruins peacefully settling. And four or five minutes from now they would hit Groundside's atmosphere, still falling almost straight downwards . . . Entry velocity only three or four kilometers per second. Would they burn up? Maybe. Flashes pricked bright above the cloud-decks.

The junk around them was mostly dark, just shadows against the sky show above. But the shape directly below was large and regular . . . the *OOB*, bow on! The ship was falling with them. Every few seconds a trim jet fired, a faint reddish glow. The ship was closing with them. If it had a nose hatch, they would land right on it.

Its docking lights flicked on, bright upon them. Ten meters separation. Five. There *was* a hatch, and open! She could see a very ordinary airlock within . . .

Whatever hit them was big. Ravna saw a vague expanse of plastic rising over her shoulder. The rogue was slowly turning, and it scarcely brushed them – but that was enough. Pham Nuwen was jarred from her grasp. His body was lost in shadow, then suddenly lit bright as the ship's spotlight tracked after him. Simultaneously the air gusted out of Ravna's lungs. They were down to three pocket pressure fields now, failing fields; it was not enough. Ravna could feel consciousness slipping away, her vision tunneling. So *close*.

The Riders unlatched from each other. She grabbed at the skrode hulls and they drifted, strung out, over the ship's lock. Blueshell's skrode jerked against her as he made fast to the hatch. The jolt twisted her around, whipping Greenstalk upwards. Things were getting dreamy now. Where was panic when you needed it? *Hold tight, hold tight, hold tight*, sang the little voice, all that was left of consciousness. Bump, jerk. The Riders pushed and pulled at her. Or maybe it was the ship jerking all of them around. They were puppets, dancing off a single string.

. . . Deep in the tunnel of her vision, a Rider grabbed at the tumbling figure of Pham Nuwen.

Ravna wasn't aware of losing consciousness, but the next she knew she was breathing air and choking on vomit – and was inside the airlock. Solid green walls closed in comfortingly on all sides. Pham Nuwen lay on the far wall, strapped into a first aid canister. His face had a bluish cast.

She pushed awkwardly across the lock toward Pham Nuwen's wall. The place was a confused jumble, unlike the passenger and sporting ships she'd been on before. Besides, this was a Rider design. Stickem patches were scattered around the walls; Greenstalk had mounted her skrode on one cluster.

They were accelerating, maybe a twentieth of a gee. 'We're still going down?'

'Yes. If we hover or rise, we'll crash,' *into all the junk that still rains from above*. 'Blueshell is trying to fly us out.' They were falling with the rest, but trying to drift out from under – before they hit Groundside. There was an occasional rattle/ping against the hull. Sometimes the acceleration ceased, or shifted in a new direction. Blueshell was actively avoiding the big pieces.

. . . Not with complete success. There was a long, rasping sound that ended with a bang, and the room turned slowly around her. '*Brrap!* Just lost an ultradrive spine,' came Blueshell's voice. 'Two others already damaged. Please strap down, my lady.'

They touched atmosphere a hundred seconds later. The sound was a barely perceptible humming beyond the hull. It was the sound of death for a ship like this. It could no more aerobrake than a dog could jump over the moon. The noise came louder. Blueshell was actually *diving*, trying to get deep enough to shed the junk that surrounded the ship. Two more spines broke. Then came a long surge of main axis acceleration. *Out of Band II* arced out of the Docks' death shadow, drove out and out, into inertial orbit.

Ravna looked over Blueshell's fronds at the outside windows. They had just passed Groundside's terminator, and were flying an inertial orbit. They were in free fall again, but *this* trajectory curved back on itself without whacking into big hard things – like Groundside.

Ravna didn't know much more about space travel than you'd expect of a frequent passenger and an adventure fan. But it was obvious that Blueshell had pulled off a new miracle. When she tried to thank him, the Rider rolled back and forth across the stick-patches, buzzing faintly to himself. Embarrassed? or just Riderly inattentive?

Greenstalk spoke, sounding a little shy, a little proud: 'Far trading is our life, you know. If we are cautious, life will be mostly safe and placid, but there will be close passages. Blueshell practices all the time, programming his skrode with every wit he can imagine. He is a master.' In everyday life indecision seemed to dominate the Riders. But in a crunch, they didn't hesitate to bet everything. She wondered how much of that was the skrode overriding its rider?

'Grump,' said Blueshell. 'I have simply postponed the close passage. I broke several of our drive spines. What if they do not self-repair? What do we do then? Everything around Groundside is destroyed. There is junk everywhere out to a hundred radii. Not dense like around the Docks, but of much higher velocity.' You can't inject billions of tonnes of wreckage into buckshot orbits and expect safe navigation.

'And any second, the Perversion's creatures will be here, eating whoever survives.'

'Urk.' Greenstalk's tendrils froze in comical disarray. She chittered to herself for a second. 'You're right . . . I forgot. I thought we had found an open space, but . . .'

Open space all right, but in a shooting gallery. Ravna looked back at the command deck windows. They were on the dayside now, perhaps five hundred kilometers above Groundside's principal ocean. The space above the hazy blue horizon was free of flash and glow. 'I don't see any fighting,' Ravna said hopefully.

'Sorry.' Blueshell switched the windows to a more significant view. Most of it was navigation and ultratrace information, meaningless to Ravna. Her eye caught on a medstat: Pham Nuwen was breathing again. The ship's surgeon thought it could save him. But there was also a communication status window; on it the attack was dreadfully clear. The local net had broken into hundreds of screaming fragments. There were only automatic voices from the planetary surface, and they were calling for medical aid. Grondr had been down there. Somehow she suspected that not even his Marketing ops people had survived. Whatever hit Groundside was even deadlier than the failures at the Docks. In near planetary space, there were a few survivors in ships and fragments of habitats, most on doomed trajectories. Without massive and coordinated help, they would be dead in minutes – hours at the outside. The directors of Vrinimi Org were gone, destroyed before they ever figured out quite what had happened.

Go, Grondr had said, *go*.

Out-system, there was fighting. Ravna saw message traffic from Vrinimi defense units. Even without control or coordination, some still opposed the Perversion's fleet. The light from their battles would arrive well after the defeat, well after the enemy arrived here in person. *How long do we have? Minutes?*

'Brrap. Look at those traces,' said Blueshell. 'The Perversion has almost four thousand vessels. They are bypassing the defenders.'

'But now there is scarcely anyone left out there,' said Greenstalk. 'I hope they're not all dead.'

'Not all. I see several thousand ships departing, everyone with the means and any sense.' Blueshell rolled back and forth. 'Alas! We have the good sense . . . but look at this repair report.' One window spread large, filled with colored patterns that meant less than zip to Ravna. 'Two spines still broken, unrepairable. Three partially repaired. If they don't heal, we'll be stuck here. *This is unacceptable!*' His voder voice buzzed up shrilly. Greenstalk drove close to him, and they rattled their fronds at each other.

Several minutes passed. When Blueshell spoke Samnorsk again, his voice was quieter. 'One spine repaired. Maybe, maybe, maybe . . .' He opened a natural view. The *OOB* was coasting across Groundside's south pole, back into night. Their orbit should take them over the worst of the Docks junk, but the ride was a constant jigging as the ship avoided other debris. The cries of battle horror from out-system dwindled. The Vrinimi Organization was one vast, twitching corpse . . . and very soon its killer would come snuffling.

'Two repaired.' Blueshell became very quiet . . . 'Three! Three are repaired! Fifteen seconds to recalibrate and we can jump!'

It seemed longer . . . but then all the windows changed to a natural view. Groundside and its sun were gone. Stars and dark stretched all around.

Three hours later and Relay was a hundred and fifty light-years behind them. The *OOB* was in with the main body of fleeing ships. What with the archives and the tourism, there had been an extraordinary number of interstellar ships at Relay: ten thousand vehicles were spread across the light-years around them. But stars were rare this far off the galactic plane and they were at least a hundred hours flying time from the nearest refuge.

For Ravna, it was the start of a new battle. She glared across the deck at Blueshell. The Skroderider dithered, its fronds twisting on themselves in a way she had not seen before. 'See here, my lady Bergsndot, High Point is a lovely civilization, with some bipedal participants. It is safe. It is nearby. You could adapt.' He paused. *Reading my expression is he?* 'But – but if that is not acceptable, we will take you further. Give us a chance to contract the proper cargo, and – and we'll take you all the way back to Sjandra Kei. How about that?'

'No. You already have a contract, Blueshell. With Vrinimi Organization. The three of us –' *and whatever has become of Pham Nuwen* '– are going to the Bottom of the Beyond.'

'I am shaking my head in disbelief! We received a preliminary retainer, true. But now that Vrinimi Org is dead, there is no one to make good on the rest of the agreement. Hence we are free of its also.'

'Vrinimi is not dead. You heard Grondr 'Kalir. The Org had – *has* – branch offices all across the Beyond. The obligation stands.'

'On a technicality. We both know that those branches could never make the final payment.'

Ravna didn't have a good answer to that. 'You have an obligation,' she said, but without the proper forcefulness. She had never been good at bluster.

'My lady, are you truly speaking from Org ethics, or from simple humanity?'

'I –' In fact, Ravna had never completely understood Org ethics. That was one reason why she had intended to return to Sjandra Kei after her 'prenticeship, and one reason the Org had dealt cautiously with the human race. 'It doesn't matter which I speak from! There is a contract. You were happy to honor it when things looked safe. Well, things turned deadly – but that possibility was part of the deal.' Ravna glanced at Greenstalk. She had been silent so far, not even rustling at her mate. Her fronds were tightly held against her central stalk. Maybe – 'listen, there *are* other reasons besides contract obligation. The Perversion is more powerful than anyone thought. *It killed a Power today.* And it's operating in the Middle Beyond . . . The Riders have a long history, Blueshell, longer than most races' entire existence. The Perversion may be strong enough to put an end to all of that.'

Greenstalk rolled toward her and opened slightly. 'You –

you really think we might find something on that ship at the Bottom, something that could harm a Power among Powers?'

Ravna paused. 'Yes. And Old One himself thought so, just before he died.'

Blueshell wrapped even tighter around himself, twisting. In anguish? 'My Lady, we are traders. We have lived long and traveled far . . . and survived by minding our own business. No matter what romantics may think, traders do not go on quests. What you ask . . . is impossible, mere Beyonders seeking to subvert a Power.'

Yet that was a risk you signed for. But Ravna didn't say it aloud. Perhaps Greenstalk did: her fronds rustled, and Blueshell scrinched even more. Greenstalk was silent for a second, then she did something funny with her axles, bumping free of the stickem. Her wheels spun on nothing as she floated through a slow arc, till she was upside down, her fronds reaching down to brush Blueshell's. They rattled back and forth for almost five minutes. Blueshell slowly untwisted, the fronds relaxing and patting back at his mate.

Finally he said. 'Very well . . . One quest. But mark you! Never another.'

Part 2

17

Spring came wet and cold, and excruciatingly slow. It had been raining the last eight days. How Johanna wished for something else, even the dark of winter back again.

She slogged across mud that had been moss. It was midday; the gloomy light would last another three hours. Scarbutt claimed that without the overcast, they would be seeing a bit of direct sunlight nowadays. Sometimes she wondered if she would ever see the sun again.

The castle's great yard was on a hillside. Mud and sullen snow spread down the hill, piled against the wooden buildings. Last summer there had been a glorious view from here. And in the winter, the aurora had spilled green and blue across the snow, glinted on the frozen harbor, and outlined the far hills against the sky. Now: The rain was a close mist; she couldn't even see the city beyond the walls. The clouds were a low and ragged ceiling above her head. She knew there were guards on the stone walls of the castle curtain, but today they must be huddled behind watch slits. Not a single animal, not a single pack was visible. The Tines' world was an empty place compared to Straum – but not like the High Lab either. High Lab was a airless rock orbiting a red dwarf. The Tines' world was *alive*, moving; sometimes it looked as beautiful and friendly as a holiday resort on Straum. Indeed, Johanna realized that it was kindlier than most worlds the human race had settled – certainly a gentler world than Nyjora, and perhaps as nice as Old Earth.

Johanna had reached her bungalow. She paused for a second under its outcurving walls and looked across the courtyard. Yes, it looked a little like medieval Nyjora. But the stories from the Age of Princesses hadn't conveyed the implacable power in such a world: The rain went on for as far as she could see. Without decent technology, even a cold rain could be a deadly thing. So could the wind. And the sea was not something for an afternoon's fun sailing, she thought of surging hillocks of coldness, puckered with rain . . . going on and on. Even the forests around the town were threatening. It was easy to wander into them, but there were no radio finders, no refresh stalls disguised as tree trunks. Once lost, you would simply die. Nyjoran fairy tales had a special meaning for her now: no great imagination was needed to invent the elementals of wind and rain and sea. This was the pretech experience, that even if you had no enemies the world itself could kill you.

And she *did* have plenty of enemies. Johanna pulled open the tiny door and went inside.

A pack of Tines was sitting around the fire. It scrambled to its feet and helped Johanna out of her rainjacket. She didn't shrink from the fine-toothed muzzles anymore. This was one of her usual helpers; she could almost think of the jaws as hands, deftly pulling the oilskin jacket down her arms and hanging it near the fire.

Johanna chucked her boots and pants, and accepted the quilted wrap that the pack 'handed' her.

'Dinner. Now,' she said to the pack.

'Okay.'

Johanna settled on a pillow by the fire pit. In fact the Tines were *more* primitive than the humans on Nyjora: The Tines' world was not a fallen colony. They didn't even have legend to guide them. Sanitation was a sometime thing. Before Woodcarver, Tinish doctors bled their patients/victims . . . She knew now that she was living in the Tines' equivalent of a luxury apartment. The deep-polished wood was not a normal thing. The designs painted on the pillars and walls were the result of many hours' labor.

Johanna rested her chin on her hands and stared into the flames. She was vaguely aware of the pack prancing around the pit, hanging pots over the fire. This one spoke very little Samnorsk; it wasn't in on Woodcarver's dataset project. Many weeks ago, Scarbutt had asked to move in here – what better way to speed the learning process? Johanna shivered at the memory. She knew the scarred one was just a single member, that the *pack* that killed Dad had itself died. Johanna understood, but every time she saw 'Peregrine,' she saw her father's murderer sitting fat and happy, thinking to hide itself behind its three smaller fellows. Johanna smiled into the flames, remembering the whack she had landed on Scarbutt when he made the suggestion. She'd lost control, but it had been worth it. No one else suggested that 'friends' should share this house with her. Most evenings they left her alone. And some nights . . . Dad and Mom seemed so near, maybe just outside, waiting for her to notice. Even though she had seen them die, something inside her refused to let them go.

Cooking smells slipped past the familiar daydream. Tonight it was meat and beans, with something like onions. Surprise. The stuff smelled good; if there had been any variety, she would have enjoyed it. But Johanna hadn't seen fresh fruit in sixty days. Salted meat and veggies were the only winter fare. If Jefri were here, he'd throw a fit. It was months past that the word came from Woodcarver's spies up north: Jefri had died in the ambush . . . Johanna was getting over it, she really was. And in some ways, being all alone made things . . . simpler.

The pack put a plate of meat and beans before her, along with a kind of knife. *Oh, well.* Johanna grabbed the crooked hilt (bent sideways to be held by Tinish jaws) and dug in.

She was almost finished when there was a polite scratching at the door. Her servant gobbled something. The visitor replied, then said in rather good Samnorsk (and a voice that was eerily like her own), 'Hello there, my name is Scriber. I would like a small talk, okay?'

One of the servants turned to look at her; the rest were watching the door. Scriber was the one she thought of as Pompous Clown. He'd been with Scarbutt at the ambush, but he was such a fool that she scarcely felt threatened by him.

'Okay,' she said, starting toward the door. Her servant (guard) grabbed crossbows in its jaws, and all five members snaked up the staircase to the loft; there wasn't space for more than one pack down here.

The cold and wet blew into the room along with her visitor. Johanna retreated to the other side of the fire while Scriber took off his rain slickers. The pack members shook themselves the way dogs do, a noisy, amusing sight – and you didn't want to be near when it happened.

Finally Scriber sauntered over to the fire pit. Under the slickers he wore jackets with the usual stirrups and the open spaces behind the shoulders and at the haunches. But Scriber's appeared to be padded above the shoulders to make his members look heavier than they really were. One of him sniffed at her plate, while the other heads looked this way and that . . . but never directly at her.

Johanna looked down at the pack. She still had trouble talking to more than one face; usually she picked on whichever was looking back at her. 'Well? What did you come to talk about?'

One of the heads finally looked at her. It licked its lips. 'Okay. Yes. I thought to see how do you do? I mean . . .' *gobble.* Her servant answered from upstairs, probably reporting what kind of mood she was in. Scriber straightened up. Four of his six heads looked at Johanna. His other two members paced back and forth, as if contemplating something important. 'Look here. You are the only human I know, but I have always been a big student of character. I know you are not happy here –'

Pompous Clown was also master of the obvious.

'– and I understand. But we do the best to help you. We are not the bad people who killed your parents and brother.'

Johanna put a hand on the low ceiling and leaned forward. *You're all thugs; you just happen to have the same enemies I do.* 'I know that, and I am cooperating. You'd still be playing the dataset's kindermode if it weren't for me. I've shown you the reading courses; if you guys have any brains, you'll have gunpowder by summer.' The Oliphaunt was an heirloom toy, a huggable favorite thing she should have outgrown years ago.

196

But there was history in it – stories of the queens and princesses of the Dark Ages, and how they had struggled to triumph over the jungles, to rebuild the cities and then the spaceships. Half-hidden on obscure reference paths there were also hard numbers, the history of technology. Gunpowder was one of the easiest things. When the weather cleared up, there would be some prospecting expeditions; Woodcarver had known about sulfur, but didn't have quantities in town. Making cannon would be harder. But then . . .

'Then your enemies will be killed. Your people are getting what they want from me. So what's your complaint?'

'Complaint?' Pompous Clown's heads bobbed up and down in alternation. Such distributed gestures seemed to be the equivalent of facial expressions, though Johanna hadn't figured many of them out. This one might mean embarrassment. 'I have no complaint. You are helping us, I know. But, but . . .' Three of his members were pacing around now. 'It's just that I see more than most people, perhaps a little like Woodcarver did in oldendays. I am a – I've seen your word for it – a "dilettante." You know, a person who studies all things and who is talented at everything. I am only thirty years old, but I have read almost every book in the world, and –' the heads bowed, perhaps in shyness? '– I'm even planning to write one, perhaps the true story of your adventure.'

Johanna found herself smiling. Most often she saw the Tines as barbarian strangers, inhuman in spirit as well as form. But if she closed her eyes, she could almost imagine that Scriber was a fellow Straumer. Mom had a few friends just as brainless and innocently self-convinced as this one, men and women with a hundred grandiose projects that would never ever amount to anything. Back on Straum, they had been boring perils that she avoided. Now . . . well, Scriber's foolishness was almost like being back home again.

'You're here to study me for your book?'

More alternating nods. 'Well, yes. And also, I wanted to talk to you about my other plans. I've always been something of an inventor, you see. I know that doesn't mean much now. It seems that everything that can be invented is already in Dataset. I've seen many of my best ideas there.' He sighed, or made the sound of a sigh. Now he was imitating one of the pop science voices in the dataset. Sound was the easiest thing for the Tines; it could be darn confusing.

'In any case, I was just wondering how to improve some of those ideas –' four of Scriber's members bellied down on the bench by the fire pit; it looked like he was settling in for a long conversation. His other two walked around the pit to give her a stack of paper threaded with brass hoops. While one on the other side of the fire continued to talk, the two carefully turned the pages and pointed at where she should look.

Well, he did have plenty of ideas: Tethered birds to hoist flying boats, giant lenses that would concentrate the sun's light on enemies and set them afire. From some of the pictures, it appeared he thought the atmosphere extended beyond the moon. Scriber explained each idea in numbing detail, pointing at the drawings and patting her hands enthusiastically. 'So you see the possibilities? My unique slant combined with the proven inventions in Dataset. Who knows where it could lead?'

Johanna giggled, overcome by the vision of Scriber's giant birds hauling kilometer-wide lenses to the moon. He seemed to take the sound for approval.

'Yes! It's brilliant, okay? My latest idea, I never would have thought it except for Dataset. This "radio," it projects sound very far and fast, okay? Why not combine it with the power of our Tinish thoughts? A pack could think as one even spread across hundreds of, um, kilometers.'

Now that almost made sense! But if gunpowder took months to make – even given the exact formula – how many *decades* would it be before the packs had radio? Scriber was an immense fountain of half-baked ideas. She let his words wash over her for more than an hour. It was insanity, but less alien than most of what she had endured this last year.

Finally he seemed to run down; there were longer pauses and he asked her opinion more often. Finally he said, 'Well, that was certainly fun, okay?'

'Unh, yes, fascinating.'

'I knew you would like it. You're just like my people, I really think. You're not all angry, not all the time . . .'

'Just what do you mean by that?' Johanna pushed a soft muzzle away and stood. The dogthing rocked back on its haunches to look up at her.

'I, well . . . you have much to hate, I know. But you seem so angry at *us* all the time, and we're the ones who are trying to help you! After the day work you stay here, you don't want to talk with people – though now I see that was our fault. You wanted us to come here but were too proud to say it. I have these insights into character, you see. My friend, the one you call Scarbutt: he is truly a nice fellow. I know I can tell you that honestly, and that as my new friend you will believe. He would very much like to come to visit you, too . . . *urk*.'

Johanna walked slowly around the fire pit, forcing the two members to back away from her. All of Scriber was looking up at her now, the necks arching around one another, the eyes wide.

'I'm *not* like you. I *don't* need your talk, or your stupid ideas.' She threw Scriber's notebook into the pit. Scriber leaped to the fire's edge, desperately reached for the burning notes. He pulled most of them back and clutched them to his chests.

Johanna kept walking toward him, kicking at his legs. Scriber retreated, backing and sprawling. 'Stupid, dirty, butchers. I'm not like you.' She slapped her hand on a ceiling beam. 'Humans don't *like* to live like animals. We don't adopt killers. You tell Scarbutt, you tell him. If he ever comes by for a friendly chat, I-I'll smash in his head; I'll smash in all of them!'

Scriber was backed into the wall now. His heads turned wildly this way and that. He was making plenty of noise. Some of it was Samnorsk, but too high-pitched to understand. One of his mouths found the door pole. He pushed open the door, and all six members raced into the twilight, their rain slickers forgotten.

Johanna knelt and stuck her head through the doorway. The air was a wind-driven mist. In an instant, her face was so cold and wet that she couldn't feel the tears. Scriber was six shadows in the darkening grayness, shadows that raced down the hillside, sometimes tumbling in their haste. In a second, he was gone. There was nothing but the vague forms of nearby cabins and the yellow light that spilled out around her from the fire.

Strange. Right after the ambush, she had felt terror. The Tines had been unstoppable killers. Then, on the boat, when she smashed Scarbutt . . . it had been so wonderful: the whole pack collapsed, and suddenly she knew that she could fight back, that she could break their bones. She didn't have to be at their mercy . . . Tonight she had learned something more. Even without touching them, she could hurt them. Some of them, anyway. Her dislike alone had undone Pompous Clown.

Johanna backed into the smoky warmth and shut the door. She should feel triumph.

18

Scriber Jaqueramaphan didn't tell anyone about his meeting with the Two-Legs. Of course, Vendacious's guard had overheard everything. The fellow might not speak much Samnorsk, but he had surely gotten the drift of the argument. People would hear about it eventually.

He moped around the castle for a few days, spent a number of hours hunched over the remains of his notebook, trying to recreate the diagrams. It would be a while before he attended any more sessions with Dataset, especially when Johanna was around. Scriber knew he seemed brash to the outside world, but in fact it had taken a lot of courage to walk in on Johanna like that. He *knew* his ideas had genius, but all his life unimaginative people had been telling him otherwise.

In most ways Scriber was a very fortunate person. He had been born a fission pack in Rangathir, at the eastern edge of the Republic. His parent had been a wealthy merchant. Jaqueramaphan had some of his parent's traits, but the dull patience necessary for day-to-day business work had been lost to him. His sibling pack more than retained that faculty;

the family business grew, and – in the first years – his sib didn't begrudge Scriber his share of the wealth. From his earliest days, Scriber had been an intellectual. He read everything: natural history, biography, brood kenning. In the end he had the largest library in Rangathir, more than two hundred books.

Even then Scriber had tremendous ideas, insights which – if properly executed – would have made them the wealthiest merchants in all the eastern provinces. Alas, bad luck and his sib's lack of imagination had doomed his early ideas. In the end, his sib bought out the business, and Jaqueramaphan moved to the Capital. It was all for the best. By this time Scriber had fleshed himself out to six members; he needed to see more of the world. Besides . . . there were *five thousand* books in the library there, the experience of all history and all the world! His own notebooks became a library in themselves. Yet still the packs at the university had no time for him. His outline for a summation of natural history was rejected by all the stationers, though he paid to have small parts of it published. It was clear that success in the world of action was necessary before his ideas could get the attention they deserved, hence his spy mission; Parliament itself would thank him when he returned with the secrets of Flenser's Hidden Island.

That was almost a year ago. What had happened since – with the flying house and Johanna and Dataset – went beyond his wildest dreams (and Scriber granted that those dreams were already pretty extreme). The library in Dataset contained *millions* of books. With Johanna to help him polish his ideas, they would sweep Flenserism from the face of the world. They would regain her flying house. Not even the *sky* would be a limit.

So to have her throw it all back at him . . . it made him wonder about himself. Maybe she was just mad at him for trying to explain Peregrine. She would like Peregrine if she let herself; he was sure of it. But then again . . . maybe his ideas just weren't that good, at least by comparison with humans'.

That thought left him pretty low. But he finished redrawing

the diagrams, and even got some new ideas. Maybe he should get some more silkpaper.

Peregrine stopped by and persuaded him to go into town.

Jaqueramaphan had made up a dozen explanations why he wasn't participating in the sessions with Johanna anymore. He tried out two or three as he and Peregrine descended Castle Street toward the harbor.

After a minute or two, his friend turned a head back. 'It's okay, Scriber. When you feel like it, we'd like to have you back.'

Scriber had always been a very good judge of attitude; in particular, he could tell when he was being patronized. He must have scowled a little, because Peregrine went on. 'I mean it. Even Woodcarver has been asking about you. She likes your ideas.'

Comforting lies or not, Scriber brightened. 'Really?' The Woodcarver of today was a sad case, but the Woodcarver of the history books was one of Jaqueramaphan's great heroes. 'No one's mad at me?'

'Well, Vendacious is a bit peeved. Being responsible for the Two-Legs' safety makes him very nervous. But you only tried something we've all wanted to do.'

'Yeah.' Even if there had been no Dataset, even if Johanna Olsndot had not come from the stars, she would still be the most fascinating creature in the world: a pack-equivalent mind in a single body. You could walk right up to her, you could *touch* her, without the least confusion. It was frightening at first, but all of them quickly felt the attraction. For packs, closeness had always meant mindlessness – whether for sex or battle. Imagine being able to sit by the fire with a friend and carry on an intelligent conversation! Woodcarver had a theory that the Two-Legs' civilization might be *innately* more effective than any Packish one, that collaboration was so easy for humans that they learned and built much faster than packs could. The only problem with that theory was Johanna Olsndot. If Johanna was a normal human, it was a surprise that the race could cooperate on anything. Sometimes she was friendly – usually in the sessions with Woodcarver; she seemed to realize that

Woodcarver was frail and failing. More often she was patronizing, sarcastic, and seemed to think the best they could do for her insulting . . . And sometimes she was like last night. 'How goes it with Dataset?' he asked after a moment.

Peregrine shrugged. 'About like before. Both Woodcarver and I can read Samnorsk pretty well now. Johanna has taught us – me via Woodcarver, I should say – how to use most of Dataset's powers. There's so much there that will change the world. But for now we have to concentrate on making *gunpowder* and *cannons*. It's that, the actual doing, that's going slow.'

Scriber nodded knowingly. That had been the central problem in his life too.

'Anyway, if we can do all that by midsummer, maybe we can face Flenser's army and recapture the flying house before next winter.' Peregrine made a grin that stretched from face to face. 'And then, my friend, Johanna can call her people for rescue . . . and we'll have all our lives to study the outsiders. I may pilgrimage to worlds around other stars.'

It was an idea they had talked of before. Peregrine had thought of it even before Scriber.

They turned off Castle Street onto Edgerow. Scriber was feeling more enthusiastic about visiting the stationer's; there must be some way he could help. He looked around with an interest that had been lacking the last few days. Woodcarvers was a fair-sized city, almost as big as Rangathir – maybe twenty thousand packs lived within its walls and in the homes immediately around. This day was a bit colder than the last few, but it wasn't raining. A cold, clean wind swept the market street, carrying faint smells of mildew and sewage, of spices and fresh-sawn wood. Dark clouds hung low, misting the hills around the harbor. Spring was definitely in the air. Scriber kicked playfully at the slush along the curb.

Peregrine led them to a side street. The place was jammed, strangers getting as close as seven or eight yards. The stalls at the stationer's were even worse. The felt dividers weren't that thick, and there seemed to be more interest in literature at Woodcarvers than any place Scriber had ever been. He could hardly hear himself think as he haggled with the stationer.

The merchant sat on a raised platform with thick padding; *he* wasn't much bothered by the racket. Scriber kept his heads close together, concentrating on the prices and the product. From his past life, he was pretty good at this sort of thing.

Eventually he got his paper, and at a decent price.

'Let's go back on Packweal,' he said. That was the long way, through the center of the market. When he was in a good mood, Scriber rather liked crowds; he was a great student of people. Woodcarvers was not as cosmopolitan as some cities by the Long Lakes, but there were traders from all over. He saw several packs wearing the bonnets of a tropic collective. At one intersection a redjackets from East Home was chatting cozily with a labormaster.

When packs came this close, and in these numbers, the world seemed to teeter on the edge of a choir. Each person hung near to himself, trying to keep his own thoughts intact. It was hard to walk without stumbling over your own feet. And sometimes the background thought sounds would surge, a moment where several packs would somehow synchronize. Your consciousness wavered and for an instant you were one with many, a superpack that might be a god. Jaqueramaphan shivered. That was the essential attraction of the Tropics. The crowds there were *mobs*, vast group minds as stupid as they were ecstatic. If the stories were true, some of the southern cities were nonstop orgies.

They had roamed the marketplace almost an hour when it hit him. Scriber shook his heads abruptly. He turned and walked in lockstep off Packweal, and up a side street. Peregrine followed. 'Is the crowd too much?' he asked.

'I just had an idea,' said Scriber. That wasn't unusual in a close crowd, but this was a *very* interesting idea . . . He said nothing more for several minutes. The side street climbed steeply, then jinked back and forth across Castle Hill. The upslope side was lined with burghers' homes. On the harbor side, they were looking out over the steep tile roofs of houses on the next switchback down. These were large homes, elegant with rosemaling. Only a few had shops on the street.

Scriber slowed down and spread out enough that he wasn't stepping on himself. He saw now that he'd been quite wrong in trying to contribute creative expertise to Johanna. There was simply too much invention in Dataset. But they still needed him, Johanna most of all. The problem was, they didn't know it yet. Finally he said to Peregrine, 'Haven't you wondered that the Flenserists haven't attacked the city? You and I embarrassed the Lords of Hidden Island more than ever in their history. We hold the keys to their total defeat.' *Johanna and Dataset.*

Peregrine hesitated. 'Hmm. I assumed their army wasn't up to it. I should think if they were, they'd have knocked over Woodcarvers long before.'

'Perhaps they could, but at great cost. Now the cost is worth it.' He gave Peregrine a serious look. 'No, I think there's another reason . . . They have the flying house, but they have no idea how to use it. They want Johanna back alive – almost as much as they want to kill all of us.'

Peregrine made a bitter sound. 'If Steel hadn't been so eager to massacre everything on two legs, he could have had all sorts of help.'

'True, and the Flenserists must know that. I'll bet they've always had spies among the townspeople here, *but now more than ever*. Did you see all the East Home packs?' East Home was a hotbed of Flenser sentiment. Even before the Movement they had been a hard folk, routinely sacrificing pups that didn't meet their brood standards.

'One anyway. Talking to a labormaster.'

'Right. Who knows what's coming in disguised as special purpose packs? I'd bet my life they're planning to kidnap Johanna. If they guess what we're planning with her, they may just try to kill her. Don't you see? We must alert Woodcarver and Vendacious, organize the people to watch for spies.'

'You noticed all this on one walk through Packweal?' There was wonder or disbelief in his voice, Scriber couldn't tell which.

'Well, um, no. The inspiration wasn't anything so direct. But it stands to reason, don't you think?'

They walked in silence for several minutes. Up here the wind was stronger, and the view more spectacular. Where there wasn't the sea, forest spread endless gray and green.

Everything was very peaceful . . . because *this was a game of stealth*. Fortunately Scriber had a talent for such games. After all, hadn't it been the very Political Police of the Republic who commissioned him to survey Hidden Island? It had taken him several tendays of patient persuasion, but in the end they had been enthusiastic. *Anything you can discover we would be most happy to review*. Those were their exact words.

Peregrine waffled around the road, seemingly very taken aback by Scriber's suggestion. Finally he said, 'I think there is . . . something you should know, something that must remain an absolute secret.'

'*Upon my soul!* Peregrine, I do not blab secrets.' Scriber was a little hurt – at the lack of trust, and also that the other might have discovered something he had not. The second should not bother him. He had guessed that Peregrine and Woodcarver were into each other. No telling what she might have confided, or what might have leaked across.

'Okay . . . You've tripped onto something that should not be noised about. You know Vendacious is in charge of Woodcarver's security?'

'Of course.' That was implicit in the office of Lord Chamberlain. 'And considering the number of outsiders wandering around, I can't say he's doing a very good job.'

'In fact, he's doing a marvelously effective job. Vendacious has agents right at the top at Hidden Island – one step removed from Lord Steel himself.'

Scriber felt his eyes widening.

'Yes, you understand what that means. Through Vendacious, Woodcarver knows for a certainty *everything* their high council plans. With clever misinformation, we can lead the Flenserists around like froghens at a thinning. Next to Johanna herself, this may be Woodcarver's greatest advantage.'

'I –' *I had no idea*. 'So the incompetent local security is just a cover.'

'Not exactly. It's supposed to look solid and intelligent, but with just enough exploitable weakness so the Movement will postpone a frontal attack in favor of espionage.' He smiled. 'I think Vendacious will be very taken aback to hear your critique.'

Scriber gave a weak laugh. He was flattered and boggled at the same time. Vendacious must count as the greatest spymaster of the age – yet he, Scriber Jaqueramaphan, had almost seen through him. Scriber was mostly quiet the rest of the way back to the castle, but his mind was racing. Peregrine was more right than he knew; secrecy was vital. Unnecessary discussion – even between old friends – must be avoided. Yes! He would offer his services to Vendacious. His new role might keep him in the background, but it was where he could make the greatest contribution. And eventually even Johanna would see how helpful he could be.

Down the well of the night. Even when Ravna wasn't looking out the windows, that was the image in her mind. Relay was far off the galactic disk. The *OOB* was descending toward that disk – and ever deeper into slowness.

But they had escaped. The *OOB* was crippled, but they had left Relay at almost fifty light-years per hour. Each hour they were deeper in the Beyond and the computation time for the microjumps increased, and their pseudovelocity declined. Nevertheless, they were making progress. They were deep into the Middle of the Beyond now. And there was no sign of pursuit, thank goodness. Whatever had brought the Blight to Relay, it had not been a specific knowledge of the *OOB*.

Hope. Ravna felt it growing in her. The ship's medieval automation claimed that Pham Nuwen could be saved, that there was brain activity. The terrible wounds in his back had been Old One's implants, organic machinery that had made Pham close-linked to Relay's local network – and thence to the Power above. And when that Power died somehow the gear in Pham became a putrescent ruin. *So Pham the person should still exist. Pray he still exists.* The surgeon thought it would be three days before his back was healed enough to attempt resuscitation.

In the meantime . . . Ravna was learning more about the apocalypse that had swept over her. Every twenty hours, Greenstalk and Blueshell jigged the ship sideways a few light-years, into some major trunk line of the Known Net to soak up the News. It was a common practice on any voyage of more than a few days; an easy way for merchants and travelers to keep track of events that might affect their success at voyage's end.

According to the News (that is, according to the vast majority of the opinions expressed), the fall of Relay was complete. *Oh, Grondr. Oh Egravan and Sarale. Are you dead or owned now?*

Parts of the Known Net were temporarily out of contact; some of the extra-galactic links might not be replaced for years. For the first time in millennia, a Power was known to have been murdered. There were tens of thousands of claims about the motive for the attack and tens of thousands of predictions about what would happen next. Ravna had the ship filter the avalanche, trying to distill the essence of the speculations.

The one coming from Straumli Realm itself made as much sense as any: the Perversion's thralls gloated solemnly about the new era, the marriage of a Transcendent being with races of the Beyond. If Relay could be destroyed – if a Power could be murdered – then nothing could stop the spread of victory.

Some senders thought that Relay was the ancestral target of whatever had perverted Straumli Realm. Maybe the attack was just the tail end of some long-ago war, a misbegotten tragedy for the descendents of forgotten races. If so, then the thralls at Straumli Realm might just wither away and the original human culture there reappear.

A number of items suggested that the attack had been aimed at stealing Relay's archives, but only one or two claimed that the Blight sought to recover an artifact, or prevent the Relayers from recovering one. Those assertions came from chronic theorizers, the sort of civilizations that get surcharged by news group automation. Nevertheless, Ravna looked through those messages carefully. None of them suggested an artifact in the Low Beyond; if anything, they claimed the Blight was searching for something in the High Beyond or Low Transcend.

There was network traffic coming out of the Blight. Its high protocol messages were rejected by all but the suicidal, and no one as getting paid to forward anything. Yet horror and curiosity spread some of the messages far. There was the Blighter 'video': almost four hundred seconds of pan-sensual data with no compression. That incredibly expensive message might be the most-forwarded hog in all Net history. Blueshell held the *OOB* on the trunk path of nearly two days to receive the whole thing.

The Perversion's thralls all appeared to be human. About half the news items coming out of the Realm were video evocations, though none this long, all showed human speakers. Ravna watched the big one again and again: She even recognized the speaker. Øvn Nilsndot had been Straumli Realm's champion trael runner. He had no title now, and probably no name. Nilsndot spoke from an office that might have been a garden. If Ravna stepped to the side of the image, she could see over his shoulder to ground level. The city there looked like the Straumli Main of record. Years ago, Ravna and her sister had dreamed about that city, the heart of mankind's adventure into the Transcend. The central square had been a replica of the Field of Princesses on Nyjora, and the immigration advertising claimed that no matter how far the Straumers went, the fountain in the Field would always flow, would always show their loyalty to humankind's beginnings.

There was no fountain now, and Ravna felt deadness behind Nilsndot's gaze. 'This one speaks as the Power that Helps,' said the erstwhile hero. 'I want all to see what I can do for even a third-rate civilization. Look upon my Helping . . .' The viewpoint swung skywards. It was sunset, and the ranked agrav structures hung against the light, megameter upon megameter. It was a more grandiose use of the agrav material than Ravna had ever seen, even on the Docks. Certainly no world in the Middle Beyond could ever afford to import the material in such quantities. 'What you see above me is just the work barracks for the construction that I will soon begin in the Straumli system. When complete, five star systems will be a single habitat, their planets and excess stellar mass distributed to support life and technology as never before seen at these depths – and as rarely seen in the Transcend itself.'

The view returned to Nilsndot, a single human, mouthpiece for a god. 'Some of you may rebel against the idea of dedicating yourselves to me. In the long run it does not matter. The symbiosis of my Power with the hands of races in the Beyond is more than any can resist. But I speak now to diminish your fear. What you see in Straumli Realm is as much a joy as a wonder. Never again will races in the Beyond be left behind by transcendence. Those who join me – and all will join eventually – will be part of the Power. You will have access to imports from across the Top and Lower Transcend. You will reproduce beyond the limits your own technology could sustain. You will absorb all that oppose me. You will bring the new stability.'

The third or fourth time she watched the item, Ravna tried to ignore the words, concentrate on Nilsndot's expression, comparing it to speeches she had in her personal dataset. There was a difference; it wasn't her imagination. The creature she watched was soul-dead. Somehow, the Blight didn't care that that was obvious . . . maybe it wasn't obvious except to human viewers, and they were a vanishingly small fraction of the audience. The viewpoint closed in on Nilsndot's ordinary dark face, his ordinary violet eyes:

'Some of you may wonder how all this is possible, and why billions of years of anarchy have passed without such help from a Power. The answer is . . . complex. Like many sensible developments, this one has a high threshold. On one side of that threshold, the development appears impossibly unlikely; on the other, inevitable. The symbiosis of the Helping depends on efficient, high-bandwidth communication between myself and the beings I Help. Creatures such as the one now speaking my words must respond as quickly and faithfully as a hand or a mouth. Their eyes and ears must report across light-years. This has been hard to achieve – especially since the system must essentially be in place before it can function. *But*, now that the symbiosis exists, progress will come much faster. Almost any race can be modified to receive Help.'

Almost any race can be modified. The words came from a familiar face, and in Ravna's birth language . . . but the origin was monstrously far away.

There was plenty of analysis. A whole news group had been formed: Threat of the Blight was spawned from Threats Group, Homo Sapiens Interest Group, and Close-Coupled Automation. These days it was busier than any five other groups. In this part of the galaxy, a significant fraction of all message traffic belonged to the new group. More bits were sent analyzing poor Øvn Nilsndot's mouthing than had been in the original. Judging from the flames and contradictions, the signal-to-noise ratio was very low:

Crypto: 0
As received by: *OOB* shipboard ad hoc
Language path: Acquileron→Triskweline, SjK units
From: Khurvark University
   [Claimed to be habitat-based university, in the
   Middle Beyond]
Subject: Blighter Video
Summary: The message shows fraud
Distribution:
   War Trackers Interest Group
   Where are they now Interest Group
   Threat of the Blight
Date: 7.06 days since Fall of Relay
Text of message:
   It's obvious that this 'Helper' is a fraud. We've researched the matter carefully. .Though he is not named, the speaker is a high official in the former Straumli regime. Now why – if the "Helper" " simply runs the hunans as teleoperated robots – why is the earlier social structure preserved? The answer should be clear to any idiot: The Helper does not have the power to teleoperate large numbers of sentients. Evidently, the Fall of Straumli Realm consisted of taking over key elements in that civilization's power structure. It's business as usual for the rest of the race. Our conclusion: this Helper Symbiosis is just another messianic religion; another screwball empire excusing its excesses and attempting to trick those it cannot

directly coerce. *Don't be fooled!*

Crypto: 0
As received by: *OOB* shipboard ad hoc
Language path: Optima→Acquileron→Triskweline,
    SjK units
From: Society for Rational Investigation [Probably a
    single system in Middle Beyond, 5700 light-years
    antispinward of Sjandra Kei]
Subject: Blighter Video thread, Khurvark University 1
Key phrases: [Probable obscenity] waste of our valu-
    able time
Distribution:
    Society for Rational Network Management
    Threat of the Blight
Date: 7.91 days since Fall of Relay
Text of message:
    Who is a fool? [probable obscenity] [probable ob-
scenity] Idiots who don't follow all the threads in de-
veloping news should not waste my precious ears
with their [clear obscenity] garbage. So you think the
'Helper Symbiosis' is a fraud of Straumli Realm? And
what do you think caused the fall of Relay? In case your
head is totally stuck up your rear [<–probable
insult], there was a *Power* allied with Relay. That
Power is now dead. You think maybe it just committed
suicide? Look it up, Flat Head [<–probable insult].
No Power has ever fallen to anything from the
Beyond. The Blight is something new and interesting. I
think it's time that [obscenity] jerks like Khurvark
University stick to the noise groups, and let the rest of
us have some intelligent discussion.

And some messages were patent nonsense. One thing
about the Net: the multiple, automatic translations often
disguised the fundamental alienness of participants. Behind
the chatty, colloquial postings, there were faraway realms, so
misted by distance and difference that communication was
impossible – even though it might take a while to realize the

fact. For instance:

Crypto: 0
As received by: *OOB* shipboard ad hoc
Language path: Arbwyth→Trade 24→Cherguelen
　→Triskweline, SjK units
From: Twirlip of the Mists
　[Perhaps an organization of cloud fliers in a single
　jovian system. Very sparse priors.]
Subject: Blighter Video thread
Key phrases: Hexapodia as the key insight
Distribution:
　Threat of the Blight
Date: 8.68 days since Fall of Relay
Text of message:
　I haven't had a chance to see the famous video from
Straumli Realm, except as an evocation. (My only
gateway onto the Net is very expensive.) Is it true that
humans have six legs? I wasn't sure from the evoca-
tion. If these humans have three pairs of legs, then I
think there is an easy explanation for —

Hexapodia: Six legs? Three pairs of legs? Probably none of
these translations was close to what the bewildered creature
of Twirlip had in its mind. Ravna didn't read any more of that
posting.

Crypto: 0
As received by: *OOB* shipboard ad hoc
Language path: Triskweline, SjK units
From: Hanse
　[No references prior to the Fall of Relay. No probable
　source. This is someone being very cautious]
Subject: Blighter Video thread, Khurvark University 1
Distribution:
　War Trackers Interest Group
　Threat of the Blight
Date: 8.68 days since Fall of Relay
Text of message:

Khurvark University thinks the Blight is a fraud because elements of the former regime have survived on Straum. There is another explanation. Suppose the Blight is indeed a Power, and that its claims of effective symbiosis are generally true. That means that the creature being 'Helped' is no more than a remotely controlled device, his brain simply a local processor supporting the communication. Would *you* want to be helped like that? My question isn't completely rhetorical; the readership is wide enough that there may be some of you who would answer 'yes.' However, the vast majority of naturally evolved, sentient beings would be revolted by the notion. Surely the Blight knows this. My guess is that the Blight is *not* a fraud – but that the notion of surviving culture in Straumli Realm *is*. Subtly, the Blight wants to convey the impression that only some are directly enslaved, that cultures as a whole will survive. Combine that with Blight's claim that not all races can be teleoperated. We're left with the subtext that immense riches are available to races that associate themselves with this Power, yet the biological and intellectual imperatives of these races will still be satisfied.

So, the question remains. Just how thorough is the Blight's control over conquered races? I don't know. There may not be any self-aware minds left in the Blight's Beyond, only billions of teleoperated devices. One thing is clear: The Blight needs something from us that it cannot yet *take*.

And so it went. Tens of thousands of messages, hundreds of points of view. It was not called the Net of a Million Lies for nothing. Ravna talked with Blueshell and Greenstalk about it every day, trying to put it all together, trying to decide which interpretation to believe.

The Riders knew humans well, but even they weren't sure of the deadness in Øvn Nilsndot's face. And Greenstalk knew humans well enough to see that there was no answer that would comfort Ravna. She rolled back and forth in front of the News window, finally reached a frond out to touch the human. 'Perhaps Sir Pham can say, once he is well.'

Blueshell was bustling, clinical. 'If you're right, that means that somehow the Blight doesn't care what humans and those close to humans know. In a way that makes sense, but . . .' His voder buzzed absentmindedly for a moment. 'I mistrust this message. Four hundred seconds of broad-band, so rich that it gives full-sense imagery for many different races. That's an enormous amount of information, and no compression whatsoever . . . Maybe it's sweetened bait, forwarded by us poor Beyonders back to our every nest.' That suspicion had been in the News too. But there were no obvious patterns in the message, and nothing that talked to network automation. Such subtle poison might work at the Top of the Beyond, but not down here. And that left a simpler explanation, one that would make perfect sense even on Nyjora or Old Earth: the video masked a message to agents already in place.

Vendacious was well-known to the people of Woodcarvers – but for mostly the wrong reasons. He was about a century old, the fusion offspring of Woodcarver on two of his strategists. In his early decades, Vendacious had managed the city's wood mills. Along the way he devised some clever improvements on the waterwheel. Vendacious had had his own romantic entanglements – mostly with politicians and speech-makers. More and more, his replacement members inclined him toward public life. For the last thirty years he had been one of the strongest voices on Woodcarver's Council; for the last ten, Lord Chamberlain. In both roles he had stood for the guilds and for fair trade. There were rumors that if Woodcarver should ever abdicate or wholly die, Vendacious would be the next Lord of Council. Many thought that might be the best that could be made of such a disaster – though Vendacious's pompous speeches were already the bane of the Council.

That was the public's view of Vendacious. Anyone who understood the ways of security would also guess that the chamberlain managed Woodcarver's spies. No doubt he had dozens of informants in the mills and on the docks. But now Scriber knew that even *that* was just a cover. Imagine – having agents in the Flenserist inner circle, knowing the Flenserist plans, their fears, their weaknesses, and being able to manipulate them! Vendacious was simply incredible. Rue-fully, Scriber must acknowledge the other's stark genius.

And yet . . . this knowledge did not guarantee victory. Not *all* the Flenserist schemes could be directly managed from the top. Some of the enemy's low-level operations might proceed unknown and quite successfully . . . and it would only take a single arrow to totally kill Johanna Olsndot.

Here was where Scriber Jaqueramaphan could prove his value.

He asked to move into the castle curtain, on the third floor. No problem getting permission; his new quarters were smaller, the walls rudely quilted. A single arrow loop gave an uninspired view across the castle grounds. For Scriber's new purpose, the room was perfect. Over the next few days, he took to lurking in the promenades. The main walls were laced with tunnels, fifteen inches wide by thirty tall. Scriber could get almost anywhere in the curtain without being seen from outside. He padded single file from one tunnel to the next, emerging for a few moments on a rampart to flit from merlon to embrasure to merlon, a head poking out here, a head poking out there.

Of course he ran into guards, but Jaqueramaphan was cleared to be in the walls . . . and he had studied the guards' routine. They knew he was around, but Scriber was confident they had no idea of the extent of his effort. It was hard, cold work, but worth the effort. Scriber's great goal in life was to do something spectacular and valuable. The problem was, most of his ideas were so deep that other packs – even people he respected immensely – didn't understand. That had been the problem with Johanna. Well, after a few more days he could go to Vendacious and then . . .

As he peeked around corners and through arrow slots, two of Scriber's members huddled down, taking notes. After ten days he had enough to impress even Vendacious.

*

216

Vendacious's official residence was surrounded by rooms for assistants and guards. It was not the place to make a secret offer. Besides, Scriber had had bad luck with the direct approach before. You could wait days for an appointment, and the more patient you were, the more you followed the rules, the more the bureaucrats considered you a nonentity.

But Vendacious was sometimes alone. There was this turret on the old wall, on the forest side of the castle . . . Late on the eleventh day of his investigation, Scriber stationed himself on that turret and waited. An hour passed. The wind eased. Heavy fog washed in from the harbor. It oozed up the old wall like slow-moving sea foam. Everything became very, very quiet – the way it always does in a thick fog. Scriber nosed moodily around the turret platform; it really was decrepit. The mortar crumbled under his claws. It felt like you could pull some of the stones right out of the wall. *Damn.* Maybe Vendacious was going to break the pattern and not come up here today.

But Scriber waited another half hour . . . and his patience paid off. He heard the click of steel on the spiral stairs. There was no sound of thought; it was just too foggy for that. A minute passed. The trapdoor popped up and a head stuck through.

Even in the fog, Vendacious's surprise was a fierce hiss.

'Peace, sir! It is only I, loyal Jaqueramaphan.'

The head came further out. 'What would a loyal citizen be doing up here?'

'Why, I am here to see you,' Scriber said, laughing, 'at this, your secret office. Come on up, sir. With this fog, there is enough room for both of us.'

One after another, Vendacious's members hoisted themselves through the trapdoor. Some barely made it, their knives and jewelry catching on the door frame; Vendacious was not the slimmest of packs. The security chief ranged himself along the far side of the turret, a posture that bespoke suspicion. He was nothing like the pompous, patronizing pack of their public encounters. Scriber grinned to himself. He certainly had the other's attention.

'Well?' Vendacious said in a flat voice.

'Sir. I wish to offer my services. I believe that my very presence here shows I can be of value to Woodcarver's security. Who but a talented professional could have determined that you use this place as your secret den?'

Vendacious seemed to untense a little. He smiled wryly. 'Who indeed? I come here precisely because this part of the old wall can't be seen from anywhere in the castle. Here I can . . . commune with the hills, and be free of bureaucratic trivia.'

Jaqueramaphan nodded. 'I understand, sir. But you are wrong in one detail.' He pointed past the security chief. 'You can't see it through all this fog, but on the harbor side of the castle there is a single spot that has a line of sight on your turret.'

'So? Who could see much from – ah, the eye-tools you brought from the Republic!'

'Exactly.' Scriber reached into a pocket and brought out a *telescope*. 'Even from across the yard, I could recognize you.' The eye-tools could have made Scriber famous. Woodcarver and Scrupilo had been enchanted by them. Unfortunately, honesty had required to him admit that he bought the devices from an inventor in Rangathir. Never mind that it was *he* who recognized the value of the invention, that it was he who used it to help rescue Johanna. When they discovered that he did not know quite how the lenses worked, they had accepted his gift of one . . . and turned to their own glass makers. Oh well, he was still the best eye-tool *user* in this part of the world.

'It's not just you I've been watching, my lord. That's been the smallest part of my investigation. Over the last ten days I've spent many hours on the castle walks.'

Vendacious's lips quirked. 'Indeed.'

'I daresay not many noticed me, and I was very careful that no one saw me using the eye-tool. In any case,' he pulled his book from another pocket, 'I've compiled extensive notes. I know who goes where and when during almost all the hours of light. You can imagine the power of my technique during the summer!' He set the book on the floor and slid it toward Vendacious. After a moment, the other reached a member forward and dragged it toward himself. He didn't seem very enthusiastic.

'Please understand, sir. I know that you tell Woodcarver what goes on in the highest Flenser councils. Without your sources we would be helpless against those lords, but —'

'*Who told you such things?*'

Scriber gulped. *Brazen it out.* He grinned weakly. 'No one had to tell me. I'm a professional, like yourself; and I know how to keep a secret. But think: there might be others of my ability within the castle, and some might be traitors. You might never hear of them from your high-placed sources. Think of the damage they could do. You need my help. With my approach, you can keep track of everyone. I would be happy to train a corps of investigators. We could even operate in the city, watching from the market towers.'

The security chief sidled around the parapet; he kicked idly at stones in the rotted mortar. 'The idea has its attractions. Mind you, I think we have all Flenser's agents identified; we feed them well . . . with lies. It's interesting to hear the lies come back from our sources up there.' He laughed shortly, and glanced over the parapet, thinking. 'But you're right. If we are missing anyone with access to the Two-Legs or Dataset . . . it could be disastrous.' He turned more heads at Scriber. 'You've got a deal. I can get you four or five people to, ah, train in your methods.'

Scriber couldn't control his expression; he almost bounced in enthusiasm, all eyes on Vendacious. 'You won't regret this, sir!'

Vendacious shrugged. 'Probably not. Now, how many others have you told about your investigation? We'll want to bring them in, swear them to secrecy.'

Scriber drew himself up. 'My Lord! I told you that I am a professional. I have kept this completely to myself, waiting for this conversation.'

Vendacious smiled and relaxed to an almost genial posture. 'Excellent. Then we can begin.'

Maybe it was Vendacious's voice — a trifle too loud — or maybe it was some small sound behind him. Whatever the reason, Scriber turned a head from the other and saw swift shadows coming over the forest side of the parapet. Too late he heard the attacker's mind noise.

Arrows hissed, and fire burned through his Phan's throat. He gagged, but kept himself together and raced around the turret toward Vendacious. 'Help me!' The scream was a waste of speech. Scriber *knew*, even before the other drew his knives and backed away.

Vendacious stood clear as his assassin jumped into Scriber's midst. Rational thought dimmed in a frenzy of noise and slashing pain. *Tell Peregrine! Tell Johanna!* The butchering continued for timeless instants and then –

Part of him was drowning in sticky red. Part of him was blinded. Jaquerama's thought came in ragged fragments. At least one of him was dead: Phan lay beheaded in a spreading pool of blood. It steamed in the cold air. Pain and cold and . . . drowning, choking . . . *tell Johanna*.

The assassin and his boss had retreated from him. Vendacious. Security chief. Traitor-in-chief. *Tell Johanna.* They stood quietly . . . watching him bleed to death. Too prissy to mess their thoughts with his. They'd wait. They'd wait . . . till his mind noise dimmed, then finish the job.

Quiet. So quiet. The killers' distant thoughts. Sounds of gagging, moaning. No one would ever know . . .

Almost all gone. Ja stared dumbly at the two strange packs. One came toward him, steel claws on his feet, blades in its mouth. *No!* Ja jumped up, slipping and skidding on the wet. The pack lunged, but Ja was already standing on the parapet. He leaped backwards and fell and fell . . .

. . . and shattered on rocks far below. Ja pulled himself away from the wall. There was pain across his back, then numbness. Where am I? Where am I? Fog everywhere. High above him there were muttering voices. Memories of knives and tines floated in his small mind, all jumbled. *Tell Johanna!* He remembered . . . something . . . from before. A hidden trail through deep brush. If he went that way far enough, he would find Johanna.

Ja dragged himself slowly up the path. Something was wrong with his rear legs; he couldn't feel them. *Tell Johanna.*

19

Johanna coughed; things just seemed to go from bad to worse around here. She'd had a sore throat and sniffles the last three days. She didn't know whether to be frightened or not. Diseases were an everyday thing in medieval times. *Yeah, and lots of people* died *of them, too!* She wiped her nose and tried to concentrate on what Woodcarver was saying.

'Scrupilo has already made some gunpowder. It works just as Dataset predicted. Unfortunately, he nearly lost a member trying to use it in a wooden cannon. If we can't make cannon, I'm afraid –'

A week ago, Woodcarver wouldn't have been welcome here; all their meetings had been down in the castle halls. But then Johanna got sick – it was a 'cold,' she was sure – and hadn't felt like running around out of doors. Besides, Scriber's visit had kind of . . . shamed her. Some of the packs were decent enough. She had decided to try and get along with Woodcarver – and Pompous Clown too, if he'd ever come around again. As long as creatures like Scarbutt stayed out of her way . . . Johanna leaned a little closer to the fire and waved away Woodcarver's objections; sometimes this pack seemed like her eldest grandmother. 'Assume we can make them. We have lots of time till summer. Tell Scrupilo to study the dataset more carefully, and quit trying shortcuts. The question is how to use them to rescue my starship.'

Woodcarver brightened. The drooler broke off wiping its muzzle to join the others in a head bob. 'I've talked about this with Peregr— with several people, especially Vendacious. Ordinarily, getting an army to Hidden Island would be a terrible problem. Going by sea is fast, but there are some deadly choke points along the way. Going through the forest is slow, and the other side would have plenty of warning. But great good luck: Vendacious has found some safe trails. We may be able to sneak –'

Someone was scratching at the door.

Woodcarver cocked a pair of heads. 'That's strange,' she said.

'Why?' Johanna asked absently. She hiked the quilt around her shoulders and stood. Two of Woodcarver went with her to the door.

Johanna opened the door and looked into the fog. Suddenly Woodcarver was talking loudly, all gobble. Their visitor had retreated. Something *was* strange, and for an instant she couldn't figure what it was. *This was the first time she had seen a dogthing all by itself.* The point barely registered when most of Woodcarver spilled past her, out the doorway. Then Johanna's servant, up in the loft, began screaming. The sound jabbed pain through Johanna's ears.

The lone Tine twisted awkwardly on its rear and tried to drag itself away, but Woodcarver had it surrounded. She shouted something and the screeching in the loft stopped. There was the thump of paws on wooden stairs, and the servant bounded into the open, its crossbows cocked. From down the hill, she heard the rattle of weapons as guards raced toward them.

Johanna ran to Woodcarver, ready to add her fists to any defense. But the pack was *nuzzling* the stranger, licking its neck. After a moment, Woodcarver caught the Tine by its jacket. 'Help me carry him inside, Johanna please.'

The girl lifted the Tine's flanks. The fur was damp with mist . . . and sticky with blood.

Then they were through the doorway and laying the member on a pillow by the fire. The creature was making that breathy whistling, the sound of ultimate pain. It looked up at her, its eyes so wide she could see the white all around. For an instant she thought it was terrified of *her*, but when she stepped back, it just made the sound louder and stretched its neck toward her. She knelt beside the pillow. It lay its muzzle on her hand.

'W-what is it?' She looked back along its body, past the padded jacket. The Tine's haunches were twisted at an odd angle, one leg dangling near the fire.

'Don't you know –' began Woodcarver. 'This is part of

Jaqueramaphan.' She pushed a nose under the dangling leg and raised it onto the pillow.

There was loud talk between the guards and Johanna's servant. Through the door she saw members holding torches; they rested their forepaws on their fellows' shoulders, and held the lights high. No one tried to come in; there'd be no room.

Johanna looked back at the injured Tine. *Scriber?* Then she recognized the jacket. The creature looked back at her, still wheezing its pain. 'Can't you get a doctor!'

Woodcarver was all around her. She answered, 'I am a doctor, Johanna.' She nodded at the dataset and continued softly, 'At least, what passes for one here.'

Johanna wiped blood from the creature's neck. More kept oozing. 'Well, can you save him?'

'This fragment maybe, but –' One of Woodcarver went to the door and talked to the packs beyond. 'My people are searching for the rest of him . . . I think he is mostly murdered, Johanna. If there were others . . . well, even fragments stick together.'

'Has he said anything?' It was another voice, speaking Samnorsk. *Scarbutt.* His big ugly snout was stuck through the doorway.

'No,' said Woodcarver. 'And his mind noise is a complete jumble.'

, 'Let me listen to him,' said Scarbutt.

'*You stay back, you!*' Johanna's voice was a scream; the creature in her arms twitched.

'Johanna! This is Scriber's friend. Let him help.' As the Scarbutt pack sidled into the room, Woodcarver climbed into the loft, giving him room.

Johanna eased her arm from under the injured Tine and backed away, ending up at the doorway herself. There were lots more packs outside than she had imagined, and they were standing closer than she had ever seen. Their torches glowed like soft fluorescents in the foggy dark.

Her gaze snapped back to the fire pit. 'I'm watching you!'

Scarbutt's members clustered around the pillow. The big one lay its head next to the injured Tine's. For a moment, the

Tine continued its breathy whistling. Scarbutt gobbled at it. The reply was a steady warbling, almost beautiful. From up in the loft, Woodcarver said something. She and Scarbutt talked back and forth.

'Well?' said Johanna.

'*Ja* – the fragment – is not a "talker,"' came Woodcarver's voice.

'Worse,' said Scarbutt. 'For now at least, I can't match his mind sounds. I'm not getting sense or image from him; I can't tell who murdered Scriber.'

Johanna stepped back into the room, and walked slowly to the pillow. Scarbutt moved aside, but did not leave the wounded Tine. She knelt between two of him and petted the long, bloodied neck. 'Will – Ja' – she spoke the sound as best she could – 'live?'

Scarbutt ran three noses down the length of the body. They pressed gently at the wounds. Ja twisted and whistled . . . except when Scarbutt pressed his haunches. 'I don't know. Most of this blood is just splatter, probably from the other members. But his spine is broken. Even if the fragment lives, he'll have only two usable legs.'

Johanna thought for a moment, trying to see things from a Tinish perspective. She didn't like the view. It might not make sense, but to her, this 'Ja' was still Scriber. To Scarbutt, the creature was a fragment, an organ from a fresh corpse. A damaged one at that. She looked at Scarbutt, at the big, killer member. 'So what does your kind do with such . . . garbage?'

Three of his heads turned toward her, and she could see his hackles rise. His synthetic voice became high-pitched and staccato. 'Scriber was a good friend. We could build a two-wheel cart for Ja's rear; he'd be able to move around some. The hard part will be finding a pack for him. You know we're looking for other fragments; we may be able to patch something up. If not . . . well, I have only four members. I will try to adopt him.' As he spoke one head patted the wounded member. 'I'm not sure it will work. Scriber was not a loose-souled person, not in any way a pilgrim. And right now, I don't match him at all.'

Johanna slumped back. Scarbutt wasn't responsible for

everything that went wrong in the universe.

'Woodcarver has excellent brood kenners. Maybe some other match can be found. But understand . . . it's hard for adult members to remerge, especially non-talkers. Single fragments like Ja often die of their own accord; they just stop eating. Or sometimes . . . Go down to the harbor sometime, look at the workers. You'll see some big packs there . . . but with the minds of idiots. They can't hold together; the smallest problem and they run in all directions. That's how the unlucky repacks end . . .' Scarbutt's voice traded back and forth between two of his members, and dribbled into silence. All his heads turned to Ja. The member had closed his eyes. Sleeping? He was still breathing, but it sounded kind of burbly.

Johanna looked across the room at the trapdoor to the loft. Woodcarver had stuck a single head down through the hole. The upside-down face looked back at Johanna. Anther time, her appearance would have been comical. 'Unless a miracle happens, Scriber died today. Understand that, Johanna. But if the fragment lives, even a short time, we'll likely find the murderer.'

'How, if he can't communicate?'

'Yes, but he can still *show* us. I've ordered Vendacious's men to confine the staff to quarters. When Ja is calmer, we'll march every pack in the castle past him. The fragment certainly remembers what happened to Scriber, and *wants* to tell us. If any of the killers are our own people, he'll see them.'

'And he'll make a fuss.' *Just like a dog.*

'Right. So the main thing is to provide him with security right now . . . and hope our doctors can save him.'

They found the rest of Scriber a couple of hours later, on a turret of the old wall. Vendacious said it looked like one or two packs had come out of the forest and climbed the turret, perhaps in an attempt to see onto the grounds. It had all the markings of an incompetent, first-time probe: nothing of value could be seen from that turret, even on a clear day. But for Scriber it had been fatally bad luck. Apparently he had surprised the intruders. Five of his members had been variously arrowed, hacked, decapitated. The sixth – Ja – had broken his back on the sloping stonework at the base of the wall. Johanna walked out to the turret the next day. Even from the ground she could see brownish stains on the parapet. She was glad she couldn't go to the top.

Ja died during the night, though not from any further enemy action; he was under Vendacious's protection the whole time.

Johanna went the next few days without saying much. At night she cried a little. *God damn their 'doctoring.'* A broken back they could diagnose, but hidden injuries, internal bleeding – of such they were completely ignorant. Apparently, Woodcarver was famous for her theory that the heart pumped the blood around the body. Give her another thousand years and maybe she could do better than a butcher!

For a while she hated them all: Scarbutt for all the old reasons, Woodcarver for her ignorance, Vendacious for letting Flenserists get so close to the castle . . . and Johanna Olsndot for rejecting Scriber when he had tried to be a friend.

What would Scriber say now? He had wanted her to trust them. He said that Scarbutt and the others were good people. One night, about a week later, she came close to making peace with herself. She was lying on her pallet, the quilt heavy and warm upon her. The designs painted on the walls glimmered dim in the emberlight. *All right, Scriber. For you . . . I will trust them.*

20

Pham Nuwen remembered almost nothing of the first days after dying, after the pain of the Old One's ending. Ghostly figures, anonymous words. Someone said he'd been kept alive in the ship's surgeon. He remembered none of it. Why they kept the body breathing was a mystery and an affront. Eventually the animal reflexes had revived. The body began breathing of its own accord. The eyes opened. No brain damage, Greenstalk(?) said, a full recovery. The husk that had been a living being spoke no contradiction.

What was left of Pham Nuwen spent a lot of time on the *OOB*'s bridge. From before, the ship reminded him of a fat sowbug. The bugs had been common in the straw laid across the floor of the Great Hall of his father's castle on Canberra. The little kids had played with them. The critters didn't have real legs, just a dozen feathery spines sticking out from a chitinous thorax. No matter how you tumbled them, those spines/antennas would twitch the bug around and it would scuttle on its way, unmindful that it might be upside down from before. Yes, the *OOB*'s ultradrive spines looked a lot like a sowbug's, though not as articulated. And the body itself was fat and sleek, slightly narrowed in the middle.

So Pham Nuwen had ended inside of a sowbug. How fitting for a dead man.

And now he sat on the bridge. The woman brought him there often; she seemed to know it should fascinate him. The walls were displays, better than he had ever seen in merchantman days. When the windows looked out the ship's exterior cameras, the view was as good as from any crystal-canopy bridge in the Qeng Ho fleet.

It was like something out of the crudest fantasy – or a graphics simulation. If he sat long enough, he could actually see the stars *move* in the sky. The ship was doing about ten ultrajumps per second: jump, recompute and jump again. In this part of The Beyond they could go a thousandth of a light-year on each jump – farther, but then the recompute time would be substantially worse. At ten per second that added up to more than thirty light-years per hour. The jumps themselves were imperceptible to human senses, and between the jumps they were in free fall, carrying the same intrinsic velocity they'd had on departing Relay. So there was none of the doppler shifting of relativistic flight; the stars were as pure as seen from some desert sky, or in low-speed transit. Without any fuss, they simply slid across the sky, the closer ones the faster. In half an hour he went farther than he had in half a century with the Qeng Ho.

Greenstalk drifted onto the bridge one day and began

changing the windows. As usual she spoke to Pham as she did so, chatting almost as if there were a real person here to listen:

'See. The center window is an ultrawave map of the region directly behind us.' Greenstalk waved a tendril over the controls. The multicolored pictures appeared on the other walls. 'Similarly for the other five points of direction.'

The words were noise in Pham's ears, understood but of no interest. The Rider paused, then continued with something like the futile persistence of the Ravna woman.

'When ships make a jump . . . when they reenter, there's a kind of an ultrawave *splash*. I'm checking if we're being followed.'

Colors on the windows all around, even in front of Pham's eyes. There were smooth gradations, no bright spots, no linear features.

'I know, I know,' she said, making up both sides of the conversation. 'The ship's analyzers are still massaging the data. But if anyone's pacing us closer than one hundred light-years, we'll see them. And if they're farther than that – well, then they probably can't detect *us*.'

It doesn't matter. Pham almost shut the question out of his mind. But there were no stars to look at; he stared at the glowing colors and actually thought about the problem. *Thought*. A joke: no one Down Here ever really thought about anything. Perhaps ten thousand starships had escaped the Fall of Relay. Most likely the Enemy had not cataloged those departures. The attack on Relay had been a minor adjunct to the murder of Old One. Most likely the *OOB* had escaped unnoticed. Why should the Enemy care where the last of Old One's memories might be hiding? Why should it care about where their little ship might be bound?

A tremor passed through his body; animal reflex, surely.

Panic was slowly rising in Ravna Bergsndot, every day a little stronger. It was not any particular disaster, just the slow dying of hope. She tried to be near Pham Nuwen part of every day, to talk to him, to hold his hand. He never responded, not even – except perhaps by accident – to look at her. Greenstalk tried too. Alien though Greenstalk was, the Pham of before had seemed truly attracted to the Riders. He was off all medical support now, but he might as well have been a vegetable.

And all the while their descent was slowing, always a little worse than what Blueshell had predicted.

And when she turned too the News . . . in some ways that was the most horrifying of all. The 'death race' theory was getting popular. More and more, there were folk who seemed to think that the human race was spreading the Blight:

Crypto: 0
As received by: *OOB* shipboard ad hoc
Language path: Baeloresk→Triskweline, SjK units
From: Alliance for the Defense
  [Claimed cooperative of five polyspecific empires in the Beyond below Straumli Realm. No record of existence before the Fall of the Realm.]
Subject: Blighter Video thread
Distribution:
  Threat of the Blight
  War Trackers Interest Group
  Homo Sapiens Interest Group
Date: 17.95 days since Fall of Relay
Test of message:
  So far we've processed half a million messages about this creature's video, and read a goodly fraction of them. Most of you are missing the point. The principle of the 'Helper's' operation is clear. This is a Transcendent Power using ultralight communication to operate through a race in the Beyond. It would be fairly easy to do in the Transcend – there are a number of stories about thralls of Powers there. But for such communication to be effective within the Beyond, truly extensive design changes must be made in the minds of the controlled race. *It could not have happened naturally*, and it can not be quickly done to new races – no matter what the Blight says.
  We've watched the Homo Sapiens interest group since the first appearance of the Blight. Where is this 'Earth' the humans claim to be from? 'Half way around

the galaxy,' they say, and deep in the Slow Zone. Even their proximate origin, Nyjora, is conveniently in the Slowness. We see an alternative theory: Sometime, maybe further back than the last consistent archives, there was a battle between Powers. The blueprint for this 'human race' was written, complete with communication interfaces. Long after the original contestants and their stories had vanished, this race happened to get in position where it could Transcend. And that Transcending was tailor-made, too, re-establishing the Power that had set the trap to begin with.

We're not sure of the details, but a scenario such as this is inevitable. What we must do is also clear. Straumli Realm is at the heart of the Blight, obviously beyond all attack. But there are other human colonies. We ask the Net to help in identifying all of them. We ourselves are not a large civilization, but we would be happy to coordinate the information gathering, and the military action that is required to prevent the Blight's spread in the Middle Beyond.

For nearly seventeen weeks, we've been calling for action. Had you listened in the beginning, a concerted strike might have been sufficient to destroy the Straumli Realm. Isn't the Fall of Relay enough to wake you up? Friends, if we act together we still have a chance.

Death to vermin.

The bastards even played on humanity's foundling nature. Foundling races were rare, but scarcely unknown. Now these Death-to-Vermin creatures were turning the Miracle of Nyjora into something deadly evil.

Death to Vermin were the only ones to call for pogroms, but even respected posters were saying things that indirectly might support such action:

Crypto: 0
As received by: *OOB* shipboard ad hoc

Language path: Triskweline, SjK units
From: Sandor Arbitration Intelligence at the Zoo [A
    known military corporation of the High Beyond. If
    this is a masquerade, somebody is living danger-
    ously.]
Subject: Blighter Video thread, Hanse subthread
Key phrases: limits on the Blight; the Blight is search-
    ing for something
Distribution:
    Threat of the Blight
    Close-coupled Automation Interest Group
    War Trackers Interest Group
Date: 11.94 days since Fall of Relay
Text of message:

The Blight admits that it is a Power that tele-
operates sophonts in the Beyond. But consider how
difficult it is to have a close-coupled automation with
time lags of more than a few milliseconds. The Known
Net is a perfect illustration of this: Lags range between
five milliseconds for systems that are a couple of light-
years apart – to (at least) several hundred seconds
when messages must pass through intermediate
nodes. This, combined with the low bandwidth available across interstellar distances, makes the Known
Net a loose forum for the exchange of information and
lies. And these restrictions are *inherent* in the nature of
the Beyond, part of the same restrictions that make it
impossible for the Powers to exist down here.

We conclude that even the Blight can't attain close-
coupled control except in the High Beyond. At the top,
the Blight's sophont agents are literally its limbs. In the
Middle Beyond, we believe mental 'possession' is
possible but that considerable preprocessing must be
done in the controlled mind. Furthermore, considerable external equipment (the bulky items characteristic of those depths) is needed to support the
communication. Direct, millisecond-by-millisecond,
control is normally impractical in the Middle Beyond.
Combat at this level would involve hierarchical control.

Long-term operations would also use intimidation, fraud, and traitors.

These are the threats that you of the Middle and Low Beyond should recognize.

These are the Blight's tools in the Middle and Low Beyond, and what you should guard against for the immediate future. We don't see imperial takeovers; there's no profit [sustenance] in it. Even the destruction of Relay was probably just a byplay to the murder it was simultaneously committing in the Transcend. The greatest tragedies will continue to be at the Top and in the Low Transcend. But we know that the Blight is searching for something; it has attacked at great distances where major archives were the target. Beware of traitors and spies.

Even some of humanity's supporters sent a chill through Ravna:

Crypto: 0
As received by: *OOB* shipboard ad hoc
Language path: Triskweline, SjK units
From: Hanse
Subject: Blighter Video thread, Alliance for the
    Defense subthread
Key phrases: Death Race Theory
Distribution:
    Threat of the Blight
    War Trackers Interest Group
    Homo Sapiens Interest Group
Date: 18.29 days since Fall of Relay
Text of message:
    I have obtained specimens from the human worlds in our volume. Detailed analysis is available in Homo sapiens interest group archive. My conclusions: previous (but less intensive) analysis of human phys/psych is correct. The race has *no* built-in structures to support remote control. Experiments with living subjects showed no special inclination toward submission. I

found little or no evidence of artificial optimization. (There was evidence of DNA surgery to improve disease resistance: drift timing dated the hackwork at two thousand years Before Present. The blood of Straumli Realm subjects carried an optigens, Thirault [a cheap medical recipe that can be tailored across a wide mammalian range].) This race — as represented by my specimens — looks like something that arrived from the Slow Zone quite recently, probably from a single origin world.

Has anyone done such retesting on more distant human worlds?

Crypto: 0
As received by: *OOB* shipboard ad hoc
Language path: Baeloresk→Triskweline, SjK units
From: Alliance for the Defense
　　[Claimed cooperative of five polyspecific empires in the Beyond below Straumli Realm. No record of existence before the Fall of the Realm.]
Subject: Blighter Video thread, Hanse 1
Distribution:
　　Threat of the Blight
　　War Trackers Interest Group
　　Homo Sapiens Interest Group
Date: 19.43 days since Fall of Relay
Text of message:

Who is this 'Hanse'? It makes objective, tough-sounding noises about testing human specimens, but it keeps its own nature secret. Don't be fooled by humans telling you about themselves! In fact, we have no way of testing the creatures that dwell in Straumli Realm; their protector will see to that.

Death to vermin.

And there was a little boy trapped at the bottom of the well. Some days, no communication was possible. Other days, when the *OOB* antenna swarm was tuned in exactly the right direction and when the vagaries of the zone favored it — then

Ravna could hear his ship. Even then the signal was so faint, so distorted, that the effective transmission rate was just a few bits per second.

Jefri and his problems might be only the smallest footnote to the story of the Blight (less than that, since no one knew of him), but to Ravna Bergsndot these conversations were the only bright thing in her life just now.

The kid was very lonely, but less so now, she thought. She learned about his friend Amdi, about the stern Tyrathect and the heroic Mr Steel and the proud Tines. Ravna smiled to herself, at herself. The walls of her cabin displayed a flat mural of jungle. Deep in the drippy murk lay regular shadows – a castle built in the roots of a giant mangrove tree. The mural was a famous one; the original had been an analog work from two thousand years ago. It showed life at an even further remove, during the Dark Ages on Nyjora. She and Lynne had spent much of their childhood imagining that they were transported to such a time. Little Jefri was trapped in the real thing. Woodcarver's butchers were no interstellar threat, but they were a deadly horror to those around them. Thank goodness Jefri had not seen the killings.

This was a real medieval world. A tough and unforgiving place, even if Jefri had fallen in with fair-minded people. And the Nyjoran comparison was only vaguely appropriate. These Tines were pack minds; even old Grondr Kalir had been surprised at that.

All through Jefri's mail, Ravna could see the panic among Steel's people:

Mister Steel asked me again if theres any way we can make our ship to fly even a little. I dont know. We almost crashed, I think. We need guns. That would save us, least till you get here. They have bows and arrows just like in Nyjoran days, but no guns. Hes asking me, can you teach us to make guns?

Woodcarver's raiders would return, and this time in enough force to overrun Steel's little kingdom. Back when they thought OOB's flight would be only forty days, that had

234

not seemed a great risk, but now . . . Ravna might arrive to find Woodcarver's murdering complete.

Oh Pham, dear Pham. If you ever really were, please come back now. Pham Nuwen of medieval Canberra. Pham Nuwen, trader from the Slowness . . . *What would someone such as you make of this? Hmm.*

21

Ravna knew that – under his bluster – Blueshell was at least as much a worrier as she. Worse, he was a nitpicker. The next time Ravna asked him about their progress, he retreated into technicalities.

Finally Ravna broke in, 'Look. The kid is sitting on something that *just might* blow the Blight sky high, and all he has are bows and arrows. How long will it be till we get down there, Blueshell?'

Blueshell rolled nervously back and forth across the ceiling. The Skroderiders had reaction jets; they could maneuver in free fall more adroitly than most humans. Instead they used stick-patches, and rolled around on the walls. In a way, it was kind of cute. Just now, it was irritating.

, At least they could talk; she glanced across the bridge to where Pham Nuwen sat facing the bridge's main display. As usual, all his attention was fixed on the slowly moving stars. He was unshaven, his reddish beard bright on his skin; his long hair floated snarled and uncombed. Physically he was cured of his injuries. Ship's surgeon had even replaced the muscle mass that Old One's communication equipment had usurped. Pham could dress and feed himself now, but he still lived in a private dreamworld.

The two riders twittered at each other. It was Greenstalk who finally answered her question: 'Truly, we're not sure how long. The quality of the Beyond changes as we descend. Each jump is taking us a fraction longer than the one before.'

'I know that. We're moving toward the Slow Zone. But the

ship is designed for that; it should be an easy matter to extrapolate the slowing.'

Blueshell extended a tendril from ceiling to floor. He diddled with the matte corrugations for a second and then his voder made a sound of human embarrassment. 'Ordinarily you would be correct, my lady Ravna. But this is a special case . . . For one thing, it appears that the zones themselves are in flux.'

'What?'

'It's not that unheard of. Small shifts are going on all the time. That's a major purpose for bottom-lugger ships: to track the changes. We're having the bad luck to run through the middle of the uncertainty.'

Actually, Ravna had known that interface turbulence was high at the Bottom below here. She just didn't think of it in grandiose terms like 'zone shifting'; she also hadn't realized it was serious enough to affect them yet.

'Okay. How bad can it get then? How much can it slow us?'

'Oh my.' Blueshell rolled to the far wall; he was standing on starry sky now. 'It would be nice to be a Lesser Skroderider. So many problems my high calling brings me. I wish I could be deep in surf right now, thinking on olden memories.' Of other days in the surf.

Greenstalk carried on for him: 'It's not "the tide, how high can it rise?" It's "this storm, how bad can it get?" Right now it is worse than anything in this region during the last thousand-years. However, we have been following the local news; most agree that the storm has peaked. If our other problem gets no worse, we should arrive in about one hundred and twenty days.'

Our other problem. Ravna drifted to the center of the bridge and strapped onto a saddle. 'You're talking about the damage we took getting out of Relay. The ultradrive spines, right? How are they holding up?'

'Quite well, apparently. We've not tried to jump faster than eighty percent of design max. On the other hand, we lack good diagnostics. It's conceivable that serious degradation might happen rather suddenly.'

'Conceivable, but unlikely,' put in Greenstalk.

Ravna nodded. Considering all their other problems, there was no point in contemplating possibilities beyond their control. Back on Relay, this had looked like a thirty or forty day trip. Now . . . the boy in the well might have to be brave for a long time yet, no matter how much she wished otherwise. *Hmm. Time for Plan B then. Time for what someone like Pham Nuwen might suggest.* She pushed off the floor and settled by Greenstalk. 'Okay, so the best we can plan on is one hundred and twenty days. If the Zone surge gets worse or if we have to get repairs . . .' Get repairs where? That might be only a delay, not an impossibility. The rebuilt *OOB* was supposed to be repairable even in the Low Beyond. 'Maybe even two hundred days.' She glanced at Blueshell, but he didn't interrupt with his usual amendments and qualifications. 'You've both read the messages we're getting from the boy. He says the locals are going to be overrun, probably in less than one hundred days. Somehow, we have to help him . . . before we actually arrive there.'

Greenstalk rattled her fronds in a way Ravna took for puzzlement.

She looked across the deck at Pham and raised her voice a trifle. *Hey you, you should be an expert on this!* 'You Skroderiders may not recognize it, but this is a problem that's been seen a million times in the Slow Zone: civilizations are separated by years – centuries – of travel time. They fall into dark ages. They become just as primitive as the pack creatures, these "Tines." Then they get visited from outside. In a short time, they have technology back again.' Pham's head did not turn; he just looked out across the starscape.

The Skroderiders rattled at each other, then:

'But how can that help us? Doesn't rebuilding a civilization take dozens of years?'

'And besides, there's nothing to rebuild on the Tines' world. According to the child, this is a world without antecedents. How long does it take to start a new civilization from scratch?'

Ravna waved a hand at the objections. *Don't stop me, I'm on a roll.* 'That's not the point. *We* are in communication with them. We have a good general library on board. Original

237

inventors don't know where they're going; they're groping in the dark. Even the archaeologist/engineers of Nyjora had to reinvent much. But we know everything about making airplanes and such; we know hundreds of ways of going at it.' Now faced with necessity, Ravna was suddenly sure they could do it. 'We can study all the development paths, eliminate the deads ends. Even more, we can find the quickest way to go from medieval to specific inventions, things that can beat whatever barbarians are attacking Jefri's friends.'

Ravna's speech tumbled to a stop. She stared, grinning, first at Greenstalk and then at Blueshell. But a silent Skroderider is one of the universe's more impassive audiences. It was hard even to tell if they were looking at her. After a moment Greenstalk said, 'Yes, I see. And rediscovery being so common in the Slow Zone, most of this may already be worked out in the ship's library.'

That's when it happened: Pham turned from the window. He looked across the deck at Ravna and the Riders. For the first time since Relay, he spoke. Even more, the words weren't nonsense, though it took her a moment to understand. 'Guns and radios,' he said.

'Ah . . . yes.' She looked back at him. *Think of something to make him say more.* 'Why those in particular?'

Pham Nuwen shrugged. 'It worked on Canberra.'

Then damn Blueshell started talking, something about doing a library search. Pham stared at them for a moment, his face expressionless. He turned back to watch the stars, and the moment was lost.

22

'Pham?' He heard Ravna's voice just behind him. She had stayed on the bridge after the Riders left, departing on whatever meaningless preparations their meeting had ordained. He didn't reply, and after a moment she drifted

around and blocked his view of the stars. Almost automatically, he found himself focussing on her face.

'Thank you for talking to us . . . We need you more than
ever.'

He could still see lots of stars. They were all around her,
slowly moving. Ravna cocked her head, the way she did when
she meant friendly puzzlement. 'We can help . . .'

He didn't answer. What *had* made him speak just now?
Then: 'You can't help the dead,' he said, vaguely surprised at
his own speaking. Like eye focussing, the speech must be a
reflex.

'You're not dead. You're as alive as I am.'

Then words tumbled from him; more than in all the days
since Relay. 'True. The illusion of self-awareness. Happy
automatons, running on trivial programs. I'll bet you never
guess. From the inside, how can you? From the outside, from
Old One's view −' He looked away from her, dizzy with a
doubled vision.

Ravna drifted closer till her face was just centimeters from
his. She floated free, except for one foot tucked into the floor.
'Dear Pham, you are wrong. You've been at the Bottom, and
at the Top, but never in between . . . "The illusion of self
awareness"? That's a commonplace of any practical
philosophy in the Beyond. It has some beautiful consequences, and some scary ones. All you know are the scary
ones. Think: the illusion must apply just as surely to the
Powers.'

'No. He could *make* devices like you and I.'

'Being dead is a choice, Pham.' She reached out to pass her
hand down his shoulder and arm. He had a typical o-gee
change of perspective; 'down' seemed to rotate sideways, and
he was looking up at her. Suddenly he was aware of his
splotchy beard, his tangled hair floating all about. He looked
up at Ravna, remembering everything he'd thought about
her. Back on Relay she'd seemed bright; maybe not smarter
than he, but as smart as most competitors of the Qeng Ho.
But there were other memories, how Old One had seen her.
As usual, His memories were overwhelming. As usual, they
were mostly unintelligible. Even His emotions were hard to

interpret. But . . . He had thought of Ravna a little like . . . a favored dog. Old One could see right through her. Ravna Bergsndot was a little manipulative; He had been pleased/amused(?) by that fact. But behind her talk and argument, He'd seen a great deal of . . . 'goodness' might be the human word. Old One had wished her well. *In the end, He had even tried to help.* Insight flitted past him, too fast to catch. Ravna was talking again:

'What happened to you is terrible enough, Pham, but it's happened to others. I've read of cases. Even the Powers are not immortal. Sometimes they fight among themselves, and someone gets killed. Sometimes, one commits suicide. There's a star system, Gods' Doom it's called in the story: A million years ago, it was in the Transcend. It was visited by a party of the Powers. There was a Zone surge. Suddenly the system was twenty light-years deep in the Beyond. That's about the biggest surge there is firm record of. The Powers at God's Doom didn't have a chance. They all died, some to rot and rusted ruin . . . others to the level of mere human minds.'

'W-what became of those?'

She hesitated, took one of his hands between hers. 'You can look it up. The point is, it happens. To the victims, it's the end of the world. But from *our* side, the human side . . . Well, the human Pham Nuwen was lucky; Greenstalk says the failure of Old One's connections didn't do gross organic damage. Maybe there's subtle damage; sometimes the remnants just destroy themselves, whatever is left.'

Pham felt tears leaking from his eyes. And knew that part of the deadness inside had been grief for His own death. 'Subtle damage!' He shook his head and the tears drifted into the air. 'My head is stuffed with Him, with His memories.' Memories? They towered over everything else. *Yet he could not understand them.* He could not understand the details. He could not even understand the emotions, except as inane simplifications – joy, laughter, wonder, fear and icy-steel determination. Now he was lost in those memories, wandering like an idiot in a cathedral. Not understanding, cowering before icons.

She pivoted around their clasped hands. After a moment

her knee bumped gently against his. 'You're still human, you still have your own –', her own voice broke as she saw the look in his eyes.

'My own memories.' Scattered amid the unintelligible he would stumble on: Himself at five years, sitting on the straw in the great hall, alert for the appearance of any adult; royals were not supposed to play in the filth. Ten years later, making love to Cindi for the first time. A year after that, seeing his first flying machine, the orbital ferry that landed on his father's parade field. The decades aspace. 'Yes, the Qeng Ho. Pham Nuwen, the great Trader of the Slowness. All the memories are still there. And for all I know, it's all the Old One's lie, an afternoon's fraud to fool the Relayers.'

Ravna bit her lip, but didn't say anything. She was too honest to lie, even now.

He reached with his free hand to brush her hair away from her face. 'I know you said that too, Rav. Don't feel bad: I would have suspected by now anyway.'

'Yeah,' she said softly. Then she was looking him straight in the eye. 'But know this. One human to another: You *are* a human now. And there could have been a Qeng Ho, and you could have been exactly what you remember. And whatever the past, you could be great in the future.'

Ghostly echoes, more than memory and less than reason: For an instant he saw her with wiser eyes. *She loves you, foolish one.* Almost laughter, kindly laughter.

He slid his arms around her, drawing her tight against him. She was so real. He felt her slip her leg between his. To laugh. Like heart massage, unthinking reflex bringing a mind back to life. So foolish, so trivial, but, 'I – I want to come back.' The words came out strangled in sobs. 'There's so much inside me now, so much I can't understand. I'm lost inside my own head.'

She didn't say anything, probably couldn't even understand his speech. For a moment all he knew was the feel of her in his arms, hugging back. *Oh please, I do want to come back.*

Making it on the bridge of a starship was something Ravna

had never done before. But then she'd never had her own starship before, either. *They don't call this a bottom-lugger for nothing.* In the excitement, Pham lost his tiedown. They floated free, occasionally bumping into walls and discarded clothing, or drifting through tears. After many minutes, they ended up with their heads just a few centimeters off the floor, the rest of them angled off toward the ceiling. She was vaguely aware that her pants were flying like a banner from where they had caught on her ankle. The affair wasn't quite the stuff of romance fiction. For one thing, floating free you just couldn't get any leverage. For another . . . Pham leaned back from her, relaxing his grip on her back. She brushed aside his red hair and looked into bloodshot eyes. 'You know,' he said shakily, 'I never guessed I could cry so hard my face hurt.'

She smiled back. 'You've led a charmed life then.' She arched her back against his hands, then drew him gently close. They floated in silence for several minutes, their bodies relaxing into each other's curves, sensing nothing but each other.

Then: 'Thank you, Ravna.'

'. . . my pleasure,' her voice came dreamy serious, and she hugged him tighter. Strange, all the things he had been to her, some frightening, some endearing, some enraging. And some she couldn't have admitted – even to herself – till now. For the first time since the fall of Relay, she felt real hope. A silly physical reaction maybe . . . but maybe not. Here in her arms was a guy who might be the equal of any story book adventurer, and more: someone who had been part of a Power.

'Pham . . . what do you think really happened back on Relay? Why was Old One murdered?'

Pham's chuckle seemed unforced, but his arms stiffened around her. 'You're asking me? I was dying at the time, remember . . . No, that's wrong. Old One, *He* was dying at the time.' He was silent for a minute. The bridge turned slowly around them, silent views on the stars beyond. 'My godself was in pain, I know that. He was desperate, panicked . . . But He was also trying to do something to me before He died.'

His voice went soft, wondering. 'Yes. It was like I was some cheap piece of luggage, and He was stuffing me with every piece of crap that he could move. You know, ten kilos in a nine kilo sack. He knew it was hurting me – I was part of Him, after all – but that didn't matter.' He twisted back from her, his face getting a little wild again. 'I'm not a sadist; I don't believe He was either I –'

Ravna shook her head. 'I . . . I think he was downloading.'

Pham was silent an instant, trying to fit the idea into his situation. 'That doesn't make sense. There's not *room* in me to be superhuman.' Fear chased hope in tight circles.

'No, no, wait. You're right. Even if the dying Power figures reincarnation is possible, there's not enough space in a normal brain to store much. But Old One was trying for something else . . . Remember how I begged Him to help with our trip to the Bottom?'

'Yes. I – He – was sympathetic, the way you might be with animals that are confronting some new predator. He never considered that the Perversion might be a threat to him, not until –'

'Right. Not until he was under attack. That was a complete surprise to the Powers; suddenly the Perversion was more than a curious problem for underminds. *Then* Old One really did try to help. He jammed plans and automation down into you. He jammed so much, you nearly died, so much you can't make sense of it. I've read about things like that in Applied Theology –' as much legend as fact. 'Godshatter, it's called.'

'Godshatter?' He seemed to play with the word, wondering. 'What a strange name. I remember His panic. But if He was doing what you say, why didn't He just *tell* me? And if I'm filled with good advice, how come all I see inside is . . .' his gaze became a little like days past, 'darkness . . . dark statues with sharp edges, crowding.'

Again a long silence. But now she could almost feel Pham thinking. His arms twitched tight and an occasional shudder swept his body. 'Yes . . . yes. Lots of things fit. Most of it I still don't understand, never will. Old One discovered something right there at the end.' His arms tightened again, and he

243

buried his face against her neck. 'It was a very . . . personal . . . sort of murder the Perversion committed on Him. Even dying, Old One learned.' More silence. 'The Perversion is something very old, Ravna. Probably billions of years. A threat Old One could only theorize before it actually killed Him. But . . .'

One minute. Two. Yet Pham did not continue. 'Don't worry, Pham. Give it time.'

'Yeah.' He backed off far enough to look her square in the face. 'But I know this much now: Old One did this for a reason. We *aren't* on a fool's chase. There's something on the Bottom, in that Straumer ship, that Old One thought could make a difference.'

He ran his hand lightly across her face, and his smile was sad where there should have been joy. 'But don't you see, Ravna? If you're right, today may be the most human I'll ever be. I'm full of Old One's download, this godshatter. Most of it I'll never consciously understand, but if things work properly, it will eventually come exploding out. His remote device; His robot at the Bottom of the Beyond.'

No! But she made herself shrug. 'Maybe. But you're human, and we're working for the same things . . . and I'm not letting you go.'

Ravna had known that 'jumpstarting' technology must be a topic in the ship's library. It turned out the subject was a major academic specialty. Besides ten thousand case studies, there were customizing programs and lots of very dull-looking theory. Though the 'rediscovery problem' was trivial in the Beyond, down in the Slow Zone almost every conceivable combination of events had happened. Civilizations in the Slowness could not last more than a few thousand years. Their collapse was sometimes a short eclipse, a few decades spent recovering from war or atmosphere-bashing. Others drove themselves back to medievalism. And of course, most races eventually exterminated themselves, at least within their single solar system. Those that didn't exterminate themselves (and even a few of those that did) eventually struggled back to their original heights.

The study of these variations was called the Applied History of Technology. Unfortunately for both academicians and the civilizations in the Slow Zone, true applications were a bit rare: The events of the case studies were centuries old before news of them reached the Beyond, and few researchers were willing to do field work in the Slow Zone, where finding and conducting a single experiment could cost them much of their lives. In any case, it was a nice hobby for millions of university departments. One of the favorite games was to devise minimal paths from a given level of technology back to the highest level that could be supported in the Slowness. The details depended on many things, including the initial level of primitiveness, the amount of residual scientific awareness (or tolerance), and the physical nature of the race. The historians' theories were captured in programs whose inputs were facts about the civilization's plight and the desired results, and whose outputs were the steps that would most quickly produce those results.

Two days later the four of them were back on the *OOB*'s bridge. *And this time we're all talking.* 'So we must decide what inventions to shoot for, something that will defend the Hidden Island Kingdom –'

'– and something "Mister Steel" can make in less than one hundred days,' said Blueshell. He had spent most of the last two days fiddling with the development programs in *OOB*'s library.

'I still say guns and radios,' said Pham.

Firepower and communications. Ravna grinned at him. Pham's human memories alone would be enough to save the kids on Tines' World. He hadn't talked any more of Old One's plans. Old One's plans . . . in Ravna's mind those were something like fate, perhaps good, perhaps terrible, but unknown for now. *And even fate can be weaseled.* 'How about it Blueshell?' she said. 'Is radio something they can produce quickly, from a standing start?' On Nyjora, radio had come almost contemporary with orbital flight – a good century into the renaissance.

'Indeed, my lady Ravna. There are simple tricks that are almost never noticed till a very high technology is attained.

For instance, quantum torsion antennas can be built from silver and cobalt steel arrays, if the geometry is correct. Unfortunately, finding the proper geometry involves lots of theory and the ability to solve some large partial differential equations. There are many Slow Zoners who never discover the principle.'

'Okay,' said Pham. 'But there's still a translation problem. Jefri has probably heard the word "cobalt" before, but how can he describe it to people who don't have the referent? Without knowing a lot more about their world, we couldn't even describe how to find cobalt-bearing ore.'

'That will slow things down,' Blueshell admitted. 'But the program accounts for it. Mr Steel seems to understand the concept of experimentation. For cobalt, we can provide him with a tree of experiments based on descriptions of likely ores and appropriate chemical tests.'

'It's not quite that simple,' said Greenstalk. 'Some of the chemical tests themselves involve search/test trees. And there are other experiments needed to check toxicity. We know far less about the pack creatures than is usual with this program.'

Pham smiled. 'I hope these creatures are properly grateful; I never heard of "quantum torsional antennas." The Tines are ending up with comm gear that Qeng Ho never had.'

But the gift could be made. The question was, could it be done in time to save Jefri and his ship from the Woodcarvers? The four of them ran the program again and again. They knew so little about the pack creatures themselves. The Hidden Island Kingdom appeared fairly flexible. *If* they were willing to go all out to follow the directions, and *if* they had good luck in finding nearby sources for critical materials, then it looked like they might have limited supplies of firearms and radios inside of one hundred days. On the other hand, if the packs of Hidden Island ended up chasing down some worst-case branches of the search trees, things might stretch out to a few years.

Ravna found it hard to accept that no matter what the four of them did, saving Jefri from the Woodcarvers would be partly a matter of luck. *Sigh*. In the end, she took the best scheme they could produce, translated it into Samnorsk, and sent it down.

23

Steel had always admired military architecture. Now he was adding a new chapter to the book, building a castle that protected against the *sky* as well as the land around. By now the boxy 'ship' on stilts was known across the continent. Before another summer passed, there would be enemy armies here, trying to take – or at least destroy – the prize that had come to him. Far more deadly: the Star People would be here. He must be ready.

Steel inspected the work almost every day now. The stone replacement for the palisade was in place all across the south perimeter. On the cliffside, overlooking Hidden Island, his new den was almost complete . . . *had been complete for some time*, a part of him grumbled. He really should move over here; the safety of Hidden Island was fast becoming illusion. Starship Hill was already the center of the Movement – and that wasn't just propaganda. What the Flenser embassies abroad called 'the oracle on Starship Hill' was more than a glib liar could dream. Whoever stood nearest that oracle would ultimately rule, no matter how clever Steel might be otherwise. He had already transferred or exectued several attendants, packs who seemed just a little *too* friendly with Amdijefri.

Starship Hill: When the aliens landed, it had been heather and rock. Through the winter, there'd been a palisade and a wooden shelter. But now construction had resumed on the castle, the crown whose jewel was the starship. Soon this hill would be the capital of the continent and the world. And after that . . . Steel looked into the blue depths of the sky. How much further his rule extended would depend on saying just the right thing, on building this castle in a very special way. *Enough dreaming.* Lord Steel pulled himself together and descended from the new wall along fresh-cut stone stairs. The yard within was twelve acres, mostly mud. The muck was cold on his paws, but the snow and slush was confined to dwindling piles away from the work routes. Spring was well-advanced, and the sun was warm in the chill air. He could see for miles, out over Hidden Island all the way to the Ocean, and down the coast along the fjord country. Steel walked the last hundred yards up the hill to the starship. His guards paced him on either side, with Shreck bringing up the rear. There was enough room that the workers didn't have to back away – and he had given orders that no one was to stop because of his presence. That was partly to maintain the fraud with Amdijefri, and partly because the Movement needed this fortress soon. Just how soon was a question that gnawed.

Steel was still looking in all directions, but his attention was where it should be now, on the construction work. The yard was piled with cut stone and construction timbers. Now that the ground was thawing, the foundations for the inner wall were being dug. Where it was still hard, Steel's engineers were injecting boiling water. Steam rose from the holes, obscuring the windlasses and the diggers below. The place was louder than a battlefield: windlasses creaking, blades hacking at dirt, leaders shouting to work teams. It was also as crowded as close combat, though not nearly so chaotic.

Steel watched a digger pack at the bottom of one of the trenches. There were thirty members, so close to each other their shoulders sometimes touched. It was an enormous mob, but there was nothing of an orgy about the association. Even before Woodcarver, construction and factory guilds had been doing this sort of thing: The thirty-member pack below was probably not as bright as a threesome. The front rank of ten swung mattocks in unison, carving steadily into the wall of dirt. When their heads and mattocks were extended high, the ten members behind them darted forward to scoop back the dirt and rocks that had just been freed. Behind them, a third tier of members hauled the dirt from the pit. Making it work was a complicated bit of timing – the rock and dirt was not homogeneous – but it was well within the mental ability of the pack. They could go on like this for hours, shifting first and second ranks every few minutes. In years past, the guilds jealously guarded the secret of each special melding. After a hard day's work, such a team would split into normally intelligent packs – each going home very well paid. Steel smiled to himself. Woodcarver had improved on the old guild tricks, but Flenser had provided an essential refinement (actually a borrowing from the Tropics). Why let the team break up at the end of a work shift? Flenser work teams stayed together indefinitely, housed in barracks so small they could never recover their separate pack minds. It worked well. After a year or two, and with proper culling, the original packs in such teams were dull things that scarcely wanted to break away.

For a moment Steel watched the cut stone being lowered into the new hole and mortared into place. Then he nodded at the whitejackets in charge and walked on. The foundation holes continued right up to the walls of the starship compound. This was the trickiest construction of all, the part that would turn the castle into a beautiful snare. A little more information via Amdijefri and he would know just what to build.

The door to the starship compound was open just now, and a whitejackets was sitting back to back in the opening. That guard heard the noise an instant before Steel: two of its members broke ranks to look around the side of the compound. Almost inaudibly, there came high screams, then honking attack calls. The whitejackets leaped from the stairs and raced around the building. Steel and his guards weren't far behind.

He skidded to a stop at the foundation trench on the far side of the ship. The immediate source of the racket was obvious. Three packs of whitejackets were putting a team's talker to the question. They had separated out the verbal member and were beating it with truncheon whips. This close, the mental screams were almost as loud as the shouting. The rest of the digger team was coming out of the trench, breaking into functional packs and attacking the whitejackets with their mattocks. How could things get so bloody screwed up? He could guess. These inner foundations were to contain the most secret tunnels of the entire castle, and the even more secret devices he planned to use against the Two-Legs. Of course, all of the workers on such sensitive areas would be disposed of after the job was done. Stupid though they were, maybe they had guessed their fate.

Under other circumstances, Steel might have backed off and simply watched. Failures like this could be enlightening; they let him identify the weaknesses in his subordinates, who was too bad (and too good) to continue in their jobs. *This time was different*. Amdi and Jefri were aboard the starship. There was no view through the wooden walls, and surely there was another whitejackets on guard within, but . . . even as he lunged forward, shouting to his servants, Steel's back-looking member caught sight of Jefri coming out of the compound. Two of the pups were on his shoulders, the rest of Amdi spilling out around him.

'*Stay back!*' he yelled at them, and in his sparse Samnorsk, '*Danger! Stay back!*' Amdi paused, but the Two-Legs kept coming. Two soldier packs scattered out of his way. They had standing orders: *never* touch the alien. Another second and the careful work of a year would be destroyed. Another second and Steel might lose the world – *all on account of stupidity and bad luck*.

But even as his back members were shouting at the Two-Legs, his forward ones leaped atop a pile of stone. He pointed at the teams coming out of the trench. 'Kill the invaders!'

His personal guards moved close around him as Shreck and several troopers streamed by. Steel's consciousness sagged in the bloody noise. This was not the controlled mayhem of experiments beneath Hidden Island. This was random death flying in all directions: arrows, spears, mattocks. Members of the digger team ran about, flailing and crying. They never had a chance, but they killed a number of others in their dying.

Steel backed away from the melee, toward Jefri. The Two-Legs was still running toward him. Amdi followed, shouting in Samnorsk. A single mindless team member, a single misaimed arrow, and the Two-Legs would die and all would be lost. Never in his life had Steel felt such panic for the safety of another. He raced to the human, surrounding him. The Two-Legs fell to his knees and grabbed Steel by a neck. Only a lifetime of discipline kept Steel from slashing back: the alien wasn't attacking, he was *hugging*.

The digger team was almost all dead now, and Shreck had pushed the surviving members too far away to be a threat. Steel's guards were securely around him only five or ten yards away. Amdi was all clumped together, cowering in the mind noise, but still shouting to Jefri. Steel tried to untangle himself from the human, but Jefri just grabbed one neck after another, sometimes two at a time. He was making burbling noises that didn't sound like Samnorsk. Steel trembled under the assault. *Don't show the revulsion.* The human would not recognize it, but Amdi might. Jefri had done this before, and Steel had taken advantage even though it cost him. The mantis child needed physical contact; it was the basis for the relationship between Amdi and Jefri. Similar trust must come from letting this thing touch him. Steel slid a head and neck across the creature's back the way he had seen parents do with pups down in the dungeon laboratories. Jefri hugged him harder, and swept his long articulate paws across Steel's pelt. Revulsion aside, it was a very strange experience. Ordinarily such close contact with another intelligent being could only come in battle or in sex – and in either case, there wasn't much room for rational thought. But with this human – well, the creature responded with obvious intelligence – but there wasn't a trace of mind noise. You could think and feel both at the same time. Steel bit down on a lip, trying to stifle his shivering. It was . . . it was like having sex with a corpse.

Finally Jefri stepped back, holding his hand up. He said something very fast, and Amdi said, 'Oh Lord Steel, you're hurt. See the blood.' There was red on the human's paw; Steel looked at himself. Sure enough, one rump had taken a nick. He hadn't even felt it in all the excitement. Steel backed away from the mantis and said to Amdi, 'It's nothing. Are you and Jefri unhurt?'

There was a rattling exchange between the two children, almost unintelligible to Steel. 'We're fine. Thank you for protecting us.'

Fast thinking was something that Flenser had carved into Steel with knives: 'Yes. But it never should have happened. The Woodcarvers disguised themselves as workers. I think they've been at this for days waiting for a chance at you. When we guessed the fraud, it was almost too late ... You really should have stayed inside when you heard the fighting.'

Amdi hung his heads ashamedly, and translated to Jefri. 'We're sorry. We got excited, and t-then we thought you might get hurt.'

Steel made comforting noises. At the same time, two of him looked around at the carnage. Where was the white-jackets that had deserted the stairs right at the beginning? That pack would pay – His line of thought crashed to a halt as he noticed: *Tyrathect.* The Flenser Fragment was watching from the meeting hall. Now that he thought about it, he'd been watching since right after the battle began. To others his posture might seem impassive, but Steel could see the grim amusement in the Fragment's expression. He nodded briefly at the other, but inside Steel cringed; he had been so close to losing everything ... *and the Flenser had noticed.*

'Well let's get you two back to Hidden Island.' He signaled to the keepers that had come up behind the starship.

'Not yet, Lord Steel!' said Amdi. 'We just got here. A reply from Ravna should arrive very soon.'

Teeth grated, but out of sight of the children. 'Yes, please do stay. But we'll all be more careful now, right?'

'Yes, yes!' Amdi explained to the human. Steel stood forelegs-on-shoulders and patted Jefri on the head.

Steel had Shreck take the children back into the compound. Till they were out of sight, all his members looked on with an expression of pride and affection. Then he turned and walked across the pinkish mud. Where was that stupid whitejackets?

The meeting hall on Starship Hill was a small, temporary thing. It had been good enough to keep the cold out during the winter, but for a conference of more than three people it was a real madhouse. Steel stomped past the Flenser Fragment and collected himself on the loft with the best view of the construction work. After a polite moment, Tyrathect entered and climbed to the facing loft.

But all the decorum was an act for the groundlings outside; now Flenser's soft laughter hissed across the air to him, just loud enough for him to hear. 'Dear Steel. Sometimes I wonder if you are truly my student . . . or perhaps some changeling inserted after my departure. Are you *trying* to screw us up?'

Steel glared back. He was sure there was no uneasiness in his posture, all that was held within. 'Accidents happen. The incompetent will be culled.'

'Quite so. But that appears to be your response to *all* problems. If you hadn't been so bent on silencing the digger teams, they might not have rioted . . . and you would have had one less "accident."'

'The flaw was in their guessing. Such executions are a necessary part of military construction.'

'Oh? You really think I had to kill all those who built the halls under Hidden Island?'

'*What?* You mean you didn't? How –?'

The Flenser Fragment smiled the old, fanged smile. 'Think on it, Steel. An exercise.'

Steel arranged his notes on the desk and pretended to study them. Then all of him looked back at the other pack. 'Tyrathect. I honor you because of the Flenser in you. But remember: You survive on my sufferance. You are not the Flenser-in-Waiting.' The news had come late last fall, just before winter closed the last pass over the Icefangs: The packs bearing the rest of the Master hadn't made it out of Parliament Bowl. The fullness of Flenser was gone forever. That had been an indescribable relief to Steel, and for a time afterward the Fragment had been quite tractable. 'Not one of my lieutenants would blink if I killed all of you – even the Flenser members.' *And I'll do it, if you push me hard enough, I swear I will.*

'Of course, dear Steel. You command.'

For an instant the other's fear showed through. *Remember,* Steel thought to himself, *always remember: This is just a fragment of the Master. Most of it is a little school teacher, not the*

Great Teacher with a Knife. True, its two Flenser members totally dominated the pack. The spirit of the Master was right here in this room, but gentled. Tyrathect could be managed, and the power of the Master used for Steel's ends.

'Good,' Steel said smoothly. 'As long as you understand this, you can be of great use to the Movement. In particular,' he riffled through the papers, 'I want to review the Visitor situation with you.' *I want some advice.*

'Yes.'

'We've convinced "Ravna" that her precious Jefri is in imminent danger. Amdijefri has told her about all the Woodcarver attacks and how we fear an overwhelming assault.'

'And that may really happen.'

'Yes. Woodcarver really *is* planning an attack, and she has her own source of "magical" help. We have something much better.' He tapped the papers; the advice had been coming down since early winter. He remembered when Amdijefri had brought in the first pages, pages of numerical tables, of directions and diagrams, all drawn in neat but childish style. Steel and the Fragment had spent days trying to understand. Some of the references were obvious. The Visitor's recipes required silver and gold in quantities that would otherwise finance a war. But what was this 'liquid silver'? Tyrathect had recognized it; the Master had used such a thing in his labs in the Republic. Eventually they acquired the amount specified. But many of the ingredients were given only as methods for creating them. Steel remembered the Fragment musing over those, scheming against nature as if it were just another foe. The recipes of mystics were full of 'horn of squid' and 'frozen moonlight.' The directions from Ravna were sometimes even stranger. There were directions within directions, long detours spent in testing common materials to decide which really fit the greater plan. Building, testing, building. It was like the Master's own method but without the dead ends.

Some of it made sense early on. They would have the explosives and guns that Woodcarver thought were her secret weapons. But so much was still unintelligible – and it never got easier.

Steel and the Fragment worked through the afternoon, planning how to set up the latest tests, deciding where to search for the new ingredients that Ravna demanded.

Tyrathect leaned back, hissing a wondering sigh. 'Stage built upon stage. And soon we'll have our own *radios*. Old Woodcarver won't have a chance . . . You are right, Steel. With this you can rule the world. Imagine knowing instantly what is happening in the Republic's Capital and being able to coordinate armies around that knowledge. The Movement will be the Mind of God.' That was an old slogan, and now it could be true. 'I salute you, Steel. You have a grasp worthy of the Movement.' Was there the Teacher's contempt in his smile? '*Radio* and *guns* can give us the world. But clearly these are crumbs from the Visitors' table. When do they arrive?'

'Between one hundred and one hundred twenty days from now; Ravna has revised her estimate again. Apparently even the Two-Legs have problems flying between the stars.'

'So we have that long to enjoy the Movement's triumph. And then we are nothing, less than savages. It might have been safer to forego the gifts, and persuade the Visitors that there is nothing here worth rescuing.'

Steel looked out through the window slits that cut horizontally between timbers. He could see part of the starship compound, and the castle foundations, and beyond that the islands of the fjord country. He was suddenly more confident, more *at peace*, than he'd been in a long time. It felt right to reveal his dream. 'You really don't see it, do you Tyrathect? I wonder if the whole Master would understand, or whether I have exceeded him, too. In the beginning, we had no choice. The Starship was automatically sending some sort of signal to Ravna. We could have destroyed it; maybe Ravna would have lost interest . . . *And maybe not*, in which case we would be taken like a fish gilled from a stream. Perhaps I took the greater risk, but if I win, the prize will be far more than you imagine.' The Fragment was watching him, heads cocked. 'I've studied these humans, Jefri and – through my spies – the one down at Woodcarvers. Their race may be older than ours, and the tricks they've learned make them seem all-powerful. But the race is flawed. As singletons, they work with handicaps we can scarcely imagine. If I can use those weaknesses . . .

'You know the average Tines cares for its pups. We've manipulated parental sentiments often enough. Imagine how it must be for the humans. To them, a single pup is also an entire child. Think of the leverage that gives us.'

'You're seriously betting everything on this? Ravna isn't even Jefri's parent.'

Steel made an irritated gesture. 'You haven't seen all of Amdi's translations.' Innocent Amdi, the perfect spy. 'But you're right, saving the one child is not the main reason for this Visit. I've tried to find out their real motive. There are one hundred fifty-one children in some kind of deathly stupor, all stacked up in coffins within the ship. The Visitors are desperate to save the children, but there's something else they want. They never quite talk about it . . . I think it's in the machinery of the ship itself.'

'For all we know the children are a brood force, part of an invasion.'

That was an old fear and – after watching Amdijefri – Steel saw no chance of it. There could be other traps, but, 'If the Visitors are lying to us, then there is really nothing we can do to win. We'll be hunted animals; maybe generations from now we'll learn their tricks, but it will be the end of *us*. On the other hand, we have good reason to believe that the Two-Legs are weak, and whatever their goals, they do not involve us directly. You were there the day of the landing, much closer than I. You saw how easy it was to ambush them, even though their ship is impregnable and their single weapon a match for a small army. It is obvious that they do not consider us a threat. No matter how powerful their tools, their real fears are elsewhere. *And in the Starship, we have something they need.*

'Look at the foundations of our new castle, Tyrathect. I've told Amdijefri that it is to protect the Starship against Woodcarver. It will do that – later in the Summer when I shatter Woodcarver upon its ramparts. But see the foundations of the curtain around the Starship. By the time our Visitors arrive, the ship will be envaulted. I've done some quiet tests on its hull. It can be breached; a few dozen tons of

256

stone falling on it would quite nicely crush it. But Ravna is not to worry; this is all for the protection of her prize. And there will be an open courtyard nearby, surrounded by strangely high walls. I've asked Jefri to get Ravna's help on this. The courtyard will be just large enough to enclose Ravna's ship, protecting it, too.

'There are many details still to be settled. We must make the tools Ravna describes. We must arrange the demise of Woodcarver, well before the Visitors arrive. I need your help in all those things, and I expect to receive it. In the end, if the Visitors are treacherous, we will make the best stand that can be. And if they are not . . . well I think you'll agree that my reach has at least matched my teacher's.'

For once, the Flenser Fragment had no reply.

The ship's control cabin was Jefri and Amdi's favorite place in all of Lord Steel's Domain. Being here could still make Jefri very sad, but now the good memories seemed the stronger . . . and here was the best hope for the future. Amdi was still entranced by the window displays – even if the views were all of wooden walls. By their second visit they had already come to regard the place as their private kingdom, like Jefri's treehouse back on Straum. And in fact the cabin was much too small to hold more than a single pack. Usually a member of their bodyguard would sit just inside the entrance to the main hold, but even that seemed to be uncomfortable duty. This was a place where they were important.

For all their rambunctiousness, Amdi and Jefri realized the trust that Lord Steel and Ravna were placing in them. The two kids might race around out-of-doors, driving their guards to distraction, but the equipment in this command cabin was to be treated as cautiously as when Mom and Dad were here. In some ways, there was not much left in the ship. The datasets were destroyed; Jefri's parents had them outside when Woodcarver attacked. During the winter, Mr Steel had carried out most of the loose items to study. The coldsleep boxes were now safe in cool chambers nearby. Every day Amdijefri inspected the boxes, looked at each familiar face, checked the diag displays. No sleeper had died since the ambush.

What was left on the ship was hard-fastened to the hull. Jefri had pointed out the control boards and status elements that managed the container shell's rocket; they stayed strictly away from those.

Mr Steel's quilting shrouded the walls. Jefri's folks' baggage and sleeping bags and exercisers were gone, but there were still the acc webbing and hard-fastened equipment. And over the months, Amdijefri had brought in paper and pens and blankets and other junk. There was always a light breeze from the fans sweeping through the cabin.

It was a happy place, strangely carefree even with all the memories it brought. This was where they would save the Tines and all the sleepers. And this was the only place in the world where Amdijefri could talk to another human being. In some ways the means of talking seemed as medieval as Lord Steel's castle: They had one flat display – no depth, no color, no *pictures*. All they could coax from it were alphanumerics. But it was connected to the ship's ultrawave comm, and that was still programmed to track their rescuers. There was no voice recognition attached to the display; Jefri had almost panicked before he realized that the lower part of the screen worked as a keyboard. It was a laborious job typing in every letter of every word – though Amdi had gotten pretty good at it, using two noses to peck at the keys. And nowadays he could read Samnorsk even better than Jefri.

Amdijefri spent many afternoons here. If there was a message waiting from the previous day, they would bring it up page by page and Amdi would copy and translate it. Then they would enter the questions and answers that Mr Steel had talked to them about. Then there was a lot of waiting. Even if Ravna was watching at the other end, it could take several hours to get a reply. But the link was so much better than during the winter; they could almost feel Ravna getting close. The unofficial conversations with her were often the high point of their day.

So far, *this* day had been quite different. After the false workers attacked, Amdijefri had the shakes for about half an hour. Mr Steel had been wounded trying to protect them.

Maybe there was nowhere that was safe. They messed with the outside displays, trying to peek through cracks in the rough planking of the compound's walks.

'If we'd been able to see out, we could have warned Mr Steel,' said Jefri.

'We should ask him to put some holes in the walls. We could be like sentries.'

They batted the idea around a bit. Then the latest message started coming in from the rescue ship. Jefri jumped into the acc webbing by the display. This was his dad's old spot, and there was plenty of room. Two of Amdi slid in beside him. Another member hopped on the armrest and braced its paws on Jefri's shoulders. Its slender neck extended toward the screen to get a good view. The rest scrambled to arrange paper and pens. It was easy to play back messages, but Amdijefri got a certain thrill out of seeing the stuff coming down 'live.'

There was the initial header stuff – that wasn't so interesting after about the thousandth time you saw it – then Ravna's actual words. Only this time it was just tabular data, something to support the radio design.

'Nuts. It's numbers,' said Jefri.

'Numbers!' said Amdi. He climbed a free member onto the boy's lap. It stuck its nose close to the screen, cross-checking what the one by Jefri's shoulder was seeing. The four on the floor were busy scratching away, translating the decimal digits on the screen into the X's and O's and I's and deltas of Tines' base four notation. Almost from the beginning Jefri had realized that Amdi was really *good* at math. Jefri wasn't envious. Amdi said that hardly any of the Tines were that good, either; Amdi was a very special pack. Jefri was proud that he had such a neat friend. Mom and Dad would have liked Amdi. Still . . . Jefri sighed, and relaxed in the webbing. This number stuff was happening more and more often. Mom had read him a story once, 'Lost in the Slow Zone,' about how some marooned explorers brought civilization to a lost colony. In *that*, the heros just collected the right materials and built what they needed. There had been no talk of precision or ratios or design.

259

He looked away from the screen, and petted the two of Amdi that were sitting beside him. One of them wriggled under his hand. Their whole bodies hummed back at him. Their eyes were closed. If Jefri didn't know better, he would have assumed they were asleep. These were the parts of Amdi that specialized in talking.

'Anything interesting?' Jefri said after a while. The one on his left opened its eyes and looked at him.

'This is that bandwidth idea Ravna was talking about. If we don't make things just right, we'll just get *clicks* and *clacks*.'

'Oh, right.' Jefri knew that the initial reinventions of radio were usually not good for much more than Morse code. Ravna seemed to think they could jump that stage. 'What do you think Ravna is like?'

'What?' The scritching of pens on paper stopped for an instant; he had all of Amdi's attention, even though they'd talked of this before. 'Well, like you . . . only bigger and older?'

'Yeah, but –' Jefri knew Ravna was from Sjandra Kei. She was a grownup, somewhere older than Johanna and younger than Mom. *What exactly does she look like?* 'I mean, she's coming all this way just to rescue us and finish what Mom and Dad were trying to do. She must really be a great person.'

The scritching stopped again, and the display scrolled heedlessly on. They would have to reply it. 'Yes,' Amdi said after a moment. 'She – she must be a lot like Mr Steel. It will be nice to meet someone I can hug, the way you do Mr Steel.'

Jefri was a little miffed by that. 'Well *wait*, you can hug me!'

The parts of Amdi next to him purred loudly. 'I know. But I mean someone that's a grownup . . . like a parent.'

'Yeah.'

They got the tables translated and checked in about an hour. Then it was time to send up the latest things that Mr Steel was asking about. There were about four pages, all neatly printed in Samnorsk by Amdi. Usually he liked to do the typing, too, all bunched up over the keyboard and display. Today he wasn't interested. He lay all over Jefri, but didn't pay any special attention to checking what was being keyed in. Every so often Jefri felt a buzzing through his chest, or the screen mounting would make a strange sound – all in sympathy to the unhearable sounds that Amdi was making between his members. Jefri recognized the signs of deep thought.

He finished typing in the latest message, adding a few small questions of his own. Things like, 'How old are you and Pham? Are you married? What are Skroderiders like?'

Daylight had faded from the cracks in the walls. Soon the digger teams would be turning in their hoes and marching off to the barracks over the edge of the hill. Across the straits, the towers on Hidden Island would be golden in the mist, like something in a fairy tale. Their whitejackets would be calling Amdi and Jefri out for supper any minute now.

Two of Amdi jumped off the acc webbing and began chasing each other around the chair. 'I've been thinking! I've been thinking! Ravna's radio thing: why is it just for talking? She says all sound is just different frequencies of the same thing. But sound is all that thought is. If we could change some of the tables, and make the receivers and transmitters to cover my tympana, why couldn't I *think* over the radio?'

'I don't know.' Bandwidth was a familiar constraint on many everyday activities, though Jefri had only a vague notion of exactly what it was. He looked at the last of the tables, still displayed on the screen. He had a sudden insight, something that many adults in technical cultures never attain. 'I use these things all the time, but I don't know exactly how they work. We can follow these directions, but how would we know what to change?'

Amdi was getting all excited now, the way he did when he'd thought of some great prank. 'No, no, no. We don't have to understand everything.' Three more of him jumped to the floor; he waved random sheets of paper up at Jefri. 'Ravna doesn't know for sure how we make sound. The directions include options for making small changes. I've been thinking. I can see how the changes relate.' He paused and made a high-pitched squealing noise. 'Darn. I can't explain it exactly. But I think we can expand the tables, and that will change the machine in ob-obvious ways. And *then* . . .' Amdi was beside himself for a moment, and speechless. 'Oh Jefri, I wish you could be a pack, too! Imagine putting one of yourself each on a different mountain top, and then using radio to think. We could be as big as the world!'

Just then there was the sound of interpack gobbling from outside the cabin, and then the Samnorsk: 'Dinner time. We go now, Amdijefri. Okay?' It was Mr Shreck; he spoke a fair amount of Samnorsk, though not so well as Mr Steel. Amdijefri picked up the scattered sheets and carefully slipped them into the pockets on the back of Amdi's jackets. They powered down the display equipment and crawled into the main hold.

'Do you think Mr Steel will let us make the changes?'

'Maybe we should also send them back to Ravna.'

The whitejackets' member retreated from the hatch, and Amdijefri descended. A minute later they were out in the slanting sunlight. The two kids scarcely noticed; they were both caught up in Amdi's vision.

24

For Johanna, lots of things changed in the weeks after Scriber Jaqueramaphan died. Most were for the better, things that might never have happened but for the murder . . . and that made Johanna very sad.

She let Woodcarver live in her cabin and take the place of the helper pack. Apparently Woodcarver had wanted to do this from the beginning, but had been afraid of the human's anger. Now they kept the dataset in the cabin. There were never less than four packs of Vendacious's security surrounding the place, and there was talk of building barracks around it.

She saw the others during the day at meetings, and individually when they needed help with the dataset. Scrupilo, Vendacious, and Scarbutt – the 'Pilgrim' – all spoke fluent Samnorsk now, more than good enough so that she could see the character behind their inhuman forms:

Scrupilo, prissy and very bright. Vendacious, as pompous as Scriber had ever seemed, but without the playfulness and imagination. Pilgrim Wickwrackscar. She felt a chill every time she saw his big, scarred one. It always sat in the back, hunching down to look nonthreatening. Pilgrim obviously knew how the sight affected her and tried not to offend, but even after Scriber's death she couldn't do more than tolerate that pack ... And after all, there could be traitors in the Woodcarver castle. It was only Vendacious's theory that the murder had been a raid from outside. She kept a suspicious eye on Pilgrim.

At night, Woodcarver chased the other packs away. She huddled around the firepit, and asked the dataset questions that had no conceivable connection with fighting the Flenserists. Johanna sat with her and tried to explain things that Woodcarver didn't understand. It was strange. Woodcarver was something very like the Queen of these people. She had this enormous (primitive, uncomfortable, ugly – yet still enormous) castle. She had dozens of servants. Yet she spent most of each night in this little wood lodge with Johanna, and helped with the fire and the food at least as much as did the pack who had been here before.

So it was that Woodcarver became Johanna's second friend among the Tines. (Scriber was the first, though she hadn't known it till after he was dead.) Woodcarver was very smart and very strange. In some ways she was the smartest person Johanna had ever known, though that conclusion came slowly. She hadn't really been surprised when the Tines mastered Samnorsk quickly – that's the way it was in most adventures, and more to the point, they had the language learning programs in the dataset. But night after night Johanna watched Woodcarver play with the set. The pack showed no interest in the military tactics and chemistry that preoccupied them all during the day. Instead she read about the Slow Zone and the Beyond and the history of Straumli Realm. She had mastered nonlinear reading faster than any of the others. Sometimes Johanna would just sit and stare over her shoulders. The screen was split into windows, the main one scrolling much faster than Johanna could follow. A dozen times a minute, Woodcarver might come upon words she didn't recognize. Most were just unfamiliar Samnorsk: she'd tap a nose on the offending word and the definition would flicker briefly in a dictionary window. Other things were conceptual, and the new windows would lead the pack off into other fields, sometimes for just a few seconds, sometimes for many minutes – and sometimes the detour would become her new main path. In a way, she was everything that Scriber had wanted to be.

Many times she had questions the dataset couldn't really answer. She and Johanna would talk late into the night. What was a human family like? What had Straumli Realm thought to make at the High Lab? Johanna no longer thought of most packs as gange of snake-necked rats. Deep past midnight, the dataset's screen was brighter than the gray light from the firepit. It painted the backs of Woodcarver in cheerful colors. The pack gathered round her, looking up, almost like children listening to a teacher.

But Woodcarver was no child. Almost from the first, she had seemed old. Those late night talks were beginning to teach Johanna about the Tines too. The pack said things she never did during the day. They were mostly things that must be obvious to other Tines, but never talked about. The human girl wondered if Woodcarver the Queen had anyone to confide in.

Only one of Woodcarver's members was physically old; two were scarcely more than puppies. It was the pattern of the pack that was half a thousand years old. And that showed. Woodcarver's soul was held together by little more than will power. The price of immortality had been inbreeding. The original stock had been healthy, but after six hundred years . . . One of her youngest members couldn't stop drooling; it was constantly patting a kerchief to its muzzle. Another had milky white in its eyes where there should have been deep brown. Woodcarver said it was stone blind, but healthy and her best talker. Her oldest member was visibly feeble; it was panting all the time. Unfortunately, Woodcarver said it was the most alert and creative of all. When it died . . .

Once she started looking for it, Johanna could see

weakness in all of Woodcarver. Even the two healthiest members, strong and with plush fur, walked a little strangely compared to normal pack members. Was that due to spinal deformities? The two were also gaining weight, which wasn't helping the problem.

Johanna didn't learn this all at once. Woodcarver had told her about various Tinish affairs, and gradually her own story came out, too. She seemed glad to have someone to confide in, but Johanna saw little self-pity in her. Woodcarver had chosen this path – apparently it was perversion to some – and had beaten the odds for longer than any other pack in recorded history. She was more wistful than anything else that her luck had finally run out.

Tines architecture tended to extremes – grotesquely over-sized, or too cramped for human use. Woodcarver's council chamber was at the large extreme; it was not a cozy place. You could get three hundred humans into the bowl-shaped cavity with room to spare. The separated balconies that ran around its upper circumference could have held another hundred more.

Johanna had been here often enough before; this was where most work was done with the dataset. Usually there was herself and Woodcarver and whoever else needed information. Today was different, not a day to consult the dataset at all: This was Johanna's first council meeting. There were twelve packs in the High Council, and they were all here. Every balcony contained a pack, and there were three on the floor. Johanna knew enough about Tines now to see that for all the empty space, the place was hideously crowded. There was the mind noise of fifteen packs. Even with all the padded tapestries, she felt an occasional buzzing in her head or through her hands from the railing.

Johanna stood with Woodcarver on the largest balcony. When they arrived, Vendacious was already down on the main floor, arranging diagrams. As the packs of the council came to their feet, he looked up and said something to Woodcarver. The Queen replied in Samnorsk: 'I know it will slow things down, but perhaps that's a good thing.' She made a human laughing sound.

Peregrine Wickwrackscar was standing on the next balcony over, just like some council pack. Strange. Johanna had not yet figured out why, but Scarbutt seemed to be one of Woodcarver's favorites. 'Pilgrim, would you translate for Johanna?'

Pilgrim bobbed several heads. 'Is, is that okay, Johanna?'

The girl hesitated an instant, then nodded back. It made sense. Next to Woodcarver, Pilgrim spoke better Samnorsk than any of them. As Woodcarver sat down, she took the dataset from Johanna and popped it open. Johanna glanced at the figures on the screen. *She's made notes*. Her surprise didn't have a chance to register before the Queen was talking again – this time in the gobble sounds of interpack talk. After a second, Pilgrim began translating:

'Everyone please sit. Hunker down. This meeting is crowded enough as it is.' Johanna almost smiled. Pilgrim Wickwrackscar was pretty good. He was imitating Woodcarver's human voice perfectly. His translation even captured the wry authority of her speech.

After some shuffling around, only one or two heads were visible sticking up from each balcony. Most stray thought noise should now be caught in the padding around the balcony or absorbed by the quilted canopy that hung over the room. 'Vendacious, you may proceed.'

On the main floor, Vendacious stood and looked up in all directions. He started talking. 'Thank you,' same the translation, now imitating the security chief's tones. 'The Woodcarver asked me to call this meeting because of urgent developments in the North. Our sources there report that Steel is fortifying the region around Johanna's starship.'

Gobble gobble interruption. Scrupilo? 'That's not news. That's what our cannon and gunpowder are for.'

Vendacious: 'Yes, we've known of the plans for some time. Nevertheless the completion date has been advanced, and the final version will have walls a good deal thicker than we had figured. It also appears that once the enclosure is complete, Steel intends to break apart the starship and distribute its cargo through his various laboratories.'

For Johanna the words came like a kick in the stomach. Before there had been a chance: If they fought hard enough, they might recapture the ship. She might finish her parents' mission, perhaps even get rescued.

Pilgrim said something on his own account, translating: 'So what's the new deadline?'

'They're confident of having the main walls complete in just under ten tendays.'

Woodcarver bent a pair of noses to the keyboard, tapped in a note. At the same time she stuck a head over the railing and looked down at the security chief. 'I've noticed before that Steel tends to be a bit over-optimstic. Do you have an objective estimate?'

'Yes. The walls will be complete between eight and eleven tendays from now.'

Woodcarver: 'We had been counting on at least fifteen. Is this a response to our plans?'

On the floor below, Vendacious drew himself together. 'That was our first suspicion, your majesty. But . . . as you know, we have a number of very special sources of informa- tion . . . sources we shouldn't discuss even here.'

'What a braggart. Sometimes I wonder if he knows anything. I've never seen him stick *his* asses out in the field.' *Huh?* It took Johanna a second to realize that this was Pilgrim editorializing. She glanced across the railing. Three of Pilgrim's heads were visible, two looking her way. They bore an expression she recognized as a silly smile. No one else seemed to react to his comment; apparently he could focus his translation on Johanna alone. She glared at him, and after a moment he resumed his businesslike translation:

'Steel knows we plan to attack, but he does *not* know about our special weapons. This change in schedule appears to be a matter of random suspicion. Unfortunately we are the worse for it.'

Three or four Councillors began talking at once. 'Much loud unhappiness,' came Pilgrim's voice, summing up. 'They're full of "I knew this plan would never work" and "Why did we ever agree to attack the Flenserists in the first place."'

Right next to Johanna, Woodcarver emitted a shrill whistle. The recriminations dribbled to a halt. 'Some of you forget your courage. We agreed to attack Hidden Island because it has been a deadly threat, one we thought we could destroy with Johanna's cannons – and one that could surely destroy *us* if Steel ever learns to use the starship.' One of Woodcarver's members, crouching on the floor, reached out to brush Johanna's knee.

Pilgrim's focused voice chuckled in her ear. 'And there's also the little matter of getting you home and making contact with the stars, but she can't say that aloud to the "pragmatic" types. In case you haven't guessed, that's one reason you're here – to remind the chuckleheads there's more in heaven than they have dreamed.' He paused, and switched back to translating Woodcarver:

'No mistake was made in undertaking this campaign: avoiding it would be as deadly as fighting and losing. So . . . do we have any chance of getting an effective army up the coast in time?' She jabbed a nose in the direction of a balcony across the room. 'Scrupilo. Please be brief.'

'The last thing Scrupilo can be is brief – oops, sorry.' More editorializing from Peregrine.

Scrupilo stuck a couple more heads into view. 'I've already discussed this with Vendacious, Your Majesty. Raising an army, traveling up the coast – those all could be done in well under ten tendays. It's the cannon, and perhaps training packs to use cannon, that is the problem. That is my special area of responsibility.'

Woodcarver said something abrupt.

'Yes, majesty. We have the gunpowder. It is every bit as powerful as Dataset says. The gun tubes have been a much greater problem. Till very recently, the metal cracked at the breech as it cooled. Now I think I have that fixed. At least I have two unblemished gun tubes. I had hoped for several tendays of testing –'

Woodcarver interrupted, '– but that is something we can't afford now.' She came completely to her feet and looked all around the council room. 'I want full-size testing immediately. If it's successful, we'll start making gun tubes as fast as we can.' *And if not . . .*

Two days later . . .

The funniest thing was that Scrupilo expected Johanna to inspect the gun tube before he fired it. The pack walked excitedly around the rig, explaining things in awkward Samnorsk. Johanna followed, frowning seriously. Some meters off, mostly hidden behind a berm, Woodcarver and her High Council were watching the exercise. Well, the thing *looked* real enough. They'd mounted it on a small cart that could roll back into a pile of dirt under the recoil force. The tube itself was a single cast piece of metal about a meter long with a ten-centimeter bore. Gunpowder and shot went in the front end. The powder was ignited through a tiny firehole at the rear.

Johanna ran her hand along the barrel. The leaden surface was bumpy, and there seemed to be pieces of dirt caught in the metal. Even the walls of the bore were not completely smooth; would that make a difference? Scrupilo was explaining how he had used straw in the molds to keep the metal from cracking as it cooled. *Yecco.* 'You should try it out with small amounts of gunpowder first,' she said.

Scrupilo's voice became bit conspiratorial, more focused. 'Just between you me, I did that. It went very good. Now for big test.'

Hmm. So you're not a complete flake. She smiled at the nearest of him, a member with no black at all in his head fur. In a kooky way, Scrupilo reminded her of some of the scientists at the High Lab.

Scrupilo stepped back from the cannon and said loudly, 'It is all okay to go now?' Two of him were looking nervously at the High Councillors beyond the berm.

'Um, yes, it looks fine to me.' And of course it should. The design was copied straight from Nyjoran models in Johanna's history files. 'But be careful – if it doesn't work right, it could kill anybody nearby.'

'Yes, yes.' Having gotten her official endorsement, Scrupilo swept around the piece and shooed Johanna toward the sidelines. As she walked back to Woodcarver, he continued in Tinish, no doubt explaining the test.

'Do you think it will work?' Woodcarver asked her quietly. She seemed even more feeble than usual. They had spread a woven mat for her on the mossy heather behind the berm. Most of her lay quietly, heads between paws. The blind one looked asleep; the young drooler cuddled against it, twitching nervously. As usual Peregrine Wickwrackscar was nearby, but he wasn't translating now. All his attention was on Scrupilo.

Johanna thought of the straw that Scrupilo had used in the molds. Woodcarver's people were really trying to help, but . . . She shook her head. 'I – who knows.' She came to her knees and looked over the berm. The whole thing looked like a circus act from a history file. There were the performing animals, the cannon. There was even the circus tent: Vendacious had insisted on hiding the operation from possible spies in the hills. The enemy might see something, but the longer Steel lacked details the better.

The Scrupilo pack hustled around the cannon, talking all the time. Two of him hauled up a keg of black powder and he began pushing the stuff down the barrel. A wad of silkpaper followed the powder down the barrel. He tamped it into place, then loaded the cannon ball. At the same time, the rest of him pushed the cart around to point out of the tent.

They were on the forest side of the castle yard, between the old and new walls. Johanna could see a patch of green hillside, drizzly clouds hanging low. About a hundred meters away was the old wall. In fact this was the same stretch of stone where Scriber had been killed. Even if the damn cannon didn't blow up, no one had any idea how far the shot would go. Johanna was betting it wouldn't even get to the wall.

Scrupilo was on this side of the gun now, trying to light a long wooden firing wand. With a sinking feeling in her stomach, Johanna knew this couldn't work. They were all fools and amateurs, she as much as they. *And this poor guy is going to get killed for nothing.*

Johanna came to her feet. *Gotta stop it.* Something grabbed her belt and pulled her down. It was one of Woodcarver's members, one of the fat ones that couldn't walk quite right.

'We have to try,' the pack said softly.

Scrupilo had the wand alight now. Suddenly he stopped talking. All of him but the white-headed one ran for the protection of the berm. For an instant it seemed like strange cowardice, and then Johanna understood: A human playing with something explosive would also try to shield his body – except for the hand that held the match. Scrupilo was risking a maiming, but not death.

The white-headed one looked across the trampled heather to the rest of Scrupilo. It didn't seem upset so much as attentively listening. At this distance it couldn't be part of Scrupilo's mind, but the creature was probably smarter than any dog – and apparently it was getting some kind of directions from the rest.

White-head turned and walked toward the cannon. It belly-crawled the last meter, taking what cover there was in the dirt behind the gun cart. It held the wand to the flame as its tip came slowly down on the fire hole. Johanna ducked behind the berm . . .

The explosion was a sharp snapping sound. Woodcarver shuddered against her, and whistles of pain came from all around the tent. Poor Scrupilo! Johanna felt tears starting. *I have to look; I'm partly responsible.* Slowly she stood and forced herself to look across the field to where a minute ago the cannon had been – *and still is!* Thick smoke floated from both ends, but the tube was intact. And more, White-head was wobbling dazedly around the cart, his white fur now covered with soot.

The rest of Scrupilo raced out to White-head. The five of him ran round and round the cannon, bounding over each other in triumph. For a long moment, the rest of the audience just stared. The gun was in one piece. The gunner had survived. And, almost as a side effect . . . Johanna looked over the gun, up the hillside: There was a meter-wide notch in the top of the old wall where none had been before. Vendacious would have a hard time hiding *that* from enemy view!

Dumb silence gave way to the noisiest affair Johanna had seen yet. There was the usual gobbling, and other sounds – hissing that hovered right at the edge of sensibility. On the other side of the tent, two Tines she didn't know ran *into* each other: for a moment of mindless jubilation, they were an enormous pack of nine or ten members.

We'll get the ship back yet! Johanna turned to hug Woodcarver. But the Queen was not shouting with the others. She huddled with her heads close together, shivering. 'Woodcarver?' She petted the neck of one of the big, fat ones. It jerked away, its body spasming.

Stroke? Heart attack? The names of oldenday killers popped into her mind. Just how would they apply to a pack? Something was terribly wrong, and nobody else had noticed. Johanna bounced back to her feet. *'Pilgrim!'* she screamed.

Five minutes later they had Woodcarver out of the tent. The place was still a madhouse, but gone deathly quiet to Johanna's ears. She'd helped the Queen onto her carriage, but after that no one would let her near. Even Pilgrim, so eager to translate everything the day before, brushed her aside. 'It will be okay,' was all he said as he ran to the front of the carriage and grabbed the reins of the shaggy Whatsits. The carriage pulled out, surrounded by several packs of guards. For an instant, the weirdness of the Tines world came crashing back on Johanna. This was obviously a great emergency. A person might be dying. People were rushing this way and that. And yet . . . The packs drew into themselves. No one crowded close. No one could touch another.

The instant passed, and Johanna was running out of the tent after the carriage. She tried to keep to the heather along the muddy path, and almost caught up. Everything was wet and chill, gunmetal gray. Everyone had been so intent on the test – could this be more Flenser treachery? Johanna stumbled, went down on her knees in the mud. The carriage turned a corner, onto cobblestones. Now it was lost to sight. She got up and slogged on through the wet, but a little slower now. There was nothing she could do, nothing she could do. She had made friends with Scriber, and Scriber had been killed. She had made friends with Woodcarver, and now . . .

She walked along the cobbled alley between the castle's storehouses. The carriage was out of sight, but she could hear its clatter on ahead. Vendacious's security packs ran in both directions past her, stopping briefly in side niches to allow opposing traffic by. Nobody answered her questions – probably none of them even spoke Samnorsk.

Johanna almost got lost. She could hear the carriage, but it had turned somewhere. She heard it again behind her. They were taking Woodcarver to Johanna's place! She went back, and a few minutes later was climbing the path to the two-storey cabin she had shared with Woodcarver these last weeks. Johanna was too pooped to run anymore. She walked slowly up the hillside, vaguely aware of her wet and muddy state. The carriage was stopped about five meters short of the door. Guard packs were strung out along the hill, but their bows weren't nocked.

The afternoon sunlight found a break in the western clouds and shone for a moment on the damp heather and glistening timbers, lighting them bright against dark sky above the hills. It was a combination of light and dark that had always seemed especially beautiful to Johanna. *Please let her be okay*.

The guards let her pass. Peregrine Wickwrackscar was standing around the entrance, three of him watching her approach. The fourth, Scarbutt, had its long neck stuck through the doorway, watching whatever was inside. 'She wanted to be back here when it happened,' he said.

'What h-happened?' said Johanna.

Pilgrim made the equivalent of a shrug. 'It was the shock of that cannon going off. But almost anything could have done it.' There was something odd about the way his heads were bobbing around. With a shock Johanna realized the pack was *smiling*, full of glee.

'I want to see her!' Scarbutt backed hastily away as she started for the door.

Inside there was only the light from the door and the high window slits. It took a second for Johanna's eyes to adjust. Something smelled . . . wet. Woodcarver was lying in a circle on the quilted mattress she used every evening. She crossed the room and went to her knees beside the pack. The pack edged nervously away from her touch. There was blood, and what looked like a pile of guts, in the middle of the mattress. Johanna felt vomit rising in her. 'W-Woodcarver?' she said very softly.

One of the Queen moved back toward Johanna and put its muzzle in the girl's hand. 'Hello, Johanna. It's . . . so strange . . . to have someone next to me at a time like this.'

'You're bleeding. What's the matter?'

Soft, human-sounding laughter. 'I'm hurt, but it's good . . . See.' The blind one was holding something small and wet in its jaws. One of the others was licking it. Whatever it was, it was wiggling, alive. And Johanna remembered how strangely plump and awkward parts of Woodcarver had become.

'*A baby?*'

'Yes. And I'm going to have another in a day or two.'

Johanna sat back on the floor timbers, covering her face with her hands. She was going to start crying again. 'Why didn't you tell me?'

Woodcarver didn't say anything for a moment. She licked the little one all around, then set it against the tummy of the member that must be its mother. The newborn snuggled close, nuzzling into the belly fur. It didn't make any noise that Johanna could hear. Finally the Queen said, 'I . . . don't know if I can make you understand. This has been very hard for me.'

'Having babies?' Johanna's hands were sticky with the blood on the quilt. Obviously this had been hard, *but that's how all lives must start on a world like this.* It was pain that needed the support of friends, pain that led to joy.

'No. Having the babies isn't it. I've borne more than a hundred in my memory's time.. But these two . . . are the ending of me. How can you understand? You humans don't even have the choice to keep on living; your offspring can never be you. But for me, it's the end of a soul six hundred years old. You see, I'm going to keep these two to be part of me . . . and for the first time in all the centuries, I am not both the mother and the father. A newby I'll become.'

Johanna looked at the blind one and the drooler. Six hundred years of incest. How much longer could Woodcarver have continued before the mind itself decayed?

Not both the mother and the father. 'But then who is father?' she blurted out.

'Who do you think?' The voice came from just beyond the door. One of Peregrine Wickwrackscar's heads peered around the corner just far enough to show an eye. 'When Woodcarver makes a decision, she goes for extremes. She's been the most tightly held soul of all time. But now she has blood – genes, Dataset would say – from packs all over the world, from one of the flakiest pilgrims who ever cast his soul upon the wind.'

'Also from one of the smartest,' said Woodcarver, her voice wry and wistful at the same time. 'The new soul will be at least as intelligent as before, and probably a lot more flexible.'

'And I'm a little bit pregnant, myself,' said Pilgrim. 'But I'm not the least bit sad. I've been a foursome for too long. Imagine, having pups by Woodcarver herself! Maybe I'll turn all conservative and settle down.'

'Hah! Even two from me is not enough to slow your pilgrim soul.'

Johanna listened to the banter. The ideas were so *alien*, and yet the overtones of affection and humor were somehow very familiar. Somewhere . . . then she had it: When Johanna was just five years old, and Mom and Dad brought little Jefri home. Johanna couldn't remember the words, or even the sense of what they'd said – but the tone was the same as what went between Woodcarver and Pilgrim.

Johanna slid back to a sitting position, the tension of the day evaporating. Scrupilo's artillery really worked; there was a chance of getting the ship. And even if they failed . . . she felt a little bit like she was back home.

'C-can I pet your puppy?'

25

The voyage of the *Out of Band II* had begun in catastrophe, where life and death were a difference of hours or minutes. In the first weeks there had been terror and loneliness and the resurrection of Pham. The *OOB* had fallen quickly toward the galactic plane, away from Relay. Day by day the whorl of stars tilted up to meet them, till it was a single band of light, the Milky Way as seen from the perspective of Nyjora and Old Earth – and from most all the habitable planets of the Galaxy.

Twenty thousand light-years in three weeks. But that had been on a path through the Middle Beyond. Now in the galactic plane, they were still several thousand light-years from their goal at the Bottom of the Beyond. The Zone interfaces roughly followed surfaces of constant mean density; on a galactic scale, the Bottom was a vaguely lens-shaped surface, surrounding much of the galactic disk. The *OOB* was moving in the plane of the disk now, more or less toward the galactic center. Every week took them deeper toward the Slowness. Worse, their path, and all variants that made any progress, extended right through a region of massive Zone shifting. The Net News had called it the Great Zone Storm, though of course there was not the slightest physical feeling of turbulence within the volume. But some days their progress was less than eighty percent what they'd expected.

Early on they'd known that it was not only the storm that was slowing them. Blueshell had gone outside, looking over the damage that still remained from their escape.

'So it's the ship itself?' Ravna had glared out from the bridge, watching the now imperceptible crawl of near stars across the heavens. The confirmation was no revelation. But what to do?

Blueshell trundled back and forth across the ceiling. Every time he reached the far wall, he'd query ship's management about the pressure seal on the nose lock. Ravna glared at him. 'Hey, that was the nth time you've checked status in the last three minutes. If you really think something is wrong, then *fix* it.'

The Skroderider's wheeled progress came to an abrupt halt. Fronds waved uncertainly. 'But I was just outside. I want to be sure I shut the port correctly . . . Oh, you mean I've already checked it?'

Ravna looked up at him, and tried to get the sting out of her voice. Blueshell wasn't the proper target for her frustration. 'Yup. At least five times.'

'I'm sorry.' He paused, going into the stillness of complete concentration. 'I've committed the memory.' Sometimes the habit was cute, and sometimes just irritating: When the Riders tried to think on more than one thing at a time, their Skrodes were sometimes unable to maintain short-term memory. Blueshell especially got trapped into cycles of behavior, repeating an action and immediately forgetting the accomplishment.

Pham grinned, looking a lot cooler than Ravna felt. 'What I don't see is why you Riders put up with it.'

'What?'

'Well, according to the ship's library, you've had these Skrode gadgets since before there was a Net. So how come you haven't improved the design, gotten rid of the silly wheels, upgraded the memory tracking? I bet that even a Slow Zone combat programmer like me could come up with a better design than the one you're riding.'

'It's really a matter of tradition,' Blueshell said primly, 'We're grateful to Whatever gave us wheels and memory in the first place.'

'Hmm.'

Ravna almost smiled. By now she knew Pham well enough to guess what he was thinking – namely that plenty of Riders might have gone on to better things in the Transcend. Those remaining were likely to have self-imposed limitations.

'Yes. Tradition. Many who once were Riders have changed – even Transcended. But we persist.' Greenstalk paused, and when she continued sounded even more shy than usual. 'You've heard of the Rider Myth?'

'No,' said Ravna, distracted in spite of herself. In the time ahead she would know as much about these Riders as about any human friends, but for now there were still surprises.

'Not many have. Not that it's a secret; it's just we don't make much of it. It comes close to being religion, but one we don't proselytize. Four or five billion years ago, Someone built the first skrodes and raised the first Riders to sentience. That much is verified fact. The Myth is that something destroyed our Creator and all its works . . . A catastrophe so great that from this distance it is not even understood as an act of Mind.'

There were plenty of theories about what the galaxy had been like in the distant past, in the time of the Ur-Partition. But the Net couldn't be forever. There had to be a beginning. Ravna had never been a big believer in Ancient Wars and Catastrophes.

'So in a sense,' Greenstalk said, 'we Riders are the faithful ones, waiting for What created us to return. The traditional skrode and the traditional interface are a standard. Staying with it has made our patience possible.'

'Quite so,' said Blueshell. 'And the design itself is very subtle, my lady, even if the function is simple.' He rolled to the center of the ceiling. 'The skrode of tradition imposes a good discipline – concentration on what's truly important. Just now I was trying to worry about too many things . . .' Abruptly he returned to the topic at hand: 'Two of our drive spines never recovered from the damage at Relay. Three more appear to be degrading. We thought this slow progress was just the storm, but now I've studied the spines up close. The diagnostic warnings were no false alarm.'

' . . . and it's still getting worse?'

'Unfortunately so.'

'So how bad will it get?'

Blueshell drew all his tendrils together. 'My Lady Ravna, we can't be certain of the extrapolations yet. It may not get much worse than now, or – You know the *OOB* was not fully ready for departure. There were the final consistency checks still to do. In a way, I worry about that more than anything. We don't know what bugs may lurk, especially when we reach the Bottom and our normal automation must be retired. We must watch the drives very carefully . . . and hope.'

It was the nightmare that haunted travelers, especially at the Bottom of the Beyond: with ultradrive gone, suddenly a light-year was not a matter of minutes but of years. Even if they fired up the ramscoop and went into cold sleep, Jefri

Olsndot would be a thousand years dead before they reached him, and the secret of his parents' ship buried in some medieval midden.

Pham Nuwen waved at the slowly shifting star fields. 'Still, this is the Beyond. Every hour we go farther than the fleet of Qeng Ho could in a decade.' He shrugged. 'Surely there's some place we can get repairs?'

'Several.'

So much for 'a quick flight, all unobserved.' Ravna sighed. The final fitting at Relay was to include spares and tested, Bottom-compatible software. All that was faraway might-have-beens now. She looked at Greenstalk. 'Do you have any ideas?'

'About what?' Greenstalk said.

Ravna bit her lip in frustration. Some said the Riders were a race of comedians; they were indeed, but it was mostly unintentional.

Blueshell rattled at his mate.

'*Oh!* You mean where can we get help. Yes, there are several possibilities. Sjandra Kei is thirty-nine hundred lights spinward from here, but outside this storm. We –'

'Too far,' Blueshell and Ravna spoke almost in chorus.

'Yes, yes, but remember. The Sjandra Kei worlds are mainly human, your home, my Lady Ravna. And Blueshell and I know them well; after all, they were the source of the crypto shipment we brought to Relay. We have friends there and you a family. Even Blueshell agrees that we can get the work done without notice there.'

'Yes, *if* we could get there.' Blueshell's voder voice sounded petulant.

'Okay, what are the other choices?'

'They are not so well-known. I'll make a list.' Her fronds drifted across a console. 'Our last chance for choice is rather near our planned course. It's a single system civilization. The Net name is . . . it translates as Harmonious Repose.'

'Rest in Peace, eh?' said Pham.

But they had agreed to voyage on quietly, always watching the bad drive spines, postponing the decision to stop for help.

*

The days became weeks, and weeks slowly counted into months. Four voyagers on a quest toward the Bottom. The drive became worse, but slowly, right on *OOB*'s diagnostic projections.

The Blight continued to spread across the Top of the Beyond, and its attacks on Network archives extended far beyond its direct reach.

Communication with Jefri was improving. Messages trickled in at the rate of one or two a day. Sometimes, when *OOB*'s antenna swarm was tuned just right, he and Ravna would talk almost in real time. Progress was being made on the Tines' world faster than she had expected – perhaps fast enough that the boy could save himself.

It should have been a hard time, locked up in the single ship with just three others, with only a thread of conversation with the outside, and that with a lost child.

In any case, it was rarely boring. Ravna found that each of them had plenty to do. For herself it was managing the ship's library, coaxing out of it the plans that would help Mr Steel and Jefri. *OOB*'s library was nothing compared to the Archive at Relay, or even the university libraries at Sjandra Kei, but without proper search automation it could be just as unknowable. And as their voyage proceeded, that automation needed more and more special care.

And . . . things could never be boring with Pham around. He had a dozen projects, and curiosity about everything. 'Voyaging time can be a gift,' he'd say. 'Now we have time to catch ourselves up, time to get ready for whatever we find ahead.' He was learning Samnorsk. It went slower than his faked learning on Relay, but the guy had a natural bent for languages, and Ravna gave him plenty of practice.

He spent several hours each day in the *OOB*'s workshop, often with Blueshell. Reality graphics were a new thing to him, but after a few weeks he was beyond toy prototypes. The pressure suits he built had power packs and weapons stores. 'We don't know what things may be like when we arrive; powered armor could be real useful.'

At the end of each work day they would all meet on the command deck to compare notes, to consider the latest from

Jefri and Mr Steel, to review the drive status. For Ravna this could be the happiest time of the day . . . and sometimes the hardest. Pham had rigged the display automation to show castle walls all around. A huge fireplace replaced the normal window on comm status. The sound of it was almost perfect; he had even coaxed a small amount of 'fire' heat from that wall. This was a castle hall out of Pham's memory, from Canberra he said. But it wasn't that different from the Age of Princesses on Nyjora (though most of *those* castles had been in tropical swamps where big fireplaces were rarely used). For some perverse reason, even the Riders seemed to enjoy it; Greenstalk said it reminded her of a trading stop from her first years with Blueshell. Like travelers who have walked through a long day, the four of them rested in the coziness of a phantom lodge. And when the new business was settled, Pham and the Riders would trade stories, often late into the 'night'.

Ravna sat beside him, the least talkative of the four. She joined in the laughter and sometimes the discussion: There was the time Blueshell had a humor fit at Pham's faith in public key encryption, and Ravna knew some stories of her own to illustrate the Rider's opinion. But this was also the hardest time for her. Yes, the stories were wonderful. Blueshell and Greenstalk had been so many places, and at heart they were traders. Swindles and bargains and good done were all part of their lives. Pham listened to his friends, almost enraptured . . . and then told his own stories, of being a prince on Canberra, of being a Slow Zone trader and explorer. And for all the limitations of the Slowness, his life's adventures surpassed even the Skroderiders'. Ravna smiled and tried to pretend enthusiasm.

For Pham's stories were too much. He honestly believed them, but she couldn't imagine one human seeing so much, doing so much. Back on Relay, she had claimed his memories were synthetic, a little joke of Old One. She had been very angry when she said it, and more than anything she wished she never had . . . because it was so clearly the truth. Greenstalk and Blueshell never noticed, but sometimes in the middle of a story Pham would stumble on his memories and a look of barely concealed panic would come to his eyes. Somewhere inside, he knew the truth too, and she suddenly wanted to hug him, comfort him. It was like having a terribly wounded friend, with whom you can talk but never mutually admit the scope of the injuries. Instead she pretended the lapses didn't exist, smiling and laughing at the rest of his story.

And Old One's jape was all so unnecessary. Pham didn't have to be a great hero. He was a decent person, though egotistical and kind of a rule breaker. He had every bit as much persistence as she, and more courage.

What craft Old One must have had to make such a person, what . . . Power. And how she hated Him for making a joke of such a person.

Of Pham's godshatter there was scarcely a sign. For that Ravna was very grateful. Once or twice a month he had a dreamy spell. For a day or two after he would go nuts with some new project, often something he couldn't clearly explain. But it wasn't getting worse; he wasn't drifting away from her.

'And the godshatter may save us in the end,' he would say when she had the courage to ask him about it. 'No, I don't know how.' He tapped his forehead. 'It's still god's own crowded attic up here. And it's more than memory. Sometimes the godshatter needs all my mind to think with and there's no room left for self-awareness, and afterwards I can't explain, but . . . sometimes I have a glimmer. Whatever Jefri's parents brought to the Tines' world: it can hurt the Blight. Call it an antidote – better yet, a countermeasure. Something taken from the Perversion as it was aborning in the Straumli lab. Something the Perversion didn't even suspect was gone until much later.'

Ravna sighed. It was hard to imagine good news that was also so frightening. 'The Straumers could sneak something like that right out from the Perversion's heart?'

'Maybe. Or maybe, Countermeasure used the Straumers to escape the Perversion. To hide inaccessibly deep, and wait to strike. And I think the plan might work, Rav, at least if I – if

282

Old One's godshatter – can get down there and help it. Look at the News. The Blight is turning the top of the Beyond upside down – hunting for *something*. Hitting Relay was the least of it, a small by-product of its murdering Old One. But it's looking in all the wrong places. We'll have our chance at Countermeasure.'

She thought of Jefri's messages. 'The rot on the walls of Jefri's ship. You think that's what it is?' ·

Pham's eyes went vague. 'Yes. It seems completely passive, but he says it was there from the beginning, that his parents kept him away from it. He seems a little disgusted by it . . . That's good, probably keeps his Tinish friends away from it.'

A thousand questions flitted up. Surely they must in Pham's mind too. And they could know the answer to none of them now. Yet someday they would stand before that unknown and Old One's dead hand would act . . . through Pham. Ravna shivered, and didn't say anything more for a time.

Month by month, the gunpowder project stayed right on the schedule of the library's development program. The Tines had been able to make the stuff easily; there had been very little backtracking through the development tree. Alloy testing had been the critical event that slowed things, but they were over the hump there too. The packs of 'Hidden Island' had built the first three prototypes: breech-loading cannon that were small enough to be carried by a single pack. Jefri guessed they could begin mass production in another ten days.

The radio project was the weird one. In one sense it was behind schedule; in another, it had become something more than Ravna had ever imagined. After a long period of normal progress, Jefri had come back with a counterplan. It consisted of a complete reworking of the tables for the acoustic interface.

'I thought these jokers were first-time medievals,' Pham Nuwen said when he saw Jefri's message.

'That's right. Apparently, they just reasoned out consequences to what we sent them. They want to support pack-

thought across the radio.'

'Hunh. Yes. We described how the tables specified the transducer grid – all in nontechnical Samnorsk. That included showing how small table changes would make the grid different. But look, our design would give them a three kilohertz band – a nice, voice-grade connection. You're telling me that implementing this new table would give 'em two hundred kilohertz.'

'Yes. That's what my dataset says.'

He grinned his cocky smile. 'Ha! And that's my point. Sure, *in principle* we gave them enough information to do the mod. It looks to me like making this expanded spec table is equivalent to solving a, hmm,' he counted rows and columns, 'a five-hundred-node numerical PDE. And little Jefri claims that all his datasets are destroyed, and that his ship computer is not generally usable.'

Ravna leaned back from the display. 'Sorry. I see what you mean.' You get so used to everyday tools, sometimes you forget what it must be like without them. 'You . . . you think this might be, uh, Countermeasure's doing?'

Pham Nuwen hesitated, as if he hadn't even considered the possibility. Then, 'No . . . no, it's not that. I think this "Mister Steel" is playing games with our heads. All we have is a byte stream from "Jefri." What do we *really* know about what's going on?'

'Well, I'll tell you some things *I* know. We are talking to a young human child who was raised in Straumli Realm. You've been reading most of his messages in Trisk translation. That loses a lot of the colloquialisms and the little errors of a child who is a native speaker of Samnorsk. The only way this might be faked is by human adults . . . And after twenty plus weeks of knowing Jefri, I'll tell you even that is unlikely.'

'Okay. So suppose Jefri is for real. We have this eight-year-old kid down on the Tines' world. He's telling us what he considers to be the truth. I'm saying it looks like someone is lying to him. Maybe we can trust what he sees with his own eyes. He says these creatures aren't sapient except in groups of five or so. Okay. We'll believe that.' Pham rolled his eyes. Apparently his reading had shown how rare group intelligences were this side of the Transcend. 'The kid says they didn't see anything but small towns from space, and that everything on the ground is medieval. Okay, we'll buy that. *But*. What are the chances that this race is smart enough to do partial differential equations in their heads, and do them from just the implications in your message?'

'Well, there have been some humans that smart.' She could name one case in Nyjoran history, another couple from Old Earth. If such abilities were common among the packs, they were smarter than any natural race she had heard of. 'So this isn't first-time medievalism?'

'Right. I bet this is some colony fallen on hard times – like your Nyjora and my Canberra, except that they have the good luck of being in the Beyond. These dog packs have a working computer somewhere. Maybe it's under control of their priest class; maybe they don't have much else. But they're holding out on us.'

'But *why?* We'd be helping them in any case. And Jefri has told us how this group saved him.'

Pham started to smile again, the old supercilious smile. Then he sobered. He was really trying to break that habit. 'You've been on a dozen different worlds, Ravna. And I know you've read about thousands more, at least in survey. You probably know of varieties of medievalism I've never guessed. But remember, I've actually *been* there . . . I think.' The last was a nervous mutter.

'I've read about the Age of Princesses,' Ravna said mildly.

'Yes . . . and I'm sorry for belittling that. In any medieval politics, the blade and the thought are closely connected. But they become much more so to someone who's lived through it. Look, even if we believe everything that Jefri says he has seen, this Hidden Island Kingdom is a sinister thing.'

'You mean the names?'

'Like Flensers, Steel, Tines? Harsh names aren't necessarily meaningful.' Pham laughed. 'I mean, when *I* was eight years old, one of my titles was already "Lord Master Disemboweler."' He saw the look on Ravna's face and hurriedly added, 'And at that age, I hadn't even *witnessed* more than a couple of executions! No, the names are only a small part of it. I'm thinking of the kid's description of the castle – which seems to be close by the ship – and this ambush he thinks he was rescued from. It doesn't add up. You asked "what could they gain from betraying us." I can see that question from their point of view. If they are a fallen colony, they have a clear idea what they've lost. They probably have some remnant technology, and are paranoid as hell. If I were them, I'd seriously consider ambushing the rescuers if those rescuers seemed weak or careless. And even if we come on strong . . . look at the questions Jefri asks for Steel. The guy is fishing, trying to figure out what we really value: the refugee ship, Jefri and the coldsleepers, or something on the ship. By the time we arrive, Steel will probably have wiped the local opposition – thanks to us. My guess is we're in for some heavy blackmail when we get to Tines' world.'

I thought we were talking about the good *news.* Ravna paged back through recent messages. Pham was right. The boy was telling the truth as he knew it, but . . . 'I don't see how we can play things any differently. If we don't help Steel against the Woodcarvers –'

'Yeah. We don't know enough to do much else. Whatever else is true, the Woodcarvers seem a valid threat to Jefri and the ship. I'm just saying we should be thinking about all the possibilities. One thing we absolutely mustn't do is show interest in Countermeasure. If the locals know how desperate we are for that, we don't have a chance.

'And it may be time to start planting a few lies of our own. Steel's been talking about building a landing place for us – inside his castle. There no way *OOB* could fit, but I think we should play along, tell Jefri that we can separate from our ultradrive, something like his container ship. Let Steel concentrate on building harmless traps . . .

He hummed one of his strange little 'marching' tunes. 'About the radio thing: why don't we just compliment the Tines real casually for improving our design. I wonder what they'd say?'

Pham Nuwen got his answer less than three days later. Jefri Olsndot said that *he* had done the optimization. So if you believed the kid, there was no evidence for hidden computers. Pham was not at all convinced: 'So just by coincidence, we have Isaac Newton on the other end of the line?' Ravna didn't argue the point. It *was* an enormous bit of luck, yet . . . She went over the earlier messages. In language and general knowledge, the boy seemed very ordinary for his age. But occasionally there were situations involving mathematical insight – not formal, taught math – where Jefri said striking things. Some of those conversations had been under fine conditions, with turnaround times of less than a minute. It all seemed too consistent to be the lie Pham Nuwen thought.

Jefri Olsndot, you are someone I want very much to meet.

There was always something: problems with the Tines' developments, fears that the murderous Woodcarvers might overrun Mr Steel, worries about the steadily degrading drive spines and the Zone turbulence that slowed *OOB*'s progress even further. Life was by turns and at once frustrating, boring, frightening. And yet . . .

One night about four months into the flight, Ravna woke in the cabin she had come to share with Pham. Maybe she had been dreaming, but she couldn't remember anything except that it had been no nightmare. There was no special noise in the room, nothing to wake her. Beside her, Pham was sleeping soundly in their hammock net. She eased her arm down his back, drawing him gently toward her. His breathing changed; he mumbled something placid and unintelligible. In Ravna's opinion, sex in zero-gee was not the experience some people bragged it up to be; but really *sleeping* with someone . . . that was much nicer in free fall. An embrace could be light and enduring and effortless.

Ravna looked around the dimly-lit cabin, trying to imagine what had awakened her. Maybe it had just been the problems of the day – Powers knew there had been enough of those. She nestled her face against Pham's shoulder. Yes, always problems, but . . . in a way she was more content than she had been in years. Sure there were problems. Poor Jefri's situation. All the people lost at Straum and Relay. But she had three friends, and a love. Alone in a tiny ship bound for the Bottom, she was less lonely than she'd been since leaving

Sjandra Kei. More than ever in her life, maybe she could do something to help with the problems.

And then she guessed, part in sadness, part in joy, that years from now she might look back on these months as goldenly happy.

26

And finally, almost five months out, it was clear there was no hope of going on without repairing the drive spines. The *OOB* was suddenly doing only a quarter of a light-year per hour in a volume that tested good for two. And things were getting worse. They would have no trouble making it to Harmonious Repose, but beyond that . . .

Harmonious Repose. An ugly name, thought Ravna. Pham's 'lighthearted' translation was worse: Rest in Peace. In the Beyond, almost everything habitable was in use. Civilizations were transient and races faded . . . but there were always new people moving up from Below. The result was most often patchwork, polyspecific systems. Young races just up from the Slowness lived uneasily with the remnants of older peoples. According to the ship's library, RIP had been in the Beyond for a *long* time. It had been continuously inhabited for at least two hundred million years, time for ten thousand species to call it home. The most recent notes showed better than one hundred racial terranes. Even the youngest was the residue of a dozen emigrations. The place should be peaceful to the point of being moribund.

So be it. They jigged the *OOB* three light-years spinward. Now they were flying down the main Net trunk towards RIP: they'd be able to listen to the News the whole way in.

Harmonious Repose advertised. At least one species valued external goods, specializing in ship outfitting and repair. An industrious, hard-footed(?) race, the ads said. Eventually, she saw some video: the creatures walked on ivory tusks and had a froth of short arms growing from just below their necks. The ads included Net addresses of satisfied users. *Too bad we can't follow up on those.* Instead Ravna sent a short message in Triskweline, requesting generic drive replacements and listing possible methods of payment.

Meantime, the bad news kept rolling in:

Crypto: 0
As received by: *OOB* shipboard ad hoc
Language path: Baeloresk→Triskweline, SjK units
From: Alliance for the Defense
    [Claimed cooperative of five polyspecific empires in
    the Beyond below Straumli Realm. No record of
    existence before the Fall of the Realm.]
Subject: Call to action
Distribution:
    Threat of the Blight
    War Trackers Interest Group
    Homo Sapiens Interest Group
Date: 158.00 days since Fall of Relay
Key phrases: Action, not talk
Text of message:
    Alliance Forces are preparing for action against the tools of the Perversion. It is time for our friends to declare themselves. At the moment we do not need your military pledges, but in the very near future we will need support services including free Net time.
    In the coming seconds we will be watching closely to see who supports our action and who may be enslaved to the Perversion. If you live with the human infestation, you have a choice: act now with a good possibility of victory – or wait, and be destroyed.
    Death to vermin.

There were plenty of secondary messages, including speculation about who Death to Vermin (aka the 'Alliance for the Defense') had in mind. There were also rumors of military movement. This wasn't making the splash the fall of Relay had, but it did have the attention of several News groups. Ravna swallowed hard and looked away from the display. 'Well, they're still making big noises.' She tried for a light tone, but it didn't come out that way.

Pham Nuwen touched her shoulder. 'Quite true. And real killers generally don't advertise beforehand.' But there was more sympathy than conviction in his voice. 'We still don't know that this is more than a single loudmouth. There's no definite word of ship movements. What can they do after all?'

Ravna pushed herself up from the table. 'Not much, I hope. There are hundreds of civilizations with small human settlements. Surely they've taken precautions since this Death to Vermin stuff began . . . *By the Powers*, I wish I knew Sjandra Kei was safe.' It had been more than two years since she'd seen Lynne and her parents. Sometimes Sjandra Kei seemed something from another life, but just knowing it was there had been more comfort than she realized. Now . . .

On the other side of the command deck, the Skroderiders had been working on the repair specs. Now Blueshell rolled toward them. 'I do fear for the small settlements, but the humans at Sjandra Kei are the driving force of that civilization; even the name is a human one. Any attack on them would be an attack on the entire civilization. Greenstalk and I have traded there often enough, and with their commercial security forces. Only fools or bluffers would announce an invasion beforehand.'

Ravna thought a moment, brightened. The Dirokimes and Lophers would stand against any threat to humankind at Sjandra Kei. 'Yeah. We're not a ghetto there.' Things might be very bad for isolated humans, but Sjandra Kei would be okay. 'Bluffers. Well it's not called the Net of a Million Lies for nothing.' She pulled her mind back from worries beyond her control. 'But one thing is clear. Stopping at Harmonious Repose, we must be damn sure not to look like anything human.'

And of course, part of not looking human was that there be no sign of Ravna and Pham. The Riders would do all the 'talking.' Ravna and the Riders went through all the ship's exterior programs, weeding out human nuances that had crept in since they left Relay. And if they were actually boarded? Well, they would never survive a determined search, but they isolated things human in a fake jovian hold. The two humans would slip in there if necessary.

Pham Nuwen checked what they did – and found more than one slipup. For a barbarian programmer, he wasn't bad. But then they were rapidly reaching the depths where the best computer equipment wasn't that much more sophisticated than what he had known.

Ironically, there was one thing they could not disguise: that the *OOB* was from the Top of the Beyond. True, the ship was a bottom-lugger and based on a Mid Beyond design. But there was an *elegance* to the refit that screamed of nearly superhuman competence. 'The damn thing has the feel of a hand axe built in a factory,' was how Pham Nuwen put it.

RIPer security was an encouraging thing: a perfunctory velocity check and no boarding. *OOB* hopped into the system and finished a rocket burn to match position/velocity vector with the heart of Harmonious Repose and 'Saint(?) Rihndell's Repair Harbor.' (Pham: 'If you're a "saint", you gotta be honest, right?')

Out of Band was above the ecliptic and some eighty million kilometers from RIP's single star. Even knowing what to expect, the view was spectacular: The inner system was as dusty/gassy as a stellar nursery, even though the primary was a three-billion-year-old G star. That sun was surrounded by millions of rings, more spectacular than those around any planet. The largest and brightest resolved into myriads more. Even in the natural view there was bright color here, threads of green and red and violet. Warping of the ring plane laid lakes of shadow between colored hillsides, hillsides a million kilometers across. There were occasional objects – structures? – sticking far enough up from the ring plane to cast needle-like shadows out-system. Infrared and proper motion windows showed more conventional features: Beyond the rings lay a massive asteroid belt, and far beyond that a single jovian planet, its own million-klick ring system a puny afterthought. There were no other planets, either detected or on file. The largest objects in the main ring system were three hundred kilometers across ... but there appeared to be thousands of them.

At Saint Rihndell's direction they brought the ship down to the ring plane and matched velocities with the local junk. That last was a big impulsive burn: three gees for almost five minutes. 'Just like old, *old* times,' Pham Nuwen said.

In free fall again, they looked out upon their harbor: Up close it looked like planetary ring systems Ravna had known all her life. There were objects of all sizes down to less than a handspan across, uncounted globs of icy froth – gently touching, sticking, separating. The debris hung nearly motionless all about them; this was chaos that had been tamed long ago. In the plane of the rings, they couldn't see more than a few hundred meters. The debris blocked further views. And it wasn't all loose. Greenstalk pointed to a line of white that seemed to curve from infinity, pass close by them, and then retreat forever in the other direction. 'Looks like a single structure,' she said.

Ravna stepped up the magnification. In planetary ring systems, the 'frothy snowballs' sometimes accreted into strings thousands of klicks long ... The white thread spread wide beyond the window. The display said it was almost a kilometer across. This arc was definitely not made of snowballs. She could see ship locks and communications nodes. Checking with images from their approach, Ravna could see that the whole thing was better than forty million kilometers long. There were a number of breaks scattered along the arc. That figured: The scaled tensile strength of such a structure could be near zero. Depending on local distortions, it would pull apart briefly, then gently come together some time later. The whole affair was vaguely reminiscent of train cars coupling and uncoupling on some old-time Nyjoran railway.

Over the next hour, they moved carefully in to dock at the ring arc. The only thing regular about the structure was its linearity. Some of the modules were clearly designed for linking fore and aft. Others were jumbled heaps of oddball equipment meshed in dirty ice. The last few kilometers, they drifted through a forest of ultradrive spines. Two thirds of the berths were occupied.

Blueshell opened a window on Saint Rihndell's business specs. 'Hmm. Hm. Sir Rihndell seems extraordinarily busy.' He angled some fronds back at the ships in the exterior view.

Pham: 'Maybe he's running a junkyard.'

Blueshell and Greenstalk went down to the cargo lock to prepare for their first trip ashore. The Skroderiders had been together for two hundred years, and Blueshell came from a star trader tradition before that. Yet the two argued back and forth about the best approach to take with 'Saint Rihndell.'

'Of course, Harmonious Repose is typical, dear Blueshell; I would remember the type even if I'd never ridden a Skrode. But *our* business here is not like anything we've done before.'

Blueshell grumped wordlessly, and pushed another trade packet under his cargo scarf. The scarf was more than pretty. The material was tough, elastic stuff that protected what it covered.

This was the same procedure they had always followed in new ring systems, and it had worked well before. Finally he replied, 'Certainly, there are differences, mainly that we have very little to trade for the repairs and no previous commercial contacts. If we don't use hard business sense we'll get nothing here!' He checked the various sensors strung across his Skrode, then spoke to the humans. 'Do you want me to move any of the cameras? Do they all have a clear view?' Saint Rihndell was a miser when it came to renting bandwidth – or maybe it was simply cautious.

Pham Nuwen's voice came back. 'No. They're okay. Can you hear me?' He was speaking through a microphone inside their skrodes. The link itself was encrypted.

'Yes.'

The Skroderiders passed through *OOB*'s locks into Saint Rihndell's arc habitat.

From within, transparency arched around them, lines of natural windows that dwindled into the distance. They looked out upon Saint Rihndell's current customers and the ring fluff beyond. The sun was dimmed in the view, but there was a haze of brightness, a super corona. That was a power satellite's swarm no doubt; ring systems did not naturally make good use of the central fire. For a moment the Riders stopped in their tracks, taken by the image of a sea greater than any sea: The light might have been sunset through shallow surf. And to them, the drifting of thousands of nearby particles looked like food in a slow tidal surge.

The concourse was crowded. The creatures here had ordinary enough body plans, though none were of species Greenstalk recognized for certain. The tusk-leg type that ran Saint Rihndell's was most numerous. After a moment, one such drifted out from the wall near the *OOB*'s lock. It buzzed something that came out as Triskweline: 'For trading, we go this way.' Its ivory legs moved agilely across netting into an open car. The Skroderiders settled behind and they accelerated along the arc. Blueshell waggled at Greenstalk, 'The old story, eh; what good are their legs now?' It was the oldest Rider humor, but it was always worth a laugh: Two legs or four legs – evolved from flippers or jaws or whatever – were all very good for movement on land. But in space it scarcely mattered.

The car was making about one hundred meters per second, swaying slightly whenever they passed from one ring segment to the next. Blueshell kept up a steady patter of conversation with their guide, the sort of pitch that Greenstalk knew was one of his great joys in life. 'Where are we going? What are those creatures there? What sort of things are they in search of at Saint Rihndell's?' All jovial, and almost humanly brisk. Where short-term memory was failing him, he depended on his skrode.

Tusk-legs spoke only reduced-grammar Triskweline, and didn't seem to understand some of the questions: 'We go to the Master Seller . . . helper creatures those are . . . allies of big new customer . . .' Their guide's limited speech bothered dear Blueshell not at all; he was collecting responses more than answers. Most races had interests that were obscure to the likes of Blueshell and Greenstalk. No doubt there were billions of creatures in Harmonious Repose who were totally inscrutable to Riders or Humans or Dirokimes. Yet simple dialogue often gave insight on the two most important questions: *What do you have that might be useful to me, and how can I persuade you to part with it?* Dear Blueshell's questions were sounding out the other, trying to find the parameters of personality and interest and ability.

It was a team game the two Skroderiders played. While Blueshell chattered, Greenstalk watched everything around them, running her skrode's recorders on all bands, trying to place this environment in the context of others they had known. Technology: What would these people need? What could work? In space this flat, there would be little use for agrav fabric. And this low in the Beyond, a lot of the most sophisticated imports from above would spoil almost immediately. Workers outside the long windows wore articulated pressure suits – the force-field suits of the High Beyond would last only a few weeks down here.

They passed trees that grew like vines. Some of the trunks circled the wall of the arc; others trailed along their path for hundreds of meters. Tusk-leg gardeners floated everywhere about the plants, yet there was no evidence of agriculture. All this was ornament. In the ring plane beyond the windows there were occasional towers, structures that sprouted a thousand kilometers above the plane and cast the pointy shadows they had seen on their final approach to the system. Ravna's voice and Pham's buzzed against her stalk, softly asking Greenstalk about the towers, and speculating on the purpose of such unstable contraptions. She stored their theories away for later consideration . . . but she doubted them; some would work only in the High Beyond, and others were simply uneconomical.

Greenstalk had visited eight ring system civilizations in her life. They were a common consequence of accidents and wars (and occasionally, of deliberate habitat design). According to *OOB*'s library, Harmonious Repose had been a normal planetary system up till ten million years ago. Then there'd been a real estate dispute: A young race from Below had thought to colonize and exterminate the moribund inhabitants. The attack had been a miscalculation, for the moribund could still kill and the system was reduced to rubble. Perhaps the young race survived. But after ten million years, if there were any of those young killers left they would now be the most frail of the systems' elder races. Perhaps a thousand new races had passed through in that time, and almost every one had done something to tailor the rings and the gas cloud left from the debacle. What was left was not a ruin at all, but old . . . old. The ship's library claimed that no race had transcended from Harmonious Repose in a thousand years. That fact was more important than all the others. The current civilizations were in their twilight, refining mediocrity. More than anything else, the system had the feel of an old and beautiful tide pool, groomed and tended, shielded from the exciting waves that might upset its bansai plumes. Most likely the tusk-legs were the liveliest species about, perhaps the only one interested in trade with the outside.

Their car slowed and spiraled into a small tower.

'By the Fleet, what I wouldn't give to be out there with them!' Pham Nuwen waved at the views coming in from the skrode cameras. Ever since the Riders left he'd been at the windows, alternately gaping wide-eyed at the ringscape and bouncing abstractedly between the command deck's floor and ceiling. Ravna had never seen him so absorbed, so intense. However fraudulent his memories of trading days, he truly thought he could make a difference. *And he may be right.*

Pham came down from the ceiling, pulled close to the screen. It looked like serious bargaining was about to begin. The Skroderiders had arrived in a spherical room perhaps fifty meters across. Apparently they were floating near the center of it. A forest grew inward from all directions, and the Riders seemed to float just a few meters from the tree tops. Here and there between the branches they could see the ground, a mosaic of flowers.

Saint Rihndell's sales creatures were scattered all about the tallest trees. Each sat with its ivory limbs grasping a tree top. Tusk-leg races were a common thing in the galaxy, but these were the first Ravna had known. The body plan was totally unlike anything from home, and even now she didn't have a clear idea of their appearance. Sitting in the trees, their legs had more of the aspect of skeletal fingers grasping around the trunk. Their chief rep – who claimed to be Saint Rihndell itself – had scrimshaw covering two-thirds of its ivory. Two of the windows showed the carving close up; Pham seemed to think that understanding the artwork might be useful.

Progress was slow. Triskweline was the common language, but good interpreting devices didn't work this deep in the Beyond, and Saint Rihndell's people were only marginally familiar with the trade talk. Ravna was used to clean translations. Even the Net messages she dealt with were usually intelligible, though sometimes misleadingly so.

They'd been talking for twenty minutes and had only just established that Saint Rihndell might have the ability to repair *OOB*. It was the usual Riderly driftiness, and something more. The tedium seemed to please Pham Nuwen. 'Rav, this is almost like a Qeng Ho operation, face to face with critters and scarcely a common language.'

'We sent them a description of our repair problem hours ago. Why should it take so long for a simple yes or no?'

'Because they're haggling,' said Pham, his grin broadening. '"Honest" Saint Rihndell here –' he waved at the scrimshawed local, '– wants to convince us just how hard the job is . . . Lord I wish I was out there.'

Even Blueshell and Greenstalk seemed a little strange now. Their Triskweline was stripped down, barely more complex than Saint Rihndell's. And much of the discussion seemed very roundabout. Working for Vrinimi, Ravna had had some experience with sales and trading. But *haggling?* You had your pricing databases and strategy support, and directions from Grondr's people. You either had a deal or you didn't. What was going on between the Riders and Saint Rihndell was one of the more alien things Ravna had ever seen.

'Actually, things are going pretty well . . . I think. You saw when we arrived, the bone legs took away Blueshell's samples. By now they know precisely what we have. There's something in those samples that they want.'

'Yeah?'

'Sure. Saint Rihndell isn't bad-mouthing our stuff for his health.'

'Damn it, it's possible we don't have anything on board they could want. This was never intended to be a trade expedition.' Blueshell and Greenstalk had scavenged 'product samples' from the ship's supplies, things that the *OOB* could survive without. These included sensoria and some Low Beyond computer gear. Some of that would be a serious loss. *But one way or another, we need the repairs.*

Pham chuckled. 'No. There's something there Saint Rihndell wants. Otherwise he wouldn't still be jawing . . . And see how he keeps needling us about his "other customers' needs"? Saint Rihndell is a human kind of a guy.'

Something like human song came over the link to the Riders. Ravna phased Greenstalk's cameras toward the sound. From the forest 'floor' on the far side of Blueshell, three new creatures had appeared.

'Why . . . they're beautiful. Butterflies,' said Ravna.

'Huh?'

'I mean they look like butterflies. You know? Um. Insects with large colored wings.'

Giant butterflies, actually. The newcomers had a generally humanoid body plan. They were about 150 centimeters tall and covered with soft-looking brown fur. Their wings sprouted from behind their shoulder blades. At full spread they were almost two meters across, soft blues and yellows, some more intricately patterned than others. Surely they were artificial, or a gengineered affectation; they would have been useless for flying about in any reasonable gravity. But here in zero-gee . . . The three floated at the entrance for just a moment, their huge, soft eyes looking up at the Riders. Then they moved their wings in measured sweeps, and drifted gracefully into the air above the forest. The entire effect was like something out of a children's video. They had pert, button noses, like pet jorakorns, and eyes as wide and bashful as any human animator ever drew. Their voices sounded like youngsters singing.

Saint Rihndell and his buddies sidled around their tree

tops. The tallest visitor sang on, its wings gently flexing. After a moment Ravna realized it was speaking fluent Trisk with a front end adapted to the creature's natural speech:

'Saint Rihndell, greetings! Our ships are ready for your repairs. We have made fair payment, and we are in a great hurry. Your work must begin at once!' Saint Rihndell's Trisk specialist translated the speech for his boss.

Ravna leaned across Pham's back. 'So maybe our friendly repairman really is overbooked,' she said.

'. . . Yeah.'

Saint Rihndell came back around his tree top. His little arms picked at the green needles as he made a reply. 'Honored Customers. You made offer of payment, not fully accepted. What you ask is in short supply, difficult to . . . do.'

The cuddly butterfly made a squeaking noise that might have passed for joyous laughter in a human child. The sense behind its singing was different: 'Times are changing, Rihndell creature! Your people must learn: We will not be stymied. You know my fleet's sacred mission. We count every passing hour against you. Think on the fleet you will face if your lack of cooperation is ever known – is ever even *suspected*.' There was a sweep of blue and yellow wings, and the butterfly turned. Its dark, bashful eyes rested on the Riders. 'And these potted plants, they are customers? Dismiss them. Till we are gone, you have no other customers.'

Ravna sucked in a breath. The three had no visible weapons, but she was suddenly afraid for Blueshell and Greenstalk.

'Well, what do you know,' Pham said. 'Butterflies in jackboots.'

27

According to the clock, it took less than half an hour for the Skroderiders to make it back. It seemed a lot longer to Pham

Nuwen, even though he tried to keep up a casual front with Ravna. Maybe they were both keeping up a front; he knew she still considered him a fragile case.

But the Riders' cameras showed no more signs of the killer butterflies. Finally the cargo lock cracked open and Blueshell and Greenstalk were back.

'I was sure the wily tusk-legs was just pretending about the strong demand,' said Blueshell. He seemed as eager to rehash the story as Pham was.

'Yeah, I thought so too. In fact, I still think those butterflies might just be part of an act. It's all too melodramatic.'

Blueshell's fronds rattled in a way that Pham recognized as a kind of shiver. 'I wager not, Sir Pham. Those were Aprahanti. Just the look of them fills you with dread, does it not? They're rare these days, but a star trader knows the stories. Still . . . this is a little much even for Aprahanti. Their Hegemony has been on the wane for several centuries.' He rattled something at the ship, and the windows were filled with views of nearby berths in the repair harbor. There was more Rider rattling, this time between Greenstalk and Blueshell. 'Those other ships are a uniform type, you know. A High Beyond design like ours, but more, um . . . *militant.*'

Greenstalk moved close to a window. 'There are twenty of them. Why would so many need drive repairs all at once?'

Militant? Pham looked at the ships with a critical eye. He knew the major features of Beyonder vessels by now. These appeared to have rather large cargo capacity. Elaborate sensoria too. *Hm.* 'Okay, so the Butterflies are hard types. How scared is Saint Rihndell and company?'

The Skroderiders were silent for a long moment. Pham couldn't tell if his question was being given serious consideration or if they had simultaneously lost track of the conversation. He looked at Ravna. 'How about the local net? I'd like to get some background.'

She was already running comm routines. 'They weren't accessible earlier. We couldn't even get the News.' That was something Pham could understand, even if it was damned irritating. The 'local net' was a RIP-wide ultrawave computer and communication network, more complex than anything

Pham had known – but conceptually similar to organizations in the Slow Zone. And Pham Nuwen had seen what vandals could do to such structures; Qeng Ho had dealt with at least one obnoxious civilization by perverting its computer net. Not surprisingly, Saint Rihndell hadn't provided them with links to the RIP net. And as long as they were in harbor, the *OOB*'s antenna swarm was necessarily down, so they were also cut off from the Known Net and the newsgroups.

A grin lit Ravna's face. 'Hei! Now we've got read access, maybe more. *Greenstalk. Blueshell.* Wake up!'

Rattle. 'I wasn't asleep,' claimed Blueshell, 'just thinking on Sir Pham's question. Saint Rihndell is obviously afraid.'

As usual, Greenstalk didn't make excuses. She rolled around her mate to get a better look at Ravna's newly opened comm window. There was an iterated-triangle design with Trisk annotations. It meant nothing to Pham. 'That's interesting,' said Greenstalk.

'I am chuckling,' said Blueshell. 'It is more than interesting. Saint Rihndell is a hard-trading type. But look, he is making no charge for this service, not even a percentage of barter. He is afraid, but he still wants to deal with us.'

Hmm, so something from their High Beyond samples was enough to make him risk Aprahanti violence. *Just hope it's not something we really need too.* 'Okay, Rav, see if –'

'Just a second,' the woman said. 'I want to check the News.' She started a search program. Her eyes flickered quickly across her console window . . . and after a second she choked, and her face paled. 'By the Powers, *no!*'

'What is it?'

But Ravna didn't reply, or put the news to a main window. Pham grabbed the rail in front of her console and pulled himself around so he could see what she was reading:

Crypto: 0
As received by: Harmonious Repose Communication
    Synod
Language path: Baeloresk→Triskweline, SjK units
From: Alliance for the Defense
    [Claimed cooperative of five polyspecific empires in

the Beyond below Straumli Realm. No record of
existence before the Fall of the Realm.]
Subject: Bold victory over the Perversion
Distribution:
  Threat of the Blight
  War Trackers Interest Group
  Homo Sapiens Interest Group
Date: 159.06 days since fall of Relay
Key phrases: Action, not talk; A promising beginning
Text of message:
  One hundred seconds ago, Allilance Forces began
action against the tools of the Blight. By the time you
read this, the Homo sapiens worlds known as Sjandra
Kei will have been destroyed.
  Note well: for all the talk and theories that have
flown about the Blight, this is the first time anyone has
successfully *acted*. Sjandra Kei was one of only three
systems outside of Straumli Realm known to harbor
humans in large numbers. In one stroke we have
destroyed a third of the Perversion's potential for
expansion.
  Updates will follow.
  Death to vermin.

There was one other message in the window, an update of
sorts, but not from Death to Vermin:

Crypto: 0
Billing: charity/general interest
As received by: Harmonious Repose Communication
  Synod
Language path: Samnorsk→Triskweline, SjK units
From:
  [Note from lower protocol layer: This message was
  received at Sneerot Down along the Sjandra Kei
  bearing. The transmission was very weak, perhaps
  from a shipboard transmitter]
Subject: Please help
Distribution:

Threats Interest Group
Date: 5.33 hours since disaster at Sjandra Kei
Text of message:
Earlier today, relativistic projectiles struck our main habitations. Fatalities cannot be less than twenty-five billion. Three billion may still live, in transit and in smaller habitats.
We are still under attack.
Enemy craft are in the inner system. We see glow bombs. They are killing everyone.
Please. We need help.

'Nei nei *nei!*' Ravna drove up against him, her arms tight around him, her face buried in his shoulder. She sobbed incoherent Samnorsk. Her whole body shuddered against him. He felt tears coming to his own eyes. So strange. She had been the strong one, and he the fragile crazy. Now it was turned all around, and what could he do? 'Father, mother, sister – gone, gone.'

It was the disaster they thought could not happen, and now it had. In one minute she had lost everything she grew up with, and was suddenly alone in the universe. *For me, that happened long ago*, the thought came strangely dispassionate. He hooked a foot into the deck and gently rocked Ravna back and forth, trying to comfort her.

The sounds of grief gradually quieted, though he could still feel her sobs through his chest. She didn't raise her face from the tear-soaked place on his shirt. Pham looked over her head at Blueshell and Greenstalk. Their fronds looked strange . . . almost wilted.

'Look, I want to take Ravna away for a bit. Learn what you can, and I'll be back.'

'Yes, Sir Pham.' And they seemed to droop even more.

It was an hour before Pham returned to the command deck. When he did, he found the Riders deep in rattling conference with the *OOB*. All the windows were filled with flickering strangeness. Here and there Pham recognized a pattern or a printed legend, enough to guess that he was seeing ordinary ship displays, but optimized to Rider senses.

Blueshell noticed him first; he rolled abruptly toward him and his voder voice came out a little squeaky. 'Is she all right?'

Pham gave a little nod. 'She's sleeping now.' *Sedated, and with the ship watching her in case I've misjudged her.* 'Look, she'll be okay. She's been hit hard . . . but she's the toughest one of us all.'

Greenstalk's fronds rattled a smile. 'I have often thought that.'

Blueshell was motionless for an instant. Then, 'Well, to business, to business.' He said something to the ship, and the windows reformatted in the compromise usable by both humans and Riders. 'We've learned a lot while you were gone. Saint Rihndell indeed has something to fear. The Aprahanti ships are a small fragment of the Death to Vermin extermination fleets. These are stragglers still on their way to Sjandra Kei!'

All dressed up for a massacre, and no place to go. 'So now they want some action of their own.'

'Yes. Apparently Sjandra Kei put up some resistance and there were some escapes. The commander of this fleetlet thinks he can intercept some of these – if he can get prompt repairs.'

'What kind of extortion is really possible? Could these twenty ships destroy RIP?'

'No. It's the reputation of the greater force these ships are part of – and the great killing at Sjandra Kei. So Saint Rihndell is very timid with them, and what they need for repairs is the same class of regrowth agent that we need. We really are in competition with them for Rihndell's business.' Blueshell's fronds slapped together, the sort of 'go get 'em' enthusiasm he displayed when a hot deal was remembered. 'But it turns out we have something Saint Rihndell really, *really* wants, something he'll even risk tricking the Aprahanti to get.' He paused dramatically.

Pham thought back over the things they had offered the RIPers. *Lord, not the low zone ultrawave gear.* 'Okay, I'll bite. What do we have to give 'em?'

'A set of flamed trellises! Ha ha.'

'Huh?' Pham remembered the name from the list of odds and ends the Skroderiders had scrounged up. 'What's a "flamed trellis"?'

Blueshell poked a frond into his cargo scarf and extended something stubby and black to Pham: an irregular solid, about forty centimeters by fifteen, smooth to the touch. For all its size, its didn't mass more than a couple of grams. An artfully smoothed ... cinder. Pham's curiosity triumphed over greater concerns: 'But what's it good for?'

Blueshell dithered. After a moment, Greenstalk said a little shyly, 'There are theories. It's pure carbon, a fractal polymer. We know it's very common in Transcendent cargoes. We think it's used as packing material for some kinds of sentient property.'

'Or perhaps the excrement of such property,' Blueshell buzz-muttered. 'Ah, but that's not important. What is, is that occasional races in the Middle Beyond prize them. And why that? Again, we don't know. Saint Rihndell's folk are certainly not the final user. The Tusk-legs are far too sensible to be ordinary trellis customers. So. We have three hundred of these wonderful things ... more than enough to overcome Saint Rihndell's fears of the Aprahanti.'

While Pham had been away with Ravna, Saint Rihndell had come up with a plan. Applying the regrowth agent would be too obvious in the same harbor with the Aprahanti ships. Besides, the chief Butterfly had demanded the *OOB* move out. Saint Rihndell had a small harbor about sixteen million klicks around the RIP system. The move was even plausible, for it happened that there was a Skroderider terrane in the Harmonious Repose system – and currently it was just a few hundred kilometers from Rihndell's second harbor. They would rendezvous with the tusk-legs, exchanging repairs for two hundred seventeen flamed trellises. And if the trellises were perfectly matched, Rihndell promised to throw in an agrav refit. After the Fall of Relay, that would be very welcome ... *Hunh.* Ol' Blueshell just never stopped wheeling and dealing.

The *OOB* slipped free of its moorings and carefully drifted up from the ring plane. *Tiptoeing out.* Pham kept a close watch on the EM and ultrawave windows. But there were no target-locking emanations from the Aprahanti vessels, nothing more than casual radar contact. No one followed. Little *OOB* and its 'potted plants' were beneath the notice of the great warriors.

One thousand meters above the ring plane. Ten. The Skroderiders' chatter – both with Pham and between themselves – dwindled to naught. Their stalks and fronds angled so the sensing surfaces looked out in all directions. The sun and its power cloud was a blaze of light on one side of the deck. They were above the rings, but still so close . . . It was like standing at sunset on a beach of colored sands . . . that stretched to an infinite horizon. The Skroderiders stared into it, their fronds gently swaying.

Twenty kilometers above the rings. One thousand. They lit the *OOB*'s main torch and accelerated across the system. The Skroderiders came slowly out of their trance. Once they arrived at the second harbor, the regrowth would take about five hours – assuming Rihndell's agent had not deteriorated; the Saint claimed it was recently imported from the Top, and undiluted.

'Okay, so when do we deliver the trellises?'

'On completion of the repairs. We can't depart until Saint Rihndell – or *his* customers – are satisfied that all the pieces are genuine.'

Pham drummed his fingers on the comm console. This operation brought back a lot of memories, some of them hair-raising. 'So they get the goods while we're still in the middle of RIP. I don't like it.'

'See here, Sir Pham. Your experience with star trading was in the Slow Zone, where exchanges were separated by decades or centuries of travel time. I admire you for that, more than I can say – but it gives you a twisted view of things. Up here in the Beyond, the notion of return business is important. We know very little of Saint Rihndell's inner motivation, but we do know his repair business has existed for at least forty years. Sharp dealing we can expect from him, but if he robbed or murdered very many, trader groups would know, and his little business would starve.'

'Hmf.' No point in arguing it right now, but Pham guessed that this situation was special. Rihndell – and the RIPers in general – had Death to Vermin sitting on their doorstep, and stories of major chaos coming from the direction of Sjandra Kei. With that background they might just lose their courage once they had the trellises. Some precautions were in order. He drifted off to the ship's machine shop.

28

Ravna came to the cargo deck as Blueshell and Greenstalk were preparing the trellises for delivery. She moved hesitantly, pushing awkwardly from point to point. There were dark rings, almost bruises, beneath her eyes. She returned Pham's hug almost tentatively, but didn't let go. 'I want to help. Is there anything I can do to help?'

The Skroderiders left their trellises and rolled over. Blueshell ran a frond gently across Ravna's arm. 'Nothing for you to do now, my Lady Ravna. We have everything well, ah, in hand. We'll be back in less than an hour, and then we can be rid of here.'

, But they let her check their cameras and the cargo strap-downs. Pham drifted close by her as she inspected the trellises. The twisted carbon blocks looked stranger than the one alone had. Properly stacked, they fit perfectly. More than a meter across, the stack looked like a three-dimensional jigsaw puzzle carved from coal. Counting a separate bag of loose spares, they totaled less than half a kilogram. *Huh*. Damn things should be flammable as hell. Pham resolved to play with the remaining hundred-odd trellises after they were safely back in deep space.

Then the Skroderiders were through the cargo lock with their delivery, and they could only follow along on their cameras.

This secondary harbor was not really part of the tusk-leg

race's terrane. The inside of the arc was far different from what they had seen on the Skroderiders' first trip. There were no exterior views. Cramped passages wound between irregular walls pocked with dark holes. Insects flew everywhere, often covering parts of the camera balls. To Pham, the place looked filthy. There was no evidence of the terrane's owners – unless they were the pallid worms that sometimes stuck a featureless head up from a burrow hole. Over his voice link, Blueshell opined that these were very ancient tenants of the RIP system. After a million years and a hundred transcendent emigrations, the residue might still be sentient, but stranger than anything evolved in the Slow Zone. Such a people would be protected from physical extinction by ancient automation, but they would also be inward-turning, totally cautious, absorbed in concerns that were inane by any outside standard. It was the type that most often lusted after trellis work.

Pham tried to keep an eye on everything. The Riders had to travel almost four kilometers from the harbor lock to reach the place where the trellises would be 'validated.' Pham counted two exterior locks along the way, and nothing that looked especially threatening – but then how would he know what 'threatening' looked like here? He had the *OOB* mount an exterior watch. A large shepherd satellite floated on the outer side of the ring, but there were no other ships in this harbor. The EM and ultra-environment seemed placid, and what could be seen on the local net did not make the ship's traffic analysis suspicious.

Pham looked up from the reports. Ravna had drifted across the deck to the outside view. The repair work was visible, though not spectacular. A pale greenish aura hung around the damaged spines. It was scarcely brighter than the glow you often see on ship hulls in low planetary orbit. She turned and said softly, 'Is it really getting fixed?'

'As far as we can – I mean yes.' Ship's automation was monitoring the regrowth, but they wouldn't know for sure till they tried to fly with it.

Pham was never sure why Rihndell had the Skroderiders pass

through the wormheads' terrane; maybe, if the creatures were the ultimate trellis users, they wanted a look at the sellers. Or maybe it had some connection with the treachery that ultimately followed. In any case the Riders were soon out of it, and into a polyspecific concourse as crowded as any low-tech bazaar.

Pham's jaw sagged. Everywhere he looked there was a different class of sophont. Intelligent life is a rare development in the universe; in all his life in the Slow Zone, he had known three nonhuman races. But the universe is a big place, and with ultradrive it was easy to find other life. The Beyond collected the detritus of countless migrations, an accumulation that finally made civilization ubiquitous. For a moment he lost track of his surveillance programs and his general suspicions, drowned in the wonder of it. Ten species? Twelve? Individuals brushed familiarly by one another. Even Relay had not been like this. But then Harmonious Repose was a civilization lost in stagnation. These races had been part of the RIP complex for thousands of years. The ones that could interact had long since learned to do so.

And nowhere did he see butterfly wings on creatures with large, compassionate eyes.

He heard a small sound of surprise from the far side of the deck. Ravna was standing close by a window that looked out from one of Greenstalk's side cameras. 'What is it, Rav?'

'Skroderiders. See?' She pointed into the mob and zoomed the view. For a moment the images towered over her. Through the passing chaos he had a glimpse of hull forms and graceful fronds. Except for cosmetic stripes and tassles, they looked very familiar indeed.

'Yeah, there's a small colony of them hereabouts.' He opened the channel to Greenstalk and told her about the sighting.

'I know. We . . . smelled them. Sigh. I wish we had time to visit them after this. Finding friends in far places . . . always nice.' She helped Blueshell push the trellises around a balloon aquarium. They could see Rihndell's people just ahead. Six tusk-legs sat on the wall around what might be test equipment.

Blueshell and Greenstalk pushed their ball of frothy carbon into the group. The scrimshawed one leaned close to the pile and reached out to fondle the pieces with its tiny arms. One after another the trellises were placed in the tester. Blueshell moved in close to watch, and Pham set the main windows to look through his cameras. Twenty seconds passed. Rihndell's Trisk interpreter said, 'First seven test true, make an interlocked septet.'

Only then did Pham realize he had been holding his breath. The next three 'septets' passed too. Another sixty seconds. He glanced at the ship's repair status. *OOB* considered the job done but for sign-off commit from the local net. *Another few minutes and we can kiss this place goodbye!*

But there are always problems. Saint Rihndell bitched about the twelfth and fifteenth sets. Blueshell argued at length, grudgingly produced replacement pieces from his bag of spares. Pham couldn't tell if the Skroderider was debating for the fun of it, or if he really was short on good replacements.

Twenty-five sets okayed.

'Where is Greenstalk going?' said Ravna.

'What?' Pham called up the view from Greenstalk's cameras. She was five meters from Blueshell and moving away. He panned wildly about. A local Skroderider was on her left and another floated inverted above her. Its fronds touched hers in apparently amiable conversation. *'Greenstalk!'* There was no reply.

'Blueshell! What's happening?' But that Rider was in gesticulating argument with the tusk-legs. Still another set of trellises had failed their examination. *'Blueshell!'* After a moment the Rider's voice came over their private channel. He sounded drifty, the way he often did when he was jammed or overloaded. 'Not to bother me now, Sir Pham. I'm down to three perfect replacements. I must persuade these fellows to settle for what they already have.'

Ravna broke in, 'But what about Greenstalk? What's happening to her?' The cameras had lost sight of each other. Greenstalk and her companions emerged from a dense crowd and floated across the middle of the concourse. They were using gas jets instead of wheels. Someone was in a hurry.

The seriousness of events finally got through to Blueshell. The view from his skrode turned wildly as he rolled back and forth around Saint Rihndell's people. There was the rattle of Rider talk and then his voice came back on the inside channel, plaintive and confused. 'She's gone. She's gone. I must . . . I have to . . .' Abruptly he rolled back to the tusk-legs and resumed the argument that had just been interrupted. After a couple of seconds his voice came back on the inside channel. 'What should I do, Sir Pham? I have a sale here still incomplete, yet my Greenstalk has wandered off.'

Or been kidnapped. 'Get us the sale, Blueshell. Greenstalk will be okay . . . *OOB*: Plan B.' He grabbed a headset and pushed off from the console.

Ravna rose with him. 'Where are you going?'

He grinned. 'Out. I thought Saint Rihndell might lose his halo when the crunch came – and I made plans.' She followed him as he glided toward the floor hatch. 'Look. I want you to stay on deck. I can only carry so much snoop equipment; I'll need your coordination.'

'But –'

He went through the hatch headfirst, missing the rest of her objection. She didn't follow, but a second later her voice was back, in his headset. Some of the tremor was gone from her voice; the old Ravna was there, fighting out from under her other problems. 'Okay, I'll back you . . . but what can we *do?*'

Pham pulled himself hand over hand down the passageway, accelerating to a speed that would have left a lubber caroming off the walls. Ahead loomed the uncompromising wall of the cargo lock. He swatted a hand gently at the wall and flipped head over heels. He dragged his hands precisely against the wall flanges, slowing just enough so the impact with the hatch did not break his ankles. Inside the lock, the ship had his suit already powered up.

'Pham, you can't go out.' Evidently she was watching through the lock's cameras. 'They'll know we're a human expedition.'

His head and shoulders were already in the suit's top shell. He felt the bottom pushing up around him, the seals fastening. 'Not necessarily.' *And by now it probably doesn't matter.* 'There are plenty of two-arm/two-leg critters around, and I've glued some camouflage to this outfit.' He cupped his chin in the helmet controls and reset the displays. The armored pressure suit was a very primitive thing compared to the field suits of Relay. Yet the Qeng Ho would have given a starship for this gear. He'd originally put the thing together to impress the Tines, *but it's going to get some early testing.*

He chinned up the outside view, what Ravna was seeing: his figure was unrelieved black, more than two meters tall. The hands were backed with carapace-claws and every edge of his figure was razor-sharp and spined. These most recent additions should break the lines of the strictly human form, and hopefully be intimidating as hell.

Pham cycled the lock and pushed off into the wormheads' terrane. Walls of mud stood all around, misty in humid air and swarms of insects.

Ravna's voice was in his ear. 'I've got a low-level query, probably automatic: "Why you send third negotiator?"'

'Ignore it.'

'Pham, be careful. These Middle Beyond cultures, the old ones, they keep nasty things in reserve. Otherwise they wouldn't still be around.'

'I'll be a good citizen.' *As long as I'm treated nice.* He was already halfway to the concourse gate. He chinned up a small window from Blueshell's camera. All this high-bandwidth comm was courtesy of the local net. Strange that Rihndell was still providing the service. Blueshell seemed to be negotiating still. Maybe there *wasn't* a scam . . . or anyway, not one that Saint Rihndell was in on.

'Pham, I've lost the video from Greenstalk, just as she went into some kind of tunnel. Her location beacon is still clear.'

The concourse gate made an opening for him, and then Pham was in the crowded market volume. He heard the raucous hubbub even through his armor. He moved slowly, sticking to the most uncrowded paths, following the guide ropes that threaded the space. The mob was no problem. Everyone made way, some with almost panicky haste. Pham didn't know whether it was his razor spines or the trace of

312

chlorine his suit 'leaked'. *Maybe that last touch was a bit much.* But the whole point was to look nonhuman. He slowed even more, doing his best not to nick anyone. Something awfully like a target-designation laser flickered in his rear window. He ducked quickly around an aquarium as Ravna said, 'The terrane just complained to your suit: "You are in violation of dress-code" is how the translation comes out.'

Is it my chlorine B.O., or have they detected the guns? 'What about outside? Any Butterflies in sight?'

'No. Ship activity hasn't changed much during the last five hours. No Aprahanti movement or change in comm status.' Long pause. Indirectly from the *OOB* bridge he could hear Blueshell talking with Ravna, the words indistinct but excited. He jabbed around, trying to find the direct connection. Then Ravna was talking to him again. 'Hei! Blueshell says Rihndell has accepted the shipment! He's onloading the agrav fabric right now. And *OOB* just got a commit on the repairs!' So they were ready to fly – except that three of them were still ashore, and one of them was missing.

Pham floated over the top of the aquarium and finally caught direct sight of Blueshell. He tweaked the suit's gas jets very carefully and settled down beside the Rider.

His arrival was about as welcome as finger-mites at a picnic. The scrimshawed one had been chattering away, tapping his articulated artwork on the wall as his helper translated into Trisk. Now the creature drew in his tusks, and the neck arms folded themselves. The others followed suit. All of them sidled up the wall, away from Blueshell and Pham. 'Our business is now complete. We don't know where your friend has gone,' said the Trisk interpreter.

Blueshell's fronds extended after them, wavering. 'B-but just a little guidance is all we need. Who –' It was no use. Saint Rihndell and his merry crew kept going. Blueshell rattled in abrupt frustration. His fronds angled slightly, turning all attention on Pham Nuwen. 'Sir Pham, I am doubting now your expertise as a trader. Saint Rihndell might have helped.'

'Maybe.' Pham watched the tusk-legs disappear into the crowd, pulling the trellises behind them like a big black balloon. Ugh. Maybe Rihndell was simply an honest trader. 'What are the chances that Greenstalk would abandon you in the middle of something like that?'

Blueshell dithered for a moment. 'In an ordinary trade stop, she might have noticed some extraordinary profit opportunity. But here, I –'

Ravna's voice interrupted sympathetically, 'Maybe she just, uh, forgot the context?'

'No.' Blueshell was definite. 'The skrode would never permit such a failure, not in the middle of a hard trade.'

Pham shifted windows around inside his helmet, looking in all directions. The crowd was still keeping an open space around them. There was no evidence of cops. *Would I know them if I saw them?* 'Okay,' said Pham. 'We have a problem, whether I'd come out or not. I suggest we take a little walk, see if we can find where Greenstalk went.'

Rattle. 'We have little choice now. My Lady Ravna, do please try to reach the tusk-legs interpreter. Perhaps he can link us to the local Skroderiders.' He came off the wall, rotated on gas jets. 'Come along, Sir Pham.'

Blueshell led the way across the concourse, vaguely in the direction Greenstalk had gone. Their path was anything but straight, more a drunkard's walk that once took them almost back to their starting place. 'Delicately delicately,' the Skroderider responded when Pham complained about the pace. The Rider never insisted on passage through clots of critters. If they did not respond to the gentle waving of his fronds, he detoured all around them. And he kept Pham directly behind him so the intimidation factor of the razored armor was of no use. 'These people may look very peaceable to you, Sir Pham, easy to push around. But note, this is among themselves. These races have had thousands of years to accommodate to one another, to achieve local commensality. To outsiders they will necessarily be less tolerant, else they would have been overrun long ago.' Pham remembered the 'dress-code' warning and decided not to argue.

The next twenty minutes would have been the experience of a lifetime for a Qeng Ho trader, to be within arm's reach of a dozen different intelligent species. But when they finally reached the far wall, Pham was grinding his teeth. Twice more he received a dress-code warning. The only bright spot: Saint Rihndell was still extending the courtesy of local net support, and Ravna had more information: 'The local Skroderider colony is about a hundred kilometers from the concourse. There's some kind of transport station beyond the wall you're at.'

And the tunnel Greenstalk had entered was just ahead of them. From this angle they could see the dark of space beyond it. For the first time there was no problem with crowds; scarcely anyone was entering or leaving the hole.

Laser light twinkled in his rear windows. 'Dress code violation. Fourth warning. It says to "please leave the volume at once."'

'We're going. We're going.'

Darkness, and Pham boosted the gain on his helmet windows. At first he thought the 'transport station' was open to space, that the locals had restraint fields as in the High Beyond. Then he noticed the pillars merged into transparent walls. They were still indoors in the old-fashioned way, but the view ... They were on the starward side of the arc. The ring particles were like dark fish floating silently a few tens of meters out from him. In the further distance, structures stuck out of the ring plane far enough to get sundazzle. But the brightest object was almost overhead: the blue of ocean, the white of cloud. Its soft light flooded the ground around him. However far the Qeng Ho fared, such a sight had been welcome. Yet this was not quite the real thing. This was only approximately spherical, and its face was bisected by the shadow of the ring. It was a small object, not more than a few hundred klicks above him, one of the shepherd satellites they had seen on the way in. The shepherd's haze of atmosphere was crisply bounded by the sides of some vast canopy.

He dragged his attention down from the sight. 'Ten to one that's the Skroderiders' terrane.'

'Of course,' Blueshell replied. 'It's typical. The surf in such minigravity can never be what I prefer, but –'

'Dear Blueshell! Sir Pham! Over here.' It was Greenstalk's

voice. According to Pham's suit, it was a local connection, not relayed through the *OOB*.

Blueshell's fronds angled in all directions. 'Are you all right, Greenstalk?' They rattled back and forth at each other for a few seconds. Then Greenstalk resumed in Trisk: 'Sir Pham. Yes, I'm all right. I'm sorry to upset you all so much. But I could tell the deal with Rihndell was going to work out, and then these local Riders stopped by. They are wonderful people, Sir Pham. They have invited us across to their terrane. Just for a day or so. It will be a wonderful rest before we go on our way. And I think they may be able to help us.'

Like the quest romances he'd found in Ravna's bedtime library: the weary travelers, partway to their goal, find a friendly haven and some special gift. Pham switched to a private line to Blueshell: 'Is that really Greenstalk? Is she under duress?'

'It's her, and free, Sir Pham. You heard us speaking. I've been with her two hundred years. No one's twisting her fronds.'

'Then why the *hell* did she skip out on us? Pham surprised himself, almost hissing the words.

Long pause. 'That *is* strange. My guess: these local Riders somehow know something very important to us. Come, Sir Pham. But carefully.' He rolled away in what seemed a random direction.

'Rav, what do you —' Pham noticed the red light blinking on his comm status panel, and his irritation chilled. How long had the link to Ravna been down?

Pham followed Blueshell, floating low behind the other, using his gas jets to pace the Skroderider. This entire area was covered with the stickem that Riders liked for zero-gee rolling. Yet right now the place seemed deserted. Nobody in sight where just a hundred meters away there were bustling crowds. The whole thing screamed ambush, yet it didn't make sense. If Death to Vermin — or their stooges — had spotted them, a simple alarm would have served. Some Rihndell game . . . ? Pham powered up the suit's beam weapons and enabled countermeasures; midge cameras flitted off in all directions. So much for dress codes.

The bluish moonlight washed the plain, showing soft mounds and angular arrays of unknown equipment. The surface was pocked with holes (tunnel entrances?). Blueshell said something muddled about the 'beautiful night,' how much fun it would be to sit on the seashore a hundred kilometers above them. Pham scanned in all directions, trying to identify fields of fire and killing zones.

The view from one of his midges showed a forest of leafless fronds – Skroderiders standing silent in the moonlight. They were two hillocks away. Silent, motionless, without any lights . . . perhaps just enjoying the moonlight. In the midge's amplified view, Pham had no trouble identifying Greenstalk; she was standing at one end of a line of five Riders, her hull stripes clearly visible. There was a hump on the front of her skrode, and a rod-like projection. Some kind of restraint? He floated a couple of midges near. *A weapon*. All those Riders were armed.

'We're already aboard the transport, Blueshell,' came Greenstalk's voice. 'You'll see it in a few more meters, just on the other side of a ventilator pile,' apparently referring to the mound that he and the Skroderider were approaching. But Pham knew there was no flier there; Greenstalk and her guns were to the side of their progress. Treachery, very workman-like but also very low tech. Pham almost shouted out to Blueshell. Then he noticed the flat ceramic rectangle mounted in the hill just a few meters behind the Rider. The nearest midge reported it was some kind of explosive, probably a directional mine. A low-resolution camera, barely more than a motion sensor, was mounted beside it. Blueshell had rolled nonchalantly past the thing, all the while chattering with Greenstalk. *They let him past.* New suspicions rose dark and grim. Pham broke to a stop, backing quickly; never touching ground, the only sounds he made were the quiet hisses of his gas jets. He detached one of his wrist claws and had a midge fly it close past the mine's sensor . . .

There was a flash of pale fire and a loud noise. Even five meters to the side, the shock wave pushed him back. He had a glimpse of Blueshell thrown frond over wheels on the far side of the mine. Edged metal whizzed about, but mindlessly:

nothing came back to attack again. Several midges were destroyed by the blast.

Pham took advantage of the racket to accelerate hard, scooting up a nearby 'hill' and into a shallow valley (alley?) that looked down on the Skroderiders. The ambushers rolled forward around the hill, rattling happily at one another. Pham held his fire, curious. After a moment, Blueshell floated into the air a hundred meters away. 'Pham?' he said plaintively. 'Pham?'

The ambushers ignored Blueshell. Three of them disappeared around the hill. Pham's midges saw them stop in consternation, fronds erect – they had realized he'd gotten away. The five spread out, searching the area, hunting him down. There was no persuasive talk from Greenstalk anymore.

There was a sharp cracking sound and blaster fire glowed from behind a hill. Somebody was a little nervous on the trigger.

Above it all floated Blueshell, the perfect target, yet still untouched. His speech was a combination of Trisk and Rider rattle now, and where Pham could understand it, he heard fear. 'Why are you shooting? What is the problem? Greenstalk, please!'

The paranoid in Pham Nuwen was not deceived. *I don't want you up there looking down.* He sighted his main beam gun on the Rider, then shifted his aim and fired. The blast was not in visible wavelengths, but there were gigajoules in the pulse. Plasma coruscated along the beam, missing Blueshell by less than five meters. Well above the Skroderider, the beam struck hull crystal. The explosion was spectacular, an actinic glare that sent glowing fragments in a thousand rays.

Pham flew sideways even as the ceiling flared. He saw Blueshell spin off, regain control – and move precipitously for cover. Where Pham's beam had hit, a corona of light was dimming from blue through orange and red, its light still brighter than the shepherd moon overhead.

His warning shot had been like a great finger pointing back toward his location. In the next fifteen seconds, four of the ambushers fired on the place Pham had been. There was

318

silence, then faint rustling. In a game of stealth, the five might think themselves easy winners. They still hadn't realized how well-equipped he was. Pham smiled at the pictures coming in from his midges. He had every one of them in sight, and Blueshell too.

If it were just these four – five?, there would be no problem. But surely reinforcements, or at least complications, were on the way. The wound in the ceiling had cooled to darkness, but there was a *hole* there now, half a meter across. The sound of hissing wind came from it, a sound that brought reflex fear to Pham even in his armor. It might take a while before the leak affected the Skroderiders, but it was an emergency nevertheless. It would attract notice. He stared at the hole. Down here it was stirring a breeze, but in the few meters right below the hole there was a miniature tornado of dust and loose junk, hurtling up and out . . .

And beyond the transparent hull, in space:

A gap of dark and then a glittering plume, where the debris emerged from the arc's shadow into the sunlight. A neat idea struggled for his attention.

Oops. The five Riders had roughly encircled him. Now one blundered into view, saw him, and snapped a shot. Pham returned fire and the other exploded in a cloud of super-heated water and charred flesh. Its undamaged skrode sailed across the space between the hills, collecting panicky fire from the others. Pham changed position again, moving in the direction he knew was farthest from his enemies' positions.

A few more minutes of peace. He looked up at the crystal plume. There was something . . . *yes*. If reinforcements should come, why not for him? He sighted on the plume and shunted his voice line through the gun's trigger circuit. He almost started talking, then thought . . . *Better lower the power on this one*. Details. He aimed again, fired continuously, and said, 'Ravna, I sure as hell hope you have your eyes open. I need help . . .' and briefly described the crazy events of the last ten minutes.

This time his beam was putting out less than ten thousand joules per second, not enough to glow the air. But reflecting off the plume beyond the hull, the modulation should be visible for thousands of klicks, in particular to the *OOB* on the other side of the habitat.

The Skroderiders were closing in again. Damn. No way he could leave *this* message on automatic send; he needed the 'transmitter' for more important things. Pham flew from valley to valley, maneuvering behind the Rider that was farthest from the others. One against three – four? He had superior firepower and information, but one piece of bad luck and he was dead. He floated up on his next target. Quietly, carefully . . .

A seat of light brushed his arm, flaring the armor incandescent. White hot drops of metal sprayed as he twisted out of the way. He boosted straight across the space between three hillocks, firing down on the Rider there. Lights crisscrossed around him, and then he was under cover again. They were *fast*, almost as if they had automatic aiming gear. Maybe they did: their skrodes.

Then the pain hit. Pham folded on himself, gasping. If this were like wounds he remembered, there would be char to the bone. Tears floated in his eyes and consciousness disappeared in a nauseated faint. He came to. It could only be a second or two later – else he'd never have wakened. The others were a lot closer now, but the one he'd fired on was just a glowing crater and random skrode fragments. His suit's automation brought the damaged armor in close to his side. He felt the chill of local anesthetic and the pain dimmed. Pham eased around the hill, trying to keep all three of his antagonists simultaneously out of sight. They had caught on to his midges; every few seconds a glow erupted or a hill top turned to glowing slag. It was overkill, but the midges were dying . . . and he was losing his greatest advantage.

Where is Blueshell? Pham cycled through the views from his remaining midges, then his own. The bastard was back in the air, high above the combat – untouched by his fellow Riders. *Reporting everything I do.* Pham rolled over, awkwardly bringing his gun to bear on the tiny figure. He hesitated. *You're getting soft, Nuwen.* Blueshell abruptly accelerated downwards, his cargo scarf billowing out behind him. Evidently he was using his gas jets' full power. Against the background noise of bubbling metal and blast beam thunder, his fall was totally silent. He was driving straight for the nearest of the attackers.

Thirty meters up, the Rider released something large and angular. The two separated, Blueshell braking and diving to the side. He disappeared behind the hills. At the same time, much nearer, came a solid *thud/crunch*. Pham spent his next to last midge for a peek around the hillside. He had a glimpse of a skrode, and fronds splayed all about a squashed stalk. There was a flash of light, and the midge was gone.

Only two ambushers left. One was Greenstalk.

For ten seconds there was no more firing. Yet things were not completely silent. The slumped, glowing metal of his arm popped and sputtered as it cooled. High above was the susurrus of air escaping the hull. Fitful breezes whispered around ground level, making it impossible to keep position without constant tweaking at his jets. He paused, letting the current carry him silently out of his little valley. *There.* A ghostly hiss that was not his own. *Another.* The two were closing in on him from different directions. They might not know his exact position, but they could obviously coordinate their own.

The pain faded in and out, along with consciousness. Short pulses of agony and darkness. He dared not fool with any more anesthetic. Pham saw frond tips peeping over a nearby hill. He halted, watched the fronds. Most likely, there was just enough vision area in the tips to sense motion . . . Two seconds passed. Pham's last midge showed the other attacker floating silently in from the side. Any second now, the two would pop up. At that instant, Pham would have given anything for an armed midge. In all his stupid hacking, he'd never gotten around to that. *No help for it.* He waited for a moment of clear consciousness, long enough to boost over the enemy and shoot.

There was a rattle of fronds, loud self-announcement. Pham's midge caught sight of Blueshell rolling behind slatted walls a hundred meters away. The Skroderider rushed from protection to protection, but always closer to Greenstalk's position. And the rattling? Was it a pleading? Even after five months with the Riders, Pham had only the vaguest sense of their rattle-talk. Greenstalk – the Greenstalk who had always been the shy one, the compulsively honest one – rattled nothing back. She swung her beamer around, raking the slats with fire. The third Rider popped up just far enough to shoot at the slats. His angle would have been just right to fry Blueshell where he stood – except that the movement took him directly in front of Pham Nuwen's gun.

Even as Pham fired, he was boosting out of his hole. Now was his only chance. If he could turn, fire back on Greenstalk before she was done with Blueshell –

The maneuver was an easy head-over-heels that should have left him upside down and facing back upon Greenstalk. But nothing was easy for him now, and Pham came around spinning too fast, the landscape dwindling beneath him. But there was Greenstalk all right, swinging her weapon back toward him.

And there was Blueshell, racing from between pillars that glowed white in the heat of Greenstalk's fire. His voice was loud in Pham's ear: 'I beg you, don't kill her. Don't kill –'

Greenstalk hesitated, then turned the weapon back on the advancing Blueshell. Pham triggered his gun, letting his spin drag the beam across the ground. Consciousness ebbed. *Aim! Aim right!* He furrowed the land below with a glowing, molten arrow, that ended at something dark and slumped. Blueshell's tiny figure was still rolling across the wreckage, trying to reach her. Then Pham had turned too far and could not remember how to change the view. The sky swung slowly past his eyes:

A bluish moon with a sharp shadow 'cross its middle. A ship floating close, with feathery spines, like some giant bug. What in the Qeng Ho . . . *where am I?* . . . and consciousness fled.

29

There were dreams. He'd lost a captaincy once again, been busted down to tending potted plants in the ship's greenhouse. Sigh. Pham's job was to water them and make them bloom. But then he noticed the pots had wheels and moved behind his back, waiting, softly rattling. What had been beautiful was now sinister. Pham had been willing to water and weed the creatures; he had always admired them.

Now he was the only one who knew they were the enemy of life.

More than once in his life, Pham Nuwen had wakened inside medical automation. He was almost used to coffin-close tanks, plain green walls, wires and tubes. This was different, and it took him a while to realize just where he was. Willowy trees bent close around him, swaying just a little in the warm breeze. He seemed to be lying on softest moss in a tiny glade above a pond. Summer haze hung in the air above the water. It was all very nice, except that the leaves were *furry*, and not quite the green of anything he had ever seen. This was someone else's notion of home. He reached up toward the nearest branch, and his hand hit something unyielding just fifty centimeters above his face. A curved wall. For all the trick pictures, this was about the same size as the surgeons he remembered.

Something clicked behind his head; the idyll slid past him, taking its warm breeze with it. Somebody – *Ravna* – floated just beyond the cyclinder 'Hi, Pham.' She reached past the surgeon's hull to squeeze his hand. Her kiss was tremulous, and she looked haunted, as if she'd been crying a lot.

'Hi, yourself,' he said. Memory came back in jagged pieces. He tried to push off the bed, and found another similarity between this surgeon and ones of the Qeng Ho: he was securely plugged in.

Ravna laughed a little weakly. 'Surgeon. Disconnect.' After a moment Pham drifted free.

'It's still holding my arm.'

'No, that's the sling. Your left arm is going to take a while to regrow. It almost got burned off, Pham.'

'Oh.' He looked down at the white cocoon that meshed his arm against his side. He remembered the gunfight now . . . and realized that parts of his dream were deadly real. 'How long have I been out?' The anxiety spilled into his voice.

'About thirty hours. We're more than sixty light-years out from Harmonious Repose. We're doing okay, except that now everyone in creation seems to be chasing us.'

The dream. His free hand clamped hard on Ravna's arm. 'The Skroderiders, where are they?' *Not on board, pray the Fleet.*

'W-what's left of Greenstalk is in the other surgeon. Blueshell is –'

Why have they let me live? Pham's eyes roved the room. .They were in a utility cabin. Any weapons were at least twenty meters away. Hm. More important than guns: get command console privileges with the *OOB* . . . if it was not already too late. He pushed off from the surgeon and drifted out of the room.

Ravna followed. 'Take it easy, Pham. You just came out of a surgeon.'

'What have they said about the shoot-out?'

'Poor Greenstalk's not in a position to say anything, Pham. Blueshell says pretty much what you did: Greenstalk was grabbed by the rogue Riders, forced to lure you two into a trap.'

'Hmhm, hmhm,' Pham strove for a noncommittal tone. So maybe there was a chance; maybe Blueshell was not yet perverted. He continued his one-handed progress up the ship's axis corridor. A minute later he was on the bridge, Ravna tagging behind.

'Pham. What's the matter? There's a lot we have to decide, but –'

How right you are. He dived onto the command deck and made for the command console. '*Ship.* Do you recognize my

324

voice?'

Ravna began, 'Pham, What's this –'

'Yes, sir.'

'– all about?'

'Command privileges,' he said. Capabilities granted while the Riders were ashore. Would they still be in place?

'Granted.'

The Skroderiders had had thirty hours to plan their defense. This was all too easy, too easy. 'Suspend command privileges for the Skroderiders. Isolate them.'

'Yes, sir,' came the ship's reply. *Liar!* But what more could he do? The sweep toward panic crested, and suddenly he felt very cool. He was Qeng Ho . . . and he was also godshatter.

Both Riders were in the same cabin, Greenstalk in the other copy of the ship's surgeon. Pham opened a window on the room. Blueshell sat on a wall beside the surgeon. He looked wilted, as when they heard about Sjandra Kei. He angled his fronds at the video pickup. 'Sir Pham. The ship tells me you've suspended our privileges?'

'*What* is going on, Pham?' Ravna had dug a foot into the floor, and stood glaring at him.

Pham ignored both questions. 'How is Greenstalk doing?' he said.

The fronds turned away, seemed to become even more limp. 'She lives . . . I thank you, Sir Pham. It took great skill to do what you did. Considering everything, I could not have asked for more.'

What did I do? He remembered firing on Greenstalk. Had he pulled his aim? He looked inside the surgeon. This was quite different from the human configuration: This one was mostly water-filled, with turbulent aeration along the patient's fronds. Asleep(?), Greenstalk looked frailer than he remembered, her fronds waving randomly in the water. Some were nicked, but her body seemed whole. His eyes traveled downwards toward the base of the stalk, where a Rider is normally attached to its skrode. The stump ended in a cloud of surgical tubing. And Pham remembered the last instant of the firefight, blasting the skrode out from under Greenstalk. *What is a Rider like without anything to ride?*

325

He pulled his eyes away from the wreckage. 'I've deleted your command privileges because I don't trust you.' *My former friend, tool of my enemy.*

Blueshell didn't answer. After a moment Ravna spoke. 'Pham. Without Blueshell, I'd never have gotten you out of that habitat. Even then – we were stuck in the middle of the RIP system. The shepherd satellite was screaming for our blood; they had figured out we were human. The Aprahanti were trying to break harbor and come down on us. Without Blueshell, we'd never have convinced local security to let us go ultra – we'd probably have been blown away the second we cleared the ring plane. We'd all be *dead* now, Pham.'

'Don't you know what happened down there?'

Some of the indignation left Ravna's face. 'Yes. But understand about skrodes. They are a mechanical contrivance. It's easy enough to disconnect the cyber part from the mechanical linkages. These guys were controlling the wheels and aiming the gun.'

Hmm. On the window behind Ravna, he could see Blueshell standing with his fronds motionless, not rushing to agree. Triumphant? 'That doesn't explain Greenstalk's sucking us in to the trap.' He raised a hand. 'Yeah, I know, she was bludgeoned into doing it. Only problem, Ravna, she had no hesitation. She was enthusiastic, bubbly.' He stared over the woman's shoulder. 'She was under no compulsion, *didn't you tell me that, Blueshell.*'

A long pause. Finally, 'Yes, Sir Pham.'

Ravna turned, drifting back so she could see both of them. 'But, but . . . it's still absurd. Greenstalk has been with us from the beginning. A thousand times she could have destroyed the ship – or gotten word to the outside. Why chance this stupid ambush?'

'Yes. Why didn't they betray us before . . .' Up until she asked the question, Pham had not known. He knew the *facts*, but had no coherent theory to hang them on. Now it all came together: the ambush, his dreams in the surgeon, even the paradoxes. 'Maybe she wasn't a traitor before. We really did escape from Relay without pursuit, without anyone knowing of us, much less our exact destination. Certainly no one expected humans to show up at Harmonious Repose.' He paused, trying to get it all together. The ambush, 'The ambush, it wasn't stupid – but it was completely ad hoc. The enemy had no backup. Their weapons were dumb, simple things –' *insight* '– why, I'll bet if you look at the wreckage of Greenstalk's skrode you'll find her beam gun was some sort of cutter tool. And the only sensor on the claymore mine was a motion detector: it had some civil use. All the gadgets were pulled together on very short notice by people who had not been expecting a fight. No, our enemy was very surprised by our appearance.'

'You think the Aprahanti could –'

'Not the Aprahanti. From what you said, they didn't break moorage till after the gunfight, when the Rider moon started screaming about us. Whoever's behind this is indepedent of the Butterflies, and must be spread in very small numbers across many star systems – a vast set of tripwires, listening for things of interest. They noticed us, and weak as their outpost was they tried to grab our ship. Only when we were getting away did they advertise us. One way or another, they didn't want us to get away.' He jerked a hand at the ultratrace window. 'If I read that right, we've got more than five hundred ships on our tail.'

Ravna's eyes flicked to the display and back. Her voice was abstracted, 'Yes. That's part of the main Aprahanti fleet and . . .'

'There will be lots more, only they won't all be Butterflies.'

'. . . what are you saying then? Why would Skroderiders wish us ill? A conspiracy is senseless. They've never had a nation-state, much less an interstellar empire.'

Pham nodded. 'Just peaceful settlements – like that shepherd moon – in polyspecific civilizations all across the Beyond.' His voice softened. 'No, Rav, the Skroderiders are not the real enemy here . . . it's the thing behind them. The Straumli Perversion.'

Incredulous silence, but he noticed how tightly Blueshell held his fronds now. That one knew.

'It's the only explanation, Ravna. Greenstalk really was our friend, and loyal. My guess is that only a small minority of the

Riders are under the Perversion's control. When Greenstalk fell in with them she was converted too.'

'T-that's impossible! This is the Middle of the Beyond, Pham. Greenstalk had courage, stubbornness. No brain-washing could have changed her so quickly.' A frightened desperation had come into her eyes. One explanation or another, some terrible thing must be true.

And I'm still here, alive and talking. A datum for godshatter; maybe there was yet a chance! He spoke almost as the understanding hit him. 'Greenstalk was loyal, yet she was totally converted in seconds. It wasn't just a perversion of her skrode, or some drug. It was as if both Rider and skrode had been designed from the beginning to respond.' He looked across at Blueshell, trying to gauge his reaction to what he would say next. 'The Riders have awaited their creator a long time. Their race is very old, far older than anyone except the senescent. They're everywhere, but in small numbers, always practical and peaceful. And somewhere in the beginning – a few *billion* years ago – their precursors were trapped in an evolutionary cul-de-sac. Their creator built the first skrodes, and made the first Riders. Now I think we know the who and the why.

'Yes, yes. I know there have been other upliftings. What's marvelous about this one is how stable it turned out to be. The greater skrodes are "tradition" Blueshell says, but that's a word I apply to cultures and to much shorter time scales. The greater skrodes of today are identical to ones a billion years ago. And they are devices that can be made anywhere in the Beyond . . . yet the design is clearly High Beyond or Transcendent.' That had been one his earliest humiliations about the Beyond. He had looked at the design diagram – dissections really – of skrodes. On the outside, the thing was a mechanical device, with moving parts even. And the text claimed that the whole thing would be made with the simplest of factories, scarcely more than what existed in some places in the Slow Zone. And yet the electronics was a seemingly random mass of components without any trace of hierarchical design or modularity. It worked, and far more efficiently than something designed by human-equivalent minds, but repair and debugging – of the cyber component – was out of the question. 'No one in the Beyond understands all the potentials of skrodes, much less the adaptations forced on their Riders. Isn't that so, Blueshell?'

The Rider clapped his fronds hard against his central stalk. Again a furious rattling. It was something Pham had never seen before. Rage? Terror? Blueshell's voder voice was distorted with nonlinearities: 'You ask? You *ask*? It's monstrous to ask me to help you in this –' the voice skeetered into high frequencies and he stood mute, his body shivering.

Pham of the Qeng Ho felt a stab of shame. The other knew and understood . . . and deserved better than this. The Riders must be destroyed, but they should not have to listen to his judging. His hand swept toward the communications cutoff, stopped. No. *This is your last chance to observe the Perversion's . . . work.*

Ravna's glance snapped back and forth between human and Skroderider, and he could tell that she understood. Her face had the same stricken look as when she learned about Sjandra Kei. 'You're saying the Perversion *made* the original skrodes.'

'And modified the Riders too. It was long ago, and certainly not the same instance of the Perversion that the Straumers created, but . . .'

The 'Blight,' that was the other common name for the Perversion, and closer to Old One's view. For all the Perversion's transcendence, its life style was more similar to a disease than anything else. Maybe that had helped to fool Old One. But now Pham could see: the Blight lived in pieces, across extraordinary reaches of time. It hid in archives, waiting for ideal conditions. And it had created helpers for its blooming . . .

He looked at Ravna, and suddenly realized a little more. 'You've had thirty hours to think about this, Rav. You saw the record from my suit. Surely you must have guessed some of this.'

Her gaze dropped from his. 'A little,' she finally said. At least she was no longer denying.

'You know what we have to do,' he said softly. Now that he

understood what must be done, the godshatter eased its grip. Its will would be done.

'What is that?' said Ravna, as if she didn't know.

'Two things: Post this to the Net.'

'Who would believe?' The Net of a Million Lies.

'Enough would. Once they look, most folk will be able to see the truth here . . . and take the proper action.'

Ravna shook her head. 'No,' barely audible.

'The Net *must* be told, Ravna. We've discovered something that could save a thousand worlds. This is the Blight's hidden edge,' at least in the Middle and Low Beyond.

She just shook her head again. 'But screaming this truth would itself kill billions.'

'In honest defense!' He bounced slowly toward the ceiling, pushed himself back to the deck.

There were tears in her eyes now. 'These are exactly the arguments used to kill m-my family, my worlds . . . A-and I will not be part of it.'

'But the claims are *true* this time!'

'I've had enough of pogroms, Pham.'

Gentle toughness . . . and almost unbelievable. 'You would make this decision yourself, Rav? We know something that *others* – leaders wiser than either of us – should be free to decide upon. You would keep them from making that choice?'

She hesitated, and for an instant Pham thought the civilized rule-follower in her would bring her around. But then her chin came up, 'Yes, Pham. I would deny them the choice.'

He made a noncommittal noise and drifted back toward the command console. No point in talking to her about what else must be done.

'And Pham, we will not kill Blueshell and Greenstalk.'

'There's no choice, Rav.' His hands played with the touch controls. 'Greenstalk was perverted; we have no idea how much of that survived the destruction of her skrode, or how long it will be before Blueshell goes bad. We can't take them along, or release them, either.'

Ravna drifted sideways, her eyes fixed on his hands. 'B-be careful who you kill, Pham,' she said softly. 'As you say, I've had thirty hours to think about my decisions, thirty hours to think about yours.'

'So.' Pham raised his hands from the controls. Rage (godshatter?) chased briefly through this mind. *Ravna, Ravna, Ravna*, a voice saying goodbye inside his head. Then all became very cold. He had been so afraid that the Riders had perverted the ship. Instead, this stupid fool had acted for them, *voluntarily*. He drifted slowly toward her. Almost unthinking, he held his arm and hand at combat ready. 'How do you intend to prevent me from doing what has to be done?' But he already guessed.

She didn't back away, even when his hand was centimeters from her throat. Her face held courage and tears. 'W-what do you think, Pham? While you were in the surgeon ... I rearranged things. Hurt me, and you will be hurt worse.' Her eyes swept the walls behind him. 'Kill the Riders, and . . . and you will die.'

They stared at each other for a long moment, measuring. Maybe there weren't weapons buried in the walls. He probably could kill her before she could defend. But then there were a thousand ways the ship could have been programmed to kill him. And all that would be left would be the Riders . . . flying down to the Bottom, to their prize. 'So what do we do, then?' he finally said.

'As b-before, we go to rescue Jefri. We go to recover the Countermeasure. I'm willing to put some restrictions on the Riders.'

A truce with monsters, mediated by a fool.

He pushed off, sailing around her back down the axis corridor. Behind him he heard a sob.

They stayed well clear of each other the next few days. Pham was allowed shallow access to ship controls. He found suicide programs threaded through the applications layers. But a strange thing, and reason for chagrin if he had been capable of it: The changes dated from hours after his confrontation with Ravna. She'd had nothing when she stood against him. *Thank the Powers, I didn't know.* The thought was forgotten almost before he formed it.

So. The charade would proceed right to the end, a continuing game of lie and subterfuge. Grimly, he set himself to winning that game. Fleets behind them, traitors surrounding him. By the Qeng Ho and his own godshatter, the Perversion would lose. The Skroderiders would lose. And for all her courage and goodness, Ravna Bergsndot would lose.

30

Tyrathect was losing the battle within herself, her battle with the Flenser. Oh, it wasn't near ended; better perhaps to say that the tide had turned. In the beginning there had been little triumphs, as when she let Amdijefri play alone with the commset without even the children guessing she was responsible. But such were many tendays past, and now . . . Some days she would be entirely in control of herself. Others – and these often seemed the happiest – would begin with her *seeming* in control.

It was not yet clear the sort of day today would be.

Tyrathect paced along the hoardings that topped the new castle's walls. The place was certainly new, but hardly yet a castle. Steel had built in panicky haste. The south and west walls were very thick, with embedded tunnels. But there were spots on the north side that were simply palisades backed by stony rubble. Nothing more could be done in the time that Steel had been given. She stopped for a moment, smelling fresh-sawn timber. The view down Starship Hill was as beautiful as she had ever seen it. The days were getting longer. Now there was only twilight between the setting and the rising of the sun. The local snow had retreated to its summer patches, leaving heather to turn green in the warmth. From here she could see miles, to where bluish sea haze clamped down on the offshore islands.

By the conventional wisdom, it would be suicide to attack the new castle – even in its present ramshackle state – with less than a horde. Tyrathect smiled bitterly to herself. Of course, Woodcarver would ignore that wisdom. Old Woodcarver thought she had a secret weapon that would breach these walls from hundreds of feet away. Even now Steel's spies were reporting that the Woodcarvers had taken the bait, that their small army and their crude cannon had begun the overland trek up the coast.

She descended the wall stairs to the yard. She heard faint thunder. Somewhere north of Streamsdell, Steel's own cannoneers were beginning their morning practice. When the air was just right, you could hear it. There was to be no testing near the farmlands, and none but high Servants and isolated workers knew of the weapons. But by now Steel had thirty of the devices and gunpowder to match. The greatest lack was gunners. Up close the noise of firing was hellish. Sustained firing could deafen. Ah, but the weapons themselves: they had a range of almost eight miles, three times as great as Woodcarver's. They could deliver gunpowder 'bombs' that exploded on impact. There were places beyond the northern hills where the forest was gouged bare and slumping landslides showed naked rock – all from sustained barrages of gunfire.

And soon – perhaps today – the Flenserists would have radio too.

God damn you, Woodcarver! Of course Tyrathect had never met the Woodcarver, but Flenser had known that pack well: Flenser was mostly Woodcarver's offspring. The 'Gentle Woodcarver' had borne him and raised him to power. It had been Woodcarver who taught him about freedom of thought and experiment. Woodcarver should have known the pride that lived in Flenser, should have known that he would go to extremes his parent never dared. And when the new one's monstrous nature became clear, when his first 'experiments' were discovered, Woodcarver should have had him killed – or at the very least, fragmented. Instead, Flenser had been allowed to take exile . . . to create things like Steel, and they to create their own monsters, ultimately to build this hierarchy of madness.

And now, a century overdue, Woodcarver was coming to correct her mistake. She came with her toy guns, as overconfident and idealistic as ever. She came into a trap of steel and fire that none of her people would survive. If only there were some way to warn the Woodcarver. Tyrathect's only reason for being here was the oath she had sworn herself to bring down Flenser's Movement. If Woodcarver knew what awaited her here, if she even knew of the traitors in her own camp, there might be a chance. Last fall, Tyrathect had come close to sending an anonymous message south. There were traders who visited both kingdoms. Her Flenser memories told her which were likely independent. She almost passed one a note, a single piece of silkpaper, reporting the starship's landing and Jefri's survival. In that she had missed death by less than a day: Steel had shown her a report from the South, about the other human and Woodcarver's progress with the 'dataset.' There were things in the report that could only be known by someone at the top at Woodcarvers. Who? She didn't ask, but she guessed it was Vendacious; the Flenser in Tyrathect remembered that sibling pack well. They'd had . . . dealings. Vendacious had none of the raw genius of their joint parent, but there was a broad streak of opportunism in him.

Steel had shown her the report only to puff himself up, to prove to Tyrathect that he had succeeded in something that Flenser had never attempted. And it *was* a coup. Tyrathect had complimented Steel with more than usual sincerity . . . and quietly shelved her plans of warning. With a spy at the top at Woodcarver's, any message would be pointless suicide.

Now Tyrathect padded across the castle's outer yard. There was still plenty of construction going on, but the teams were smaller. Steel was building timber lodges all over the yard. Many were empty shells. Steel hoped to persuade Ravna to land at a special spot near the inner keep.

The inner keep. *That* was the only thing about this castle built to the standards of Hidden Island. It was a beautiful structure. It really could be what Steel told Amdijefri: a shrine to honor Jefri's ship and protect it from Woodcarver attack. The central dome was a smooth sweep of cantilevers and fitted stone, as wide as the main meeting hall on Hidden Island. Tyrathect watched it with one pair of eyes as she trotted round it. Steel intended to face the dome with the finest pink marble. It would be visible for dozens of miles into the sky. The deadfalls built into its structure were the centerpiece of Steel's plan, even if the rescuers didn't land in his other trap.

Shreck and two other high Servants stood on the steps of the castle's meeting hall. They came to attention as she approached. The three backed quickly away, bellies scraping stone . . . but not as quickly as last fall. They knew that the other Flenser Fragments had been destroyed. As Tyrathect swept past them, she almost smiled. For all her weakness and all her problems, she knew she could best these three.

Steel was already inside, alone. The most important meetings were all like this, just Steel and herself. She understood the relationship. In the beginning, Steel had been simply terrified of her – the one person he believed he could never kill. For ten days, he had teetered between grovelling before her and dismembering her. It was amusing to see the bonds Flenser had installed years before still having force. Then had come word of the death of the other Fragments. Tyrathect was no longer Flenser-in-Waiting. She had half expected death to come then. But in a way this made her safer. Now Steel was less afraid, and his need for intimate advice could be satisfied in ways he saw less threatening. She was his bottled demon: Flenser wisdom without the Flenser threat.

This afternoon he seemed almost relaxed, nodding casually to Tyrathect as she entered. She nodded back. In many ways Steel was her – Flenser's – finest creation. So much effort had been spent honing Steel. How many packs-worth of members had been sacrificed to get just the combination that was Steel. She – Flenser – had wanted brilliance, ruthlessness. As Tyrathect she could see the truth. With all the flensing, Flenser had created a poor, sad thing. It was strange, but . . . sometimes Steel seemed like Flenser's most pitiable victim.

'Ready for the big test?' Tyrathect said. At long last, the *radios* seemed complete.

'In a moment. I wanted to ask you about timing. My sources tell me Woodcarver's army is on its way. If they make reasonable progress, they should be here in five tendays.

'That's at least three tendays before Ravna's ship arrives.'

'Quite. We will have your old enemy disposed of long before we go for the high stakes. But . . . something is strange about the Two-Legs' recent messages. How much do you think they suspect? Is it possible that Amdijefri are telling them more than we know?'

It was an uncertainty Steel would have masked back when Tyrathect had been Flenser-in-Waiting. She slid to a seated position before replying. 'You might know the answer if you had bothered to learn more of the Two-Legs' language, dear Steel, or let me learn more.' Through the winter, Tyrathect had been desperate to talk to the children alone, to get warning to the ship. She was of two minds about that now. Amdijefri were so transparent, so innocent. If they glimpsed anything of Steel's treachery, they couldn't hide it. And what might the rescuers do if they knew Steel's villainy? Tyrathect had seen one starship in flight. Just its landing could be a terrible weapon. Besides . . . *If Steel's plan succeeds, we won't need the aliens' goodwill.*

Aloud, Tyrathect continued, 'As long as you can continue your magnificent performance, you have nothing to fear from the child. Can't you see that he loves you?'

For an instant Steel seemed pleased, and then the suspicion returned. 'I don't know. Amdi seems always to taunt me, as though he sees through my act.'

Poor Steel. Amdiranifani was his greatest success, and he would never understand it. In this one thing Steel had truly exceeded his Master, had discovered and honed a technique that had once been Woodcarver's. The Flenser eyed his former student almost hungrily. If only he could do him all over again; there must be a way to combine the fear and the flensing with love and affection. The resulting tool would truly merit the name Steel. Tyrathect shrugged. 'Take my word for it. *If* you can continue your kindness act, both children will be faithful. As for the rest of your question: I have noticed some change in Ravna's messages. She seems

336

much more confident of their arrival time, yet something has gone wrong for them. I don't think they're any more suspicious than before; they seemed to accept that Jefri was responsible for Amdi's idea about the *radios*. That lie was a good move, by the way. It played to their sense of superiority. On a fair battlefield, we are probably their betters – and they *must not* guess that.'

'But what are they suddenly so tense about?'

The Fragment shrugged. 'Patience, dear Steel. Patience and observation. Perhaps Amdijefri have noticed this too. You might subtly inspire them to ask about it. My guess is the Two-Legs have their own politics to worry about.' He stopped and turned all his heads on Steel. 'Could you have your "source" down at Woodcarver's ferret about with the question?'

'Perhaps I will. That Dataset is Woodcarver's one great advantage.' Steel sat in silence for a moment, nervously chewing at his lips. Abruptly, he shook himself all over, as if to drive off the manifold threats he saw encroaching. 'Shreck!'

There was the sound of paws. The hatch creaked open and Shreck stuck a head inside. 'Sir?'

'Bring the *radio* outfits in here. Then ask Amdijefri if he can come down to talk to us.'

The *radios* were beautiful things. Ravna claimed that the basic device could be invented by civilizations scarcely more advanced than Flenser's. That was hard to believe. There were so many steps in the making, so many meaningless detours. The final result: eight, one-yard squares of night-darkness. Glints of gold and silver showed in the strange material. That, at least, was no mystery: a part of Flenser's gold and silver had gone into the construction.

Amdijefri arrived. They raced around the central floor, poked at the radios, shouted to Steel and the Flenser Fragment. Sometimes it was hard to believe they were not truly one pack, that the Two-Legs was not another member: They clung to each other as a single pack might. As often as not, Amdi answered questions about Two-Legs before Jefri had a chance to speak, using the 'I-pack' pronoun to identify both of them.

Today, however, there seemed to be a disagreement. 'Oh, *please* my lord, let me be the one to try it!'

Jefri rattled off something in Samnorsk. When Amdi didn't translate, he repeated the words more slowly, speaking directly to Steel. 'No. It is [something something] dangerous. Amdi is [something] small. And also, time [something] narrow.'

The Flenser strained for the meaning. *Damn.* Sooner or later their ignorance of the Two-Legs' language was going to cost them.

Steel listened to the human, then sighed the most marvelously patient sigh. 'Please. Amdi. Jefri. What is problem?' He spoke in Samnorsk, making more sense to the Flenser Fragment than the human child had.

Amdi dithered for a moment. 'Jefri thinks the radio jackets are too big for me. But look, it doesn't fit so badly!' Amdi jumped all around one of the night-dark squares, dragging it heedlessly off its velvet pallet onto the floor. He pulled the fabric over the back and shoulders of his largest member.

Now the *radio* was roughly the shape of a greatcloak; Steel's tailors had added clasps at the shoulders and gut. But the thing was vastly outsized for little Amdi. It stood like a tent around one of him. 'See? See?' The tiny head poked out, looking first at Steel and then at Tyrathect, willing their belief.

Jefri said something. The Amdi pack squeaked back angrily. Then, 'Jefri worries about everything, but *somebody* has to test the *radios*. There's this little problem with speed. *Radio* goes much faster than sound. Jefri's just afraid it's so fast it might confuse the pack using it. That's foolish. How much faster could it be than heads-together thought?' He asked it as a question. Tyrathect/Flenser smiled. The pack of puppies couldn't quite lie, but he guessed that Amdi knew the answer to his question – and that it did not support his argument.

On the other side of the hall, Steel listened with heads cocked – the picture of benign tolerance. 'I'm sorry, Amdi. It's just too dangerous for you to be the first.'

'But I am brave! And I want to help.'

'I'm sorry. After we know it's safe –'

Amdi gave a shriek of outrage, much higher than normal interpack talk, almost in the range of thought. He swarmed around Jefri, whacking at the human's legs with his butt ends. 'Hideous traitor!' he cried, and continued the insults in Samnorsk.

It took about ten minutes to get him calmed down to a sulk. He and Jefri sat on the floor, grumbling at each other in Samnorsk. Tyrathect watched the two, and Steel on the other side of the room. If irony were something that made sound, they would all be deaf by now. All their lives, Flenser and Steel had experimented on others – usually unto death. Now they had a victim who literally begged to be victimized . . . and he must be rejected. There was no question about the rejection. Even if Jefri had not raised objections, the Amdi pack was too valuable to be risked. Furthermore, Amdi was an eightsome. It was a miracle that such a large pack could function at all. Whatever dangers there were with *radio* would be much greater for him.

So a proper victim would be found. A proper wretch. Surely there were plenty of those in the dungeons beneath Hidden Island. Tyrathect thought back on all the packs she remembered killing. How she hated Flenser, his calculating cruelty. *I am so much worse than Steel. I made Steel.* She remembered where her thoughts had been the last hour. This was one of the bad days, one of the days when Flenser sneaked out from the recesses of her mind, when she rode the power of his reason higher and higher, till it became rationalization and she became him. Still, for a few more seconds she might be in control. What could she do with it? A soul that was strong enough might deny itself, might become a different person . . . might at the very least end itself.

'I-I will try the *radio.*' The words were spoken almost before he thought them. *Weak, silly frill.*

'What?' said Steel.

But the words had been clear, and Steel had heard. The Flenser Fragment smiled dryly. 'I want to see what this *radio* can do. Let me try it, dear Steel.'

*

They took the radios out into the yard, on the side of the starship that was hidden from general view. Here it would just be Amdijefri, Steel, and *whoever I am at the moment.* The Flenser Fragment laughed at the upwelling fear. Discipline, she had thought! Perhaps that was best. He stood in the middle of the yard and let the human help him with the radio gear. Strange to see another intelligent being so close, and towering over him.

Jefri's incredibly articulate paws arranged the jackets loosely on his backs. The inside material was soft, deadening. And unlike normal clothing, the *radios* covered the wearer's tympana. The boy tried to explain what he was doing. 'See? This thing,' he pulled at the corner of the greatcloak, 'goes over your head. The inside has [something] that makes sound into *radio.*'

The Fragment shrugged away as the boy tried to pull the cover forward. 'No. I can't think with these cloaks on.' Only by standing just so, all members facing inward, could the Fragment maintain full consciousness. Already the weaker parts of him were edging toward isolation panic. The conscience that was Tyrathect would learn something today.

'Oh. I'm sorry.' Jefri turned and spoke to Amdi, something about using the old design.

Amdi was heads-together just thirty feet away. He had been all frowns, sullen at being denied, nervous to be apart from the Two-Legs. But as the preparations continued, the frowns eased. The puppies' eyes grew wide with happy fascination. The Fragment felt a wave of affection for the puppies that came and went almost too fast to be noticed.

Now Amdi edged nearer, taking advantage of the fact that the cloaks muffled much of the Fragment's thought sounds. 'Jefri says maybe we shouldn't have tried to make the mind-size *radio,*' he said. 'But this will be so much better. I know it! And,' he said with transparent slyness, 'you could still let me test it instead.'

'No, Amdi. This is the way it must be.' Steel's voice was all soft sympathy. Only the Flenser Fragment could see the broad grin on a couple of the lord's members.

'Well, okay.' The puppies crept a little nearer. 'Don't be

afraid, Lord Tyrathect. We've had the *radios* in sunlight for some time. They should have lots of power. To make them work you just pull all the belts tight, even the ones at your neck.'

'All of them *at once?*'

Amdi fidgeted. 'That's probably best. Otherwise, there will be such a mismatch of speeds that –' He said something to the Two-Legs.

Jefri leaned close. 'This belt goes here, and this here.' He pointed to the braid-bone straps that drew the head covering close. 'Then just pull this with your mouth.'

'The harder you pull, the louder the *radio*, 'Amdi added.

'Okay.' The Fragment drew himself together. He shrugged the jackets into place, tightening the shoulder and gut belts. *Deadly muffling.* The jackets almost seemed to mold themselves to his tympana. He looked at himself, and grasped desperately for what was left of consciousness. The jackets were beautiful, magic darkness yet with a hint of the golden-silver of a Flenserist Lord. Beautiful instruments of torture. Even Steel had not imagined such twisted revenge. Had he?

The Fragment grabbed the head straps and pulled.

Twenty years ago, when Tyrathect was new, she had loved to hike with her fission parent on the grassy dunes along Lake Kitcherri. That was before their great falling out, before loneliness drove Tyrathect to the Republic's Capital and her search for 'meaning.' Not all of the shore of Lake Kitcherri was beaches and dunes. Farther south there was the Rockness, where streams cut through stone to the water. Sometimes, especially when she and her parent had fought, Tyrathect would walk up from the shore along streams bordered by sheer, smooth cliffs. It was a sort of punishment: there were places where the stone had a glassy haze, and it didn't absorb sound at all. *Everything* was echoed, right up to the top of thought. It was if she were surrounded by copies of herself, and copies beyond them, all thinking the same sounds but out of step.

Of course, echoes are often a problem with unquilted stone walls, especially if the size and geometry are wrong. But the cliffs were such perfect reflectors, a quarrier's nightmare. And there were places where the shape of the Rockness conspired with the sounds . . . When Tyrathect walked there, she couldn't tell her own thought from the echoes. Everything was garbled with barely offset resonance. At first it had been a great pain that sent her running. But she forced herself back again and again, and finally learned to think even in the worst of the narrows.

Amdijefri's radio was just a little like the Kitcherri cliffs. *Enough to save me, maybe.* Tyrathect came to consciousness all piled in a heap. At most seconds had passed since she brought the *radios* to life; Amdi and Steel were simply staring at her. The human was rocking one of her bodies, talking to her. Tyrathect licked the boy's paw, then stood partly up. She heard only her own thoughts, but they had some of the jarring difference of the stone echoes.

She was back on her bellies again. Part of her was vomiting in the dirt. The world shimmered, out of tune. *Thought is there. Grab it! Grab it!* All a matter of coordination, of timing. She remembered Amdijefri talking about how fast the radio was. In a way, this was the reverse of the problem of the screaming cliffs.

She shook her heads, mastering the weirdness. 'Give me a moment,' she said, and her voice was almost calm. She looked around. Slowly. If she concentrated, didn't move fast, she could think. Suddenly she was aware of the greatcloaks, pressing in on all her tympana. She should have been deafened, isolated. Yet her thoughts were no muzzier than after a bad sleep.

She got to her feet again and walked slowly around the open space between Amdi and Steel. 'Can you hear me?' she asked.

'Yes,' said Steel. He edged nervously away from her.

Of course. The cloaks muffled sound like any heavy quilt: anything in the range of thought would be totally absorbed. But interpack speech and Samnorsk were low-pitched sound – they would scarcely be affected. She stopped, holding all her breath. She could hear birds and the sounds of timber being sawn somewhere on the far side of the inner yard. Yet

Steel was only thirty feet from her. His thought noise should have been a loud intrusion, even confusing. She strained to hear . . . There was nothing but her own thoughts and a *stickety* buzzing noise that seemed to come from all directions.

'And we thought this would just give us control in battle,' she said, wonderingly. All of her turned, walking toward Amdi. He was twenty feet away, ten feet. Still no thought noise. Amdi's eyes were wide. The puppies held their ground; in fact all eight of him seemed to lean toward her. 'You knew about this all along, didn't you?' Tyrathect said.

'I hoped. Oh, I hoped.' He stepped closer. Five feet. The eight of him looked at the five of her from a distance of inches. He extended a nose, brushing muzzles with Tyrathect. His thought sounds came only faintly through the cloak, no louder than if he were fifty feet away. For a moment they looked at each other in stark astonishment. Nose to nose, and they both could still think! Amdi gave a whoop of glee and bounded in among Tyrathect, rubbing back and forth across her legs. 'See, Jefri,' he shouted in Samnorsk. 'It works. It works!'

Tyrathect wobbled under the assault, almost lost hold of her thoughts. What had just happened . . . In all the history of the world there had never been such a thing. If thinking packs could work paw by jowl . . . There were consequences and consequences, and she got dizzy all over again.

, Steel moved a little closer, and suffered a flying hug from Jefri Olsndot. Steel was trying his best to join the celebration, but he wasn't quite sure what had happened. He hadn't lived the consequences like Tyrathect. 'Wonderful progress for the first try,' he said. 'But it must be painful even so.' Two of him looked sharply at her. 'We should get that gear off you, and give you a rest.'

'No!' Tyrathect and Amdi said almost together. She smiled back at Steel. 'We haven't really tested it yet, have we? The whole purpose was long-distance communications.' *We thought that was the purpose, anyway*. In fact, even if it had no better range than talk sounds, it was already a towering success in Tyrathect's mind.

'Oh.' Steel smiled weakly at Amdi and glared hidden faces

343

at Tyrathect. Jefri was still hanging on two of his necks. Steel was a picture of barely concealed anguish. 'Well, go slowly then. We don't know what might happen if you run out of range.'

Tyrathect disentangled two of herself from Amdi and stepped a few feet away. Thought was as clear – and as potentially confusing – as before. By now she was beginning to get the feel of it though. She had very little trouble keeping her balance. She walked the two another thirty feet, about the maximum range a pack could coordinate in the quietest conditions. 'It's like I'm still heads-together,' she said wonderingly. Ordinarily at thirty feet, thoughts were faint and the time lag so bad that coordination was difficult.

'How far can I go?' she murmured the question to Amdi.

He made a human giggling sound and slid a head close to hers. 'I'm not sure. It should be good at least to the outer walls.'

'Well,' she said in a normal voice, for Steel, 'let's see if I can spread a little bit further.' The two of her walked another ten yards. She was more than sixty feet across!

Steel was wide-eyed. 'And now?'

Tyrathect laughed. 'My thought's as crisp as before.' She turned her two and walked away.

'*Wait!*' roared Steel, bounding to his feet. '*That's far* –' then he remembered his audience, and his fury became more a frightened concern for her welfare. 'That's far too dangerous for the first experiment. Come back!'

From where she sat with Amdi, Tyrathect smiled brightly. 'But Steel, I never left,' she said in Samnorsk.

Amdijefri laughed and laughed.

She was one hundred fifty feet across. Her two broke into a careful trot – and she watched Steel swallow back foam. Her thought still had the sharp, abrupt quality of closer than heads-together. *How fast* is *this radio thing?*

She passed close by Shreck and the guards posted at the edge of the field. 'Hey, hey, Shreck! What do you say?' one of her said at his stupefied faces. Back with Amdi and the rest of her, Steel was shouting at Shreck, telling him to follow her.

Her trot became an easy run. She split, one going north of

344

the inner yard, the other south. Shreck and company followed, clumsy with shock. The dome of inner keep was between her, a sweeping hulk of stone. Her *radio* thoughts faded into the *stickety* buzzing.

'Can't think,' she mumbled to Amdi.

'Pull on the mouth straps. Make your thoughts louder.'

Tyrathect pulled, and the buzzing faded. She regained her balance and raced around the starship. One of her was in a construction area now. Artisans looked up in shock. A loose member usually meant a fatal accident or a pack run amok. In either case the singleton must be restrained. But Tyrathect's member was wearing a greatcloak that sparkled here and there of gold. And behind her Shreck and his guards were shouting for everyone to stand back.

She turned a head to Steel, and her voice was joy. 'I *soar!*' She ran through the cowering workers, ran toward the walls. She was *everywhere*, spreading and spreading. These seconds would make memories that woud outlast her soul, that would be legends in the minds of her descendants a thousand years from now.

Steel hunkered down. Things were totally out of his control now; Shreck's people were all on the far side of inner keep. All that he and Amdijefri could know came from Tyrathect – and the clamor of alarms.

Amdi bounced around her. 'Where are you now? Where?'

'Almost to the outer wall.'

'Don't go beyond that,' Steel said quietly.

Tyrathect scarcely heard. For a few more seconds she would drink this glorious power. She charged up the inside stairs. Guards scuttled back, some members jumping back into the yard. Shreck still followed, shouting for her safety.

One of her reached the parapet, then the other.

She gasped.

'Are you all right?' said Amdi.

'I –' Tyrathect looked about her. From her place on the south wall she could see herselves back in the castle yard: a tiny clump of gold and black that was her three and Amdi. Beyond the northeast walls stretched forest and valleys, the trails up into the Icefang mountains. To the west was Hidden

Island and the misty inner waters. These were things she had seen a thousand times as Flenser. How he had loved them, his domain. But now . . . she was seeing as if in a dream. Her eyes were so far apart. Her pack was almost as wide as the castle itself. The parallax view made Hidden Island seem just a few paces away. Newcastle was like a model spread out around her. Almighty Pack of Packs – this was God's view.

Shreck's troopers were edging closer. He had sent a couple of packs back to get directions. 'A couple of minutes. I'll come down in a couple of minutes.' She spoke the words to the troopers on the palisade and to Steel back in the yard. Then she turned to survey her domain.

She had only extended two of herself across less than a quarter of a mile. But there was no perceptible time lag; coordination had the same abrupt feel it did when she was all together. And there was plenty more pull in the braid-bone straps. What if all five of her spread out, moved *miles* apart. All of the northland would be her private room.

And Flenser? Ah, Flenser. Where was he? The memories were still there, but . . . Tyrathect remembered the loss of consciousness right when the *radios* began working. It took a special skill of coordination to think in the face of such terrible speed. Perhaps Lord Flenser had never walked between close cliffs when he was new. Tyrathect smiled. Perhaps only her mindset could hold when using the *radios*. In that case . . . Tyrathect looked again across the landscape. Flenser had made a great empire. If these new developments were managed properly, then the coming victories could make it infinitely grander.

He turned to Shreck's troopers. 'Very well, I'm ready to return to Lord Steel.'

31

It was high summer when Woodcarver's army left for the north. The preparations had been frantic, with Vendacious driving himself and everyone else to the point of exhaustion. There had been thirty cannons to make – Scrupilo cast seventy tubes before getting thirty that would fire reliably. There had been cannoneers to train – and safe methods of firing to discover. There had been wagons to build and kherhogs to buy.

Surely word of the preparations had long ago filtered north. Woodcarvers was a port city; they could not close down the commerce that moved through it. Vendacious warned them of this in more than one inner council meeting: Steel knew they were coming. The trick was in keeping the Flenserists uncertain as to numbers and timing and exact purpose. 'We have one great advantage over the enemy,' he said. 'We have agents in his highest councils. We know what *he* knows of us.' They couldn't disguise the obvious from the spies, but the details were a different matter.

The army departed along inland routes, a dozen wagons here, a few squads there. In all there were a thousand packs in the expedition, but they would never be together till they reached deep forest. It would have been easier to take the first part of the trip by sea, but the Flenserists had spotters hidden high in the fjordlands. Any ship movement – even deep in Woodcarver territory – would be known in the north. So they traveled on forest paths, through areas that Vendacious had cleared of enemy agents.

At first the going was very easy, at least for those with the wagons. Johanna rode in one of the rear ones with Woodcarver and Dataset. *Even I'm beginning to treat the thing like an oracle*, thought Johanna. Too bad it couldn't really predict the future.

The weather was as beautiful as Johanna had ever seen it on Tines' world, an endless afternoon. It was strange that such unending fairness should make her so nervous, but she couldn't help it. This was so much like her first time on this world, when everything had . . . gone wrong.

During the first dayarounds of the journey, while they were still in home territory, Woodcarver pointed out every peak that came into view and tried to translate its name into Samnorsk for her. After six hundred years the Queen knew

347

her land well. Even the patches of snow – the ones that lasted all through the summer – were known to her. She showed Johanna a sketchbook she had brought along. Each page was from a different year, and showed her special snowpatches as they had appeared on the same day of the summer. Riffling through the leaves, it was almost like a crude piece of animation. Johanna could see the patches moving, growing over a period of decades, then retreating. 'Most packs don't live long enough to feel it,' said Woodcarver, 'but to me, the patches that last all summer are like living things. See how they move? They are like wolves, held off from our lands by our fire that is the sun. They circle about, grow. Sometimes they link together and a new glacier starts toward the sea.'

Johanna had laughed a little nervously. 'Are they winning?'

'For the last four centuries, no. The summers have often been hot and windy. In the long run? I don't know. And it doesn't matter quite so much to me anymore.' She rocked her two little puppies for a moment and laughed gently. 'Peregrine's little ones are not even thinking yet, and I'm already losing my long view!'

Johanna reached out to stroke her neck. 'But they are your puppies too.'

'I know. Most of my pups have been with other packs, but these are the first that I have kept to be with me.' Her blind one nuzzled at one of the puppies. It wriggled and made a sound that warbled at the top of Johanna's hearing. Johanna held the other on her lap. Tine pups looked more like baby sea'mals than dogs. Their necks were so long compared to their bodies. And they seemed to develop much more slowly than the puppy she and Jefri had raised. Even now they seemed to have trouble focusing. She moved her fingers slowly back and forth in front of one puppy's head; its efforts to track were comical.

And after sixty days, Woodcarver's pups couldn't really walk. The Queen wore two special jackets with carrying pouches on the sides. Most of the waking day, her little ones stayed there, suckling through the fur on her tummy. In some ways, Woodcarver treated her offspring as a human would. She was very nervous when they were taken from her sight.

She liked to cuddle them and play little games of coordination with them. Often she would lay both of them on their backs and pat their paws in a sequence of eight, then abruptly tap the one or the other on the belly. The two wriggled furiously at the attack, their little legs waving in all directions. 'I nibble the one whose paw was last touched. Peregrine is worthy of me. These two are already thinking a little. See?' She pointed to the puppy that had convulsed into a ball, avoiding most of her surprise tickle.

In other ways Tinish parenting was alien, almost scary. Neither Woodcarver nor Peregrine ever talked to their pups in audible tones, but their ultrasonic 'thoughts' seemed to be constantly probing the little ones. Some of it was so simple and regular that it set sympathetic vibrations through the walls of the little wagon. The wood buzzed under Johanna's hands. It was like a mother humming a lullaby, but she could see it had another purpose. The little creatures responded to the sounds, twitching in complicated rhythms. Peregrine said it would be another thirty days before the pups could contribute conscious thought to the pack, but they were already being trained and exercised for the function.

They camped part of each dayaround, the troops standing turns as sentry lines. Even during the traveling part of the day they stopped numerous times, to clear the trail, or await the return of a patrol, or simply to rest. At one such, Johanna sat with Peregrine in the shade of a tree that looked like pine but smelled of honey. Pilgrim played with his young ones, helping them to stand up and walk a few steps. She could tell by the buzzing in her head that he was thinking at the pups. And suddenly they seemed more like marionettes than children to her. 'Why don't you let them play by themselves, or with their –' *Brothers? Sisters? What do you call siblings born to the other pack?* '– with Woodcarver's pups?'

Even more than Woodcarver, the pilgrim had tried to learn human customs. He was by far the most flexible pack she knew . . . after all, if you can accommodate a murderer in your own mind, you *must* be flexible. But Pilgrim was visibly startled by her question. The buzzing in her head stopped abruptly. He laughed weakly. It was a very human laugh, though a bit theatrical. Peregrine had spent hours at interactive comedy on Dataset – whether for entertaiment or insight, she didn't know. 'Play? By themselves? Yes . . . I see how natural that would seem to you. To us, it would be a kind of perversion . . . No, *worse* than that, since perversions are at least fun for some people some of the time. But if a pup were raised a singleton, or even a duo – it would be making an *animal* of what could be sturdy member.'

'You mean that pups never have life of their own?'

Peregrine cocked his heads and scrunched close to the ground. One of him continued to nose around the puppies, but Johanna had his attention. He loved to puzzle over human exotica. 'Well, sometimes there is a tragedy – an orphan pup left to itself. Often there is no cure for it; the creature, becomes too independent to meld with any pack. In any case, it is a very lonely, empty life. I have personal memories of just how unpleasant.'

'You're missing a lot. I know you've watched children's stories on Dataset. It's sad you can never be young and foolish.'

'Hei! I never said that. I've been young and foolish lots; it's my way of life. And most packs are that way when they have several young members by different parents.' As they talked, one of Peregrine's pups had struggled to the edge of the blanket they sat on. Now it awkwardly extended its neck into the flowers that grew from the roots of a nearby tree. As it scruffed around in the green and purple, Johanna felt the buzzing begin again. The pup's movement became a tad more organized. 'Wow! I can smell the flowers with him. I bet we'll be seeing through each other's eyes well before we get to Flenser's Hidden Island.' The pup backed up, and the two did a little dance on the blanket. Peregrine's heads bobbed in time with the movement. 'They are such bright little ones!' He grinned. 'Oh, we are not so different from you, Johanna. I know humans are proud of their young ones. Both Woodcarver and I wonder what ours will become. She is so brilliant, and I am – well, a bit mad. Will these two make me a scientific genius? Will Woodcarver's turn *her* into an adventurer? Heh, heh. Woodcarver's a great brood kenner, but even she's not sure what our new souls will be like. Oh, I can't wait to be six again!'

It had taken Scriber and Pilgrim and Johanna only three days to sail from Flenser's Domain to the harbor at Woodcarver's. It would take this army almost thirty days to walk back to where Johanna's adventure began. On the map it had looked a tortuous path, wiggling this way and that through the fjordland. Yet the first ten days were amazingly easy. The weather stayed dry and warm. It was like the day of the ambush stretched out forever and ever. A dry winds summer, Woodcarver called it. In summer, there should be occasional storms, at least cloudiness. Instead the sun circled endlessly above the forest canopy, and when they broke into the open – never for long, and then only when Vendacious was sure that it was safe – the sky was clear and almost cloudless.

In fact, there was already uneasiness about the weather. At noon it could get downright hot. The wind was constant, drying. The forest itself was drying out; they must be careful with fires. And with the sun always up and no clouds, they might be seen by lookouts many kilometers away. Scrupilo was especially bothered. He hadn't expected to fire his cannons en route, but he had wanted to drill 'his' troops more in the open.

Scrupilo was a council member and the Queen's chief engineer. Since his experiment with the cannon, he had insisted on the title 'Commander of Cannoneers.' To Johanna, the engineer had always seemed curt and impatient. His members were almost always moving, and with jerky abruptness. He spent almost as much time with the Dataset as did the Queen or Peregrine Wickwrackscar, yet he had very little interest in people-oriented subjects. 'He has a blindness for all but machines,' Woodcarver once said of him, 'but that's how I made him. He's invented much, even before you came.'

Scrupilo had fallen in love with the cannons. For most packs, firing the things was a painful experience. Since that first test, Scrupilo had fired the things again and again, trying to improve the tubes, the powder, and the explosive rounds.

His fur was scored with dozens of powder burns. He claimed that nearby gun thunder cleared the mind – but most everybody else agreed it made you daft.

During rest stops Scrup was a familiar figure, strutting up and down the line, haranguing his cannoneers. He claimed even the shortest stop was an opportunity for training, since in real combat speed would be essential. He had designed special epaulets, based on Nyjoran gunners' ear muffs. They didn't cover the low-sound ears at all, but instead the forehead and shoulder tympana of the trigger member. Actually tying the muffs down was a mind-numbing thing to do, but for the moments right around firing it was worth it. Scrupilo wore his own muffs all the time, but unsnugged. They looked like silly little wings sticking out from his head and shoulders. He obviously thought the effect was raffish – and in fact, his gunner crews also made a big thing of wearing the gear at all times. After a while, even Johanna could see that the drill was paying off. At least, they could swing the gun tubes around at an instant's notice, stuff them with fake powder and ball, and shout the Tinish equivalent of 'BANG!'

The army carried much more gunpowder than food. The packs were to live off the forest. Johanna had little experience with camping in an atmosphere. Were forests usually this rich? It was certainly nothing like the urban forests of Straum, where you needed a special license to walk off marked paths, and most of the wild life were mechanical imitations of Nyjoran originals. This place was wilder than even the stories of Nyjora. After all, that world had been well settled before it fell to medievalism. The Tines had never been civilized, had never spread cities across continents. Pilgrim guessed there were fewer than thirty million packs in all the world. The Northwest was only beginning to be settled. Game was everywhere. In their hunting, the Tines were like animals. Troopers raced through the underforest. The favorite hunt was one of sheer endurance, where the prey was chased until it dropped. That was rarely practical here, but they got almost as much pleasure from chasing the unwary into ambushes.

Johanna didn't like it. Was this a medieval perversion or a

peculiarly Tinish one? If allowed the time, the troops didn't use their bows and knives. The pleasure of the hunt included slashing at throats and bellies with teeth and claws. Not that the forest creatures were without defenses: for millions of years threat and counterthreat had evolved here. Almost every animal could generate ultrasonic screeching that totally drowned the thought of any nearby pack. There were parts of the forest that seemed silent to Johanna, but through which the army drove at a cautious gallop, troops and drivers writhing in agony from the unseen assault.

Some of the forest animals were more sophisticated.

Twenty-five days out, the army was stuck trying to get across the biggest valley yet. In the middle – mostly hidden by the forest – a river flowed down to the western sea. The walls of these valleys were like nothing Johanna had seen in the parks of Straum: If you took a cross-section at right angles to the river, the walls made a 'U' shape. They were cliff-like steep at the high edges, then became slopes and finally a gentle plain where the river ran. 'That's how the ice gouges it,' explained Woodcarver. 'There are places further up where I've actually watched it happen,' and she showed Johanna explanations in the Dataset. That was happening more and more; Pilgrim and Woodcarver and sometimes even Scrupilo seemed to know more of a child's modern education than Johanna.

They had already been across a number of smaller valleys. Getting down the steep parts was always tedious, but so far the paths had been good. Vendacious took them to the edge of this latest valley.

Woodcarver and staff stood under the forest cover just short of the dropoff. Some meters back, Johanna sat surrounded by Peregrine Wickwrackscar. The trees at this elevation reminded Johanna a little of pines. The leaves were narrow and sharp and lasted all year. But the bark was blistered white and the wood itself was pale blond. Strangest of all were the flowers. They sprouted purple and violet from the exposed roots of the trees. Tines' world had no analog of honeybees, but there was constant motion among the flowers as thumb-sized mammals climbed from plant to plant. There were thousands of them, but they seemed to have no interest in anything except the flowers and the sweetness that oozed from them. She leaned back among the flowers and admired the view while the Queen gobbled with Vendacious. How many kilometers could you see from here? The air was clear as she had ever known it on Tines' world. East and west the valley seemed to stretch forever. The river was a silver thread where it occasionally showed through the forest of the valley floor.

Pilgrim nudged her with a nose and nodded toward the Queen. Woodcarver was pointing this way and that over the dropoff. 'Argument is in the air. You want a translation?'

'Yeah.'

'Woodcarver doesn't like this path,' Pilgrim's voice changed to the tone the Queen used when speaking Samnorsk: 'The path is completely exposed. Anyone on the other side can sit and count our every wagon. Even from miles away. [A mile is a fat kilometer.]'

Vendacious whipped his heads around in that indignant way of his. He gobbled something that Johanna knew was angry. Pilgrim chuckled and changed his voice to imitate the security chief's: 'Your majesty! My scouts have scoured the valley and far wall. There is no threat.'

'You've done miracles, I know, but do you seriously claim to have covered that entire north face? That's five miles away, and I know from my youth that there are dozens of cavelets – you have those memories yourself.'

'*That* stopped him!' said Pilgrim, laughing.

'C'mon. Just translate.' She was quite capable of inter-preting body language and tone by now. Sometimes even the Tinish chords made sense.

'Hmph. Okay.'

The Queen hiked her baby packs around and sat down. Her tone became conciliatory. 'If this weather weren't so clear, or if there were night times, we might try it, but – You remember the old path? Twenty miles inland from here? That should be overgrown by now. And the road coming back is –'

Gobble-hiss from Vendacious, angry. 'I tell you, this is safe! We'll lose days on the other path. If we arrive late at

Flenser's, all my work will be for nothing. You must go forward here.'

'Oops,' Pilgrim whispered, unable to resist a little editorializing, 'Ol' Vendacious may have gone too far with that.' The Queen's heads arched back. Pilgrim's imitation of her human voice said, 'I understand, your anxiety, pack of my blood. But we go forward where I say. If that is intolerable to you, I will regretfully accept your resignation.'

'But you need me!'

'Not *that* much.'

Johanna suddenly realized that the whole mission could fall apart right here, without even a shot being fired. *Where would we be without Vendacious?* She held her breath and watched the two packs. Parts of Vendacious walked in quick circles, stopping for angry instants to stare at Woodcarver. Finally all his necks drooped. 'Um. My apologies, your majesty. As long as you find me of use, I beg to continue in your service.'

Now Woodcarver relaxed, too. She reached to pet her puppies. They had responded with her mood, thrashing in their carriers and hissing. 'Forgiven. I want your independent advice, Vendacious. It has been miraculously good.'

Vendacious smiled weakly.

'I didn't think the jerk had it in him,' Pilgrim said near Johanna's ear.

It took two dayarounds to reach the old path. As Woodcarver had predicted, it was overgrown. More: In places there was no sign of the path at all. It would take *days* to get down the valley side this way. If Woodcarver had any misgivings about the decision, she didn't mention them to Johanna. The Queen was six hundred years old; she talked often enough about the inflexibility of age. Now Johanna was getting a clear example of what that meant.

When they came to a washout, trees were cut down and a bridge constructed on the spot. It took a day to get by each such spot. But progress was agonizingly slow even where the path was still in place. No one rode in the carts now. The edge of the path had worn away, and the cart wheels sometimes turned on nothingness. On Johanna's right she could look down at tree crowns that were a few meters from her feet.

They ran into the wolves six days along the detour, when they had almost reached the valley floor. Wolves. That's what Pilgrim called them anyway; what Johanna saw looked like gerbils.

They had just completed a kilometer stretch of easy going. Even under the trees they could feel the wind, dry and warm and moving ceaselessly down the valley. The last patches of snow between the trees were being sucked to nothingness, and there was a haze of smoke beyond the north wall of the valley.

Johanna was walking alongside Woodcarver's cart. Pilgrim was about ten meters behind, chatting occasionally with them. (The Queen herself had been very quiet these last days.) Suddenly there was a screech of Tinish alarm from above them.

A second later Vendacious shouted from a hundred meters ahead. Through gaps in the trees, Johanna could see troopers on the next switchback above them unlimbering crossbows, firing into the hillside above them. The sunlight came dappled through the forest cover, bringing plenty of light but in splotches that broke and moved as the soldiers hustled about. Chaos, but . . . there were things up there that weren't Tines! Small, brown or gray, they flitted through the shadows and the splotches of light. They swept up the hillside, coming upon the soldiers from the *opposite* direction that they were shooting.

'Turn around! Turn around!' Johanna screamed, but her voice was lost in the turmoil. Besides, who there could understand her? All of Woodcarver was peering up at the battle. She grabbed Johanna's sleeve. 'You see something up there? Where?'

Johanna stuttered an explanation, but now Pilgrim had seen something too. His gobbled shouting came loud over the battle. He raced back up the trail to where Scrupilo was trying to get a cannon unlimbered. 'Johanna! Help me.'

Woodcarver hesitated, then said, 'Yes. It may be that bad. Help with the cannon, Johanna.'

It was only fifty meters to the gun cart, but uphill. She ran.

Something heavy smashed into the path just behind her. Part of a soldier! It twisted and screamed. Half a dozen gerbil-sized hunks of fur were attached to the body, and its pelt was streaked with red. Another member fell past her. Another. Johanna stumbled but kept running.

Wickwrackscar was standing heads-together, just a few meters from Scrupilo. He was armed in every adult member – mouth knives and steel tines. He waved Johanna down next to him. 'We run on a nest of, of wolves.' His speech was awkward, slurred. 'It must be between here and path above. A lump, like a l'il castle tower. Gotta kill nest. Can you see it?' Evidently he could not; he was looking all over. Johanna looked back up the hillside. There seemed to be less fighting now, just sounds of Tinish agony.

Johanna pointed. 'You mean there, that dark thing?'

Pilgrim didn't answer. His members were twitching, his mouth knives waving randomly. She leaped away from the flashing metal. He had already cut himself. *Sound attack*. She looked back along the path. She'd had more than a year to know the packs, and what she was seeing now was . . . madness. Some packs were exploding, racing in all directions to distances where thought couldn't possibly be sustained. Others – Woodcarver on her cart – huddled in heaps, with scarcely a head showing.

Just beyond the nearest uphill trees she could see a gray tide. *The wolves*. Each furry lump looked innocent enough. All together . . . Johanna froze for an instant, watching them tear out the throat of a trooper's member.

Johanna was the only sane person left, and all it would mean is she would *know* she was dying.

Kill the nest.

On the gun cart beside her only one of Scrupilo was left, old White Head. Daffy as ever, it had pulled down its gunner's muffs and was nosing around under the gun tube. *Kill the nest*. Maybe not so daffy after all!

Johanna jumped up on the wagon. It rolled back toward the dropoff, banging against a tree; she scarcely noticed. She pulled up the gun barrel, just as she had seen in all the drills. The white-headed one pulled at the powder bag, but with just his one pair of jaws he couldn't handle it. Without the rest of its pack it had neither hands nor brains. It looked up at her, its eyes wide and desperate.

She grabbed the other end of the bag, and the two of them got the powder into the barrel. White Head dived back into the equipment, nosing around for a cannonball. *Smarter than a dog, and trained.* Between them, maybe they had a chance!

Just half a meter beneath her feet, the wolves were running by. One or two she could have fought off herself. But there were dozens down there, worrying and tearing at random members. Three of Pilgrim were standing around Scarbutt and the pups, but their defense was unthinking slashing. The pack had dropped its mouth knives and tines.

She and White Head got the round down the barrel. White Head whipped back to the rear, began playing with the little wick-lighter the gunners used. It was something that could be held in a single mouth, since only one member actually fired the weapon.

'Wait, you idiot!' Johanna kicked him back. 'We gotta aim this thing!'

White Head looked hurt for an instant. The complaint wasn't completely clear to him. He had dropped the standoff wand, but still held the lighter. He flicked on the flame, and circled determinedly back, tried to worm past Johanna's legs. She pushed him back again, and looked uphill. *The dark thing. That must be the nest.* She tilted the gun tube on its mounting and sighted down the top. Her face ended up just centimeters from the persistent White Head and his flame. His muffed head darted forward, and the flame touched the fire-hole.

The blast almost knocked Johanna off the cart. For a moment she could think of nothing but the pain that stabbed into her ears. She rolled to a sitting position, coughing in the smoke. She couldn't hear *anything* beyond a high-pitched ringing that went on and on. Their little wagon was teetering, one wheel hanging over dropoff. White Head was flopping around under the butt of the cannon. She pushed it off him and patted the muffed head. He was bleeding – or she was. She just sat dazed for a few seconds, mystified by the blood, trying to imagine how she had ever ended up here.

A voice somewhere in the back of her head was screaming. *No time, no time.* She forced herself to her knees and looked around, memories coming back painfully slow.

There were splintered trees uphill of them; the blond wood glinted among the leaves. Beyond them where the nest had been, she saw a splash of fresh turned earth. They had 'killed' it, but . . . the fighting continued.

There were still wolves on the path, but now they were the ones running in all directions. As she watched, dozens of them catapulted off the edge of trail into the trees and rocks below. And the Tines were actually fighting now. Pilgrim had picked up his knives. The blades and his muzzles dripped red and he slashed. Something gray and bleeding flew over the edge of the cart and landed by Johanna's leg. The 'wolf' couldn't have been more than twenty centimeters long, its hair dirty gray brown. It really did look like a pet, but the tiny jaws clicked at her ankles with murderous intent. Johanna dropped a cannonball on it.

During the next three days, while Woodcarver's people struggled to bring their equipment and themselves back together, Johanna learned quite a bit about the wolves. What she and Scrupilo's White Head did with the cannon had stopped the attack cold. Without doubt, knocking out the nest had saved a lot of lives and the expedition itself. The 'wolves' were a type of hive creature, only a little like the packs. The Tines race used group thought to reach high intelligence; Johanna had never seen a rational pack of more than six members. The wolf nests didn't care about high intelligence. Woodcarver claimed that a nest might have thousands of members – certainly the one they'd tripped over was huge. Such a mob couldn't be as smart as a human. In terms of raw reasoning power, it probably wasn't much brighter than a single pack member. On the other hand, it could be a lot more flexible. Wolves could operate alone at great distances. When within a hundred meters of the home nest they were appendages of the 'queen' members of the nest, and no one doubted their canniness then. Pilgrim had legends of nests with almost packish intelligence, of foresters who made treaties with nearby nests for protection in return for food. As long as the high-powered noises in the nest lived, the worker wolves could coordinate almost like Tine members. But kill the nest, and the creature fell apart like some cheap, center-topology network.

Certainly this nest had done a number on Woodcarver's army. It had waited quietly until the troopers were within its inner loudness. Then outlying wolves had used synchronized mimicry to create sonic 'ghosts,' tricking the packs into turning from the nest and shooting uselessly into the trees. And when the ambush actually began, the nest had screamed concentrated confusion down on the Tines. That attack had been a far more powerful thing than the 'stink noise' they'd encountered in other parts of the forest. To the Tines, the stinkers had been painfully loud and sometimes even frightening, but not the mind-destroying chaos of the wolf-nest attack.

More than one hundred packs had been knocked out in the ambush. Some, mostly packs with pups, had huddled. Others, like Scrupilo, had been 'blasted apart.' In the hours following the attack, many of these fragments straggled back and reassembled. The resulting Tines were shaken but unharmed. Intact soldiers hunted up and down the forested cliffs for injured members of their comrades. There were places along the dropoff that were more than twenty meters deep. Where their fall wasn't cushioned by tree boughs, members landed on naked rock. Five dead ones were eventually found, and another twenty seriously injured. Two carts had fallen. They were kindling, and their kherhogs were too badly injured to survive. By great good luck, the gunshot had not started a forest fire.

Three times the sun made its vast, tilted course around the sky. Woodcarver's army recovered in a camp in the depths of the valley forest, by the river. Vendacious had posted lookouts with signaling mirrors on the northern valley wall. This place was about as safe as any they could find so far north. It was certainly one of the most beautiful. It didn't have the view of the high forest, but there was the sound of the river nearby, so loud it drowned the sighing of the dry wind. The lowland trees didn't have root flowers, but they were still different from what Johanna had known. There was no underbrush, just a soft, bluish 'moss' that Pilgrim claimed was actually part of the trees. It stretched like mown parkland to the edge of the river.

On the last day of their rest, the Queen called a meeting of all the packs not at guard or lookout. It was the largest collection of Tines Johanna had seen in one place since her family was killed. Only these packs weren't fighting. As far as Johanna could see across the bluish moss, there were packs, each at least eight meters from its nearest neighbor. For an absurd instant she was reminded of Settlers Park at Overby: Families picnicking on the grass, each with its own traditional blanket and food lockers. But these 'families' were each a pack, and this was a military formation. The rows were gently curving arcs, all facing toward the Queen. Peregrine Wickwrackscar was ten meters behind her, in shadow; being Queen's consort didn't count for anything official. On Woodcarver's left lay the living casualties of the ambush, members with bandages and splints. In some ways, such visible damage wasn't the most horrifying. There were also what Pilgrim called the 'walking wounded.' These were singletons and duos and trios that were all that was left of whole packs. Some of these tried to maintain a posture of attention, but others mooned about, occasionally breaking into the Queen's speech with aimless words. It was like Scriber Jaqueramaphan all over again, but most of these would live. Some were already melding, trying to make new individuals. Some of these might even work out, as Peregrine Wickwrackscar had done. For most, it would be a long time before they were fully people again.

Johanna sat with Scrupilo in the first rank of troopers before the Queen. The Commander of Cannoneers stood at Tinish parade rest: rumps on the ground, chest high, most heads facing front. Scrup had come through it without serious damage. His white head had a few more scorch marks, and one of the other members had sprained a shoulder falling off the path. He wore his flying cannoneer muffs as flamboyantly as always, but there was something subdued

361

about him – maybe it was just the military formation and getting a medal for heroism.

The Queen was wearing her special jackets. Each head looked out at a different section of her audience. Johanna still couldn't understand Tinish, and would certainly never speak it without mechanical assistance. But the sounds were mostly within her range of hearing – low frequencies carry a lot better than high ones. Even without memory aides and grammar generators she was learning a little. She could recognize emotional tone easily, and things like the raucous *ark ark ark* that passed for applause around here. As for individual words – well, they were more like *chords*, single syllables that had meaning. Nowadays, if she listened really carefully (and Pilgrim weren't nearby to give a running translation) she could even recognize some of those.

... Just now, for instance, Woodcarver was saying good things about her audience. Approving *ark ark*s came from all directions. They sounded like a bunch of sea'mals. One of the Queen's heads dipped into a bowl, coming up with a small carven doodad in its mouth. She spoke a pack's name, a multichord *tumptititum* that if Johanna heard often enough she might be able to repeat as 'Jaqueramaphan' – or even see meaning in, as 'Wickwrackscar.'

From the front rank of the audience, *a single member* trotted toward the Queen. It stopped practically nose to nose with the Queen's nearest member. Woodcarver said something about bravery, and then two of her fastened the wooden – broach? – to the member's jacket. It turned smartly and returned to its pack.

Woodcarver picked out another decoration, and called on another pack. Johanna leaned over toward Scrupilo. 'What's going on?' she said wonderingly. 'Why are single members getting medals?' *And how can they stand to get so near another pack?*

Scrupilo had been standing more stiffly at attention than most packs, and was pretty much ignoring her. Now he turned one head in her direction. 'Shh!' He started to turn back, but she grabbed him by one of his jackets. 'Foolish one,' he finally replied. 'The award is for the whole pack. One member is extended to accept. More would be madness.'

Hmm. One after another, three more packs 'extended a member' to take their decorations. Some were full of precision, like human soldiers in stories. Others started out smartly, then became timid and confused as they approached Woodcarver.

Finally Johanna said, 'Ssst. Scrupilo! When do we get ours?'

This time he didn't even look at her; all his heads faced rigidly toward the Queen. 'Last, of course. You and I killed the nest, and saved Woodcarver herself.' His bodies were almost shaking with the intensity of their brace. *He's scared witless.* And suddenly Johanna guessed why. Apparently Woodcarver had no problem maintaining her mind with one outside member nearby. But the reverse would not be true. Sending one of yourself into another pack meant losing some consciousness and placing trust in that other pack. Looking at it that way . . . well, it reminded Johanna of the historical novels she used to play. On Nyjora during the Dark Age, ladies traditionally gave their sword to their queen when granted audience, and then knelt. It was a way to swear loyalty. Same thing here, except that looking at Scrupilo, Johanna realized that even as a matter of form, the ceremony might be damn frightening.

Three more medals bestowed, and then Woodcarver gobbled the chords that were Scrupilo's name. The Commander of Cannoneers went absolutely rigid, made faint whistling noises through his mouths. 'Johanna Olsndot,' said Woodcarver, then more Tinish, something about coming forward.

Johanna stood up, but not one of Scrupilo moved.

The Queen made a human laugh. She was holding two polished broaches. 'I'll explain all in Samnorsk later, Johanna. Just come forward with one of Scrupilo. Scrupilo?'

Suddenly they were the center of attenton, with thousands of eyes watching. There was no more *ark*ing or background chatter. Johanna hadn't felt so exposed since she played First Colonist in her school's Landing Play. She leaned down so that her head was close to one of Scrupilo's. 'Come *on*, guy.

We're the big heroes.'

The eyes that looked back at her were wide. 'I can't.' The words were almost inaudible. For all his jaunty cannoneer muffs and standoffish manner, Scrupilo was terrified. But for him it wasn't stage fright. 'I can't tear me apart so soon. I *can't.*'

There was murmured gobbling in the ranks behind them, Scrupilo's own cannoneers. By all the Powers, would they hold this against him? Welcome to the middle ages. *Stupid people. Even cut to pieces, Scrupilo had saved their behinds, and now –*

She put her hands on two of his shoulders. 'We did it before, you and I. Remember?'

The heads nodded. 'Some. That one part of me alone . . . could never have done it.'

'Right. And neither could I. But together we killed a wolf-nest.'

Scrupilo stared at her a second, eyes wavering, 'Yes, we really did.' He came to his feet, frisked his heads so the cannoneer muffs flapped. 'Yes!' And he moved his white-headed one closer to her.

Johanna straightened. She and White Head walked out into the open space. Four meters. Six. She kept the fingertips of one hand lightly on his neck. When they were about twelve meters from the rest of Scrupilo, White Head's pace faltered. He looked sideways up at Johanna, then continued more slowly.

Johanna didn't remember much of the ceremony, so much of her attention was on White Head. Woodcarver said something long and unintelligible. Somehow they both ended up with intricately carven decorations on their collars, and were headed back toward the rest of Scrupilo. *Then* she was aware of the crowd once more. They stretched as far as she could see under the forest canopy – and every one of them seemed to be cheering, Scrup's cannoneers loudest of all.

Midnight. Here at the bottom of the valley there were three or four hours of the dayaround when the sun dipped behind the high north wall. It didn't much feel like night, or even twilight.

The smoke from the fires to the north seemed to be getting worse. She could smell it now.

Johanna walked back from the cannoneers section toward the center of camp, and Woodcarver's tent. It was quiet; she could hear little creatures scritching in the root bushes. The celebrating might have gone on longer, except that everyone knew that in another few hours they would be preparing for the climb up the valley's north wall. So now there was only occasional laughter, an occasional pack walking about. Johanna walked barefoot, her shoes slung over her shoulders. Even in the dry weather, the moss was wonderfully soft between her toes. Above her the forest canopy was shifting green and patches of hazy sky. She could almost forget what had gone before, and what lay ahead.

The guards around Woodcarver's tent didn't challenge her, just called softly ahead. After all, there weren't that many humans running around. The Queen stuck out a head. 'Come inside, Johanna.'

Inside she was sitting in her usual circle, the puppies protected in the middle. It was quite dark, the only light being what came through the entrance. Johanna flopped down on the pillows where she usually slept. Ever since this afternoon, the big award thing, she had been planning to give Woodcarver a piece of her mind. Now . . . well the party at the cannoneers had been a happy thing. It seemed kind of a shame to break the mood.

Woodcarver cocked a head at her. Simultaneously, the two puppies duplicated the gesture. 'I saw you at the party. You are a sober one. You eat most of our foods now, but none of the beer.'

Johanna shrugged. *Yes, why?* 'Kids aren't supposed to drink before they're eighteen years old.' That was the custom, and her parents had agreed with it. Johanna had turned fourteen a couple of months ago; Dataset had reminded her of the exact hour. She wondered. If none of this had happened, if she were still back at the High Lab or Straumli Realm: Would she be sneaking out with friends to try such forbidden things? Probably. Yet here, where she was entirely on her own, where she was currently a big hero, she hadn't tried a drop . . . Maybe it was because Mom and Dad *weren't* here, and following their wishes seemed to keep them closer. She felt tears coming to her eyes.

'Hmm.' Woodcarver didn't seem to notice. 'That's what Pilgrim said was the reason.' She tapped at her puppies and smiled. 'I guess it makes sense. These two don't get beer till they're older – though I know they got some second-hand partying from *me* tonight.' There was a hint of beer breath in the tent.

Johanna wiped roughly at her face. She really did not want to talk about being a teenager just now. 'You know, that was kind of a mean trick you pulled on Scrupilo this afternoon.'

'I – Yes. I talked to him about it beforehand. He didn't want it, but I thought he was just being . . . is stiff-necked the word? If I had known how upset he was, well –'

'He practically fell apart out there in front of everybody. If I understand how things work, that would have been his disgrace, right?'

'. . . Yes. Exchanging honor for loyalty in front of peers, it's an important thing. At least the way I run things; I'm sure Pilgrim or Dataset can say a dozen other ways to lead. Look Johanna, I needed that Exchange, and I needed you and Scrupilo to be there.'

'Yeah, I know. "We two saved the day."'

'Silence!' He voice was suddenly edged, and Johanna remembered that this was a medieval queen. 'We are two hundred miles north of my borders, almost to the heart of the Flenser Domain. In a few days we will meet the enemy, and many more of us will die for we-know-not-quite-what.'

The bottom dropped out of Johanna's stomach. If she couldn't get back to the ship, couldn't finish what Mom and Dad had started . . . '*Please*, Woodcarver! It *is* worth it!'

'I know that. Pilgrim knows it. The majority of my council agrees, though grudgingly. But we of the council have talked with Dataset. We've seen your worlds and what your science can do. On the other hand, most of my people here,' she waved a head at the camp beyond the tent, 'are here on faith, and out of loyalty to me. For *them*, the situation is deadly and the goal is vague.' She paused, though her two pups

366

continued gesturing forcefully for a second. 'Now I don't know how you would persuade your kind to take such risks. Dataset talks of military conscription.'

'That was Nyjora, long ago.'

'Never mind. The point is, my troops are here out of loyalty, mostly to me personally. For six hundred years, I have protected my people well; their memories and legends are clear on it. More than once, I was the only one who saw a peril, and it was my advice that saved all those who heeded it. *That* is what keeps most of the soldiers, most of the cannoneers going. Each of them is free to turn back. So. What should they think when our first "combat" is to fall like ignorant . . . tourists . . . onto a nest of wolves? Without the great good luck of you and part of Scrupilo being at the right place and alert, I would have been killed. Pilgrim would have been killed. Perhaps a third of the soldiers would have died.'

'If not us, perhaps someone else,' Johanna said in a small voice.

'Perhaps. I don't think anyone else came close to firing on the nest. You see the effect on my people? "If bad luck in the forest can kill our Queen and destroy our marvelous weapons, what will it be like when we face a *thinking* enemy?" That was the question in many minds. Unless I could answer it, we'd never make it out of this valley – at least not going northward.'

'So you gave the medals. Loyalty for honor.'

, 'Yes. You missed the sense of it, not understanding Tinish. I made a big thing of how well they had done. I gave silverwood accolades to packs who showed any competence in the ambush. That helped some. I repeated my reasons for this expedition – the wonders that Dataset describes and how much we will lose if Steel gets his way. But they've heard that argument before, and it points to far away things they can scarcely imagine. The *new* thing I showed them today was you and Scrupilo.'

'*Us?*'

'I praised you beyond the skies. Singletons often do brave things. Sometimes they are halfway clever, or talk as though they are. But alone, Scrupilo's fragment wouldn't be much more than a good knife fighter. He knew about using the cannon, but he didn't have the paws or mouths to do anything with it. And by himself, he would never have figured out where to shoot it. You, on the other hand, are a Two-Legs. In many ways you are helpless. The *only* way you can think is by yourself, but you can do it without interfering with those around you. Together you did what no pack could do in the middle of a wolf-nest attack. So I told my army what a team our two races could become, how each makes up for the age-old failings of the other. Together, we are one step closer to being the Pack of Packs. How is Scrupilo?'

Johanna smiled faintly. 'Things turned out okay. Once he was able to get out there and accept his medal,' she fingered the broach that was pinned to her own collar; it was a beautiful thing, a landscape of Woodcarver's city, 'once he'd done that, he was totally changed. You should have seen him with the cannoneers afterwards. They did their own loyalty/honor thing, and then they drank a lot of beer. Scrupilo was telling them all about what we were doing. He even had me help demonstrate . . . You really think the army bought what you said about humans and Tines?'

'I think so. In my own language, I can be very eloquent. I've bred myself to be.' Woodcarver was silent for a moment. Her puppies scrambled across the carpet, and patted their muzzles at Johanna's hands. 'Besides . . . it may even be true. Pilgrim is sure of it. You can sleep in this same tent with me and still think. That's something that he and I can't do; in our own ways, we've each lived a long time and I think we are each at least as smart as the humans and other creatures that Dataset talks about in the Beyond. But you singleton creatures can stand next to each other, and think and build. Compared to us, I'll bet singleton races developed the sciences very fast. But now, with your help, maybe things will change fast for us too.' The two puppies retreated, and Woodcarver lowered heads to paws. 'That's what I told my people, anyway . . . You should try to get some sleep now.'

On the ground beyond the tent's entrance there were already splashes of sunlight. 'Okay.' Johanna slipped off her outer clothes. She lay down and dragged a light quilt across herself. Most of Woodcarver already looked asleep. As usual,

368

one or two pairs of eyes were open, but their intelligence would be limited – and just now, even they looked tired. Funny, Woodcarver had worked with Dataset so much, her human voice had come to capture emotion as well as pronunciation. Just now she had sounded so tired, so sad.

Johanna reached out from under her quilt to brush the neck of Woodcarver's nearest, the blind one. 'Do *you* believe what you told everyone?' she said softly.

One of the 'sentry' heads looked at her, and a very human sigh seemed to come from all directions. Woodcarver's voice was very faint. 'Yes . . . but I am very afraid that it doesn't matter anymore. For six hundred years, I have had proper confidence in myself. But what happened on the south wall . . . should not have happened. It would not if I had followed Vendacious's advice, and come down on the New Road.'

'But we might have been seen –'

'Yes. A failure either way, don't you see? Vendacious has precise information from the highest councils of the Flenser. But he's something of a careless fool in everyday matters. I knew that, and thought I could compensate. But the Old Road was in far worse condition than I remembered: the wolf-nest could never have settled by it if there had been any traffic during the last few years. If Vendacious had managed his patrols properly, or if I had been managing *him* properly, we would never have been surprised. Instead we were nearly overrun . . . and my only remaining talent appears to be in fooling those who trust me into thinking I still know what I'm doing.' She opened another pair of eyes and made the smile gesture. 'Strange. I haven't said these things even to Pilgrim. Is this another "advantage" of human relations?'

Johanna patted the blind one's neck. 'Maybe.'

'Anyway, I believe what I said about things that *could* be, but I fear that my soul may not be strong enough to make them so. Perhaps I should turn things over to Pilgrim or Vendacious; that's something I must think on.' Woodcarver *shh*ed Johanna's surprised protests.

'Now sleep, please.'

32

There was a time when Ravna thought their tiny ship might fly all the way to the Bottom unnoticed. Along with everything else, that had changed. At the moment, *Out of Band II* might be the most famous starship known to the Net. A million races watched the chase. In the Middle Beyond there were vast antenna swarms beaming in their direction and listening to the stories – mostly lies – sent from the ships that pursued the *OOB*. She couldn't hear those lies directly of course, but the transmissions she received were as clear as if they were on a main trunk.

Ravna spent part of each day reading the News, trying to find hope, trying to prove to herself that she was doing the right thing. By now, she was pretty sure what was chasing them. No doubt even Pham and Blueshell would have agreed on that. *Why* they were being chased, and *what* they might find at the end was now the subject of endless speculation on the Net. As usual, whatever the truth might be was well hidden among the lies.

Crypto: 0
As received by: *OOB* shipboard ad hoc
Language path: Triskweline, SjK units
From: Hanse
   [No references prior to the fall of Relay. No probable
   source. This is someone being very cautious.]
Subject: Alliance for the Defense fraudulent?
Distribution:
   Threat of the Blight
   War Trackers Interest Group
   Homo Sapiens Interest Group
Date: 5.80 days since Fall of Sjandra Kei
Key phrases: Fools' errand, unnecessary genocide
Text of message:

Earlier I speculated that there had been no destruction at Sjandra Kei. Apologies. That was based on a catalog identification error. I agree with the messages (13123 as of a few seconds ago) assuring me that the habitations of Sjandra Kei suffered collisional damage within the last six days..

So apparently the 'Alliance for the Defense' has taken the military action they claimed earlier. And apparently, they are powerful enough to destroy small civilizations in the Middle Beyond. The question still remains: 'Why?' I have already posted arguments showing it unlikely that Homo sapiens is especially controllable by the Blight (though they were *stupid* enough to create that entity). Even the Alliance's own reports admit that less than half of Sjandra Kei's sophonts were of that race.

Now a large part of the Alliance fleet is chasing into the Bottom of the Beyond after a *single ship*. What conceivable damage can the Alliance do to the Blight down there? The Blight is a great threat, perhaps the most novel and threatening in well-recorded history. Nevertheless, Alliance behavior appears destructive and pointless. Now that the Alliance has revealed some of its sponsoring organizations (see messages [id numbers]), I think we know its real motives. I see connections between the Alliance and the old Aprahant Hegemony. A thousand years ago, that group undertook a similar jihad, grabbing real estate left vacant by recent Transcendences. Stopping the Hegemony was an exciting bit of action in that part of the galaxy. I think these people are back, taking advantage of the general panic attending the Blight (which is admittedly a much greater threat).

My advice: Beware of the Alliance and its claims of heroic efforts.

Crypto: 0
As received by: *OOB* shipboard ad hoc
Language path: Schirachene→Rondralip→

Triskweline, SjK units
From: Harmonious Repose Communications Synod
Subject: Encounter with agents of the Perversion
Distribution:
   Threat of the Blight
Date: 6.37 days since Fall of Sjandra Kei
Key phrases: Hanse fraudulent?
Test of message:

   We have no special inclination toward any of the
posters on this thread. Nevertheless, it's remarkable
that an entity that has not revealed its location or
special interests – namely 'Hanse' – should be
smearing the efforts of the Alliance for the Defense.
The Alliance kept its constituents secret only during
that period when its forces were being gathered,
when a single stroke of the Perversion's power might
destroy it entirely. Since that time, it has been quite
open in its efforts.

   Hanse wonders how a single starship could be
worth the Alliance's attention. As Harmonious Repose
was the site of the latest turn of events, we are in a
position to give some explanation. The ship in question, the *Out of Band II*, is clearly designed for operations at the Bottom of the Beyond – and is even
capable of limited operations within the Slow Zone.
The ship presented itself as a special zonographic
flight commissioned to study the recent turbulence at
the Bottom. In fact, this ship's mission is a very
different one. In the aftermath of its violent departure,
we have pieced together some extraordinary facts:

   At least one of the ship's crew was human. Though
they made great efforts to stay out of the view and
used Skroderider traders as intermediaries, we have
recordings. A biosequence of one individual was
obtained, and it maches the patterns maintained by
two out of three of the Homo sapiens archives. (It's
well known that the third archive, on Sneerot Down, is
in the control of Human sympathizers.) Some might
say this deception was founded in fear. After all, these

events happened after the destruction of Sjandra Kei. We think otherwise: The ship's initial contact with us occurred before the Sjandra Kei incident.

We have since made a careful analysis of the repair work our yards performed on this vessel. Ultradrive automation is a deep and complex thing; even the cleverest of cloaking cannot mask all the memories in it. We now know that the *Out of Band II* was from the Relay system and that it left there *after* the Perversion's attack. Think what this means.

The crew of the *Out of Band II* brought weapons into a habitat, kill several local sophonts, and escaped before our musicians [harmonizers? police?] were properly notified. We have good reason to wish them ill.

Yet our misfortune is a small thing compared to the unmasking of this secret mission. We are very grateful that the Alliance is willing to risk so much in following this lead.

There's more than the usual number of unsubstantiated assertions floating around on this news thread. We hope our facts will wake some people up. In particular, consider what '"Hanse"' may really be. The Perversion is very visible in the High Beyond, where it has great power and can speak with its own voice. Down here, it is more likely that deception and covert propaganda will be its tools. Think on this when you read postings from unidentified entities such as 'Hanse'!

Ravna gritted her teeth. The hell of it was, the facts in the posting were correct. It was the inferences that were vicious and false. And she couldn't guess if this were some shade of black propaganda or simply Saint Rihndell expressing honest conclusions (though Rihndell had never seemed so trusting of the butterflies).

One thing all the News seemed to agree on: Much more than the Alliance fleet was chasing the *OOB*. The swarm of ultradrive traces could be seen by anyone within a thousand light-years. The best guess was that three fleets pursued the *OOB*. Three! The Alliance for the Defense, still loud and boastful, even though suspected (by some) of being opportunistic genocides. Behind them, Sjandra Kei . . . and what was left of Ravna's motherland; in all the universe perhaps the only folk she could trust. And just behind them, the silent fleet. Diverse news posters claimed it was from the High Beyond. That fleet might have problems at the Bottom, but for now it was gaining. Few doubted that it was the Perversion's child. More than anything, it convinced the universe that the *OOB* or its destination was cosmically important. Just why it was important was the big question. Speculation was drifting in at the rate of five thousand messages per hour. A million different viewpoints were considering the mystery. Some of those viewpoints were so alien that they made Skroderiders and Humans look like the same species. At least five participants on this News thread were gaseous inhabitants of stellar coronas. There were one or two others that Ravna suspected were uncataloged races, beings so shy that this might be their first active use of the Net ever.

The *OOB*'s computer was a lot dumber than it had been in the Middle Beyond. She couldn't ask it to sift through the messages looking for nuance and insight. In fact, if an incoming message didn't have a Triskweline text, it was often unreadable. The ship's translator programs still worked fairly well with the major trade languages, but even there the translation was slow and full of alternative meanings and jabberwocky. It was just another sign that they were approaching the Bottom of the Beyond. Effective translation of natural languages comes awfully close to requiring a sentient translator program.

Nevertheless, with proper design, things might have been better. The automation might have degraded gracefully under the restrictions imposed by their depth. Instead, gear just stopped working; what remained was slow and error-prone. If only the refitting had been completed before the Fall of Relay. *And just how many times have I wished for that?* She hoped things were as bad aboard the pursuing ships.

So Ravna used the ship to do light culling on the Threats newsgroup. Much of what was left was inane, as from people who see 'portents in the weather' —

Crypto: 0
Syntax: 43
As received by: *OOB* shipboard ad hoc
Language path: Arbwyth→Trade 24→
Cherguelen→Triskweline, SjK units
From: Twirlip of the Mists
    [Perhaps an organization of cloud fliers in a single jovian system. Very sparse priors before this thread began. Appears to be seriously out of touch. Program recommendation: delete this poster from presentation.]
Subject: The Blight's goal at the Bottom
Distribution:
    Threat of the Blight
    Great Secrets of Creation
Date: 4.54 days since Fall of Sjandra Kei
Key phrases: Zone Instability and the Blight,
    Hexapodia as the key insight
Text of message:
    Apologies first if I am repeating obvious conclusions. My only gateway onto the Net is very expensive, and I miss many important postings. I think that anyone following both Great Secrets of Creation and Threat of the Blight would see an important pattern. Since the events reported by Harmonious Repose information service, most agree that something important to the Perversion exists at the Bottom of the Beyond in region [. . .]. I see a possible connection here with the Great Secrets. During the last two hundred and twenty days, there have been increasing reports of zone interface instability in the region below Harmonious Repose. As the Blight threat has grown and its attacks against advanced races and other Powers continued, this instability has increased. Could there not be some connection? I urge all to consult

375

their information on the Great Secrets (or the nearest archive maintained by that gorup). Events such as this prove once again that the universe is all ronzelle between.

Some of the postings were tantalizing —

Crypto: 0
Syntax: 43
As received by: *OOB* shipboard ad hoc
Language path: Wobblings→Baeloresk→Trisk-
   weline, Sjk units
From: Cricketsong under the High Willow
   [Cricketsong is a synthetic race created as a jape/
   experiment/instrument by the High Willow upon its
   Transcendence. Cricketsong has been on the Net
   for more than ten thousand years. Apparently it is a
   fanatical studier of paths to Transcendence. For
   eight thousand years it has been the heaviest poster
   on 'Where are they now' and related groups. There
   is no evidence that any Cricketsong settlement has
   itself Transcended. Cricketsong is sufficiently peculiar that there is a large news group for speculation
   concerning the race itself. Consensus is that
   Cricketsong was designed by High Willow as a
   probe back into the Beyond, that the race is somehow incapable of attempting its own Trans-
   cendence.]
Subject: The Blight's goal at the Bottom
Distribution:
   Threat of the Blight
   War Trackers Special Interest Group
   Where are they now Special Interest Group
Date: 5.12 days since Fall of Sjandra Kei
Key phrases: On becoming Transcendent
Text of message:
   Contrary to other postings, there are a number of
reasons why a Power might install artifacts at the
Bottom of the Beyond. The Abselor's message on this

376

thread cites some: some Powers have documented curiosity about the Slow Zone and, even more, about the Unthinking Depths. In rare cases, expeditions have been dispatched (though any return from the Depths would occur long after the dispatching Power lost interest in all local questions).

However, none of these motives are likely here. To those who are familiar with Fast Burn transcendence, it is clear that the Blight is a creature seeking stasis. Its interest in the Bottom is very sudden, provoked, we think, by the revelations at Harmonious Repose. There is something at the Bottom that is critical to the Perversion's welfare.

Consider the notion of ablative dissonance (see the Where Are They Now group archive): No one knows what setup procedures the humans of Straumli Realm were using. The Fast Burn may itself have had Transcendent intelligence. What if *it* became dissatisfied with the direction of the channedring? In that case it might try to hide the jumpoff birthinghel. The Bottom would not be a place where the algorithm itself could normally execute, but avatars might still be created from it and briefly run.

Up to a point, Ravna could almost make sense of it; ablative dissonance was a commonplace of Applied Theology. But then, like one of those dreams where the secret of life is about to be revealed, the posting just drifted into nonsense.

There were postings that were neither asinine nor obscure. As usual, Sandor at the Zoo had a lot of things dead right:

Crypto: 0
As received by: *OOB* shipboard ad hoc
Language path: Triskweline, SjK units
From: Sandor Arbitration Intelligence at the Zoo [A known military corporation of the High Beyond. If this is a masquerade, somebody is living dangerously.]
Subject: The Blight's goal at the Bottom

Key phrases: Sudden change in Blight's tactics
Distribution:
  Threat of the Blight
  War Trackers Interest Group
  Homo Sapiens Interest Group
Date: 8.15 days since Fall of Sjandra Kei
Text of message:

In case you don't know, Sandor Intelligence has a number of different Net feeds. We can collect messages on paths that have no intermediate nodes in common. Thus we can detect and correct tampering done en route. (There remain the lies and misunderstandings that were present to begin with, but that's something that makes the intelligence business interesting.)

The Blight has been our top priority since its instantiation a year ago. This is not just because of the Blight's obvious strength, the destruction and the deicides it has committed. We fear that all this is the lesser part of the Threat. There have been perversions almost as powerful in the recorded past. What truly distinguishes this one is its stability. We see no evidence of internal evolution; in some ways it is *less* than a Power. It may never lose interest in controlling the High Beyond. We may be witnessing a massive and permanent change in the nature of things. Imagine: a stable necrosis, where the only sentience in the High Beyond is the Blight.

Thus, studying the Blight has been a matter of life and death for us (even though we are powerful and widely distributed). We've reached a number of conclusions. Some of these may be obvious to you, others may sound like flagrant speculation. All take on a new coloring with the events reported from Harmonious Repose:

Almost from the beginning, the Blight has been searching for something. This search has extended far beyond its aggressive physical expansion. Its automatic agents have tried to penetrate virtually every

378

node in the Top of the Beyond; the High Network is in shambles, reduced to protocols scarcely more efficient than those known below. At the same time, the Blight has physically stolen several archives. We have evidence of very large fleets searching for off-Net archives at the Top and in the Low Transcend. At least three Powers have been murdered in this rampage.

And now, suddenly, this assault has ended. The Blight's physical expansion continues, with no end in sight, but it no longer searches the High Beyond. As near as we can tell, the change occurred about two thousand seconds before the escape of the human vessel from Harmonious Repose. Less than six hours later, we saw the beginnings of the silent fleet that so many are now speculating about. That fleet is indeed the creature of the Blight.

In other times, the destruction of Sjandra Kei and the motives of the Alliance for the Defense would all be important issues (and our organization might have interest in doing business with those affected). But all that is dwarfed by the fact of this fleet and the ship it pursues. And we disagree with the analysis from Harmonious Repose: it is obvious to us that the Blight did not know of the *Out of Band II* until its discovery at Harmonious Repose.

That ship is not a tool of the Blight, but it contains or is bound for something of enormous importance *to* the Blight. And what might that be? Here we begin frank speculation. And since we are speculating, we'll use those powerful pseudo-laws, the Principles of Mediocrity and Minimal Assumption. If the Blight has the potential for taking over all the Top in a permanent stability, then why has this not happened before? Our guess is that the Blight has been instantiated before (with such dire consequence that the event marks the beginning of recorded time), but it has its own peculiar natural enemy.

The order of events even suggests a particular scenario, one familiar from network security. Once upon a time (very long ago), there was another instance of the Blight. A successful defense was mounted, and all known copies of the Blight's recipe were destroyed. Of course, on a wide net, one can never be sure that *all* copies of a badness are gone. No doubt, the defense was distributed in enormous numbers. But even if a harboring archive were reached by such a distribution, there might be no effect if the Blight were not currently active there.

The luckless humans of Straumli Realm chanced on such an archive, no doubt a ruin long off the Net. They instantiated the Blight and incidentally – perhaps a little later – the defense program. Somehow that Blight's enemy escaped destruction. And the Blight has been searching for it ever since – *in all the wrong places*. In its weakness, the new instance of the defense retreated to depths no Power would think of penetrating, whence it could never return without outside help. Speculation on top of speculation: we can't guess the nature of this defense, except that its retreat is a discouraging sign. And now even that sacrifice has gone for naught, since the Blight has seen through the deception.

The Blight's fleet is clearly an ad hoc thing, hastily thrown together from forces that happened to be closest to the discovery. Without such haste, the quarry might have been lost to it. Thus the chase equipment is probably ill-suited to the depths, and its performance will degrade as the descent progresses. However, we estimate that it will remain stronger than any force that can reach the scene in the near future.

We may learn more after the Blight reaches the *Out of Band II*'s destination. If it destroys that destination immediately, we'll know that something truly dangerous to the Blight existed there (and may exist elsewhere, at least in recipe form). If it does not, then perhaps the Blight was looking for something that will make it even more dangerous than before.

*

Ravna sat back, stared at the display for some time. Sandor Arbitration Intelligence was one of the sharpest posters in this newsgroup . . . But now even their predictions were just different flavors of doom. And all so damn cool they were, so analytical. She knew that Sandor was polyspecific, with branch offices scattered through the High Beyond. But they were no Power. If the Perversion could knock over Relay and kill Old One, then all of Sandor's resources wouldn't help it if the enemy decided to gobble them up. Their analysis had the tone of the pilot of a crashing ship, intent on understanding the danger, not taking time out for terror.

Oh Pham, how I wish I could talk to you like before! She curled gently in on herself, the way you can in zero gee. The sobs came softly, but without hope. They had not exchanged a hundred words in the last five days. They lived as if with guns at each others' heads. And that was the literal truth – *she* had made it so. When she and he and the Skroderiders had been together, at least the danger had been a shared burden. Now they were split apart and their enemies were slowly gaining on them. What good could Pham's godshatter be against a thousand enemy ships and the Blight behind them?

She floated for a timeless while, the sobs fading into despairing silence. And again she wondered if what she'd done could possibly be right. She had threatened Pham's life to protect Blueshell and Greenstalk and their kind. In doing so she had kept secret what might be the greatest treachery in the history of the Known Net. *Can one person make such a decision?* Pham had asked her that, and she had answered *yes* but . . .

The question toyed with her every day. And every day she tried to see some way out. She wiped her face silently. She didn't doubt what Pham had discovered.

There were some smug posters on the Net who argued that something as vast as the Blight was simply a tragic disaster, and not an evil. Evil, they argued, could only have meaning on smaller scales, in the hurt that one sophont does to another. Before RIP, the argument had seemed a frivolous playing with words. Now she saw that it was meaningful – and dead wrong. The Blight had created the Riders, a marvelous and peaceful race. Their presence on a billion worlds had been a good. And behind it all was the potential for converting the sovereign minds of friends into monsters. When she thought of Blueshell and Greenstalk, and the fear welled up and she knew the poison that was there – *even though they were good people* – then she knew she'd glimpsed evil on the Transcendent scale.

She had gotten Blueshell and Greenstalk into this mission; they had not asked for it. They were friends and allies, and she *would not* harm them because of what they could become.

Maybe it was the latest news items. Maybe it was confronting the same impossibilities for the nth time: Ravna gradually straightened, looking at those last messages. So. She believed Pham about the Skroderider threat. She also believed these two were only enemies in potential. She had thrown away everything to save them and their kind. Maybe it was a mistake, *but take what advantage there is in it. If they are to be saved because you think they are allies, then treat them as allies. Treat them as the friends they are. We are all pawns together.*

Ravna pushed gently toward her cabin's doorway.

The Skroderiders' cabin was just behind the command deck. Since the debacle at RIP, the two had not left it. As she drifted down the passage toward their door, Ravna half-expected to see Pham's handiwork lurking in the shadows. She knew he was doing his best to 'protect himself.' Yet there was nothing unusual. *What will he think of my visiting them?*

She announced herself. After a moment Blueshell appeared. His skrode was wiped clean of cosmetic stripes, and the room behind him was a jumble. He waved her in with quick jerks of his fronds.

'My lady.'

'Blueshell.' She nodded at him. Half the time she cursed herself for trusting the Riders; the other half, she was mortally embarrassed for having left them alone. 'H-how is Greenstalk?'

Surprisingly, Blueshell's fronds snapped together in a smile. 'You guessed? This is the first day with her new skrode . . . I will show you, if you'd like.'

He threaded around equipment that was scattered in a lattice across the room. It was similar to the shop equipment Pham had used to build his powered armor. And if Pham had seen it, he might have lost all self-control.

'I've worked on it every minute since . . . Pham locked us in here.'

Greenstalk was in the other room. Her stalk and fronds rose from a silver pot. There were no wheels. It looked nothing like a traditional skrode. Blueshell rolled across the ceiling and extended a front down to his mate. He rustled something at her, and after a moment she replied.

'The skrodeling is very limited, no mobility, no redundant power supplies. I copied it off a Lesser Skroderider design, a simple thing designed by Dirokimes. It's not meant for more than sitting in one place, facing in one direction. But it provides her with short-term memory support, and attention focusers . . . She is back with me.' He fussed around her, some fronds caressing hers, others pointing to the gadget he had built for her. 'She herself was not badly injured. Sometimes I wonder – whatever Pham says, maybe at the last second he could not kill her.'

He spoke nervously, as though afraid of what Ravna might say.

'The first few days I was very worried. But the surgeon is good. It gave her plenty of time to stand in strong surf. To think slowly. Since I've added on this skrodeling, she has practiced the calesthenics of memory, repeating what the surgeon or I say to her. With the skrodeling she can hold on to a new memory for almost five hundred seconds. That's usually long enough for her natural mind to commit a thought to long-term memory.'

Ravna drifted close. There were some new creases in Greenstalk's fronds. Those would be scars healing. Her visual surfaces followed Ravna's approach. The Rider knew she was here; her whole posture was friendly.

'Can she talk Trisk, Blueshell? Do you have a voder hooked up?'

'What?' Buzz. He was forgetful or nervous, Ravna couldn't tell which. 'Yes, yes. Just give me a minute . . . There was no need before. No one wanted to talk to us.' He fiddled with something on the homemade skrode.

After a moment, 'Hello, Ravna I . . . recognize you.' Her fronds rustled in time with the words.

'I know you, too. We, I am glad that you are back.'

The voder voice was faint, wistful? 'Yes. It's hard for me to tell. I do want to talk, but I'm not sure . . . am I'm making sense?'

Out of Greenstalk's sight, Blueshell flicked a long tendril, a gesture: *say yes*.

'Yes, I understand you, Greenstalk.' And Ravna resolved never again to get angry with Greenstalk about not remembering.

'Good.' Her fronds straightened and she didn't say anything more.

'See?' came Blueshell's voder voice. 'I am brightly cheerful. Even now, Greenstalk is committing this conversation to long-term memory. It goes slowly for now, but I am improving the skrodeling. I'm sure her slowness is mainly emotional shock.' He continued to brush at Greenstalk's fronds, but she didn't say anything more. Ravna wondered just how brightly cheerful he could be.

Behind the Riders were a set of display windows, customized now for the Rider outlook. 'You've been following the News?' Ravna asked.

'Yes, indeed.'

'I-I feel so helpless.' *I feel so foolish saying that to you.*

But Blueshell didn't take offense. He seemed grateful for the change of topic, preferring the gloom at a distance. 'Yes. We certainly are famous now. Three fleets chasing us down, my lady. Ha ha.'

'They don't seem to be gaining very fast.'

Frond shrug. 'Sir Pham has turned out to be a competent ship's master. I'm afraid things will change as we descend. The ship's higher automation will gradually fail. What you call "manual control" will become very important. *OOB* was designed for my race, my lady. No matter what Sir Pham thinks of us, at bottom we can fly it better than any. So bit by bit the others will gain – at least those who truly understand their own ships.'

'S-surely Pham must know this?'

'I think he must. But he is trapped in his own fears. What can he do? If not for you, my lady Ravna, he might have killed us already. Maybe when the choice comes down to dying in the next hour against trusting us, maybe then there will be a chance.'

'By then it will be too late. Look, even if he doesn't trust — even though he believes the worst of Riders — there must still be a way.' And it came to her that sometimes you don't have to change the way people think, or even whom they may hate. 'Pham wants to get to the Bottom, to recover this Countermeasure. He thinks you may be from the Blight, and after the same thing. But up to a point —' Up to a point he *can* cooperate, postpone the showdown he imagines till perhaps it won't matter.

Even as she started to say it, Blueshell was already shouting back at her. 'I'm *not* of the Blight! Greenstalk is not! The Rider race is not!' He swept around his mate, rolled across the ceiling till his fronds rattled right before Ravna's face.

'I'm sorry. It's just the potential —'

'*Nonsense!*' His voder buzzed off-scale. 'We ran into an evil few. Every race has such, people who will kill for trade. They forced Greenstalk, substituted data at her voder. Pham Nuwen would kill our billions for the sake of this fantasy.' He waved, inarticulate. Something she had never seen in a Skroderider: his fronds actually changed tone, darkened.

The motion ceased, yet he said nothing more. And then Ravna heard it, a keening that might have come from a voder. The sound was steadily growing, a howl that made all Blueshell's sound effects friendly nonsense. It was Greenstalk.

The scream reached a threshold just below pain, then broke into choppy Triskweline: '*It's true!* Oh, by all our trading, Blueshell, it's true . . .' and staticky noise came from her voder. Her fronds started shaking, random turning that must be like a human's eyes wildly staring, like a human's mouth mumbling hysteria.

Blueshell was already back by the wall, reaching to adjust

her new skrode. Greenstalk's fronds brushed him away, and her voder voice continued, '*I was horrorstruck, Blueshell.* I was horrorstruck, struck by horror. And it would not stop . . .' She was silent for a moment. Blueshell stood frozen. 'I remember everything up till the last five minutes. And everything Pham says is true, dear love. Loyal as you are, and I have seen that loyalty now for two hundred years, you would be turned in an instant . . . just as I was.' Now that the dam broke, her words came quickly, mostly making sense. The horrors she could remember were graven deep, and she was finally coming out of ghastly shock. 'I was right behind you, remember, Blueshell? You were deep in your trading with the tusk-legs, so deep you did not really see. I noticed the other Riders coming toward us. No matter: a friendly meeting, so far from home. Then one touched my Skrode. I –' Greenstalk hesitated. Her fronds rattled and she began again, 'horrorstruck, horrorstruck . . .'

After a moment: 'It was like suddenly new memories in the skrode, Blueshell. New memories, new attitudes. But thousands of years deep. *And not mine.* Instantly, instantly. I never even lost consciousness. I thought just as clearly, I remembered all I had before.

'And when you resisted?' Ravna said softly.

'. . . Resisted? My Lady Ravna, *I did not resist,* I was theirs . . . No. Not theirs, for they were owned too. We were things, our intelligence in service to another's goal. Dead, and alive to see our death. I would kill you. I would kill Pham, I would kill Blueshell. You know I tried. And when I did, I wanted to succeed. You could not imagine, Ravna. You humans speak of violation. You could never know . . .' Long pause. 'That's not quite right. At the Top of the Beyond, within the Blight itself – perhaps there, *everyone* lives as I did.'

The shuddering did not subside, but her gestures were no longer aimless. The fronds were saying something in her own language, and brusthing gently against Blueshell.

'Our whole race, dear love. Just as Pham says it.'

Blueshell wilted, and Ravna felt the sort of gut-tearing she had when they learned of Sjandra Kei. That had been her worlds, her family, her life. Blueshell was hearing worse.

Ravna pushed a little closer, near enough to run her hand up the side of Greenstalk's fronds. 'Pham says it's the greater skrodes that are the cause.' Sabotage hidden billion of years deep.

'Yes, it is mainly the skrodes. The "great gift" we Riders love so . . . It is a design for control, but I fear we were remade for it, too. When they touched my skrode, I was converted instantly. Instantly, everything I cared for was meaningless. We are like smart bombs, scattered by the trillions through space that everyone thinks is safe. We will be used sparingly. We are the Blight's hidden weapon, especially in the Low Beyond.'

Blueshell twitched, and his voice came out jerkily: 'And everything Pham claims is correct.'

'No, Blueshell, not everything.' Ravna remembered that last chilling standoff with Pham Nuwen. 'He has the facts, but he weighs them wrong. As long as your skrodes are not perverted, you are the same folk that I trusted to fly me to the Bottom.'

Blueshell angled his look away from her, an angry shrug. Greenstalk's voice came instead. 'As long as the skrode has not been perverted . . . But look how easy it was done, how sudden I became the Blight's.'

'Yes, but could it happen except by direct touch? Could you be "changed" by reading the Net News?' She meant the question as ghastly sarcasm, but poor Greenstalk took it seriously:

'Not by a News item, nor by standard protocol messages. But accepting a transmission targeted on skrode utilities might do it.'

'Then we are safe here. You, because you no longer ride a greater skrode, Blueshell because –'

'Because I was never touched – but how can you know that?' His anger was still there, deep within shame, but now it was a hopeless anger, directed at something very far away.

'No, dear love, you have not been touched. I would know.'

'Yes, but why should Ravna believe *you*?'

Everything could be a lie, thought Ravna, . . . *but I believe Greenstalk. I believe we four are the only ones in all the Beyond who can hurt the Blight*. If only Pham could see it. And that brought her back to: 'You say we will start losing our lead?'

Blueshell waved an affirmative. 'As soon as we are a little lower. They should have us in a matter of weeks.'

And then it won't matter who was perverted and who was not. 'I think we should have a little chat with Pham Nuwen.' Godshatter and all.

Beforehand Ravna couldn't imagine how the confrontation would turn out. Just possibly – if he'd lost all touch with reality – Pham might try to kill them when they appeared on the command deck. More likely there would be rage and argument and threats, and they would be back to square one.

Instead . . . it was almost like the old Pham, from before Harmonious Repose. He let them enter the command deck, he made no comment when Ravna set herself carefully between himself and the Riders. He listened without interruption while Ravna explained what Greenstalk had said. 'These two are safe, Pham. And without their help we'll not make it to the Bottom.'

He nodded, looked away at the windows. Some showed natural starscape; most were ultratrace displays, the closest thing to a picture of the enemies that were closing on the *OOB*. His calm expression broke for just an instant, and the Pham that loved her seemed to stare out, desperate: 'And you really believe all this, Rav? *How?*' Then the lid was back on, his expression distant and neutral. 'Never mind. Certainly it's true: without all of us working together we'll never make it to Tines' World. Blueshell, I accept your offer. Subject to cautious safeguards, we work together.' *Till I can safely dispose of you*, Ravna could feel the unsaid words behind his blandness. Showdown deferred.

33

They were less than eight weeks from Tines' World, both Pham and Blueshell said. If the Zone conditions remained stable. If they were not overtaken in the meantime.

Less than two months after the six already voyaged. But the days were not like before. Every one was a challenge, a standoff sometimes cloaked in civility, sometimes flaring into threats of sudden death – as when Pham retrieved Blueshell's shop equipment.

Pham was living on the command deck now; when he left it, the hatch was locked on his ID. He had destroyed, or thought he had destroyed, all other privileged links to the ship's automation. He and Blueshell were in almost constant collaboration . . . but not like before. Every step was slow, Blueshell explaining everything, allowed to demonstrate nothing. That's where the arguments came closest to deadly force, when Pham must give in to one peril or the other. For every day the pursuing fleets were a little bit closer: two bands of killers, and what was left of Sjandra Kei. Evidently some of the SjK Commercial Security fleet could still fight, wanted revenge on the Alliance. Once Ravna suggested to Pham that they contact Commercial Security, try to persuade them to attack the Blight fleet. Pham had given her a blank look. 'Not yet, maybe not ever,' he said, and turned away. In a way his answer was a relief: Such a battle would be a suicidal long shot. Ravna didn't want the last of her kinsfolk dying for her.

So the *OOB* might arrive at Tines' World before the enemy, but with what little time to spare! Some days Ravna withdrew in tears and despair. What brought her back was Jefri and Greenstalk. They both needed her, and for a few weeks more she could still help.

Mr Steel's defense plans were proceeding. The Tines were even having some success with their wideband radio. Steel reported that Woodcarver's main force was on its way north; there was more than one race against time. She spent many hours with *OOB*'s library, devising more gifts for Jefri's friends. Some things – like telescopes – were easy; but others . . . It wasn't wasted effort. Even if the Blight won, its fleet might ignore the natives, might settle for killing the *OOB* and winning back the Countermeasure.

Greenstalk was slowly improving. At first Ravna was afraid the improvement might be in her own imagination. Ravna was spending a good part of each day sitting with the Rider, trying to see progress in her responses. Greenstalk was very 'far away,' almost like a human with stroke damage and prosthesis. In fact, she seemed regressed from the articulate horror of her first conversations. Maybe her recent progress was just a mirror to Ravna's sensitivity, to the fact that Ravna was with her so much. Blueshell insisted there was progress, but with that stubborn inflexibility of his. Two weeks, three – and there was no doubt: Something was healing at the boundary between Rider and skrodeling. Greenstalk consistently made sense, consistently committed important rememberings . . . Now as often as not it was *she* helping Ravna. Greenstalk saw things that Ravna had missed: 'Sir Pham isn't the only one who is afraid of us Skroderiders. Blueshell is frightened too, and it is tearing him apart. He can't admit it even to me, but he thinks it's possible that we're infected independently of our skrodes. He desperately wants to convince Pham that this is not true – and so to convince himself.' She was silent for a long moment, one frond brushing against Ravna's arm. Sea sounds surrounded them in the cabin, but ship's automation could no longer produce surging water. 'Sigh. We must pretend the surf, dear Ravna. Somewhere it will always be, no matter what happened at Sjandra Kei, no matter what happens here.'

Blueshell was hearty gentleness around his mate, but alone with Ravna his rage showed through: 'No, no, I don't object to Sir Pham's navigation, at least not now. Perhaps we could be a little further ahead with me directly at the helm, but the fastest ships behind us would still be closing. It's the other things, My Lady. You know how untrustworthy our automation is down here. Pham is hurting it further. He's written his own security overrides. He's turning the ship's environment automation into a system of boobytraps.'

Ravna had seen evidence of this. The areas around *OOB*'s command deck and ship's workshop looked like military checkpoints. 'You know his fears. If this makes him feel safer –'

'That's not the point, My Lady. I would do anything to

persuade him to accept my help. But what he's doing is deadly dangerous. Our Bottom automation is not reliable, and he's making it actively worse. If we get some sudden stress, the environment programs will likely have a bizarre crash – atmosphere dump, thermal runaway, anything.'

'I –'

'Doesn't he understand? Pham controls *nothing*.' His voder broke into a nonlinear squawk. 'He has the ability to destroy, but that is all. He needs my help. He was my friend. Doesn't he understand?'

Pham understood . . . oh, Pham understood. He and Ravna still talked. Their arguments were the hardest thing in her life. And sometimes they didn't exactly argue; sometimes it was almost like rational discussion:

'I haven't been taken over, Ravna. Not like the Blight takes over Riders, anyway. I still have charge of my soul.' He turned away from the console and flashed a wan smile in her direction, acknowledging the flaw in such self-conviction. And from things like that smile, Ravna was convinced that Pham Nuwen still lived, and sometimes spoke.

'What about the godshatter state? I see you for hours just staring at the tracking display, or mucking around in the library and the News,' scanning faster than any human could consciously read.

, Pham shrugged. 'It's studying the ships that are chasing us, trying to figure out just what belongs to whom, just what capabilities each might have. I don't know the details. Self-awareness is on vacation then,' when all Pham's mind was turned into a processor for whatever programs Old One had downloaded. A few hours of fugue state might yield an instant of Power-grade thought – and even that he didn't consciously remember. 'But I know this. Whatever the godshatter is, it's a very narrow thing. It's not alive; in some ways it may not even be very smart. For everyday matters like ship piloting, there's just good old Pham Nuwen.'

'. . . there's the rest of us, Pham. Blueshell would like to help,' Ravna spoke softly. This was the place where Pham would close into icy silence – or blow up in rage. This day, he just cocked his head. 'Ravna, Ravna. I know I need him . . . And, and I'm glad I need him. That I don't have to kill him.' *Yet.* Pham's lips quivered for a second, and she thought he might start crying.

'The godshatter can't know Blueshell –'

'*Not* the godshatter. It's not making me act this way – I'm doing what any person should do when the stakes are this high.' The words were spoken without anger. Maybe there was a chance. Maybe she could reason:

'Blueshell and Greenstalk are loyal, Pham. Except at Harmonious Repose –'

Pham sighed, 'Yeah. I've thought about that a lot. They *came* to Relay from Straumli Realm. They got Vrinimi looking for the refugee ship. That smells of setup, but probably unknowing – maybe even a setup by something opposing the Blight. In any case they were innocent then, else the Blight would have known about Tines' World right from the beginning. The Blight knew nothing till RIP, till Greenstalk was converted. And I know Blueshell was loyal even then. He knew things about my armor – the remotes, for instance – that he could have warned the others about.'

Hope came as a surprise to Ravna. He really had thought things out, and – 'It's just the skrodes, Pham. They're traps waiting to be sprung. But we're isolated here, and you destroyed the one that Greenstalk –'

Pham was shaking his head. 'It's more than the skrodes. The Blight had its hand in Rider design too, at least to some degree. I can't imagine the takeover of Greenstalk's being so smooth otherwise.'

'Y-yes. A risk. A very small risk compared to –'

Pham didn't move, but something in him seemed to draw away from her, denying the support she could offer. 'A small risk? We don't know. The stakes are so *high*. I'm walking a tightrope. If I don't use Blueshell now, we'll be shot out of space by the Blighter fleet. If I let him do too much, if I trust him, then he or some part of him could betray us. All I have is the godshatter, and a bunch of memories that . . . that may be the biggest fakes of all.' These last words were nearly inaudible. He looked up at her, a look that was both cold and terribly lost. 'But I'm going to use what I have, Rav, and whatever it is I am. Somehow I'm going to get us to Tines' World. Somehow I'm going to get Old One's godshatter to whatever is there.'

It was another three weeks before Blueshell's predictions came true.

The *OOB* had seemed a sturdy beast up in the Middle Beyond; even its damaged ultradrive had failed gracefully. Now the ship was leaking bugs in all directions. Much of it had nothing to do with Pham's meddling. Without those final consistency checks, none of *OOB*'s Bottom automation was really trustworthy. But its failures were compounded by Pham's desperate security 'fixes.'

The ship's library had source code for generic Bottom automation. Pham spent several days revising it for the *OOB*. All four of them were on the command deck during the installation, Blueshell trying to help, Pham suspiciously examining every suggestion. Thirty minutes into the installation, there were muffled banging noises down the main corridor. Ravna might have ignored them, except that she'd never heard the like aboard the *OOB*.

Pham and the Riders reacted with near panic; spacers don't like unexplained bumps in the night. Blueshell raced to the hatch, floated fronds-first through the hole. 'I see nothing, Sir Pham.'

Pham was paging quickly through the diagnostic displays, mixed format things partly from the new setup. 'I've got some warning lights here, but –'

Greenstalk started to say something, but Blueshell was back and talking fast; 'I don't believe it. Anything like this should make pictures, a detailed report. Something is terribly wrong.'

Pham stared at him a second, then returned to his diagnostics. Five seconds passed. 'You're right. Status is just looping through stale reports.' He began grabbing views from cameras all over the *OOB*'s interior. Barely half of them reported, but what they showed . . .

The ship's water reservoir was a foggy, icy cavern. That

was the banging sound – tonnes of water, spaced. A dozen other support services had gone bizarre, and –

– the armed checkpoint outside the workshop had slagged down. The beamers were firing continuously on low power. And for all the destruction, the diagnostics still showed green or amber or no report. Pham got a camera in the workshop itself. *The place was on fire.*

Pham jumped up from his saddle and bounced off the ceiling. For an instant she thought he might go racing off the bridge. Then he tied himself down and grimly began trying to put out the fire.

For the next few minutes the bridge was almost quiet, just Pham quietly swearing as none of the obvious things worked. 'Interlocking failures,' he mumbled the phrase a couple of times. 'The firesnuff automation is down . . . I can't dump atmosphere from the shop. My beamers have melted everything shut.'

Ship fire. Ravna had seen pictures of such disasters, but they had always seemed an improbable thing. In the midst of universal vacuum, how could a fire survive? And in zero-gee, surely a fire would choke itself even if the crew couldn't dump atmosphere. The workshop camera had a hazy view on the real thing: True, the flames ate the oxygen around them. There were sheets of construction foam that were only lightly scorched, protected for the moment by dead air. But the fire spread out, moving steadily into still-fresh air. In places, heat-driven turbulence enriched the mix, and previously burned areas blazed up.

'It's still got ventilation, Sir Pham.'

'I *know*. I can't shut it. The vents must be melted open.'

'It's as likely software.' Blueshell was silent for a second. 'Try this –' The directions were meaningless to Ravna, some low-level workaround.

But Pham nodded, and his fingers danced across the console.

In the workshop, the surface-hugging flames crept farther across the construction foam. Now they licked at the innards of the armor Pham had spent so much time on. This latest revision was only half finished. Ravna remembered he was working on reactive armor now . . . *There would be oxidizers there.* 'Pham, is the armor sealed –'

The fire was sixty meters aft and behind a dozen bulkheads. The explosion came as a distant thump, almost innocent. But in the camera view, the armor dismembered itself, and the fire blazed triumphant.

Seconds later, Pham got Blueshell's suggestion working, and the workshop's vents closed. The fire in the wrecked armor continued for another half hour, but did not spread beyond the shop.

It took two days to clean up, to estimate the damage, and to have some confidence that no new disaster was on the way. Most of the workshop was destroyed. They would have no armor on Tines' World. Pham salvaged one of the beamers that had been guarding the entrance to the shop. Disaster was scattered all across the ship, the classic random ruin of interlocking failures: They had lost fifty percent of their water. The ship's landing boat had lost its higher automation.

OOB's rocket drive was massively degraded. That was unimportant here in interstellar space, but their final velocity matching would be done at only 0.4 gees. Thank goodness the agrav worked; they would have no trouble maneuvering in steep gravitational wells – that is, landing on Tines' World.

Ravna knew how close they were to losing the ship, but she watched Pham with even greater dread. She was so afraid that he would take this as final evidence of Rider treachery, that this would drive him over the edge. Strangely, almost the opposite happened. His pain and devastation were obvious, but he didn't lash out, just doggedly went about gathering up the pieces. He was talking to Blueshell more now, not letting him modify the automation, but cautiously accepting more of his advice. Together they restored the ship to something like its pre-fire state.

She asked Pham about it. 'No change of heart,' he finally said. 'I had to balance the risks, and I messed up . . . And maybe there is no balance. Maybe the Blight will win.'

The godshatter had bet too much on Pham's doing it all himself. Now it was turning down the paranoia a little.

Seven weeks out from Harmonious Repose, less than one week from whatever waited at Tines' World, Pham went into a multiday fugue. Before, he had been busy, a futile attempt to run handmade checks on all the automation they might need at Tines' World. Now – Ravna couldn't even get him to eat.

The nav display showed the three fleets as identified by the News and Pham's intuition: the Blight's agents, the Alliance for the Defense, and what was left of Sjandra Kei Commercial Security: deadly-monsters and the remains of a victim. The Alliance still proclaimed itself with regular bulletins on the News. SjK Commercial Security had posted a few terse refutations, but was mostly silent; they were unused to propaganda, or – as likely – uninterested in it. A private revenge was all that remained to Commercial Security. And the Blighter fleet? The News hadn't heard anything from them. Piecing together departures and lost ships, War Trackers Newsgroup concluded they were a wildly ad hoc assembly, whatever the Blight had controlled down here at the time of the RIP debacle. Ravna knew that the War Trackers analysis was wrong about one thing: The Blighter fleet was not silent. Thirty times over the last weeks, they had sent messages at the *OOB* . . . in skrode maintenance format. Pham had had the ship reject the messages unread – and then worried about whether the order was really followed. After all, the *OOB* was of Rider design.

But now the torment in him was submerged. Pham sat for hours, staring at the display. Soon Sjandra Kei would close with the Alliance fleet. At least one set of villains would pay. But the Blighter fleet and at least part of the Alliance would survive . . . Maybe this fugue was just godshatter getting desperate.

Three days passed; Pham snapped out of it. Except for the new thinness in his face, he seemed more normal than he had in weeks. He asked Ravna to bring the Riders up to the bridge.

Pham waved at the ultradrive traces that floated in the window. The three fleets were spread through a rough cylinder, five light-years deep and three across. The display captured only the heart of that volume, where the fastest of the pursuers had clustered. The current position of each ship was a fleck of light trailing an unending stream of fainter lights – the ultradrive trace left by that vehicle's drive. 'I've used red, blue, and green to mark my best guess as to the fleet affiliation of each trace.' The fastest ships were collected in a blob so dense that it looked white at this scale, but with colored streamers diverging behind. There were other tags, annotations he had set but which he admitted once to Ravna he didn't understand.

'The front edge of that mob – the fastest of the fast – is still gaining.'

Blueshell said hesitantly. 'We might get a little more speed if you would grant me direct control. Not much, but –'

Pham's response was civil, at least. 'No, I'm thinking of something else, something Ravna suggested a while back. It's always been a possibility and . . . I . . . think the time may have come for it.'

Ravna moved closer to the display, stared at the green traces. Their distribution was in near agreement with what the News claimed to be the remnants of Sjandra Kei Commercial Security. *All that's left of my people*. 'They've been trying to engage with the Alliance for a hundred hours now.'

Pham's glance touched hers. 'Yeah,' he said softly. 'Poor bastards. They're literally the fleet from Port Despair. If I were them, I'd –' His expression smoothed over again. 'Any idea how well-armed they are?' That was surely a rhetorical question, but it put the topic on the table.

'War Trackers thinks that Sjandra Kei had been expecting something unpleasant ever since the Alliance started talking "death to vermin." Commercial Security was providing deep space defense. Their fleet is converted freighters armed with locally designed weapons. War Trackers claims they weren't really a match for what the other side could field, *if* the Alliance was willing to take some heavy casualties. Trouble is, Sjandra Kei never expected the planet-smasher attack. So when the Alliance fleet showed up, ours moved out to meet it –'

'– and meantime the KE bombs were coming straight in to the heart of Sjandra Kei.'

Into my heart. 'Yes. The Alliance must have been running those bombs for weeks.'

Pham Nuwen laughed shortly. 'If I were shipping with the Alliance fleet, I'd be a bit nervous now. They're down in numbers, and those retread freighters seem about as fast as anything here . . . I'll bet every pilot out of Sjandra Kei is dead set on revenge.' The emotion faded. 'Hmm. There's no way they could kill all the Alliance ships or all the Blight's, much less all of both. It would be pointless to . . .

His gaze abruptly focused on her. 'So if we leave things as they are, the Sjandra Kei fleet will eventually match position with the Alliance and try to blow them out of existence.'

Ravna just nodded. 'In twelve hours or so, they say.'

'And then all that will be left is the Blight's own fleet on our tail. But if we could talk your people into fighting the right enemies . . .'

It was Ravna's nightmare scheme. All that was left of Sjandra Kei dying to save the *OOB* . . . trying to save them. There was little chance the Sjandra Kei fleet could destroy all Blighter ships. *But they're here to fight. Why not a vengeance that means something?* That was the nightmare's message. Now somehow it fit the godshatter's plans. 'There are problems. They don't know what we're doing or the purpose of the third fleet. Anything we shout back to them will be overheard.' Ultrawave was directional, but most of their pursuers were closely mingled.

Pham nodded. 'Somehow we have to talk to them, and them alone. Somehow we have to persuade them to fight.' Faint smile. 'And I think we may have just the . . . equipment . . . to do all that. Blueshell: Remember that night on the High Docks. You told us about your "rotted cargo" from Sjandra Kei?'

'Indeed, Sir Pham. We carried one third of a cipher generated by SjK Commercial Security for the razor-jaws. It's still in the ship's safe, though worthless without the other two thirds.' Gram for gram, crypto materials were about the most valuable thing shipped between the stars – and once compromised, about the most valueless. Somewhere in *Out of Band*'s cargo files there was an SjK one-time communications pad. Part of a pad.

'Worthless? Maybe not. Even one third would provide us with secure communications.'

Blueshell dithered. 'I must not mislead you. No competent customer would accept such. Certainly it provides secure communication, but the other side has no verification that *you* are who you claim.'

Pham's glance slid sideways toward Ravna. There was that smile again. 'If they'll listen, I think we can convince them . . . The hard part is, I only want one of them to hear us.' Pham explained what he had in mind. The Riders rustled faintly behind his words. After all their time together, Ravna could almost get some sense of their talk – or maybe she just understood their personalities. As usual, Blueshell was worrying about how impossible the idea was, and Greenstalk was urging him to listen.

But when Pham finished, the large Rider did not launch into objections. 'Across seventy light-years, ultrawave comm between ships is practical; we could even have live video. But you are right, the beam spread would include all the ships in the central cluster of fleets. If we could reliably identify an outlying vessel as belonging to Sjandra Kei, then what you are asking might be done; that ship could use internal fleet codes to relay to the others. But in honesty I must warn you,' continued Blueshell, brushing back Greenstalk's gentle remonstrance, 'professional communications folk would not honor your request for talk – would probably not even recognize it as such.'

'Silly.' Greenstalk finally spoke, her voder-voice gentle but clear. 'You always say things like that – except when we are talking to paying customers.'

'*Brap*. Yes. Desperate times, desperate measures. I want to try it, but I fear . . . I want there to be no accusation of Rider treachery, Sir Pham. I want you to handle this.'

Pham Nuwen smiled back. 'My thought exactly.'

'The Aniara Fleet.' That's what some of the crew of Commercial Security were calling themselves. Aniara was the ship of an old human myth, older than Nyjora, perhaps going back to the Tuvo-Norsk cooperatives in the asteroids of Earth's solar system. In the story, Aniara was a large ship launched into interstellar depths just before the death of its parent civilization. The crew watched the death agonies of the home system, and then over the following years – as their ship fell out and out into the endless dark – died themselves, their life-support systems slowly failing. The image was a haunting one, which was probably the reason it was known across millennia. With the destruction of Sjandra Kei and the escape of Commercial Security, the story seemed suddenly come true.

But we will not play it to the end. Group Captain Kjet Svensndot stared into the tracking display. This time the death of civilization had been a murder, and the murderers were almost within vengeance's reach. For days, fleet HQ had been maneuvering them to close with the Alliance. The display showed that success was very, very near. The majority of Alliance and Sjandra Kei ships were bound in a glowing ball of drive traces – which also included the third, silent fleet. From that display you might think that battle was already possible. In fact, opposing ships were passing through almost the same space – sometimes less than a billion kilometers apart – but still separated by milliseconds of time. All the vessels were on ultradrive, jumping perhaps a dozen times a second. And even here at the Bottom of the Beyond that came to a measurable fraction of a light-year on each jump. To fight an uncooperative enemy meant matching their jumps perfectly and flooding the common space with weapon drones.

Group Captain Svensndot changed the display to show ships that had exactly matched their pace with the Alliance. Almost a third of the fleet was in synch now. Another few hours and ... 'Damnation!' He slapped his display board, sending it spinning across the deck.

His first officer retrieved the display, sent it sailing back. 'Is this a new damnation, or the usual?' Tirolle asked.

'It was the usual. Sorry.' And he really was. Tirolle and Glimfrelle had their own problems. No doubt there were still pockets of humanity in the Beyond, hidden from the Alliance.

But of the Dirokimes, there might be no more than those on Commercial Security's fleet. Except for adventurous souls like Tirolle and Glimfrelle, all that was left of their kind had been in the dream terranes at Sjandra Kei.

Kjet Svensndot had been with Commercial Security for twenty-five years, back when the company had been just a small fleet of rent-a-cops. He had spent thousands of hours learning to be the very best combat pilot in the organization. Only twice had he ever been in a shootout. Some might have regretted that. Svensndot and his superiors took it as the reward for being the best. His competence had won him the best fighting equipment in Commercial Security's fleet, culminating with the ship he commanded now. The *Ølvira* was purchased with part of the enormous premium that Sjandra Kei paid out when the Alliance first started making threatening noises. *Ølvira* was not a rebuilt freighter, but a fighting machine from the keel out. The ship was equipped with the smartest processors and the smartest ultra drive that could operate Sjandra Kei's altitude in the Beyond. It needed only a three-person crew – and combat could be managed by the pilot alone with his AI associates. Its holds contained more than ten thousand seeker bombs, each smarter than the average freighter's entire drive unit. Quite a reward for twenty-five years of solid performance. They even let Svensndot name his new ship.

And now . . . Well, the true Ølvira was surely dead. Along with billions of others they had been hired to protect, she had been at Herte, in the inner system. Glow bombs leave no survivors.

And his beautiful ship with the same name, it had been a half light-year out-system, seeking enemies that weren't there. In any honest battle, Kjet Svensndot and this *Ølvira* could have done very well. Instead they were chasing down into the Bottom of the Beyond. Every light-year took them further from the regions *Ølvira* was built for. Every light-year the processors worked a bit more slowly (or not at all). Down here the converted freighters were almost an optimum design. Clumsy and stupid, with crews of dozens, but they kept on working. Already *Ølvira* was lagging five light-years behind them. It was the freighters that would make the attack on the Alliance fleet. And once again Kjet would stand powerless while his friends died.

For the hundredth time, Svensndot glared at the trace display and contemplated mutiny. There were Alliance stragglers too – 'high performance' vehicles left behind the central pack. But his orders were to maintain position, to be a tactical coordinator for the fleet's swifter combatants. Well, he would do as he was hired . . . this one last time. But when the battle was done, when the fleet was dead, along with as many of the Alliance as they could take with them – then he would think of his own revenge. Some of that depended on Tirolle and Glimfrelle. Could he persuade them to leave the remnants of the Alliance fleet and ascend to the Middle Beyond, up where the *Ølvira* was the best of her kind? There was solid evidence about which star systems were behind the 'Alliance for the Defense.' The murderers were boasting to the News. Apparently they thought that would bring them new support. It might also bring them visitors like *Ølvira*. The bombs in her belly could destroy worlds, though not as swiftly sure as what had been used on Sjandra Kei. And even now Svensndot's mind shrank from that sort of revenge. No. They would choose their targets carefully: ships coming to form new Alliance fleets, underprotected convoys. *Ølvira* might last a long time if he always struck from ambush and never left survivors. He stared and stared at the display, and ignored the wetness that floated at the corners of his eyes. All his life he had lived by the law. Often his job had been to stop acts of revenge . . . And now revenge was all that life had left for him.

'I'm getting something peculiar, Kjet.' Glimfrelle was monitoring signals this watch. It was the sort of thing that should *have* been totally automated – and had been in *Ølvira*'s natural environment – but which was now a boring and exhausting enterprise.

'What? More Net lies?' said Tirolle.

'No. This is on the bearing of that bottom-lugger everyone is chasing. It can't be anyone else.'

Svensndot's eyebrows rose. He turned on the mystery with enormous, scarcely realized, pleasure. 'Characteristics?'

'Ship's signal processor says it's probably a narrow beam. *We* are its only likely target. The signal is strong and the bandwidth is at least enough to support flat video. If our *snarfling* digital signal processor was working right, I'd know –' 'Frelle sang a little song that was impatient humming among his kind. '– *Iiae!* It's encrypted, but at a high layer. This stuff is syntax 45 video. In fact, it claims to be using one third of a cipher the Company made a year back.' For an instant Svensndot thought 'Frelle was claiming the message itself was smart; that should be absolutely impossible here at the Bottom. The second officer must have caught his look: 'Just sloppy language, Boss. I read this out of the frame format . . .' Something flashed on his display. 'Okay, here's the story on the cipher: the Company made it and its peers to cover shipping security.' Back before the Alliance, that had been the highest crypto level in the organization. 'This is the third that never got delivered. The whole was assumed compromised, but miracle of miracles, we still have a copy.' Both 'Frelle and 'Rolle were looking at Svensndot expectantly, their eyes large and dark. Standard policy – standard *orders* – were that transmissions on compromised keys were to be ignored. If the Company's signals people had been doing a proper job, the rotted cipher wouldn't even have been aboard and the policy would have enforced itself.

'Decrypt the thing,' Svensndot said shortly. The last weeks had demonstrated that his company was a dismal failure when it came to military intelligence and signals. They might as well get some benefit from that incompetence.

'Yes sir!' Glimfrelle tapped a single key. Somewhere inside *Ølvira*'s signal processor, a long segment of 'random' noise was broken into frames and laid precisely down on the 'random' noise in the data frames incoming. There was a perceptible pause (*damn the Bottom*) and then the comm window lit with a flat video picture.

'– fourth repetition of this message.' The words were Samnorsk, and a dialect of pure *Herte i Sjandra*. The speaker was . . . for a heartstopping instant he was seing Ølvira again, alive. He exhaled slowly, trying to relax. Black-haired, slim, violet-eyed – just like Ølvira. And just like a million other women of Sjandra Kei. The resemblance was there, but so vague he would never have been taken by it before. For an instant he imagined a universe beyond their lost fleet, and goals beyond vengeance. Then he forced his attention back to business, to seeing everything he could in the images in the window.

The woman was saying, 'We'll repeat three more times. If by then you have still not responded, we will attempt a different target.' She pushed back from the camera pickup, giving them a view of the room behind her. It was low-ceilinged, deep. An ultradrive trace display dominated the background, but Svensndot paid it little attention. There were two Skroderiders in the background. One wore stripes on its skrode that meant a trade history with Sjandra Kei. The other must be a lesser Rider; its skrode was small and wheelless. The pickup turned, centered on the fourth figure. Human? Probably, but of no Nyjoran heritage. In another time his appearance would have been big news across all human civilizations in the Beyond. Now the point only registered on Svensndot's mind as another cause for suspicion.

The woman continued, 'You can see that we are human and Rider. We are the entire crew of the *Out of Band II*. We are not part of the Alliance for the Defense nor agents of the Blight . . . But we *are* the reason their fleets are down here. If you can read this, we're betting that you are of Sjandra Kei. We must talk. Please reply using the tail of the pad that is decrypting this message.' The picture jigged and the woman's face was back in the foreground. 'This is the fifth repetition of this message,' she said. 'We'll repeat two more –'

Glimfrelle cut the audio. 'If she means it, we have about one hundred seconds. What next, Captain?'

Suddenly the *Ølvira* was not an irrelevant straggler. 'We talk,' said Svensndot.

Response and counter-response took a matter of seconds. After that . . . five minutes of conversation with Ravna Bergsndot was enough to convince Kjet that what she had to say must be heard by Fleet Central. His ship would be a mere relay, but at least he had something very important to pass on.

Fleet Central refused the full video link coming from the *Out of Band*. Someone on the flagship was dead set on following standard procedures – and using compromised cipher keys stuck in their craw. Even Kjet had to settle for a combat link: The screen showed a color image with high resolution. Looking at it carefully, one realized the thing was a poor evocation . . . Kjet recognized Owner Limmende and Jan Skrits, her chief of staff, but they looked several years out of style: old video matched with the transmitted animation cues. The actual communication channel was less than four thousand bits per second; Central was taking no chances.

God only knew what they were seeing as the evocation of Pham Nuwen. The smokey-skinned human had already explained his point several times. He was having as little success as Ravna Bergsndot before him. His cool, manner had graduallly deserted him. Desperation was beginning to show on his face. '– and I'm telling you, they are *both* your enemies. Sure, Alliance for the Defense destroyed Sjandra Kei, but the Blight is responsible for the situation that made that possible.'

The half-cartoonish figure of Jan Skrits glanced at Owner Limmende. *Lord, evocations are crappy at the Bottom*, Svensndot thought to himself. When Skrits spoke, his voice didn't even match his lip movements: 'We do read Threats, Mr Nuwen. The threat of the Blight was used as an excuse to destroy our worlds. We will *not* go on random killing sprees, especially against an organization that is clearly the enemy of our enemy . . . Or are you claiming the Blight is secretly in league with the Allilance for the Defense?'

Pham gave an angry shrug. 'No. I have no idea how the Blight regards the Alliance. But you should know the evil the Blight has been up to, things on a scale far grander than this "Alliance."'

'Ah yes. That's what it says on the Net, Mr Nuwen. But those events are thousands of light-years away. They've been through multiple hops and unknown interpretations before they ever arrived in the Middle Beyond – even if the stories were true to begin with. It is not called the Net of a Million Lies for nothing.'

The stranger's face darkened. He said something loud and angry, in a language that was totally unlike anything from Nyjora. The tones jumped up and down, almost like Dirokime twittering. He calmed himself with a visible effort, but when he continued his Samnorsk was even more heavily accented than before. 'Yes. But I'm telling you. I was at the Fall of Relay. The Blight is more than the worst horrors you've heard. The murder of Sjandra Kei was its smallest side-effect. Will you help us against the Blighter fleet?'

Owner Limmende pushed her massive form back into her chair webbing. She looked at her chief of staff, and the two talked inaudibly. Kjet's gaze drifted beyond them; the flagship's command deck extended a dozen meters behind Limmende. Underofficers moved quietly about, some watching the conversation. The picture was crisp and clear, but when the figures moved it was with cartoonlike awkwardness. And some of the faces belonged to people Kjet knew had been transferred before the fall of Sjandra Kei. The processors here on the *Ølvira* were taking the narrow-band signal from Fleet Central, fleshing it out with detailed (and out of date) background and evoking the image shown. *No more evocations after this*, Svensndot promised himself, *at least while we're down here.*

Owner Limmende looked back at the camera. 'Forgive a paranoid old cop, but I think it's possible that you might be of the Blight.' Limmende raised her hand as if to ward off interruptions, but the redhead just gaped in surprise. 'If we believe you, then we must accept that there is something useful and dangerous on the star system we're all heading towards. Furthermore, we must accept that both you and the "Blighter fleet" are peculiarly qualified to take advantage of this prize. If we fight them as you ask, there will likely be few of us alive afterwards. You alone will have the prize. We fear what you might turn out to be.'

For a long moment, Pham Nuwen was silent. The wildness slowly left his face. 'You have a point. Owner Limmende. And a dilemma. Is there any way out?'

'Skrits and I have been discussing it. No matter what we do, both we and you must take big chances ... It's only the alternatives that are more terrible. We are willing to accept your guidance in battle, *if* you will first maneuver your ship back toward us and allow us to board.'

'Give up the lead in this chase, you mean?'

Limmende nodded.

Pham's mouth opened and closed, but no words emerged. He seemed to be having trouble breathing. Ravna said, 'Then if you don't succeed, everything is lost. At least now, we have a sixty-hour lead. That might be enough to get word out about this artifact, even if the Blighter fleet survives.'

Skrits' face twisted, a cartoonish smile. 'You can't have it both ways. You want us to risk everything on your assurances. We are willing to die for this, but not to be pawns in a game of monsters.' The last words had a strange tone, the angry delivery shading away. And now there was no motion in the picture from Fleet Central except for ill-synched lip movement. Glimfrelle caught Svensndot's eye and pointed at the failure lights on his comm panel.

Skrits' voice continued, 'And Group Captain Svensndot: It's imperative that all further communications with this unknown vessel be channeled –' the image froze, and there were no more words.

Ravna: 'What happened?'

Glimfrelle made a twitter-snort. 'We're losing the link with Fleet Central. Our effective bandwidth is down to twenty bits per second, and dropping Skrits' last transmission was scarcely a hundred bits,' *padded out to apparent legibility by the Ølvira's software.*

Kjet waved angrily at the screen. 'Cut the damn thing off.' At least he wouldn't have to put up with the evocation any further. And he didn't want to hear what he guessed was Jan Skrits' last order.

Tirolle said, 'Hei, why not leave it on? We might not notice much difference.' Glimfrelle snickered at his brother's wit, but his longfingers danced across the comm panel, and the display became a window on the stars. The two Dirokimes had a thing about bureaucrats.

Svensndot ignored them and looked at the remaining comm window. The channel to Pham and Ravna was wideband video with scarcely any interpretation; there would be no perverse subtleties if it went down. 'Sorry about that. The last few days, we've had a lot of problems with comm. Apparently, this Zone storm is the worst in centuries.' In fact, it was getting still worse: half the ultratrace displays were showing random garbage.

'You've lost contact with your command?' asked Ravna.

'For the moment . . .' He glanced at Pham. The redhead's eyes were still a bit glassy. 'Look . . . I'm even more sorry about how things have turned out, but Limmende and Skrits are bright people. You can see their point of view.'

'Strange,' interrupted Pham. 'The pictures were strange.' His tone was drifty.

'You mean our relay from Fleet Central?' Svensndot explained about the narrow bandwidth and the crummy performance of his ship's processors down here at the Bottom.

'And so their picture of us must have been equally bad . . . I wonder what they thought I was?'

'Unh . . .' *Good question.* Consider Pham Nuwen: bristly red hair, smoke-gray skin, singsong voice. If cues such as those were sent, like as not the display at Fleet Central would show something quite different from the human Kjet saw. '. . . wait a minute. That's not how evocations work. I'm sure they got a pretty clear view of you. See, a few high-resolution pics would get sent at the beginning of the session. Then those would be used as the base for the animation.'

Pham stared back lumpishly, almost as though he didn't buy it and was daring Kjet to think things through. Well damn it, the explanation was correct; there was no doubt that Limmende and Skrits had seen the redhead as a human. Yet there *was* something here that bothered Kjet . . . *Limmende and Skrits had both looked out of date.*

'Glimfrelle! Check the raw stream we got from Central. Did they send us any sync pictures?'

It took Glimfrelle only seconds. He whistled a sharp tone of surprise. 'No, Boss. And since it was all properly encrypted, our end just made do with old ad animation.' He said something to Tirolle, and the two twittered rapidly. 'Nothing seems to work down here. Maybe this is just another bug.' But Glimfrelle didn't sound very confident of his assertion.

Svensndot turned back to the picture from the *Out of Band*. 'Look. The channel to Fleet Central was fully encrypted, using one-time schemes I trust more than what we're talking with now. I can't believe it was a masquerade.' *But nausea was creeping up Kjet's guts.* This was like the first minutes of the Battle for Sjandra Kei, when he guessed how thoroughly they had been outmaneuvered, when he realized that everyone he was trying to protect would be murdered. 'Hei, we'll contact other vessels. We'll verify Central's location –'

Pham Nuwen raised an eyebrow. 'Maybe it wasn't a masquerade.' Before he could say more, one of the Riders – the one with the greater skrode – was shouting at them. It rolled across the room's apparent ceiling, pushing the humans aside to get close to the camera. 'I have a question!' The voder speech was burred, nearly unintelligible. The creature's tendrils rattled dryly against each other, as distressed as Kjet Svensndot had ever heard. 'My question: Are there Skroderiders aboard your fleet's command vessel?'

'Why do you –'

'Answer the question!'

'How should I know?' Kjet tried to think. 'Tirolle. You have friends on Skrits' staff. Are there any Riders aboard?'

Tirolle stuttered a few bars. *'A'a'a'a.* Yes. Emergency hires – rescues actually – right after the battle.'

'That's the best we can do, friend.'

The Skroderider trembled, unspeaking. Then its tendrils seemed to wilt. 'Thank you,' it said softly. It rolled back and out of camera range.

Pham Nuwen disappeared from view. Ravna looked wildly around, 'Wait please!' she said to the camera, and Kjet was looking at the abandoned command deck of the *Out of Band*. At the limit of the pickup's hearing came sounds of mumbled conversation, voder and human. Then she was back.

'What was *that* all about?' Svensndot to Ravna.

'N-nothing any of us can help anymore ... Captain Svensndot, it looks to me like your fleet is no longer run by the people you think.'

'Maybe.' *Probably.* 'It's something I've got to think about.'

She nodded. For a moment they looked at each other, unspeaking. So strange, so far from home and after all the heartbreak ... to see someone so familiar. 'You were truly at Relay?' The question sounded stupid in his ears. Yet in a way she was a bridge from what he knew and trusted to the deadly weirdness of the present situation.

Ravna Bergsndot nodded. 'Yes ... and it was like everything you've read. We even had direct contact with a Power ... And yet it was not enough, Group Captain. The Blight destroyed it all. That part of the News is no lie.'

Tirolle pushed back from his nav station. 'Then how can anything you do down here hurt the Blight?' The words were blunt, but 'Rolle's eyes were wide and serious. In fact, he was pleading for some sense behind all the death. Dirokimes had not been the greatest part of the Sjandra Kei civilization, but they had been by far its oldest member race. A million years ago they had burst out of the Slow Zone, colonizing the three systems that humans one day would call Sjandra Kei. Long before the humans arrived, they were a race of inward dreamers. They protected their star systems with ancient automation and friendly younger races. Another half million years and their race might be gone from the Beyond, extinct or evolved into something else. It was a common pattern, something like death and old age, but gentler.

There is a common misconception about such senescent races: that their members are senescent too. In any large population, there will be variation. There will always be those who want to see the outside world and play there for a while. Humankind had gotten on very well with the likes of Glimfrelle and Tirolle.

And Bergsndot seemed to understand. 'Have any of you heard of godshatter?'

Kjet said, 'No,' then noticed that both Dirokimes had started. They whistled at each other for several seconds. 'Yes,' 'Rolle spoke at last in Samnorsk, his voice as close to awe as Kjet had ever heard. 'You know we Dirokimes have been in the Beyond for a long time. We've sent many colonies into the Transcend; some became Powers ... And once ... Something came back. It wasn't a Power of course. In fact, it was more like a mind-crippling Dirokime. But it knew things and did things that made great changes for us.'

'Fentrollar?' Kjet asked wonderingly, suddenly recognizing the story. It had happened one hundred thousand years before humankind arrived at Sjandra Kei, yet it was a central contradiction of the Dirokime terranes.

'Yes.' Tirolle said. 'Even now people don't agree if Fentrollar was a gift or a curse, but he founded the dream habitats and the Old Religion.'

Ravna nodded. 'That's the case most familiar to us of Sjandra Kei. Maybe it's not a happy example considering all its effects ...' And she told them about the fall of Relay, what had happened to Old One, and what had become of Pham Nuwen. The Dirokimes side chat dwindled to zero and they were very still.

Finally Kjet said, 'So what does Nu –' he stumbled over the name, as strange as everything else about this fellow, 'Nuwen know about the thing he seeks at the Bottom? What can he do with it?'

'I-I don't know, Group Captain. Pham Nuwen himself doesn't now. A little bit at a time, the insight comes. I believe, because I was there for some of it ... but I don't know how to make you believe.' She drew a shuddering breath. Kjet suddenly guessed what a tortured place the *Out of Band* must be. Somehow that made the story more credible. Anything that really could destroy the Blight would be unwholesomely weird. Kjet wondered how he would do, locked up with such a thing.

'My Lady Ravna,' he said, the words stilted and formal. *After all, I'm suggesting treason.* 'I, uh, I've got a number of friends in the Commercial Security fleet. I can check on the suspicions you've raised, and ...' *say it!* 'It's possible we can give you support in spite of my HQ.'

'Thank you, sir. Thank you.'

Glimfrelle broke the silence. 'We're getting a poor signal

on the *Out of Band*'s channel now.'

Kjet's eyes swept the windows. All the ultratrace displays looked like random noise. Whatever this storm was, it was bad.

'Looks like we won't be talking much longer, Ravna Bergsndot.'

'Yes. We're losing signal . . . Group Captain, if none of this works, if you can't fight for us . . . Your people are all that's left of Sjandra Kei. It's been good to see you and the Dirokimes . . . after so long to see familiar faces, people I really understand. I –' as she spoke, her image square-blurred into low-frequency components.

'*Huui!*' said Glimfrelle. 'Bandwidth just dropped through the floor.' There was nothing sophisticated about their link to the *Out of Band*. Given communications problems, the ship's processors just switched to low-rate coding.

'Hello, *Out of Band*. We've got problems on this channel now. Suggest we sign off.'

The window turned gray, and printed Samnorsk flickered across it:

Yes. It is more than a communicati

Glimfrelle diddled his comm panel. 'Zip. Zero,' he said. 'No detectable signal.'

Tirolle looked up from his navigation tank. 'This is a lot more than a communications problem. Our computers haven't been able to commit on an ultradrive jump in more than twenty seconds.' They had been doing five jumps a second, and just over a light-year per hour. Now . . .

Glimfrelle leaned back from his panel. 'Hei – so welcome to the Slow Zone.'

The Slow Zone. Ravna Bergsndot looked across the deck of the *Out of Band II*. Somewhere in the dark of her mind, she had always had a vision of the Slowness as a stifling darkness lit at best by torches, the domain of cretins and mechanical calculators. In fact, things didn't look much different from before. The ceilings and walls glowed just as before. The stars still shone through the windows (only now, it might be a *very* long time before any of them moved).

It was on the *OOB*'s other displays that the change was most obvious. The ultratrace tank blinked monotonously, a red legend displaying elapsed time since the last update. Navigation windows were filled with output from the diagnostics exercising the drive processors. An audible message in Triskweline was repeating over and over, 'Warning. Transition to Slowness detected. Execute back jump at once! Warning. Transition to Slowness detected. Execute . . .'

'Turn that off!' Ravna grabbed a saddle and strapped herself down. She was actually feeling dizzy, though that could only be (a very natural) panic. 'Some bottom-lugger this is. We run right into the Slow Zone, and all it can do is spout warnings after the fact!'

Greenstalk drifted closer, 'tiptoeing' off the ceiling with her tendrils. 'Even bottom-luggers can't avoid things like this, my Lady Ravna.'

Pham said something at the ship and most of the displays cleared.

Blueshell: 'Even a huge Zone storm doesn't normally extend more than a few light-years. We were two hundred light-years above the Zone boundary. What hit us must be a monster surge, the sort of thing you only read about in archives.'

Small consolation. 'We knew something like this could happen,' Pham said. 'Things have been getting awfully rough the last few weeks.' For a change, *he* didn't seem too upset.

'Yes,' she said. 'We expected a slowing maybe, but not The Slowness.' *We are trapped.* 'Where's the nearest habitable system? Ten light-years? Fifty?' The vision of darkness had a new reality, and the starscape beyond the ship's walls was no longer a friendly, steadying thing. They were surrounded by unending nothingness, moving at some vanishing fraction of the speed of light . . . entombed; all the courage of Kjet Svensndot and his fleet, for nothing; Jefri Olsndot, forever unrescued.

Pham's hand touched her shoulder, the first touch in . . . days? 'We can still make it to the Tines' world. This is a bottom-lugger, remember? We are not trapped. Hell, the ramscoop on this buggy is better than anything I ever had in the Qeng Ho. And I thought I was the freest man in the universe back then.'

Decades of travel time, mostly in coldsleep. Such had been the world of the Qeng Ho, the world of Pham's memories. Ravna let out a shuddering breath that ended in weak laughter. For Pham, the terrible pressure was abated, at least temporarily. He could be human.

'What's so funny?' said Pham.

She shook her head. 'All of us. Never mind.' She took a couple of slow breaths. 'Okay. I think I can make rational conversation. So the Zone has surged. Something that normally takes a thousand years – even in a storm – to move a single light-year, has suddenly shifted two hundred. Hunh! There'll be people a million years from now reading about this in the archives. I'm not sure I want the honor . . . We knew there was a storm, but I never expected to be drowned,' buried beneath the sea, light-years deep.

'The sea storm analogy is not perfect,' said Blueshell. The Skroderider was still on the far side of the deck, where he had retreated after questioning the Sjandra Kei captain. He still looked upset, though he was back to sounding precise and picky. Blueshell was studying a nav display, evidently a recording from right before the surge. He dumped the picture to a display flat and rolled slowly across the ceiling toward them. Greenstalk's fronds brushed him gently as he passed.

He sailed the display flat into Ravna's hands, and continued in a lecturing tone. 'Even in a sea storm, the water's surface is never as roiled as in a big interface disturbance. The most recent News reports showed it as a fractal surface with dimension close to three . . . Like foam and spray.' Even he could not avoid the storm analogy. The starscapes hung serene beyond crystal walls, and the loudest sound was from the ship's ventilators. Yet they had been swallowed in a maelstrom. Blueshell waved a frond at the display flat. 'We could be back in the Beyond in a few hours.'

'What?'

'See. The plane of the display is determined by the positions of the supposed Sjandra Kei command vessel, the outflying craft that we contacted directly, and ourselves.' The three formed a narrow triangle, the Limmende and Svensndot vertices close together. 'I've marked the times that contact was lost with the others. Notice: the link to Commercial Security HQ went down 150 seconds before we were hit. From the incoming signal and its requests for protocol changes, I believe that *both* we and the outflyer were enveloped at about the same time.'

Pham nodded. 'Yeah. The most distant sites losing contact last. That must mean the surge moved in from the side.'

'Exactly!' From his perch on the ceiling, Blueshell reached to tap the display. 'The three ships were like probes in the standard Zone mapping technique. Replaying the trace displays will no doubt confirm the conclusion.'

Ravna looked at the plot. The long point of the triangle – tipped by the *OOB* – pointed almost directly toward the heart of the galaxy. 'It must have been a huge, clifflike thing perpendicular to the rest of the surface.'

'A monster wave sweeping sideways!' said Greenstalk. 'And that's also why it won't last long.'

'Yes. It's the radial changes that are most often long term. This thing must have a trailing edge. We should pass through it in a few hours – and back into the Beyond.'

, So there was still a race to be won . . . or lost.

The first hours were strange. 'A few hours,' had been Blueshell's estimate of when they would be back in the Beyond. They hung around the bridge, alternately watching the clock and stewing about the strange conversations just completed. Pham was building himself back to trigger tension. Any time now, they would be back in the Beyond. What to do then? If only a few ships were perverted, perhaps Svensndot could still coordinate an attack. Would that do any good? Pham played the ultratrace recordings over and over, studying every detectable ship in all the fleets. 'But when we get out, when we get out . . . I'll know what to do. Not *why* I must do it, but what.' And he couldn't explain more.

Any time now... There was scarcely any reason to do much about resetting equipment that would need another initialization right away.

But after eight hours: 'It really could be longer, even a day.' They had been scrounging around in some of the historical literature. 'Maybe we should do a little housekeeping.' The *Out of Band II* had been designed for both the Beyond and the Slowness, but that second environment was regarded as an unlikely, emergency one. There were special-purpose processors for the Slow Zone, but they hadn't come up automatically. With Blueshell's advice, Pham took the high-performance automation off-line; that wasn't too difficult, except for a couple of voice-actuated independents that were no longer bright enough to understand the quitting commands.

Using the new automation gave Ravna a chill that, in a subtle way, was almost as frightening as the original loss of the ultradrive. Her image of the Slowness as darkness and torchlight – that was just nightmare fantasy. On the other hand, the Slowness as the domain of cretins and mechanical calculators, there was something to that. The *OOB*'s performance had degraded steadily during their voyage to the Bottom, but now... Gone were the voice-driven graphics generators; they were just a bit too complex to be supported by the new *OOB*, at least in full interpretive mode. Gone were the intelligent context analyzers that made the ship's library almost as accessible as one's own memories. Eventually Ravna even turned off the art and music units; without mood and context response, they seemed so wooden... constant reminders that there were no brains behind them. Even the simplest things were corrupted. Take voice and gesture controls: They no longer responded consistently to sarcasm and casual slang. It took a certain *discipline* to use them effectively. (Pham actually seemed to like this. It reminded him of the Qeng Ho).

Twenty hours. Fifty. Everyone was still telling each other there was nothing to worry about. But now Blueshell said that talk of 'hours' had been unrealistic. Considering the height of the 'tsunami' (at least two hundred light-years), it would likely be several hundred light-years across – that in keeping with the scaling laws of historical precedent. There was only one trouble with this reasoning: they were beyond all precedent. For the most part, zone boundaries followed galactic mean density. There was virtually no change from year to year, just the aeons' long shrinkage that might someday – after the death of all but the smallest stars – expose the galactic core to the Beyond. At any given time, perhaps one billionth of that boundary might qualify as being in a 'storm state.' In an ordinary storm, the surface might move in or out a light-year in a decade or so. Such storms were common enough to affect the fortunes of many worlds every year.

Much rarer – perhaps once in a hundred thousand years in the whole galaxy – there would be a storm where the boundary became seriously distorted, and where surges might move at a high multiple of light speed. *These* were the transverse surges that Pham and Blueshell made their scale estimates from. The fastest moved at about a light-year per second, across a distance of less than three lights; the largest were thirty light-years high and moved at scarcely a light-year per day.

So what was known of monsters like the thing that had engulfed them? Not much. Third-hand stories in the Ship's library told of surges perhaps as big as theirs, but the quoted dimensions and propagation rates were not clear. Stories more than a hundred million years old are hard to trust; there are scarcely any intermediate languages. (And even if there were, it wouldn't have helped. The new, dumb version of the *OOB* absolutely could not do mechanical translation of natural languages. Dredging the library was pointless.)

When Ravna complained about this to Pham, he said, 'Things could be worse. What was the Ur-Partition really?'

Five billion years ago. 'No one's sure.'

Pham jerked a thumb at his library display. 'Some people think it was a "super supersurge," you know. Something so big it swallowed the races that might have recorded it. Sometimes the biggest disasters aren't noticed at all – no one's around to write horror stories.'

Great.

'I'm sorry, Ravna. Honestly, if we're in anything like most past disasters, we'll come out of it in another day or two. The best thing is to *plan* for things that way. This is like a "time-out" in the battle. Take advantage of it to have a little peace. Figure out how to get the unperverted parts of Commercial Security to help us.'

'. . . Yeah.' Depending on the shape of the surge's trailing edge the *OOB* might have lost a good part of its lead . . . *But I'll bet the Alliance fleet is completely panicked by all this*. Such opportunists would likely run for safety as soon as they're back in the Beyond.

The advice kept her busy for another twenty hours, fighting with the half-witted things that claimed to be strategy planners on the new version of the *OOB*. Even if the surge passed right this instant, it might be too late. There were players in this game for whom the surge was not a time-out: Jefri Olsndot and his Tinish allies. It had been seventy hours now since their last contact; Ravna had missed three comm sessions with them. If *she* were panicked, what must it be like for Jefri? Even if Steel could hold off his enemies, time – and trust – would be running out at Tines' world.

One hundred hours into the surge, Ravna noticed that Blueshell and Pham were doing power tests on the *OOB*'s ramscoop drive . . . Some time-outs last forever.

34

The summer hot spell broke for a time; in fact, it was almost chilly. There was still the smoke and the air was still dry, but the winds seemed less driven. Inside their cubby aboard the ship, Amdijefri weren't taking much notice of the nice weather.

'They've been slow in answering before,' said Amdi. 'She's explained how the ultrawave –'

'Ravna's never been *this* late!' Not since the winter, anyway. Jefri's tone hovered between fear and petulance. In fact, there was supposed to be a transmission in the middle of the night, technical data for them to pass on to Mr Steel. It hadn't arrived by this morning, and now Ravna had also missed their afternoon session, the time when normally they could just chat for a bit.

The two children reviewed all the comm settings. The previous fall, they had laboriously copied those and the first level diagnostics. It all looked the same now . . . except for something called 'carrier detect.' If they only had a dataset, they might have looked up what that meant.

They had even very carefully reset some of the comm parameters . . . then nervously set them back when nothing happened. Maybe they hadn't given the changes enough of a chance to work. Maybe now they had *really* messed something up.

They stayed in the command cubby all through the afternoon, their minds cycling through fear and boredom and frustration. After four hours, boredom had at least a temporary victory. Jefri was napping uneasily in his father's hammock with two of Amdi curled up in his arms.

Amdi poked idly around the room, looked at the rocket controls. No . . . not even his self-confidence was up to playing with those. Another of him jerked at the wall quilting. He could always watch the fungus grow for a while. Things were that slow.

Actually, the gray stuff had spread a lot farther than the last time he looked. Behind the quilt, it was quite thick. He sent a chain of himself squirreling back between the wall and the fabric. It was dark, but some light spilled through the gap at the ceiling. In most places the mold was scarcely an inch thick, but back here it was five or six – *wow*. Just above his exploring nose, a huge lump of it grew from the wall. This was as big as some of the ornamental moss lumps that decorated castle meeting halls. Slender gray filaments grew down from the fungus. He almost called out to Jefri, but the two of him in the hammock were so comfortable.

He brought a couple of heads close to the strangeness. The wall behind it looked a little odd, too . . . as though part of its substance had been taken by the mold. And the gray itself:

like smoke – he felt the filaments with his nose. They were solid, dry. His nose tickled. Amdi froze in shocked surprise. Watching himself from behind, he saw that two of the filaments had actually passed through his member's head! And yet there was no pain, just that tickling feeling.

'What – what?' Jefri had been jostled into wakefulness as Amdi tensed around him.

'I found something really strange behind the quilts. I touched this big hunk of fungus and –'

As he spoke, Amdi gently backed away from the thing on the wall. The touch didn't hurt, but it made him more nervous than curious. He felt the filaments sliding slowly out.

'I told you, we aren't supposed to play with that stuff. It's dirty. The only good thing is, it doesn't smell.' Jefri was out of the hammock. He stepped across the cubby and lifted the quilting, Amdi's tip member lost its balance and jerked away from the fungus. There was a snapping sound, and a sharp pain in his lip.

'Geez, that thing is big!' Then, hearing Amdi's pain whistle. 'You okay?'

Amdi backed away from the wall. 'I think so.' The tip of one last filament was still stuck in his lip. It didn't hurt as much as the nettles he'd sampled a few days earlier. Amdijefri looked over the wound. What was left of the smoky spine seemd hard and brittle. Jefri's fingers gently worked it free. Then the two of them turned to wonder at the thing in the wall.

'It really has spread. Looks like it's hurt the wall, too.'

Amdi dabbed at his bloodied muzzle. 'Yeah. I see why your folks told you to stay away from it.'

'Maybe we should have Mr Steel scrub it all out.'

The two spent half an hour crawling around behind all the quilting. The grayness had spread far, but there was only the one marvelous flowering. They came back to stare at it, even sticking articles of clothing into the wisps. Neither risked fingers or noses on further contact.

Staring at the fungus on the wall was by far the most exciting thing that happened that afternoon; there was no message from the *OOB*.

The next day the hot weather was back.

Two more days passed . . . and still there was no word from Ravna.

Lord Steel paced the walls atop Starship Hill. It was near the middle of the night, and the sun hung about fifteen degrees above the northern horizon. Sweat filmed his fur; this was the warmest summer in ten years. The drywind was into its thirtieth dayaround. It was no longer a welcome break in the chill of the northland. The crops were dying in the fields. Smoke from fjord fires was visible as brownish haze both north and south of the castle. At first the reddish color had been a novelty, a change from the unending blue of sky and distance and the whitish haze of the sea fogs. Only at first. When fire struck East Streamsdell, the entire sky had been dipped in red. Ash had rained all the dayaround, and the only smell had been that of burning. Some said it was worse than the filthy air of the southern cities.

The troops on the walls backed far out of his way. This was more than courtesy, more than their fear of Steel. His troops were still not used to the cloaked ones, and the cover story Shreck was spreading did nothing to ease their minds: Lord Steel was accompanied by a singleton – in the colors of a Lord. The creature made no mind sounds. It walked incredibly close to its master.

Steel said to the singleton, 'Success is a matter of meeting a schedule. I remember you teaching me that,' *cutting it into me, in fact.*

The member looked back at him, cocked its head. 'As I remember, I said that success was a matter of adapting to changes in schedules.' The words were perfectly articulated. There were singletons that could talk that well – but even the most verbal could not carry on intelligent conversation. Shreck had had no trouble convincing the troops that Flenser science had created a race of superpacks, that the cloaked ones were individually as smart as any ordinary pack. It was a good cover for what the cloaks really were. It both inspired fear and obscured the truth.

The member stepped a little closer – nearer to Steel than anyone had been except during murders and rapes and the beatings of the past. Involuntarily, Steel licked his lips and spread out from around the threat. Yet in some ways the dark-cloaked one was like a corpse, without a trace of mind sound. Steel snapped his jaws shut and said, 'Yes. The genius is in winning even when the schedules have fallen down the garderobe.' He looked all away from the Flenser member, scanning the red-shrouded southern horizon. 'What's the latest estimate of Woodcarver's progress?'

'She's still camped about five days southeast of here.'

'The damned incompetent. It's hard to believe she's your parent! Vendacious made things so easy for her; her soldiers and toy cannon should have been here almost a tenday past –'

'And been well-butchered, on schedule.'

'Yes! Long before our sky friends arrived. Instead, she wanders inland and then balks.'

The Flenser member shrugged in its dark cloak. Steel knew the radio was as heavy as it looked. It consoled him that the other was paying a price for his omniscience. Just think, in heat like this, to have every part of oneself muffled to the tympana. He could imagine the discomfort . . . Indoors, he could smell it.

They walked past one of the wall cannon. The barrel gleamed of layered metal. The thing had thrice the range of Woodcarver's pitiful invention. While Woodcarver had been working with Dataset and a human child's intuition, he had had the direct advice of Ravna and company. At first he'd feared their largesse, thinking it meant the Visitors were superior beyond need for care. Now . . . the more he heard of Ravna and the others, the more clearly he understood their weakness. They could not experiment with themselves, improve themselves. Inflexible, slow-changing dullards. Sometimes they showed a low cunning – Ravna's coyness about what she wanted from the first starship – but their desperation was loud in all their messages, as was their attachment to the human child.

Everything had been going so well till just a few days ago. As they walked out of earshot of the gunner pack, Steel said to the Flenser member, 'And still no word from our "rescuers."'

'Quite so.' That was the other botched schedule, the

important one, which they could not control. 'Ravna has missed four sessions. Two of me is down with Amdijefri right now.' The singleton jabbed its snout toward the dome of the inner keep. The gesture was an awkward abortion. Without other muzzles and other eyes, body language was a limited thing. *We just aren't built to wander around a piece here, a piece there.* 'Another few minutes and the space folk will have missed a fifth talk session. The children are getting desperate, you know.'

The member's voice sounded sympathetic. Almost unconsciously, Lord Steel sidled a little farther out from around it. Steel remembered that tone from his own early existence. He also remembered the cutting and death that had always followed. 'I want them kept happy, Tyrathect. We're assuming communication will resume; when it does we'll need them.' Steel bared six pairs of jaws at the surrounded singleton. *'None of your old tricks.'*

The member flinched, an almost imperceptible twitch that pleased Steel more than the grovelling of ten thousand. 'Of course not. I'm just saying that you should visit them, try to help them with their fear.'

'You do it.'

'Ah . . . they don't fully trust me. I've told you before, Steel; they love you.'

'Ah! And they've seen through to your meanness, eh?' The situation made Steel proud. He had succeeded where Flenser's own methods would have failed. He had manipulated without threats or pain. It had been Steel's craziest experiment, and certainly his most profitable. But '– Look, I don't have time to wetnurse anyone. It's a tiresome thing to talk to those two.' And it was very tiresome to hold his temper, to suffer Jefri's 'petting' and Amdi's pranks. In the beginning, Steel had insisted that no one else have close contact with the children. They were too important to expose to others; the most casual slipup might show them the truth and ruin them. Even now, Tyrathect was the only pack besides himself who had regular contact. But for Steel, every meeting was worse than the last, an ultimate test of his self control. It was hard to think straight in a killing rage, and that's how almost every conversation with them ended for Steel. How wonderful it would be when the space folk landed. *Then* he could use the other end of the tool that was Amdijefri. *Then* there would be no need to have their trust and friendship. *Then* he would have a lever, something to torture and kill to enforce his demands.

Of course, if the aliens never landed, or if . . . 'We must do something! I will not be flotsam on the wave of the future.' Steel lashed at the scaffolding that ran along the inner side of the parapet, shredding the wood with his gleaming tines. 'We can't do anything about the aliens, so let's deal with Woodcarver. Yes!' He smiled at the Flenser member. 'Ironic, isn't it? For a hundred years, you sought her destruction. Now I can succeed. What would have been your great triumph is for me just an annoying detour, undertaken because greater projects are temporarily delayed.'

The cloaked one did not look impressed. 'There is a little matter of gifts falling out of the sky.'

'Yes, into my open jaws. And that is *my* good fortune, isn't it?' He walked on several paces, chuckling to himself. 'Yes. It's time to have Vendacious bring his trusting Queen in for the slaughter. Maybe it will interfere with other events, but . . . I know, we'll have the battle east of here.'

'The Margrum Climb?'

'Correct. Woodcarver's forces should be well concentrated coming up the defile. We'll move our cannon over there, set them behind the ridgeline at the top of the Climb. It will be easy to destroy all her people. And it's far enough from Starship Hill; even if the space folk arrive at the same time, we can keep the two projects separate.' The singleton didn't say anything, and after a moment Steel glared at him. 'Yes dear teacher, I know there is a risk. I know it splits our forces. But we've got an army sitting on our doorstep. They've arrived inconveniently late, but even Vendacious can't make them turn around and go home. And if he tries to stall things, the Queen might . . . Can you predict just what she would do?'

'. . . No. She has always had a way with the unexpected.'

'She might even see through Vendacious' fraud. So. We take a small chance, and destroy her now. You are with

Farscout Rangolith?'

'Yes. Two of me.'

'Tell him to get word to Vendacious. He is to have the Queen's army coming up Margrum Climb not less than two days from now. Feel free to elaborate; you know the region better than I. We'll work out final details when both sides are in position.' It was a wonderful thing to be the effective commander of both sides in a battle! 'One more thing. It's important and Vendacious must see to it within the day-around: I want Woodcarver's human dead.'

'What harm can she do?'

'That's a stupid question,' *especially coming from you.* 'We don't know when Ravna and Pham may reach us. Till we have them safe in our jaws, the Johanna creature is a dangerous thing to have nearby. Tell Vendacious to make it look like an accident, but I want that Two-Legs dead.'

Flenser was everywhere. It was a form of godhood he'd dreamed of since he'd been Woodcarver's newby. While one of him talked to Steel, two others lounged about the Starship with Amdijefri, and two more padded through light forest just north of Woodcarver's encampment.

Paradise can also be an agony, and each day the torment was a little harder to bear. In the first place, this summer was as insufferably hot as any in the North. And the radio cloaks were not merely hot and heavy. They necessarily covered his members' tympana. And unlike other uncomfortable costumes, the price of taking these off *for even a moment* was mindlessness. His first trials had lasted just an hour or two. Then had come a five-day expedition with Farscout Rangolith, providing Steel with instant information and instant command of the country around Starship Hill. It had taken a couple dayarounds to recover from the sores and aches of the radio cloaks.

This latest exercise in omniscience had lasted twelve days. Wearing the cloaks all the time was impossible. Every day in a rotation, one of his members threw off its radio, was bathed, and had its cloak's liner changed. It was Flenser's hour of daily madness, when sometimes the weak-willed Tyrathect would come back to mind, vainly trying to reestablish her dominance. It didn't matter. With one of his members disconnected, the remaining pack was only four. There are foursomes of normal intelligence, but none existed in Flenser/Tyrathect. The bathing and recloaking were all done in a confused haze.

And of course, even though Flenser was 'everywhere at once,' he wasn't any smarter than before. After the first jarring experiments, he got the hang of seeing/hearing scenes that were radically different – but it was as difficult as ever to carry on multiple conversations. When he was bantering with Steel, his other members had very little to say to Amdijefri or to Rangolith's scouts.

Lord Steel was done with him. Flenser walked along the parapets with his former student, but if Steel had said anything to him it would have taken him away from his current conversation. Flenser smiled (carefully so the one with Steel would not show it). Steel thought he was talking to Farscout Rangolith just now. Oh, he would do that . . . in a few minutes. One advantage of his situation was that no one could know for sure everything Flenser was up to. If he was careful, he would eventually rule here again. It was a dangerous game, and the cloaks were themselves dangerous devices. Keep a cloak out of the sunlight for a few hours and it lost power, and the member wearing it was cut off from the pack. Worse was the problem of *static* – that was the mantis word. The second set of cloaks had killed its user, and the spacers weren't sure of the cause, except that it was some sort of 'interference problem.'

Flenser had experienced nothing so extreme. But sometimes on his farthest hikes with Rangolith, or when a cloak's power faded . . . there was an incredible shrieking in his mind, like a dozen packs crowding close, sounds that scaled between sex madness and killing frenzy. Tyrathect seemed to like times like that; she'd come bounding out of the confusion, swamping him with her soft hate. Normally she lurked around the edges of his consciousness, tweaking a word here, a motive there. After the *static*, she was much worse; on one occasion she'd held control for almost a dayaround. Given a year without crises, Flenser could have studied Ty and Ra and Thect and done a proper excision. Thect, the member with the white-tipped ears, was probably the one to kill: it wasn't bright, but it was likely the capstone of the trio. With a precisely crafted replacement, Flenser might be even greater than before the massacre at Parliament Bowl. But for now, Flenser was stuck; soul surgery on one's self was an awesome challenge – even to The Master.

So. Careful. Careful. Keep the cloaks well-charged, take no long trips, and don't let any one person see all the threads of your plan. While Steel thought he was seeking Rangolith, Flenser was talking to Amdi and Jefri.

The human's face was wet with tears. 'F-four times we've missed R-ravna. *What has happened to her?*' His voice screeched up. Flenser hadn't realized there was such flexibility in the belching mechanism that humans use to make sound.

Most of Amdi clustered round the boy. He licked Jefri's cheeks. 'It could be our ultrawave. Maybe it's broken.' He looked beseechingly at Flenser. There were tears in the puppies' eyes, too. 'Tyrathect, please ask Steel again. Let us stay in the ship all the dayaround. Maybe there are messages that have come through and not been recorded.'

Flenser with Steel descended the northern stairs, crossed the parade ground. He gave a sliver of attention to the other's complaints about the sloppy maintenance around the practice stands. At least Steel was smart enough to keep the discipline scaffolds over on Hidden Island.

Flenser with Rangolith's troopers splashed through a mountain stream. Even in high summer, in the middle of a Drywind, there were still snow patches, and the streams running from under them were icy cold.

Flenser with Amdijefri edged forward, let two of Amdi rest against his sides. Both children liked physical contact, and he was the only one they had besides each other. It was all perversion of course, but Flenser had based his life on manipulating others' weakness, and – but for the pain – welcomed it. Flenser buzzed a deep purring sound through his shoulders, caressing the puppy next to him. 'I'll ask our

427

Lord Steel the very next time I see him.'

'Thank you.' A puppy nuzzled at his cloak, then mercifully moved away; Flenser was a mass of sores beneath that cover. Perhaps Amdi realized that, or perhaps . . . more and more Flenser saw a reticence in the two. His comment to Steel had been a slip into the truth: these two really didn't trust him. That was Tyrathect's fault. On his own, Flenser would have had no trouble winning Amdijefri's love. Flenser had none of Steel's killing temper and fragile dignity. Flenser could chat for casual pleasure, all the while mixing truth with lies. One of his greatest talents was empathy; no sadist can aspire to perfection without that diagnostic ability. But just when he was doing well, when they seemed about to open to him – then Ty or Ra or Thect would pop up, twisting his expression or poisoning his choice of phrase. Perhaps he should content himself with undermining the children's respect for Steel (without, of course, ever saying anything directly against him). Flenser sighed, and patted Jefri's arm comfortingly. 'Ravna will be back. I'm sure of it.' The human sniffled a little, then reached out to pet the part of Flenser's head that was not shrouded by the cloak. They sat in companionable silence for a moment, and his attention drifted back to –

–*the forest and Rangolith's troops*. The group had been moving uphill for almost ten minutes. The others were lightly burdened and used to this sort of exercise. Flenser's two members were lagging. He hissed at the group leader.

The group leader sidled back, his squad shifting briskly out of his way. He stopped when his nearest was fifteen feet from Flenser's. The soldier's heads cocked this way and that. 'Your wishes . . . my lord?' This one was new; he had been briefed about the cloaks, but Flenser knew the fellow didn't understand the new rules. The gold and silver that glinted in the darkness of the cloaks – those colors were reserved for the Lords of the Domain. Yet there were only two of Flenser here; normally such a fragment could barely carry on a conversation, much less give reasonable orders. Just as disconcerting, Flenser knew, was his lack of mind sound. 'Zombie' was the word some of the troops used when they thought themselves alone.

Flenser pointed up the hill; the timberline was only a few yards away. 'Farscout Rangolith is on the other side. We will take a short cut,' he said weakly.

Part of the other was already looking up the hill. 'That is not good, sir.' The trooper spoke slowly. *Stupid damn duo*, his posture said. 'The bad ones will see us.'

Flenser glowered at the other, a hard thing to do properly when you are just two. 'Soldier, do you see the gold on my shoulders? Even one of me is worth *all* of you. If I say take a short cut, we do it – even if it means walking belly-deep through brimstone.' Actually, Flenser knew exactly where Vendacious had put lookouts. There was no risk in crossing the open ground here. And he was *so* tired.

The group leader still didn't know quite what Flenser was, but he saw the dark-cloaks were at least as dangerous as any full-pack lord. He backed off humbly, bellies dragging on the ground. The group turned uphill and a few minutes later were walking across open heather.

Rangolith's command post was less than a half mile away along this path –

Flenser with Steel walked into the inner keep. The stone was freshly cut, the walls thrown up with the feverish speed of all this castle's construction. Thirty feet over their heads, where vault met buttresses, there were small holes set in the stonework. Those holes would soon be filled with gunpowder – as would slots in the wall surrounding the landing field. Steel called those the Jaws of Welcome. Now he turned a head back to Flenser. 'So what does Rangolith say?'

'Sorry. He's been out on patrol. He should be here – I mean, he should be in camp – any minute.' Flenser did his best to conceal his own trips with the scouts. Such recons were not forbidden, but Steel would have demanded explanations if he knew.

Flenser with Rangolith's troops sloshed through water-soaked heather. The air over the snowmelt was delightfully chill, and the breeze pushed cool tongues partway under his wretched cloaks.

Rangolith had chosen the site for his command post well. His tents were in a slight depression at the edge of a large

429

summer pond. A hundred yards away, a huge patch of snow covered the hill above them, fed the pond, and kept the air pleasantly cool. The tents were out of view from below, yet the site was so high in the hills that from the edge of the depression there was a clear view across three points of the compass, centered on the south. Resupply could be accomplished from the north with little chance of detection, and even if the damn fires struck the forests below, this post would be untouched.

Farscout Rangolith was lounging about his signal mirrors, oiling the aiming gears. One of his subordinates lay with snouts stuck over the lip of the hill, scanning the landscape with its telescopes. Rangolith came to attention at the sight of Flenser, but his gaze wasn't full of fear. Like most long-range scouts, he wasn't completely terrorized by castle politics. Besides, Flenser had cultivated an 'us against the prigs' relationship with the fellow. Now Rangolith growled at the group leader: 'The next time you come prancing across the open like that, your asses go on report.'

'My fault, Farscout,' put in Flenser. 'I have some important news.' They walked away from the others, down toward Rangolith's tent.

'See something interesting, did you?' Rangolith was smiling oddly. He had long ago figured out that Flenser was not a brilliant duo, but part of a pack with members back at the castle.

'When is your next session with Craddleheads?' That was the fieldname for Vendacious.

'Just past noon. He hasn't missed in four days. The Southerners seem to be on one big squat.'

'That will change.' Flenser repeated Steel's orders for Vendacious. The words came hard. The traitor within him was restive; he felt the beginnings of a major attack.

'Wow! You're going to move everything over to Margrum Climb in less than two – Never mind, that's something I'd best not know.'

Under his cloaks, Flenser bristled. There are limits to chumminess. Rangolith had his points, but maybe after all this was over he could be smoothed into something less . . . ad hoc.

'Is that all, my lord?'

'Yes – No.' Flenser shivered with uncharacteristic puzzlement. The trouble with these cloaks, sometimes they made it hard to remember things. *By the Great Pack, no!* It was that Tyrathect again. Steel had ordered the killing of Woodcarver's human – all things considered, a perfectly sensible move, but . . .

Flenser with Steel shook his head angrily, his teeth clicking together. 'Something the matter?' said Lord Steel. He really seemed to love the pain that the radio cloaks caused Flenser.

'Nothing, my lord. Just a touch of the *static*.' In fact there was no *static*, yet Flenser felt himself disintegrating. What had given the other such sudden power?

Flenser with Amdijefri snapped his jaws open and shut, open and shut. The children jumped back from him, eyes wide. 'It's okay,' he said grimly, even as his two bodies thrashed against each other. There really were lots of good reasons why they should keep Johanna Olsndot alive: In the long run, it assured Jefri's good will. And it could be Flenser's secret human. Perhaps he could fake the Two-Leg's death to Steel and – *No. No. No!* Flenser grabbed back control, jamming the rationalizations out of mind. The very tricks he had used against Tyrathect she thought to turn against him. *It won't work on me. I am the master of lies.*

And then her attack twisted again, became a massive bludgeoning that destroyed all thought.

With Flenser, with Rangolith, with Amdijefri – all of him was making little gibbering noises now. Lord Steel danced around him, unsure whether to laugh or be concerned. Rangolith goggled at him in frank amazement.

The two children edged back to touch him. 'Are you hurt? Are you hurt?' The human slipped those remarkable *hands* under the radio cloak and brushed softly at Flenser's bleeding fur. The world blurred in a surge of *static*. 'No. Don't do that. It might hurt him more,' came Amdi's voice. The puppies' tiny muzzles reached out, trying to help with the cloaks.

Flenser felt his being pushed downwards towards oblivion. Tyrathect's final attack was a frontal assault, without rationalizations or sly infiltration, and . . .

. . . And she looked out upon herself in astonishment. *After so many days, I am me. And in control. Enough butchering of innocents. If anyone is to die, it is Steel and Flenser.* Her head followed Steel's prancing forms, picked out the most articulate member. She gathered her legs beneath her, and prepared to leap at its throat. *Come just a little closer . . . and die.*

Tyrathect's last moment of consciousness probably didn't last longer than five seconds. Her attack on the Flenser within her was a desperate, all-out thing that left her without reserves or internal defense. Even as she tensed to leap upon Steel, she felt her soul being pulled back and down, and Flenser rising up from the darkness. She felt the member's legs spasm and collapse, the ground smash into its face . . .

. . . And Flenser was back in control. The weakling's attack had been astonishing. She really had *cared* for the ones who were to be destroyed, cared so much she was willing to sacrifice herself if it would kill Flenser. And that had been her undoing. Suicide is never something to hang pack dominance on. Her very resolve had weakened her hold on the hindmind – and given The Master his chance. He was back in control, and with a great opportunity. Tyrathect's assault had left her defenseless. The innermost mental barriers around her three members were suddenly as thin as the skin of an overripe fruit. Flenser slashed through the membrane, pawed at the flesh of her mind, spattering it across his own. The three who had been her core would still live, but never again would they have a soul separate from his.

Flenser with Steel sprawled as though unconscious, his convulsions subsiding. Let Steel think him incapacitated. It would give him time to think of the most advantageous explanation.

Flenser with Rangolith came slowly to his feet, though the two members were still in a posture of confusion. Flenser pulled them together. No explanations were due here, but it would be best if Farscout didn't suspect soulstrife. 'The cloaks are powerful tools, dear Rangolith; sometimes a bit too powerful.'

'Yes, my lord.'

Flenser let a smile spread across his features. For a moment he was silent, savoring what he would say next. No, there was no sign of the weak-willed one. This had been her last, best try at domination – her last and biggest mistake. Flenser's smile spread further, all the way to the two with Amdijefri. It suddenly occurred to him that Johanna Olsndot would be the first person he had ordered killed since his return to Hidden Island. Johanna Olsndot would therefore be the first blood on three of his muzzles.

'There's one more item for Craddleheads, Farscout. An execution . . .' As he spoke the details, the warmth of a decision well-made spread through his members.

35

The only good thing about all the waiting had been the chance it gave the wounded. Now that Vendacious had found a way past the Flenserist defenses, everyone was anxious to break camp, but . . .

Johanna spent the last afternoon at the field hospital. The hospital was laid off in rough rectangles, each about six meters across. Some of the plots had ragged tents – those belonging to wounded who were still smart enough to care for themselves. Others were surrounded by stranded fencing; inside each of those was a single member, the survivor of what had once been an entire pack. The singletons could easily have jumped the fences, but most seemed to recognize their purpose, and stayed within.

Johanna pulled the foodcart through the area, stopping at first one patient and then another. The cart was a bit too large for her, and sometimes it got caught in the roots that grew across the forest floor. Yet this was a job that she could do better than any pack, and it was nice to find a way she could help.

In the forest around the hospital there was the sound of kherhogs being coaxed up to wagon ties, the shouts of crews securing the cannons and getting the camp gear stowed. From the maps Vendacious had shown at the meeting, it was clear the next two days would be an exhausting time – but at the end of it they would have the high ground behind unsuspecting Flenserists.

She stopped at the first little tent. The threesome inside had heard her coming and was outside now, running little circles around her cart. 'Johanna! Johanna!' it said in her own voice. This was all that was left of one of Woodcarver's minor strategists; once upon a time, it had known some Samnorsk. The pack had originally been six; three had been killed by the wolves. What was left was the 'talker' part – about as bright as a five year old, though with an odd vocabulary. 'Thank you for food. Thank you.' Its muzzles pushed at her. She patted the heads before reaching into the cart and pulling out bowls of lukewarm stew. Two of them dug in right away, but the third sat back for a moment and chatted. 'I hear, we fight soon.'

Not you anymore, but 'Yes. We are going up by the dry fall, just east of here.'

'Uh, oh.' It said. 'Uh, oh. That's *bad*. Poor seeing, no control, ambush scary.' Apparently the fragment had some memories of its own tactical work. But there was no way Johanna could explain Vendacious's reasoning to it. 'Don't worry, we will make it okay.'

'You sure? You promise?'

Johanna smiled gently at what was left of a rather nice fellow. 'Yes. I promise.'

'Ah-ah-ah . . . Okay.' Now all three had their muzzles stuck into stew bowls. This was one of the lucky ones, really. It showed plenty of interest in what went on around it. Just as important, it had childlike enthusiasms. Pilgrim said that fragments like this could grow back easily if they were just treated right long enough to bear a puppy or two.

She pushed the cart a few meters further, to the fenced square that was the symbolic corral for a singleton. There was a faint odor of shit in the air. Some of the singletons and duos were not housebroken; in any case, the camp latrines were a hundred meters away.

'Here, Blacky, Blacky?' Johanna banged an empty bowl

against the side of the cart. A single head eased up from behind some root bushes; sometimes this one didn't respond even that much. Johanna got on her knees so her eyes weren't much higher than the black-faced one. 'Blacky?'

The creature pulled himself out of the bushes and slowly approached. This was all that was left of one of Scrupilo's cannoneers. She vaguely remembered the pack, a handsome sixsome all large and fast. But now even 'Blacky' wasn't whole: a falling gun had crushed his rear legs. He dragged his legless rear on a little wagon with thirty centimeter wheels . . . sort of like a Skroderider with forelegs. She pushed a bowl of stew toward him, and made the noises that Pilgrim coached her in. Blacky had refused food the last three days, but today he rolled and walked close enough that she could pet his head. After a moment he lowered his muzzle to the stew.

Johanna grinned in surprised pleasure. This hospital was a strange place. A year ago she would have been horrified by it; even now she didn't have the proper Tinish outlook on the wounded. As she continued to pet Blacky's lowered head, Johanna looked across the forest floor at the crude tents, the patients and parts of patients. It really was a hospital. The surgeons did try to save lives, even if the medical science was a horrifying process of cutting and splinting without anesthetics. In that regard, it was quite comparable to the medieval human medicine that Johanna had seen on Dataset. But with the Tines there was something more. This place was almost a spare parts warehouse. The medics were interested in the welfare of *packs*. To them, singletons were pieces that might have a use in making larger fragments workable, at least temporarily. *Injured* singletons were at the bottom of all medical priorities. 'There's not much left to save in such cases,' one medic had said to her, via Pilgrim. 'And even if there was, would you want a crippled, loose-bonded member in your self?' The fellow had been too tired to notice the absurdity of his question. His muzzles had been dripping blood; he'd been working for hours to save wounded members of whole packs.

Besides, most wounded singletons just stopped eating and died in less than a tenday. Even after a year with Tines,

Johanna couldn't quite accept it. Every singleton reminded her of dear Scriber; she wanted them to have a better chance than his last remnant had. She had taken over the food cart and spent as much time with the wounded singletons as she did with any of the other patients. It had worked out well. She could get close to each patient without mindsound interference. Her help gave the brood kenners more time to study the fragments and singletons, and try to build working packs from the wreckage.

And now maybe this one wouldn't starve. She'd tell Pilgrim. He'd done miracles with some of the other match-ups, and seemed to be the only pack who shared some of her feelings for damaged singletons. 'If they don't starve it often means a strength of mind. Even crippled, they could be an advantage to a pack,' he'd said to her. 'I've been crippled off and on in my travels; you can't always pick and choose when you're down to three and you're a thousand miles into an unknown land.'

Johanna set a bowl of water beside the stew. After a moment, the crippled member turned on his axle and took some shallow sips. 'Hang on, Blacky, we'll find someone for you to be.'

Chitiratte was where he was supposed to be, walking his post exactly as expected. Nevertheless, he felt a thrill of nervousness. He always kept at leat one head gazing at the mantis creature, the Two-Legs. Nothing suspicious about that posture either. He was *supposed* to be doing security duty here, and that meant keeping a lookout in all directions. He shifted his crossbow nervously about from jaws to field pack and back to jaws. Just a few more minutes . . .

Chitiratte circled the hospital compound once more. It was soft duty. Even though this stretch of wood had been spared, the drywind fires had chased the bigger wildlife downstream. This close to the river, the ground was covered with softbush, and there was scarcely a thorn to be found. Pacing around the hospital was like a walk on Woodcarver's Green down south. A few hundred yards east was harder work – getting the wagons and supplies in shape for the climb.

The fragments knew that something was up. Here and there, heads stuck up from pallets and burrows. They watched the wagons being loaded, heard the familiar voices of friends. The dumbest ones felt a call to duty; he had chased three able-bodied singles back into the compound. No way such feebs could be of any help. When the army marched up Margrum Climb, the hospital would stay behind. Chitiratte wished he could too. He'd been working for the Boss long enough to guess whence his orders ultimately came; Chitiratte suspected that not many would be coming back from Margrum Climb.

He turned three pairs of eyes toward the mantis creature. This latest job was the riskiest thing he'd been a part of. If it worked out he might just demand that the Boss leave him with the hospital. *Just be careful, old fellow. Vendacious didn't get where he is by leaving loose ends.* Chitiratte had seen what happened to that easterner who nosed a little too close into the Boss's business.

Damn but the human was slow! She'd been grunting at that one singleton for five minutes. You'd think she was having sex with these frags for all the time she spent with them. Well, she'd pay for the familiarity very soon. He started to cock his bow, then thought better of it. *Accident, accident.* It must all look like an accident.

Aha. The Two-Legs was collecting food and water bowls and stowing them on the meal cart. Chitiratte made unobtrusive haste around the hospital perimeter, positioning himself in view of the Kratzi duo – the fragment that would actually do the killing.

Kratzinissinari had been a foot trooper before losing the Nissinari parts of himself. He had no connection with the Boss or Security. But he'd been known as a crazy-headed get of bitches, a pack that was always on the edge of combat rage. Getting killed back to two members normally had a gentling influence. In this case – well, the Boss claimed that Kratzi was specially prepared, a trap ready to be sprung. All Chitiratte need do was give the signal, and the duo would tear the mantis apart. A great tragedy. Of course, Chitiratte would be there, the alert hospital warden. He would quickly put arrows through Kratzi's brains . . . but alas, not in time to save the Two-Legs.

The human dragged the meal cart awkwardly around root bushes toward Kratzi, her next patient. The duo came out of its burrow, speaking half-witted greetings that even Chitiratte could not understand. There were undertones though, a killing anger that edged its friendly mien. Of course, the mantis thing didn't notice. She stopped the cart, began filling food and water bowls, all the time grunting away at the twosome. In a moment, she would bend down to put the food on the ground . . . For half an instant, Chitiratte considered shooting the mantis himself if Kratzi were not immediately successful. He could claim it was a tragic miss. He really didn't like the Two-Legs. The mantis creature was a menacing thing; it was so tall and moved so weirdly. By now he knew it was fragile compared to packs, but it was scary to think of a single animal so smart as this. He shelved the temptation even faster than he had thought it. No telling what price he might pay for that, even if they believed his shot was an accident. No altruism today, thank you very much; Kratzi's jaws and claws would have to do.

One of Kratzi's heads was looking in Chitiratte's general direction. Now the mantis picked up the bowls and turned from the meal cart –

'Hei, Johanna! How is it going?'

Johanna looked up from the stew to see Peregrine Wickwrackscar walking along the edge of the hospital. He was moving to get as close as possible without invading the mind sounds of the patients. The guard who had stopped there a moment before retreated before his advance and stopped a few meters further on. 'Pretty good,' she called back. 'You know the one on wheels? He actually ate some stew tonight.'

'Good. I've been thinking about him and the threesome on the other side of the hospital.'

'The wounded medic?'

'Yes. What's left of Trellelak is all female, you know. I've been listening to mind sounds and –' Pilgrim's explanation

438

was delivered in fluent Samnorsk, but it didn't make much sense to Johanna. Brood kenning had *so* many concepts without referents in human language that even Pilgrim couldn't make it clear. The only obvious part was that since Blacky was a male, there was a chance that he and the medic threesome might have pups early enough to bind the group. The rest was talk of 'mood resonance' and 'meshing weak points with strong.' Pilgrim claimed to be an amateur at brood kenning, but it was interesting the way the docs – and even Woodcarver sometimes – deferred to him. In his travels he had been through a lot. His matchups seemed to 'take' more often than anybody's. She waved him to silence. 'Okay. We'll try it soon as I've fed everybody.'

Pilgrim cocked a head or two at the nearby hospital plots. 'Something strange is going on. Can't quite "put my finger on it," but . . . all the fragments are watching you. Even more than usual. Do you feel it?'

Johanna shrugged. 'No.' She knelt to set the water and stew bowls before the twosome patient. The pair had been vibrating with eagerness, though they had been quite polite in not interrupting. Out of the corner of her eye, she noticed the hospital guard make a strange dipping motion with its two middle heads, and –

The blows were like two great fists smashing into her chest and face. Johanna fell to the ground, and they were on her. She raised bloody arms against the slashing jaws and claws.

When Chitiratte gave the signal, both of Kratzi leaped into action – *crashing into each other*, almost incidentally knocking the mantis on her back. Their claws and teeth were tearing at empty air and each other as much as the Two-Legs. For an instant, Chitiratte was struck motionless with surprise. *She might not be dead.* Then he remembered himself and jumped over the fence, at the same time cocking and loading his bow. Maybe he could miss the first shot. Kratzi was shredding the mantis, but slow –

Suddenly, there was no possibility of shooting the twosome. A wave of snarling black and white surged over Kratzi and the mantis. Every able-bodied fragment in the hospital seemed to be running to the attack. It was instant killing rage, far wilder than anything that could come from whole packs. Chitiratte fell back in astonishment before the sight and the mindsound of it.

Even the pilgrim seemed caught up in it; the pack raced past Chitiratte and circled the melee. The pilgrim never quite plunged in, but nipped here and there, screaming words that were lost in the general uproar.

A splash of coordinated mindsound boomed out from the mob, so loud it numbed Chitiratte twenty yards away. The mob seemed to shrink in on itself, the frenzy gone from most of its members. What had been near a single beast with two dozen bodies was suddenly a confused and bloody crowd of random members.

The pilgrim still ran around the edge, somehow keeping his mind and purpose. His huge, scarred member dived in and out of the remaining crowd, clawing at anything that still fought.

The patients dragged themselves away from the killing ground. Some that had gone in as threesomes or duos came out single. Others seemed more numerous than before. The ground that was left was soaked with blood. At least five members had died. Near the middle, a pair of prosthetic wheels lay incongruously.

The pilgrim paid it all no attention; the four of him stood around and over the bloody mound at the center.

Chitiratte smiled to himself. *Mantis splatter.* Such a tragedy.

Johanna never quite lost consciousness, but the pain and the suffocating weight of dozens of bodies left no room for thought. Now the pressure eased. Somewhere beyond the local din she could hear shouts of normal Tinish talk. She looked up and saw Pilgrim standing all around her. Scarbutt was straddling her, its muzzle centimeters away. It reached down and licked her face. Johanna smiled and tried to speak.

Vendacious had arranged to be in conference with Scrupilo and Woodcarver. Just now the 'Commander of Cannoneers' was deep into tactics, using Dataset to illustrate his scheme for Margrum Climb.

Squalls of rage sounded from down by the river.

Scrupilo looked up peevishly from the Pink Oliphaunt: 'What the muddy hell –'

The sounds continued, more than a casual brawl. Woodcarver and Vendacious exchanged worried glances even as they arched necks to see among the trees. 'A fight in the hospital?' said the Queen.

Vendacious dropped his note board and lunged out of the meeting area, shouting for the local guards to guard the Queen. As he raced across the camp, he could see that his roving guards were already converging on the hospital. Everything seemed as smooth as a program on Dataset . . . except, why so *much* noise?

The last few hundred yards, Scrupilo caught up with him and pulled ahead. The cannoneer raced into the hospital and stumbled over himself in abrupt horror. Vendacious burst into the clearing all prepared to display his own shock combined with alert resolve.

Peregrine Wickwrackscar was standing by a meal cart, Chitiratte not far behind him. The pilgrim was standing over the Two-Legs in a litter of carnage. *By the Pack of Packs, what happened?* There was too much blood by far. 'Everybody back except the doctors,' Vendacious bellowed at the soldiers who crowded at the edge of the compound. He picked his way along a path that avoided the loudest-minded patients. There were a lot of fresh wounds, and here and there speckles of blood dark on the pale tree trunks. Something had gone wrong.

Meanwhile Scrupilo had run around the edge of the hospital and was standing just a few dozen yards from the Pilgrim. Most of him was staring at the ground under Wickwrackscar. 'It's Johanna! Johanna!' For a moment it looked like the fool would jump over the fence.

'I think she's okay, Scrupilo.' Wickwrackscar said. 'She was just feeding one of the duos and it went nuts – attacked her.'

One of the doctors looked over the carnage. There were

three corpses on the ground, and blood enough for more. 'I wonder what she did to provoke them.'

'Nothing, I tell you! But when she went down, half the hospital went after Whatsits here.' He waggled a nose at unidentifiable remains.

Vendacious looked at Chitiratte, at the same time saw Woodcarver arrive. 'What about it, Soldier?' he asked. *Don't screw up, Chitiratte.*

'I-it's just like the pilgrim says, my lord. I've never seen anything like it.' He sounded properly astounded by the whole affair.

Vendacious stepped a little closer to the Pilgrim. 'If you'll let me take a closer look, Pilgrim?'

Wickwrackscar hesitated. He had been snuffling around the girl, looking for wounds that might need immediate attention. Then the girl nodded weakly to him, and he backed off.

Vendacious approached, all solemn and solicitous. Inside he raged. He'd never heard of anything like this. But even if the whole damn hospital had come to her aid, she should still be dead; the Kratzi duo could have ripped her throat out in half a second. His plan had seemed fool-proof (and even now the failure would cause no lasting damage), but he was just beginning to understand what had gone wrong: For days, the human had been in contact with these patients, even Kratzi. No Tinish doctor could approach and touch them like the Two-Legs. Even some whole packs felt the effect; for fragments it must be overwhelming. In their inner soul, most of the patients considered the alien part of themselves.

He looked at the Two-Legs from three sides, mindful that the eyes of fifty packs were watching his every move. Very little of the blood was from the Two-Legs. The cuts on her neck and arms were long and shallow, aimless slashings. At the last minute, Kratzi's conditioning had failed before the notion of the human as pack member. Even now, a quick flick of a forepaw would rip the girl's throat open. He briefly considered putting her under Security medical protection. The ploy had worked well with Scriber, but it would be very risky here. Pilgrim had been nose to nose with Johanna; he would be suspicious of any claims about 'unexpected complications.' *No. Even good plans sometimes fail. Count it as experience for the future.* He smiled at the girl and spoke in Samnorsk, 'You're quite safe now,' *for the moment and quite unfortunately.* The human's head turned to the side, looking off in the direction of Chitiratte.

Scrupilo had been pacing back and forth along the fence, so close to Chitiratte and Pilgrim that the two had been forced back. 'I won't have it!' The cannoneer said loudly. 'Our most important person attacked like this. It smells of enemy action!'

Wickwrackscar goggled at him. 'But how?'

'I don't *know!*' Scrupilo said, his voice a desperate shout. 'But she needs protection as much as nursing. Vendacious must find some place to keep her.'

The pilgrim pack was clearly impressed by the argument – and unnerved. He inclined a head at Vendacious and spoke with uncharacteristic respect, 'What do you think, Vendacious?'

Of course, Vendacious had been watching the Two-Legs. It was interesting how little humans could disguise their point of attention. Johanna had been staring at Chitiratte, now she was looking up at Vendacious, her shifty little close-set eyes narrowing. Vendacious had made a project this last year of studying human expressions, both on Johanna and in stories in Dataset. She suspected something. And she also must have understood part of Scrupilo's speech. Her back arched and raised one hand weakly. Fortunately for Vendacious, her shout came out a whisper that even he could scarcely hear. 'No . . . not like Scriber.'

Vendacious was a pack who believed in careful planning. He also knew that the best-made schemes must be altered by circumstances. He looked down at Johanna and smiled with the gentlest public sympathy. It would be risky to kill her like Scriber's frag, but – now he saw that the alternatives were far more dangerous. Thank goodness Woodcarver was stuck with her limper on the other side of the camp. He nodded at Pilgrim and drew himself together. 'I fear Scrupilo is right. Just how it might have been done, I don't know, but we can't

take a chance. We'll take Johanna to my den. Tell the Queen.'
He pulled cloaks from his backs and began gently to wrap the
human for the last trip she would ever make. Only her eyes
protested.

Johanna drifted in and out of consciousness, horrified at her
inability to scream her fears. Her strongest cries were less
than whispers. Her arms and legs responded with little more
than twitches, even that lost in Vendacious's swaddling.
Concussion, maybe, something like that, the explanation came
from some absurdly rational corner of her mind. Everything
seemed so far away, so dark . . .

Johanna woke in her cabin at Woodcarvers. What a terrible
dream! That she had been so cut up, unable to move, and
then thinking Vendacious was a traitor. She tried to shrug
herself to a sitting position, but nothing moved. *Darn sheets are
all wrapped around me.* She lay quiet for a second, still
massively disoriented by the dream. 'Woodcarver?' she tried
to say, but only a little moan came out. Somemember moved
gently around the firepit. The room was only dimly lit, and
something was wrong with it. Johanna wasn't lying in her
usual place. There was a moment of puzzled lassitude as she
tried to make sense of the orientation of the dark walls.
Funny. The ceiling was awfully low. Everything smelled like
raw meat. The side of her face *hurt*, and she tasted blood on
her lips. She wasn't at Woodcarvers and that terrible dream
was —

Three Tinish heads drifted in silhouette nearby. One came
closer, and in the dim light she recognized the pattern of
white and black on its face. *Vendacious.*

'Good,' he said. 'You are awake.'

'Where am I?' the words came out slurred and weak. The
terror was back.

'The abandoned cotter's hut at the east end of the camp.
I've taken it over. As a security den, you know.' His Samnorsk
was quiet and fluent, spoken in one of the generic voices of
Dataset. One of his jaws carried a dagger, the blade a glint in
the dimness.

Johanna twisted in the tied cloaks and whispered screams. Something was wrong with her; it was like shouting on empty breath.

One of Vendacious paced the hut's upper level. Daylight splashed across its muzzle as it peered out first one and then another of the narrow slits cut in the timbers. 'Ah, it's good that you don't pretend. I could see that you somehow guessed about my . . . second career. My hobby. But screaming – even loud – won't help either. We have only a brief time to chat. I'm sure the Queen will come visiting soon . . . and I will kill you just before she arrives. So sad. Your hidden wounds were tragically severe . . .'

Johanna wasn't sure of all he said. Her vision blurred every time she moved her head. Even now she couldn't remember the details of what had happened back in the hospital compound. Somehow Vendacious *was* a traitor, but how . . . memories wriggled past the pain. 'You did murder Scriber, didn't you? *Why?*' Her voice came louder than before, and she choked on blood dribbling back down her throat.

Soft, *human*, laughter came from all around her. 'He learned the truth about me. Ironic that such an incompetent would be the only one to see through me . . . Or do you mean a larger why?' The three nearby muzzles moved closer still, and the blade in one's jaw patted the side of Johanna's cheek. 'Poor Two-Legs, I'm not sure you could ever understand. Some of it, the will to power maybe. I've read what Dataset has to say about human motivation, the "freudian" stuff. We Tines are much more complicated. I am almost entirely male, did you know that? A dangerous thing to be, all one sex. Madness lurks. Yet it was my decision. I was tired of being an indifferently good inventor, of living in Woodcarver's shadow. So many of us are her get, and she dominates most all of us. She was quite happy about my going into Security, you know. She doesn't quite have the combination of members for it. She thought that all male but one would make me controllably devious.'

His sentry member made another round of the window slits. Again there was a human chuckle. 'I've been planning a long time. It's not just Woodcarver I'm up against. The power-side of her soul is scattered all over the arctic coast; Flenser had almost a century headstart on me; Steel is new, but he has the empire Flenser built. I made myself indispensable to all of them: I'm Woodcarver's chief of security . . . and Steel's most valued spy. Played aright, I will end up with Dataset and all the others will be dead.'

His blade tapped her face again. 'Do you think you can help me?' Eyes peered close into her terror. 'I doubt it very much. If my proper plan had succeeded, you would be neatly dead now.' A sigh breathed around the room. 'But that failed, and I'm stuck with carving you up myself. Perhaps it will turn out for the best. Dataset is a torrent of information about most things, but it scarcely acknowledges the existence of torture. In some ways, your race seems so fragile, so easily killable. You die before your minds can be dismembered. Yet I know you can feel pain and terror; the trick is to apply force without quite killing.'

The three nearby members snuggled into more comfortable positions, like a human settling down for serious talk. 'And there *are* some questions you may be able to answer, things I couldn't really ask before. Steel is very confident, you know, and it's not because he has me with Woodcarver. That pack has some other advantage. Could he have his own Dataset?'

Vendacious paused. Johanna didn't answer, her silence a combination of terror and stubbornness. This was the monster that killed Scriber.

The muzzle with the knife slid between the blankets and Johanna's skin, and pain shot up Johanna's arm. She screamed. 'Ah, Dataset said a human could be hurt there. No need to answer that one, Johanna. Do you know what I think is Steel's secret? I think one of your family survived – most likely your little brother, considering what you've told us about the massacre.'

Jefri? *Alive?* For an instant she forgot the pain, almost forgot the fear. 'How . . .?'

Vendacious gave a Tinish shrug. 'You never saw him dead. You can be sure Steel wanted a live Two-Legs, and after reading about cold sleep in Dataset, I doubt he could have

446

revived any of the others. And he's got *something* up there. He's been eager for information from Dataset, but he's never demanded that I steal the device for him.'

Johanna closed her eyes, denying the traitor pack's existence. *Jefri lives!* Memories rose before her; Jefri's playful joy, his childish tears, his trusting courage aboard the refugee ship . . . things she had thought forever lost to her. For a moment they seemed more real than the slashing violence of the last few minutes. But what could Jefri do to help the Flenserists? The other datasets had surely burned. *There's something more here, something that Vendacious still is missing.*

Vendacious grabbed her chin, and gave her head a little shake. 'Open your eyes; I've learned to read them, and I want to see . . . Hmm, I don't know if you believe me or not. No matter. If we have time, I will learn just what he might have done for Steel. There are other, sharper questions. Dataset is clearly the key to all. In less than half a year, I and Woodcarver and Pilgrim have learned an enormous amount about your race and civilization. I daresay we know your people better than you do. When all the violence is over, the winner will be the pack that still controls Dataset. I intend to be that pack. And I've often wondered if there are other passwords, or programs I can run that would actually watch for my safety –'

The babysitter code.

The watching heads bobbed a grin. 'Aha, so there is such a thing! Perhaps this morning's bad luck is all for the best. I might never have learned –' his voice broke into dischords. Two of Vendacious jumped up to join the one already at the window slits. Softly by her ear, the voice continued, 'It's the Pilgrim, still far away, but coming toward us . . . I don't know. You would be much better safely dead. One deep wound, all out of sight.' The knife slid further down. Johanna arched futilely back from the point. Then the blade withdrew, the point poised gently against her skin. 'Let's hear what Pilgrim has to say. No point in killing you this instant if he doesn't insist on seeing you.' He pushed a cloth into her mouth and tied it tight.

There was a moment of silence, maybe the crunch of paws in the brush right around the cabin. Then she heard a pack warble loud from beyond the timbered walls. Johanna doubted that she would ever learn to recognize packs by their voices, but . . . her mind stumbled through the sounds, trying to decode the Tinish chords that were words piled on top of one another:

> '*Johanna*
> *something* interrogative
> *screech* safe.'

Vendacious gobbled back,

> 'Hail Peregrine Wickwrackscar
> Johanna *trill*
> not visible hurts
> sad uncertain *squeak*.'

And the traitor murmured in her ear: 'Now he'll ask if I need medical help, and if he insists . . . our chat will have an early end.'

But the only reply Pilgrim made was a chorus of sympathetic worry. 'Damn assholes are just sitting down out there,' came Vendacious's irritated whisper.

The silence stretched on a moment, and then Peregrine's human voice, the Joker from Dataset, said in clear Samnorsk. 'Don't do anything foolish, Vendacious, old man.'

Vendacious made a sound of polite surprise – and tensed around her. His knife jabbed a centimeter deep between Johanna's ribs, a thorn of pain. She could feel the blade trembling, could feel his member's breath on her bloody skin.

Pilgrim's voice continued, confident and knowing: 'I mean we know what you're up to. Your pack at the hospital has gone completely to pieces, confessed what little he knew to Woodcarver. Do you think your lies can get by *her?* If Johanna is dead, you'll be bloody shreds.' He hummed an ominous tune from Dataset. 'I know her well, the Queen. She seems such a gracious pack . . . but where do you think Flenser got his gruesome creativity? Kill Johanna and you'll find just how far her genius in that exceeds Flenser's.'

448

The knife pulled back. One more of Vendacious leaped to the window slits, and the two by Johanna loosened their grip. He stroked the blade gently across her skin. Thinking? *Is Woodcarver really that fearsome?* The four at the windows were looking in all directions; no doubt Vendacious was counting guard packs and planning furiously. When he finally replied, it was in Samnorsk: 'The threat would be more credible if it were not at second hand.'

Pilgrim chuckled. 'True. But we guessed what would happen if she approached. You're a cautious fellow; you'd have killed Johanna instantly, and been full of lying explanation before you even heard what the Queen knows. But seeing a poor pilgrim amble over . . . I know you think me a fool, only one step better than Scriber Jaqueramaphan.' Peregrine stumbled on the name, and for an instant lost his flippant tone. 'Anyway, now you know the situation. If you doubt, send your guards beyond the brush; look at what the Queen has surrounding you. Johanna dead only kills you. Speaking of which, I assume this conversation has some point?'

'Yes. She lives.' Vendacious slipped the gag from Johanna's mouth. She turned her head, choking. There were tears running down the sides of her face. 'Pilgrim, oh Pilgrim!' The words were scarcely more than a whisper. She drew a painful breath, concentrated on making noise. Bright spots danced before her eyes. 'Hei, Pilgrim!'

'Hei Johanna. Has he hurt you?'

'Some, I –'

'That's enough. She's alive, Pilgrim, but that's easily corrected.' Vendacious didn't jam the gag back in her mouth. Johanna could see him rubbing heads nervously as he paced round and round the ledge. He trilled something about 'stalemated game.'

Peregrine replied, 'Speak Samnorsk, Vendacious. I want Johanna to understand – and you can't talk quite as slick as in pack talk.'

'Whatever.' The traitor's voice was unconcerned, but his members kept up their nervous pacing. 'The Queen must realize we have a standoff here. Certainly I'll kill Johanna if I'm not treated properly. But even then, Woodcarver could not afford to hurt me. Do you realize the trap Steel has set on Margrum Climb? I'm the only one who knows how to avoid it.'

'Big deal. I never wanted to go up Margrum anyway.'

'Yes, but you don't count, Pilgrim. You're a mongrel patchwork. Woodcarver will understand how dangerous this situation is. Steel's forces are everything I said they weren't, and I've been sending them every secret I could write down from my investigations of Dataset.'

'My brother is alive, Pilgrim,' Johanna said.

'Oh . . . You're kind of a record setter for treason aren't you. Vendacious? Everything to us was a lie, while Steel learned all the truth about us. You figure that means we daren't kill you now?'

Laughter, and Vendacious's pacing stopped. *He sees control coming back to him.* 'More, you need my full-membered cooperation. See, I exaggerated the number of enemy agents in Woodcarver's troops, but I do have a few – and maybe Steel has planted others I don't know about. If you even arrest me, word will get back to the Flenser armies. Much of what I know will be useless – and you'll face an immediate, overwhelming attack. You see? The Queen *needs* me.'

'And how do we know this is not more lies?'

'That is a problem, isn't it? Matched only by how I can be guaranteed safety once I've saved the expedition. No doubt it's beyond your mongrel mind. Woodcarver and I must have a talk, someplace mutually safe and unseen. Carry *that* message back to her. She can't have this traitor's hides, but if she cooperates she may be able to save her own!'

There was silence from outside, punctuated by the squeaking of animals in the nearer trees. Finally, surprisingly, Pilgrim laughed. 'Mongrel mind, eh? Well, you have me in one thing, Vendacious. I've been all the world round, and I remember back half a thousand years – but of all the villains and traitors and geniuses, you take the record for bald impudence!'

Vendacious gave a Tinish chord, untranslatable but as a sign of smug pleasure. 'I'm honored.'

'Very well, I'll take your points back to the Queen. I hope

the two of you are clever enough to work something out . . . One thing more: the Queen requires that Johanna come with me.'

'The Queen requires? That sounds more like your mongrel sentiment to me.'

'Perhaps. But it will prove you are serious in your confidence. View it as *my* price for cooperation.'

Vendacious turned all his heads toward Johanna, silently regarding. Then he scanned out all the windows one last time. 'Very well, you may have her.' Two jumped down to the cabin's hatch while another pair pulled her toward it. His voice was soft and near her ear. 'Damn Pilgrim. Alive, you're just going to cause me trouble with the Queen.' His knife slid across her field of view. 'Don't oppose me with her. I am going to survive this affair still powerful.'

He lifted back the hatch and daylight spilled blindingly across her face. She squinted; there was a sweep of branches and the side of the hut. Vendacious pushed and pulled her cot onto the forest floor, and the same time gobbling at his guards to keep their positions. He and Peregrine chatted politely, agreeing on when the pilgrim would return.

One by one, Vendacious trotted back through the cabin's hatch. Pilgrim advanced and grabbed the handles at the front of the cot. One of his pups reached out from his jacket to nuzzled her face. 'You okay?'

, 'I'm not sure. I got bashed in the head . . . and it seems kind of hard to breathe.'

He loosened the blankets from around her chest as the rest of him dragged the cot away from the hut. The forest shade was peaceful and deep, and . . . Vendacious's guards were stationed here and there about the area. How many were really in on the treason? Two hours ago, Johanna had looked to them for protection. Now their every glance sent a shiver through her. She rolled back to the center of the cot, dizzy again, and stared up into the branches and leaves and patches of smoke-stained sky. Things like Straumli tree squigglies chased each other back and forth, chittering in seeming debate.

Funny. Almost a year ago Pilgrim and Scriber were dragging me

*around, and I was even worse hurt, and terrified of everything –
including them..* And now . . . she had never been so glad to see
another person. Even Scarbutt was a reassuring strength
walking beside her.

The waves of terror slowly subsided. What was left was an
anger as intense, though more reasoning, than the year
before. She *knew* what had happened here; the players were
not strangers, the betrayal was not random murder. After all
Vendacious's treachery, after all his murders, and his planning to kill them all . . . he was going to go *free!* Pilgrim and
Woodcarver were just going to *overlook* that. 'He killed
Scriber, Pilgrim. He killed Scriber . . .' *He cut Scriber to pieces,
then chased down what was left and killed that right out of our
arms.* 'And Woodcarver is going to let him go free? How can
she do it? How can you do it?' The tears were coming again.

'Sh, sh.' Two of Pilgrim's heads came into view. They
looked down at her, then swiveled around almost nervously.
She reached out, touching the short plush fur. Pilgrim was
shivering! One of him dipped close; his voice didn't sound
jaunty at all. 'I don't know what the Queen will do, Johanna.
She doesn't know about any of this.'

'Wha –'

'Sh.' And his voice became scarcely a buzzing through her
hand. 'His people can still see us. He could still figure things
out . . . Only you and I know, Johanna. I don't think anyone
else suspects.'

'But the pack that confessed . . . ? '

'Bluff, all bluff. I've done some crazy things in my life but
next to following Scriber down to your starship, this takes the
prize . . . After Vendacious took you away, I began to think.
You weren't that badly injured. It was all too much like what
happened to Jaqueramaphan, but I had no proof.'

'And you haven't told anyone?'

'No. Foolish as poor Scriber, aren't I?' His heads looked in
all directions 'If I was right, he'd be silly not to kill you
immediately. I was so afraid I was already too late . . .'

*You would have been, if Vendacious weren't quite the monster I
know he is.*

'Anyway, I learned the truth just like poor Scriber – almost

452

by accident. But if we can get another seventy meters away, we won't die like him. And everything I claimed to Vendacious will be *true*.'

She patted his nearest shoulder and looked back. The tiny cabin and its ring of guards disappeared behind the forest brush.

. . . and Jefri *lives!*

Crypto: 0
  [95 encrypted packets have been discarded]
As received by: *Ølvira* shipboard ad hoc
Language path: Tredeschk→Triskweline, SjK units
From: Zonograph Eidolon
  [Co-op (or religious order) in the Middle Beyond
  maintained by subscription of several thousand Low
  Beyond civilizations, in particular those threatened
  by immersion]
Subject: Surge Bulletin Update and Ping
Distribution:
  Zonograph Eidolon Subscribers
  Zonometric Interest Group
  Threats Interest Group, subgroup: navigational Ping
  participants
Date: 1087892301 seconds since Calibration Event
  239011, Eidolon Frame
  [66.91 days since Fall of Sjandra Kei]
Key phrases: galactic scale event, superluminal,
  charitable emergency announcement
Text of message:
  (Please include accurate local time in any ping
responses.)
  If you receive this, you know that the monster surge
has receded. The new zone surface appears to be a
stable froth of low dimensionality (between 2.1 and
2.3). At least five civilizations are trapped in the new
configuration. Thirty virgin solar systems have
achieved the Beyond. (Subscribers may find specifics
in the encrypted data that follow this bulletin.)
  The change corresponds to what is seen in a normal

period of two years across the whole galaxy's Slow Zone surface. Yet this surge happened in less than two hundred hours and on less than one thousandth of that surface.

Even these numbers do not show the scale of the event. (The following can only be estimates, since so many sites were destroyed, and no instruments were calibrated for this size event.) At its maximum, the surge reached 1000 light-years above Zone Surface Standard. Surge rates of more than thirty million times lightspeed [about one light-year per second] were sustained for periods of more than 100 seconds. Reports from subscribers show more than ten billion sophont deaths directly attributable to the Surge (local network failures, failures leading to environment collapse, medical collapse, vehicle crashes, security failures). Posted economic damage is much greater.

The important question now is what can we expect in aftersurges. Our predictions are based on instrumented sites and zonometric surveys, combined with historical data from our archives. Except for long-term trends, predicting zone changes has never been a science, but we have served our subscribers well in advising of aftersurges and in identifying available new worlds. Unfortunately, the present situation makes all previous work almost useless. We have precise documentation going back ten million years. Faster than light surges happen about every twenty thousand years (usually with speed under 7.0c). Nothing like this monster is on file. The surge just seen is the kind described at third-hand in old and glutted databases: Sculptor had one this size fifty million years ago. The [Perseus Arm] in our galaxy probably suffered something like this half a billion years ago.

This uncertainty makes our Mission nearly impossible, and is an important reason for this public message to the Zonometry newsgroup and others: Everyone interested in zonometry and navigation must pool resources on this problem. Ideas, archive access, algorithms – all these things could help. We pledge significant contributions to non-subscribers, and one-for-one trades to those with important information. Note: We are also addressing this message to the Swndwp oracle, and direct beaming it to points in the Transcend thought to be inhabited. Surely an event such as this must be of interest even there? We appeal to the Powers Above: Let us send you what we know. Give us some hint if you have ideas about this event.

To demonstrate our good faith, here are the estimates we have currently. These are based on naïve scale-up of well-documented surges in this region. Details are in the non-crypted appendix to this sending. Over the next year there will be five or six aftersurges, of diminishing speed and range. During this time at least two more civilizations (see risk list) will likely be permanently immersed. Zone storm conditions will prevail even when aftersurges are not in progress. Navigation in the volume [coordinate specification] will be extremely dangerous during this period; we recommend that shipping in the volume be suspended. The time line is probably too short to admit feasible rescue plans for the civilizations at risk. Our long-range prediction (probably the least uncertain of all): The million-year-scale secular shrinkage will not be affected at all. The next hundred thousand years will however show a retardation in the shrinkage of the Slow Zone boundary in this portion of the galaxy.

Finally, a philosophical note. We of Zonographic Eidolon watch the zone boundary and the orbits of border stars. For the most part, the zone changes are very slow: 700 meters per second in the case of the long-term secular shrinkage. Yet these changes together with orbital motion affect billions of lives each year. Just as the glaciers and droughts of a pretechnical world must affect a people, so must we accept these long-term changes. Storms and surges are obvious tragedies, near-instant death for some civilizations. Yet these are as far beyond our control as the slower movements. Over the last few weeks, some newsgroups have been full of tales of war and battle fleets, of billions dying in the clash of species. To all such – and those living more peaceably around them – we say: Look out on the universe. It does not care, and even with all our science there are some disasters that we can not avert. All evil and good is petty before Nature. Personally, we take comfort from this, that there is a universe to admire that cannot be twisted to villainy or good, but which simply *is*.

Crypto: 0
As received by: *Ølvira* shipboard ad hoc
Language path: Arbwyth→Trade 24→
    Cherguelin→Triskweline, SjK units
From: Twirlip of the Mists
    [Who knows what this is, though probably not a
    propaganda voice. Very sparse priors.]
Subject: The cause of the recent Great Surge
Distribution:
    Threat of the Blight
    Great Secrets of Creation
    Zonometric Interest Group
Date: 66.47 days since Fall of Sjandra Kei
Key phrases: Zone Instability and the Blight,
    Hexapodia as the key insight
Test of message:
    Apologies if I am repeating obvious conclusions. My only gateway onto the Net is very expensive, and I miss many important postings. The Great Surge now in progress appears by all accounts to be an event of cosmic scope and rarity. Furthermore, the other posters put its epicenter less than 6,000 light-years from recent warfare related to the Blight. Can this be mere coincidence? As has long been theorized [citations from various sources, three unknown to *Ølvira*; the theories cited are of long standing and nondisprovable], the Zones themselves may be an artifact,

456

perhaps created by something beyond Transcendence for the protection of lesser forms or [hypothetical] sentient gas clouds in galactic cores.

Now for the first time in Net history we have a Transcendent form, the Blight, that can effectively dominate the Beyond. Many on the Net [cites Hanse and Sandor at the Zoo] believe that it is searching for an artifact near the Bottom. Is it no wonder that this could upset the Natural Balance and provoke the recent Event?

Please write to me and tell me what you think. I don't get much mail.

Crypto: 0
As received by: *Ølvira* shipboard ad hoc
Language path: Baeloresk→Triskweline, SjK units
From: Alliance for the Defense
    [Claimed union of five empires below Straumli
    Realm. No references prior to the Fall of the Straumli
    Realm. Numerous counter claims (including from
    Out of Band II) that this Alliance is a front for the old
    Aprahant Hegemony. Cf, *Butterfly Terror*.]
Subject: Courageous Mission Accomplished
Distribution:
    Threat of the Blight
    War Trackers Interest Group
    Homo Sapiens Interest Group
Date: 67.07 days since Fall of Sjandra Kei
Key phrases: Action, not talk
Text of message:
    Subsequent to our action against the human nest at [Sjandra Kei] a part of our fleet pursued human and other Blight-controlled forces toward the Bottom of the Beyond. Evidently, the Perversion hoped to protect these forces by putting them in an environment too dangerous to challenge. That thinking did not count on the courage of Alliance commanders and crews. We can now report the substantial destruction of

those escaping forces.

The first major operation of your Alliance has been an enormous success. With the extermination of their most important supporters, Blight encroachment on the Middle Beyond has been brought to a standstill. Yet much remains to be done:

The Alliance Fleet is returning to the Middle Beyond. We've suffered some casualties and need substantial reprovisioning. We know that there are still scattered pockets of humanity in the Beyond, and we've identified secondary races that are aiding humanity. The defense of the Middle Beyond must be the goal of every sophont of good will. Elements of your Alliance Fleet will soon visit systems in the volume [parameter specification]. We ask for your aid and support against what is left of this terrible enemy.

Death to vermin.

36

Kjet Svensndot was alone on *Ølvira*'s bridge when the Surge passed. They had long since done all the preparations that were meaningful, and the ship had no realistic means of propulsion in the Slowness that surrounded it. Yet the Group Captain spent much of his time up here, trying to program some sort of responsiveness into the automation that remained. Half-assed programming was a time-filler that, like knitting, must date to the beginning of the human experience.

Of course, the actual transition out of Slowness would have been totally unnoticed if not for all the alarms he and the Dirokimes had installed. As it was, the noise and lights blew him out of a half-drowse into hair-raised wakefulness. He punched the ship's comm: 'Glimfrelle! Tirolle! Get your tails up here.'

By the time the brothers reached the command deck, preliminary nav displays had been computed and a jump sequence was awaiting confirmation. The two were grinning from ear to ear as they bounced in and strapped themselves down at action posts. For a few moments there was little chitchat, only an occasional whistle of pleasure from the Dirokimes. They had rehearsed this over and over during the last hundred plus hours, and with the poor automation there was a lot for them to do. Gradually the view from the deck's windows sharpened. Where at first there had only been vague blurs, the ultrawave sensors were posting individual traces with steadily improving information on range and rates. The communication window showed the queue of fleet comm messages getting longer and longer.

Tirolle looked up from his work 'Hei, Boss, these jump figures look okay – at least as a first cut.'

'Good. Commit and allow autocommit.' In the hours after the Surge, they had decided that their initial priority should be to continue with the pursuit. What they did then . . . they had talked long on that, and Group Captain Svensndot had thought even longer. Nothing was routine any more.

'Yes, *sir!*' The Dirokime's longfingers danced across the controls, and 'Rolle added some verbal control. 'Bingo!'

Status showed five jumps completed, ten. Kjet stared out the true-view window for a few seconds. No change, no change . . . then he noticed that one of the brightest stars in the field had moved, was sliding imperceptibly across the sky. Like a juggler getting her pace, *Ølvira* was coming up to speed.

'Hei, hei!' Glimfrelle leaned over to see his brother's work. 'We're making 1.2 light-years per hour. That's better than before the Surge.'

'Good. Comm and Surveillance?' Where was everybody *else* and what were they up to?

'Yup. Yup. I'm on it.' Glimfrelle bent his slender frame back to the console. For some seconds, he was almost silent. Svensndot began paging through the mail. There was nothing yet from Owner Limmende. Twenty-five years Kjet had worked for Limmende and SjK Commercial Security. Could he mutiny? And if he did, would any follow?

'Okay. Here's the situation, Boss.' Glimfrelle shifted the

main window to show his interpretation of the ship's reports. 'It's like we guessed, maybe a little more extreme.' They had realized almost from the beginning that the surge was bigger than anything in recorded history; that's not what the Dirokime meant by 'extreme.' He swept his shortfingers down, making a hazy blue line across the window. 'We guessed that the leading edge of the Surge moved normal to this line. That would account for it taking Boss Limmende out four hundred seconds before it hit the *Out of Band*, and hitting us ten seconds after that . . . Now if the trailing edge were similar to ordinary surges' – upgraded a million times – 'then we, and then the rest of the pursuing fleets should come out well before *Out of Band*.' He pointed at a single glowing dot that represented the *Ølvira*. Around and just ahead of it dozens of points of light were popping into existence as the ship's detectors reported seeing the initiation of ultradrive jumps. It was like a cold fire sweeping away from them into the darkness. Eventually Limmende and the heart of the anonymous fleet would all be back in business. 'Our pickup log shows that's about what happened. Most all the pursuing fleets will be out of the surge before the *Out of Band*.'

'Hm. So it'll lose part of its lead.'

'Yup. But if it's going where we think –' a G-star eighty light-years ahead of the fugitive. '– it'll still get there before they kill it.' He paused, pointed at a haze that was spreading sideways from the growing knot of light. 'Not everybody is still chasing.'

'Yeah . . .' Svensndot had been reading the News even as he listened to 'Frelle's summary. '. . . according to the Net, that's the Alliance for the Defense departing the battle field, victorious.'

'Say *what?*' Tirolle twisted abruptly in his harness. His large, dark eyes held none of their usual humor.

'You heard me.' Kjet put the item where the brothers could see it. The two read rapidly, 'Frelle mumbling phrases aloud, '. . . *courage* of Alliance commanders . . . *substantial* destruction of escaping forces . . .'

Glimfrelle shuddered, all flippany departed. 'They don't even mention the Surge. Everything they say is a cowardly lie!

his voice shifted up to its normal speaking range and he continued in his own language. Kjet could understand parts of it. The Dirokimes that left their dream habitats were normally lighthearted folk, full of whimsy and gentle sarcasm. Glimfrelle sounded almost that way now, except for the high edges to his whistling and the insults more colorful than Svensndot had ever heard from them: '. . . get from a verminous cow-pie . . . killers of innocent dreams . . .' even in Samnorsk the words were strong, but in Dirokime 'verminous cow-pie' was drenched in explicit imagery that almost brought the smell of such a thing into the room. Glimfrelle's voice went higher and higher, then beyond the human register. Abruptly he collapsed, shuddering and moaning low. Dirokimes could cry, though Svensndot had never seen such a thing before. Glimfrelle rocked in his brother's arms.

Tirolle looked over Glimfrelle's shoulder at Kjet. 'Where does revenge take us now, Group Captain?'

For a moment, Kjet looked back silently. 'I'll let you know, Lieutenant.' He looked at the displays. *Listen and watch a little longer, and maybe we'll know.* 'Meantime, get us nearer the center of pursuit,' he said gently.

'Aye, sir.' Tirolle patted his brother's back gently and returned to his console.

During the next five hours, *Ølvira*'s crew watched the Alliance fleet race helter-skelter for the higher spaces. It could not even be called a retreat, more a panicked dissolution. Great opportunists, they had not hesitated to kill by treachery, and to give chase when they thought there might be treasure at the end. Now that they were confronted with the possibility of being trapped in the Slowness, of dying between the stars, they raced for their separate safety. Their bulletins to the newsgroups were full of bravado, but their maneuver couldn't be disguised. Former neutrals pointed to the discrepancy; more and more it was accepted that the Alliance was built around the Aprahanti Hegemony and perhaps had other motives than altruistic opposition to the Blight. There was nervous speculation about who might next receive

Alliance attention.

Major transceivers still targeted the fleets. They might as well have been on a network trunk. The news traffic was a vast waterfall, totally beyond *Ølvira*'s present ability to receive. Nevertheless, Svensndot kept an eye on it. Somewhere there might be some clue, some insight . . . The majority of War Trackers and Threats seemed to have little interest in the Alliance or the death of Sjandra Kei, per se. Most were terrified of the Blight that was still spreading through the Top of the Beyond. None of the Highest had successfully resisted, and there were rumors that two more interfering Powers had been destroyed. There were some (secret mouths of the Blight?) who welcomed the new stability at the Top, even one based on permanent parasitization.

In fact, the chase down here at the Bottom, the flight of the *Out of Band* and its pursuers, seemed the only place where the Blight was not completely triumphant. No wonder they were the subject of 10,000 messages an hour.

The geometry of emergence was enormously favorable to *Ølvira*. They had been on the outskirts of the action, but now they had hours headstart on the main fleets. Glimfrelle and Tirolle were busier than they had ever been in their lives, monitoring the fleets' emergence and establishing *Ølvira*'s identity with the other vessels of Commercial Security. Until Scrits and Limmende emerged from the Slowness, Kjet Svensndot was the ranking officer of the organization. Furthermore, he was personally known to most of the commanders. Kjet had never been the admiral type; his Group Captaincy had been a reward for piloting skills, in a Sjandra Kei at peace. He had always been content to defer to his employers. But now . . .

The Group Captain used his ranking status. The Alliance vessels were not pursued. ('Wait till we can all act together,' ordered Svensndot.) Possible game plans bounced back and forth across the emerging fleet, including schemes that assumed HQ was destroyed. With certain commanders, Kjet hinted that this last might be the case, that Limmende's flag ship was in enemy hands, and that the Alliance was somehow just a side effect of that true enemy. Very soon Kjet would be committed to the 'treason' he planned.

The Limmende flag ships and the core of the Blighter fleet came out of the Slowness almost simultaneously. Comm alarms went off across *Ølvira*'s deck as priority mail arrived and passed through the ship's crypto. 'Source: Limmende at HQ. Star Breaker Priority,' said the ship's voice.

Glimfrelle put the message on the main window, and Svensndot felt a chill certainty spread up his neck.

> . . . All units are to pursue fleeing vessels. These are the enemy, the killers of our people. WARNING: Masquerades suspected. Destroy any vessels countermanding these orders. Order of Battle and validation codes follow . . .

Order of Battle was simple, even by Commercial Security standards. Limmende wanted them to split up and be gone, staying only long enough to destroy 'masqueraders.' Kjet said to Glimfrelle, 'How about the validation codes?'

The Dirokime seemed his usual self again: 'They're clean. We wouldn't be receiving the message at all unless the sender had today's one-time pad . . . We're beginning to receive queries from the others, Boss. Audio and video channels. They want to know what to do.'

If he hadn't prepared the ground during the last few hours, Kjet's mutiny wouldn't have had a chance. If Commercial Security had been a real military organization, the Limmende order might have been obeyed without question. As it was, the other commanders pondered the questions that Svensndot had raised: At these ranges, video communication was easy and the fleet had one-time ciphers large enough to support enormous amounts of it. Yet 'Limmende' had chosen printed mail for her priority message. It made perfect military sense given that the encryption was correct, but it was also what Svensndot had predicted: The supposed HQ was not quite willing to show its face down here where perfect visual masquerades were not possible. Their commands would be by mail, or evocations that any sharp observer might suspect.

Such a slender thread of reason Kjet and his friends were

hanging from.

Kjet eyed the knot of light that represented the Blighter fleet. *It* was suffering from no indecision. None of *its* vessels were straggling back toward safer heights. Whatever commanded there had discipline beyond most human militaries. It would sacrifice everything in its single-minded pursuit of one small starship. *What next, Group Captain?*

Just ahead of that cold smear of light, a single tiny gleam appeared. 'The *Out of Band*!' said Glimfrelle. 'Sixty-five light-years out now.'

'I'm getting encrypted video from them, Boss. The same half-crocked xor pad as before.' He put the signal on the main window without waiting for Kjet's direction.

It was Ravna Bergsndot. The background was a jumble of motion and shouting, the strange human and a Skroderider arguing. Bergsndot was facing away from the pickup and doing her share of shouting. Things looked even worse than Kjet's recollection of the first moments of his ship's emergence.

'It doesn't *matter* just now, I tell you! Let him be. We've got to contact –' she must have seen the signal Glimfrelle was sending back to her. 'They're here! By the Powers, Pham, please –' She waved her hand angrily and turned to the camera. 'Group Captain. We're –'

'I know. We've been out of the surge for hours. We're near the center of the pursuit now.'

She caught her breath. Even with a hundred hours of planning, events were moving too fast for her. *And for me too*. 'That's something,' she said after an instant. 'Everything we said before holds, Group Captain. We need your help. That's the Blight that's coming behind us. Please!'

Svensndot noticed a telltale by the window. Sassy Glimfrelle was retransmitting this to all the fleet they could trust. *Good*. He had talked about the situation with the others these last hours, but it meant something more to see Ravna Bergsndot on the comm, to see someone from Straumli who still survived and needed their help. *You can spend the rest of your life chasing revenge in the Middle Beyond, but all you kill will be the vultures. What's chasing Ravna Bergsndot may be the first cause.*

The Butterflies were long gone, still singing their courage across the Net. Less than one percent of Commercial Security had followed 'Limmende's' order to chase after them. Those were not the problem: it was the ten percent that stayed behind and arrayed themselves with the Blight's forces that bothered Kjet Svensndot. Some of those ships might not be subverted, might simply be loyal to orders they believed. It would be very hard to fire on them.

And there would be fighting, no doubt of that. Maneuvering for conflict while under ultradrive was difficult – if the other side attempted to evade. But the Blight's fleet was unwavering in its pursuit of the *Out of Band*. Slowly, slowly the two fleets were coming to occupy the same volume. At present they were scattered across cubic light-years, but with every jump the Group Captain's Aniara fleet was more finely tuned to the stutter of their quarries' drives. Some ships were actually within a few hundred million kilometers of the enemy – or where the enemy had been or would be. Targeting tactics were set. First fire was only a few hundred seconds away.

'With the Aprahanti gone, we have numerical superiority. A normal enemy would back off now –'

'But of course, that is one thing the Blight fleet is *not*.' It was the red-haired guy who was doing the talking now. It was a good thing Glimfrelle hadn't relayed *his* face to the rest of Svensndot's fleet. The guy acted edgy and alien most of the time. Just now he seemed intent on bashing every idea Svensndot advanced. 'The Blight doesn't care what its losses are as long as it arrives with the upper hand.'

Svensndot shrugged. 'Look, we'll do our best. First fire is one hundred and fifty seconds off. If they don't have any secret advantage, we may win this one.' He looked sharply at the other. 'Or is that your point? Could the Blight –' Stories were still coming down about the Blight's progress across the Top of the Beyond. Without a doubt it was a transhuman intelligence. An unarmed man might be outnumbered by a pack of dogs, yet still defeat them. So might the Blight . . . ?

Pham Nuwen shook his head. 'No, no, no. The Blight's

tactics down here will probably be *inferior* to yours. Its great advantage is at the Top, where it can control its slaves like fingers on a hand. Its creatures down here are like badly-synched waldos.' Nuwen frowned at something off camera. 'No, what we have to fear is its strategic cleverness.' His voice suddenly had a detached quality that was more unsettling than the earlier impatience. It wasn't the calm of someone facing up to a threat; it was more the calm of the demented. 'One hundred seconds to contact... Group Captain, we have a chance, if you concentrate your forces on the right points.' Ravna floated down from the top of the picture, put one hand on the red-head's shoulder. Godshatter, she said he was, their secret edge against the enemy. Godshatter, a Power's dying message; garbage or treasure, who really knew?

Damn. If the other guys are badly-synched waldos, what does following Pham Nuwen make us? But he motioned Tirolle to mark the targets that Nuwen was saying. Ninety seconds. Decision time. Kjet pointed at the red marks Tirolle had scattered through the enemy fleet. 'Anything special about those targets, 'Rolle?'

The Dirokime whistled for a moment. Correlations popped up agonizingly slowly on the windows before him. 'The ships he's targetting aren't the biggest or the fastest. It's gonna take extra time to position on them.' Command vessels? 'One other thing. Some of 'em show high real velocities, not natural residuals at all.' Ships with ram drives? Planet busters?

'Hm.' Svensndot looked at the display just a second more. Thirty seconds and Jo Haugen's ship *Lynsnar* would be in contact, but not with one of Nuwen's targets. 'Get on the comm, Glimfrelle. Tell *Lynsnar* to back off, retarget.' Retarget everything.

The lights that were Aniara fleet slid slowly around the core of the Blighter fleet, searching for their new targets. Twenty minutes passed, and not a few arguments with the other captains. Commercial Security was not built for military combat. What had made Kjet Svensndot's appeal successful was also the cause of constant questioning and counter-

466

suggestions. And then there were the threats that came from Owner Limmende's channel: kill the mutineers, death to all those disloyal to the company. The encryption was valid but the tone was totally alien to the mild, profit-oriented Giske Limmende. Everyone could now see that disbelieving Limmende was one correct decision, anyway.

Johanna Haugen was the first to achieve synch with the new targets. Glimfrelle opened the main window on the *Lynsnar*'s data stream: The view was almost natural, a night sky of slowly shifting stars. The target was less than thirty million kilometers from *Lynsnar*, but about a millisecond out of synch. Haugen was arriving just before or just after the other had jumped.

'Drones away,' Haugen's voice said. Now they had a true view of *Lynsnar* from a few meters away, from a camera aboard one of the first drones launched. The ship was barely visible, a darkness obscuring the stars beyond – a great fish in the depths of an endless sea. A fish that was now giving spawn. The picture flickered, *Lynsnar* disappearing and reappearing as the drone lost synch momentarily. A swarm of blue lights spilled from the ship's hold. Weapon drones. The swarm hung by *Lynsnar*, calibrating itself orienting on the enemy.

The light faded from around *Lynsnar* as the drones moved fractionally out of synch in space and time. Tirolle opened a window on a hundred-million klick sphere centered at *Lynsnar*. The target vessel was a red dot that flickered around the sphere like a maddened insect. *Lynsnar* was stalking prey at eight thousand times the speed of light. Sometimes the target disappeared for a second, synch almost lost; other times *Lynsnar* and the target merged for an instant as the two craft spent a tenth of a second at less than a million kilometers remove. What could not be accurately displayed was the disposition of the drones. The spawn diffused on a myriad trajectories, their sensors extended for sign of the enemy ship.

'What about the target, is it swarming back? Do you need backup?' said Svensndot. Tirolle gave a Dirokime shrug. What they were watching was three light-years away. No way he could know.

But Jo Haugen replied, 'I don't think my bogie is swarming. I've lost only five drones, no more'n you'd expect from near misses. We'll see –' She paused, but *Lynsnar's* trace and signal remained strong. Kjet looked out the other windows. Five of Aniara were already engaged and three had completed swarm deploy. Nuwen looked on silently from *Out of Band*. The godshatter had had its way, and now Kjet and his people were committed.

And now good news and bad came in very fast:

'Got him!' from Jo Haugen. The red dot in *Lynsnar's* swarm was no more. It had passed within a few thousand kilometers of one of the drones. In the milliseconds necessary to compute a new jump, the drone had discovered its presence and detonated. Even that would not have been fatal if the target had jumped before the blast front hit it; there had been several near misses in earlier seconds. This time the jump did not reach commit in time. A mini-star was born, one whose light would be years in reaching the rest of the battle volume.

Glimfrelle gave a rasping whistle, an untranslatable curse. 'We just lost *Ablsndot* and *Holder*, Boss. Their target must have counter-swarmed.'

'Send in *Gliwing* and *Trance*.' Something in the back of his head curled up in a knot of horror. These were his friends who were dying. Kjet had seen death before, but never like this. In police action no one took lethal chances except in a rescue. And yet . . . he turned from the field summary to order more ships on a target that had acquired defending vessels. Tirolle was moving in others on his own. Ganging up a few nonessential targets might lose in the long run, but in the short term . . . the enemy was being hurt. For the first time since the fall of Sjandra Kei, Commercial Security was hurting someone back.

Haugen: 'Powers, that guy was moving! Secondary drone got EM spectrum on the kill. Target was going 15,000 kps true speed.' A rocket bomb ramping up? Damn. They should be postponing those till *after* they controlled the battlefield.

Tirolle: 'More kills, far side of battle volume. The enemy is repositioning. Somehow they've guessed which we're after –'

Glimfrelle: *Triumph whistle.* 'Get 'em, get 'em – oops. Boss, I think Limmende has figured we're coordinating things –'

A new window had opened over Tirolle's post. It showed the five million kilometers around *Ølvira*. Two other ships were there now: the window identified them as Limmende's flag and one of the vessels that had not responded to Svensndot's recruiting.

There was an instant of stillness on *Ølvira*'s command deck. The voices of triumph and panic coming from the rest of the fleet seemed suddenly far away. Svensndot and his crew looked at death close up. 'Tirolle! How long till swarm –'

'They're on us already – just missed a drone by ten milliseconds.'

'Tirolle! Finish running current engagements. Glimfrelle, tell *Lynsnar* and *Trance* to chain command if we lose contact.' Those ships had already spent their drones, and Jo Haugen was known to all the other captains.

Then the thought was gone, and he was busy coordinating *Ølvira*'s own battle swarm. The local tactics window showed the cloud dissipating, taking on colors coded by whether they were lagging or leading relative to *Ølvira*.

Their two attackers had matched pseudospeeds perfectly. Ten times per second all three ships jumped a tiny fraction of a light-year. Like rocks skipping across the surface of a pond, they appeared in real space in perfectly measured hops – and the distance between them at every emergence was less than five million kilometers. The only thing that separated them now were millisecond differences in jump times and the fact the light itself could not pass between them in the brief time they spent at each jump point.

Three actinic flashes lit the deck, casting shadows back from Svensndot and the Dirokimes. It was second-hand light, the display's emergency signal of nearby detonation. *Run like hell* was the message any rational person should take from that awful light. It would be easy enough to break synch . . . and lose tactical control of Aniara fleet. Tirolle and Glimfrelle bent their heads away from the local window, shying from the glare of nearby death. Their whistling voices scarcely broke cadence, and the commands from *Ølvira* to the others continued. There were dozens of other battles going on out there. Just now *Ølvira* was the only source of precision and control available to their side. Every second they remained on station meant protection and advantage to Aniara. Breaking off would mean minutes of chaos till *Lynsnar* or *Trance* could pick up control.

Nearly two thirds of Pham Nuwen's targets were destroyed now. The price had been high, half of Svensndot's friends. The enemy had lost much to protect those targets, yet much of its fleet survived.

An unseen hand smashed *Ølvira*, driving Svensndot hard against his combat harness. The lights went out, even the glow from the windows. Then dim red light came from the floor. The Dirokimes were silhouetted by one small monitor. 'Rolle whistled softly, 'We're out of the game, Boss, least while it counts. I didn't know you could get misses that near.'

Maybe it wasn't a miss. Kjet scrambled out of his harness and boosted across the room to float head-down over the tiny monitor. *Maybe we're already dead.* Somewhere very close by a drone had detonated, the wave front reaching *Ølvira* before she jumped. The concussion had been the outer part of the ship's hull exploding as it absorbed the soft-x-ray component of the enemy ordnance. He stared at the red letters marching slowly across the damage display. Most likely, the electronics was permanently dead; chances were they had all received a fatal dose of gamma. The smell of burnt insulation floated across the room on the ventilator's breeze.

'*Iiya!* Look at that. Five nanoseconds more and we wouldn't have been clipped at all. We actually jumped *after* the front hit!' And somehow the electronics had survived long enough to complete the jump. The gamma flux through the command deck had been 200 rem, nothing that would slow them down over the next few hours, and easily managed by a ship's surgeon. As for the surgeon and all the rest of the *Ølvira*'s automation . . .

Tirolle typed several long queries at the box; there was no voice recognition left. Several seconds passed before a response marched across the screen. 'Central automation suspended. Display management suspended. Drive computation suspended.' Tirolle dug an elbow at his brother. 'Hei, 'Frelle, it looks like *'Vira* managed a clean disconnect. We can bring most of this back!'

Dirokimes were known for being drifty optimists, but in this case Tirolle wasn't far from the truth. Their encounter with the drone bomb had been a one-in-a-billion thing, the tiniest fraction of an exposure. Over the next hour and a half the Dirokimes ran reboots off the monitor's hardened processor, bringing up first one utility and then another. Some things were beyond recovery: parsing intelligence was gone from the comm automation, and the ultradrive spines on one side of the craft were partially melted. (Absurdly, the burning smell had been a vagrant diagnostic, something that should have been disabled along with all the rest of *Økvira*'s automation.) They were far behind the Blighter fleet.

. . . and there *was* still a Blighter fleet. The knot of enemy lights was smaller than before, but on the same unwavering trajectory. The battle was long over. What was left of Commercial Security was scattered across four light-years of abandoned battlefield; they had started the battle with numerical superiority. If they'd fought properly, they might have won. Instead they'd destroyed the vessels with significant real velocities – and knocked out only about half the others. Some of the largest vessels survived. These outnumbered the corresponding Aniara survivors by more than four to one. The Blight could have easily destroyed all that remained of Commercial Security. But that would have meant a detour from the pursuit, and that pursuit was the one constant in the enemy's behavior.

Tirolle and Glimfrelle spent hours reestablishing communications and trying to discover who had died and who might be rescued. Five ships had lost all drive capability but still had surviving crew. Some ships had been hit at known locations, and Svensndot dispatched vessels with drone swarms to find the wrecks. Ship-to-ship warfare was a sanitary, intellectual exercise for most of the survivors, but the rubble and the destruction were as real as in any ground war, only spread over a trillion times more space.

Finally the time for miracle rescues and sad discoveries was passed. The SjK commanders gathered on a common channel to decide a common future. It might better have been a wake – for Sjandra Kei and Aniara fleet. Partway through the meeting a new window appeared, a view onto the bridge of the *Out of Band*. Ravna Bergsndot watched the proceedings silently. The erstwhile 'godshatter' was nowhere in evidence.

'What more to do?' said Johanna Haugen. 'The damn Butterflies are long gone.'

'Are we sure we have rescued everyone?' asked Jan Trenglets. Svensndot bit back an angry reply. The commander of *Trance* had become a recording loop on that issue. He had lost too many friends in the battle; all the rest of his life Jan Trenglets would live with nightmares of ships slowly dying in the deep night.

'We've accounted for everything, even to vapor,' Haugen spoke as gently as the words allowed. 'The question is where to go now.'

Ravna made a small throat-clearing sound. 'Gentlemen and ladies, if –'

Trenglets looked up at her transceived image. All his hurt transformed into a blaze of anger. 'We're not *your* gentlemen, slut! You're not some princess we happily die for. You deserve our deadly fire now, nothing more.'

The woman shrank from Trenglets' rage. 'I –'

'*You* put us into this suicidal battle,' shouted Trenglets. 'You made us attack secondary targets. And then you did nothing to help. The Blight is locked on you like a dumshark on a squid. If you had just altered your course the tiniest fraction, you could have thrown the Blighters off our path.'

'I doubt that would have helped, sir,' said Ravna. 'The Blight seems most interested in where we're bound.' The solar system a few dozen light-years beyond the *Out of Band*. The fugitives would arrive there just over two days before their pursuers.

Jo Haugen shrugged. 'You must realize what your friend's

crazy battle plan has done. If we had attacked rationally, the enemy would be a fraction of its present size. If it chose to continue, we might have been able to protect you at this, this Tines' world.' She seemed to taste the strange name, wondering at its meaning. 'Now . . . no way am I going to chase them there. What's left of the enemy could wipe us out.' She glanced at Svensndot's viewpoint. Kjet forced himself to look back. No matter who might blame the *Out of Band*, it had been Group Captain Kjet Svensndot's word that had persuaded the fleet to fight as they did. Aniara's sacrifice had been ill-spent, and he wondered that Haugen and Trenglets and the others talked to him at all now. 'Suggest we continue the business meeting later. Rendezvous in one thousand seconds, Kjet.'

'I'll be ready.'

'Good.' Jo cut the link without saying anything more to Ravna Bergsndot. Seconds later, Trenglets and the other commanders were gone. It was just Svensndot and the two Dirokimes – and Ravna Bergsndot looking out her window from the *Out of Band*.

Finally, Bergsndot said, 'When I was a little girl on Herte, sometimes we would play kidnappers and Commercial Security. I always dreamed of being rescued from fates worse than death by your company.'

Kjet smiled bleakly, 'Well, you got the rescue attempt,' and you're not even a currently subscribed customer. 'This was far the biggest gun fight we've ever been in.'

'I'm sorry, Kje – Group Captain.'

He looked into her dark features. A lass from Sjandra Kei, down to the violet eyes. No way this could be a simulation, not here. He had bet everything that she was not; he still believed she was not. Yet – 'What does your friend say about all this?' Pham Nuwen had not been seen since his so-impressive godshatter act at the beginning of the battle.

Ravna's glance shifted to something off-camera. 'He's not saying much, Group Captain. He's wandering around even more upset than your Captain Trenglets. Pham remembers being absolutely convinced he was demanding the right thing, but now he can't figure out why it was right.'

'Hmm.' A little late for second thoughts. 'What are you going to do now? Haugen is right, you know. It would be useless suicide for us to follow the Blighters to your destination. I daresay it's useless suicide for you, too. You'll arrive maybe fifty-five hours before them. What can you do in that time?'

Ravna Bergsndot looked back at him, and her expression slowly collapsed into sobbing grief. 'I don't know. I . . . don't know.' She shook her head, her face hidden behind her hands and a sweep of black hair. Finally she looked up and brushed back her hair. Her voice was calm but very quiet.

'I . . . don't know. But we are going ahead. It's what we came for. Things could still work out . . . You know there's something down there, something the Blight wants desperately. Maybe fifty-five hours is enough to figure out what it is and tell the Net. And . . . and we'll still have Pham's godshatter.'

Your worst enemy? Quite possibly this Pham Nuwen was a construct of the Powers. He certainly *looked* like something built from a second-hand description of humanity. But how can you tell godshatter from simple nuttery?

She shrugged, as if acknowledging the doubts – and accepting them. 'So what will you and Commercial Security do?'

'There is no Commercial Security anymore. Virtually all our customers got shot out from under us. Now we've killed our company's owner – or at least destroyed her ship and those supporting her. We are Aniara Fleet now. 'It was the official name chosen at the fleet conference just ended. There was a certain grim pleasure in embracing it, the ghost from before Sjandra Kei and before Nyjora, from the earliest times of the human race. For they were truly cast away now, from their worlds and their customers and their former leaders. One hundred ships bound for . . . 'We talked it over. A few still wanted to follow you to Tines' world. Some of the crews want to return to the Middle Beyond, spend the rest of their lives killing Butterflies. The majority want to start the races of Sjandra Kei over again, some place where we won't be noticed, some place where no one cares if we live.'

And the one thing everyone agreed on was that Aniara must be split no further, must make no further sacrifices outside of itself. Once that was clear, it was easy to decide what to do. In the wake of the Great Surge, this part of the Bottom was an incredible froth of Slowness and Beyond. It would be centuries before the zonographic vessels from above had reasonable maps of the new interface. Hidden away in the folds and interstices were worlds fresh from the Slowness, worlds where Sjandra Kei could be born again. *Ny Sjandra Kei?*

He looked across the bridge at Tirolle and Glimfrelle. They were busy bringing the main navigation processors out of suspension. That wasn't absolutely necessary for the rendezvous with *Lynsnar*, but things would be a lot more convenient if both ships could maneuver. The brothers seemed oblivious to Kjet's conversation with Ravna. And maybe they weren't paying attention. In a way, the Aniara decision meant more to them than to the humans of the fleet: No one doubted that millions of humans survived in the Beyond (and who knew how many human worlds might still exist in the Slowness, distant cousins of Nyjora, distant children of Old Earth). But this side of the Transcend, the Dirokimes of Aniara were the only ones that existed. The dream habitats of Sjandra Kei were gone, and with them the race. There were at least a thousand Dirokimes left aboard Aniara, pairs of sisters and brothers scattered across a hundred vessels. These were the most adventurous of their race's latter days, and now they were faced with their greatest challenge. The two on *Ølvira* had already been scouting among the survivors, looking for friends and dreaming a new reality.

Ravna listened solemnly to his explanations. 'Group Captain, zonography is a tedious thing . . . and your ships are near their limits. In this froth you might search for years and not find a new home.'

'We're taking precautions. We're abandoning all our ships except the ones with ramscoop and coldsleep capability. We'll operate in coordinated nets; no one should be lost for more than a few years.' He shrugged. 'And if we never find what we seek –' *if we die between the stars as our life support finally fails* '– well then, we will have still lived true to our name.' *Aniara*. 'I think we have a chance.' More than can be said for you.

Ravna nodded slowly. 'Yes, well. It . . . helps me to know that.'

They talked a few minutes more, Tirolle and Glimfrelle joining in. They had been at the center of something vast, but as usual with the affairs of the Powers, no one knew quite what had happened, nor the result of the strivings.

'Rendezvous *Lynsnar* two hundred seconds,' said the ship's voice.

Ravna heard it, nodded. She raised her hand. 'Fare you well, Kjet Svensndot and Tirolle and Glimfrelle.'

The Dirokimes whistled back the common farewell, and Svensndot raised his hand. The window on Ravna Bergsndot closed.

. . . Kjet Svensndot remembered her face all the rest of his life, though in later years it seemed more and more to be the same as Ølvira's.

Part 3

37

'Tines' world. I can *see* it, Pham!'

The main window showed a true view upon the system: a sun less than two hundred million kilometers away, daylight across the command deck. The positions of identified planets were marked with blinking red arrows. But one of those – just twenty million kilometers off – was labeled 'terrestrial.' Coming off an interstellar jump, you couldn't get positioning much better than that.

Pham didn't reply, just glared out the window as if there were something wrong with what they were seeing. Something had broken in him after the battle with the Blight. He'd been so sure of his godshatter– and so bewildered by the consequences. Afterwards he had retreated more than ever. Now he seemed to think that if they moved fast enough, the surviving enemy could do them no harm. More than ever he was suspicious of Blueshell and Greenstalk, as if somehow they were greater threats than the ships that still pursued.

'*Damn*,' Pham said finally. 'Look at the relative velocity.' Seventy kilometers per second.

Position matching was no problem, but 'Matching velocities will cost us time, Sir Pham.'

Pham's stare turned on Blueshell. 'We talked this out with the locals three weeks ago, remember? You managed the burn.'

'And you checked my work, Sir Pham. This must be another nav system bug . . . though I didn't expect anything was wrong in simple ballistics.' A sign inverted, seventy kicks per second closing velocity instead of zero. Blueshell drifted

479

toward the secondary console.

'Maybe,' said Pham. 'Just now, I want you off the deck, Blueshell.'

'But I can help! We should be contacting Jefri, and rematching velocities, and –'

'*Get off the deck, Blueshell.* I don't have time to watch you anymore.' Pham dived across the intervening space and was met by Ravna, just short of the Rider.

She floated between the two, talking fast. 'It's okay, Pham. He'll go.' She brushed her hand across one of Blueshell's wildly vibrating fronds. After a second, Blueshell wilted. 'I'll go. I'll go.' She kept an encouraging touch on him – and kept herself between him and Pham as the Skroderider made a dejected exit.

When the Rider was gone, she turned to Pham. 'Couldn't it have been a nav bug, Pham?'

The other didn't seem to hear the question. The instant the hatch had closed, he had returned to the command console. *OOB*'s latest estimate put the Blight's arrival less than fifty-three hours away. And now they must waste time redoing a velocity match supposedly accomplished three weeks earlier. 'Somebody, something, screwed us over . . .' Pham was muttering, even as he finished with the control sequence. 'Maybe it was a bug. This next damn burn is going to be as manual as it can be.' Acceleration alarms echoed down the core of the *OOB*. Pham flipped through monitor windows, searching for loose items that might be big enough to be dangerous. 'You tie down too.' He reached out to override the five minute timer.

Ravna dived back across the deck, unfolding the free-fall saddle into a seat and strapping in. She heard Pham speaking on the general announce channel, warning of the timer override. Then the impulse drive cut in, a lazy pressure back into the webbing. Four tenths of a gee – all the poor *OOB* could still manage.

When Pham said manual, he meant it. The main window appeared to be bore-centered now. The view didn't drift at the whim of the pilot, and there were no helpful legends and

480

schematics. As much as possible, they were seeing true view along *OOB*'s main axis. Peripheral windows were held in fixed geometry with main. Pham's eyes flickered from one to another as his hands played over the command board. As near as could be, he was flying by his own senses and trusting no one else.

But Pham still had use for the ultradrive. They were twenty million klicks off target, a submicroscopic jump. Pham Nuwen fiddled with the drive parameters, trying to make an accurate jump smaller than the standard interval. Every few seconds the sunlight would shift a fraction, coming first over Ravna's left shoulder and then her right. It made reestablishing comm with Jefri nearly impossible.

Suddenly the window below their feet was filled by a world, huge and gibbous, blue and swirling white. The Tines' world was as Jefri Olsndot advertised, a normal terrestrial planet. After the months aspace and the loss of Sjandra Kei, the sight caught Ravna short. Ocean, the world was mostly ocean, but near the terminator there were the darker shades of land. A single tiny moon was visible beyond the limb.

Pham sucked in his breath. 'It's about ten thousand kilometers off. Perfect. Except we're closing at seventy klicks per second.' Even as she watched, the world seemed to grow, falling toward them. Pham watched it for a few seconds more. 'Don't worry, we're going to miss, fly right past the, um, north limb.'

The globe swelled below them, eclipsing the moon. She had always loved the appearance of Herte at Sjandra Kei. But that world had smaller oceans and was criss-crossed with Dirokime Paths. This place was as beautiful as Relay, and seemed truly untouched. The small polar cap was in sunlight, and she could follow the coastline that came south from it toward the terminator. *I'm seeing the northwest coast. Jefri's right down there!* Ravna reached for her keyboard, asking the ship to attempt both ultrawave comm and a radio link.

'Ultrawave contact,' she said after a second.

'What does it say?'

'It's garbled. Probably just a ping response,' acknowledgment to *OOB*'s signal, the most that had been possible since the surge. Jefri was housed very near the ship these days; sometimes she had gotten responses almost immediately, even during his night time. It would be good to talk to him again even if . . .

Tines' World filled half the windows now, its limb a barely curving horizon. Sky colors stood before them, fading to the black of space. Icecap and icebergs showed detail within detail against the sea. She could see cloud shadows. She followed the coast southwards, islands and peninsulas so closely fit that she could not be sure of one from the other. Blackish mountains and black-striped glaciers. Green and brown valleys. She tried to remember the geography they had learned from Jefri. *Hidden Island?* But there were so many islands.

'I have radio contact from the planet's surface,' came the ship's voice. Simultaneously a blinking arrow pointed at a spot just in from the coast. 'Do you want the audio in real time?'

'Yes. Yes!' said Ravna, then punched at her keyboard when the ship did not respond immediately.

'Hei, Ravna. Oh, Ravna!' The little boy's voice bounced excitement around the deck. He sounded just as she had imagined.

Ravna keyed in a request for two-way. They were less than five thousand klicks from Jefri now, even if they were sweeping by at seventy kilometers per second. Plenty close enough for a radio conversation. 'Hei, Jefri!' she said. 'We're here at last, but we need –' *We need all the cooperation your four-legged friends can give us. How to say that quickly and effectively?*

But the boy on the ground already had an agenda: '– need help *now*, Ravna! The Woodcarvers are attacking *now*.'

There was a thumping, as if the transmitter was bouncing around. Another voice spoke, high-pitched and weirdly inarticulate. 'This Steel, Ravna. Jefri right. Woodcarver –' the almost human voice dissolved into a hissing gobble. After a moment she heard Jefri's voice: '"Ambush," the word is "ambush."'

'Yes . . . Woodcarver has done big, big ambush. They all

around now. We die in hours if you not help.'

Woodcarver had never wanted to be a warrior. But ruling for half a thousand years requires a range of skills, and she had learned about making war. Some of that – such as trusting to staff – she had temporarily *un*learned these last few days. There had indeed been an ambush on Margrum Climb, but not the one that Lord Steel had planned.

She looked across the tented field at Vendacious. That pack was half-hidden by noise baffles, but she could see he wasn't so jaunty as before. Being put to the question will loosen anyone's control . . . Vendacious knew his survival now depended on her keeping a promise. Yet . . . it was awful to think that Vendacious would live after he had killed and betrayed so many. She realized that two of herself were keening rage, lips curled back from clenched teeth. Her puppies huddled back from threats unseen. The tented area stank of sweat and the mindnoise of too many people in too small a space. It took a real effort of will to calm herself. She licked the puppies, and daydreamed peaceful thoughts for a moment.

Yes, she would keep her promises to him. And maybe it would be worth the price. Vendacious had only speculations about Steel's inner secrets, but he had learned far more about Steel's tactical situation than the other side could have guessed. Vendacious had known just where the Flenserists were hiding and in what numbers. Steel's folk had been overconfident about their super guns and their secret traitor. When Woodcarver's troops surprised them, victory had been easy – and now the Queen had some of the marvelous guns.

From behind the hills, those cannons were still pounding away, eating through the stocks of ammunition the captured gunners had revealed. Vendacious the traitor had cost her much, but Vendacious the prisoner might yet bring her victory.

'Woodcarver?' It was Scrupilo. She waved him closer. Her chief gunner edged out of the sun, sitting down an intimate twenty-five feet away. Battle conditions had blown away all notions of decorum.

483

Scrupilo's mind noise was an anxious jumble. He looked by parts exhausted and exhilarated and discouraged. 'It's safe to advance up the castle hill, your majesty,' he said. 'Answering fire is almost extinguished. Parts of the castle walls have been breached. There is an end to castles here, my queen. Even our own poor cannons would make it so.'

She bobbed agreement. Scrupilo spent most of his time with Dataset in learning to *make* – cannons in particular. Woodcarver spent her time learning what those inventions ultimately created. By now she knew far more than even Johanna about the social effects of weapons, from the most primitive to ones so strange that they seemed not weapons at all. A thousand million times, castle technologies had fallen to things like cannon; why should her world be different?

'We'll move up then –'

From beyond the shade of the tent there was a faint whistle, a rare, incoming round. She folded the puppies within herself, and paused a moment. Twenty yards away, Vendacious shrank down in a great cower. But when it came, the explosion was a muffled thump above them on the hill. *It might even have been one of our own.* 'Now our troops must take advantage of the destruction. I want Steel to know that the old games of ransom and torture will only win him worse.' *We'll most likely win the starship and the child.* The question was, would either be alive when they got them? She hoped Johanna would never know the threats and the risks she planned for the next few hours.

'Yes, majesty.' But Scrupilo made no move to depart, and suddenly seemed more bedraggled and worried than ever. 'Woodcarver, I fear . . .'

'What? We have the tide. We must rush to sail on it.'

'Yes, majesty . . . But while we move forward, there are serious dangers coming up on our flanks and rear. The enemy's far scouts and the fires.'

Scrupilo was right. The Flenserists who operated behind her lines were deadly. There weren't many of them; the enemy troops at Margrum Climb had been mostly killed or dispersed. The few that ate at Woodcarver's flanks were equipped with ordinary crossbows and axes . . . but they were extraordinarily well-coordinated. And their tactics were brilliant; she saw the snouts and tines of Flenser himself in that brilliance. Somehow her evil child lived. Like a plague of years past, he was slipping back upon the world. Given time, those guerrilla packs would seriously hurt Woodcarver's ability to supply her forces. Given time. Two of her stood and looked Scrupilo in the eyes, emphasizing the point: 'All the more reason to move now, my friend. We are the ones far from home. We are the ones with limited numbers and food. If we don't win soon, then we will be cut up a bit at a time.' *Flensed.*

Scrupilo stood up, nodding submission. 'That's what Peregrine says, too. And Johanna wants to chase right through the castle walls . . . But there's something else, your majesty. Even if we must lunge all forward: I worked for a ten of tendays, using every clue I could understand from Dataset, to make our cannon. Majesty, *I know* how hard it is to do such. Yet the guns we captured on Margrum have three times the range and one quarter the weight. *How could they do it?*' There were chords of anger and humiliation in his voice. 'The traitor,' Scrupilo jerked a snout in the direction of Vendacious, 'thinks they may have Johanna's brother, but Johanna says they have nothing like Dataset. Majesty, Steel has some advantage we don't yet know.'

Even the executions were not helping. Day by day, Steel felt his rage growing. Alone on the parapet, he whipped back and forth upon himself, barely conscious of anything but his anger. Not since he had been under Flenser's knife had the anger been such a radiant thing. *Get back control before he cuts you more*, the voice of some early Steel seemed to say.

He hung on the thought, pulled himself together. He stared down a bloody drool and tasted ashes. Three of his shoulders were streaked with tooth cuts – he'd been hurting himself, another habit Flenser had cured him of long ago. *Hurt outwards, never toward yourself.* Steel licked mechanically at the gashes and walked closer to the parapet's edge:

At the horizon, gray-black haze obscured the sea and the islands. The last few days, the summer winds had been a hot breath, tasting of smoke. Now the winds were like fire themselves, whipping past the castle, carrying ash and smoke. All last dayaround the far side of Bitter Gorge had been a haze of fire, today he could see the hillsides: they were black and brown, crowned with smoke that swept toward the sea's horizon. There were often brush and forest fires in the High Summer. But this year, as if nature was a godly pack of war, the fires had been everywhere. The wretched guns had done it. And this year he couldn't retreat to the cool of Hidden Island and leave the coastlings to suffer.

Steel ignored his smarting shoulders and paced the stones more thoughtfully, almost analytical for a change. The creature Vendacious had not stayed bought; he had turned traitor to his treason. Steel had anticipated that Vendacious might be discovered; he had other spies who should have reported such a thing. But there had been no sign . . . until the disaster at Margrum Climb. Now the twist of Vendacious's knife had turned all his plans on their heads. Woodcarver would be here very soon, and not as a victim.

Who would have guessed that he would really need the Spacers to rescue him from Woodcarver? He had worked so hard to confront the Southerners before Ravna arrived. But now he did need that help from the sky – and it was more than five hours away. Steel almost slipped back into rage state at the thought. In the end, would all the cozening of Amdijefri be for nothing? *Oh, when this is over, how much will I enjoy killing those two.* More than any of the others, they deserved death. They had caused so much inconvenience. They had consistently required his kindliest behavior, as though *they* ruled *him*. They had showered him with more insolence than ten thousand normal subjects.

From the castle yard there was the sound of laboring packs, straining winches, the screech and groan of rock being moved about. The professional core of Flenser's Empire survived. Given a few more hours, the breaches in the walls would be repaired and new guns would be brought in from the north. *And the grand scheme can still succeed. As long as I am together, no matter what else is lost, it can succeed.*

Almost lost in the racket, he heard the click of claws on the

486

inward steps. Steel drew back, turned all heads toward the sound. Shreck? But Shreck would have announced himself first. Then he relaxed; there was only one set of claw sounds. It was a singleton coming up the stairs.

Flenser's member cleared the steps and bowed to Steel, an incomplete gesture without other members to mirror it. The member's radio cloak shone clean and dark. The army was in awe of those cloaks, and of the singletons and duos who seemed smarter than the brightest pack. Even Steel's lieutenants who understood what the cloaks really were – even Shreck – were cautious and tentative around them. And now Steel needed the Flenser Fragment more than anyone, more than *anything* except Starfolk gullibility. 'What news?'

'Leave to sit?' Was the sardonic Flenser smile behind that request?

'Granted,' snapped Steel.

The singleton eased itself onto the stones. But Steel saw when the other winced; the Fragment had been dispersed across the Domain for almost twenty days now. Except for brief periods, he had been wrapped in the radio cloaks that whole time. Dark and golden torture. Steel had seen this member without its cloak, when it was bathed. Its pelt was rubbed raw at shoulder and haunch, where the weight of the radio was greatest. Bleeding sores had opened at the center of the bald spots. Alone without its cloak, the mindless singleton had blabbered its pain. Steel enjoyed those sessions, even if this one was not especially verbal. It was almost as if he, Steel, were now the One who Teaches with a Knife, and Flenser were his pupil.

The singleton was silent for a moment. Steel could hear its ill-concealed panting. 'The last dayaround has gone well, my lord.'

'Not here! We've lost almost all our cannon. We're trapped inside these walls.' And the starfolk may arrive too late.

'I mean out there.' The singleton poked its nose toward the open spaces beyond the parapet. 'Your scouts are well-trained, my lord, and have some bright commanders. Right now, I am spread round Woodcarver's rear and flanks.' The singleton made its part of a laughing gesture. '"Rear and flanks." Funny. To me Woodcarver's entire army is like a single enemy pack. Our Attack Infantries are like tines on my own paws. We are cutting the Queen deep, my lord. I set the fire in Bitter Gorge. Only I could see exactly where it was spreading, exactly how to kill with it. In another four dayarounds there will be nothing left of the Queen's supplies. She will be ours.'

'Too long, if we're dead this afternoon.'

'Yes.' The singleton cocked its head at Steel. *He's laughing at me.* Just like all those times under Flenser's knife when a problem would be posed and death was the penalty for failure. 'But Ravna and company should be back here in five hours, no?' Steel nodded. 'Well, I guarantee you that will be hours ahead of Woodcarver's main assault. You have Amdijefri's confidence. It seems you need only advance and compress your previous schedule. If Ravna is sufficiently desperate –'

'The starfolk are desperate. I know that.' Ravna might mask her precise motives, but her desperation was clear. 'And if you can slow Woodcarver –' Steel settled all of himself down to concentrate on the scheming at hand. He was half-conscious of his fears retreating. Planning was always a comfort. 'The problem is that we have to do two things now, and perfectly coordinated. Before, it was simply a matter of *feigning* a siege and tricking the starship into our castle's Jaws.' He turned a head in the direction of the courtyard. The stone dome over the landed starship had been in place since midspring. It showed some artillery damage now, the marble facing chipped away, but it hadn't taken direct hits. Beside it lay the field of the Jaws: large enough to accept the rescue ship, but surrounded by pillars of stone, the teeth of the Jaws. With the proper use of gunpowder, the teeth would fall on the rescuers. That would be a last resort, if they didn't kill and capture the humans as they came out to meet dear Jefri. That scheme had been lovingly honed over many tendays, aided by Amdijefri's admissions about human psychology and his knowledge of how spaceships normally land. But now: '– Now we really need their help. What I ask them must do double duty, to fool them and to destroy Woodcarver.'

'Hard to do all at once,' agreed the Cloak. 'Why not play it in two steps, the first more or less undeceitful: Have them destroy Woodcarver, *then* worry about taking them over?'

Steel clicked a tine thoughtfully on stone. 'Yes. Trouble is, if they see too much . . . They can't possibly be as naïve as Jefri. He says that humankind has a history that includes castles and warfare. If they fly around too much, they'll see things that Jefri never saw, or never understood . . . Maybe I could get them to land inside the castle and mount weapons on the walls. We'll have them hostage the moment that they stand between our Jaws. *Damn.* That would take some clever work with Amdijefri.' The bliss of abstract planning foundered for a moment on rage. 'It's getting harder and harder for me to deal with those two.'

'They're both wholly puppies, for Pack's sake.' The Fragment paused a second. 'Of course, Amdiranifani may have more raw intelligence than any pack I've ever seen. You think he may even be smart enough to see past his *childishness*,' he used the Samnorsk word, 'and see the deception?'

'No, not that. I have their necks in my jaws, and they still don't see it. You're right, Tyrathect; they do love me.' *And how I hate them for it.* 'When I'm around him, the mantis thing is all over me, close enough to cut my throat or poke out my eyes, but hugging and petting. And expecting me to love him back. Yes, they believe everything I say, but the price is accepting unending insolence.'

'Be cool, dear student. The heart of manipulation is to empathize without being touched.' The Fragment stopped, as always, just short of the brink. But this time, Steel felt himself hissing at the words even before he was consciously aware of his reaction.

'Don't . . . lecture . . . *me!* You are *not* Flenser. You are a fragment. Shit! You are a fragment of a fragment now. A word and you will be cut up, dead in a thousand pieces.' He tried to suppress the trembling that spread through his members. *Why haven't I killed him before now? I hate Flenser more than anything in the world, and it would be so easy.* Yet the fragment was always so indispensable, somehow the only thing between

489

Steel and failure. And he *was* under Steel's control.

And the singleton was doing a very good terrified cower. 'Sit up, you! Give me your counsel and not your lectures, and you will live . . . Whatever the reason, it's impossible for me to carry on the charade with these puppies. Perhaps for a few minutes at a time I can do it, or if there are other packs to keep them away from me, but none of this unending loving. Another hour of that and I-I know I'll start killing them. So. I want you to talk with Amdijefri. Explain the "situation." Explain —'

'But —' The singleton was looking at him in astonishment.

'I'll be watching; I'm not giving up those two to your possession. Just handle the close diplomacy.'

The Fragment drooped, the pain in its shoulders undisguised. 'If that is your wish, my lord.'

Steel showed all his teeth. 'It is indeed. Just remember, I'll be present for everything important, especially direct radio communication.' He waved the singleton off the parapet. 'Now go and cuddle up to the children; learn something of self-control yourself.'

After the Cloak was gone, he called Shreck up to the parapet. The next few hours were spent touring the defenses and planning with his staff. Steel was very surprised how much clearing up the puppy problem improved his quality of mind. His advisors seemed to pick up on it, relaxed to the point of offering substantive suggestions. Where the breaches in the walls could not be repaired, they would build deadfalls. The cannon from the northern shops would arrive before the end of the dayaround, and one of Shreck's people had worked out an alternate plan for food and water resupply. Reports from the far scouts showed steady progress, a withering of the enemy's rear; they would lose most of their ammunition before they reached Starship Hill. Even now there was scarcely any shot falling on the hill.

As the sun rose in the south, Steel was back on the parapets, scheming on just what to say to the Starfolk.

This was almost like earlier days, when plans went well and success was wondrous yet achievable. And yet . . . at the back of his mind all the hours since talking with the singleton, there had been the little claws of fear. Steel had the appearance of ruling. The Flenser Fragment gave the appearance of following. But even though it was spread across miles, the pack seemed more together than ever before. Oh, in earlier times, the Fragment often pretended equilibrium, but its internal tension always showed. Lately it seemed self-satisfied, almost . . . smug. The Flenser Fragment was responsible for the Domain's forces south of Starship Hill, and after today – after Steel had *forced* the responsibility upon him – the Cloaks would be with Amdijefri every day. Never mind that the motivation had come from within Steel. Never mind that the Fragment was in an obvious state of agonized exhaustion. In its full genius, the Great One could have charmed a forest wolf into thinking Flenser its queen. *And do I really know what he's saying to the packs beyond my hearing? Could my spies be feeding me lies about him?*

Now that he had a moment away from immediate concerns, these little claws dug deeper. *I need him, yes. But the margin for error is smaller now.* After a moment, he grated a happy chord, accepting the risk. If necessary, he would use what he had learned with the second set of cloaks, something he had artfully concealed from Flenser Tyrathect. If necesary, the Fragment would find that death can be *radio* swift.

Even as he flew the velocity match, Pham was working the ultradrive. This would save them hours of fly back time, but it was a chancy game, one the ship had never been designed for. *OOB* bounced all around the solar system. One really lucky jump was all they needed, and one really unlucky jump, *into* the planet, would kill them – a good reason why this game was not normally played.

After hours of hacking the flight automation, of playing ultradrive roulette, poor Pham's hands were faintly trembling. Whenever Tines' world came back into view – often no more than a far point of blue light – he would glare for a second at it. Ravna could see the doubts rising within him: His memories told him he should be good with low-tech automation, yet some of the *OOB* primitives were almost impenetrable. Or maybe his memories of competence, of the

Qeng Ho, were cheap fakes.

'The Blighter fleet. How long?' asked Pham.

Greenstalk was watching the nav window from the Riders' cabin. It was the fifth time the question had been asked in the last hour, yet her voice came back calm and patient. Maybe the repeated questions even seemed a natural thing. 'Range forty-nine light-years. Estimated time of arrival forty-eight hours. Seven more ships have dropped out.' Ravna could subtract: one hundred and fifty-two were still coming.

Blueshell's voder sounded over his mate's, 'During the last two hundred seconds, they have made slightly better time than before, but I think that is local variance in Bottom conditions. Sir Pham, you are doing well, but I know my ship. We could get a little more time if only you'd allow me control. Please –'

'Shut up.' Pham's voice was sharp, but the words were almost automatic. It was a conversation – or the abortion of one – that occurred almost as often as Pham's demand for status info on the Blighter fleet.

In the early weeks of their journey, she had assumed that godshatter was somehow superhuman. Instead it was parts and pieces, automation loaded in a great panic. Maybe it was working right, or maybe it had run amok and was tearing Pham apart with its errors.

The old cycle of fear and doubt was suddenly broken by soft blue light. Tines' World! At last, a wondrously accurate jump, almost as good as the shocker of five hours before: Twenty thousand kilometers away hung a vast narrow crescent, the edge of planetary daylight. The rest was a dark blot against the stars, except where the auroral ring hung a faint green glow around the south pole. Jefri Olsndot was on the other side of the world from them, in the arctic day. They wouldn't have radio communication until they arrived – and she hadn't figured out how to recalibrate the ultrawave for shortrange transmission.

She turned back from the view. Pham still stared upward into the sky behind her. '. . . Pham, what good is forty-eight hours? Will we just destroy the Countermeasure?' *What of Jefri and Mr Steel's people?*

'Maybe. But there are other possibilities. There must be.'
That last softly. 'I've been chased before. I've been in bigger
jams before.' His eyes avoided hers.

38

Jefri hadn't seen the sky for more than an hour in the last two
days. He and Amdi were safe enough in the great stone dome
that sheltered the refugee ship, but there was no way to see
outside. *If it weren't for Amdi, I couldn't have stood it a minute.* In
some ways it was worse even than his first days on Hidden
Island. The ones who killed Mom and Dad and Johanna were
just a few kilometers away. They had captured some of Mr
Steel's guns and the last few days the explosions had gone on
for hours, a booming that shook the ground beneath them and
sometimes even smashed at the walls of the dome.

Their food was brought in to them, and when they weren't
sitting in the ship's command cabin, the two wandered
outside the ship to the rooms with the sleeping children. Jefri
had kept up with the simple maintenance procedures he
remembered, but looking through the chill transp of the cold
sleep coffins, he was terribly afraid. Some of them weren't
breathing very much. The inside temperature seemed too
high. And he and Amdi didn't know how to help.

Nothing had changed here, but now there was joy. Ravna's
long silence had ended. Amdijefri and Mr Steel had actually
talked to her in *voice!* Three more hours and her ship would
be here! Even the bombardment had ended, almost as if
Woodcarver realized that her time was near to ending.

Three more hours. Left to himself, Jefri would have spent
the time in a state of wall-climbing anxiety. After all, he was
nine years old now, a grown-up with grown-up problems. But
then there was Amdi. The pack was much smarter than Jefri
in some ways, but he was such a little kid – about five years
old, as near as Amdijefri could figure it. Except when he was
into heavy thinking, he could not stay still. After the call from

Ravna, Jefri wanted to sit down for serious worrying, but Amdi began chasing himself around the pylons. He shouted back and forth in Jefri's voice and Ravna's, and bumped into the boy accidentally on purpose. Jefri hopped up and glared at the careening puppies. *Just a little kid*. And suddenly, happy and so sad all at once: *Is this how Johanna saw me?* And so he had responsibilities now too. Like being patient. As one of Amdi came rushing past his knees, Jefri swept down to grab the wriggling form. He raised it to shoulder level as the rest of the pack converged gleefully, pounding on him from all directions.

They fell to the dry moss and wrestled for a few seconds. 'Let's explore, let's explore!'

'We have to be here for Ravna and Mr Steel.'

'Don't worry. We'll remember when.'

'Okay.' Where was there really to go?

The two walked through the torchlit dimness to the clerestory that ringed the inner edge of the dome. As far as Jefri could see, they were alone. That was not unusual. Mr Steel was very worried that Woodcarver spies might get into the ship. Even his own soldiers rarely came here.

Amdijefri had investigated the inside wall before. Behind the quilts, the stone felt cool and damp. There were some holes to the outside – for ventilation – but they were almost ten meters up, where the wall was already curving inwards toward the apex of the dome. The stone was rough cut, not yet polished. Mr Steel's workers had been in a frantic hurry to complete the protection before Woodcarver's army arrived. Nothing was polished, and the quilts were undecorated.

Ahead and behind him, Amdi was sniffing at the cracks and fresh mortar. The one in Jefri's arms gave a concerted wiggle. 'Ha! Up ahead. I knew that mortar was coming loose,' the pack said. Jefri let all of his friend rush forward to a nook in the wall. It didn't look any different than before, but Amdi was scratching with five pairs of paws.

'Even if you can get it loose, what good does it do you?' Jefri had seen these blocks as they were lowered into place. They were almost fifty centimeters across, laid in alternating rows. Getting past one would just bring them to more stone.

'Heh heh, I don't know. I've been saving this up till we had some time to kill . . . Yech. This mortar burns my lips.' More scratching, and the pack passed back a fragment as big as Jefri's head. There really was a hole between the blocks, and it was big enough for Amdi. One of him darted into the tiny cave.

'Satisfied?' Jefri plunked himself down by the hole and tried to look in.

'Guess what!' Amdi's shrill voice came from a member right by his ear. 'There's a tunnel back here, not just another layer of stone!' A member wriggled past Jefri and disappeared into the dark. Secret tunnels? That was too much like a Nyjoran fairy tale. 'These are big enough for a full-grown member, Jefri. You could get through these on hands 'n' knees.' Two more of Amdi disappeared into the hole.

The tunnel he had discovered might be large enough for a human child, but the entrance hole was a tight fit even for the puppies. Jefri had nothing to do but stare into the darkness. The parts of Amdi that remained at the entrance talked about what he had found. '– Goes on for a long, long way. I've doubled back a couple of times. The top of me is about five meters up, way over your head. This is kooky. I'm getting all strung out.' Amdi sounded even sillier than his normal playfulness. Two more of him went into the hole. This was developing into serious adventure – that Jefri could have no part of.

'Don't go too far; it might be dangerous.'

One of the pair that remained looked up at him. 'Don't worry. Don't worry. The tunnel isn't an accident. It feels like it was cut as grooves in the stones when they were laid. This is some special escape route Mister Steel made. I'm all right. I'm all right. Ha ha, hoohooo.' One more disappeared into the hole. After a moment the last remaining one ran in, but stayed near enough to the entrance so Amdi could still talk to Jefri. The pack was having a high old time, singing and screeching to itself. Jefri knew exactly what the other was up to; it was another of the games he could never play. In this posture, Amdi's thoughts would be the weirdest rippling things. *Darn*. Now that he was playing within stone, it must be even neater than before, since he was totally cut off from all thoughts except from member to adjacent member.

The stupid singing went on a little longer, and then Amdi spoke in an almost reasonable tone. 'Hei, this tunnel actually splits off in places. The front of me has come to a fork. One side is heading down . . . Wish I had enough members to go both ways!'

'Well, you don't!'

'Hei ho, I'll take the upper tunnel today.' A few seconds of silence. 'There's a little door here! Like a member-size room door. Not locked.' Amdi relayed the sounds of stone scritching against stone. 'Ha! I can see light! Up just a few more meters, it opens onto a window. Hear the wind.' He relayed wind sound and the keening of the sea birds that soared up from Hidden Island. It sounded wonderful. 'Oh oh, this is stretching things, but I wanna look out . . . Jefri, I can see the sun! I'm outdoors, sitting way up on the side of the dome. I can see all round to the south. Boy, it's smoky down there.'

'What about the hillside?' Jefri asked the nearest member; its white-splotched pelt was barely visible through the entrance hole. At least Amdi was staying in touch.

'A little browner than last tenday. I don't see any soldiers out there.' Jefri heard the relayed sound of a cannon firing. 'Yipes. There's shooting though . . . It hit just on this side of the crest. Someone's out there, just below my line of sight.' Woodcarver, come at last. Jefri shivered, angry that he couldn't see, frightened of what might be seen. He often had nightmares about what Woodcarver must truly be, how she had done it to Mom and Dad and Johanna. Images never fully formed . . . yet almost memories. *Mister Steel will get Woodcarver.*

'Uh-oh. Old Tyrathect is coming across the castle yard this way.' Thumping sounds came from the hole as Amdi blundered back down. No point in letting Tyrathect know that there was a tunnel hidden in the wall. He'd probably just order them to stay away from it. One, two, three, four – half of Amdi popped out of the wall. The four wandered around a little dazedly. Jefri couldn't tell if it was because of their stretched-out experience or if they were temporarily split from the other half of the pack. 'Act natural. Act natural.'

Then the other four arrived, and Amdi began to settle down. He led Jefri away from the wall at a fast trot. 'Let's get the commset. We'll pretend we've been trying to raise Ravna with it.' Amdi knew well that the starship couldn't be back for another thirty minutes or so. In fact, he had been the one who verified the deceleration math for Mister Steel. Nevertheless, he chased up the ship's steps and dragged down the radio. The two were already plugging the antenna into a signal booster when the public doors on the west side of the dome were unlatched. Silhouetted against the daylight were parts of a guard pack and a single member of Tyrathect. The guard retired, sliding the doors shut, and the Cloak walked slowly across the moss towards them.

Amdi rushed over and chattered about their attempts to use the radio. It was a little forced, Jefri thought. The puppies were still confused by their trip through the walls.

The singleton looked at the powdering of mortar dust on Amdi's pelt. 'You've been climbing in the walls, haven't you?'

'What?' Amdi looked himself over, noticed the dust. Usually he was more clever. 'Yes,' he said shamefacedly. He brushed the powder away. 'You won't tell, will you?'

Fat chance he'll help us, thought Jefri. Mr Tyrathect had learned Samnorsk better than Mr Steel, and besides Steel was the only one who had much time to talk with them. But even before the radio cloaks, he'd been a short-tempered, bossy sort. Jefri had had baby-sitters like him. Tyrathect was nice up to a point, and then would get sarcastic or say something mean. Lately that had improved, but Jefri still didn't like him much.

But Mr Tyrathect didn't say anything right away. He sat down slowly, as if his rump hurt. '. . .No, I won't tell.'

Jefri exchanged a surprised glance with one of Amdi. 'What is the tunnel for?' he asked timidly.

'All castles have hidden tunnels, especially in my . . . in the domain of Mr Steel. You want ways to escape, ways to spy on your enemies.' The singleton shook its head. 'Never mind. Is your radio properly receiving, Amdijefri?'

Amdi cocked a head at the comm's display. 'I think so, but there's nothing yet to receive. See, Ravna's ship had to decelerate and um, I could show you the arithmetic . . . ? ' But Mr Tyrathect was obviously not interested in playing with chalk boards. '. . . well, depending on their luck with the ultradrive, we should have radio contact with them real soon.'

But the little window on the comm showed no incoming signal. They watched it for several minutes. Mr Tyrathect lowered his muzzle and seemed to sleep. Every few seconds his body twitched. Jefri wondered what the rest of him was doing.

Then the comm window was glowing green. There was a garble of sound as it tried to sort signal from background noise. '. . . over you in five minutes,' came Ravna's voice. 'Jefri? Are you listening?'

'Yes! We're here.'

'Let me talk to Mr Steel, please.'

Mr Tyrathect stepped nearer to the comm. 'He is not here now. Ravna.'

'Who is this?'

Tyrathect's laugh was a giggle; he had never heard any other kind. 'I?' He made the Tinish chord that sounded like 'Tyrathect' to Jefri. 'Or do you mean a taken name, like Steel? I don't know the exact word. You may call me . . . Mr Skinner.' Tyrathect laughed again. 'For now, I can speak for Steel.'

'Jefri, are you all right?'

'Yes, yes. Listen to Mr Skinner.' What a strange name.

The sounds from the comm became muffled. There was a male voice arguing. Then Ravna was back, her voice kind of tight, like Mom when she was mad. 'Jefri . . . what's the volume of a ball ten centimeters across?'

Amdi had been fidgeting impatiently through the conversation. All through the last year he had been hearing stories of humans from Jefri, and dreaming what Ravna might really be like. Now he had a chance to show off. He jumped for the comm, and grinned at Jefri. 'That's easy, Ravna.' His voice was perfect Jefri – and completely fluent. 'It's 523.598 cubic centimeters . . . or do you want more digits?'

Muffled conversation. '. . . No, that's fine. Okay, Mr Skinner. We have pictures from our earlier pass and a general radio fix. Where exactly are you?'

'Under the castle dome at the top of Starship Hill. It's right at the coast by a –'

A man's voice cut in. Pham? He had a funny accent. 'I got it on the map. We still can't see you direct. Too much haze.'

'That's smoke,' said the Cloak. 'The enemy is almost upon us from the south. We need your help immediately –' The singleton lowered its head from the commset. Its eyes closed and opened a couple of times. Thinking? 'Hmm, yes. Without your help, we and Jefri and this ship are lost. Please land within the castle courtyard. You know we've specially reinforced it for your arrival. Once down we can use your weapons to –'

'No way.' The guy replied immediately. 'Just separate the friendlies from the bad guys and let us take care of things.'

Tyrathect's voice took on a wheedling tone, like a little kid complaining. *He really has been studying us.* 'No, no, didn't mean to be impolite. Certainly, do it your own way. About the enemy force: everyone close to the castle on the south side of the hill are enemy. A single pass with your ship's . . . um, torch . . . would send them running.'

'I can't fly that torch inside an atmosphere. Did your Pop really land with the main jet, Jefri? No agrav?'

, 'Yes, sir. All we had was the jet.'

'He was a lucky genius.'

Ravna: 'Maybe we could just float across, a few thousand meters up. That might scare them away.'

Tyrathect began, 'Yes, that might –'

The public doors on the north side of the dome slid open. Mr Steel stood silhouetted against the daylight beyond. 'Let me talk to them,' he said.

The goal of all their voyaging lay just twenty kilometers below *OOB*. They were so *close*, yet those twenty thousand meters might be as hard to bridge as the twenty thousand light-years they had come so far.

They floated on agrav directly over 'Starship Hill.' *OOB*'s multispectral wasn't working very well, but where smoke did not obscure, the ship's optics could count the needles on the trees below. Ravna could see the forces of 'Woodcarver' ranged across the slopes south of the castle. There were other troops, and apparently cannon, hidden in the forests that lined the fjord south of that. Given a little more time they would be able to locate them too. Time was the one thing they did not have.

Time and trust.

'Forty-eight hours, Pham. Then the fleet will be here, all around us.' Maybe, *maybe* godshatter could work a miracle; they'd never know stewing about it up here. *Try*: 'You've got to trust somebody, Pham.'

Pham glared back at her, and for an instant she feared he might go completely to pieces. 'You'd hand yourself over to that Steel? Medieval villains are just as smart as any you've seen in the Beyond, Rav. They could teach the Butterflies a thing or two. An arrow in the head will kill you as sure as an antimatter bomb.'

More fake memories? But Pham was right on this: She thought about the just-concluded conversation. The second pack – Steel – had been a bit too insistent. He had been good to Jefri, but he was clearly desperate. And she believed him when he said that a high fly-by wouldn't scare the Woodcarvers off. They needed to come down near the ground with firepower. Just now, about all the firepower they had was Pham's beam gun. 'Okay, then! Do what you and Steel talked about. Fly the lander past Woodcarver's lines, laser blast them.'

'God damn it, you know I can't fly that. The landing boat is like nothing either of us know, and without the automation I –'

Softly: 'Without the automation, you need Blueshell, Pham.' There was horror on Pham's face. She reached out to him. He was silent for a long moment, not seeming to notice.

'Yeah.' His voice was low, strangled. Then: 'Blueshell! Get up here.'

OOB's lander had more than enough room for the

Skroderider and Pham Nuwen. The craft had been built specifically for Rider use. With higher automation working, it would have been easy for Pham – for even a child – to fly. Now the craft could not provide stable flight, and the 'manual' controls were something that gave even Blueshell a hard time. *Damn automation. Damn optimization.* For most of his adult life Pham had lived in the Slowness. All those decades, he had managed spacecraft and weapons that could have reduced the feudal empire below to slag. Yet now, with equipment that should have been enormously more powerful, he couldn't even fly a damn landing boat.

Across the crew compartment, Blueshell was at the pilot's position. His fronds stretched across a web of supports and controls. He had turned off all display automation; only the main window was alive, a natural view from the boat's bow camera. *OOB* floated some hundred meters ahead, drifting up and out of view as their craft slid backwards and down.

Blueshell's fidgety nervousness – furtiveness, it seemed to Pham – had disappeared as he got into piloting the craft. His voder voice became terse and preoccupied, and the edges of his fronds writhed across the controls, an exercise that would have been impossible to Pham even if he had a lifetime of experience with the gear. 'Thank you, Sir Pham . . . I'll prove you can trust . . .' The nose lurched downwards and they were staring almost straight into the fjord-carven coastline twenty kilometers below. They fell free for half a minute while the Rider's fronds writhed on their supports. Hot piloting? No: 'Sorry, sorry.' Acceleration, and Pham sank into his restraints under a grav load that wobbled between a tenth gee and an intolerable crush. The landscape rotated and they had a brief glimpse of *OOB*, now like a tiny moth above them.

'Is it necessary to kill, Sir Pham? Perhaps simply our appearance over the battle . . .'

Nuwen gritted his teeth. 'Just get us down.' The Steel creature had been adamant that they fry the entire hillside. Despite all Pham's suspicions, the pack might be right on that. They were up against a crew of murderers that had not hesitated to ambush a starship; the Woodcarvers needed a real demonstration.

Their boat fluttered down the kilometers. Steel's fortifications were clearly visible even in the natural view: the rough polygon that guarded the refugee ship, the much larger structure that rambled across an island several kilometers westward. *I wonder if this is how my Father's castle looked to the Qeng Ho landers?* Those walls were high and unsloping. Clearly the Tines had had no idea of gunpowder till Ravna had clued them to it.

The valley south of the castle was a blot of dark smoke smoothly streaming toward the sea. Even without data enhancement, he could see hot spots, fringes of orange edging the black.

'You're at two thousand meters,' came Ravna's voice. 'Jefri says he can see you.'

'Patch me through to them.'

'I will try, Sir Pham.' Blueshell fiddled, his lack of attention spinning the boat through a complete loop. Pham had seen falling leaves with more control.

A child's piping voice: 'A-are you okay? Don't *crash*!'

And then the Steel pack's hybrid of Ravna and the kid: 'South to go! South to go! Use fire gun. Burn them quick.'

Blueshell had them down in the smoke already. For seconds they were flying blind. A break in the smoke showed the hillside less than two hundred meters off, coming up fast. Before Pham could curse at Blueshell, the Rider had turned them around and floated the boat into clearer air. Then he pitched over so they might see directly down.

After thirty weeks of talk and planning, Pham had his first glimpse of the Tines. Even from here, it was obvious they were different from any sophonts Pham had encountered: Clusters of four or five or six members hung together so close they seemed a single spiderlike being. And each pack stood separated from the others by ten or fifteen meters.

A cannon flashed in the murk. The pack crewing it moved like a single, coordinated hand to rock the barrel back and ram another charge down the muzzle.

'But if these are the enemy, Sir Pham, where did they get the guns?'

'They stole 'em.' *But muzzle loaders?* He didn't have time to pursue the thought.

'You're right over them, Pham! I can see you in and out of the smoke. You're drifting south at fifteen meters per second, losing altitude.' It was the kid, speaking with his usual incredible precision.

'Kill them! Kill them!'

Pham wriggled out of his restraints and crawled back to the hatch where they had mounted his beam gun. It was about the only thing salvaged from the workshop fire, but by God this *was* something he could operate.

'Keep us steady, Blueshell. Bounce me around and I'll fry you as likely as anything!' He pushed open the hatch, and gagged on spicy smoke. Then Blueshell's agravs wafted them into a clear space and Pham lined the beamer down the ranks of packfolk.

Originally Woodcarver had demanded Johanna stay at the base camp. Johanna's response had been explosive. Even now the girl was a little surprised at herself. Not since the first days on Tines' World had she come so close to attacking a pack. No way was anyone going to keep her from finding out about Jefri. In the end they had compromised: Johanna would accept Pilgrim as her guard. She could follow the army into the field, as long as she obeyed his direction.

Johanna looked up through the drifting smoke. *Damn.* Pilgrim was always such a carefree joker. By his own telling, he had gotten himself killed over and over again through the years. And now he wouldn't even let her go up to Scrupilo's cannons. The two of them paced across a terrace in the hillside. The brush fire had swept through here hours before, and the spicy smell of moss ash was thick around them. And with that smell came the bright memory of horror, of a year ago, right here . . .

Trusted guard packs paced their course twenty meters on either side. This area was supposedly safe from infiltration, and there had been no artillery fire from the Flenserists for hours. But Peregrine absolutely refused to let her get any closer.

It's nothing like last year. Then all had been sunny blue skies and clean air – and her parents' murder. Now she and Pilgrim had returned, and the blue sky was yellow-gray and the sweeps of mossy hillside were black. And now the packs around her were fighting *with* her. And now there was a chance . . .

'Lemme closer, damn it! Woodcarver will have the Oliphaunt no matter what happens to me.'

Peregrine shook himself, a Tinish negative. One of his puppies reached out from a jacket pouch to catch at her sleeve. 'A little longer,' Pilgrim said for the tenth time. 'Wait for Woodcarver's messenger. Then we can –'

'I want to be up there! I'm the only one who knows the ship!' *Jefri, Jefri. If only Vendacious was right about you . . .*

She was twisting about to slap at Scarbutt when it happened: A glare of heat on her back, and the smoke flashed bright. Again. Again. And then the impact of rapid thunder marching across the sky.

Pilgrim shuddered against her. 'That's not gunfire!' he shouted. 'Two of me are almost blinded. C'mon.' He surrounded her, almost knocking her off her feet as he pushed/dragged her down the hill.

For a second Johanna went along, more dazed than cooperative. Somehow they had lost their escort.

From up the hill the shouts of battle had stopped. The sharp thunder had silenced all. Where the smoke thinned she could see one of Scrupilo's cannons, the barrel extending from a puddle of melted steel. The cannoneer had been blown to bits. Not gunfire. Johanna spasmed out of Pilgrim's grip. *Not gunfire.*

'Spacers! Pilgrim, that must be a drive torch.'

Peregrine grabbed her, continuing down the hill. 'Not a drive torch! That I've heard. This is quieter – and somebody's *aiming* it.'

There had been a long stutter of separate blasts. How many of Woodcarver's people had just died? 'They must think we're attacking the ship, Pilgrim. If we don't do something, they'll wipe out everyone.'

His jaws eased their grip on her sleeves and pants. 'What can we do? Hanging around here will just get us killed.'

504

Johanna stared into the sky. No sign of fliers, but there was so much smoke. The sun was a dull bloody ball. If only the rescuers knew they were killing her friends. If only they could see . . . She dug her feet into the ground. 'If I can get where they can see me . . . Let go of me, Pilgrim! I'm going uphill, out of the smoke.'

He'd stopped moving but his grip was fiercely tight. Four adult faces and two puppy ones looked up at her, and indecision was in every look. 'Please, Pilgrim. It's the only way.' Packs were straggling down, some bleeding, some in fragments.

His frightened eyes stared at her an instant longer. Then he let go and touched her hand with a nose. 'I guess this hill will always be the death of me. First Scriber, now you – you're all crazy.' The old Pilgrim smile flickered across his members. 'Okay. Let's try it!' The two without puppies went up the hillside, scouting for the safest route.

Johanna and the rest of him followed. They were moving across a sloping terrace. The summer drought had drained the chill swamp water she remembered from the landing, and the blackened moss was firm under her. The going should have been easy, but Peregrine wound through the deepest hummocks, hunkering down every few seconds to look in all directions. They reached the end of the terrace and began climbing. There were places so steep she had to grab the epaulet stirrups on two of Peregrine and let him hoist her up. They passed the nearest cannon, what was left of it. Johanna had never seen such things except in stories, but the splash of metal and the carbonized flesh could only mean some kind of beam weapon. Running across the hill were similar craters, destruction punched into the already burned land.

Johanna leaned against a smooth rounding of rock. 'Just pull over this one and we're on the next terrace,' Pilgrim's voice came in her ear. 'Hurry, I hear shouting.' He leaned two of himself down, tilting his epaulets toward her hands. She grabbed them, pushing off with her feet. For a moment she and the pack teetered over a four-meter fall, and then she was lying on brownish, unburned moss. Pilgrim clustered around her, hiding her. She peeked out between his legs. The

505

outermost walls of Steel's castle were visible from here. Tinish archers stood boldly on the ramparts, taking advantage of the chaos among Woodcarver's troops. In fact, the Queen's force had not lost many packs in the air attack, but even the unwounded were milling around. The Queen's soldiers were no cowards – Johanna knew that by now – but they had just been confronted by force beyond all defense.

Overhead the smoke faded into blue. The battlefield ahead of her lay under clear sky. In the years before the High Lab, Johanna and her mother had often gone on nature trips over Bigby Marsh at Straum. With the sensors on their camper packs they'd had no trouble watching the skyggwings there: even if this flier's automation was not specifically looking for a human on the ground, it should notice her. 'Do you see anything?'

The four adult heads angled back and forth in coordinated pairs. 'No. The flier must be very far away or behind the smoke.'

Nuts. Johanna came off her knees, trotted toward the castle walls. They must be watching there!

'Woodcarver's not going to like this.'

Two of the Queen's soldiers were already running toward them, attracted by their purposeful movement or the sight of Johanna. Pilgrim waved them back.

Alone on an open field less than two hundred meters from the castle wall. Even with normal vision, how could they be overlooked? In fact, they were noticed: There was a soft hissing, and a meter-long arrow thunked into the turf on their left. Scarbutt grabbed her shoulder, pulling her to a crouch. The puppies shifted his shields into position: Pilgrim made a barricade of himself on the castle side and started back out of range. Back into the smoke.

'No! Run parallel! I want to be seen.'

'Okay, okay.' Soft sounds of death whispered down. Johanna kept one hand on his shoulder as they ran across the field. She felt Scarbutt falter. The arrow had caught him in the thick of his shoulder, centimeters from a tympanum. 'I'm okay! Stay down, stay down.'

The front line of Woodcarver's force was rallying toward

them now, a dozen packs racing across the terrace. Pilgrim bounced up and down, shouting with a voice that punched like physical force. Something about staying back and danger from the sky. It didn't stop their advance. 'They want you away from the arrows.'

And suddenly they noticed that the fire from the castle had stopped. Pilgrim scanned the sky. 'It's back! Coming from the east, maybe a kilometer out.'

She looked in the direction he was pointing. It was a lumpy thing, probably space-based though it had no ultradrive spines. It bobbled and staggered. There was no sign of jets. Some kind of agrav? Nonhumans? The thoughts skittered through her mind, alongside the joy.

Pale light flickered from a mast on its belly and dirt geysered around the troops who were racing to protect her. Again the stuttering thunder, only now the light was marching right across her friends toward her.

Amdijefri was on the battlements. Steel hid his glares from the two. There simply was no help for it; Ravna had demanded Jefri be by the radio to guide the strike. The human was not completely stupid. It shouldn't make any difference. An Army looks like an army whether it is foe or friend. Very soon the army beyond these walls would cease to exist.

'How did the first run go?' Ravna's voice came clearly from the comm set. But it wasn't Jefri who answered: all eight of Amdiranifani was poking around the battlements, some of him sitting on the crenellations practicing stereo vision, others eyeing Steel and the radio. Telling him to stay back had no effect. Now Amdi answered the question with Jefri's voice. 'Okay. I counted fifteen pulses. Only ten hit anything. I bet I could shoot better than that.'

'Damn it, that's the best I can do with this [unknown words].' The voice was not Ravna's. Steel heard the irritation in it. *Everybody can find something to hate in these pups.* The thought warmed him.

'Please,' said Steel. 'Fire again. Again.' He looked over the stonework. The air attack had taken out a band of enemy by

507

the edge of the near terrace. It was spectacular destruction, like enormous cannon blows, or the separate landing of twenty starships. And all from a little craft that fluttered like a falling leaf. The enemy front line was dissolving in panic. Up and down the ramparts, his own troops danced about their stations. Things had been bleak since their cannon were knocked out; they needed something to cheer about. 'The archers, Shreck! Shoot upon the survivors.' Then, continuing in Samnorsk: 'The front ranks are still coming. They are – they are –' *Damn, what's the word for 'confident'?* 'They will kill us without more help.'

The human child looked at Steel in puzzlement. If he called that a lie, then . . . A moment later Ravna said. 'I don't know. They're well back from your walls, at least all that I can see. I don't want to butcher . . .' Rapid fire conversation with the human in the flier, perhaps not even in Samnorsk. The gunner did not sound pleased. 'Pham will pull back a few kilometers,' she said. 'We can come back instantly if your enemy advances.'

'*Sssst!*' Shreck's Hightalk hiss was like a physical jab. Steel wheeled, glaring. *How dare* – But his lieutenant was wide-eyed, pointing toward the center of the battlefield. Of course Steel had had a pair of eyes on that direction, but he hadn't been paying attention: *The other Two-Legs!*

The mantis figure dropped behind an accompanying pack, mercifully before Amdijefri noticed. Thank the Pack of Packs that puppies are nearsighted. Steel swept forward, surrounding some of Amdi, shouting at the others to get off the parapet. Both of Tyrathect ran in close, physically grabbing for the disobedient wretches. 'Get below!' Steel screamed in Tinish. For a second all was confusion, as his own mind sounds mixed with the puppies'. Amdi tumbled away from him, thoroughly distracted by the noise and the rough pushing. And then in Samnorsk, Steel said, 'There are more cannons out there. Get below before you're hurt!'

Jefri started for the parapet. 'But I don't see –' And fortunately there *was* nothing special to see. Now. The other Two-Legs was still crouched behind one of Woodcarver's packs. Shreck took the human child in paw and jaw. He and one of Tyrathect hustled the protesting children down the stairs. As they departed, Tyrathect was already embellishing on Steel's story, reporting on the troops it could see from below the crest of the hill.

'Blow up the lesser powder dump,' Steel hissed at the departing Shreck. That dump was nearly empty, but its destruction might persuade the spacers where words could not.

After they were gone, Steel stood for an instant, silent and shivering. He had never seen disaster so narrowly avoided. Along the ramparts, his archers were showering arrows upon the enemy pack and the Two-Legs. *Damn*. They were almost out of range.

In the castle yard, Shreck detonated the lesser dump. The explosion was a satisfying one, much louder than an artillery hit; one of the inner towers was blown apart. Flying rock showered the yard, the smallest pieces reaching all the way to where Steel stood on the ramparts.

Ravna's voice was shouting in swift Samnorsk, too fast for Steel to understand. Now all the planning, all the hopes, all balanced on a knife edge. He must bet everything: Steel leaned a shoulder close to the comm and said, 'Sorry. Things go fast here. Many more Woodcarver come up under smoke. Can you kill all on hillside?' Could the mantises see through smoke? That was part of the gamble.

The gunner's voice came back, 'I can try. Watch this.'

A third voice, thready and narrow even by human standards: 'It will be fifty seconds more, Sir Steel. We've having trouble turning.'

Good. Concentrate on your flying and your killing. Don't look at your victims too carefully. The archers had driven the human back, part way under the cover of smoke. Other packs were rushing out to protect her. By the time the Visitors circled back, there would be lots of targets, the human lost among them.

Two of him caught sight of the spacer floating down through the haze. The Visitors would have no clear view of what they were shooting at. Pale light flickered from beneath the craft. A scythe swept across the hillside toward

Woodcarver's troops.

Pham was bounced around his perch as Blueshell turned the boat back to the target. They weren't moving fast; the airstream couldn't have been more than thirty meters per second. But every second was full of the damnedest jerks and tumbles. At one point Pham's grip on the gun mount was all that kept him indoors. *Forty some hours from now, the deadliest thing in the universe is going to arrive, and I'm taking potshots at dogs.*

How to take out the hillside? Steel's whiney voice still echoed in his ears. And Ravna wasn't sure what *OOB* was seeing beneath all the smoke. *We might do better without automation than with this bastard mix.* At least his beamer had a manual control. Pham embraced the barrel with one arm while he reached with the other. At wide dispersion the beam was useless against armor, but could burst eyes and set skin and hair afire – and the beam width would be dozens of meters across at ground level.

'Fifteen seconds, Sir Pham,' Blueshell's voice came in his ear.

They were low this time. Gaps in the smoke flickered past like stop-action art. Most of the ground was burned-over black, but there were precipices of naked rock and even sooty patches of snow trapped in crannies and shadowed pits . . . Here and there was a pile of doggy bodies, an occasional gun tube.

'There's a crowd of them ahead, Sir Pham. Running near the castle.'

Pham leaned down and looked forward. The mob was about four hundred meters ahead. They were running parallel to the castle walls, through a field that was a spinehide of arrowshafts. He pressed the firing stud, swept the beam out from below the boat. There was plenty of water under that dried cover; it exploded in steam as the beam passed over it . . . But further out, the wide dispersion wasn't doing much. It would be another few seconds before he'd have a good shot at the hapless packs.

Time for the little suspicions. So how come the enemy had

muzzle-loading cannon? *Those* they must have made themselves – in a world with no evidence of firearms. Steel was the classic medieval manipulator; Pham had spotted the type from a thousand light-years out. They were doing the critter's dirty work, that was obvious. *Shut up. Deal with Steel later.*

Slanting in on the packs, Pham fired again, sweeping through living flesh this time. He fired ahead of them and on the castle side; maybe they wouldn't all die. He stuck his head further into the slipstream, trying for a better view. Ahead of the packs was a hundred meters of open field, a single pack of four and – *a human figure, black-haired and slim, jumping and waving.*

Pham smashed the barrel up against the hull, safing it at the same time. The back flash was a surge of heat that crisped his eyebrows. 'Blueshell! Get us down! Get us down!'

39

'A bad understanding. She was lied to.'

Ravna tried to read something behind the voice. Steel's Samnorsk was as creaky as ever, the tones childish and whiney. He sounded no different than before. But his story was stretched very thin by what had just happened . . . He was either a galactic master of impudence – or his story was actually true.

'The human must have been hurt, then lied to by Woodcarver. This explains a lot, Ravna. Without her, Woodcarver could not attack. Without her, all may be safe.'

Pham's voice came to Ravna on a private channel. 'The girl *was* unconscious during part of the ambush, Rav. But she practically scratched my eyes out when I suggested she might be wrong about Steel and Woodcarver. And the pack with her is a lot more convincing than Steel.'

Ravna looked questioningly across the deck at Greenstalk. Pham didn't know she was here. *Tough.* Greenstalk was an island of sanity amidst the madness – and she knew the *OOB* infinitely better than Ravna.

Steel spoke into her hesitation: 'See now, nothing has changed, except for the better. One more human lives. How can you doubt us? Speak to Jefri; he understands. We have done the best for the children in . . .' a gobbling noise, and (another?) voice said, 'coldsleep.'

'Certainly we must speak to him again, Steel. He's our best proof of your good intentions.'

'Okay. In a few minutes, Ravna. But see, he is also my good protection against tricks from you. I know how powerful you Visitors are. I . . . fear you. We need to –' gobbling consultation '– accommodate each other in our fears.'

'Um. We'll work something out. Just let us speak to Jefri now.'

'Yes.'

Ravna switched channels. 'What do you think, Pham?'

'There's no question in my mind. This Johanna is not a naïve kid like Jefri. We've always known Steel was a tough critter. We just had some other facts wrong. The landing site is in the middle of his territory. He's the killer.' Pham's voice became quieter, almost a whisper. 'Hell of it is, this may not change anything. Steel does have the ship. I've got to get in there.'

'It will be another ambush.'

'. . . I know. But does it matter? If we can get me time with the Countermeasure, it could be – it will be – worth it.' What matter a suicide mission within a suicide mission?

'I'm not sure, Pham. If we give him everything, he'll kill us before we ever get near the ship.'

'He'll try. Look, just keep him talking. Maybe we can get a directional on his radio, blow the bastard away.' He did not sound optimistic.

Tyrathect didn't take them back to the ship, or to their rooms. They descended stairs within the outer walls, part of Amdi first, then Jefri with the rest of Amdi, then the singleton from Tyrathect.

Amdi was still complaining. 'I don't understand, I don't understand. We can help.'

Jefri: 'I didn't see any enemy cannons.'

The singleton was full of explanations, though it sounded even more preoccupied than usual. 'I saw them from one of my other members, out in the valley. We're pulling in all our soldiers. We must make a stand, or none of us will be alive to be rescued. For now, this is the best place for you to be.'

'How do you know?' said Jefri. 'Can you talk to Steel right now?'

'Yes, one of me is still up there with him.'

'Well, tell him we have to help. We can talk better Samnorsk even than you.'

'I'll tell him right now,' was the Cloak's quick reply.

There were no more window slots cut in the walls. The only light came from wick torches set every ten meters along the tunnel. The air was cool and musty; wetness glistened on unquilted stone. The tiny doors were not of polished wood. Instead there were bars, and darkness beyond. *Where are we going?* Jefri was suddenly reminded of the dungeons in stories, the treachery that befell the Greater Two and the Countess of the Lake. Amdi didn't seem to feel it. For all his mischievous nature, Puppies was basically trusting; he had always depended on Mr Steel. But Jefri's parents had never acted quite like this, even during the escape from High Lab. Mr Steel suddenly seemed so different, as if he couldn't be bothered pretending to be nice anymore. And Jefri had never really trusted the sullen Tyrathect; now that one was acting downright sneaky.

There had been no new threat on the hillside.

Fear and stubbornness and suspicion all came together: Jefri spun around, confronting the Cloak. 'We're not going any farther. This isn't where we're supposed to go. We want to talk to Ravna and Mr Steel.' A sudden, liberating realization: 'And you're not big enough to stop us!'

The singleton backed up abruptly, then sat down. It lowered its head, blinked. 'So you don't trust me? You are right not to. There is no one here but yourselves that you can trust.' Its gaze drifted from Jefri to the range of Amdi, and then down the hall. 'Steel doesn't know I've brought you here.'

The confession was so quick, so easily made. Jefri

swallowed hard. 'You brought us down here to k-kill us.' All of Amdi was staring at him and Tyrathect, every eye wide with shock.

The singleton bobbed its head in part of a smile. 'You think I am traitor? After all this time, some healthy suspicion. I am proud of you.' Mr Tyrathect continued smoothly, 'You are surrounded by traitors, Amdijefri. But I am not one of them. I am here to help you.'

'I know that.' Amdi reached forward to touch a muzzle to the singleton's. 'You're no traitor. You're the only person besides Jefri that I can touch. We've always wanted to like you, but –'

'Ah, but you should be suspicious. You will all die if you aren't.' Tyrathect looked over the puppies, at the frowning Jefri. 'Your sister is alive Jefri. She's out there now, and Steel has known all along. He killed your parents; he did almost everything he said Woodcarver did.' Amdi backed away, shaking himself in frightened negations. 'You don't believe me? That's funny. Once upon a time I was such a good liar; I could talk the fish right into my mouths. But now, when only the truth will work, I can't convince you . . . Listen:'

Suddenly it was Steel's human-speaking voice that came from the singleton, Steel talking with Ravna about Johanna being alive, excusing the attack he had just ordered on her.

Johanna. Jefri rushed forward, fell on his knees before the Cloak. Almost without thought, he grabbed the singleton by the throat, shaking it. Teeth snapped at his hands as the other tried to shake free. Amdi rushed forward, pulled hard on his sleeves. After a moment, Jefri let go. Centimeters away from his face, the singleton peered back at him, the torchlight glinting in its dark eyes. Amdi was saying: 'Human voices are easy to fake –'

The fragment was disdainful. 'Of course. And I'm not claiming that was a direct relay. What you heard is several minutes old. Here's what Steel and I are planning this very second.' His Samnorsk abruptly stopped, and the hallway was filled with the gobbling chords of Pack talk. Even after a year, Jefri could only extract vague sense from the conversation. It did sound like two packs. One of them wanted the other to do

514

something, bring Amdijefri – that chord was clear – up.

Amdiranifani went suddenly still, every member straining at the relayed sounds. 'Stop it!' he shrilled. And the hallway was as quiet as a tomb. 'Mr Steel, oh Mr Steel.' All of Amdi huddled against Jefri. 'He's talking about hurting you if Ravna doesn't obey. He wants to kill the Visitors when they land.' The wide eyes were ringed with tears. 'I don't understand.'

Jefri jabbed a hand at the Cloak. 'Maybe he's faking that, too.'

'I don't know. I could never fake two packs that well . . .' The tiny bodies shuddered against Jefri, and there was the sound of human weeping, the eerily familiar sound of a small child desolated . . . 'What are we going to do, Jefri?'

But Jefri was silent, remembering and finally understanding, the first few minutes after Steel's troops had rescued – captured? – him. Memories suppressed by later kindness crept out from the corners of his mind. *Mom, Dad, Johanna. But Johanna still lived, just beyond these walls . . .*

'Jefri?'

'I don't know either. H-hide maybe?'

For a moment they just stared at each other. Finally the fragment spoke. 'You can do better than hide. You already know about the passages through these walls. If you know the entrance points – and I do – you can get to almost anywhere you want. You can even get outside.'

Johanna.

Amdi's crying stopped. Three of him watched Tyrathect front, aft, and sideways. The rest still clung to Jefri. 'We still don't trust *you*, Tyrathect,' said Jefri.

'Good, good. I am a pack of various parts. Perhaps not entirely trustable.'

'Show us all the holes.' Let us decide.

'There won't be time –'

'Okay, but start showing us. And while you do, keep relaying what Mr Steel is saying.'

The singleton bobbed its head, and the multiple streams of Pack talk resumed. The Cloak got painfully to its feet and led the two children down a side tunnel, one where the wick

515

torches were mostly burned out. The loudest sound down here was the soft dripping of water. The place was less than a year old, yet – except for the jagged edges of the cut stone – it seemed ancient.

Puppies was crying again. Jefri stroked the back of the one that clung to his shoulder, 'Please Amdi, translate for me.'

After a moment Amdi's voice came hesitantly in his ear. 'M-Mr Steel is asking again where we are. Tyrathect says we're trapped by a ceiling fall in the inner wing.' In fact, they had heard the masonry shift a few minutes before, but it sounded far away. 'Mr Steel just sent the rest of Tyrathect to get Mr Shreck and dig us out. Mr Steel sounds so . . . different.'

'Maybe it's not really him,' Jefri whispered back.

Long silence. 'No. It's him. He just seems so angry, and he's using strange words.'

'Big words?'

'No. Scary ones. About cutting and killing . . . Ravna and you and me. He . . . he doesn't like us, Jefri.'

The singleton stopped. They were beyond the last wall torch, and it was too dark to see anything but shadowy forms. He was pointed at a spot on the wall. Amdi reached forward and pushed at the rock. All the while Mr Tyrathect continued talking, reporting from outside.

'Okay,' said Amdi, 'that opens. And it's big enough for you, Jefri. I think –'

Tyrathect's human voice said, 'The Spacers are back. I can see their little boat . . . I got away just in time. Steel is getting suspicious. A few more seconds and he will be searching everywhere.'

Amdi looked into the dark hole. 'I say we go,' he said softly, sadly.

'Yeah.' Jefri reached down to touch one of Amdi's shoulders. The member led him to a hole cut in sharp-edged stone. If he scrunched his shoulders there would be enough room to crawl in. One of Amdi entered just ahead of him. The rest would follow. 'I hope it doesn't get any narrower than this.'

Tyrathect: 'It shouldn't. All these passages are designed

for packs in light armor. The important thing: keep to upward curving passages. Keep moving and you'll eventually get outside. Pham's flying craft is less than, uh, five hundred meters from the walls.

Jefri couldn't even look over his shoulder to talk to the Cloak. 'What if Mr Steel chases us into the walls?'

There was a brief silence. 'He probably won't do that, if he doesn't now where you entered. It would take too long to find you. But,' the voice was suddenly gentler, 'but there are openings on the top of the walls. In case enemy soldiers tried to sneak in from the outside, there has to be some way to kill them in the tunnels. He could pour oil down the tunnels.'

The possibility did not frighten Jefri. At the moment it just sounded bizarre. 'We've got to hurry then.'

Jefri scrabbled forward as the rest of Amdi crawled in behind him. He was already several meters deep in stone when he heard Amdi's voice back at the entrance, the last one to enter: 'Will you be okay, Mr Tyrathect?'

Or is this all another lie? thought Jefri.

The other's voice had its usual, cynical tone. 'I expect to land on my feet. Please do remember that I helped you.'

And then the hatch was shut and they scrambled forward, into the dark.

Negotiations, shit. It was obvious to Pham that Steel's idea of 'mutually safe meeting' was a cover for mayhem. Even Ravna wasn't fooled by the pack's new proposals. At least it meant that Steel was ad libbing now – that he was beyond all the scripts and schemes. The trouble was, he still wasn't giving them any openings. Pham would have cheerfully died for a few undisturbed hours with the Countermeasure, but Steel's setup would have them dead before they ever saw the inside of the refugee ship.

'Keep moving around, Blueshell. I want Steel to have us weighing on his mind, without being a good target.'

The Rider waved a frond in agreement and the boat bounced briefly up from the moss, drifted a hundred meters parallel to the castle walls, and descended again. They were in the no-man's land between the forces of Woodcarver and

Steel.

Johanna Olsndot twisted around to look at him. The boat was a very crowded place now, Blueshell stretched across the Riderish controls at the bow, Pham and Johanna jammed into the seats behind him – and a pack called Pilgrim in every empty space in between. 'Even if you can locate the commset, don't fire. Jefri could be close by.' For twenty minutes Steel had been promising the momentary reappearance of Jefri Olsndot.

Pham eyed her smudged face. 'Yeah, we won't fire unless we can see exactly what we'll hit.' The girl nodded briefly. She couldn't have been more than fourteen, but she was a good trooper. Half the people he had known in Qeng Ho would have been in limp hysterics after this pickup. And of the rest, few could have given a better status report than Johanna and her friend.

He glanced at the pack. It would take a while to get used to these critters. At first he'd thought that two of the dogs were sprouting extra heads – then he noticed the small ones were just puppies carried in jacket pockets. The 'Pilgrim' was all over the boat; just what part of him should he talk to? He picked the head that was looking in his direction. 'Any theories how to deal with Steel?'

The pack's Samnorsk was better than Pham's. 'Steel and Flenser are as tricky as anything I've seen in Johanna's dataset. And Flenser is cool.'

'Flenser? Hadn't realized there was a person with that name . . . There was a "Mr Skinner" we talked to. Some kind of assistant to Steel.'

'Hmm. He's tricky enough to play flunky . . . wish we could drop back and chat with Woodcarver about this.' The request was artfully contained in his intonation. Pham wondered briefly what percentage of Packfolk were so flexible. They might be one hell of a trading race if they ever reached space.

'Sorry, we don't have time for that. In fact, if we can't get in right away, we've lost everything. I just hope Steel doesn't guess that.'

The heads subtly rearranged themselves. The biggest member, the one with a broken arrow shaft sticking up from its jacket, moved closer to the girl. 'Well, if Steel is in charge, there's a chance. He's very smart, but we think he runs amok when things get tough. Your finding Johanna has probably put him to chasing his tails. Keep him off balance, and you can expect some big mistakes.'

Johanna spoke abruptly, 'He might kill Jefri.'

Or blow up the starship. 'Ravna, any luck with Steel?'

Her voice came back over the comm: 'No. The threats are a bit more transparent now, and his Samnorsk is getting harder to understand. He's trying to bring cannon in from north of the Castle; I don't think he knows how much I can see . . . He still hasn't brought Jefri back to the radio.'

The girl paled, but she didn't say anything. Her hand stole up to grasp one of Pilgrim's paws.

Blueshell had been very quiet all through the rescue, first because he had his fronds full with flying, then because the girl and the Pack had so much to say. Pham had noticed that part of Pilgrim had been politely nosing around the Rider. Blueshell hadn't seemed upset by the attention; his race had plenty of experience with others.

But now the Rider made a *brap* for attention. 'Sir Pham, there is action in front of the castle.'

Pilgrim was on it at almost the same instant, one head helping another look through a telescope. 'Yes. That's the main sally port that's coming open. But why would Steel send packs out now? Woodcarver will chew them up.' The enemy was indeed fielding infantry. The packs spewed out the wide hole in a headlong dash, much like troops of Pham's recollection. But once they cleared the entrance they broke off into clumps of four to six dogs each and spread across the castle perimeter.

Pham leaned forward, trying to see as far along the walls as possible. 'Maybe not. These guys aren't advancing. They're staying in range of the archers on the walls.'

'Yeah. But we still have cannons.' Pilgrim's perfect imitation of humanity broke for a second, and a Tinish chord filled the cockpit. 'Something is really strange. It's like they're trying to keep someone from getting *out*.'

'Are there other entrances?'

'Probably. And lots of little tunnels, just one member wide.'

'Ravna?'

'Steel's not talking at all now. He said something about traitors infiltrating the castle. Now all I'm getting is Tinish gobble.' From embrasure to embrasure along the battlements, Pham could see enemy soldiers moving above those on the ground. Something had upset the rats' nest.

Johanna Olsndot was a vision of horrified concentration, her free hand gathered into a fist, her lips faintly trembling. 'All this time I thought he was dead. If they kill him now, I . . .' Her voice suddenly scaled up: 'What are they doing?' Cast iron kettles had been dragged to the top of the walls.

Pham could guess. Siege fighting on Canberra had involved similar things. He looked at the girl, and kept his mout h shut. *There's nothing we can do.*

The Pilgrim pack was not so kind – or not so patronizing: 'It's oil, Johanna. They want to kill someone in the walls. But if he can get out . . . Blueshell, I've read about loudspeakers. Can I use one? If Jefri is in the walls, Woodcarver can safely scrape Steel's troops off the field and battlements.'

Pham opened his mouth to object, but the Rider had already opened a channel. Pilgrim's Tinish voice echoed across the hillside. Along the castle walls heads turned. To them, the voice must have sounded like a god's. The chords and trills continued a moment longer, then ceased.

Ravna's voice was on the line an instant later, 'Whatever you did just now, it pushed Steel over the edge. I can barely understand him; He seems to be describing how he'll torture Jefri if we don't pull the Woodcarvers back.'

Pham grunted. 'Okay then. Get us in the air, Blueshell.' It felt good to kiss subtlety goodbye.

Blueshell wobbled the boat aloft. They moved forward, scarcely faster than a man can run. Behind them more of Woodcarver's troops were coming over the military crest of the hill. Those fellows had been pulled well back after Pham's strafing run: things might be decided before they got to the castle . . . But Woodcarver's reach was still long and deadly: splashes of smoke and fire appeared along the battlements, followed by sharp popping noises. Killing Jefri Olsndot was going to be a very expensive proposition for Steel.

'Can you use the beamer to clear Steel's troops away from the wall?' asked Johanna.

Pham started to nod, then noticed what was happening by the castle. 'See the oil.' Dark pools were growing between the enemy packs and the walls they guarded. Until they knew where the kid was coming out, it would be best not to start fires.

Pilgrim: 'Oops.' Then he was shouting something more on the loudspeakers. Woodcarver's artillery ceased.

'Okay,' said Pham, 'for now, all eyes on the castle wall. Circle the perimeter, Blueshell. If we can see the kid before Steel's guys, we may have a chance.'

Ravna: 'They're spread evenly around every side except the North, Pham. I don't think Steel has any idea where the boy is.'

When you challenge Heaven, the stakes are high. *And I could have won. If he had not betrayed me. I could have won.* But now the masks were down, and the enemy's brute physical power was all that counted. Steel brought himself down from the hysterical blackout of the last few minutes. *If I can not have Heaven, at least I can still take them to Hell.* Kill Amdijefri, destroy the ship the Visitors wanted so . . . most of all, destroy his traitorous teacher.

'My lord?' It was Shreck.

Steel turned a head in Shreck's direction. The time for hysteria was past. 'How goes the flooding?' he said mildly. He wouldn't ask about Tyrathect again.

'All but complete. The oil is pooling beyond the castle walls.' The two packs crouched as one of Woodcarver's bombs exploded just beyond the battlement. Her troops were already halfway back across the field – and Steel's archers were preoccupied with flooding the tunnels and watching the exits. 'We may have flushed out the traitors, my lord. Just before Woodcarver resumed fire, we heard something by the southeast wall. But I fear the Spacers will see whatever we do there.' His heads bobbed spastically.

Strange to see Shreck coming apart, Steel thought vaguely. Shreck's was the loyalty of clockwork, but now his orderly world was failing and there was nothing left to support him. The madness he was born from was all that was left.

If Shreck was close to breaking, then the siege of Starship Hill was nearly at an end. *Just a little longer, that is all I ask now*. Steel forced a confident expression upon his members. 'I understand. You have done well, Shreck. We may still win. I know how these mantises think. If you can kill the child, especially before their eyes, it will break their spirit – just as puppies can be broken by the right terrors.'

'Yes, sir.' There was dull incredulity in Shreck's eyes, but this would hold him, a plausible excuse to continue the charade.

'Light the oil beyond the walls. Move the troops in front of where you think Amdijefri will exit. The Visitors must see this if it is to have proper effect. And –' *and blow up the refugee ship!* The words almost slipped out, but he caught himself in time. The explosives built into the Jaws and the Starship dome would bring down everything interior to the outerwalls and would kill most of the packs within. Ordering Shreck to do that would make Steel's real goal all too clear. '– And move quickly before Woodcarver's troops can close. This is the Movement's last hope, Shreck.'

The pack bowed its way back down the steps. Steel maintained an expansive posture, boldly looking across the battlefield until the other was out of sight. Then he reached across the battlements and slammed the radio into the stone walkway. This one didn't break, and now the Ravna mantis's voice came querulously from it. Steel bounded down the stairs. 'You get nothing,' he shrieked back at her in Tines' talk. 'Everything you want will die!'

And then he was down the stairs and running across the courtyard. He ducked out of sight, into the hallway that circled the Jaws of Welcome. He could blow those easily, but very likely the main dome and the ship within would survive. No, he must go to the heart. Kill the ship and all the sleeping mantises. He stepped into a secret room, picked up two crossbows – and the extra *radio* cloak he had prepared. Inside that cloak was a small bomb. He had tested the idea with the second set of *radios*; the wearer had died instantly.

Down another set of stairs, into a supply corridor. The sounds of battle were lost behind him. His own tines' clatter was the loudest noise. Around him loomed bits of gunpowder, food supplies, fresh timber. The fuses and set charges were only fifty yards further on. And Steel slowed to a walk, curled his paws so the metal on them made no noise. Listening. Looking in every direction. Somehow he knew the other would be here. The Flenser Fragment. Flenser had haunted him from the beginning of his existence, had haunted him even after Flenser had mostly died. But not until this clear treason had Steel been able to free his hate. Most likely the Master thought to escape with the children, but there was a chance that Flenser schemed to win *everything*. There was a chance that he had returned. Steel knew his own death would come soon. And yet there might still be triumph. If, by his own jaws and claws, he could kill the Master . . . *Please, please be here, dear Master. Be here thinking you can trick me one more time.*

A wish granted. He heard faint mind sounds. Close. Heads rose from behind the bins above him. Two of the Fragment showed themselves in the corridor ahead.

'Student.'

'Master.' Steel smiled. All five of the others were here; the Fragment had smuggled himself all back. *But gone were the radio cloaks.* The members stood naked, their pelts covered with oozing sores. The radio bomb would be useless. Perhaps it didn't matter; Steel had seen corpses that looked healthier than these. Out of sight he raised his bows. 'I have come to kill you.'

The death's heads shrugged. 'You have come to try.'

Jaws on claws, Steel would have had no trouble killing the other. But the Fragment had positioned three of himself above, by cargo bins that looked strangely off-balance. A straight forward rush could be fatal. But if he could get good bow shots . . . Steel eased forward, to just short of where the cargo bins would fall. 'Do you really expect to live, Fragment? I am not your only enemy.' He waved a nose back up the corridor. 'There are thousands out there who hunger for your death.'

The other bobbed its heads in a ghastly smile. New blood oozed from the wounds that were opened. 'Dear Steel, you never seem to understand. *You* have made it possible for me to survive. Don't you see? I have saved the children. Even now, I am preventing you from harming the starship. In the end this will win me a conditional surrender. I will be weak for a few years, but I will survive.'

The old Flenser glittered through the pain of the wounds. The old opportunism.

'But you are a *fragment*. Three-fifths of you is –'

'The little school teacher?' Flenser lowered his heads, blinked shyly. 'She was stronger than I expected. For a while she ruled this pack, but bit by bit I forced my way back. In the end, even without the others, I am whole.'

Flenser whole once more. Steel edged back, almost in retreat. Yet there was something strange here. Yes, the Flenser was at peace with himself, self-satisfied. But now that Steel could see the pack all together, he saw something in its body language that . . . Insight came then, and with it a flash of intense pride. *For once in my life, I understand better than the Master.* 'Whole, you say? Think. We both know how souls do battle within, the little rationalizations, the great unknowings. You think you've killed the other, but whence comes your recent confidence? What you're doing is exactly what Tyrathect would do now. All thought is yours now, but the foundation is her soul. And whatever you *think*, it's the little school teacher who won!'

The Fragment hesitated, understanding. Its inattention lasted only a fraction of a second, but Steel was ready: he leaped into the open, loosing his arrows, lunging across the open space for the other's throats.

40

Any time before now, the climb through the walls would have been fun. Even though it was pitch dark, Amdi was in front and behind him, and his noses gave him a good feel for the way. Any time before now, there would have been the thrill of discovery, of giggling at Amdi's strung-out mental state.

But now Amdi's confusion was simply scary. He kept bumping into Jefri's heels. 'I'm going as fast as I can.' The fabric of Jefri's pants' knees was already torn apart on the rough stone. He hustled faster, the stabbing beat of rock on knees barely penetrating his consciousness. He bumped into the puppy ahead of him. The puppy had stopped, seemed to be twisting sideways. 'There's a fork. I say we . . . what should I say, Jefri?'

Jefri rolled back, knocking his head on top of the wormhole. For most of a year it had been Amdi's confidence, his cheeky cleverness, that had kept him going. Now . . . Suddenly he was aware of the tonnes of rock that were pressing in from all directions. If the tunnel narrowed just a few centimeters, they would be stuck here forever.

'Jefri?'

'I –' *Think!* 'Which side seems to be going up?'

'Just a second.' The lead member ran off a little ways down one fork.

'Don't go too far!' Jefri shouted.

'Don't worry. I . . . he'll know to get back.' Then he heard patter of return, and the lead member was touching its nose to his cheek. 'The one on the right goes up.'

They hadn't gone more than fifteen meters before Amdi started hearing things. 'People chasing us?' asked Jefri.

'No. I mean, I'm not sure. Stop. Listen . . . Hear that? Gluppy, syrupy.' *Oil.*

No more stopping. Jefri moved faster than ever up the tunnel. His head bumped into the ceiling and he stumbled to his elbows, recovered without thinking and raced on. A trickle of blood dripped down his cheek.

Even he could hear the oil now.

The sides of the tunnel closed down on his shoulders. Ahead of him, Amdi said, 'Dead end – or we're at an exit!' Scritching sounds. 'I can't move it.' The puppy turned around and wiggled back between Jefri's legs. 'Push at the top, Jefri. If it's like the one I found in the dome, it opens at the top.'

The darn tunnel got narrow right before the door. Jefri hunched his shoulders and squeezed forward. He pushed at the top of the door. It moved, maybe a centimeter. He crawled forward a little further, squished so tightly between the walls that he couldn't even take a deep breath. Now he pushed as hard as he could. The stone turned all the way and light spilled onto his face. It wasn't full daylight; they were still hidden from the outside behind angles of stone – but it was the happiest sight Jefri had ever seen. Half a meter more and he would be out – only now he was jammed.

He twisted forward a fraction, and things only seemed to get worse. Behind him, Amdi was piling up. 'Jefri! My rear paws are in the oil. It's filled the tunnel all up behind us.'

Panic. For a second Jefri couldn't think of anything. So close, so close. He could see color now, the bloody smears on his hands. 'Back up! I'll take off my jacket and try again.'

Backing up was itself almost impossible, so thoroughly wedged had he become. Finally he'd done it. He turned on his side, shrugged out of the jacket.

'Jefri! Two of me under . . . oil. Can't breathe.' The puppies jammed up around him, their pelts slick with oil. *Slick!*

'Jus' second!' Jefri wiped the fur, smeared his shoulders with the oil. He extended his arms straight past his head and used his heels to push back into the narrowness. Behind him, what was left of Amdi was making whistling noises. Jam. *Push. Push.* A centimeter, another. And then he was out to his armpits and it was easy.

He dropped to the ground and reached back to grab the nearest part of Amdi. The pup wriggled out of his hands. It blubbered something not Tinish and not human. Jefri could see the dark shadows of several members pulling at something out of sight. A second later, a cold, wet blob of fur rolled out of the darkness into his arms. A second more, and out came another. Jefri lowered the two to the ground and wiped goo away from their muzzles. One rolled onto its legs and began to shake itself. The other started choking and coughing.

Meanwhile the rest of Amdi dropped out of the hole. All eight were covered with some amount of oil. They straggled drunkenly into a heap, wiping at each another's tympana. Their buzzing and croaking made no sense.

Jefri turned from his friend and walked toward the light. They were hidden by a turn in the stone . . . fortunately. From around the corner he could hear the marshalling calls of Steel's troopers. He crept to the edge and peered around. For an instant he thought he and Amdi were back inside the castle yard; there were so many troopers. But then he saw the unbounded sweep of the hillside and the smoke rising out of the valley.

What next? He glanced back at Amdi, who was still frantically grooming his tympana. The chords and hums were sounding more rational now, and all of Amdi was moving. He turned back to the hillside. For an instant he almost felt like rushing out to the troops. They had been his protectors for so long.

One of Amdi bumped against his legs, and looked out for himself. 'Wow. There's a regular lake of oil between us and Mr Steel's soldiers. I –'

The booming sound was loud, but not like a gunpowder blast. It lasted almost a second, then became a background roar. Two more of Amdi stretched necks around the corner. The lake had become a roaring sea of flame.

Blueshell had maneuvered the boat within two hundred meters of the castle wall, opposite the point where the packs had bunched up. Now the lander floated just a man's height off the moss. 'Just our being here is driving the packs away,' said Pilgrim.

Pham glanced over his shoulder. Woodcarver's troops had regained the field, were racing toward the castle walls. Another sixty seconds, max, and they would be in contact with Steel's packs.

There was a loud *brap* from Blueshell's voder, and Pham looked forward. 'By the Fleet,' he said softly. Packs on the ramparts had fired some kind of flamethrowers into the pools of oil below the castle walls. Blueshell flew in a little closer. Long pools of oil lay parallel to the walls. The enemy's packs on the outside were all but cut off from their castle now. Except for one thirty-meter-wide gap, the section they had been guarding was high fire.

The boat bobbed a little higher, tilting and sliding in the fire-driven whirl of air. In most places the oil lapped the sloped base of the walls. Those walls were more intricate than the castles of Canberra – in many places it looked like there were little mazes or caves built into the base. *Looks damn stupid in a defensive structure.*

'*Jefri!*' screamed Johanna, and pointed toward the middle of the unburning section. Pham had a glimpse of something withdrawing behind the stonework.

'I saw him too.' Blueshell tilted the boat over and slid downwards, toward the wall. Johanna's hand closed on Pham's arm, pushing and shaking. He could barely hear her voice over the Pilgrim's shouting. 'Please, please, please,' she was saying.

For a moment it looked like they would make it: Steel's troops were well back from them and – though there were ponds of oil below them – they were not yet alight. Even the air seemed quieter than before. For all that, Blueshell managed to lose control. A gentle tipping went uncorrected, and the boat slid sideways into the ground. It was a slow collision, but Pham heard one of the landing pods cracking. Blueshell played with the controls and the other side of the craft settled to earth. The beamer was stuck muzzle first into the earth.

Pham's gaze snapped up at the Skroderider. He'd known it would come to this.

Ravna: 'What happened? Can you get up?'

Blueshell dithered with the controls a moment longer, then gave a Riderish shrug. 'Yes. But it will take too long – ' He was undoing his restraints, unclamping his skrode from the deck. The hatch in front of him slid open, and the noise of battle and fire came loud.

'What in hell do you think you're doing, Blueshell!'

The Rider's fronds angled attention at Pham. 'To rescue the boy. This will all be afire in a moment.'

'And this boat could fry if we leave it here. You're not going anywhere, Blueshell.' He leaned forward, far enough to grab the other by his lower fronds.

Johanna was looking wildly from one to the other in an uncomprehending panic. 'No! Please – ' And Ravna was shouting at him too. Pham tensed, all his attention on the Rider.

Blueshell rocked toward him in the cramped space and pushed his fronds close to Pham's face. The voder voice frayed into nonlinearity: 'And what will you do if I disobey? I go, Sir Pham. I prove I am not the thrall of some Power. Can you prove as much?'

He paused, and for a moment Rider and human stared at each other from centimeters apart. But Pham did not grab him.

Brap. Blueshell's fronds withdrew. He rolled back onto the lip of the hatch. The skrode's third axle reached the ground, and he descended in a controlled teeter. Still Pham had not moved. *I am not some Power's program.*

'Pham?' The girl was looking up at him, and tugging at his sleeve. Nuwen shook the nightmare away and saw again. The Pilgrim pack was already out of the boat. Short swords were held in the mouths of the four adults; steel claws gleamed on their forepaws.

'Okay.' He flipped open a panel, withdrew the pistol he'd hidden there. Since Blueshell had crashed the damn boat, there was no choice but to make the best of it.

The realization was a cool breath of freedom. He pulled free of the crash restraints and clambered down. Pilgrim stood all around him. The two with puppies were unlimbering some kind of shields. Even with all his mouths full, the critter's voice was as clear as ever: 'Maybe we can find a way closer in – ' between the flames. There were no more arrows from the ramparts. The air above the fire was just too hot for the archers.

Pham and Johanna followed Pilgrim as he skirted pools of black goo. 'Stay as far from the oil as you can.'

The packs of Mr Steel were rounding the flames. Pham couldn't tell if they were charging the lander or simply fleeing the friendlies that chased them. And maybe it didn't matter. He dropped to one knee and sprayed the oncoming packs with his handgun. It was nothing like the beamer, especially at this range, but it was not to be ignored: the front dogs tumbled. Others bounded over them. They reached the far edge of the oil. Only a few ventured into the goo – they knew what it could become. Others shifted out of Pham's sight, behind the landing boat.

Was there a dry approach? Pham ran along the edge of the oil. There had to be a gap in the 'moat,' or surely the fire would have spread. Ahead of him the flames towered ten meters into the air, the heat a physical battering on his skin. Above the top of the glow, tarry smoke swept back over the field, turning the sunlight into reddish murk. 'Can't see a thing,' came Ravna's voice in his ear, despairing.

'There's still a chance, Rav.' If he could hold them off long enough for Woodcarver's troops . . .

Steel's packs had found a safe path inwards and were coming closer. Something zipped past him – an arrow. He dropped to the ground and sprayed the enemy packs at full rate. If they had known how fast he was getting to empty they might have kept coming, but after a few seconds of ripping carnage, the advance halted. The enemy sweep broke apart and the dogthings were running away, taking their chances with Woodcarver's packs.

Pham turned, looking back at the castle. Johanna and Pilgrim stood ten meters nearer the walls. She was standing, pulling against the pack's grasp. Pham followed her gaze . . . There was the Skroderider. Blueshell had paid no attention to the packs that ran around the edge of the fire. He rolled steadily inwards, oily tracks marking his progress. The Rider had drawn in all his externals, and pulled his cargo scarf close to his central stalk. He was driving blind through the superheated air, deeper and deeper into the narrowing gap between flames.

He was less than fifteen meters from the walls. Abruptly two fronds extended out from his trunk, into the heat. *There.* Through the heat shimmer, Pham could see the kid, walking uncertainly out from the cover of stone. Small shapes sat on the boy's shoulders and walked beside him. Pham ran up the slope. He could move faster over this terrain than any Rider. Maybe there was time.

A single burst of flame arched down from the castle, into the pond of oil between him and the Rider at the wall. What had been a narrow channel of safety was gone, and the flames spread unbroken before him.

'There's still lots of clear space,' Amdi said. He reached a few meters out from their hiding place to reconnoiter around the corners. '*The flier is down!* Some . . . strange thing . . . is coming our way. Blueshell or Greenstalk?'

There were lots of Steel's packs out there too, but not close – probably because of the flier. That was a weird one, with none of the symmetry of Straumer aircraft. It looked all tilted over, almost as if it had crashed. A tall human raced across their field of view, firing at Steel's troops. Jefri looked further out, and his hand tightened almost unconsciously on the nearest puppy. Coming toward them was a wheeled vehicle, like something out of a Nyjoran historical. The sides were painted with jagged stripes. A thick pole grew up from the top.

The two children stepped a little ways out from their protection. The spacer saw them! It slewed about, spraying oil and moss from under its wheels. Two frail somethings reached out from its bluish trunk. Its voice was squeaky Samnorsk. 'Quickly, Sir Jefri. We have little time.' Behind the creature, beyond the pond of oil, Jefri could see . . . *Johanna.*

And then the pond exploded, the fire on both sides sprouting across all escape routes. Still the Spacer was waving its tendrils, urging them onto the flat of its hull. Jefri grasped at the few handholds available. The puppies jumped up after him, clinging to his shirt and pants. Up close, Jefri could see that the stalk was the person: the skin was smudged and dry, but it was soft and it moved.

Two of Amdi were still on the ground, ranging out on either side of the cart for a better view of the fire. *'Wah!'* shrieked Amdi by his ear. Even so close, he could scarcely be heard over the thunder of the fire. 'We can never get through that, Jefri. Our only chance is to stay here.'

The Spacer's voice came from a little plate at the base of its stalk. 'No. If you stay here, you *will* die. The fire is spreading.' Jefri had huddled as much behind the Rider's stalk as possible, and still he could feel the heat. Much more and the oil in Amdi's fur might catch fire.

The Rider's tendrils lifted the colored cloth that lay on its hull. 'Pull this over you.' It waggled a tendril at the rest of Amdi. *'All* of you.'

The two on the ground were crouched behind the creature's front wheels. 'Too hot, too hot,' came Amdi's voice. But the two jumped up and buried themselves under the peculiar tarpaulin.

'Cover yourself, all the way!' Jefri felt the Rider pulling the cover over them. The cart was already rolling back, toward the flames. Pain burned through every gap in the tarp. The boy reached frantically, first with one hand and then the other, trying to get the cloth over his legs. Their course was a wild bouncing ride, and Jefri could barely keep hold. Around him he felt Amdi straining with his free jaws to keep the tarpaulin in place. The sound of fire was a roaring beast, and the tarp itself was searing hot against his skin. Every new jolt bounced him up from the hull, threatening to break his grip. For a time, panic obliterated thought. It was not till much later that he remembered the tiny sounds that came from the voder plate, and understood what those sounds must mean.

Pham ran toward the new flames. Agony. He raised his arms across his face and felt the skin on his hands blistering. He backed away.

'This way, this way!' Pilgrim's voice came from behind him, guiding him out. He ran back, stumbling. The pack was in a shallow gully. It had shifted its shields around to face the new stretch of fire. Two of the pack moved out of his way as he dived behind them.

Both Johanna and the pack were slapping at his head.

'Your hair's on fire!' the girl shouted. In seconds they had the fire out. The Pilgrim looked a big singed, too. Its shoulder pouches were tucked safely shut; for the first time, no inquisitive puppy eyes peeked out.

'I still can't see anything, Pham.' It was Ravna from high above. 'What's going on?'

Quick glance behind him. 'We're okay,' he gasped. 'Woodcarver's packs are tearing up Steel's. But Blueshell – ' He peered between in the shields. It was like looking into a kiln. Right by the castle wall there might be a breathing space. A slim hope, but –

'Something is moving in there.' Pilgrim had tucked one head briefly around the shield. He withdrew it now, licking his nose from both sides.

Pham looked again through the crack. The fire had internal shadows, places of not-so-bright that wavered . . . moved? 'I see it too.' He felt Johanna stick her head close to his, peering frantically. 'It's Blueshell, Rav . . . *By the Fleet.*' This last said too softly to carry over the fire sound. There was no sign of Jefri Olsndot, but 'Blueshell's rolling through the middle of the fire, Rav.'

The skrode wheeled out of the deeper oil. Slowly, steadily making its way. And now Pham could see fire within fire, Blueshell's trunk flaring in rivulets of flame. His fronds were no longer gathered into himself. They extended, writhing with their own fire. 'He's still coming, driving straight out.'

The skrode cleared the wall of fire, rolled with jerky abandon down the slope. Blueshell didn't turn toward them, but just before he reached the landing boat, all six wheels grated to a fast stop.

Pham stood and raced back toward the Skroderider. Pilgrim was already unlimbering his shields and turning to follow him. Johanna Olsndot stood for a second, sad and slight and alone, her gaze stuck hopelessly on the fire and smoke on the castle side. One of the Pilgrim grabbed her sleeve, drawing her back from the fire.

Pham was at the Rider now. He stared silently for a second. '. . . Blueshell's dead, Rav, no way you could doubt if you could see.' The fronds were burnt away, leaving stubs along the stalk. The stalk itself had burst.

Ravna's voice in his ear was shuddery. 'He drove *through* that even while he was burning?'

'Can't be. He must have been dead after the first few meters. This must all have been on autopilot.' Pham tried to forget the agonized reaching of fronds he had seen back in the fire. He blanked out for a moment, staring at the fire-split flesh.

The skrode itself radiated heat. Pilgrim sniffed around it, shying away abruptly when a nose came too close. Abruptly he reached out a steel-tined paw and pulled hard on the scarf that covered the hull.

Johanna screamed, rushing forward faster than Pilgrim or Pham. The forms beneath the scarf were unmoving but unburned. She grabbed her brother by the shoulders, pulling him to the ground. Pham knelt down beside her. *Is the kid breathing?* He was distantly aware of Ravna shouting in his ear, and Pilgrim plucking tiny dogthings off the metal.

Seconds later the boy started coughing. His arms windmilled against his sister. 'Amdi, Amdi!' His eyes opened, widened. 'Sis!' And then again. 'Amdi?'

'I don't know,' said the Pilgrim, standing close to the seven – no, *eight* – grease-covered forms. 'There are some mind sounds but not coherent.' He nosed at three of puppies, doing something that might have been rescue breathing.

After a moment the little boy began crying, a sound lost in the fire sounds. He crawled across to the puppies, his face right next to one of Pilgrim's. Johanna was right behind him, holding his shoulders, looking first to Pilgrim and then at the still creatures.

Pham came to his knees and looked back at the castle. The fire was a little lower now. He stared a long time at the blackened stump that had been Blueshell. Wondering and remembering. Wondering if all the suspicion had been for naught. Wondering what mix of courage and autopilot had

534

been behind the rescue.

Remembering all the months he had spent with Blueshell, the liking and then the hate – *Oh, Blueshell, my friend.*

The fires slowly ebbed. Pham paced the edge of receding heat. He felt the godshatter coming finally back upon him. For once he welcomed it, welcomed the drive and the mania, the blunting of irrelevant feeling. He looked at Pilgrim and Johanna and Jefri and the recovering puppy pack. It was all a meaningless diversion. No, not quite meaningless: It had had an effect, of slowing down progress on what *was* deadly important.

He glanced upwards. There were gaps in the sooty clouds, places where he could see the reddish haze of high-level ash and occasional splotches of blue. The castle's ramparts appeared abandoned, and the battle around the walls had died. 'What news?' He said impatiently at the sky.

Ravna: 'I still can't see much around you, Pham. Large numbers of Tines – probably the enemy – are retreating northwards. Looks like a fast, coordinated retreat. Nothing like the "fight-to-the-last" that we were seeing before. There are no fires within the castle – or evidence of remaining packs either.'

Decision. Pham turned back toward the others. He struggled to turn sharp commands into reasonable-sounding requests. 'Pilgrim! Pilgrim! I need Woodcarver's help. We have to get inside the castle.'

Pilgrim didn't need any special persuasion, though he was full of questions. 'You're going to fly over the walls?' he asked as he bounded toward him.

Pham was already jogging toward the boat. He boosted Pilgrim aboard, then clambered up. No, he wasn't going to try to fly the damn thing. 'No, just use the loudspeaker to get your boss to find a way in.'

Seconds later, packtalk was echoing across the hillside. *Just minutes more. Just miutes more and I will be facing the Countermeasure.* And though he had no conscious notion what might come of that, he felt the godshatter bubbling up for one final takeover, one final act of Old One's will. 'Where is the Blighter fleet, Rav?'

Her answer came back immediately. She had watched the battle below, and the hammer coming down from above. 'Forty-eight light-years out.' Mumbled conversation off-mike. 'They've speeded up a little. They'll be in-system in forty-six hours . . . I'm sorry, Pham.'

Crypto: 0
As received by: *OOB* shipboard ad hoc
Language path: Triskweline, SjK units
Apparently From: Sandor Arbitration Intelligence
   [Not the usual originator, but verified by intermedi-
   ate sites. Originator may be a branch office or a
   back-up site.]
Subject: Our final message?
Distribution:
   Threat of the Blight
   War Trackers Interest Group
   Where Are They Now, Extinctions Log
Date: 72.78 days since the Fall of Sjandra Kei
Key phrases: vast new attack, the Fall of Sandor
   Arbitration
Text of message:
   As best we can tell, all of our High Beyond sites have been absorbed by the Blight. If you can, please ignore all messages from those sites.
   Until four hours ago, our organization comprised twenty civilizations at the Top. What is left of us doesn't know what to say or what to do. Things are so slow and murky and dull now; we were not meant to live this low. We intend to disband after this transmission.
   For those who can continue, we want to say what happened. The new attack was an abrupt thing. Our last recollections from Above are of the Blight suddenly *reaching* in all directions, sacrificing all its immediate security to acquire as much processing power as possible. We don't know if we had simply underestimated its power, or if the Blight itself is now desperate – and taking desperate risks.
   Up to 3000 seconds ago we were still under heavy

assault along our organization's internal networks.
That has ceased. Temporarily? Or is this the limit of the
attack? We don't know, but if you hear from us again,
you will know that the Blight has us.

Farewell.

Crypto: 0
As received by: *OOB* shipboard ad hoc
Language path: Optima→Acquileron→Triskweline,
  SjK units
From: Society for Rational Investigation
  [Probably a single system in the Middle Beyond,
  7500 light-years antispinward of Sjandra Kei]
Subject: The Big Picture
Key Phrases: The Blight, Nature's Beauty, Unprece-
  dented Opportunities
Summary: Life goes on
Distribution:
  Threat of the Blight
  Society for Rational Network Management
  War Trackers Interest Group
Date: 72.80 days since the Fall of Sjandra Kei
Text of message:

It's always amusing to see people who think themselves the center of the universe. Take the recent
spread of the Blight [references follow for readers not
on those threads and newsgroups]. The Blight is an
unprecedent change in a limited portion of the Top of
the Beyond – far away from most of my readers. I'm
sure it's the ultimate catastrophe for many, and I
certainly feel sympathy for such, but a little humor too,
that these people somehow think their disaster is the
end of everything. Life goes on, folks.

At the same time, it's clear that many readers are
not paying proper attention to these events – certainly
not seeing what is truly significant about them. In the
last year, we have witnessed the apparent murders of
several Powers and the establishment of a new

ecosystem in a portion of the High Beyond. Though far away, these events are without precedent.

Often before, I have called this the Net of a Million Lies. Well, people, we now have an opportunity to view things while the truth is still manifest. With luck we may solve some fundamental mysteries about the Zones and the Powers.

I urge readers to watch events below the Blight from as many angles as possible. In particular, we should take advantage of the remaining relay at Debley Down to coordinate observations on both sides of the Blight-affected region. This will be expensive and tedious, since only Middle and Low Beyond sites are available in the affected region, but it will be well worth it.

General topics to follow:

The nature of the Blight's Net communications: The creature is part Power and part High Beyond, and infinitely interesting.

The nature of the recent Great Surge in the Low Beyond beneath the Blight: This is another event without clear precedent. Now is the time to study it . . .

The nature of the Blighter fleet now closing on an off-net site in the Low Beyond: This fleet has been of great interest to War Trackers over the last weeks, but mainly for asinine reasons (who cares about Sjandra Kei and the Aprahant Hegemony; local politics is for locals). The real question should be obvious to all but the brain damaged: *Why* has the Blight made this great effort so far from its natural zone?

If there are any ships still in the vicinity of the Blight's fleet, I urge them to keep War Trackers posted. Failing that, local civilizations should be reimbursed for forwarding ultrawave traces.

This is all very expensive, but worth it, the observation of the aeon. And the expense will not continue long. The Blight's fleet should arrive at the target star momentarily. Will it stop and retrieve? Or will we see how a Power destroys the systems which oppose it? Either way, we are blessed with opportunity.

41

Ravna walked across the field toward the waiting packs. The thick smoke had been blown away, but its smell was still heavy in the air. The hillside was burned-over desolation. From above, Steel's castle had looked like the center of a great, black nipple, hectares of natural and pack-made destruction capping the hill.

The soldiers silently made way for her. More than one cast an uneasy glance at the starship grounded behind her. She walked slowly past them, toward the ones who waited. Eerie the way they sat, like picnickers but all uneasy about each other's presence. This must be the equivalent of a close staff conference for them. Ravna walked toward the pack at the center, the one sitting on silken mats. Intricate wooden filigree hung around the necks of the adults, but some of those looked sick, old. And there were two puppies sitting out front of it. They stepped precisely forward as Ravna crossed the last stretch of open ground.

'Er, you're the Woodcarver?' she asked.

A woman's voice, incredibly human, came from one of the larger members. 'Yes, Ravna. I'm Woodcarver. But it's Peregrine you want. He's up in the castle, with the children.'

'Oh.'

'We have a wagon. We can take you inwards right away.' One of them pointed at a vehicle being drawn up the hillside. 'But you could have landed much closer, could you not?'

Ravna shook her head. 'No. Not . . . anymore.' This was the best landing that she and Greenstalk could make.

The heads cocked at her, all a coordinated gesture. 'I thought you were in a terrible hurry. Peregrine says there is a fleet of spacers coming hot on your trail.'

For an instant Ravna didn't say anything. So Pham had told them of the Blight? But she was glad he had. She shook her

539

head, trying to clear it of the numbness. 'Y-yes. We are in a great hurry.' The dataset on her wrist was linked to the *OOB*. Its tiny dislay showed the steady approach of the Blight's fleet.

All the heads twisted, a gesture that Ravna couldn't interpret. 'And you despair. I fear I understand.'

How can you? And if you can, how can you forgive us? But all that Ravna said aloud was, 'I'm sorry.'

The queen mounted her wagon and they rolled across the hillside toward the castle walls. Ravna looked back once. Down slope, the *OOB* lay like a great, dying moth. Its topside drive spines arched a hundred meters into the air. They glistened a wet, metallic green. Their landing had not quite been a crash. Even now, agrav cancelled some of the craft's weight. But the drive spines on the ground side were crumpled. Beyond the ship, the hillside fell steeply away to the water and the islands. The westering sun cast hazy shadows across the islands and on the castle beyond the straits. A fantasy scene of castles and starships.

The display on her wrist serenely counted down the seconds.

'Steel put gunpowder bombs all around the dome.' Woodcarver swept a couple of noses, pointing upwards. Ravna followed her gesture. The arches were more like a Princess cathedral than military architecture: pink marble challenging the sky. And if it all came down, it would surely wreck the spacecraft parked beneath.

Woodcarver said that Pham was in there now. They rolled indoors, through dark, cool rooms. Ravna glimpsed row after row of coldsleep boxes. *How many might still be revivable? Will we ever find out?* The shadows were deep. 'You're sure that Steel's troops are gone?'

Woodcarver hesitated, her heads staring in different directions. So far, pack expresions were impossible for Ravna to read. 'Reasonably sure. Anybody still in the castle would need to be behind lots of stone, or my search parties would have found them. More important, we have what's left of Steel.' The Queen seemed to read Ravna's questioning expression perfectly. 'You didn't know? Apparently, Lord

Steel came down here to blow all the bombs. It would have been suicide, but that pack was always a crazy one. Someone stopped him. There was blood all over. Two of him are dead. We found the rest wandering around, a whimpering mess . . . Whoever did Steel in is also behind the rapid retreat. That someone is doing his best to avoid any confrontation. He won't be back soon, though I fear I'll have to face dear Flenser eventually.'

Under the circumstances, Ravna figured that was one problem that would never materialize. Her dataset showed forty-five fours till the Blight's arrival.

Jefri and Johanna were by their starship, under the main dome. They sat on the steps of the landing ramp, holding hands. When the wide doors opened and Woodcarver's wagon drove through, the girl stood and waved. Then they saw Ravna. The boy walked first quickly then more slowly across the wide floor. 'Jefri Olsndot?' Ravna called softly. He had a tentative, dignified posture that seemed much too old for a nine year old. Poor Jefri had lost much, and lived with so little for so long. She stepped down from the wagon and walked toward him.

The boy advanced out of the shadows. He was surrounded by a near mob of small-size pack members. One of them hung on his shoulder; others tumbled around his feet without ever seeming to get in his way; still others followed his path both in front and behind. Jefri stopped well back from her. 'Ravna?'

She nodded.

'Could you step a little closer? The queen's mind sound is too close' The voice was still the boy's, *but his lips hadn't moved.* She walked the few meters that still separated them. Puppies and boy advanced hesitantly. Up close she could see the rips in his clothing, and what looked like wound dressings on his shoulders and elbows and knees. His face looked recently washed, but his hair was a sticky mess. He looked up at her solemnly, then raised his arms to hug her. 'Thank you for coming.' His voice was muffled against her, but he wasn't crying. 'Yes, thank you, thank poor Mr Blueshell.' His voice again, sad but unmuffled, coming from the pack of pupppies all around them.

Johanna Olsndot had advanced to stand just behind them. *Only fourteen she is?* Ravna reached a hand toward her. 'From what I hear, you were a rescue force all by yourself.'

Woodcarver's voice came from the wagon. 'Johanna was that. She changed our world.'

Ravna gestured up the ship's ramp, at the glow of the interior lighting. 'Pham's up there?'

The girl started to nod, was preempted by the pack of puppies. 'Yes, he is. He and the Pilgrim are up there.' The pups disentangled themselves and started up the steps, one remaining behind to tug Ravna toward the ramp. She started after them, with Jefri close beside her.

'Who *is* this pack?' she said abruptly to Jefri, pointing to the puppies.

The boy stopped in surprise. 'Amdi of course.'

'I'm sorry,' Jefri's voice came from the puppies. 'I've talked to you so much, I forget you don't know – ' There was a chorus of tones and chords that ended in a human giggle. She looked down at the bobbing heads, and was certain the little devil was quite aware of his misrepresentations. Suddenly a mystery was solved. 'Pleased to meet you,' she said, angered and charmed at the same time. 'Now – '

'Right, there are much more important things now.' The pack continued to hop up stairs. 'Amdi' seemed to alternate between shy sadness and manic activity. 'I don't know what they're up to. They kicked us out as soon as we showed them around.'

Ravna followed the pack, Jefri close behind. It didn't *sound* like anything was going on. The interior of the dome was like a tomb, echoing with the talk of the few packs who guarded it. But here, halfway up the steps, even those sounds were muted, and there was nothing coming through the hatch at the top. 'Pham?'

'He's up there.' It was Johanna, at the base of the stairs. She and Woodcarver were looking up at them. She hesitated. 'I'm not sure if he's okay. After the battle, he – he seemed strange.'

Woodcarver's heads weaved about, as if she were trying to get a good look at them through the glare of the hatch lights.

'The acoustics in this ship of yours are awful. How can humans stand it?'

Amdi: 'Ah, it's not so bad. Jefri and I spent lots of time up here. I got used to it.' Two of his heads were pushing at the hatch. 'I don't know why Pham and Pilgrim kicked us out; we could have stayed in the other room and been real quiet.'

Ravna stepped carefully between the pack's lead puppies and pounded on the hull metal. It wasn't hard-latched; now she could hear the ship's ventilation. 'Pham, what progress?'

There was a rustling sound and the click of claws. The hatch slid partway back. Bright, flickering light spilled down the ramp. A single doggy head appeared. Ravna could see white all around its eyes. Did that mean anything? 'Hi,' it said. 'Uh, look. Things are a bit tense just now. Pham – I don't think Pham should be bothered.'

Ravna slipped her hand past the gap. 'I'm not here to bother him. But I am coming in.' *How long we've fought for this moment. How many billions have died along the way. And now some talking dog tells me things are a bit tense.*

The Pilgrim looked down at her hand. 'Okay.' He slid the hatch far enough open to let her through. The pups were quick around her heels, but they recoiled before the Pilgrim's glance. Ravna didn't notice . . .

The 'ship' was scarecely more than a freight container, a cargo hull. The cargo this time – the coldsleep boxes – had been removed, leaving a mostly level floor, dotted with hundreds of fittings.

All this she scarcely noticed. It was the light, the *thing*, that held her eyes. It grew out from the walls and gathered almost too bright to bear at the center of the hold. Its shape changed and changed again, its colors shifting from red to violet to green. Pham sat crosslegged by the apparition, within it. Half his hair was burned away. His hands and arms were shivering, and he mumbled in some language she didn't recognize. Godshatter. Two times it had been the companion to disaster. A dying Power's madness . . . and now it was the only hope. *Oh Pham.*

Ravna took a step toward him, felt jaws close on her sleeve.

'Please, he mustn't be disturbed.' The one that was holding her arm was a big dog, battle scarred. The rest of the pack – Pilgrim – all faced inwards on Pham. The savage stared at her, somehow saw the anger rising in her face. Then the pack said, 'Look ma'am, your Pham's in some sort of fugue state, all the normal personality traded for computation.'

Huh? This Pilgrim had the jargon, but probably not much else. Pham must have been talking to him. She made a shushing gesture. 'Yes, yes. I understand.' She stared into the light. The changing shape, so hard to look at, was something like the graphics you can generate on most displays, the silly cross-sections of high-dimensional froths. It glowed in purest monochrome, but shifted through the colors. Much of the light must be coherent: interference speckles crawled on every solid surface. In places the interference banded up, stripes of dark and light that slid across the hull as the colour changed.

She walked slowly closer, staring at Pham and . . . the Countermeasure. For what else could it be? The scum in the walls, now grown out to meet godshatter. This was not simply data, a message to be relayed. This was a Transcendent machine. Ravna had read of such things: devices made in the Transcend for use at the Bottom of the Beyond. There would be nothing sentient about it, nothing that violated the constraints of the Lower Zones – yet it would make the best possible use of nature here, to do whatever its builder had desired: *Its builder? The Blight? An enemy of the Blight?*

She stepped closer. The thing was deep in Pham's chest, but there was no blood, no torn flesh. She might have thought it all trick holography except that she could see him shudder at its writhing. The fractal arms were feathered by long teeth, twisting at him. She gasped, almost called his name. But Pham wasn't resisting. He seemed deeper into godshatter than ever before, and more at peace. The hope and fear came suddenly out of hiding: hope that maybe, even now, godshatter could do something about the Blight; and fear, that Pham would die in the process.

The artifact's twisting evolution slowed. The light hung at the pale edge of blue. Pham's eyes opened. His head turned toward her. 'The Riders' Myth is real, Ravna.' His voice was distant. She heard the whisper of a laugh. 'The Riders should know, I guess. They learned the last time. There are Things that don't like the Blight. Things my Old One only guessed at . . .'

Powers beyond the Powers? Ravna sank to the floor. The display on her wrist glowed up at her. Less than forty-five hours left.

Pham saw her downward glance, 'I know. Nothing has slowed the fleet. It's a pitiful thing so far down here . . . but more than powerful enough to destroy this world, this solar system. And that's what the Blight wants now. The Blight knows I can destroy it . . . just as it was destroyed before.'

Ravna was vaguely aware that Pilgrim had crawled in close on all sides. Every face was fixed on the blue froth and the human enmeshed within. 'How, Pham?' Ravna whispered.

Silence. Then, 'All the zone turbulence . . . that was Countermeasure trying to act, but without coordination. Now I'm guiding it. I've begun . . . the reverse surge. It's drawing on local energy sources. Can't you feel it?'

Reverse surge? What was Pham talking about? She glanced again at her wrist – and gasped. Enemy speed had jumped to twenty light-years per hour, as fast as might be expected in the Middle Beyond. What had been almost two days of grace was barely two hours . . . Now the display said twenty-five light-years per hour. Thirty.

Someone was pounding on the hatch.

Scrupilo was delinquent. He should be supervising the move up the hillside. He knew that, and really felt quite guilty – but he persevered in his dereliction. Like an addict chewing *krima* leaves, some things are too delicious to give up.

Scrupilo dawdled behind, carrying Dataset carefully between him so that its floppy pink ears would not drag on the ground. In fact, guarding Dataset was certainly more important than hassling his troopers. In any case, he was more or less close enough to give advice. And his lieutenants were more clever than he at everyday work.

During the last few hours, the coastal winds had taken the

smoke clouds inland, and the air was clean and salty. On this part of the hill, not everything was burned. There were even some flowers and fluffy seed pods. Bob-tailed birds sailed up the rising air from the sea valley, their cries a happy music, as if promising that the world would soon be as before.

Scrupilo knew it could not be. He turned all his heads to look down the hillside, at Ravna Bergsndot's starship. He estimated the surviving drive spines as one hundred meters long. The hull itself was more than one hundred and twenty. He hunkered down around Dataset, and popped open its cushioned Oliphaunt face. Dataset knew lots about space-craft. Actually, this ship was not a human design, but the overall shape was fairly ordinary; he knew that from his previous readings. Twenty to thirty thousand tonnes, equip-ped with antigravity floats and faster-than-light drive. All very ordinary for the Beyond . . . But to see it *here*, through the eyes of his very own members! Scrupilo couldn't keep his gaze from the thing. Three of him worked with Dataset while the other two stared at the irridescent green hull. The troopers and guncarts around him faded to insignificance. For all its mass, the ship seemed to rest gently on the hillside. *How long will it be before we can build such?* Centuries without outside help, the histories in Dataset claimed. *What I wouldn't give for a dayaround aboard her!*

Yet this ship was being *chased* by something mightier. Scrupilo shivered in the summer sun. He had often enough heard Pilgrim's story of the first landing, and he had seen the human's beam weapon. He had read much in Dataset about planet wrecker-bombs and the other weapons of the Beyond. While he worked on Woodcarver's cannon – the best weapons he could bring to be – he had dreamed and wondered. Until he saw the starship floating above, he had never quite felt the reality in his innermost hearts. Now he did. So a *fleet* of killers chased close behind Ravna Bergsndot. The hours of the world might be few indeed. He tabbed quickly through Dataset's search paths, looking for articles about space piloting. *If there be only hours, at least learn what there is time to learn.*

So Scrupilo was lost in the sound and vision of Dataset. He

546

had three windows open, each on a different aspect of the piloting experience.

Loud shouts from the hillside. He looked up with one head, more irritated than anything else. It wasn't a battle alarm they were calling, just a general unease. Strange, the afternoon air seemed pleasantly cool. Two of him looked high, but there was no haze. 'Scrupilo! Look, Look!'

His gunners were dancing in panic. They were pointing at the sky ... at the sun. He folded the pink covers over Dataset's face, at the same time looking sunward with shaded view. The sun was still high in the south, dazzling bright. Yet the air was cool, and the birds were making the cooing sounds of low-sun nesting. And suddenly he realized that he was looking straight at the sun's disk, had been for five seconds – without pain or even watering of his eyes. And there was still no haze that he could see. An inner chill spread across his mind.

The sunlight was fading. He could see black dots on the surface. *Sunspots*. He had seen them often enough with Scriber's telescopes. But that had been through heavy filters. *Something stood between him and the sun, something that sucked away its light and warmth.*

The packs on the hillside moaned. It was a frightened sound Scrupilo had never heard in battle, the sound of someone confronted by unknowable terror.

, Blue faded from the sky. The air was suddenly cold as deep dark night. And the sun's color was a gray luminescence, like a faded moon. Less. Scrupilo hunkered bellies to ground. Some of him was whistling deep in the throat. *Weapons, weapons. But Dataset never spoke of this.*

The stars were the brightest light on the hillside.

'Pham, Pham. They'll be here in an hour. What have you done?' A miracle, but of ill?

Pham Nuwen swayed in Countermeasure's bright embrace. His voice was almost normal, the godshatter receding. 'What have I done? N-not much. And more than any Power. Even Old One only guessed, Ravna. The thing the Straumers brought here is the Rider Myth. We – I, it –

just moved the Zone boundary back. A local change, but intense. We're in the equivalent of the High Beyond now, maybe even the Low Transcend. That's why the Blighter fleet can move so fast.'

'But – '

Pilgrim was back from the hatch. He interrupted Ravna's incoherent panic with a matter-of-fact, 'The sun just went out.' His heads bobbed in an expression she couldn't fathom.

Pham answered, 'That's temporary. Something has to power this maneuver.'

'W-why, Pham?' Even if the Blight was sure to win, why *help* it?

The man's face went blank, Pham Nuwen almost disappearing behind the other programs at work in his mind. Then, 'I'm ... focusing Countermeasure. I see now, Countermeasure, what it is ... It was designed by something beyond the Powers. Maybe there are Cloud People, maybe this is signalling them. Or maybe what it's just done is like an insect bite, something that will cause a much greater reaction. The Bottom of the Beyond has just receded, like the waterline before a tsunami.' The Countermeasure glared red-orange, its arcs and barbs embracing Pham more tightly than before. 'A-and now that we have bootstrapped to a decent Zone ... things can really happen. Oh, the ghost of Old One is amused. Seeing beyond the Powers was almost worth dying for.'

The fleet stats flowed across Ravna's wrist. The Blight was coming on even faster than before. 'Five minutes, Pham.' Even though they were still thirty light-years out.

Laughter. 'Oh, the Blight knows, too. I see this is what it feared all along. This *is* what killed it those aeons ago. It's racing forward now, but it's too late.' The glow brightened, the mask of light that was Pham's face seemed to relax. 'Something very ... far ... away has heard me, Rav. It's coming.'

'What? What's coming?'

'The Surge. So big. It makes what hit us before seem a gentle wave. This is the one nobody believes, because no one's left to record it. The Bottom will be blown out beyond

548

the fleet.

Sudden understanding. Sudden wild hope. '. . . And they'll be trapped out there, won't they?' So Kjet Svensndot had not fought in vain, and Pham's advice had not been nonsense: Now there wasn't a single ramscoop in the Blighter fleet.

'Yes. They're thirty light-years out. We killed all the speed-capable ones. They'll be a thousand years getting here . . .' The artifact abruptly contracted, and Pham moaned. 'Not much time. We're at maximum recession. When the surge comes, it will – ' Again a sound of pain. 'I can see it! By the Powers, Ravna, it will sweep high and last long.'

'How high, Pham?' Ravna said softly. She thought of all the civilizations above them. There were the Butterflies, and the treacherous types who had supported the pogrom at Sjandra Kei . . . And there were trillions who lived in peace and made their own way toward the heights.

'A thousand light-years? Ten thousand? I'm not sure. The ghosts in Countermeasure – Arne and Sjana thought it might rise so high it would punch into the Transcend, encyst the Blight right where it sits . . . That must be what happened Before.'

Arne and Sjana?

The Countermeasure's writhing had slowed. Its light flickered bright and then out. Bright and then out. She heard Pham's breath gasp with every darkness. Countermeasure, a savior that was going to kill a million civilizations. And was killing the man who had triggered it.

Almost unthinking, she dodged past the thing, reaching for Pham. But razors on razors blocked her, raking her arms.

Pham was looking up at her. He was trying to say something more.

Then the light went out for a final time. From the darkness all around came a hissing sound and a growing, bitter smell that Ravna would never forget.

For Pham·Nuwen there was no pain. The last minutes of his life were beyond any description that might be rendered in the Slowness or even in the Beyond.

549

So try metaphor and simile: It was like . . . it was like . . .
Pham stood with Old One on a vast and empty beach. Ravna
and Tines were tiny creatures at their feet. Planets and stars
were the grains of sand. And the sea had drawn briefly back,
letting the brightness of thought reach here where before had
been darkness. The Transcendence would be brief. At the
horizon, the drawn-back sea was building, a dark wall higher
than any mountain, rushing back upon them. He looked up at
the enormity of it. Pham and godshatter and Countermeasure
would not survive that submergence, not even separately.
They had triggered catastrophe beyond mind, a vast section
of the Galaxy plunged into Slowness, as deep as Old Earth
itself, and as permanent.

Arne and Sjana and Straumers and Old One were
avenged . . . and Countermeasure was complete.

And as for Pham Nuwen? A tool made, and used, and now
to be discarded. A man who never was.

The surge was upon him then, plunging depths. Down
from the Transcendent light. Outside, the Tines' world sun
would be shining bright once more, but inside Pham's mind
everything was closing down, senses returning to what eyes
can see and ears can hear. He felt Countermeasure slough
toward nonexistence, its task done without ever a conscious
thought. Old One's ghost hung on for a little longer, huddling
and retreating as thought's potential ebbed. But it let Pham's
awareness be. For once it did not push him aside. For once it
was gentle, brushing at the surface of Pham's mind, as a
human might pet a loyal dog.

More a brave wolf, you are, Pham Nuwen. There were only
seconds left before they were fully in the depths, where the
merged bodies of Countermeasure and Pham Nuwen would
die forever and all thought cease. Memories shifted. The
ghost of Old One stepped aside, revealing certainties it had
hidden all along. *Yes, I built you from several bodies in the
junkyard by Relay. But there was only one mind and one set of
memories that I could revive. A strong, brave wolf – so strong I could
never control you without first casting you into doubt . . .*

Somewhere barriers slipped aside, the final failing of Old
One's control, or a final gift. It did not matter which now, for

whatever the ghost said, the truth was obvious to Pham Nuwen and he would not be denied:

Canberra, Cindi, the centuries avoyaging with Qeng Ho, the final flight of the *Wild Goose*. It was all real.

He looked up at Ravna. She had done so much. She had put up with so much. And even disbelieving, she had loved. *It's okay. It's okay.* He tried to reach out to her, to tell her. *Oh, Ravna, I am real!*

Then the full weight of the depths was upon him, and he knew no more.

There was more pounding on the door. She heard Pilgrim walk to the hatch. A crack of light shone in. Ravna heard Jefri's piping voice: 'The sun is back! The sun is back! . . . Hei, why is it so dark in here?'

Pilgrim: 'The artifact – the thing Pham was helping – its light went out.'

'Geez, you mean you left off the main lights?' The hatch slid all the way open, and the boy's head, along with several puppies', was silhouetted against the torchlight beyond. He scrambled over the lip of the hatch. The girl was right behind him. 'The control is right over here . . . see?'

And soft white light shone on the curving walls. All was ordinary and human, except . . . Jefri stood very still, his eyes wide, his hand over his mouth. He turned to hold onto his sister. 'What is it? What is it?' his voice said from the opened hatch.

Now Ravna wished she could not see. She dropped back to her knees. 'Pham?' she said softly, knowing there would be no answer. What was left of Pham Nuwen lay amid the Countermeasure. The artifact didn't glow any more. Its tortuous boundaries were blunted and dark. More than anything it looked like rotted wood . . . but wood that embraced and impaled the man who lay with it. There was no blood, and no charring. Where the artifact had pierced Pham there was an ashy stain, and the flesh and the thing seemed to merge.

Pilgrim was close around her, his noses almost touching the still form. The bitter smell still hung in the air. It was the smell of death, but not the simple rotting of flesh; what had died here was flesh and something else.

She glanced at her wrist. The display had simplified to a few alphanumeric lines. No ultradrives could be detected. *OOB* status showed problems with attitude control. They were deep in the Slow Zone, out of reach of all help, out of reach of the Blight's fleet. She looked into Pham's face. 'You did it, Pham. You really did it.' She said the words softly, to herself.

The arches and loops of Countermeasure were a fragile, brittle thing now. The body of Pham Nuwen was part of that. How could they break those arches without breaking . . . ? Pilgrim and Johanna gently urged Ravna out of the cargo hold. She didn't remember much of the next few minutes, of them bringing out the body. Blueshell and Pham, both gone beyond all retrieval.

They left her after a while. There was no lack of compassion, but disaster and strangeness and emergency were in too abundant a supply. There were the wounded. There was the possibility of counterattack. There was great confusion, and a desperate need for order. It made scarcely any impression on her. She was at the end of her long desperate run, at the end of all her energy.

Ravna must have sat by the ramp for much of the afternoon, so deep in loss as not to think, scarcely aware of the seasong that Greenstalk shared with her through the dataset. Eventually she realized that she was not alone. Besides Greenstalk's comfort . . . sometime earlier, the little boy had returned. He sat beside her, and around them all the puppies, all silent.

Epilogs

Peace had come to what had once been Flenser's Domain. At least there was no sign of belligerent forces. Whoever had pulled them back had done it very cleverly. As the days passed, local peasantry showed themselves. Where the people weren't simply dazed, they seemed glad to be rid of the old regime. Life picked up in the farmlands, peasants doing their best to recover from the worst fire season of recent memory, compounded by the most fighting the region had ever known.

The queen had sent messengers south to report on the victory, but she seemed in no rush to return to her city. Her troops helped with some of the farm work, and did their best not to be a burden on the locals. But they also scouted through the castle on Starship Hill, and the huge old castle on Hidden Island. Down there were all the horrors that had been whispered about over the years. But still there was no sign of the forces that had escaped. The locals were eager with their own stories, and most were ominously credible: That before Flenser had undertaken his attempt upon the Republic, he had created redoubts further north. There had been reserves there – though some thought that Steel had long since used them. Peasants from the northern valley had seen the Flenserist troops retreating. Some said they had seen Flenser himself – or at least a pack wearing the colors of a lord. Even the locals did not believe all the stories, the ones about Flenser being here and there, singletons separated by kilometers, coordinating the pull out.

Ravna and the queen had reason to believe the story, but not the foolhardiness to check it out. Woodcarver's expeditionary force was not a large one, and the forests and valleys stretched on for more than one hundred kilometers to where the Icefangs curved west to meet the sea. That territory was unknown to Woodcarver. If Flenser had been preparing it for decades – as was that pack's normal method of operation – there would be deadly surprises, even for a large army hunting just a few dozens of partisans. Let Flenser be, and hope that his redoubts had been gutted by Lord Steel.

Woodcarver worried that this would be the great peril of the next century.

But things were resolved much sooner than that. It was Flenser who sought them out, and not with a counterattack: About twenty days after the battle, at the end of a day when the sun dipped just behind the northern hills, there was the sound of signal horns. Ravna and Johanna were wakened and shortly found themselves on the castle's parapet, peering into something like a sunset, all orange and gold silhouetting the hills beyond the northern fjord. Woodcarver's aides were gazing from many eyes at the ridgeline. A few had telescopes.

Ravna shared her binocs with Johanna. 'Someone's up there.' Stark against the sky glow, a pack carried a long banner with separate poles for each member.

Woodcarver was using two telescopes, probably more effective than Ravna's gear, considering the pack's eye separation. 'Yes, I see it. That's a truce flag, by the way. And I think I know who's carrying it.' She yammered something at Peregrine. 'It's been a long time since I've talked to that one.'

Johanna was still looking through the binoculars. Finally she said, 'He . . . made Steel, didn't he?'

'Yes, dear.'

The girl lowered the binocs. 'I . . . think I'll pass up meeting him.' Her voice was distant.

They met on the hillside north of the castle just eight hours later. Woodcarver's troops had spent the intervening time scouting the valley. It was only partly a matter of protecting against treachery from the other side: one very special pack of the enemy would be coming, and there were plenty of locals who would like that one dead.

Woodcarver walked to where the hill fell off precipitously toward forest. Ravna and Pilgrim followed behind her at a Tinishly close ten meters. Woodcarver wasn't saying much about this meeting, but Pilgrim had turned out to be a very talkative sort. 'This is just the way I came originally, a year ago when the first ship landed. You can see how some of the trees were burned by the torch. Good thing it wasn't as dry that summer as this.'

The forest was dense, but they were looking down over the treetops. Even in the dryness there was a sweet, resinous smell in the air. To their left was a tiny waterfall and a path that led to the valley floor – the path their truce visitor had agreed to take. Farmland, Peregrine called the valley bottom. It was undisciplined chaos to Ravna's eyes. The Tines grew different crops together in the same fields, and she saw no fences, not even to hold back livestock. Here and there were wooden lodges with steep roofs and outward curving walls; what you might expect in a region with snowy winters.

'Quite a mob down there,' said Pilgrim.

It didn't look crowded to her: little clumps, each a pack, each well-separated from the others. They clustered around the lodge buildings. More were scattered across the fields. Woodcarver packs were stationed along the little road that crossed the valley.

She felt Pilgrim tense next to her. A head extended past her waist, pointing. 'That must be him. All alone, as promised. And – ' part of him was looking through a telescope, 'now that's a surprise.'

A single pack trekked slowly down the road, past Woodcarver's guards. It was pulling a small cart – containing one of its own members, apparently. A cripple?

The peasants in the fields drifted toward the edge of the field, paralleling the lone pack's course. She heard the gobble of Tinish talk. When they wanted to be loud, they could be very, very loud. The troopers moved to chase back any local who got too close to the road.

'I thought they were grateful to us?' This was the closest thing to violence she had seen since the battle of Starship Hill.

'They are. Most of those are shouting death to Flenser.'

Flenser, Skinner, the pack who had rescued Jefri Olsndot. 'They can hate one pack so much?'

'Love and hate and fear, all together. More than a century they've been under his knife. And now he is here, half-crippled, and without his troops. Yet they are still afraid.

There are enough cotters down there to overwhelm our guard, but they're not pushing hard. This was Flenser's Domain, and he treated it like a good farmer might treat his yard. Worse, he treated the people and the land like some grand experiment. From reading Dataset, I see he is a monster ahead of his time. There are some out there who might still kill for the Master, and no one is sure who they are . . .' He paused a second, just watching.

'And you know the greatest reason for fear? That he would come here alone, so far from any help we can conceive.'

So. Ravna shifted Pham's pistol forward on her belt. It was a bulky, blatant thing . . . and she was glad to have it. She glanced westward towards Hiddden Island. *OOB* was safely grounded against the battlements on the castle there. Unless Greenstalk could do some basic reprogramming, it would not fly again. And Greenstalk was not optimistic. But she and Ravna had mounted the beam gun in one of its cargo bays, and that remote was dead simple. Flenser might have his surprises, but so did Ravna.

The fivesome disappeared beneath the steepness.

'It will be a while yet,' said Pilgrim. One of his pups stood on his shoulders and leaned against Ravna's arm. She grinned: her private information feed. She picked it up and placed in on her shoulder. The rest of Peregrine sat his rumps on the ground and watched expectantly.

Ravna looked at the others of the Queen's party. Woodcarver had posted crossbow packs to her right and left. Flenser would sit directly before her and a little downslope. Ravna thought she could see nervousness in Woodcarver. The members kept licking their lips, the narrow pink tongues slipping in and out with snake-like quickness. The Queen had arranged herself as if for a group portrait, the taller members behind and the two little ones sitting erect in front. Most of her gaze seem focused on the break in the verge, where the path from below reached the terrace they sat upon.

Finally Ravna heard the scritching of claws on stone. One head appeared over the drop off, and then more. Flenser walked out onto the moss, two of his members pulling the wheeled cart. The one in the cart sat erect, its hindquarters covered by a blanket. Except for its white-tipped ears, it seemed unremarkable.

The pack's heads peered in every direction. One stayed disconcertingly focused on Ravna as the pack proceeded up the slope toward the Queen. Skinner – Flenser – was the one who had worn the radio cloaks. None were worn now. Through gaps in its jackets Ravna could see scabby splotches where the fur had been rubbed away.

'Mangy fellow, isn't he?' came the little voice in Ravna's ear. 'But cool too. Catch his insolent look.' The queen hadn't moved. She seemed frozen, every member staring at the oncoming pack. Some of her noses were trembling.

Four of Flenser tipped the cart forward, helping the white-tipped one slide to the ground. Now Ravna could see that under the blanket, its hindquarters were unnaturally twisted and still. The five settled themselves rumps together. Their necks arched up and out, almost like the limbs of a single creature. The pack gobbled something that sounded to Ravna like strangling songbirds.

Pilgrim's translation came immediately from the puppy on Ravna's shoulder. The pup spoke in a new voice, a traditional villain voice from children's stories, a dry and sardonic voice. 'Greetings . . . Parent. It has been many years.'

Woodcarver said nothing for a moment. Then she gobbled something back, and Pilgrim translated: 'You recognize me?'

One of Flenser's heads jabbed out toward Woodcarver. 'Not the members of course, but your soul is obvious.'

Again, silence from the queen. Peregrine, annotating: 'My poor Woodcarver. I never thought she would be this flummoxed.' Abruptly he spoke loud, addressing Flenser in Samnorsk. 'Well, you are not so obvious to me, O former traveling companion. I remember you as Tyrathect, the timid teacher from the Long Lakes.'

Several of the heads turned toward Peregrine and Ravna. The creature replied in pretty good Samnorsk, but with a childish voice. 'Greetings, Peregrine. And greetings, Ravna Bergsndot? Yes. Flenser Tyrathect I am.' The heads angled downwards, eyes blinking slowly.

'Sly bugger,' Peregrine muttered.

'Is Amdijefri safe?' the Flenser suddenly asked.

'What?' said Ravna, not recognizing the name at first. Then, 'Yes, they are fine.'

'Good.' Now all the heads turned back to the queen, and the creature continued in Pack talk; 'Like a dutiful creation, I have come to make peace with my Parent, dear Woodcarver.'

'Does he really talk like that?' Ravna hissed at the puppy on her shoulder.

'Hei, would I exaggerate?'

Woodcarver gobbled back, and Pilgrim picked up the translation, now in the queen's human voice: 'Peace. I doubt it, Flenser. More likely you want breathing space to build again, to try to kill us all again.'

'I wish to build again, that is true. But I have changed. The "timid teacher" has made me a little . . . softer. Something you could never do, Parent.'

'What?' Pilgrim managed to inject a tone of injured surprise into the word.

'Woodcarver, have you never thought on it? You are the most brilliant pack to live in this part of the world, perhaps the most brilliant of all time. And the packs you made, they are mostly brilliant, too. But have you not wondered on the most successful of them? You created too brilliantly. You ignored inbreeding and [things that I can't translate easily], and you got . . . me. With all the . . . quirks that have so pained you over the last century.'

'I-I have thought on that mistake, and done better since.'

'Yes, as with Vendacious? [Oh, look at my Queen's faces. He really hurt her there.] Never mind, never mind. Vendacious may well have been a different sort of error. The point is, you made *me*. Before, I thought that your greatest act of genius. Now . . . I'm not so sure. I want to make amends. To live in peace.' One of the heads jabbed at Ravna, another at the *OOB* down by Hidden Island. 'And there are other things in the universe to point our genius at.'

'I hear the arrogance of old. Why should I trust you now?'

'I helped to save the children. I saved the ship.'

'And you were always the world's greatest opportunist.'

Flenser's flanking heads shifted back. '[That's a kind of

dismissing shrug.] You have the advantage, Parent, but some of my power is left in the north. Make peace, or you will have more decades of maneuvering and war.'

Woodcarver's response was a piercing shriek. '[And that's a sign of irritation, in case you didn't guess.] Impudence! I can kill you here and now, and have a century of certain peace.'

'I've bet that you won't harm me. You gave me safe passage, separately and in the whole. And one of the strongest things in your soul is your hate for lies.'

The back members of Woodcarver's pack hunkered down, and the little ones at the front took several quick steps toward the Flenser. 'It's been many decades since we last met, Flenser! If *you* can change, might not I?'

For an instant every one of Flenser's members was frozen. Then part of him came slowly to its feet, and slowly, slowly edged toward Woodcarver. The crossbow packs on either side of the meeting ground raised their weapons, tracking him. Flenser stopped six or seven meters from Woodcarver. His heads weaved from side to side, all attention on the queen. Finally, a wondering voice, almost abashed: 'Yes, you might. Woodcarver, after all the centuries . . . you've given up yourself? These new ones are . . .'

'Not all mine. Quite right.' For some reason, Pilgrim was chuckling in Ravna's ear.

'Oh. Well . . .' The Flenser backed to its previous position, 'I still want peace.'

'[Woodcarver looks surprised.] You sound changed, too. How many of you are really of Flenser?'

A long pause. 'Two.'

'. . . Very well. Depending on the terms, there will be peace.'

Maps were brought out. Woodcarver demanded the location of Flenser's main troops. She wanted them disarmed, with two or three of her packs assigned to each unit, reporting by heliograph. Flenser would give up the radio cloaks, and submit to observation. Hidden Island and Starship Hill would be ceded to Woodcarver. The two sketched new borders, and wrangled on the oversight the queen would have in his remaining lands.

The sun reached its noon point in the southern sky. In the fields below, the peasants had long since given up their angry vigil. The only tensely watchful people left were the queen's crossbow packs.

Finally Flenser stepped back from his end of the maps. 'Yes, yes, your folk can watch all my work. No more . . . ghastly experiments. I will be a gentle gatherer of knowledge [is this sarcasm?], like yourself.'

Woodcarver's heads bobbed in rippling synchrony. 'Perhaps so; with the Two-Legs on my side, I'm willing to chance it.'

Flenser rose again from his seated posture. He turned to help his crippled member back on the cart. Then he paused. 'Ah, one last thing, dear Woodcarver. A detail. I killed two of Steel when he tried to destroy Jefri's starship. [Squashed them like bugs, actually. Now we know how Flenser hurt himself.] Do you have the rest of him?'

'Yes.' Ravna had seen what was left of Steel. She and Johanna had visited most of the wounded; it should be possible to adapt *OOB* first aid for the Tines. But in the case of Steel, there had been a bit of vengeful curiosity; that creature had been responsible for so much unnecessary death. What was left of Steel didn't really need medical attention: There were some bloody scratches (self-inflicted, Johanna guessed) and one twisted leg. But the pack was a pitiable, almost an unnerving thing. It had cowered at the back of its pen, all shivering in terror, heads shifting this way and that. Every so often the creature's jaws would snap open and shut, or one member would make an aborted run at the fence. A pack of three was not of human intelligence, but this one could talk. When it saw Ravna and Johanna, its eyes went wide, the whites showing all around, and it rattled barely intelligible Samnorsk at them. The speech was a nightmare mix of threats and pleas that they 'not cut, not cut!' Poor Johanna started crying then. She had spent most of a year hating the pack these were from, yet – 'They seem to be victims, too. It's b-bad to be three, but no one will ever let them be more.'

'Well,' continued Flenser, 'I would like custody of what

remains, I – '

'Never! That one was almost as smart as you, even if crazy enough to defeat. You're not going to build him back.'

Flenser came together, all eyes staring at the queen. His 'voice' was soft: 'Please, Woodcarver. This is a small matter, but I will throw over everything,' he jabbed at the maps, 'rather than be denied in it.'

'[Uh-oh.]' The crossbow packs were suddenly at the ready. Woodcarver came partly around the maps, close enough to Flenser that their mind noise must collide. She brought all her heads together in a concerted glare. 'If it is so unimportant, why risk everything for it?'

Flenser bumped around for an instant, his members actually staring at one another. It was a gesture Ravna had not seen till now. 'That is *my* affair! I mean . . . Steel was my greatest creation. In a way, I am proud of him. But . . . I am also responsible for him. Don't you feel the same about Vendacious?'

'I've got my plans for Vendacious.' The response was grudging. '[In fact, Vendacious is still whole; I fear the Queen made too many promises to do much with him now.]'

'I want to make up to Steel the harm I made him. You understand.'

'I understand. I've seen Steel and I understand your methods: the knives, the fear, the pain. You're not going to get another chance at it!'

It sounded to Ravna like faint music, something from far beyond the valley, an alien blending of chords. But it was Flenser answering back. Pilgrim's translating voice held no hint of sarcasm: 'No knives, no cutting. I keep my name because it is for others to rename me when they finally accept that . . . in her way, Tyrathect *won*. Give me this chance, Woodcarver. I am begging.'

The two packs stared at each other for more than ten seconds. Ravna looked from one to the other, trying to divine their expressions. No one said anything. There was not even Pilgrim's voice in her ear to speculate on whether this was a lie or the baring of a new soul.

It was Woodcarver who decided. 'Very well. You may have

him.'

Peregrine Wickwrackscar was *flying*. A pilgrim with legends that went back almost a thousand years – and not one of them could come near to this! He would have burst into song except that it would pain his passengers. They were already unhappy enough with his rough piloting; even though they thought it was simply his inexperience.

Peregrine stepped across clouds, flew among and through them, danced with an occasional thunderstorm. How many hours of his life had he stared up at the clouds, gauging their depths – and now he was in them, exploring the caves within caves within caves, the cathedrals of light.

Between scattered clouds, the Great Western Ocean stretched forever. By the sun and the flier's instruments, he knew that they had nearly reached the equator, and were already some eight thousand kilometers southwest of Woodcarver's Domain. There were islands out here, the *OOB*'s pictures from space said so, and so did the Pilgrim's own memories. But it had been long since he ventured here, and he had not expected to see the island kingdoms in the lifetime of his current members.

Now suddenly he was going back. Flying back!

The *OOB*'s landing boat was a wonderful thing, and not nearly as strange as it had seemed in the midst of battle. True, they had not yet figured out how to program it for automatic flight. Perhaps they never would. In the meantime, this little flier worked with electronics that were barely more than glorified moving parts. The agrav itself required constant adjustment, and the controls were scattered across the bow periphery – conveniently placed for the fronds of a Skroderider, or the members of a pack. With the Spacers' help and *OOB*'s documentation, it had taken Pilgrim only a few days to get the hang of flying the thing. It was all a matter of spreading one's mind across all the various tasks. The learning had been happy hours, a little bit scary, floating nearly out of control, once in a screwball configuration that accelerated endlessly upward. But in the end, the machine was like an extension of his jaws and paws.

*

Since they descended from the purpling heights and began playing in the cloud tops, Ravna had been looking more and more uncomfortable. After a particularly stomachs-lurching bump and drop, she said, 'Will you be able to land okay? Maybe we should have postponed this till – ' *unh!* ' – you can fly better.'

'Oh yes, oh yes. We'll be past this, um, weather front real soon.' He dived beneath the clouds and swerved a few tens of kilometers eastwards. The weather was clear here, and it was actually more on a line with their destination. Secretly chastened, he resolved to do no more joy-riding . . . on the inbound leg, anyway.

His second passenger spoke up then, only the second time in the two-hour flight. 'I liked it,' said Greenstalk. Her voder voice charmed Pilgrim: mostly narrow-band, but with little frets high up, from the squarewaves. 'It was . . . it was like riding just beneath the surf, feeling your fronds moving with the sea.'

Peregrine had tried hard to know the Skroderider. The creature was the only nonhuman alien in the world, and harder to know than the Two-Legs. She seemed to dream most of the time, and forgot all but things that happened again and again to her. It was her primitive skrode that accounted for part of that, Ravna told him. Remembering the run that Greenstalk's mate had made through the flames, Pilgrim believed. Out among the stars, there were things even stranger than Two-Legs – it made Pilgrim's imagination ache.

On the horizon he saw a dark ring and another beyond. 'We'll have you in real surf very soon.'

Ravna: 'These are the islands?'

Peregrine looked over the map displays as he took a shot on the sun. 'Yes, indeed,' though it didn't really matter. The Western Ocean was over twelve thousand kilometers across, and all through the tropics it was dotted with atolls and island chains. This group was just a bit more isolated than others; the nearest Islander settlement was almost two thousand kilometers away.

They were over the nearest island. Pilgrim took a swing

around it, admiring the tropic ferns that clung to the coral. At this tide, their bony roots were exposed. Not any flat land here at all; he flew on to the next, a larger one with a pretty glade just within the ringwall. He floated the boat down in a smooth glide that touched the ground without even the tiniest bump.

Ravna Bergsndot looked at him with something like suspicion. *Oh oh.* 'Hei, I'm getting better, don't you think?' he said weakly.

An uninhabited little island surrounded by endless sea. The original memories were blurred now; it had been his Rum member who had been a native of the island kingdoms. Yet what he remembered all fit: the high sun, the intoxicating humidity of the air, the heat soaking through his paws. Paradise. The Rum aspect that still lived within him was most joyous of all. The years seemed to melt away; part of him had come home.

They helped Greenstalk down to the ground. Ravna claimed the skrode was an inferior imitation, its new wheels an ad hoc addition. Still, Pilgrim was impressed: the four balloon tyres each had a separate axle. The Rider was able to make it almost to the crest of the coral without any help from Ravna or himself. But near the top, where the tropic ferns were thickest and their roots grew across every path, there he and Ravna had to help a bit, lifting and pulling.

Then they were on the other side and could see the ocean.

Now part of Pilgrim ran ahead, partly to find the easiest descent, partly to get close to the water and smell the salt and the rotting floatweed. The tide was nearly out now, and a million little pools – some no more than stony-walled puddles – lay exposed to the sun. Three of him ran from pool to pool, eying the creatures that lay within. The strangest things in the world they had seemed to him when he first came to the islands. Creatures with shells, slugs of all dimensions and colors, animal-plants that would become tropic ferns if they ever got trapped far enough inland.

'Where would you like to sit?' he asked the Skroderider. 'If we go all the way out to the surf right now, you'll be a meter underwater at high tide.'

The Rider didn't reply. But all her fronds were angled towards the water now. The wheels on her skrode slipped and spun with a strange lack of coordination. 'Let's take her closer,' Ravna said after a moment.

They reached a fairly level stretch of coral, pocked with holes and gullies not more than a few centimeters deep. 'I'll go for a swim, find a good place,' Peregrine said. All of him ran down to where the coral broke the water; going for a swim was not something you did by parts. *Heh heh.* Fact was, damn few mainland packs could swim and think at the same time. Most mainlanders thought that there was a craziness in water. Now Peregrine knew it was simply the great difference in sound speed between air and water. Thinking with all tympana immersed must be a little like using the radio cloaks: it took discipline and practice to do it, and some were never able to learn. But the Island folk had always been great swimmers, using it for meditation. Ravna even thought the Packs might be descended from packs of whales!

Peregrine came to the edge of the coral and looked down. Suddenly the surf did not seem a completely friendly thing. He would soon find out if Rum's spirit and his own memories of swimming were up to the real thing. He pulled off his jackets.

All at once. It's best done all at once. He gathered himself and plopped awkwardly into the water. Confusion, heads out and in. *Keep all under.* He paddled about, holding all his heads down. Every few seconds, he'd poke a single nose into the air and refresh that member. *I still can do it!* The six of him slipped through swarms of squidlets, dived separately through arching green fronds. The hiss of the sea was all around, like the mindsound of a vast sleeping pack.

After a few minutes he'd found a nice level spot, sand all about and shielded from the worst fury of the sea. He paddled back to where the sea crashed against stony coral . . . and almost broke some legs scrambling out. It was just impossible to exist all at once, and for a few moments it was every member for itself. 'Hei, over here!' He shouted to Greenstalk and Ravna. He sat licking at coral cuts as they crossed the white rock. 'Found a place, more peaceful than this – ' He waved at the crash and spray.

Greenstalk rolled a little closer to the edge, then hesitated. Her fronds turned back and forth along the curving sweep of the shore. *Does she need help?* Pilgrim started forward, but Ravna just sat down beside the Rider and leaned against the wheeled platform. After a moment, Pilgrim joined them. They sat for a time, human looking out to the sea, Rider looking he wasn't sure quite where, and pack looking in most all directions . . . There was peace here, even with (or because of?) the booming surf and the haze of spray. He felt his hearts slowing, and just lazed in the sunlight. On every pelt the drying sea water was leaving a glittery powder of salt. Grooming himself tasted good at first, but . . . *yech*, too much dry salt was one of the *bad* memories. Greenstalk's fronds settled lightly across him, too fine and narrow to provide much shade, but a light and gentle comfort.

They sat for a long while – long enough so that later some of Pilgrim's noses were blistered, and even darkskinned Ravna was sunburned.

The Rider was humming now, a sort of song that after long minutes came to be speech. 'It is a good sea, a good edge. It is what I need now. To sit and think at my own pace for a while.'

And Ravna said, 'How long? We will miss you.' That was not just politeness. Everyone would miss her. Even with her mind adrift, Greenstalk was the expert on *OOB*'s surviving automation.

'Long by your measure, I fear. A few decades . . .' She watched (?) the waves a few minutes more. 'I am eager to get down there. Ha ha. Almost like a human in that . . . Ravna, you know my memories are muddled now. I had two hundred years with Blueshell. Sometimes he was petty and a little spiteful, but he was a great trader. We had many wonderful times. And at the end even you could see his courage.'

Ravna nodded.

'We found a terrible secret on this last journey. I think that hurt him as much as the final . . . burning. I am grateful to you for protecting us. Now I want to think, to let the surf and the time work with my memories and sort them out. Maybe if this poor imitation skrode is up to it, I'll even make a chronicle of our quest.'

She touched Peregrine on two of his heads. 'One thing, Sir Pilgrim. You trust much to give me freedom of your seas . . . But you should know, Blueshell and I were pregnant. I have a mist of our common eggs within me. Leave me here and there will be new Riders by this island in future years. Please do not take that as betrayal. I want to remember Blueshell with children – but modestly; our kind has shared ten million worlds and never been bad neighbors . . . except in a way that Ravna can tell you, that cannot happen here.'

In the end, Greenstalk was not at all interested in the protected stretch of water that Peregrine had discovered. She wanted – of all the places here – the one where the ocean crashed most ferociously. It took them more than an hour to find a path down to that violent place, and another half hour to get Rider and skrode safely into the water. Peregrine didn't even try to swim here. The coral rock came in close from all sides, slimy green in patches, razor jagged in others. Five minutes in that meat grinder and he might be too weak to get out. Strange that there was so much green in the water here. It was all but opaque with sea grasses and swarms of foam midges.

Ravna was a little better off; at the water's greatest height, she could still keep feet to ground – at least most of the time. She stood in the foam, bracing herself with feet and an arm, and helped the skrodeling over the lip of rock. Once in, the mechanical crashed firmly to the bottom beside the human.

Ravna looked up at Pilgrim, made an 'okay' gesture. Then she huddled down for a moment, holding to the skrode to keep her place. The surf crashed over the two, obscuring all but Greenstalk's standing fronds. When the foam moved back, he could see that the lower fronds draped across the human's back, and hear a voder buzzing that wasn't quite intelligible against all the other noise.

The human stood and slogged through the waist deep-water toward the rocks Peregrine occupied. Peregrine grabbed onto himself, reached down to give Ravna some paws. She scrambled up the slime green and coral white.

He followed the limping Two-Legs toward the crest of

tropical ferns. They stopped under the shade, and she sat down, leaned back into the mat of a fern's trunk net. Cut and bruised, she looked almost as hurt as Johanna ever had.

'You okay?'

'Yeah.' She ran her hands back through disheveled hair. Then she looked at him and laughed. 'We both look like casualties.'

Um, yes. Sometime soon he needed a fresh-water bath. He looked around and out. From the crest of the atoll ring they had a view of Greenstalk's niche. Ravna was looking down there too, minor injuries forgotten.

'How can she like that spot?' Peregrine said wonderingly. 'Imagine being smashed and smashed and smashed.'

There was a smile on Ravna's face, but she kept her two eyes on the surf. 'There are strange things in the universe, Pilgrim; I'm glad there are some you have not read about yet. Where the surf meets the shore – lots of neat things can happen there. You saw all the life that floated in that madness. Just as plants love the sun, there are creatures that can use the energy differences down at that edge. There they have the sun and the surge and the richness of the suspension . . . Still, we should keep watch a little longer.' Between each insurge of the waves, they could still see Greenstalk's fronds. He already knew that those limbs weren't strong, but he was beginning to realize that they must be very tough. 'She'll be okay, though that cheap skrode may not last long. Poor Greenstalk may end up without any automation at all . . . she and her children, the lowest of all Riders.'

Ravna turned to look at the pack . There was still that smile on her face. Wondering, yet pleased? 'You know the secret Greenstalk spoke of?'

'Woodcarver told me what you told her.'

'I'm glad – surprised – she was willing to let Greenstalk come here. Medieval minds – sorry, most any minds – would want to kill before taking even the faintest risk with something like this.

'Then why *did* you tell the queen?' About the skrode's perversion.

'It's your world. I was tired of playing god with the Secret.

And Greenstalk agreed. Even if the queen had refused, Greenstalk could have used a cold box on the *OOB*.' And likely slept forever. 'But Woodcarver didn't refuse. Somehow she understood what I was saying: it's the true skrodes that can be perverted, but Greenstalk no longer has one of those. In a decade, this island's shore will be populated with hundreds of young Riders, but they would never colonize beyond this archipelago without permission of the locals. The risk is vanishing . . . but I was still surprised Woodcarver took it.'

Peregrine settled down around Ravna, only one pair of eyes still watching the Rider's fronds down in the foam. *Best to give some explanation.* He cocked a head at Ravna. 'Oh, we are medieval, Ravna – even if changing fast, now. We admired Blueshell's courage in the fire. Such deserves reward. And medieval types are used to courting treachery. So what if the risk is of cosmic size? To us, here, it is no more deadly for that. We poor primitives live with deadly risk all the time.'

'Ha!' Her smile spread at his flippant tone.

Peregrine chuckled, heads bobbing. His explanation was the truth, but not all the truth, or even the most important part. He remembered back to the day before, when he and Woodcarver had decided what to do with Greenstalk's request. Woodcarver had been afraid at first, statecraftly cautious before an evil secret billions of years old. Even leaving such a being in cold sleep was a risk. The statecraftly . . . the *medieval* . . . thing to do, would be to grant the request, leave the Rider ashore on this distant island . . . and then sneak back a day or two later and kill it.

Peregrine had settled down by his queen, closer than any but mates and relations could ever do without losing their train of thought. 'You showed more honor to Vendacious,' he had said. Scriber's murderer still walked the earth, complete, scarcely punished at all.

Woodcarver snapped at the empty air; Peregrine knew that sparing Vendacious hurt her too. '. . . Yes. And these Skroderiders have shown us nothing but courage and honesty. I will not harm Greenstalk. Yet I am afraid. With her, there's a risk that goes beyond the stars.'

Peregrine laughed. It might be pilgrim madness but – 'And that's to be expected, my queen. Great risks for great gains. I like being around the humans; I like touching another creature and being able to think at the same time.' He darted forward to nuzzle the nearest of Woodcarver, and then retreated to a more rational distance. 'Even without their starships and their datasets, they would make our world over. Have you noticed . . . how easy it is for us to learn what they know? Even now, Ravna can't seem to accept our fluency. Even now, she doesn't understand how thoroughly we have studied Dataset. And their ship is easy, my queen. I don't mean I understand the physics behind it – few even among star folk do. But the equipment is easy to learn, even with the failures it has suffered. I suspect Ravna will never be able to fly the agrav boat as well as I.'

'Hmmf. But you can reach all the controls at once.'

'That's only part of it. I think we Tines are more flexibly minded than the poor Two-Legs. Can you imagine what it will be like when we make more radio cloaks, when we make our own flying machines?'

Woodcarver smiled, a little sadly now. 'Pilgrim, you dream. This is the Slow Zone. The agrav will wear out in a few years. Whatever we make will be far short of what you play with now.'

'So? Look at human history. It took less than two centuries for Nyjora to regain spaceflights after their dark age. And we have better records than their archaeologists. We and the humans are a wonderful team; they have freed us to be everthing we can be.' A century till their own spaceships, perhaps another century to start building sub-light-speed starships. And someday they would get out of the Slow Zone. *I wonder if packs can be bigger than eight up in the Transcend.*

The younger parts of Woodcarver were up, pacing around the rest. The Queen was intrigued. 'So you think, like Steel seemed to, that we are some kind of special race, something with a happy destiny in the Beyond? Interesting, except for one thing: These humans are all we know from Out There. How do they compare with other races there? Dataset can't fully answer that.'

'Ah, and *there*, Woodcarver, is why Greenstalk is so important. We do need experience of more than one other race. Apparently the Riders are among the most common throughout the Beyond. We need them to talk to . We need to discover if they are as much fun, as *useful*, as the Two-Legs. Even if the risk was ten times what it seems, I would still want to grant this Rider her wish.'

'. . . Yes. If we are to be all we can be, we need to know more. We need to take a few risks.' She stopped her pacing; all her eyes turned toward Peregrine in a gesture of surprise. Abruptly she laughed.

'What?'

'Something we've thought before, dear Peregrine, but now I see how true it is. You're being a little bit clever and scheming here. A good statesman and planner for the future.'

'But still for a pilgrimly goal.'

'To be sure . . . And I, now I don't care so completely about the planning and the safety. *We will visit the stars someday.*' Her puppies waggled a joyous salute. 'I've a little of the pilgrim in me now too.'

She went down all on her bellies and crept across the floor toward him. Consciousness slowly dissolved into a haze of loving lust. The last thing Peregrine remembered her saying was, 'How wonderful the luck: that I had grown old and *had* to be new, and that you were just the change we need.'

Peregrine's attention drifted back to the present, and Ravna. The human was still grinning at him. She reached a hand across to brush one of his heads. 'Medieval minds indeed.'

They sat in the fern shade for another couple of hours and watched the tide come in. The sun fell through midafternoon – even then it was as high in the sky as any noontime sun could be at Woodcarver's. In some ways, the quality of the light and the motion of the sun were the strangest things about the scene. The sun was so high, and came down *so* straight, with none of the long sliding glide of afternoon in the arctic. He had almost forgotten what it was like in the land of Short Twilight.

Now the surf was thirty yards inland of where they had put

the Rider. The crescent moon was following the sun toward the horizon; the water wouldn't rise any further. Ravna stood, shaded her eyes against the lowering sun. 'Time for us to go, I think.'

'You think she'll be safe?'

Ravna nodded. 'This was long enough for Greenstalk to notice any poisons, and most predators. Besides, she's armed.

Human and Tines picked their way to the crest of the atoll, past the tallest of the ferns. Peregrine kept one pair of eyes on the sea behind them. The surf was well past Greenstalk now. Her location was still swept by deep waves, but it was beyond the spume and spray. His last sight of her was in the trough behind a crasher: the smoothness of the sea was broken for an instant by two of her tallest fronds, the tips gently swaying.

Summer took gentle leave of the land around Hidden Island. There was some rain, and no more brush fires. There would even be a harvest, war and drought notwithstanding. Each dayaround the sun hid deeper behind the northern hills, a time of twilight that broadened with the weeks till true night held at midnight. And there were stars.

It was something of an accident that so many things came together on the last night of summer. Ravna took the kids out skygazing on the fields by Starship Castle.

No urban haze here, nor even near-space industry. Nothing to fog the view of heaven except a subtle pinkness in the north that might have been vagrant twilight – or aurora. The four of them settled on the frosty moss and looked around. Ravna took a deep breath. There was no hint of ash left in the air, just a clean chill, a promise of winter.

'The snow will be deep as your shoulders, Ravna,' said Jefri, enthusiastic about the possibility. 'You'll love it.' The pale blotch that was his face seemed to be looking back and forth across the sky.

'It can be bad,' said Johanna Olsndot. She hadn't objected to coming up here tonight, but Ravna knew that she would rather have stayed down on Hidden Island to worry about the doings of tomorrow.

Jefri picked up on her unease – no, that was Amdi talking

now; they would never cure those two of pretending to be each other. 'Don't worry, Johanna. We'll help you.'

For a moment no one said anything. Ravna looked down the hill. It was too dark to see the six hundred meter drop, too dark to see where fjord and islands lay below. But the torchlight on the ramparts of Hidden Island marked its location. Down there in Steel's old inner court – where Woodcarver now ruled – were all the working coldboxes from the ship. One hundred and fifty-one children slept there, the last survivors of the Straumer's flight. Johanna claimed that most could be revived, with best chance of success if it were done soon. The queen had been enthusiastic about the idea. Large sections of the castle had been set aside, refurbished for human needs. Hidden Island was well sheltered – if not from winter snow, at least from the worst winds. If they could be revived, the children would have no trouble living there. Ravna had come to love Jefri and Johanna and Amdi – but could she handle one hundred and fifty-one *more?* Woodcarver seemed to have no misgivings. She had plans for a school where Tines would learn of humans and the children would learn of this world . . . Watching Jefri and Amdi, Ravna was beginning to see what might become of this. Those two were closer than any children she had ever known, and in sum more competent. And that was not just the puppies' math genius; they were competent in other ways.

Humans and Packs *fit*, and old Woodcarver was clever enough to take advantage of it. Ravna liked the queen, and liked Pilgrim even more, but in the end the Packs would be the great beneficiaries. Woodcarver clearly understood the disabilities of her pack race. Tinish records went back at least ten thousand years. For all their recorded history they had been trapped in cultures not much less advanced than now. A race of sharp intelligence yet they had a single overwhelming disadvantage: they could not cooperate at close range without losing that intelligence. Their civilizations were made of isolated minds, forced introverts who could never progress beyond certain limits. The eagerness of Pilgrim and Scrupilo and the others for human contact was evidence of this. *In the long run, we can move the Tines out of this cul-de-sac.*

Amdi and Jefri were giggling about something, the Pack sending runners out almost to the limit of consciousness. These last weeks, Ravna had come to learn that pell-mell activity was the norm for Amdi, that his initial slowness had been part of his hurt over Steel. How . . . perverse – or how wonderful? – . . . that a monster like Steel could be the object of such love.

Jefri shouted, 'You watch in all directions, let me know where to look.' Silence. Then Jefri's voice again: 'There!'

'*What* are you doing?' Johanna asked with sisterly belligerence.

'Watching for meteors,' one of the two said. 'Yes, I watch in all directions and jab Jefri – *there!* – where to look when one comes by.'

Ravna didn't see anything, but the boy had twisted around abruptly at his friend's signal.

'Neat, neat,' came Jefri's voice. 'That was about forty kilometers up, speed – ' the two's voice murmured unintelligibly for a second. Even with the pack's wide vision, how could they know how high it was?

Ravna sat back in the hollow formed by the hummocky moss. It was a good parka the locals had made for her; she barely felt the chill in the ground. Overhead, the stars. Time to think, get some peace before all the things that would begin tomorrow. *Den Mother to one hundred and fifty-some kids . . . and I thought I was a librarian.*

Back home she had loved the night sky; at one glance she could see the other stars of Sjandra Kei, sometimes the other worlds. The places of her home had been in her sky. For a moment the evening chill seemed part of a winter that would never go away. Lynne and her folks and Sjandra Kei. Her whole life till three years ago. It was all gone now. *Don't think on it.* Somewhere out there was what was left of Aniara fleet, and what was left of her people. Kjet Svensndot. Tirolle and Glimfrelle. She had only known them for a few hours, but they were of Sjandra Kei – and they have saved more than they would ever know. They would still live. SjK Commercial Security had some ramscoops in its fleet. They could find a world, not here, but nearer the battle site.

Ravna tilted her head back, wondering at the sky. *Where?* Maybe not even above the horizon now. From here the galactic disk was a glow that climbed across the sky almost at right angles to the ecliptic. There was no sense of its true shape or their exact position in it; the greater picture was lost to nearby splendors, the bright knots of open clusters, frozen jewels against the fainter light. But down near the southern horizon, far from the galactic way, there were two splotchy clouds of light. The Magellanics! Suddenly the geometry clicked, and the universe above was not completely unknown. Aniara fleet would be –

'I – I wonder if we can see Straumli Realm from here,' said Johanna. For more than a year she had had to play the adult. Come tomorrow, that role would be forever. But her voice just now was wistful, childlike.

Ravna opened her mouth, about to say how unlikely that must be.

'Maybe we can, maybe we can.' It was Amdi. The pack had pulled itself together, snuggled companionably among the humans. The warmth was welcome. 'See, I've been reading Dataset about where things are, and trying to figure how it matches what we see.' A pair of noses were silhouetted against the sky for an instant, like a human waving his hands exuberantly at the heavens. 'The brightest things we see are just kind of local dazzle. They aren't good guide posts.' He pointed at a couple of open clusters, claimed they matched stuff he'd found in the Dataset. Amdi had also noticed the Magellanic galaxies, and figured out far more than Ravna. 'So anyway, Straumli Realm was' – *was! you got it kid* – 'in the High Beyond, but near the galactic disk. So, see that big square of stars?' Noses jabbed. 'We call that the Great Square. Anyway, just left of the upper corner and go six thousand light-years, and you'd be at Straumli Realm.'

Jefri came to his knees and stared silently for a second. 'But so far away, is there anything to see?'

'Not the Straumli stars, but just forty light-years from Straum there's a blue-white giant – '

'Yeah,' whispered Johanna. 'Storlys. It was so bright you could see shadows at night.'

'Well that's the fourth brightest star up from the corner; see, they almost make a straight line. I can see it, so I know you can.'

Johanna and Jefri were silent for a long time, just staring up at that patch of sky. Ravna's lips compressed in anger. These were good kids; they had been through hell. And their parents had fought to prevent that hell; they had escaped the Blight with the means of its destruction. But . . . how many million races had lived in the Beyond, had probed the Transcend and made bargains with devils? How many more had destroyed themselves there? Ah, but that had not been enough for Straumli Realm. They had gone into the Transcend and wakened Something that could take over a galaxy.

'Do you think anybody's left there?' said Jefri. 'Do you think we're *all* that's left?'

His sister put an arm around him. 'Maybe . . . maybe not Straumli Realm. But the rest of the universe – look, it's still there.' Weak laughter. 'Daddy and Mom, Ravna and Pham. They stopped the Blight.' She waved a hand against the sky. 'They saved most all of it.'

'Yes,' said Ravna. 'We're saved and safe, Jefri. To begin again.' And as far as it went, that comfort was probably true. The ship's zone probes were still working. Of course, a single measure point is of no use for precise zonography, but she could tell that they were deep in the new volume of the Slowness, the volume created by Pham's Revenge. And – much more significant – the *OOB* detected no variation in zonal intensity. Gone was the continuous trembling of the months before. This new status had the feeling of mountain roots, to be moved only by the passage of the ages.

Fifty degrees along the galactic river was another unre- markable space of sky. She didn't point it out to the kids, but what was of interest there was *much* nearer, just under thirty light-years out: the Blighter Fleet. Flies trapped in amber. At normal jump rates for the Low Beyond, they had been just hours away when Pham created the Great Surge. And now . . . ? If they had been bottom-luggers, ships with ramscoops, they could close the gap in less than fifty years. But Aniara Fleet had made their sacrifice; they had followed

Pham's godshattered advice. And though they didn't know it, they had broken the Blight fleet. There wasn't a single Slow Zone capable vessel in the approaching fleet. Perhaps they had some in-system capability – a few thousand klicks per second. But no more, not Down Here, where new construction was not a matter of waving a magic wand. The Blight's extermination force would sweep past Tines' World in . . . a few thousand years. Time enough.

Ravna leaned back against one of Amdi's shoulders. He nestled comfortably around her neck. The puppies had *grown* these last two months; apparently Steel had kept them on some sort of stunting drugs. Her gaze lost itself in the dark and glow: far upon far that were all the Zones above her. And where are the boundaries now? How awesome was Pham's Revenge. Maybe she should call it Old One's Revenge. No, it was far more even than that. 'Old One' was just a recent victim of the Blight. Old One was no more than midwife to this revenge. The first cause must be as old as the original Blight and more powerful than the Powers.

But whatever caused it, the Surge had done more than revenge. Ravna had studied the ship's measurement of zone intensity. It could only be an estimate, but she knew they were trapped between one thousand and thirty thousand light-years deep in the new Slowness. Powers only knew how far the Surge had pushed the Slowness . . . And maybe even some of the Powers were destroyed by it. This was like some vision of planetary Armageddon – the type of thing that primitive civilizations had nightmares about – but blown up to a galactic scale. A huge hunk of the Milky Way galaxy had been gobbled up by the Slowness, all in a single afternoon . Not just the Blighter Fleet were flies trapped in amber. Why, the whole vault of heaven – excepting the Magellanics faint and *far* away – might now be a tomb of Slowness. Many must still be alive out there, but how many millions of starships had been trapped between the stars? How many automated systems had failed, killing the civilizations that depended on them? Heaven was truly silent now. In some ways the Revenge was a worse thing that the Blight itself.

And what of the Blight – not the fleet that chased the *OOB*, but the Blight itself? That was a creature of the Top and the Transcend. At a very far remove, it covered much of the sky they could see this night. Could Pham's Revenge have really toppled it? If there was a point to all the sacrifice, then surely so. A surge so great that it pushed the Slowness up thousands of light-years, through the Low and Mid Beyond, past the great civilizations at the Top . . . and into the Transcend. *No wonder it was so eager to stop us.* A Power immersed in the Slowness would be a Power no more, would likely be a living thing no more. *If, if, if.* If Pham's Surge could climb so high. *And that is something I will never know.*

Crypto: 0
As received by:
Language path: Optima
From: Society for Rational Investigation
Subject: Ping
Key phrases: Help me!
Summary: Has there been a network partition, or
    what?
Distribution:
    Threat of the Blight
    Society for Rational Network Management
    War Trackers Interest Group
Date: 0.412 Msec since loss of contacts
Text of message:
    I have still not recovered contact with any network site known to be spinward of me. Apparently, I am right at the very edge of a catastrophe.
    If you receive this ping, please respond! Am I in danger?
    For your information, I have no trouble reaching sites that are antispinward. I understand an effort is being made to hop messages the long way around the galaxy. At least that would give us an idea how big the loss is. Nothing has come back as yet — not surprising, I guess, considering the great number of hops and the

expense.

In the meantime, I am sending out pings such as this. I am expending enormous resources to do this, let me tell you – but it is that important. I've beamed direct at all the hub sites that are in range to the spinward of me. No replies.

More ominous: I have tried to transmit 'over the top', that is by using known sites in the Transcend that are above the catastrophe. Most such would not normally respond, Powers being what they are. But I received *no* replies. A silence like the Depths is there. It appears that a portion of the Transcend itself has been engulfed.

Again: If you receive this message, please respond!

The End

I am grateful for the advice and help of: Jeff Allen, Robert Cademy, John Carroll, Howard L. Davidson, Michael Gannis, Gordon Garb, Corky Hansen, Dianne L. Hansen, Sharon Jarvis, Judy Lazar, and Joan D. Vinge.

I am very grateful to James R. Frenkel for the wonderful job of editing he has done with this book.

Thanks for Poul Anderson for the quote that I use as the motto of Qeng Ho.

During the summer of 1988 I visited Norway. Many things I saw there influenced the writing of this story. I am very grateful to: Johannes Berg and Heidi Lyshol and the Aniara Society for showing me Oslo and for the wonderful hospitality; the organizers of the Arctic '88 distributed systems course at the University of Tromsøy, in particular Dag Johansen. As for Tromsøy, and the surrounding lands: I had not dreamed that so pleasant and beautiful a place could exist in the arctic.

Science fiction has imagined many alien creatures; this is one of the genre's great charms. I don't know what in particular inspired me to make the Riders in this novel, but I do know that Robert Abernathy wrote about a similar race in his short story, 'Junior' (*Galaxy*, January 1956). 'Junior' is a beautiful commentary on the spirit of life.

V. V.

Vernor Steffen Vinge was born in Wisconsin in 1944. He is a retired San Diego State University Professor of Mathematics, a computer scientist and science fiction author. He is best known for his two epic space operas *A Fire Upon the Deep* (1992) and *A Deepness in the Sky* (1999), both of which won the Hugo Award and were shortlisted for the Nebula. He is the winner of 5 Hugos, 4 Prometheus Awards and the John W. Campbell Memorial Award, among many others. In addition to his works of science fiction, Vinge authored the influential 1993 essay 'The Coming Technological Singularity', in which he argued that the creation of superhuman artificial intelligence will mark the point at which 'the human era will be ended', such that no current models of reality are sufficient to predict beyond it.

A full list of SF Masterworks can be found at

www.gollancz.co.uk

ABOUT GOLLANCZ

Gollancz is the oldest SF publishing imprint in the world. Since being founded in 1927 Gollancz has continued to publish a focused selection of bestselling and award-winning authors. The front-list includes **Ben Aaronovitch**, **Joe Abercrombie**, **Charlaine Harris**, **Joanne Harris**, **Joe Hill**, **Alastair Reynolds**, **Patrick Rothfuss**, **Nalini Singh** and **Brandon Sanderson**.

As one of the largest Science Fiction and Fantasy imprints in the UK it is no surprise we have one of the most extensive backlists in the world. Find high quality SF on Gateway written by such authors as **Philip K. Dick**, **Ursula Le Guin**, **Connie Willis**, **Sir Arthur C. Clarke**, **Pat Cadigan**, **Michael Moorcock** and **George R.R. Martin**.

We also have a strand of publishing in translation, which includes French, Polish and Russian authors. Gollancz is home to more award-winning authors than any other imprint, with names including **Aliette de Bodard**, **M. John Harrison**, **Paul McAuley**, **Sarah Pinborough**, **Pierre Pevel**, **Justina Robson** and many more.

The SF Gateway
More than 3,000 classic, rare and previously out-of-print SF novels at your fingertips.
www.sfgateway.com

The Gollancz Blog
Bringing you news from our worlds to yours. Stories, interviews, articles and exclusive extracts just for you!
www.gollancz.co.uk

GOLLANCZ
LONDON

BRINGING NEWS
FROM OUR WORLDS
TO YOURS . . .

Want your news daily?

The Gollancz blog has instant updates
on the hottest SF and Fantasy books.

Prefer your updates monthly?

Sign up for our
in-depth newsletter.

www.gollancz.co.uk

Follow us  @gollancz
Find us ⓕ facebook.com/GollanczPublishing

Classic SF as you've never read it before.
Visit the SF Gateway to find out more!
www.sfgateway.com